Henry Beasley

The Book of Prescriptions

SALZWASSER
VERLAG

Henry Beasley

The Book of Prescriptions

Reprint of the original, first published in 1865.

1st Edition 2022 | ISBN: 978-3-75259-069-2

Verlag (Publisher): Salzwasser Verlag GmbH, Zeilweg 44, 60439 Frankfurt, Deutschland
Vertretungsberechtigt (Authorized to represent): E. Roepke, Zeilweg 44, 60439 Frankfurt, Deutschland
Druck (Print): Books on Demand GmbH, In de Tarpen 42, 22848 Norderstedt, Deutschland

THE

BOOK OF PRESCRIPTIONS.

THE

BOOK OF PRESCRIPTIONS,

CONTAINING

3000 PRESCRIPTIONS,

COLLECTED FROM THE PRACTICE OF THE MOST EMINENT PHYSICIANS AND SURGEONS,

English, French, and American.

COMPRISING ALSO,

A COMPENDIOUS HISTORY OF THE MATERIA MEDICA, LISTS OF THE DOSES OF ALL OFFICINAL OR ESTABLISHED PREPARATIONS,

AND AN

INDEX OF DISEASES AND REMEDIES.

BY

HENRY BEASLEY

PHILADELPHIA

1865.

PUBLISHERS' NOTICE.

In presenting to the American public a second edition of this valuable work from the recent carefully revised London edition, the publishers have endeavored to render it still more acceptable to every medical practitioner who may wish to consult its pages, by translating into plain English all the Latin directions for dispensing the prescriptions, and administering the medicines; which plan it is confidently hoped will be found quite an improvement upon the previous edition.

ADVERTISEMENT.

THE Editor trusts that this work will supply a want which has long been felt. Carefully selecting from the mass of materials at his disposal, it has been his aim to compile a volume, sufficiently comprehensive, in which both physician and druggist, prescriber and compounder, may find, under the head of each remedy, the manner in which that remedy may be most effectively administered, or combined with other medicines, in the treatment of various diseases. The alphabetical arrangement will render this easy. It is also hoped that the short description given of each medicine, and the list of the doses in which its several preparations may be prescribed, will be found useful.

In selecting the prescriptions and determining the doses reliance has been placed upon those medical authors who are generally considered as of most authority in each instance. But it will readily be imagined that the prescriptions are not all of equal merit, and the reader will find several opportunities of comparison, by which a considerable variety of opinion among medical practitioners, particularly in the matter of doses, has been forcibly illustrated. When it has been necessary to point out the mean between extremes of this nature, the Editor has been assisted in his task by competent medical advice, and he hopes that a correct judgment has been thereby arrived at.

Besides those special pharmaceutical works, of which a full list is given at the commencement of the "Medical Formulary," the author has consulted, in the compilation of this volume, a large number of standard works on Medicine, Surgery, and Midwifery, both by English and foreign practitioners. The names, which are in general appended at the foot of each prescription, will for the most part be readily recognized.

Reference must also be made to the "Formulary," by the same author, for exact information as to the composition and manner of compounding of the various preparations enumerated below in the lists of doses, or ordered in the prescriptions contained in the present work.

To the Second Edition of the Book of Prescriptions one hundred additional prescriptions have been added, collected from recent works, English, French, and American. And a want having been felt of some practical outline that should serve as a key to the whole, an Index of Diseases and Remedies has been inserted at the end, which, it is hoped, will be of use to the prescriber.

SIGNS AND ABBREVIATIONS OCCURRING IN PRESCRIPTIONS.

REFERRING TO THE OPERATION.

℞, *Recipe*, take.
M., *Misce*, mix.
F., *Fac*, *Fiat*, make, let there be made.
Div., *Divide*, divide.
Sol., *Solve*, dissolve.
F.S.A., *Fac secundum artem*, make or prepare according to the rules of the art.
M.S.D., *Misce, signa, da*, mix, write (the label or direction), and deliver to the patient.

REFERRING TO QUANTITY, WEIGHT, OR PROPORTION.

A., *āā.*, *ana*, of each.
Singulorum, of each.
Q.S., *Quantum sufficit*, as much as is sufficient.
Q.L., *Quantum lubet*, as much as you please.
C., *Cong.*, *Congius*, a gallon.
O., *Octarius*, a pint; 20 ounces.
℔., *Libra*, a pound (apothecaries' or troy weight); 12 ounces.
℥., *Uncia*, an ounce; 8 drachms.
f℥., *Fluiduncia*, a fluid ounce. (This f is often omitted.)
ʒ., *Drachma*, a drachm; 60 grains.
fʒ., *Fluidrachma*, a fluid drachm.
℈., *Scrupulus*, a scruple; 20 grains.
Gr., *Granum*, a grain.
♏., *Minimum*, a minim, or drop; also, *gtt.*, *gutta*.
SS., *Semis*, a half.

REFERRING TO THE FORM OF THE PREPARATION TO BE MIXED OR COMPOUNDED.

Co., *Comp.*, *Compositus*, compound.
P., *Pulv.*, *Pulvis*, a powder.
Pil., *Pilula*, a pill.
Extr., *Extractum*, an extract.
Elect., *Electuarium*, an electuary.
Bol., *Bolus*, a large pill.
Liq., *Liquor*, a solution.
Tinct., *Tinctura*, a tincture.
Inf., *Infusum*, an infusion.
Dec., *Decoct.*, *Decoctum*, a decoction.
Mist., *Mistura*, a mixture.
Haust., *Haustus*, a draught.
Pot., *Potus*, *Potio*, a drink.
Coll., *Collyrium*, an eye-water.
Collut., *Collutorium*, a mouth-wash.
Inj., *Injectio*, an injection.
En., *Enema*, a clyster.
Garg., *Gargarisma*, a gargle.
Lot., *Lotio*, a lotion.
Lin., *Linimentum*, a liniment.
Baln., *Balneum*, a bath.

REFERRING TO THE ADMINISTRATION.

Cap., *Sum.*, *Capiat*, *Sumat*, let the patient take.
Æg., *Æger*, *Ægra*, the patient, the sick man, or woman.
Det., *Detur*, let it be given.
Part. 3*tiam*, 4*tam*, 6*tam*, *Partem tertiam*, *quartam*, *sextam*, the third, fourth, or sixth part (accusative case).
Semel, *bis*, *ter in d.*, once, twice, thrice a day.
H., *Hora*, an hour.
H. S., *Horâ somni*, at bedtime.
O. n., *Omni nocte*, every night.
O. m., *Omni mane*, every morning.
Coch., *Cochleare*, a spoonful.
Poc., *Poculum*, a cup.
Cyath., *Cyathus*, a wineglass.

LIST OF LATIN WORDS AND PHRASES MORE OR LESS FREQUENTLY MET WITH IN PRESCRIPTIONS.

Abdomen, the belly; *abdominis*, of the belly; *abdomini*, to the belly.

Absente febre, in the absence of fever.

Accurate, accurately.

Ad duas vices, at twice taking.

Ad tertiam vicem, for three times.

Ad gratam aciditatem, to an agreeable sourness.

Ad defectionem animi, to fainting.

Ad libitum, at pleasure.

Adde, or *addantur*, add, or let be added.

Adhibendus, to be administered.

Adjacens, adjacent.

Admove, or *admoveatur*, or *admoveantur*, apply, or let it or them be applied.

Adstante febre, when the fever is on.

Adversum, against.

Aggrediente febre, while the fever is coming on.

Agitato vase, the phial being shaken.

Aliquot, some.

Alter, the other.

Alternis horis, every other hour.

Aluta, leather.

Alvo adstrictâ, when the belly is bound.

Alvus, the belly.

Amplus, large.

Ana, of each ingredient. In the Pharmacopœia the term *singulorum* is employed instead of *ana*.

Aqua, water. *Aqua astricta*, frozen water. *Aqua bulliens*, boiling water. *Aqua communis*, common water. *Aqua fluviatilis*, river water. *Aqua marina*, sea water. *Aqua nivalis*, snow water. *Aqua pluviatilis*, or *Aqua pluvialis*, rain water. *Aqua fervens*, hot water. *Aqua fontana*, or *Aqua fontis*, or *Aqua fontalis*, spring water.

Auris, the ear.

Aut, or.

Balneum Mariæ, or *Balneum maris*, a warm water bath.

Balneum vaporosum, or *Balneum vaporis*, a vapor bath.

Barbadensis, Barbadoes; as *Aloe Barbadensis*.

Bene, well.

Bibe, drink (thou).

Biduum, two days.

Bis indies, twice a day.

Bulliat, or *Bulliant*, let boil.

Butyrum, butter.

Cæruleus, blue.

Calefactus, warmed.

Calomelas, calomel, or chloride of mercury.

Capiat, let the patient take.

Cautè, cautiously.

Charta, paper.

Cochlear, or *Cochleare*, a spoonful, a tablespoonful. *Cochleatim*, by spoonfuls. *Cochleare amplum*, a large (or table) spoonful, about half an ounce. *Cochleare infantis*, a child's spoonful. *Cochleare magnum*, a large spoonful. *Cochleare medium*, *Cochleare modicum*, a middling spoonful—*i.e.* a child's, or dessertspoonful: about f℥ij. *Cochleare parvum*, a small (or tea) spoonful: about f℥j.

Cibus, food.

Coctio, boiling.

Cola, strain. *Colatus*, strained.

Colaturæ, to, or of, the strained liquor.

Coletur, let it be strained.

Colentur, let them be strained.

Coloretur, let it be colored.

Compositus, compounded.
Concisus, cut.
Congius, a gallon.
Conserva, a conserve; also, keep thou.
Continuantur remedia, let the remedies be continued.
Contusus, bruised.
Coque, boil; *coquantur*, let them be boiled. *Coque ad medietatis consumptionem*, boil to the consumption of half. *Coque in sufficiente quantitate aquæ*, boil in a sufficient quantity of water.
Cor, *Cordis*, the heart.
Cornu cervi, hartshorn.
Cornu cervi ustum, burnt hartshorn.
Cortex, bark.
Coxa, the hip.
Cras, to-morrow.
Cras vespere, to-morrow evening.
Cras mane sumendus, to be taken to-morrow morning.
Cras nocte, to-morrow night.
Crastinus, for to-morrow.
Cucurbitula cruenta, a cupping-glass with the scarificator.
Cujus, of which.
Cujuslibet, of any.
Cum, with.
Cyatho theæ, in a cup of tea.
Cyathus, vel
Cyathus vinarius, } a wineglass: from f℥iss to f℥ij.
Da, give.
De (prep.), of, or from.
Deaurentur pilulæ, let the pills be gilt.
Debita spissitudo, a proper consistence.
Debitus, due, proper.
Decanta, pour off.
Decem, ten; *decimus*, the tenth.
Decubitus, lying down.
De die in diem, from day to day.
Deglutiatur, may be (*or* let be) swallowed.

Dejectiones alvi, stools.
Detur, let it be given.
Detur in duplo, let twice as much be given.
Dexter, *dextra*, the right.
Diebus alternis, every other day.
Dilue, *dilutus*, dilute (thou), diluted.
Diluculo, at break of day.
Dimidius, one-half.
Directione propriâ, with a proper direction.
Dividatur in partes æquales, let it be divided into equal parts.
Dolor, pain.
Donec, until.
Donec alvus bis dejiciatur, until the bowels have been twice evacuated.
Donec alvus soluta fuerit, until the bowels shall be opened.
Donec dolor nephriticus exulaverit, until the nephritic pain be removed.
Dosis, a dose.
Durante dolore, while the pain lasts.
Eadem (fem.), the same.
Eburneus, made of ivory.
Edulcorata, edulcorated.
Ejusdem, of the same.
Electuarium, an electuary.
Emesis, vomiting.
Enema, a clyster; *enemata*, clysters.
Evanuerit, shall have disappeared.
Exhibeatur, let it be exhibited.
Extende super alutam mollem, spread (thou) upon soft leather.
Fac, make; *fiat*, *fiant*, let it or them be made.
Fac pilulas duodecim, make twelve pills.
Farina, flour.
Fasciculus, a bundle, which can be carried under the arm.
Febre durante, during the fever.
Febris, fever.
Femoribus internis, to the inner parts of the thighs.
Fervens, boiling.

Fiat haustus, let a draught be made.
Fiat lege artis, let it be made by the rules of art.
Fiat mistura, let a mixture be made.
Fiat secundum artis regulas, let it be made according to the rules of art.
Fiat venæsectio, bleed.
Fictilis, earthen.
Filtra, filter (thou).
Filtrum, a filter.
Fistula armata, a clyster pipe and bladder fitted for use.
Fluidus, liquid.
Formula, a prescription.
Frustillatim, in little pieces.
Fuerit, shall have been.
Gargarisma, a gargle.
Gelatinâ quâvis, in any kind of jelly.
Gradatim, by degrees.
Grana sex pondere, six grains by weight.
Granum, grain; *grana*, grains.
Gratus, pleasant.
Gutta, a drop; *guttæ*, drops.
Guttatim, by drops.
Guttis quibusdam, with a few drops.
Harum pilularum sumantur tres, let three of these pills be taken.
Haustus, a draught.
Hebdomada, a week.
Herba, a herb.
Heri, yesterday.
Hic, *hæc*, *hoc*, this.
Hirudo, a leech.
Hora, an hour.
Horâ decubitûs, at the hour of going to bed.
Horâ somni, just before going to sleep.
Horâ undecimâ matutinâ, at the eleventh hour in the morning.
Horæ unius spatio, at the expiration of an hour.
Horis intermediis, in the intermediate hours.

Idem, the same.
Idoneus, proper.
Imprimis, first.
Indies, from day to day, or daily.
Incide, cut (thou); *incisus*, being cut.
Infunde, pour in.
Injectio, an injection.
Injiciatur enema, let a clyster be given.
In pulmento, in gruel.
Instar, as big as.
Inter, between.
Internus, inner.
Jam, now, already.
Julepus, *Julepum*, *Julapium*, a julep.
Jusculum, broth.
Juxta, near to.
Kali præparatum (*Potassæ carbonas*, Ph. L.), prepared kali, or carbonate or subcarbonate of potash.
Lac, milk.
Lana, flannel.
Languor, faintness.
Lateri dolenti, to the side that is painful.
Lectus, a bed.
Linteum, lint.
Magnus, large.
Mane, in the morning.
Mane primo, very early in the morning.
Manipulus, a handful.
Manus, the hand.
Massa, a mass.
Massa pilularis, a pill mass.
Matutinus, in the morning, early.
Medius, middle.
Mica panis, crumb of bread.
Minimum, a minim.
Minutum, a minute.
Misce, mix.

Mistura, a mixture.
Mitte, send; *mittatur*, or *mittantur*, let be sent.
Mitte sanguinem ad uncias duodecim saltem, take away blood to twelve ounces at least.
Modicus, middle-sized.
Modo præscripto, in the manner prescribed.
Mora, delay.
More dicto, in the manner directed.
More solito, in the usual manner.
Mortarium, a mortar.
Necnon, also.
Nisi, unless.
Novem, nine.
Nox, *noctis*, night.
Nucha, the nape of the neck.
Numerus, number.
Nux Moschata, a nutmeg.
Octarius, a pint.
Octavus, cighth.
Octo, eight.
Oleum lini sine igne, cold drawn linseed oil.
Omni hora, every hour. *Omni biduo*, every two days. *Omni bihorio*, every two hours.
Omni mane, every morning.
Omni nocte, every night.
Omni quadrante horæ, every quarter of an hour.
Opus, need, occasion.
Ovum, an egg.
Oz., *Uncia*, the ounce avoirdupois, or common weight.
Pannus, a rag.
Pars, *partis*, a part.
Partes æquales, equal parts.
Partitis vicibus, in divided doses.
Parvulus, an infant; *Coch. parvulum*, a teaspoonful.
Parvus, little.
Pastillus, *pastillum*, a little ball of paste, to take like a lozenge, &c.

Pediluvium, a footbath.

Peractâ operatione emetici, when the operation of the emetic is finished.

Per deliquium, by deliquescence.

Pergo, pergere, to go on with.

Ph. D., *Pharmacopœia Dublinensis*. *Ph. E.*, *Pharmacopœia Edinensis*. *Ph. L.*, *Pharmacopœia Londinensis*. *Ph. U. S.*, *Pharmacopœia of the United States*.

Poculum, a cup; *pocillum*, a little cup.

Pondere, by weight.

Pondus civile, civil weight (avoirdupois weight).

Pondus medicinale, medicinal (apothecaries') weight.

Pone aurem, behind the ear.

Post singulas sedes liquidas, after every loose stool.

Potus, drink.

Præparata, prepared.

Primus, the first.

Primo mane, very early in the morning.

Pro ratione ætatis, according to the age of the patient.

Pro re natâ, according as circumstances arise (*i.e.* occasionally).

Pugillus, a pinch; a gripe between the thumb and two first fingers.

Pulvis; pulverizatus, a powder—powdered.

Pyxis, a pill-box.

Quantum lubet, }
Quantum placet, } as much as you please.

Quantum sufficiat, or *Quantum satis*, as much as is sufficient.

Quantum vis, *Quantum volueris*, as much as you will.

Quâquâ horâ, each hour.

Quartus, the fourth.

Quatuor, four.

Quinque, five.

Quintus, the fifth.

Quorum, of which.

℞, *Recipe*, take.

Ratio, proportion.

Redactus in pulverem, powdered.

Redigatur in pulverem, let it be reduced to powder.
Regio umbilici, the umbilical region.
Reliquus, remaining.
Repetatur, *repetantur*, let it or them be continued.
Respondeo, to answer.
Retineo, to keep.
Saltem, at least.
Scatula, a box.
Scilicet, namely.
Secundum artem, according to art.
Secundum naturam, according to nature.
Secundus, second.
Sedes, the alvine evacuation.
Semel, once.
Semi, *semis*, a half.
Semidrachma, half a drachm.
Semihora, half an hour.
Septem, seven.
Septimana, a week.
Sescuncia, an ounce and a half.
Sesquihora, an hour and a half.
Sex, six.
Sextus, sixth.
Si, if.
Simul, together.
Sine, without.
Singulorum, of each.
Si non valeat, if it do not answer.
Si opus sit, if there be occasion.
Si vires permittant, if the strength will bear it.
Signetur nomine proprio, let it be written upon with the proper name (not a trade name).
Sit, let it be.
Solus, alone.
Solve, *solvere*, *solutus*, to dissolve, dissolved or loosened.
Somnus, sleep.
Spiritus vini rectificatus, rectified spirit of wine.

Spiritus vini tenuis, proof spirit.
Spiritus vinosus, ardent spirit of any strength.
Statim, immediately.
Stet, let it stand; *stent*, let them stand.
Sub finem coctionis, when the boiling is nearly finished.
Subactus, subdued.
Subinde, frequently.
Sumat talem, let the patient take one like this.
Sume, *sumat*, *sumatur*, *sumantur*, *sumendus*, take thou, let him take, let it or them be taken, to be taken.
Summitates, the summits, or tops.
Supra, above.
Superbibendo haustum, drinking afterward this draught.
Tabella, (dim. of *tabula*, a table) a lozenge.
Talis, such a one.
Tempori dextro, to the right temple.
Tempus, *temporis*, time or temple.
Ter, three times.
Tero, to rub.
Tertius, third.
Tinctura, tincture.
Tinctura opii, tincture of opium.
Tinctura opii camphorata, paregoric elixir. It is now called *Tinct. camphoræ composita.*
Tres, three.
Triduum, three days.
Tritura, triturate.
Trochisci, troches or lozenges.
Tussis, a cough.
Ultimo præscriptus, the last ordered.
Una, together.
Utor, *uti*, to make use of.
Vas vitreum, a glass vessel.
Vehiculum, a vehicle.
Venæsectio brachii, bleeding in the arm.
Vesper, *vesperis*, the evening.
Vices, turns.

Vires, strength.
Vitellus, yolk.
Vitello ovi solutus, dissolved in the yolk of an egg.
Vitrum, glass.
Vomitione urgente, the vomiting being troublesome.

GAUBIUS' TABLE,

Regulating the ordinary proportion of doses according to the age of the patient.

For an adult, suppose the dose to be	1,	or	1 drachm.
Under 1 year, will require,	$\frac{1}{12}$	"	5 grains.
" 2 " "	$\frac{1}{8}$	"	8 "
" 3 " "	$\frac{1}{6}$	"	10 "
" 4 " "	$\frac{1}{4}$	"	15 "
" 7 " "	$\frac{1}{3}$	"	1 scruple.
" 14 " "	$\frac{1}{2}$	"	$\frac{1}{2}$ a drachm.
" 20 " "	$\frac{2}{3}$	"	2 scruples.
From 21–60, the full dose,	1	"	1 drachm.

Above 60, an inverse gradation should be observed.

THE

BOOK OF PRESCRIPTIONS.

ABELMOSCHUS. *Musk Seeds.*

The seeds of Hibiscus Abelmoschus (Nat. Ord. *Malvaceæ*) have the odor of musk, and are supposed to possess its nervine, stimulant, and antispasmodic properties. In South America they are used as a remedy for the bites of serpents. The only preparation used in Great Britain, (not used in U. S.,) is *Tinctura Abelmoschi;* dose, half a drachm to a drachm and a half.

1. ℞ Tincturæ Abelmoschi, ℥j.
Tincturæ Fumariæ alkalinæ, ℥ss.
Sodæ Bicarbonatis, ʒiij.
Misturæ Camphoræ, ℥vj.
Mix: three tablespoonfuls three times a day.

In Indigestion, in nervous and gouty subjects.—Dr. R. Reece.

2. ℞ Tinct. Abelmoschi, ℥j.
Tinct. Lupulinæ, ʒiij.
Liquor Potassæ, ʒij.
Infusi Buchu, ℥vj. As the last.

In Indigestion, with nervousness, and high-colored urine.
Dr. R. Reece.

Absinthium. See Artemisia.

ACACIA. *Gum Arabic.*

This gum is the product of Acacia vera, and other species. (Nat. Ord. *Leguminosæ.*) It is demulcent; and is used in the dose of a drachm or more, chiefly in solution, in irritations of the urinary and respiratory organs, of the intestinal canal, &c. Dose of *Mistura Acaciæ* (Mucilage), 2 to 8 drachms; *Emulsio*

Acaciæ; Pasta et Trochisci Acaciæ, almost *ad libitum; Syrupus Acaciæ,* 4 drachms. The powdered gum with resin is used as a styptic; and mucilage has been recommended as an application to burns.

3. ℞ Acaciæ electæ, ℥j.
Aquæ, Oiss. Dissolve; then add
Syrupi Simpl. (or Althææ) ℥ij.
Mix: a wineglassful frequently.

In Strangury, Irritant Poisoning, &c.

4. ℞ Misturæ Acaciæ, ℥iss.
Aquæ, f℥iiiss.
Syrupi, f℥ss. Mix: a tablespoonful frequently.

In Bronchial Catarrh of Children.—Dr. URE.

5. ℞ Misturæ Acaciæ, f℥ij.
Aquæ, f℥iv.
Syrupi Tolutani,
Aquæ fl. Aurantii, āā f℥j.
Make into a mixture. Take a tablespoonful every second hour.

In Irritation of Mucous Membranes.—Dr. JOY.

6. ℞ Pulv. Acaciæ,
Mellis Optimi, ana f℥ss. Mix: a teaspoonful frequently.

In Catarrhal Cough.—SAINTE MARIE.

7. ℞ Misturæ Acaciæ, f℥ij.
Syrupi Mori, f℥j.
Aquæ Rosæ, f℥iij.
Tinct. Scillæ, fʒj.
Mix: two or three tablespoonfuls to be taken frequently.

Demulcent and Expectorant.—Mr. BRENDE.

ACETUM. ACIDUM ACETICUM; ACIDUM PYROLIGNEUM. *Vinegar (common and distilled), Acetic and Pyroligneous Acid.*

Vinegar is refrigerant, antiseptic, astringent, and diuretic. Dose, from 1 fluid drachm to 4 fluid drachms, with diluent drinks in inflammatory fevers. *Oxymel, and Syrupus Aceti,* and *Syrupus Rubi Idæi,* for the same purposes, in doses of 1 to 3 drachms; generally added to water, barley water, or linseed tea, so as to make them pleasantly acid as a common drink in fevers. *Externally,* vinegar is applied as a discutient, styptic, and disinfectant.

Distilled vinegar has the same properties and uses: both may be regarded as weak acetic acid.

Acetic acid, in its more concentrated state, is caustic and rubefacient; its vapor is reviving, and is supposed to prevent infection. The most concentrated acid with aromatics and camphor, constitutes *Acetum Aromaticum* and *Acidum Aceticum Camphoratum.* Blotting paper, imbued with the strong acid, is used as a speedy vesicant. Pyroligneous acid is acetic acid, derived from the destructive distillation of wood. As employed in the following prescriptions, the name intends acetic acid from wood, which has been rectified, but not entirely freed from the creosote and other tarry products, which increase its antiseptic powers.

Diluted acetic acid does not differ from distilled vinegar, except in being free from some accidental impurities which attend the latter.

8. ℞ Aceti, f℥j.
Aquæ, f℥xv.
Sacchari, ℥ss.
Mix: to be taken as a common drink.

In fevers, and in White Urinary Deposits.

9. ℞ Syrupi Aceti, f℥ij.
Aquæ, f℥xviij
Mix: make a mixture. Take a spoonful frequently.

To allay thirst in Febrile Affections.—Dr. NELIGAN.

10. ℞ Aquæ fl. Sambuci, f℥x.
Aceti Vini acerrimi, ℥j.
Extracti Cinchonæ, ʒiij.
Succi Spiss. Sambuci, ℥j. Mix: a spoonful every hour.

In Putrid Fevers.—GESNER.

11. ℞ Aceti destillati, fʒij.
Syrupi, fʒiv.
Aquæ, f℥ij. Mix: a fourth part every three hours.

In Scarlatina (for a child of 3 years).—Mr. J. B. BROWN.

12. ℞ Aceti destillati, f℥ij.
Aquæ Lauro-cerasi, fʒij.
Syrupi Rhœados, fʒvj.
Aquæ destillati, f℥v.
Mix: two tablespoonfuls every six hours.

In Mucous Discharges, with Debility and Irritability of Stomach. Dr. NELIGAN.

13. ℞ Acidi Acetici diluti, f℥j.
Tinct. Jalapæ, ♏xv.
Tinct. Aurantii, f℥j.
Misturæ Camphoræ, f℥x.
Mix: make a draught to be taken two or three times a day.

In Rheumatism in debilitated subjects.—Mr. ATKINSON.

14. ℞ Acidi Acetici Pyrolig. ♏xxv.
Liq. Ammon. Acet., f℥iiss.
Mist. Camphoræ, f℥j.
Syrupi Zingiberis, f℥ss.
Mix: make a draught to be taken three or four times a day.

In Offensive Discharges after Abortions.—Dr. COPLAND.

15. ℞ Acidi Pyrolignei rect. ℥j.
Aquæ fl. Aurantii, ℥ij.
Syrupi Amygdalæ, ℥j.
Mix: a large teaspoonful every hour.

In Gelatiniform Softening of Stomach, &c. of Children.

PITSCHAFT.

16. ℞ Acidi Pyrolignei rectif. ℥ij.
Tinct. Calami, ℥iij.
Aquæ Menthæ, ℥iv.
Syrupi Simpl. ℥iss. Mix: a spoonful every two hours.

PHŒBUS.

17. ℞ Aceti communis, f℥j.
Aquæ, f℥vj. Mix: make an enema.

In Constipation and Typhus.—SWEDIAUR.

18. ℞ Aceti com. f℥j.
Aquæ, f℥iij–iv. Mix.

For Sponging the Body in Fevers.—BRANDE.

19. ℞ Aceti com. f℥iij.
Aquæ, f℥v. Mix: make a lotion.

In Contusions, &c.—Dr. PEREIRA.

20. ℞ Aceti, ℥ij.
Ammon. Mur. ℥j.
Mellis, ℥iss.
Aquæ, ℥xij. Mix: make a gargle.

In Sore Throat.—M. DE SANTE.

21. ℞ Aceti, f℥iiss.
Decoct. Hordei, f℥xvj.
Mel. Rosæ, f℥iss. Mix: make a gargle.

Dr. A. T. THOMSON.

22. ℞ Acidi Pyrolignei rect. ℥ss.
Aquæ Cinnamomi, f℥iv.
Syrupi Mori, ℥ij. Mix: make a mouth-wash.

PHŒBUS.

23. ℞ Acidi Pyrolignei, ℥j.
Infusi Salviæ, ℥vj.
Mix: make a gargle.

In Putrid Sore Throat.—FRANCKEL.

24. ℞ Acidi Acetici (Ph. L.), f℥j.
Spr. Camphoræ, f℥iij.
Mix: make an embrocation.

As a Rubefacient.—Mr. BRANDE.

25. ℞ Acidi Acetici, f℥j.
Aquæ, f℥iij. Mix.

The shaved scalp to be rubbed over with this acid. The red spots produced show the infected parts, and are to be each wet with *undiluted* acetic acid for three or four minutes, by means of a sponge tied on a stick. The disease is generally cured by one application.

In Tinea Capitis.—Dr. WIGAN.

26. ℞ Myrrhæ pulv. ʒj.
Ol. Cassiæ, gutt. ij.
Bals. Peruviani, gutt. iv.
Acid. Pyrolig. rectif., ʒij.
Carbonis pulv. q. s. Mix: make a confection for the gums.

As an Antiscorbutic to the Gums.—PHŒBUS.

FOR ACIDUM BENZOICUM, see BENZOINUM.

FOR ACIDUM BORACICUM, see BORAX.

ACIDUM CARBONICUM. *Carbonic Acid Gas.*

Carbonic acid introduced into the stomach (in the form of simple aerated water, soda water, effervescing draughts, &c.) is refrigerant and antiseptic; it checks vomiting, and allays thirst and gastric irritation. The gas is applied topically to the skin as a cutaneous stimulant; to ulcers, to promote suppuration and diminish fetor; it has been injected into the rectum in cancerous ulcers and dysentery; and into the uterus in a painful condition of that organ. Inhaled, it is a powerful poison.

Carbonic acid is an active ingredient in the following officinal compounds:—*Aqua Acidi Carbonici; Aqua Selterana* (and the other aerated mineral waters); *Balneum Carbonicum; Liquor Potassæ Effervescens; Liquor Sodæ Effervescens; Pilulæ Acidi Carbonici; Cataplasma Effervescens; Haustus Antiemeticus; Haustus Effervescens; Pulveres Effervescentes, &c.*

ACIDUM CITRICUM. SUCCUS LIMONIS. ACIDUM TARTARICUM.

Citric acid and lemon juice are refrigerant, allaying thirst, and diminishing febrile heat. In large doses lemon juice reduces the power of the pulse, and acts as a diuretic. It is also antiscorbutic. Dose of citric acid, 10 to 30 grains. Of lemon juice, as a refrigerant, 2 to 4 drachms; as a remedy for rheumatism, 2 to 6 ounces. Tartaric acid possesses the same refrigerant properties as citric acid, and is used for the same purposes, and in the same forms. It is, however, more irritant, and in doses of a few drachms it has proved fatal. It is often used with carbonate or bicarbonate of potash to form effervescing saline draughts. Added to salts of iron it prevents the precipitation of oxide by alkalies. Dose of tartaric acid, 10 to 25 grains; of *Syrupus Acidi Citrici et A. Tartarici*, 2 fluid drachms to an ounce; *Trochisci A. T.*, one frequently; *Pulveres Effervescentes Citrati et Tartarizati*, &c., as required; *Limonadum*, *Lim. aeratum*, *Julepum Limonis*, ad libitum; *Limonadum Siccum*, a teaspoonful in a glass of water; *Decoctum Limonum*, by small glassfuls.

27. ℞ Succi Limonis recent. f℥j–ij.
Misturæ Camphoræ, f℥j.
Mix: make a draught to be taken three times a day.

In Acute Rheumatism.—Dr. G. O. Rees.

28. ℞ Succi Limonis recent. f℥iij ad f℥vj.
To be taken three times a day.

In Acute Rheumatism.—Dr. Babington.

29. ℞ Succi Limonis, f℥iv.
Cort. Limon, recentis conc. ℥ss.
Potassæ Nitrat. ʒj.
Sacchari Albi, ℥iv.
Aquæ ferventis, Oiij.
Cool, and strain.

As a common drink in Fevers, &c.—Mr. Brande.

30. ℞ Fruct. Limonis, No. 1.
Aquæ frigidæ, Oiss.
Syrupi, f℥ij.
Make into a lemonade for a general drink.

In Fevers and Inflammations.

31. ℞ Succi Limonis recentis, ℥j.
Olei Amygdalæ dulcis, ℥iss.
Syrupi Althææ, ℥ss. Mix: a spoonful every three hours.

In Obstinate Diarrhœa.—STEINHEIM.

32. ℞ Succi Limonis, f℥j–ij.
Aquæ, f℥xv. Make an injection.

In Alkaline Leucorrhœa.—Dr. ASHWELL.

ACIDUM GALLICUM. ACIDUM TANNICUM. See GALLÆ.

ACIDUM HYDROCYANICUM. *Hydrocyanic or Prussic Acid.*

Hydrocyanic acid is a direct sedative, and so highly poisonous, that a single grain of the pure acid is sufficient to destroy life. The diluted acid, in medicinal doses, allays irritation, reduces the pulse, and lowers the sensibility of the nervous system. It is used to quiet irritable and spasmodic cough, to allay vomiting and nervous palpitations, and to relieve pain and quiet the system in neuralgic, rheumatic, and other painful affections. *Externally*, it is used in lotions, to allay itching in some cutaneous diseases. *Inhaled*, it has been tried in some affections of the lungs.

The usual dose of Acidum Hydrocyanicum Dilutum, L., is from 3 to 5 minims. That of the new DUB. Ph. is, perhaps, intended to be of the same strength, but its percentage of real acid is not stated. The process yields a product which is variable, but usually stronger than that of L. Acidum hydrocyanicum, E., is stronger than L., 3 minims of the former being equal to about 5 of the latter. *Acidum Hydrocyanicum* (*Scheelii*) is often met with in prescriptions; but there is no standard strength for it, and it possesses no advantage over the pharmacopœia preparation. The average strength, as procured from various manufacturers, seems to be about twice that of L. *Acidum Hydrocyanicum* of the United States and Prussian pharmacopœias contains, like that of L., 2 per centum of real acid.

Potassii Cyanidum has the same properties and uses as hydrocyanic acid. Dose, from one-eighth to one-fourth of a grain.

The latter dose is equal to 5 minims of diluted Hydrocyanic Acid, L.

33. ℞ Acidi Hydrocyanici dil. ♏j.
Aquæ destillatæ, f℥vij.
Syrupi simplicis, f℥j.
Mix: make a draught to be taken every second hour, until the symptoms disappear.

In Gastric Irritability, Nervous Palpitation, &c.—Dr. Neligan.

34. ℞ Acidi Hydrocyanici dil. ♏iv.
Aquæ destillatæ, f℥j.
Syrupi Aurantii, f℥ss.
Mix: make a draught to be taken every fourth hour.

Mr. Brande.

35. ℞ Acidi Hydrocyanici dil ♏ij.
Misturæ Amygdalæ, f℥ij. Mix: make a draught.

Dr. Joy.

36. ℞ Acidi Hydrocyan. dil. ♏xij.
Aquæ destillatæ, f℥vj.
Syrupi Papaveris, f℥iij.
Mix: take a large spoonful every second hour.

In Consumptive Cough, &c.—Dr. Granville.

37. ℞ Acidi Hydrocyanici dil. ♏v.
Misturæ Amygdalæ, f℥j.
Extracti Conii, gr. iij.
Mix: make a draught, to be taken twice or thrice a day.

Mr. Brande.

38. ℞ Misturæ Acaciæ, f℥j.
Aquæ destillatæ, f℥viss.
Syrupi Tolutani, f℥ss.
Acidi Hydrocy. diluti, gutt. xij.
Mix: a tablespoonful every three hours.

In Consumptive Cough.—Mr. S. G. Morton.

39. ℞ Potassæ Bicarbonatis, gr. xv.
Cocci Cacti, gr. viij.
Aquæ destillatæ, f℥vj. Rub up together, strain, and add
Acidi Hydrocyanici dil. ♏x.
Mix: a teaspoonful to be taken when the cough is troublesome.

In Hooping-Cough of Children.—Dr. Granville.

40. ℞ Acidi Hydrocyan. dil. ♏xxiv.
Bismuthi Nitratis,
Magnes. Carbonatis, ana ʒij.
Aquæ puræ ad f℥vj.
Mix: take a fluid ounce twice daily.

Dr. W. Budd.

41. ℞ Acidi Hydrocyanici, (Scheelii) ♏iss.
Sodæ Bicarbonatis, gr. xv.
Misturæ Camphoræ, f℥x.
Make a draught, to be taken three times a day, after meals.

Dr. CHAMBERS.

42. ℞ Acidi Hydrocyan. dil. ♏xij.
Aquæ Rosæ, f℥vss.
Syrupi Papaveris, f℥iij.
Mix: a teaspoonful every two or three hours.

In Croupy Cough, after Purgatives.—Dr. GRANVILLE.

43. ℞ Acidi Hydrocyan. dil. ♏v.
Spir. Ammoniæ fœtidi, f℥ss.
Tinct. Hyoscyami, ♏x.
Spiritus Anisi, f℥j.
Syrupi Aurantii, f℥ss.
Aquæ, f℥j.
Mix: take a teaspoonful thrice a day.

In Laryngismus Stridulus.—Dr. REID.

44. ℞ Misturæ Amygdalæ, f℥vss.
Acidi Hydrocyan. dil. f℥ss.
Tincturæ Opii, f℥ss.
Tinct. Lavand. comp. f℥ij.
Mix: make a mixture, of which take two tablespoonfuls every second or third hour.

In Gastrodynia with Spasms.—Dr. COPLAND.

45. ℞ Acidi Hydrocyanici dil. ♏iij
Creosoti, ♏iij.
Olei Terebinth. ♏x.
Mucil. Acaciæ, f℥j.
Aquæ Cinnamomi, f℥j.
Mix: take one-half for a dose, and, if necessary, repeat.

In Spasmodic Asthma.—Sir P. CRAMPTON.

46. ℞ Acidi Hydrocyanici dil. ♏iv.
Potas. Bicarbonatis, gr. x.
Syrupi Zingiberis, f℥ss.
Aquæ Anethi, f℥iss.
Mix: make a draught to be taken twice a day.

In Irritable and Acid Stomach.—Dr. DRUITT.

47. ℞ Acid. Hydrocyan. gtt. 32.
Liq. Mur. Morph. f℥iij.
Mist. Amygdalæ, f℥viij.
Mix: take a tablespoonful thrice daily.

In Painful Indigestion.—Dr. ROSS.

48. ℞ Acid. Hydrocyan. gtt. ij–iij.
Creosoti, gtt. j–iij.
Liq. Morph. Mur. gtt. xx.
Sodæ S.-Carb. gr. xx.
Aquæ, ℥iss. Mix: make a draught.

In Gastrodynia with Vomiting.—Dr. Ross.

49. ℞ Acidi Hydrocyanici, guttas v.
Aquæ calidæ, q. s.

Inhale the vapor by means of a suitable apparatus three times a day, lying down an hour after each; very gradually increase the dose to ten drops. After four or six weeks give steel and quinine.

In Hypertrophy of the Heart.—Dr. T. G. Hare.

50. ℞ Acidi Hydrocyanici diluti, f℥ij.
Aquæ destillatæ, f℥viij. Mix: make a lotion.

To allay Itching in Cutaneous Diseases.—Dr. Neligan.

51. ℞ Acidi Hydrocyanici dil. fʒiss.
Aquæ Rosæ, f℥viiss. Make a lotion.

For the same purpose.—Dr. A. T. Thomson.

52. ℞ Acidi Hydrocyanici diluti, ʒj–iv.
Decocti Malvæ (*vel* Althææ), lbj. Mix: make a lotion.

In Irritable Cutaneous Affections.—Dr. Joy.

53. ℞ Acidi Hydrocyanici dil. fʒiij.
Spirit. rectificati, f℥ss.
Aquæ distillatæ, f℥vij.

Make a lotion, to be applied with lint, covered with oiled silk.

In Impetigo (after the scabs have been removed by fomentations, &c). Mr. Plumbe.

54. ℞ Acidi Hydrocyanici diluti, fʒij.
Misturæ Amygdalæ, f℥viij. Make a lotion.

In Itching Cutaneous Diseases.—Dr. Hooper.

55. ℞ Liq. Ammoniæ Acetatis, f℥ij.
Acidi Hydrocyanici dil. fʒj
Tinct. Digitalis, fʒiij.
Aquæ Rosæ, f℥v.

Make a lotion: apply twice a day to the parts affected, by means of a small sponge.

In Pruriginous Diseases of old persons.—Dr. A. T. Thomson.

56. ℞ Acidi Hydrocyanici diluti, f℥j.
Liquoris Potassæ, fʒij.
Misturæ Amygdalæ, f℥viij. Mix: make a lotion.

In Lichen.—Dr. Burgess.

57. ℞ Acidi Hydrocyanici dil. f℈iss.
Aquæ destillatæ, f℥vijss.
Plumbi Acetatis, gr. xvj.
Spirit. rectificati, f℈ij. Make a lotion.

To allay Itching in Cutaneous Affections.—Dr. A. T. THOMSON.

58. ℞ Acidi Hydrocyanici dil. f℈ij.
Aquæ destillatæ, f℈vj.
Mix: to be applied by means of a camel-hair pencil.

In Acute Rheumatism.—Dr. H. W. FULLER.

59. ℞ Acidi Hydrocyanici diluti, f℈ss.
Sodæ Bicarbonatis, ℈ij.
Lactis vac. f℥viij. Mix: make a lotion.

In Milk-scall.—Dr. A. T. THOMSON.

60. ℞ Acidi Hydrocyanici dil. ℈ij.
Hydrargyri Bichloridi, gr. ij.
Emulsio. Amygd. Amaræ, f℥vj. Mix: make a lotion.

In Chronic Eruptions with Itching.—Dr. BURGESS.

61. ℞ Potassii Cyanidi, gr. j.
Aquæ destillatæ, f℥iijss.
Syrupi Limonum, f℥ss.
Mix, and divide into eight draughts, of which take one for a dose.

As a substitute for Hydrocyanic Acid.—Mr. DONOVAN.

62. ℞ Potassii Cyanidi, gr. j.
Amyli pulveris,
Syrupi Acaciæ, ana q. s.
Mix well, and divide into 4 pills. Take one every sixth hour.

In Convulsive Dyspnœa.—BAILLY.

63. ℞ Potassii Cyanidi, gr. xij.
Mist. Amygdalæ, f℥vj. Make a lotion.

In Itching Eruptions, Lichen, &c.—LOUIS.

64. ℞ Potassii Cyanidi, gr. iij.
Aquæ destillatæ, f℥j. Mix: to be applied with compresses.

To ease Rheumatic and Neuralgic pains.—LOMBARD.

65. ℞ Potassii Cyanidi, gr. xv.
Aquæ destillatæ, ℥iij.
Dissolve, and form a lotion. (Folds of linen dipped in this to be applied to the seat of pain, and renewed frequently, taking care that none of the solution enters the mouth.)

In frontal Neuralgia.—TROUSSEAU and REVEIL.

66. ℞ Cyanidi Potassii, gr. iij.
Aq. Belladonnæ, dest. ℥j. Make an eye-wash.

In extreme Photophobia, &c.—CUNIER.

67. ℞ Cyanidi Potassii, gr. xij.
Olei Amygdalæ, ʒij.
Ung. Ceræ Albæ, ℥ij. Make an ointment.

In Lichen.—Dr. Burgess.

68. ℞ Potassii Cyanidi, gr. j. ad iv.
Olei Amygdalæ, ʒij.
Cerati Galeni (cold cream), ℥ij.
Mix: make an ointment.

In Neuralgic pains.—M. Cazenave.

ACIDUM HYDROCHLORICUM. ACIDUM NITRICUM. ACIDUM NITRO-HYDROCHLORICUM. *Hydrochloric or Muriatic, Nitric, and Nitro-muriatic Acids.*

These are all tonic, in small doses properly diluted. Externally they are caustic and detergent.

Hydrochloric acid is refrigerant, tonic, antiseptic, and vermifuge. The diluted acid is used in malignant typhus and scarlet fever; in cases of phosphatic urinary deposits; and sometimes in syphilis. It is also used as a gargle in malignant sore throat, &c.

Nitric acid is tonic and antiseptic; in chronic hepatitis; in indigestion, especially when connected with mixed urinary deposits of uric acid and the phosphates; and in syphilitic affections in broken-down or scrofulous constitutions. It has also been found useful in hooping-cough, and in asthma. Dr. Arnoldi prescribes it diluted to the strength of lemon juice, and sweetened; in this way he has given as much as a drachm of the strong acid *per diem* to a child of two years old.

The *red fuming nitric acid*, commonly termed nitrous acid, is sometimes preferred, particularly in cholera.

Strong nitric acid is used locally as a caustic to warts, sloughing phagedænæ, hæmorrhoidal excrescences, &c.; and in a more diluted form to superficial ulcers which are indisposed to cicatrize, and to offensive ulcers, and caries of the bones. The vapor of nitric acid is disinfectant; but probably inferior to chlorine.

Nitro-hydrochloric (nitro-muriatic) acid is thought to act more decidedly on the liver than the preceding, especially as applied to the skin by foot-bath and sponging. It is also used in syphilitic and mercurial cachexia, cutaneous diseases, &c.

The preparations and doses are as folllows:

Acidum Hydrochloricum purum, 5 to 30 minims.
——————— *dilutum*, L 30 to 60 minims.
Julepum Acidum [Guy's H.], *ad libitum*.
Acidum Nitricum Dilutum, L. 10 to 40 minims.
Acidum Nitro-muriaticum [nitro-hydrochloricum], 5 to 20 minims.
——————— *dilutum*, 10 to 40 minims.
——— *Nitricum alcoholisatum*, 30 minims.

69. ℞ Acidi Hydrochlorici, ʒj.
Aquæ destillatæ, f℥xiv.
Syrupi, f℥ij.
Mix: take two fluid ounces frequently.

In Typhus, Scarlatina, and Angina.—Dr. Gregory.

70. ℞ Acidi Muriatici [hydrochlorici], fʒj.
Decocti Hordei, Oj.
Sacchari Albi, ℥ss.
Make a mixture. Take from two to four fluid ounces twice or three times a day.

In Typhoid Fever, and White Deposits from Urine.
Dr. Copland.

71. ℞ Acidi Hydrochlorici, fʒj.
Aquæ destillatæ, f℥vj.
Syrupi Mori, f℥j. Mix: write
A tablespoonful every four or five hours.

In Malignant Fevers and Exanthemata of Children.—Dr. Ure.

72. ℞ Acidi Hydrochlorici, fʒij.
Aquæ destillatæ, f℥viij.
Syrupi Rubi Idæi, f℥ij.
Mix: a tablespoonful every hour in water or gruel.

In Fevers, Phlebitis, &c.—Dr. Reid.

73. ℞ Acidi Hydrochlorici diluti, fʒij.
Infusi Quassiæ, f℥viiss.
Syr. Aurantii, f℥ss.
Make a mixture. Take a fourth portion, twice a day.

To prevent the generation of worms, after purgatives.
Dr. Paris.

74. ℞ Acidi Hydrochlorici, fʒij.
Infusi Calumbæ, f℥vss.
Tincturæ Lupuli, f℥ss.
Make a mixture. Take a sixth part for a dose.

In Indigestion with Phosphatic Diathesis.—Dr. Hooper.

75. ℞ Acidi Hydrochlorici, ʒij.
Ætheris Acetici, ʒss.
Decocti Althææ, ℥v.
Syrupi Rubi Idæi, ℥ij. Mix: write
A tablespoonful every two hours.

PHŒBUS.

76. ℞ Acidi Hydrochlorici diluti, ♏xx.
Infusi Aurantii, comp. fʒix.
Syrupi Zingiberis, fʒj.
Make a draught, to be taken daily two hours before dinner.

In the above cases.—Dr. PARIS.

77. ℞ Acidi Hydrochlorici, fʒij.
Sodii Chloridi, ℥ss.
Aquæ destillatæ, f℥iv.
Make a solution. Take a teaspoonful in a wineglassful of water.

In Anorexia.—Dr. CULLEN.

78. ℞ Decocti Cydonii, f℥vij.
Syrupi Mori, f℥j.
Acidi Hydrochlorici, ♏xv–xxx. Make a gargle.

In Sore Throat.—R. G. HOLLAND.

79. ℞ Acidi Hydrochlorici, fʒiss.
Decocti Cinchonæ,
Infusi Rosæ comp. ana f℥iiiss.
Mellis Rosæ, f℥j. Mix: make a gargle.

In Malignant Sore Throat.—Mr. BRANDE.

80. ℞ Acid. Hydrochlor. ♏xv.
Infusi Cinchonæ, f℥iv.
Mellis Rosæ, f℥j. M. Make a gargle.

In Relaxed and Putrid Sore Throat.—TROUSSEAU & REVEIL.

81. ℞ Acidi Hydrochlorici, fʒj–iss.
Syrupi Rosæ gallicæ, f℥j.
Decocti Hordei, f℥vij. Mix: make a gargle.

Dr. JOY.

82. ℞ Acidi Hydrochlorici, ʒj.
Infusi Cinchonæ, ℥vij.
Mellis Despumati, ℥j. Make a gargle.

In Putrid Sore Throat, Chronic Quinsy, &c.—RADIUS.

83. ℞ Infusi Salviæ, ℥viij.
Acidi Hydrochlorici, ʒiss.
Syrupi Mori, ℥ij. Mix: make a gargle.

In Malignant Sore Throat.—WENDT.

84. ℞ Acidi Hydrochlorici, fʒss.
Infusi Rosæ comp. f℥iiiss.
Mellis Rosæ, f℥ss. Mix: make a gargle.

Dr. AINSLIE.

85. ℞ Infusi Rosæ comp. f℥viss.
Acidi Muriatici dil. ℈ij.
Tinct. Capsici, fʒiss.
Mellis, fʒiij.
Make a gargle to be used frequently.

Dr. COPLAND.

86. ℞ Acidi Hydrochlorici, fʒj.
Mellis,
Aquæ Rosæ, ana f℥j.
Mix: make a thick syrup to be applied to the gums, three or four times a day.

In Scorbutic Ulceration of the Gums.—Mr. BRANDE.

87. ℞ Acidi Hydrochlorici,
Mellis, ana partes æquales. Mix.

To touch the Fauces with in Diptherite.—BRETTONNEAU.

88. ℞ Acidi Hydrochlorici, ʒij.
Syrupi Mori, ℥ij.
Mix: make a mouth-wash, to be applied to the affected parts.

In Stomatitis.—WENDT.

89. ℞ Mel. Rosæ, ʒx.
Acidi Hydrochlorici, ♏xx.
Syrupi Rhœados, ℥ij. Mix: make into a thick syrup.

90. ℞ Acidi Muriatici, ʒj.
Aquæ destillatæ, ℥ij. Mix: make a lotion.

In Chilblains, Lepra, &c.—BERAL.

91. ℞ Acidi Hydrochlorici, gutt. iij. ad vj.
Aquæ destillatæ, ℥j.
Make an eye-wash, to be applied frequently.

For removing particles of iron from the Eye.—SICHEL.

92 ℞ Acidi Hydrochlorici, gutt. viij.
Aquæ puræ, f℥iv. Mix: make an injection.

R. G. HOLLAND.

93. ℞ Acidi Hydrochlorici, ♏x.
Vini Opii, ♏xx.
Decocti Hordei, q. s. Make an injection.
To be carefully injected into the bladder, when coated with mucus and phosphates.

Dr. G. BIRD.

94. ℞ Acidi Hydrochlorici, ℥ss.
Unguenti Sambuci, ʒx.
Make a liniment, to be applied twice a day.

In Porrigo.—Dr. URE.

95. ℞ Acidi Muriatici,
Ung. Althææ, ana ℥ss.
Ung. Juniperi, ℥ij.
Mix: make an ointment, to be applied twice a day.

In Tinea Capitis.—HENKE.

96. ℞ Acidi Nitrici diluti, fʒij.
Syrupi Aurantii, f℥ij.
Aquæ, f℥xiv. Make a mixture. Dose, f℥iv.

Dr. HAMILTON.

97. ℞ Acidi Nitrici, fʒss.
Decocti Hordei, Oj.
Mix: a wineglassful to be taken three times a day.

In Papulous Eruptions.—Dr. BURGESS.

98. ℞ Acidi Nitrici diluti, fʒiss.
Aquæ, f℥xxiv.
Sacchari, ℥iss.
Make a mixture. Take f℥iij three times a day, by means of a glass tube.

In Typhoid Fevers, Chronic Hepatitis, and secondary Syphilis.

Dr. JOY.

99. ℞ Acidi Nitrici diluti, fʒij.
Spir. Ætheris Nitrici, fʒij.
Syrupi, f℥ss.
Aquæ, f℥viiss.
Mix: take a sixth part three times a day.

In Dyspepsia, with foul tongue and inactive liver.—Dr. DRUITT.

100. ℞ Acidi Nitrici diluti, fʒj.
Decocti Hordei, Oj. Mix: the whole to be taken daily.

In Coloration of the skin from taking nitrate of silver.

Dr. URE.

101. ℞ Acidi Nitrici dil. fʒj
Aquæ destillatæ, f℥xivss.
Syrupi Aurantii, f℥iss.
Make a mixture, to be taken daily, through a glass tube, in proportionate doses.

Dr. PEREIRA.

102. ℞ Acidi Nitrici diluti, fʒij.
Infusi Chiraytæ, ℥viiss.
Mix: dose, f℥jss three times a day.

As a Tonic, when the bowels are irritable.—Dr. DRUITT.

103. ℞ Acidi Nitrici dil. ♏xxx.
Decocti Cinchonæ, f℥iss.
Make a draught, to be taken every fourth hour.

In Dropsy with Diseased Liver (after a purgative).

Mr. J. S. WILKINSON.

104. ℞ Acidi Nitrici diluti, fʒj.
Aquæ destillatæ, f℥vss.
Extr. Hyoscyami, ʒss.
Syrupi Zingiberis, fʒiij. Mix: take fʒj.

Dr. COPLAND.

105. ℞ Acidi Nitrici diluti, f℥iss.
Aquæ destillatæ, Oiss.
Spir. Lavandulæ comp. f℥iv.
Syrupi Aurantii, f℥iss.
Mix: dose, a wineglassful three or four times a day.

In Secondary Syphilis, Chronic Hepatitis, Chronic Indolent Ulcers of the Leg, obstinate Cutaneous Diseases, &c.

Dr. M. RYAN.

106. ℞ Infusi Cascarillæ, f℥vj.
Potassæ Nitratis, ʒj.
Acidi Nitrici diluti, fʒiss.
Tinct. Opii, fʒj.
Make a mixture: take two tablespoonfuls three times a day.

In Oxaluria.—Dr. ALBRIDGE.

107. ℞ Acidi Nitrici rubri, fʒj.
Aquæ Menthæ piperitæ (*vel* Misturæ Camphoræ), f℥j.
Tincturæ Opii, ♏xx. Mix.
A fourth part to be taken in a cupful of gruel every three or four hours.

In Asiatic Cholera.—Mr. HOME.

108. ℞ Acidi Nitrici, ♏xij.
Aquæ destillatæ, f℥xvj. Make a lotion.

To Indolent Ulcers.—SIR E. HOPE.

109. ℞ Acidi Nitrici diluti, fʒij.
Aquæ puræ, Oj. Make a lotion.

To Indolent and Fetid Ulcers, and Caries of Bones.

Dr. A. T. THOMSON.

110. ℞ Rosæ petalæ, ℈j.
Aquæ ferventis, f℥viij.
Acidi Nitrici dil. fʒiiss.
Macerate and strain; and make a lotion.

In Lichen and Chronic Eczema.—Dr. HOOPER.

111. ℞ Acidi Nitrici diluti, fʒj.
Acidi Hydrochlorici dil. fʒss.
Aquæ destillatæ, f℥viij.
Mix: take two spoonfuls three times a day.

In Irritable Bladder, with Alkaline Urine.—Mr. COULSON.

112. ℞ Acidi Hydrochl. diluti,
Acidi Nitrici diluti, ana fʒij.
Tinct. Gentianæ comp. f℥iiiss. Make a mixture.
A teaspoonful to be taken in a wineglassful of water twice a day.

Mr. E. WILSON.

113. ℞ Acidi Nitrici diluti,
Acidi Hydrochl. diluti, ana ♏x.
Infusi Quassiæ, f℥iss.
Mix; make a draught to be taken three times a day.

In desquamative Nephritis, with general Dropsy.

Dr. G. Johnson.

114. ℞ Acidi Nitrici, ♏xij.
Acidi Hydrochlorici, ♏xij.
Aquæ Menthæ pip. f℥vss.
Syrupi Aurantii, f℥ss. Mix: one-sixth part for a dose.

Dr. Hooper.

115. ℞ Acidi Nitrici, fℨj.
Acidi Hydrochlorici, fℨiij.
Misturæ Camphoræ, f℥iiiss.
Mix: take a teaspoonful in f℥iss of infusion of chamomile flowers, three times a day; and take every night five grains of the compound calomel pill.*

In Oxaluria, with Dyspepsia, &c.—Dr. G. Bird.

116. ℞ Acidi Nitrici diluti,
Acidi Hydrochlorici diluti, ana fℨiij.
Syrupi Aurantii, f℥j.
Aquæ fl. Aurantii, f℥j.
Aquæ destillatæ, f℥xiiiss.
Make a mixture: take a wineglassful three or four times a day.

Dr. Druitt.

117. ℞ Acidi Nitrici diluti,
Acidi Hydrochlorici dil. ana ♏v.
Inf. Serpentariæ, ℥j.
Make a draught, to be taken three times a day.

In Oxaluria, with Debility and Irritability.—Dr. G. Bird.

118. ℞ Acidi Nitrici dil.
Acidi Hydrochlorici dil. ana ♏v.
Misturæ Gentianæ comp. fℨx.
Make a draught, to be taken three times a day.

Tonic and Laxative.

119. ℞ Acidi Nitrici, ♏xij.
Acidi Hydrochlorici, ♏xxiv.
Infusi Lupuli, f℥viij.
Mix: take a wineglassful three times during the day, and every night take the following pill.
Hydrarg. cum Creta, gr. iss.
Ipecacuanhæ p. gr. j. Make a pill.

In Oxaluria, &c.—Dr. G. Bird.

* Plummer's Pill.

120. ℞ Acidi Hydrochlor. diluti,
Acidi Nitrici diluti, ana ♏xxx.
Tinct. Camphoræ comp. f℥iv.
Tinct. Aurantii, f℥ss.
Syrupi Sarsæ, f℥ss.
Aquæ Rosæ, f℥vj.
Mix: take two tablespoonfuls twice a day.

H. F.

121. ℞ Acidi Hydrochlorici diluti,
Acidi Nitrici diluti, ana f℥j.
Extracti Taraxaci, ℥j.
Infusi Gentianæ comp. f℥vij.
Mix: make a mixture, of which take two tablespoonfuls twice daily, before taking food.

In Dysmenorrhœa and Amenorrhœa.—Dr. E. Rigby.

122. ℞ Acidi Nitrici diluti,
Acidi Hydrochlorici, ana f℥iss.
Syrupi Zingiberis, f℥ss.
Tinct. Aurantii, f℥ix.
Mix: take a teaspoonful in a wineglassful of water, on an empty stomach, twice every day.

B. Travers, Jun.

123. ℞ Acidi Nitrici dil. f℥ss.
Acidi Hydrochlor. dil. f℥j.
Spir. Ætheris Nitrici, f℥ss.
Syrupi Sarsæ, f℥j.
Aquæ puræ, f℥viss.
Mix: take two spoonfuls three times a day.

Alterative.—Dr. Hooper.

124. ℞ Acidi Hydrochlorici diluti,
Acidi Nitrici diluti, ana f℥j.
Liquoris Taraxaci, f℥j.
Infusi Cinchonæ flavæ, f℥vij.
Make a mixture, of which take two tablespoonfuls twice a day, before taking food.

In Dysmenorrhœa.—Dr. E. Rigby.

125. ℞ Acidi Nitrici, f℥ij.
Acidi Hydrochlorici, f℥iij.
Aquæ destillatæ, f℥viij. Mix.
For sponging the body, add f℥iij. of the above to Oj. of warm water, and apply it for a quarter of an hour.

As a foot-bath, add 6 ounces of the acid to 2 gallons of water in a deep wooden or earthen vessel; and while the feet are in the bath (the temperature of which should be 96° or 98°) the inside of the legs and thighs and arms, and the right side over the liver, should be sponged alternately. This should be continued for fifteen minutes, morning and evening. An aperient draught of salts in a bitter infusion should be taken every second morning.

In Chronic Affections of the Liver.—Mr. J. R. MARTIN.

126. ℞ Acidi Nitro-muriatici, ʒj.
Adipis preparati, ℥j.
Mix with a *wooden* spatula, and add
Olei Terebinth. rect. ʒij. Mix : make a liniment.

As a Rubefacient in Chest Affections.—Dr. GRAVES.

ACIDUM LACTICUM. *Lactic Acid.*

Lactic acid increases the appetite and promotes digestion, in cases of deficiency of the acid of the gastric juice ; it has also been recommended in the phosphatic diathesis. It is obtained as a syrupy liquid. Dose, ♏x.—xxx. diluted with water. *Trochisci Acidi Lactici* (Magendie's), 6 in the day.

127. ℞ Acidi Lactici, ʒj.
Aquæ, Oj.
Syrupi simp. (*vel* Aurantii), ℥j.
A wineglass several times a day.

In simple Indigestion.—MAGENDIE.

ACIDUM MURIATICUM. See ACIDUM HYDROCHLORICUM, &c.

ACIDUM OXALICUM. *Oxalic Acid.*

Oxalic Acid, or Acid of Sugar, is well known as one of the most rapid and fatal poisons. On the Continent it is used as a refrigerant, in very small doses, and is supposed to be useful in some inflammatory conditions of mucous membranes. Dose, ½ grain to 1 grain.

Salt of sorrel and the artificial superoxalate of potash possess the same poisonous and remedial properties.

128. ℞ Acidi Oxalici, gr. viij.
Misturæ Acaciæ, f℥iij.
Syrupi, f℥j.
Mix: a spoonful to be taken several times a day.

In Inflammation of the Fauces and Digestive Tube.

M. NARDO.

129. ℞ Acidi Oxalici, gr. iv.
Syrupi Limonis, f℥ss.
Aquæ, f℥viiss.
Mix: make a mixture, of which take two tablespoonfuls every third hour.
In Inflammation of the Stomach.—Dr. NELIGAN.

[For Trochisci Acidi Oxalici, and Troch. Potassæ Superoxalatis, see "Pocket Formulary."]

The effects of a poisonous dose are best combated by the *immediate* administration of chalk, whiting, or magnesia, in water, or any demulcent liquid.

ACIDUM PHOSPHORICUM.

Phosphoric Acid is employed as a refrigerant and general tonic, like the mineral acids, but is preferred to them in some cases; it is more efficacious in quenching thirst in diabetes, agrees better with the stomach, and is thought to possess peculiar efficacy when there is a tendency to earthy deposits in the urine, or to exostosis, or ossification of the arteries; in caries, &c. Dose of *Acidum Phosphoricum Dilutum*, 20 to 40 minims.

130. ℞ Acidi Phosphorici diluti, ʒj.
Decocti Hordei, Oij. To be used as an ordinary beverage.
In Diabetes.

131. ℞ Acidi Phosphorici diluti, ʒj.
Decocti Salep. (*vel* Avenæ), ℥vj.
Syrupi Rubi Idæi (*vel* Mori), ℥ss.
Mix: a spoonful every two hours.
In Caries, Salivation, and Hæmorrhage.—WENDT.

132. ℞ Acidi Phosphorici diluti, f℥ss.
Infusi Calumbæ, ℥viiss.
Tinct. Cardam. comp. f℥ss.
Make a mixture, of which take f℥j three times a day.
In Phosphatic Deposits from Urine.—Dr. NELIGAN.

133. ℞ Acidi Phosphorici diluti,
Acidi Hydrochlorici dil. ana fʒiss.
Tinct. Calumbæ, ʒix.
Mix: take a teaspoonful twice a day in a wineglassful of water.
In the same.

134. ℞ Acidi Phosphorici dil. f℥ss.
Infusi Uvæ Ursi, f℥iss.
Make a draught, to be taken twice a day.

In Mucous Urine, with copious earthy excretions.

Dr. G. BIRD.

135. ℞ Acidi Phosphorici dil. f℥ss.
Infusi Chimaphilæ, f℥iss.
Make a draught, to be taken twice a day.

In the same case, when the Kidneys are inactive.

Dr. G. BIRD.

136. ℞ Acidi Phosphorici dil. f℥ss.
Inf. Pareiræ, f℥iss. Make a draught.

In the same, with opaque mucus.—Dr. G. BIRD.

137. ℞ Acidi Phosphorici dil. f℥ss.
Infusi Buchu, f℥iss. Make a draught.

In the same, with Inaction of the Skin and Kidneys.

Dr. G. BIRD.

138. ℞ Acidi Phosphorici sicci,
Assafœtidæ,
Pulv. rad. Althææ, ana ʒij.
Aquæ, q. s.
Make into pills of four grains each. Three pills three times a day.

In Caries.—RUST.

139. ℞ Acidi Phosphorici sicci,
Pulv. Cinchonæ,
Extracti Cascarillæ, ana ℥j.
Testæ præparatæ, gr. xv.
Ferri pulverati, gr. xlv.
Mix with mucilage of gum arabic a sufficient quantity to form one hundred and twenty (120) pills. Five pills to be taken three times a day.

In Seminal Weakness.—WURTZER.

140. ℞ Acidi Phosphorici dil. ʒiv.
Aquæ puræ, ℥ivss. Make a lotion.

In Caries.—Dr. A. T. THOMSON.

ACIDUM SALICULOSUM. *Saliculous Acid.*

This acid is obtained by dissolving 1 part of salicine in 10 of water, mixing it with 1 part of bichromate of potash, and 2½ of oil of vitriol, diluted with 10 of water, distilling, and rectifying the oily acid from chloride of calcium. It exists also in the volatile oil of Meadow Sweet, *Spiræa Ulmaria.* It is diuretic, irritant, and narcotic, and is used in various dropsical affections, particularly in those connected with heart disease, where from the weakened state of that organ digitalis would be improper. It is administered in the form of a *tincture*, containing 1 drachm of the acid in 1 ounce of proof spirit; or of a *syrup*, made by adding 45 drops of the tincture to 1 ounce of simple syrup. By saturating the acid with potash or soda, and evaporating, salts of these alkalies are obtained which have the same effects as the acid more certainly and powerfully.

141. ℞ Tincturæ Acidi Saliculosi, gtt. xx.
Syrupi Menthæ piperitæ, ℥j.
Aquæ Hyssopi, f℥vj.
Mix: a spoonful to be taken every hour.

In Dropsy.—M. Hannon.

142. ℞ Syrupi Acidi Saliculosi, ℥j.
Aquæ Hyssopi, ℥v. Mix: as the last.

143. ℞ Potassii *vel* Sodii Salicylidi, ʒss.
Extracti Graminis (*vel* Tarax.), q. s.
Make into a hundred and twenty (120) pills. Take from two to five pills in the day.

In Dropsies.—M. Hannon.

144. ℞ Potassii *vel* Sodii Salicylidi, ʒss.
Sacchari Lactis pulv. ʒiv.
Mix well, and divide into sixty powders. Two to four packets in the day.

In Dropsies.—M. Hannon.

ACIDUM SULPHURICUM. *Sulphuric Acid.*

The concentrated acid (Oil of Vitriol) is a powerful escharotic, rapidly disorganizing the parts with which it comes in contact, and is consequently an energetic corrosive poison. Largely diluted, it is administered as an antiseptic and refrigerant in typhoid fevers; as a tonic in general debility, and in weakness of the digestive organs attended with alkaline pyrosis; as an astringent in hæmorrhages and colliquative sweats. Lately it has been used with remarkable success in many cases of epidemic diarrhœa and cholera. It is also given in some chronic cutaneous affections attended with troublesome itching; in hiccough; in chronic catarrhal diseases, &c.

The dose of the diluted acid (*Acidum Sulphuricum Dilutum,*

L.) is from 10 to 20 or 30 minims; of *Acidum Sulphuricum Aromaticum*, 5 to 15 minims.

Externally, the strong acid is used alone, carefully applied, as a caustic; or formed into a paste with saffron (*Causticum Sulphuricum*). As a rubefacient, it is combined with lard (*Unguentum Acidi Sulphurici*), or with oils (*Linimentum Ac. Sulph. Compositum*). With a large quantity of water it is used as a lotion in some skin diseases, and in injections.

145. ℞ Acidi Sul. dil. f℥ss.
Syrup. simp. ℥ij.
Aquæ, ℥xxxij.
M. (*Mineral Lemonade*, to be taken as a common drink.)

In cases requiring Mineral Acids.—TROUSSEAU and REVEIL.

146. ℞ Acidi Sulphurici, (by weight) ʒj.
Aquæ puræ, ℥xxxij.
Syrupi simplicis, ℥ij. Mix: to be taken by small cupfuls.

As a preventive of Lead Colic.—M. MARTIN SOLON.

147. ℞ Acidi Sulphurici diluti, fʒij.
Aquæ destillatæ, f℥vj.
Mix: take f℥jss immediately, and repeat in doses of f℥j after each liquid evacuation.

In Epidemic Diarrhœa.—Mr. GRIFFITH.

148. ℞ Acidi Sulphurici diluti, ʒij.
Aquæ puræ, f℥vj.
Mix: take f℥j after each liquid evacuation.

In the same.—Dr. H. W. FULLER.

149. ℞ Sacchari albi, ʒiv.
Acidi Sulphurici diluti, ʒij.
Tinct. Cardamomi comp. fʒiv.
Aquæ Menthæ pip. ad f℥vj.
Mix: take a fourth part every fourth hour.

In the same.—Mr. E. SHEPHERD.

150. ℞ Sacchari albi, ʒiv.
Acidi Sulphurici diluti, fʒiss.
Tinct. Cardamomi co. fʒiij.
Liq. Morphiæ Bimeconatis, ♏xl.
Misturæ Camphoræ, f℥vss.
Mix: a fourth part every four hours.

In Diarrhœa, with Vomiting (English Cholera).
Mr. E. SHEPHERD.

151. ℞ Acidi Sulphurici diluti, ♏xv.
Infusi Rosæ comp. f℥iss.
Syrupi, fʒj. Mix: make a draught.

In Hæmorrhage.—Dr. JOY.

152. ℞ Acidi Sulphurici diluti, f℥iv.
Syrupi Aurantii, f℥iss.
Aquæ Cinnamomi, f℥j.
Mix: a teaspoonful to be taken twice a day in a glass of water.

Dr. J. CLARK.

153. ℞ Acidi Sulphurici diluti, f℥j.
Syrupi Aurantii, f℥vj.
Aquæ puræ, f℥viiss.
Mix: a sixth portion to be taken three times a day.

In Debility, with profuse Perspiration.—Dr. DRUITT.

154. ℞ Acidi Sulphurici diluti, f℥ss to f℥j.
Syrupi Mori, f℥j.
Aquæ puræ, f℥iv. Mix: a tablespoonful three times a day.

In the advanced stage of Inflammatory and Febrile disorders of Children. Dr. URE.

155. ℞ Infusi Rosæ comp. f℥x.
Acidi Sulphurici diluti, ♏xxx.
Syrupi, f℥j.
Mix: make a draught, to be taken every hour.

In Hæmoptysis.—Dr, G. GREGORY.

156. ℞ Acidi Sulphurici dil. f℥ij.
Magnesiæ Sulphatis, ℥vj.
Infusi Rosæ comp. ℥vj.
Make a mixture, of which take f℥j every fourth hour.

In Epistaxis.—Mr. DAVIS.

157. ℞ Acidi Sulphurici diluti, ♏v–xv.
Infusi Cascarillæ, f℥x.
Syrupi Aurantii, f℥j.
Make a draught, to be taken three times a day.

Tonic.—Dr. DRUITT.

158. ℞ Infusi Rosæ comp. f℥vss.
Acidi Sulphurici dil. f℥ij.
Extracti Conii, gr. xij.
Syrupi Mori, f℥iij.
Make a mixture: take two tablespoonfuls every fourth hour.

In Hæmoptysis.—Dr. G. GREGORY.

159. ℞ Acidi Sulphurici diluti, ♏xl.
Spirit. Ætheris comp. f℥ij.
Sacchari albi, ℥ss.
Aquæ Menthæ vir. f℥vj.
Mix: take a fourth part four times a day.

As a Restorative after Illness.—Dr. DRUITT

160. ℞ Decocti Cinchonæ, f℥vj.
Acidi Sulphurici diluti, f℥iss.
Make a mixture: dose, a sixth part.

Tonic.—Dr. HOOPER

161. ℞ Infusi Cascarillæ, f℥iss.
Magnesiæ Sulphatis, ʒj.
Acidi Sulphurici dil. ♏xv.
Make a draught, to be taken twice or thrice a day.

Tonic and Laxative.—Mr. BRANDE.

162. ℞ Acidi Sulphurici diluti, f℥ss.
Syrupi Rhœados, f℥ij.
Tinct. Cardamomi, fʒij.
Make a mixture, of which take a teaspoonful every sixth hour, in some agreeable vehicle.

Dr. PEREIRA.

163. ℞ Acidi Sulphurici Aromatici, fʒiiss.
Syrupi Rosæ Gallicæ, fʒvss.
Aquæ destillatæ, f℥vij.
Mix: make a mixture; take an ounce every sixth hour.

In Passive Hæmorrhages and Colliquative Sweats.

Dr. NELIGAN.

164. ℞ Acidi Sulphurici Alcoholisati (*Eau de Rabel*), ʒss.
Aquæ puræ, ℥xij.
Syrupi simplicis, ℥ss. Mix: for a common drink.

In Low Fevers and Passive Hæmorrhages.—FRENCH HOSP.

165. ℞ Acidi Sulphurici,
Ætheris Nitrici, ana partes æquales.
Mix: take from five to ten drops in an ounce of water.

In Spasms, Hæmorrhages, &c.—VOGLER.

166. ℞ Decocti Hordei, f℥vij.
Mellis Rosæ, f℥j.
Acidi Sulphurici diluti, fʒss. vel. ♏xl.
Mix: make a gargle.

Mr. R. G. HOLLAND.

167. ℞ Acidi Sulph. ♏xv.
Syrupi simpl. ℥ss.
Aquæ, ℥iv. Mix: make a gargle.

In Relaxed Throat.—TROUSSEAU and REVEIL.

168. ℞ Mellis Optimi, ʒv.
Acidi Sulphurici (pondere), ℈j. Mix.
To be applied by means of a camel-hair pencil.

In Aphthæ.—Professor LIPPICH.

169. ℞ Acidi Sulphurici dil. fʒij.
Aquæ, Oj. Make a lotion.

In Prurigo.—Dr. GREGORY.

170. ℞ Acidi Sulphurici (by weight), ℥iv.
Acidi Acetici,
Spiritus rectificati, āā lb. ij. Mix.
Applied externally to foul ulcers, and to stop bleeding. Also 20 to 30 drops given internally in water.

Vulnerary, Styptic, Astringent.—CAMPANA.

171. ℞ Acidi Sulphurici, ʒiss.
Olei Terebinthinæ, ℥ss.
Olei Olivæ, ℥iss. Mix: make a liniment.
As a Counter-irritant.—Mr. PEARSON.

ACIDUM TARTARICUM. See ACIDUM CITRICUM.

ACIDUM TANNICUM. See GALLÆ.

ACONITUM. *Monkshood.*

Monkshood (the leaves and root of Aconitum Napellus, Nat. Ord. *Ranunculaceæ*) is a powerful poison. In medicinal doses it is anodyne, sedative, diuretic, and diaphoretic. It produces a sensation of numbness in the mouth and throat, and the parts to which it is applied. It is used, both topically and internally, to relieve neuralgic and rheumatic pains; and is also occasionally administered in hypertrophy of the heart, dropsy, consumption, gastralgia, &c. A slight increase in the quantity or frequency of the dose may be attended with fatal effects; it must therefore be exhibited with the greatest caution, and the state of the pulse ascertained before the dose is repeated. As there are several Tinctures of Aconite (the doses of which are stated below), it is of importance that the prescriber should indicate which he intends. The extract is of such variable strength, that its use requires especial caution. The following are the usual doses of the officinal preparations:

Extractum Aconiti, L. or E., $\frac{1}{2}$ grain to 2 grains.
——— *Alcohol.* U. S. & P., $\frac{1}{8}$ of a grain to $\frac{1}{3}$.
———, et *siccum*, PRUS. PH., 1 grain to 3 grains.
Succus Aconiti (*alcholisatus*) (less powerful than the tincture of the root).
Tinctura Aconiti, L. (from the root), 5 to 9 minims, but chiefly for outward use.
Tinctura Aconiti radicis, U. S., as L.
——— D., 4 to 7 minims.
——— Dr. FLEMING'S. 3 minims 3 times a day, as an anodyne, aneuralgic, and calmative; or 5 minims, repeated in not less than 4 hours, as an antiphlogistic.
Tinctura Aconiti rad. concentrata, TURNBULL'S, for outward use.
——— *foliorum*, U. S., 20 to 30 drops.
Aconitina, dose 1-120th to 1-50th gr.
Liquor Aconitinæ (Dr. HEADLAND), ♏v–xij (each drop contains 1-600th gr.).

Unguentum Aconitinæ (for outward use, made of several strengths). See below.

Lotio Aconitinæ (Dr. HEADLAND). See below.

Unguentum Aconiti, and Ung. Aconiti Ammoniatum, are also for outward use, in neuralgia, &c. *Aconitina*, the active principle of Aconite, is almost too powerful for internal administration. Its high price used to present an obstacle to its use in neuralgia. It may now be made more cheaply by Dr. Headland's process.

172. ℞ Tincturæ Aconiti (Fleming's), fʒj.
Sodæ Carbonatis, ʒiss.
Magnesiæ Sulphatis, ℥iss.
Aquæ destillatæ, f℥vj.

Make a mixture: a tablespoonful to be taken when the pain is urgent.

In Gastralgia.—Dr. FLEMING.

173. ℞ Tincturæ Aconiti (D.), ♏v.
Misturæ Camphoræ, f℥j.

Make a draught, to be taken every fourth hour until the suffering is mitigated. (Its effects must be carefully watched.)

In Acute Rheumatism and Neuralgia.—Dr. NELIGAN.

174. ℞ Extr. Aconiti Alcoholici, granum unum.
Pulveris Glycyrrhizæ, gr. xij.
Syrupi simplicis, q. s. Mix: make into six pills.

Dr. TURNBULL.

175. ℞ Extracti Aconiti, gr. j.
Antimonii Oxysulphureti, gr. j.
Magnesiæ, gr. x.

Mix: make a powder, one to be taken every four hours.

In Rheumatic Pains, &c.—VOGLER.

176. ℞ Extracti Aconiti, ʒss.
Vini Antim. Potassio-tart. ℥ss.

Mix: from 15 to 20 drops to be taken three times a day.

In Painful Gout, with Fever.—RUST.

177. ℞ Extracti Aconiti, gr. xx.
Tincturæ Guaiaci, ʒij.
Vini Colchici sem. ℥ss.

Mix: fifteen drops to be taken three times a day.

In Chronic Gout.—Dr. SOBERNHEIM.

178. ℞ Extr. Aconiti Alcoholici, gr. xv.
Extr. Taraxaci, gr. xv.
Pulv. Glycyrrhizæ, q. s.

Mix with great care, and divide the mass into forty pills, of which one or two may be taken morning and night.

In Papulous Affections of the Skin.—CAZENAVE.

179. ℞ Extracti Aconiti Alcoholici, gr. ij.
Myristicæ Adipis, gr. xviij.
Misturæ Acaciæ, q. s.

Make into a mass; divide into six pills, of which one may be taken every sixth hour.

In Chronic Rheumatism, &c.—Dr. NELIGAN.

180. ℞ Extracti Aconiti, gr. j.
Guaiaci Resinæ, gr. viij.
Olei Cajeputi, q. s.

Make into two pills; take one night and morning.

In Rheumatism, &c.—Dr. COPLAND.

181. ℞ Tincturæ Aconiti (Ph. L.), f℥x.
Linimenti Saponis, f℥vj.

Make a liniment, to be rubbed on the painful joint at bedtime.

Dr. A. T. THOMSON.

182. ℞ Tincturæ Aconiti,
Tincturæ Belladonnæ, ana f℥ij.
Aquæ Rosæ, f℥iv.

Mix: make an embrocation. Let f℥ij be rubbed over the sacrum, groins, &c.

In Threatened Abortion.—Dr. R. EADES.

183. ℞ Tincturæ Aconiti, f℥j.
Aquæ destillatæ, f℥j. Make an embrocation.

In Neuralgic Pains.—Dr. R. EADES.

184. ℞ Tincturæ Aconiti (Fleming's), f℥iv.
Extracti Belladonnæ, ℥ss.
Linim. Camphoræ comp. f℥iss. Make a liniment.

As a Counter-irritant and Sedative.—Dr. OLDHAM.

185. ℞ Linim. Saponis, ℥ij.
Tinct. Aconiti (Ph. L.), ℥j. Mix: make a liniment.

186. ℞ Extracti Aconiti, ℥j.
Liquoris Ammoniæ, gtt. viij.
Adipis præparati, ℥iij. Make an ointment.

In Old Rheumatic Pains, Neuralgia, &c.—Dr. A. TURNBULL.

187. ℞ Aconitinæ puræ, gr. ij.
Cerat. Cetacei, ℥j.

Mix with the greatest care, and make an ointment, of which rub in a moderate portion over the region affected by pain.

In Facial Neuralgia.—Dr. HEADLAND.

188. ℞ Aconitinæ puræ, gr. iv.
Cerat. Cetacci, ℥j.

Mix with great care. *A strong aconite ointment..*

In the same, to produce a more rapid and powerful effect.

Dr. HEADLAND.

189. ℞ Aconitinæ, gr. iv.
Olei Olivæ, ♏viij. Triturate together, then add
Adipis præparati, ℥ij.
Mix; to be used by friction with the finger for several minutes.

In Neuralgia, &c.—Dr. A. TURNBULL.

190. ℞ Aconitinæ, gr. v.
Olei Olivæ, ʒss. Rub together, then add
Adipis præparati, ℥viiss.
Olei Bergamii, ♏x.
Olei Santali, ♏ij. Make an ointment.

In Neuralgic Rheumatism.—Dr. H. W. FULLER.

191. ℞ Aconitinæ puræ, granum.
Spirit. rectif. ʒj.
Aquæ destillatæ, ℥ix.
Dissolve the Aconite in the Spirits, then add the water, and strain.
Add, Glycerinæ, ℥ij.
Olei Bergamotæ, ♏v. Mix: make a lotion.

The solution in spirit and water forms *Liquor Aconitinæ*, which may be prescribed internally in minute doses in acute Rheumatism. With the Glycerin, &c., a lotion is formed, which will rapidly produce numbness if rubbed on to the painful part in a quantity of about ʒss. at a time.

Anæsthetic application.—Dr. HEADLAND.

ACORUS CALAMUS. See CALAMUS.

ADANSONIA. *Baobab Tree.*

The bark of the Baobab Tree (Adansonia digitata, Nat. Ord. *Bombaceæ*, or *Sterculiaceæ*) is tonic and diaphoretic, and has been recommended as a substitute for Cinchona. It differs from it, however, in having but little taste. The decoction is mucilaginous, and soon spoils. It is taken in the same manner as Cinchona bark, usually in the form of decoction.

ADIANTUM. *Maidenhair.*

Adiantum Capillus Veneris, and A. pedatum, European and American Maidenhair, are pectoral, and are used, especially in France, in the form of Syrup (*Sirop de Capillaire*). Mixed with water, it may be taken as a common drink in catarrhal disorders.

ÆGLE MARMELOS. *Bael,* or *Bela.*

The Bael is sometimes termed the Bengal Quince, but belongs to the Nat. Ord. *Aurantiaceæ*. A decoction of the *root* is used in Malabar as a remedy for hypochondriasis, melancholy, and palpitations of the heart; and of the *leaves* in asthma. In this country the bark of the root, and the unripe fruit and the preserved fruit, have been introduced into medical use, chiefly in irritations of the mucous membrane, and to obviate costiveness arising from debility.

192. ℞ Fruct. immaturi Belæ, ℥ij.
Aquæ, Oj. Boil slowly to f℥v, and strain.
For a dose, f℥j to f℥iss two or three times a day, or every third hour.
In Dysentery and Diarrhœa.—Mr. POUND.

ÆSCULUS HIPPOCASTANUM. *Horse Chestnut.*

The bark of Horse Chestnut has been used as a substitute for Cinchona. From half an ounce to an ounce of the powder may be taken in twenty-four hours. The decoction may be used in the same way as *Decoctum Cinchonæ.*

ÆTHEREA. *Æthers.*

Æther. Sulphuric Æther is a diffusible stimulant, much employed, on account of its rapid but transient effects, for the relief of spasmodic and nervous affections not connected with inflammation; as in spasmodic asthma, angina pectoris, cramp of the stomach, spasmodic and flatulent colic, hiccough, nervous palpitation, fainting, &c. *Externally*, it is applied to produce cold by evaporation; or if the vapor is confined, as a stimulant and rubefacient. *Inhaled*, it produces insensibility to pain, and is used for this purpose in painful and protracted operations. In some cases, fatal results have followed its inhalation. The other æthers have a similar effect as diffusible stimuli, but with some differences. *Æther Nitrosus* and *Spiritus Ætheris Nitrici* are mildly stimulating, and more decidedly diuretic, or diaphoretic if the patient be kept warm. *Oleum Æthereum* is anodyne and calmative; but is seldom given alone. *Æther Aceticus* is much used on the Continent, *internally*, as a mild stimulant, diaphoretic, antispasmodic, and nervine; *externally*, in stimulating liniments; and *alone*, in gentle frictions in Gout. *Æther Hydrochloricus*, Muriatic Ether, is regarded as diuretic and diaphoretic. What has been termed *Chloric Æther* is a solution of chloroform in alcohol.

Chloroformyl, Chloroform, is classed with the Æthers; it is given as a pleasant and effective antispasmodic, in spasmodic asthma, colic, cholera, &c.; and is used *externally* as a stimulant and anodyne; and to arrest phagedænic ulceration. *Inhaled*, it is now preferred to æther for producing insensibility to pain; but requires caution. The doses of the officinal æthereal compounds are:

Æther [Sulphuricus], 20 minims to a fluid-drachm, or sometimes more.
Spiritus Ætheris compositus, from half a fluid-drachm to two.
Æther Nitrosus, 10 to 20 minims.
Spiritus Ætheris Nitrici, half a fluid-drachm to two.
Æther Aceticus, from 5 to 30 or 40 drops.
Æther Muriaticus, 10 to 30 minims.
Spiritus Ætheris Muriaticus, 20 minims to a drachm.
Chloroformyl [chloroform], 3 to 12 drops; in delirium tremens, to a drachm.
Æther Chloricus is of uncertain strength, and usually contains 1 part of chloroform to 6 or 7 parts of alcohol.

[Æther Anæstheticus (chlorinated hydrochloric ether), Amylene, Dutch liquid, and some other ethereal compounds have been used for inhaling.]

193. ℞ Ætheris Sulphurici, fʒiij.
Misturæ Camphoræ, f℥vss.
Make a mixture. Dose, a fourth part.

Dr. Hooper.

194. ℞ Ætheris, fʒj.
Cetacei, gr. ij. Rub up together, and add
Aquæ (*vel* Aq. Menthæ pip.), fʒxj. Make a draught.

In Nervous Headache, Spasmodic Colic, &c.—Durande.

195. ℞ Ætheris Sulphurici, f℥ss.
Misturæ Camphoræ, f℥vij.
Syrupi Croci, f℥ss.
Make a mixture, of which give for a dose three large spoonfuls.

In Spasms (repeated every 1, 2, or 3 hours, according to their violence). Mr. Brande.

196. ℞ Ætheris Sulphurici,
Liquoris Ammoniæ, ana fʒss.
Misturæ Camphoræ, fʒx.
Tinct. Cardamomi comp. fʒj.
Make into a draught, to be taken two or three times a day.

In Nervous Headache.—Mr. Brande.

197. ℞ Ætheris Sulphurici, ʒij.
Olei Ricini, ℥j.
Mix: a teaspoonful every one, two, or three hours.

In Tape Worms.—ALIBERT.

198. ℞ Ætheris Sulphurici, ʒiij–vj.
Olei Terebinthinæ rectif. ʒij.
Mix: ten or twelve drops to be taken in sugared water morning and evening.

In Gall Stones.—DURANDE.

199. ℞ Sp. Ætheris compositi, fʒj.
Misturæ Camphoræ, f℥j.
Tinct. Cardam. comp fʒij.
Mix: make a draught, to be taken immediately, and repeat in two hours, if the flatulence continues troublesome.

In Flatulent Colic.—Dr. NELIGAN.

200. ℞ Misturæ Camphoræ, f℥j.
Spir. Ætheris comp. fʒij.
Tinct. Cardam. comp. fʒiv.
Spir. Anisi, fʒvj.
Olei. Carui, ♏xij.
Syrupi Zingiberis, fʒij.
Aquæ Menthæ pip. f℥vss.
Mix: make a mixture; take two tablespoonfuls for troublesome flatulence.

In Flatulent Colic.—Dr. JOY.

201. ℞ Magnesiæ Carbon. ℈j.
Aquæ Anethi, fʒx.
Spir. Ætheris comp. fʒj.
Tinct. Castorei, ʒj.
Olei Anisi, ♏ij. Mix: make a draught.

Dr. COPLAND.

202. ℞ Spir. Ammoniæ Arom. fʒiss.
Spir. Ætheris Sulph. fʒj.
Syrupi Zingiberis, fʒiij.
Aquæ Anethi, f℥iiiss. Mix: dose, a third part frequently.

In Hysteria, Syncope, Tympanitis, &c.—Dr. DRUITT.

203. ℞ Spir. Ætheris comp. f℥j.
Spir. Ammoniæ Arom. f℥ss.
Spir. Cinnamomi, f℥ss.
Inf. Cascarillæ, f℥iv. Make a mixture: dose, a sixth part

Dr. HOOPER

204. ℞ Misturæ Camphoræ, f℥j.
Liq. Ammon. Acetatis, fʒij.
Sp. Ætheris comp. fʒj.
Tinct. Camphoræ comp. fʒj.
Syrupi Papaveris, fʒj. Mix: make a draught.

In Angina Pectoris.—Dr. COPLANI

205. ℞ Spiritus Ætheris Sulphurici, f℥j.
Solutionis Muriatis Morphiæ, (Ph. Ed) ♏xv.
Aquæ Menthæ piperitæ, f℥j.
Mix: make a draught to be taken immediately; and repeat, if necessary, in a quarter of an hour.

In Spasm of Stomach, and Spasmodic Colic.—Dr. NELIGAN.

206. ℞ Mist. Camphoræ, f℥x.
Sp. Ætheris Sulphurici, f℥j.
Confect. Aromaticæ, ℈j.
Tinct. Lavand. comp. f℥ss.
Mix: make a draught, and repeat in four hours, or if the symptoms are urgent.

In the sinking of Fevers, Palpitations, &c.—Dr. JOY.

207. ℞ Spirit. Ætheris comp. f℥iij.
Tinct. Abelmoschi, f℥j.
Misturæ Camphoræ, f℥vj.
Two tablespoonfuls occasionally.

To allay Nervous Excitability.—Dr. R. REECE.

208. ℞ Spir. Ætheris comp. ♏viij.
Acidi Hydrochlorici dil. ♏iv.
Misturæ Camphoræ, f℥iij.
Make a draught, to be taken every sixth hour. [For a child of five years of age.]

In the advanced stage of Fever.—Dr. WEST.

209. ℞ Spirit. Ætheris Aromatici, f℥j.
Aquæ Cinnamomi, f℥vj.
Spir. Lavand. comp. f℥j. Mix: make a cordial draught.

Dr. E. G. CLARK.

210. ℞ Ætheris Sulphurici,
Liquoris Ammoniæ Acet.
Spiritus Vini rectificati, ana f℥iss.
Aquæ Rosæ, f℥iiiss. Mix: make an evaporating lotion.

In Inflammation of the Brain.—Dr. COPLAND.

211. ℞ Ætheris Sulphurici,
Spir. Camphoræ,
Tincturæ Opii,
Tincturæ Cantharidis, ana f℥iv.
Mix: make a liniment, to be rubbed upon the affected part frequently during the day.

In Hysterical Pain in the Side.—Dr. ASHWELL.

212. ℞ Sp. Ætheris Nitrici, f℥j.
Aquæ destillatæ, f℥j. Make a draught.

Diuretic.—Dr. PARIS.

213. ℞ Spirit. Ætheris Nitrici, f℥iij.
Liq. Ammoniæ Acetatis, f℥j.
Misturæ Camphoræ, f℥ivss.
Syrupi Zingiberis, f℥ij.
Make a mixture, of which take three large spoonfuls frequently.
In Low Febrile Affections.—Mr. BRANDE.

214. ℞ Spir. Ætheris Nitrici, f℥j.
Liq. Ammoniæ Acetatis, f℥ij.
Syrupi simplicis, f℥j.
Aquæ ad. f℥iv. Mix: dose, two or three spoonfuls.
Diaphoretic.—Dr. HOOPER.

215. ℞ Spir. Ætheris Nitrici, f℥ij.
Tinct. Camphoræ comp. f℥j.
Mucilaginis Acaciæ, f℥ij.
Liq. Ammoniæ Acetatis, f℥ij.
Spirit. Anisi, f℥j.
Mist. Camphoræ, f℥j.
Syrupi Tolutani, f℥j.
Make a draught, to be taken on going to sleep.
In recent Catarrh. (To be followed by a stomachic aperient next morning.) Dr. COPLAND.

216. ℞ Aquæ destillatæ, ℥j.
Spir. Ætheris Nitrici, ♏xl.
Vini Opii, ♏xv.
Syr. Rhœados, f℥iij.
Make a draught, to be taken going to sleep.
As an Anodyne in Fevers.—Dr. E. G. CLARK.

217. ℞ Sp. Ætheris Nitrici,
Sp. Ammoniæ Arom. ana f℥j.
Mix: take a teaspoonful two or three times a day in water.
Diaphoretic and Diuretic.—Sir A. COOPER.

218. ℞ Spir. Ætheris Nitrici,
Liquoris Potassæ, ana f℥j.
Mix: take a teaspoonful in water three times a day.
H. J.

[If the Sp. Æth. Nit. is not free from Aldehyd, the mixture will be brown.]

219. ℞ Spir. Ætheris Nitrici, f℥j.
Liq. Ammoniæ Acet. f℥iv.
Ammoniæ Sesquicarb. ℨj.
Misturæ Camphoræ, f℥iiss.
Tinct. Scillæ, f℥ss.
Mix: take a tablespoonful three times daily with a tablespoonful of pure water.
J. HODGSON.

220. ℞ Spir. Ætheris Nitrici,
Syrupi Tolutani, ana f℥j.
Mix: a teaspoonful to be taken frequently while the cough is troublesome.

In Coughs.—Dr. HOOPER.

221. ℞ Ætheris Acetici, ʒj.
Liq. Ammon. Acet.
Aquæ fl. Aurantii, ana ℥j.
Syrupi Ribium (*vel* Mori), ʒiij.
Mix: a spoonful every hour.

To promote Diaphoresis.—JAHN.

222. ℞ Ætheris Acetici, ♏xxx.
Misturæ Camphoræ cum Magnesiâ, f℥j.
Make a draught, to be taken immediately, and, if necessary, repeat in an hour.

In Hysteria.—Dr. NELIGAN.

223. ℞ Ætheris Acetici, ʒss.
Acidi Acetici, ʒij.
Aquæ Rubi Idæi, ℥iv.
Syrupi ejusdem, ℥ij. Mix: a spoonful every two hours.

In Nervous Fevers.—SUNDELIN.

224 ℞ Olei Cajaputi, ♏xij.
Ætheris Acetici, ʒij.
Tincturæ Opii, ʒj.
Mix: ten, fifteen, or more drops to be taken every hour, shaking the bottle.

In Asiatic Cholera.—PHŒBUS.

225. ℞ Ætheris Acetici, gutt. xxx.
Olei Olivæ, ʒij. Mix: put a few drops in the ear at night.

H. NEIL.

226. ℞ Ætheris Acetici, ℥j.
Saponis sevi, ʒj.
Dissolve at a gentle heat, and strain. From half a dr. to 1 dr. to be used in frictions.

In Rheumatic Pains.—PELLETIER.

227. ℞ Ætheris Hydrochlorici, ʒss.
Aquæ Menthæ pip. ℥iij.
Syrupi Aurantii, ℥j. Mix: to be taken by spoonfuls.

As a Stimulant in Sinking.—BRERA.

228 ℞ Chloroformylis, gr. xv.
Syrupi flor. Aurant. ʒx.
Aquæ flor. Tiliæ, ℥iij.
Mix, according to art; dose, a dessert or tablespoonful.

In violent Colic, Neuralgia, or Asthma.
TROUSSEAU and REVEIL.

229. ℞ Chloroformi, gutt. vj.
Aquæ puræ, f℥j. Make a draught.

In Asiatic Cholera (after a pill of 5 gr. calomel, and 2 gr. opium.) Mr. J. P. OATES.

230. ℞ Chloroformi, ♏v.
Syrupi Rhœados, f℥j.
Aquæ, f℥iss.
Make a draught, to be taken when the pain is urgent.

In Spasmodic and Cancerous Diseases.—Dr. NELIGAN.

231. ℞ Chloroformi, ♏viij.
Sp. Vini Gallici, f℥iij.
Aquæ, f℥ij. Make a draught.

In Cholera.—Mr. BRADY.

232. ℞ Chloroformi, f℥j.
Sp. Ætheris comp.
Tinct. Valerianæ, ana f℥ij.
Aquæ, f℥iss. Make a draught.

In desperate cases of Delirium Tremens.
Dr. S. PRATT (U.S.).

233. ℞ Chloroformi, f℥j.
Aquæ, f℥iiss. Make a draught.

In the same.—Mr. BUTCHER.

234. ℞ Chloroformi, ♏v.
Tinct. Belladonnæ, f℥ss. [♏xv?]
Syrupi Croci, f℥j.
Aquæ destillatæ, f℥iss.
Mix: make a draught. Take such a draught three or four times a day.

In Epileptiform Hysteria, and Hysterical Neuralgia.
Dr. NELIGAN.

235. ℞ Chloroformi, part j.
Misturæ Acaciæ, p. ij.
Mix: make an injection. It produces severe pain.

In Gonorrhœa.—Mr. H. BEHRENDS.

236. ℞ Chloroformi, ℥j.
Olei Terebinthinæ, ℥iiiss. Make a liniment.

In Intermittents (rubbed on the spine).—M. ARAN.

237. ℞ Chloroformi, ♏xx.
Tinct. Aconiti rad.
Tinct. Opii, ana f℥j.
Lin. Camphoræ comp. f℥xiv. Mix: make a liniment.

In Neuralgic and Rheumatic Pains.—Dr. NELIGAN.

238. ℞ Chloroformi, ℥j.
Camphoræ, ℥j.
Adipis præp. ℥j.
Make an ointment, to be applied every night.

In Rheumatism

239. ℞ Chloroformi, ʒss.
Cerati Galeni (cold cream), ℥j. Make an ointment.

To allay Itching in Urticaria, &c.—Dr. NELIGAN.

240. ℞ Chloroformi, gutt. lx.
Adipis, ℥j.
Rub up together in a mortar, to form an ointment.

In Neuralgic and Rheumatic Pains.—M. BOUIS.

241. ℞ Chloroformi, ʒiv.
Potassii Cyanidi, ʒiij.
Ung. Ceræ Albæ, ℥iv. Make an ointment.

In Neuralgia.—CAZENAVE.

242. ℞ Pulv. Resinæ flav. ʒss.
Chloroformylis, q. s. to dissolve the resin.
Impregnate with this thick solution a small piece of cotton, and introduce it into the hollow of the tooth.

In Toothache.—TROUSSEAU and REVEIL.

243. ℞ Chloroformi, fʒj.
Zinci Oxydi, ʒss.
Ol. Olivæ, ʒj.
Cerati Cetacei, ʒiv. Mix: make an ointment.

To sensitive Ulcers of the Rectum.—Mr. CURLING.

244. ℞ Chloroformi, ♏xx.
Olei Olivæ, f℥j.
Make a liniment: to be smeared on the skin, previously well dried, after a tepid bath.

In Lichen.—Dr. NELIGAN.

245. ℞ Ætheris Chlorici, fʒj.
Pulveris Acaciæ, ʒss.
Aquæ, f℥iv.
Make a mixture, of which a third part may be given for a dose.

Antispasmodic and Stimulant.—Dr. DRUITT.

246. ℞ Ætheris Chlorici, ʒj–iij.
Aquæ destillatæ, Oj. Make a lotion.

In painful affections of the Breast.—Mr. TUSON.

ALCOHOL.

In the form of Rectified Spirit and Proof Spirit, alcohol is used in many pharmaceutical preparations, which are noticed under the several drugs. Largely diluted spirit is used in evaporating and other lotions, in gargles, collyria, &c. Ardent Spirits (brandy, rum, gin, whisky, &c.) may be regarded as diluted alcohol. Of their dietetic use it is not necessary to speak here; but we may notice Dr. Paris's opinion, that the habitual use of them induces "more than half of all our chronical diseases." Medicinally, they are sometimes prescribed, particularly brandy, to rouse the system in some cases of extreme debility, the sinking stage of typhus fever, &c. *Mistura Spiritus Vini Gallici* is given in the dose of half an ounce to an ounce, frequently repeated.

247. ℞ Infusi Thææ, Oij.
Succi Limonis, f℥j.
Spirit. Vini Gallici, ℥iv.
Sacchari albi, ℥iv. Mix: a small glassful frequently.
In Cholera, &c.—MAGENDIE.

248. ℞ Spiritus Vini rectificati,
Albuminis ovi, partes æquales.
Mix: to be applied with a feather.
To Bed Sores in their first stage.—Dr. CHRISTISON.

249. ℞ Spiritus rectificati, f℥j.
Aquæ puræ, f℥xv. Make a lotion.
To produce cold by evaporation.—Dr. DRUITT.

250. ℞ Spirit. Vini rectificati, f℥iv.
Liquoris Calcis, f℥viij. Make a lotion.
To inflamed surfaces.—Dr. REECE.

251. ℞ Spirit. Vini rectif. ℥ij.
Liq. Ammoniæ Acet. ℥vj. Mix: make a lotion.
Discutient.—R. G. HOLLAND.

252. ℞ Spirit. rectificati, f℥ij.
Aquæ (*vel* Aquæ Rosæ), ℥iv. Make an eyewash.
PHŒBUS.

ALLIUM.

Allium Sativum, Garlic; and *Allium Cepa*, Onion (Nat. Ord. *Liliaceæ*), are stimulant, diuretic, expectorant, and deobstruent; but are more suitable for cold phlegmatic constitutions than for hot and bilious ones. They are seldom prescribed; but have been recommended in chronic catarrhs, humoral asthma, worms, &c. Dr. Sydenham says he has seen dropsies cured by garlic. Epilepsy, of old standing, is said to have been cured by a strong infusion of it. *Externally*, Garlic is used as a revulsive. Onions, roasted and split, are applied as maturating cataplasms.

Dose of *Garlic*, ½ dr. to 2 dr. (a clove or two is recommended to be taken in the morning, for worms); *Syrupus Allii*, a teaspoonful; *Vinum Cepæ*, a wineglassful as a diuretic; *Unguentum Allii* is rubbed on the soles of the feet in hooping-cough.

253. ℞ Allii contusi, lb.ss.
Aquæ, lb j.

Let them stand in an oven, in a covered vessel, for some hours; then strain. Two spoonfuls to be taken before and after every meal.

In Epilepsy.—Mr. WHITE (Veterinarian).

254. ℞ Succi cepæ, ℥j.
Sacchari, ℥iss.

Make into a syrup: a teaspoonful occasionally.

In Coughs of Children, without Inflammation.—Dr. WOOD.

255. ℞ Allii sativi bulbi, ʒij–iv.
Lactis, ℥vj–viij.

Boil gently, and strain, to make an enema.

In Thread Worms.—RADIUS.

256. ℞ Bulbos Allii sativi incis. No. 3–4.
Spir. Vin. Gallici, f℥xxvij.

Macerate for 36 hours, strain, and add
Decocti Bardanæ, ℥viij. Make a lotion.

To prevent Baldness.—PHŒBUS.

ALOE. *Aloes.*

Aloes is the inspissated juice of various species of Aloe (Nat. Ord. *Liliaceæ*). In full doses it operates pretty certainly, though slowly, as a stimulant cathartic, chiefly acting on the lower bowels. In smaller doses it is stomachic and tonic. On account of its stimulating action on the rectum, aloes must be cautiously prescribed where there is a tendency to piles; and as its stimulus extends to the uterus, it is ranked among the *Emmenagogues*, and must be used with caution during pregnancy. Aloes is much used as a remedy for sluggish bowels in persons of sedentary habits; in dyspepsia, hypochondriasis, jaundice, &c. On account of its extreme bitterness it is usually given in the form of pills; in the liquid form its taste is partially concealed by liquorice. Its purgative powers are increased by the addition of bitter tonics.

The dose of Socotrine Aloes is from 1 or 2 grains (as a

stomachic and laxative), to 12 grains as a cathartic. Barbadoes and hepatic aloes are regarded as rather more powerful. The following are the principal officinal preparations in which it is the chief ingredient, with their respective doses:

Extractum Aloes (Aquosum), 3 to 12 grains.
" " Barb. 2 to 10 grains.
Pilulæ Aloes, E. 10 to 20 grains.
" " comp. 5 to 15 grains.
" " et Assafœtidæ, 10 to 15 grains.
" " cum Sapone, 5 to 15 grains.
" " cum Myrrhâ, 5 to 20 grains.
" " et Ferri, E. 1 to 3 pills.
" " et Mastiches, 6 grains.
" Aloeticæ (Guy's H.), 2 to 4 pills.
Aloina (the active principle), 1 or 2 grains.
Collyrium Aloeticum.
Decoctum Aloes comp. ½ oz. to 2 oz.
Enema Aloes.
Solutio Aperiens (Mettauer's), 1 to 2 drs.
Tinctura Aloes, 1 dr. to 1 ounce.
" " comp. ½ dr. to 1 drachm.
" Rhei et Aloes, ½ oz. to 1 oz.
" Aloes Alkalina, 1 dr. to 4 drs.
Vinum Aloes, 1 to 2 drs as a stomachic.
" " ½ oz. to 1½ oz. purgative.
Pulvis Aloes comp. 10 to 20 grains.
" " cum Canellâ, 5 to 15 grains.
" " et Ferri, 5 to 15 grains.
Suppositorium Anthelminticum.
Unguentum Aloes.

257. ℞ Aloes Socot. ℥ij.
Saponis mollis, (Ph. L.) ℥ss.
Olei Menthæ pip. ♏v.
Make into 30 pills. Take one or two occasionally, as necessary.
In Sluggish Bowels.—Dr. A. T. THOMSON.

258. ℞ Aloes Extracti, ℈j.
Pulv. Ipecacuanhæ, gr. viij.
Pulv. Zingiberis, ℥ss.
Syrupi, q. s.
Make 16 pills. One to be taken before dinner.
In Indigestion with Costiveness.—Dr. BAILLIE.

259. ℞ Pulv. Aloes comp. gr. viij.
Olei Anisi, gutt. ij.
Olei Carui, gutt. j. Make two pills.
Aperient and Carminative.—Dr. HOOPER

260. ℞ Extr. Aloes aquosi,
Pulv. Rhei,
Pulv. Ipecacuanhæ,
Saponis Hispan. sing. gr. xij.

Make a mass, to be divided into 12 pills. Take one or two for a dose.

In Indigestion.—Dr. G. GREGORY.

261. ℞ Extracti Aloes aquosi, ʒj.
Scammonii opt. ʒss.
Bals. Peruviani, gr. x.
Olei Carui, gutt. x.

Mix: make 20 pills, of which two or three may be taken, according to circumstances, occasionally.

For Indolent Bowels in Aged Persons.—Dr. ROBINSON.

262. ℞ Pulv. Aloes,
Pulv. Mastiches,
Pulv. Rhei, ana ʒss.

Water, sufficient to form a mass, which is to be divided into 20 pills, of which two or three may be taken before dinner.

In Costiveness and Flatulence in Dyspeptic Habits.
Mr. BRANDE.

263. ℞ Pil. Aloes comp.
Pil. Ferri comp. ana ʒj.
Ol. Sabinæ,
Ol. Rutæ, ana gutt. iij.
Pulv. Capsici. gr. viij.

Triturate intimately, and divide into 24 pills. One may be taken three times a day.

In Amenorrhœa.—Dr. RYAN.

264. ℞ Aloes Socotrinæ, gr. xvj.
Mastiches, gr. viij.
Extr. Gentianæ,
Pil. Galbani comp. ana gr. iij.
Olei Anisi, q. s.

Make into 12 pills. Take three every day on going to sleep.

As a warm Laxative, in Asthma, &c.—Dr. COPLAND.

265. ℞ Aloes Socotrinæ,
Zingiberis, pulv. ana ʒss.
Extr. Anthemidis, ℈ij.

Make into 20 pills. One or two an hour before dinner.

In Indigestion, with Costiveness.—Dr. HOOPER.

266. ℞ Aloes Socotrinæ,
Rhei Pulveris, ana ʒss.
Saponis, q. s.

Make a mass, and divide into 25 pills. Three or four may be taken occasionally, as may be necessary.

In Dyspepsia, with Costiveness.—DR. ELLIS (U.S.).

267. ℞ Pil. Aloes cum Myrrhâ. ℈ij.
Extracti Hyoscyami, ℈j.
Mix: and divide into 12 pills. Take one at night, frequently.

As a mild Laxative in Dyspepsia.—Dr. G. GREGORY.

268. ℞ Pil. Aloes compos ℈iiss.
Olei Crotonis, gutt. j.
Make 12 pills, of which take two at the hour of sleep, as often as may be necessary.

Dr. ELLIOTSON.

269. ℞ Aloes spicatæ, ℈ss.
Rhei pulveris. ʒss.
Extr. Gentianæ, ℈j.
Syrupi, q. s. Make 20 pills. Take two twice a day.

In Dyspepsia, with Torpid Bowels.—Dr. AINSLIE.

270. ℞ Aloes Socot. ʒiij.
Mastiches, ʒj.
Petalæ Rosæ (*vel* Pulv. Rhei), ʒj.
Fellis inspissati, ʒiss.
Mix well, and divide into 100 pills, of which take two or three before dinner.

In Indigestion.—Dr. COPLAND.

271. ℞ Pil. Aloes et Myrrhæ, ʒj.
Pil. Galbani comp ʒij.
Mix, and divide into 40 pills. Take two three times a day.

In Costiveness, with Nervous Debility.—Dr. FARRE.

272. ℞ Pulv. Aloes comp. ℈ij.
Pulv. Antimonii comp. ℈j.
Syr. Zingiberis, q s.
Make into 16 pills Take two every night.

As a Sudorific Laxative.—Dr. AINSLIE.

273. ℞ Extr. Aloes Barb. aquosi,
Saponis Hispanici,
Theriacæ (treacle),
Extr. Glycyrrhizæ, each ʒj.
Soften together in a water bath, and then divide into 48 pills. Take one on going to sleep.

Dr. MARSHALL HALL.

274. ℞ Aloes Barbad. gr. xxiv.
Acidi Sulphurici, guttas sex.
Mix well, and divide into 6 pills, of which two may be taken every fourth hour.

In Obstinate Costiveness.—Dr. DICKSON.

275. ℞ Pil. Aloes comp.
Pil. Hydrargyri, ana gr. xxv.
Syr. Zingiberis, q. s.
Mix, and divide into 10 pills; take one every night, going to sleep.

In Flatulent Indigestion, with Liver Derangement.

Dr. AINSLIE.

276. ℞ Pulv. Aloes comp. ʒj.
Pulv. Antimonii comp. gr. v.
Saponis duri, ℈ss.
Decocti Aloes comp. q. s.

Make a mass and divide into 20 pills, of which two may be taken to excite a proper action of the bowels.

Dr. PARIS.

277. ℞ Extracti Aloes aquosi,
Quinæ Disulphatis, ana ℈j.

Mix: make into 20 pills, one to be taken at bedtime.

In Costiveness from Torpor of Colon, and Deficient Bile.

PITTSCHAFT.

278. ℞ Extracti Aloes purif. gr. xviij.
Quinæ Disulphatis, gr. xij.
Pil. Hydrargyri, gr. vj.
Extracti Rhei, gr. xviij.

Mix: make 12 pills, take one at noon and one just before going to sleep.

Dr. BARON.

279. ℞ Pulv. Aloes, gr. iv. ad viij.
Syrupi simp. (vel empyreumatici), ʒj.

Make an electuary to be taken at evening.

[This is continued nightly with only 2 grains, or q. s. of aloes, for a child of 7 to 10 years.]

In Chorea.—Dr. JAMES HAMILTON.

280. ℞ Vini Aloes, f℥iss.
Spir. Ammoniæ arom. f℥ss.

Mix: dose, a tablespoonful, with water.

As a Warm Aperient.—Dr. AINSLIE.

281. ℞ Decocti Aloes comp.
Inf Gentianæ comp. ana f℥iij.
Liq. Potassæ, ʒij.

Mix: take two large spoonfuls every morning.

In Headache, with Indigestion.—Dr. G. GREGORY.

282. ℞ Decocti Aloes comp. fʒiv.
Infusi Cascarillæ, f℥j.

Make a draught, to be taken once or twice a day.

In Costiveness in Weak Hysterical Subjects.—Dr. UWINS.

283. ℞ Decocti Aloes comp. f℥iij.
Mist. Ferri comp. f℥v.

Make a mixture, take two spoonfuls twice a day.

Dr. A. T. THOMSON.

284. ℞ Decocti Aloes comp. f℥ivss.
Sodæ Bicarbon. ʒj.
Vini Aloes, fʒvj.
Extracti Taraxaci, ʒiij.
Spir. Pimentæ, f℥ss.

Mix: take a third part for a dose.

In Habitual Constipation.—Dr. COPLAND.

285. ℞ Decocti Aloes comp. f℥viss.
Tinct. Sennæ comp. f℥j.
Tinct. Scillæ, fʒiij.
Make a mixture, three tablespoonfuls to be taken occasionally.

As a Laxative, in Asthma.—Dr. R. REECE.

286. ℞ Decocti Aloes compositi, f℥ij.
Syrupi Croci,
Syrupi Rhei, ana f℥ss.
Make a mixture, to be taken in two doses.

In Torpor of the Bowels, with Chlorosis.—Dr. NELIGAN.

287. ℞ Decocti Aloes compos. f℥iss.
Extracti Glycyrrhizæ, ʒij.
Vini Aloes, fʒij.
Mix: one or two teaspoonfuls twice a day.

As a Laxative and Vermifuge for Children.

Drs. EVANSON and MAUNSELL.

[The same, with ♏xxx–lx Tinct. Ferri Sesquichloridi, is given to prevent the re-generation of worms.]

288. ℞ Decocti Aloes comp. f℥vss.
Infusi Sennæ comp. f℥ij.
Tinct. Sennæ,
Tinct. Jalapæ, ana fʒij.
Make a mixture, of which take two tablespoonfuls twice daily, morning and late in the evening.

Dr. PARIS.

289. ℞ Decocti Aloes comp. f℥iij.
Potas. Bicarbon. ʒij.
Ferri Ammonio-tart. (Aikin's), ʒss.
Sp. Ammoniæ arom. fʒiij.
Aquæ, ℥viss.
Make a mixture, take a sixth part twice a day.

Laxative and Tonic.—H. J.

290. ℞ Aloes, ʒj.
Sacchari crystallati, ʒij.
Triturate intimately, and divide into 18 equal doses; give one occasionally.

In Convalescence from Chorea.—Dr. JAS. HAMILTON.

ALTHÆA. *Marsh Mallow.*

The dried root of Marsh Mallow (Althæa officinalis, Nat. Ord. *Malvaceæ*) is used as an emollient and demulcent, in inflammations and irritations of the alimentary canal, and of the urinary and respiratory organs. The powdered root is employed to give consistence and coherence to pill-masses, &c.

The leaves and flowers of Althæa (as well as of the common mallow, Malva Sylvestris) have similar properties, but are chiefly used externally, in soothing fomentations, &c.

The powdered root, and also *Mistura Althææ*, *Syrupus Althææ*, and *Pasta Althææ*, are taken almost *ad libitum*. *Unguentum Althææ* is emollient and resolvent.

291. ℞ Decocti Althææ, f℥vj.
Syrupi simplicis, f℥j.
Make a mixture, of which give a third portion, every sixth hour.

In Calculous Disorders, and Inflammation of the Kidneys.

Dr. A. T. THOMSON.

292. ℞ Pulv. Althææ,
Pulv. Glycyrrhizæ, ana ℥iij.
Pulv. Potassæ Nitratis, ℥ss.
Pulv. Camphoræ, ʒj.
Mix, and divide into 30 powders; one powder three times a day.

293. ℞ Rad. Althææ, ℥ij.
Rad. Glycyrrhizæ, ʒiij.
Aquæ, Oiss. Boil down to a pint, and strain.

Dr. COPLAND.

294. ℞ Rad. Althææ, ℥j.
Aquæ, Oss. Coque ad f℥v. cola, et adde
Lactis, f℥iij.
Mellis, ℥iss. Make a gargle.

TROUSSEAU.

295. ℞ Fæculæ Solani tuberosi,
Decocti Althææ, ana p æq.
Mix the starch with a little of the cold decoction, then add the remainder of the decoction, and boil until it assumes a proper consistency for use as a poultice.

In Irritable Diseases of the Skin.—Dr. JOY.

296. ℞ Infusi Althææ, f℥xvj.
Liq Plumbi Diacetatis, fʒj–ij. Make a lotion.

In Lichen and Chronic Eczema.—Dr. BURGESS.

297. ℞ Decocti Althææ, Oss.
Sodæ Sulphatis, ℥j.
Olei Olivæ, f℥j. Mix: make an enema.

Dr. HOOPER.

ALUMEN. *Alum.*

Alum (Sulphate of Alumina and Potash) is astringent, and is prescribed in hæmorrhages, chronic diarrhœa, and dysentery, and in atonic discharges generally; also in hooping-cough and lead colic. *Locally*, its saturated solution is used as a styptic; and a weaker solution as a lotion, to ulcers and chilblains; as a gargle, in relaxed sore throat, excessive salivation, &c.; as a collyrium in chronic ophthalmia; as an injection in gleet, &c. The powder is blown into the throat in diphtherite, &c. Burnt alum is chiefly used as a mild caustic to repress proud flesh.

The usual dose of alum is from 5 to 30 grains for an adult, or 1 to 5 grains for children: some practitioners have given as much as a teaspoonful to children of two years old, as an emetic in croup.

Confectio Aluminis (St. Bart. H.), a drachm.

Liq. Aluminis Compositus (L.), for outward use.

298. ℞ Aluminis, gr. xlviij.
Aquæ calidæ, f℥vss.
Syrupi, f℥ss.
Mix: dose, from fʒss to fʒiv, according to the age, three or four times a day.

In Bronchitis.—Dr. ANDREWS.

299. ℞ Aluminis, gr. xxiv.
Acidi Sulphurici diluti, ♏xij.
Syrupi Rhœados, fʒiv.
Aquæ puræ, f℥iiss.
Make a mixture, take fʒiij every six hours.

In Hooping-cough.—Dr. WEST.

300. ℞ Aluminis, ʒss.
Aquæ, f℥iiiss.
Syrupi Rhœados, fʒiv.
Mix: take from a teaspoonful to a tablespoonful, according to the age of the patient, twice a day.

In Hooping-cough.—Dr. DAVIS.

301. ℞ Aluminis, gr. xxv.
Extracti Conii, gr. xij.
Syrupi Rhœados, fʒij.
Aquæ Anethi, f℥iij.
Mix: take a dessertspoonful every sixth hour.

In the second stage of Hooping-cough.—Dr. GOLDING BIRD.

302. ℞ Aluminis, ʒiss.
Syrupi Rosæ Gallicæ, f℥j.
Aquæ Rosæ, f℥vij.
Mix: make a mixture, of which let the patient take a tablespoonful every three or four hours.

In Painters' Colic and old Diarrhœas.—Dr. NELIGAN.

303. ℞ Infusi Rosæ comp. f℥viiss.
Aluminis, ʒij.
Tinct. Cardam. co. f℥ss.
Mix: give two tablespoonfuls three times a day.

In Habitual Constipation.—Dr. ALDRIDGE.

304. ℞ Aluminis, ʒij.
Magnes. Sulphatis, ℥j.
Infusi Rosæ comp. f℥viij.
Mix: give two tablespoonfuls with two wineglassfuls of water, early in the morning, every day.

In Habitual Constipation and Lead Colic.—Dr. ALDRIDGE.

305. ℞ Aluminis, ʒj.
Acidi Sulphurici dil. fʒiss.
Syrupi simpl. f℥ss.
Infusi Rosæ comp. f℥vij.
Mix: dose, one-sixth every fourth hour.

In Passive Hæmorrhages.—Dr. DRUITT.

306. ℞ Pulv. Aluminis,
P. Kino, ana ʒiiss.
Syrupi simp. q. s.
To make a mass to be divided into 100 pills; dose, 2–10 daily.

In Chronic Diarrhœa or Menorrhagia.
TROUSSEAU and REVEIL.

307. ℞ Aluminis, ʒiiss.
Syrup. Rhataniæ, ℥ij.
Aquæ, ℥vj.
Dissolve the alum in the water, and add the syrup; divide into four doses, and administer at intervals of half an hour.

In Hæmoptysis.—TROUSSEAU and REVEIL.

308. ℞ Camphoræ rasæ, gr. iv; rub up with
Mucilaginis Acaciæ, f℥ss.
Aquæ Pimentæ, f℥j.
Pulv. Aluminis, ʒss.
Spirit. Anisi, fʒj.
Syrupi Croci, fʒss.
Mix: make a draught, to be taken every fourth or fifth hour, first shaking the vial.

In Painters' Colic.—Dr. COPLAND.

309. ℞ Lactis Vaccini bullientis, Oj.
Aluminis contriti, ʒij.
Boil together until a coagulum is formed; strain the serum, and give a wineglassful frequently.

Mr. BRANDE.

310. ℞ Pulveris Aluminis, ʒiiss.
Mellis albi, ʒx.
Mix: half a spoonful to be given every hour; and powdered alum blown into the throat every four hours.

In Croup and Diphtheritis.—Dr. TROUSSEAU

311. ℞ Pulv. Aluminis, ℈j.
Pulv. Cubebæ, ℈v.
Make a powder, to be taken three times a day.
In Gonorrhœa.—M. Ricord.

312. ℞ Pulv. Aluminis, gr. viij.
Quinæ Disulph. gr. ij.
Pulv. Acaciæ,
Pulv. Sacchari albi, ana gr. xij.
Make a powder. Prepare 12 such powders, and let the patient take one powder every third hour.
In Passive Hæmorrhages, Adynamic Fevers, &c.
Dr. Copland.

313. ℞ Picis liquidæ,
Pulv. Aluminis, ana ʒv.
Pulv. Glycyrrhizæ, q. s.
Make a mass, and divide into pills of 4½ grains; take from 6 to 10 every day.
In Gonorrhœa.—M. Berton.

314. ℞ Pulv. Aluminis, gr. vj.
Pulv. Ipecacuanhæ, gr. iss.
Syrupi Papav. q. s.
Make a bolus, to be repeated in four or six hours.
In Dysentery.—Dr. Joy.

315. ℞ Pulv. Aluminis, gr. xij.
Pulv. Catechu, gr. v.
Cinnamomi, gr. iv.
Conf. Rosæ, q. s.
To make a bolus, to be taken three times a day.
In Flooding from Relaxation.—Dr. Osborne.

316. ℞ Pulv. Aluminis, gr. vj. Dissolve in
Aquæ Rosæ, f℥v. Make an eyewash.
In Chronic Ophthalmia.—Mr. Brande.

317. ℞ Pulv. Aluminis, gr. vj ad ℈j.
Aquæ Rosæ, f℥vj. Dissolve, and make an eyewash.
Mr. R. G. Holland.

318. ℞ Aluminis, ʒij.
Inf. Rosæ, Oj. Make a lotion.
In Acne, Pityriasis, Eczema, &c. (after the removal of the incrustations).
M. Cazenave.

319. ℞ Aluminis, ʒj.
Decocti Cinchonæ, f℥xij.
Mellis Rosæ, f℥iss. Mix: make a gargle.
In relaxed Sore Throat.—Sir A. Cooper.

320. ℞ Infusi Rosæ comp.
Decocti Althææ, ana f℥iij.
Aluminis, ʒj.
Mel. Rosæ, f℥ij. Make a gargle. Use frequently.

In relaxed Sore Throat and Ulcerated Mouth.—Dr. NELIGAN.

321. ℞ Aluminis, ʒj.
Acidi Sulph. diluti, ♏xx.
Tinct. Myrrhæ, fʒij.
Decocti Cinchonæ, f℥vj. Make a gargle.

Dr. HOOPER.

322. ℞ Pulv. Acaciæ, ʒss.
Pulv. Aluminis, gr. v.
Mix with great care, and make a powder. To be applied to the nipple as often as may be necessary.

To Sore Nipples (applied after suckling).
Dr. A. T. THOMSON.

323. ℞ Aluminis pulv. ℈j.
Cretæ præparatæ, ʒj.
Mix carefully, and make a powder, of which a portion may be sprinkled on the nipple as often as occasion may require.

Dr. PEREIRA.

324. ℞ Pulv. Aluminis,
Pulv. Acaciæ, ana part. æq.
Mix: to be blown into the nostrils.

In Epistaxis.—M. LECLUYSE.

325. ℞ Aluminis pulv. ʒvj.
Tinct. Capsici concent. ʒij.
Mix, and dry. A very small quantity of the powder to be applied to the tonsils.

Dr. TURNBULL.

326. ℞ Aluminis, ʒiss.
Aquæ Rosæ, f℥viij. Make an injection.

In Gonorrhœa.—BELL.

327. ℞ Liq. Aluminis comp. fʒvj.
Aquæ destillatæ, f℥vss.
Misturæ Acaciæ, f℥ss. Mix: make an injection.

In Gleet.—Mr. BRANDE.

328. ℞ Aluminis, ʒij.
Decocti fol. Juglandis, Oij. Mix: make an injection.

In Leucorrhœa.—M. TROUSSEAU.

329. ℞ Infusi Lini, f℥xv.
Aluminis, ʒij.
Tincturæ Kino, ℥j. Mix: make an injection.

In Cauliflower Excrescence of the Uterus.—Dr. CLARK.

330. ℞ Aluminis, ʒj–iv.
Decocti Quercus, Oj. Make an injection.
Sir A. COOPER.

331. ℞ Aluminis usti,
Hydrarg. Nitrico-oxydi, ana ʒj. Mix well.
As a Caustic for Fungous Growths.—Dr. KIRKLAND.

332. ℞ Aluminis, ʒj.
Butyri recentis, ℥j. Make an ointment.
In Hæmorrhoids.—M. SUNDELIN.

333. ℞ Aluminis usti,
Sodæ biboratis, ana ʒss.
Medullæ bovinæ, ℥j.
Olei Bergamiæ, gutt. vj.
Mix: make an ointment. Half a teaspoonful to be rubbed on the head night and morning.
To promote the Growth of the Hair.—FRICKE.

ALUMINA. ALUMINÆ ACETAS, &c.

Alumina, earth of Alum, or Argil, is the basis of clays and boles; but for medical use it is usually obtained from alum. It is chiefly prescribed in diarrhœa and dysentery of children, to whom it is given in some mucilaginous liquid, to the amount of 30 grains, or more, in the day. To adults, in doses of 10 to 20 grains several times a day.

Acetate of Alumina is astringent, sometimes used in injections, and more rarely given in hæmoptysis, &c.

The *simple Sulphate of Alumina* is used to preserve animal substances, and also in detergent and antiseptic lotions to foul ulcers.

334. ℞ Aluminæ puræ, ʒss.
Acaciæ pulv. ʒj.
Sacchari albi, ʒij.
Aquæ Fœniculi, f℥iij.
Mix: a teaspoonful to be given frequently.
In Diarrhœa of Children.—RIECKE.

335. ℞ Aluminæ Acetatis, gr. x–xx.
Aquæ destillatæ, f℥iij. Make an injection.
Dr. PEREIRA.

336. ℞ Aluminæ Sulphatis, ʒij.
Aquæ destillatæ, f℥viij. Make a lotion.
To Foul Ulcers.—Dr. PENNYPACKER (U.S.)

[Tannate of Alumina is commended by Mr. B. Harrison and others, in injections; but they appear to have used a *spurious salt.* We therefore omit their formulæ.]

AMMONIA. AMMONIÆ CARBONAS, &c.

Ammonia, whether in its caustic state or combined with carbonic acid, is antacid, diaphoretic, and stimulant. It stimulates the stomach and increases the action of the heart and arteries, without unduly exciting the brain. It is prescribed, in the form of some of the compounds mentioned below, in fainting, and sinking of the vital powers from hæmorrhages, &c.; in poisoning by prussic acid and other sedatives; in some cases of scarlet and typhus fever, and delirium tremens; and as an antidote to the bites and stings of venomous reptiles and insects. Ammonia has also been supposed to remedy the nervous disorders produced by alcohol and tobacco.

The *sesquicarbonate* is less irritant than the caustic ammonia (as contained in *Liquor Ammoniæ*); the *bicarbonate* is still milder.

The *Sp. Ammoniæ aromaticus, et fœtidus*, L., contain a carbonate of ammonia; the same preparations of the E. and D. Ph., and the simple *Sp. Ammoniæ*, E., contain ammonia in a caustic state, and are consequently rather more irritant.

The vapor of Ammonia is applied to the nostrils as a stimulant in faintness, nervous headache, vertigo, suspended animation, &c. It should not be used in a too concentrated form, especially when the patient is in an insensible state; as the after-effects have sometimes proved serious.

Spiritus Ammoniæ Aromaticus, L., 20 to 80 minims.
——————— E. and D., 10 to 60 minims.
——————— *Fœtidus*, L., 40 to 60 minims.
——————— E., 20 to 60 minims.
Liquor Ammoniæ, 10 to 30 minims.
——————— *fortior*, 3 to 10 minims.
Ammoniæ Sesquicarbonas, 4 to 15 grains; or as an emetic, 30 grains.
Ammoniæ Bicarbonas, 6 to 24 grains.
Liq. Ammoniæ Sesquicarbonatis, 20 to 40 minims.
——————— *Anisatus*, 5 to 20 drops.
—— *Volatilis Cornu Cervi*, 20 to 60 minims.
Tinct. Ammoniæ Composita, 5 to 10 minims.

Linimentum Ammoniæ; Lin. Ammoniæ Sesquicarbonatis; Linimentum Ammoniæ compositum; Emplastrum Ammoniæ; and Unguentum Ammoniæ, are used as local stimulants, or rubefacients, and counter-irritants.

337. ℞ Liquoris Ammoniæ, gutt. x.
Aquæ cum Saccharo, ℥iij.
Mix: to be taken in the course of the day.

To remove the ill effects of Tobacco and Alcoholic Drinks.
M. TESSIER.

338. ℞ Liquoris Ammoniæ,
Tinct. Cardamomi comp.
Tinct. Gentianæ comp. ana fʒss.
Misturæ Camphoræ, f℥iss. Make a draught.

In Fainting, Giddiness, and Acidity of the Stomach.
Mr. BRANDE.

339. ℞ Liquor. Ammoniæ, ♏xv.
Misturæ Amygdalæ, f℥ij.
Tinct. Opii, ♏vj.
Make a draught: to be taken three times a day.

In Acidity of the Primæ Viæ.—Dr. JOY.

340. ℞ Liq. Ammoniæ, ♏x.
Infusi Chiraytæ, f℥j.
Tinct. Aurantii, fʒij.
Make a draught: to be taken morning and noon.

In Dyspepsia of the Debilitated, with Acidity.—Dr. NELIGAN.

341. ℞ Liquor. Ammoniæ, gtt. x.
Syrupi Erysimi, ℥iss.
Infusi Tiliæ, ℥iij. Mix: to be taken at one dose.

Prescribed for Napoleon I, for the *immediate* cure of *Severe Hoarseness.* Dr. FOREAU.

342. ℞ Ammoniæ Sesquicarb. ʒss.
Misturæ Camphoræ, ℥vss.
Syr. Zingiberis, ʒiv.
Mix: make a mixture. Take a tablespoonful every second hour.

In Prostration of Typhus Fever.—Dr. JOY.

343. ℞ Ammoniæ Sesquicarb. ʒij.
Aquæ destillatæ, f℥v.
Two teaspoonfuls to be taken every three or four hours. When the difficulty of swallowing abates, cold water, or toast-water may be added to each dose.

In Scarlatina.—Dr. PEART.

[Mr. Wilkinson gives the same medicine also in *Erysipelas*, *Rubeola*, *Urticaria*, *Roseola*, and *Erythema.*]

344. ℞ Ammon. Sesquicarb. ʒss.
Sodæ Carbonatis, ʒj.
Infusi Quassiæ, f℥vj. Mix: take a sixth part for a dose.
In Indigestion, with Acidity.—Dr. Hooper.

345. ℞ Ammoniæ Sesquic. gr. xxv.
Aquæ destillatæ, f℥vss.
Tinct. Calumbæ, fʒij.
Tinct. Zingiberis, fʒiss.
Syr. Aurantii, fʒij.
Make a mixture: take two tablespoonfuls at 11 o'clock A.M.
Dr. Hodgkin.

346. ℞ Ammoniæ Sesquicarb. gr. v.
Sodæ Bicarbon. ʒss.
Tinct. Calumbæ, fʒj.
Inf. Gentianæ comp. f℥iss.
Mix: make a draught. To be taken twice a day.
In Cancerous Diseases.—Sir A. Cooper.

347. ℞ Ammoniæ Sesquicarb. ʒss.
Aquæ Menthæ pip. f℥vij.
Syrupi Aurantii, f℥ss.
Mix: take an eighth part in fainting spells.
Dr. Paris.

348. ℞ Ammoniæ Sesquicarb. gr. iv.
Tinct. Hyoscyami, fʒj.
Liq. Ammoniæ Acet. fʒiij.
Syrupi, fʒj.
Misturæ Camphoræ, f℥j.
Mix: make a draught. To be taken every six hours.
In Delirium Tremens.—Dr. G. Gregory.

349. ℞ Ammoniæ Sesquic. ʒiv.
Tinct. Aurantii, f℥iv.
Dissolve: take a teaspoonful twice a day in water.
G. T. G.

350. ℞ Ammon. Sesquicarb. ʒss.
Liq. Ammoniæ Acet. f℥ij.
Mist. Camphoræ, f℥iijss.
Syr. Aurantii, f℥ss. A sixth part to be taken for a dose.
Stimulant and Diaphoretic.—Dr. Hooper.

351. ℞ Ammoniæ Sesquicarb.
Potassæ Bicarbonatis, ana ʒss.
Aquæ destillatæ, f℥viiss.
Make a mixture. Dose, f℥jss twice a day, after breakfast, and just before going to sleep.
In Dyspepsia, with Acidity.—Dr. Joy.

352. ℞ Ammoniæ Sesquic. ℈ss.
Aquæ Cinnamomi, ℥j.
Tinct. Capsici, ʒss.
Syrupi Croci, ℥ss.
Make a draught: to be taken just before going to sleep.

To prevent Nightmare.—Dr. WALLER.

353. ℞ Ammoniæ Sesquicarb. ʒij.
Gummi Tragacanthæ, ℈j.
Aquæ destillatæ, f℥vij.
Make a mixture. Take a spoonful every hour.

In Vomiting from Acidity.—RUDERMACHER.

354. ℞ Ammoniæ Sesquicarb. ʒj.
Aquæ Rutæ, ℥ix.
Syrupi Papaveris, ℥j. Mix: a spoonful every ten minutes.

In Spasmodic Asthma.—VAN SWIETEN.

355. ℞ Liq. Ammoniæ Sesquic. f℥ss.
Infusi Cascarillæ, f℥vij.
Spir. Ætheris Nitrici, fʒj.
Spir. Cinnamomi, fʒiij.
Mix: make a mixture, of which two tablespoonfuls may be taken three times a day.

In Lithic Diathesis, with Debility of Stomach.—Dr. NELIGAN.

356. ℞ Ammoniæ Sesquicarb. ʒiiss.
Syrupi Sudorifici [*vel* Sarsæ], ℥viij.
Mix: a tablespoonful from once to four times a day.

In obstinate Skin Diseases.—CAZENAVE.

357. ℞ Ammoniæ Sesquicarb. ℈j.
Ipecacuanhæ, ʒss.
Tinct. Capsici, ʒj.
Aquæ Menthæ pip. f℥iij. Make an emetic draught.

In Poisoning by Narcotics.—SPRAGUE.

358. ℞ Ammoniæ Sesquicarb. ʒss.
Infusi Senegæ, f℥j.
Syrupi Croci, fʒij.
Make a draught: to be taken immediately.

In Suffocative Catarrh of Typhus.—Dr. NELIGAN.

359. ℞ Ammon. Sesquicarb. ʒss.
Spirit. Sacchari (*Rum*), ʒv.
Syrupi simpl. ʒv.
Aquæ, ℥iij. Mix: half to be taken morning and night.

In Saccharine Diabetes.—M. BOUCHARDAT

60. ℞ Ammoniæ Sesquicarb. ℈ss.
Pulv. Valerianæ, ℈j.
Aquæ Cinnamomi, f℥ij. Make a draught.

In Nervous Headache.—Dr. JOY.

361. ℞ Ammoniæ Sesquicarb.
Extracti Gentianæ, ana ʒss.
Make into a mass, and divide into 12 pills, of which one is to be taken twice or thrice a day.

Antacid, Tonic, and Stimulant.—Mr. BRANDE.

362. ℞ Ammoniæ Sesquicarb. gr. xxiv.
Fellis bov. inspissati, ʒss.
Mucilag. Acaciæ, q. s.
Make into 12 pills. Take one thrice a day.

In Dyspepsia, with Vomiting and Constipation.
Dr. NELIGAN.

363. ℞ Ammoniæ Sesquicarb. gr. viij.
Extracti Rhei, gr. viij.
Syr. Zingiberis, q. s.
Divide into 4 pills. Take one or two as occasion may require when acid is present in the stomach.

In Dyspepsia, with Acidity.—Dr. JOY.

364. ℞ Ammoniæ Sesquicarb.
Extracti Anthemidis, ana ʒss.
Make a mass, and divide into 12 pills, of which one is to be taken twice or thrice a day.

Dr. COPLAND.

365. ℞ Ammoniæ Bicarbon. gr. viij.
Infusi Calumbæ, f℥j.
Tinct. Humuli, fʒj.
Tinct. Hyoscyami, ♏xx.
Mix: make a draught. To be taken twice daily.

In Dyspepsia, with Acidity and Irritability of the Stomach.
Dr. NELIGAN.

366. ℞ Spiritus Ammoniæ aromatici, f℥j.
Aquæ Cinnamomi, f℥v.
Sodæ Bicarbonatis, ℥ss.
Olei Cinnamomi, ♏xv.
Tinct. Capsici, fʒj.
Mix: take a dessertspoonful in a wineglassful of water, after breakfast and dinner, every day.

Antacid and Stimulant.—Mr. VANCE.

367. ℞ Magnesiæ Carbon. ℈j.
Mist. Camphoræ, f℥iss.
Spir. Ammoniæ aromat. fʒss.
Tinct. Opii, ♏v.
Mix: make a draught. To be taken at bedtime.

In Acid Dyspepsia, with Languor and Irritability.
Mr. BRANDE.

368. ℞ Spirit. Ammoniæ arom.
Tinct. Cascarillæ, ana f℥j.
Mix: take a teaspoonful thrice a day in a wineglassful of water.

Dr. GOLDING BIRD.

369. ℞ Spir. Ammoniæ aromat.
Tinct. Lavandulæ comp. ana f℥j.
Mix: take a teaspoonful in water when the flatulence is excessive; or, in faintness.

Dr. JOY.

370. ℞ Spir. Ammoniæ aromat.
Liquoris Potassæ,
Tincturæ Rhei, ana f℥j.
Mix: take a teaspoonful twice a day in water.

Antacid, Stimulant, and Stomachic.—H. J.

371. ℞ Aquæ Menthæ, f℥iss.
Sp. Ammon. arom. fʒss.
Sp. Ætheris Nitrici, gutt. xij.
Sp. Lavandulæ comp. fʒj.
Syrupi simpl. ℥ss. Mix: take fʒj every second hour.

In receded Eruptions, Sinking, &c. of Children.

Drs. EVANSON and MAUNSELL.

372. ℞ Spirit. Ammon. arom. f℥ss.
Tinct. Lavandulæ comp f℥j.
Aquæ Cinnamomi, f℥iiiss.
Syrupi Aurantii, f℥j.
Take a sixth or fourth part for a dose.

Dr. HOOPER.

373. ℞ Spirit. Ammon. arom.
Spirit. Ætheris sulph. ana fʒiss.
Morphiæ Acetatis, gr. ss.
Misturæ Camphoræ, f℥ij.
Mix: a teaspoonful to be taken when occasion requires.

In Spasms of the Stomach, &c.—Dr. GRINDROD.

374. ℞ Aquæ Carui, f℥j.
Tinct. Cardam. comp fʒij.
Spir. Ammoniæ arom. ♏x.
Syrupi Croci, fʒj. Mix: make a draught.

Dr. JOY.

375. ℞ Liquoris Calcis, f℥vss.
Magnesiæ Carbon. ʒss.
Spir. Ammon. arom. fʒij.
Tinct. Rhei, fʒiij. Mix: dose, f℥j twice daily.

In Herpes Labialis, &c.—Dr. BURGESS.

376. ℞ Spir. Ammon. arom. fʒij.
Sp. Ætheris Nitrici, fʒij.
Tinct. Hyoscyami, fʒij.
Mist. Camphoræ, f℥v. Take a fourth part thrice a day.

In Irritable Bladder, with Acid Urine.

[This has been recommended when *fixed alkalies* disagree; the latter, however, are always preferable where the object is to render the urine alkaline, ammonia being decomposed before it reaches the bladder.]

377. ℞ Liquoris Ammoniæ anisati,
Vini Antim. Potassio-tart. ana fʒiss.
Decocti Althææ, f℥v.
Syr. Opii, P. [*vel* Papaveris], ℥j.
Mix: a spoonful every two hours.

In Bronchitis.—SCHUBARTH.

378. ℞ Decoct. Althææ, ℥ij.
Olei Amygd. dulcis,
Pulv. Acaciæ, ana ʒij.
Liq. Ammoniæ anisati, gutt xxv.
Sacchari conditi, ʒj.
Mix: take two teaspoonfuls every second hour.

In Colic, Diarrhœa, and Tenesmus, of Children of 2 years.
RADIUS.

379. ℞ Misturæ Camphoræ, f℥v.
Spir. Ammon. fœtidi, fʒv.
Syrupi Croci, fʒiij. Mix: take two tablespoonfuls for a dose.

In Hysteria, &c.—Dr. JOY.

380. ℞ Sp. Ammoniæ fœtidi, fʒiij.
Misturæ Camphoræ, f℥vj.
Syrupi Aurantii, fʒiij.
Spir. Lavand. comp. fʒij.
Mix: take two spoonfuls twice daily.

℞ Zinci Sulphatis, ℈ss.
Extr. Gentianæ, ℈ij.
Extr. Coloc. comp. ℈j. Make 20 pills. Take 2 every night.

In Costiveness, with Nervous Debility.—Dr. BABINGTON.

381. ℞ Infusi Valerianæ, fʒxj.
Spir. Ammon. fœtidi, fʒss.
Tinct. Castorei, fʒss.
Mix: make a draught, to be taken twice or thrice a day.

In Angina Pectoris and other Spasmodic disorders.
Dr. COPLAND.

[For other formulæ containing Sp. Ammon. Fœtidus, see ASSAFŒTIDA, VALERIAN, and CASTOR.]

EXTERNAL APPLICATIONS.

382. ℞ Liq. Ammoniæ, fʒij.
Linim. Saponis, f℥j. Make a liniment.

Rubefacient and Counter-irritant.—Dr. DRUITT.

383. ℞ Liquor. Ammoniæ, f℥j.
Glycerinæ, f℥vj.
Sp. Lavandulæ, f℥ij.
Aquæ destillatæ, f℥vj. Mix: make a lotion.

In Cutaneous Diseases, with Atony of the Skin.

DR. NELIGAN.

384. ℞ Sp. Rosmarini, f℥ij.
Liq. Ammoniæ,
Tinct. Opii, ana ℥ss.

Mix: make an embrocation, to be rubbed over the chest and along the spine.

In Spasmodic Croup and Convulsions of Children.—DR. URE.

385. ℞ Liq. Ammoniæ, f℥ss.
Olei Olivæ, ℥j.
Olei Terebinthinæ, f℥ss.
Olei Limonis, f℥ss. Shake together until well mixed.

DR. COPLAND.

386. ℞ Liq. Ammoniæ, ℥ss.
Petrolei Barbad. ℥iss. Make a liniment.

As a Counter-irritant in Diseased Joints.—DR. KIRKLAND.

[For other Ammoniacal Liniments, see under CAMPHORA, OL. TEREBINTHINÆ, &c.]

387. ℞ Liquor. Ammoniæ, ℈iv.
Lactis Vaccini, ℥iv.

Make an injection, f℥j to be injected daily.

In Amenorrhœa.—LAVAGNA.

AMMONIÆ ACETAS. AMMONIÆ CITRAS. AMMONIÆ TARTRAS. *Acetate, Citrate, and Tartrate of Ammonia.*

These neutral Salts of Ammonia are all regarded as diaphoretic, and in some cases diuretic. They are used in febrile diseases, and generally to promote diaphoresis, as in dropsy, rheumatism, &c.

The *acetate* (as well as the carbonate and pure ammonia) has also been recommended to remove the effects of intoxicating liquors.

The acetate is only employed in the form of *Liquor Ammoniæ Acetatis*, commonly termed Mindererus' Spirit. The *citrate* is very commonly given in the extemporaneous and effervescing form of sesquicarbonate of ammonia and lemon-juice. The doses are:

> *Liq. Ammoniæ Acetatis*, 3 to 12 drachms.
> *Ammoniæ Citras*, 1 to 3 scruples.
> *Liq. Ammoniæ Citratis*, L.; 2½ to 4 drachms.
> ——— *Tartratis*; the same.

Externally, Liq. Ammon. Acet. is cooling and discutient, and is used in lotions to bruises and inflammations, and as a collyrium in chronic ophthalmia.

388. ℞ Liquoris Ammoniæ Acetatis, f℥ij.
Misturæ Camphoræ, f℥vj.
Mix: take f℥ij every six hours.

As a Diaphoretic in Low Fevers.—Dr. AINSLIE.

389. ℞ Liq. Ammoniæ Acetatis, fʒix.
Vini Antim. Potassio-tart. fʒj.
Syrupi Papaveris, fʒj.
Aquæ Menthæ, fʒxij.
Make a mixture: take a tablespoonful every fourth hour, and take every night, going to bed, the following powder:
℞ Pulv. Ipecac. comp. gr. iiiss.
Hydrarg. cum Creta, gr. v. Mix.

In Dropsy, after Scarlatina.—Dr. GOLDING BIRD.

390. ℞ Liq. Ammoniæ Acet. fʒiij.
Misturæ Camphoræ,
Aquæ destillatæ, ana fʒiv.
Syrupi Rhœados, fʒj.
Make a draught, to be taken every 6 hours.

As a Diaphoretic.—Dr. G. GREGORY.

391. ℞ Liquor. Ammoniæ Acet. f℥ij.
Syrupi simplicis, f℥j.
Aquæ fl. Aurantii, f℥j.
Misturæ Camphoræ, f℥iv.
Mix: take f℥j every fourth hour.

Dr. NELIGAN.

392. ℞ Liquor. Ammon. Acet. fʒij.
Aquæ Menthæ pip.
Aquæ puræ, ana f℥ss.
Vin. Antim. Potassio-tart. ♏xx.
Syrupi, fʒj.
Make a draught, to be taken every four hours.

Dr. G. GREGORY.

393. ℞ Liq. Ammon. Acet. fʒiij.
Misturæ Camphoræ, f℥j.
Syr. Aurantii, fʒj. Make a draught.

As a Mild Diaphoretic.—Dr. JOY.

394. ℞ Misturæ Camphoræ, f℥iss.
Liq. Ammon. Acet. f℥iv.
Vini Antim. Potassio-tart. gutt. xl.
Tincturæ Opii, gutt xx.
Mix: make a draught, to be taken at the hour of retiring.

In Acute Rheumatism.—BLANE.

395. ℞ Liq. Ammon. Acet. f℥iij.
Vini Opii, ♏xv.
Mucilag. Acaciæ, f℥j.
Aquæ, Oiss.
Mix: the whole to be taken in the course of the day.

In Typhoid Fevers.—M. MICHEL.

396. ℞ Liq. Ammoniæ Acet.
Misturæ Camphoræ, ana f℥vj.
Syrupi Papaveris, f℥j.
Vini Antim. Potassio-tart. ♏xx.
Mix: make a draught. To be taken before going to bed.

In Common Catarrh.—Mr. BRANDE.

397. ℞ Misturæ Camphoræ,
Misturæ Amygdalæ, ana f℥ij.
Liq. Ammoniæ Acet. f℥iss.
Spir. Ætheris Nitrici,
Vini Antim. Potassio-tart. ana f℥iis.
Syrupi Tolutani, f℥iss.
Mix: take two tablespoonfuls every second hour.

In Bronchitis.—Dr. COPLAND.

398. ℞ Liq. Ammon. Acetatis,
Liq. Potassæ Acetatis,
Oxymellis Scillæ, ana ℥j.
Mix: dose, one to two spoonfuls every second hour.

In Dropsy, after Scarlet Fever.—JAHN.

399. ℞ Liq. Ammon. Acet. f℥vj.
Tinct. Camphoræ comp. f℥ij.
Sp. Ætheris Nitrici, f℥j.
Syrupi Tolutani, f℥j.
Aquæ puræ, f℥ij.
Take one-half one night, and the balance the next night.

Dr. C. G. BABINGTON.

400. ℞ Liq. Ammon. Acet. ℥iss.
Potass. Nitrat. ℨj.
Liq. Morph. Mur. ℨj.
Mist. Amygdalæ, ad ℥vj.
Mix: a tablespoonful three times a day, half an hour before meals.

In Inflammatory Dyspepsia.—Dr. ROSS.

401. ℞ Liq. Ammoniæ, Acet. f℥j.
Vini Antimonii P. fʒij.
Syrupi Tolutani, fʒvj.
Aquæ fontanæ, f℥iv.
Make a mixture: take ⅛th part every fourth hour.

In Catarrh.—Dr. G. Gregory.

402. ℞ Ammoniæ Sesquicarb. ℈j.
Succi Limonis recentis, fʒvj.
(*vel* Acidi Citrici, gr. xxiv.)
Aquæ destillatæ, fʒivj.
Syrupi Tolutani,
Spir. Myristicæ, ana fʒss. Make a draught.

Diaphoretic.—Mr. Brande.

403. ℞ Ammoniæ Sesquicarb. ʒj.
Aquæ puræ, f℥iiiss.
Succi Limonis, f℥ij. (or sufficient to saturate).
Syrupi Aurantii, f℥ss.
Make a mixture: two spoonfuls to be taken every third or fourth hour.

In Fevers.—Dr. Cheyne.

404. ℞ Ammoniæ Sesquicarb. ℈j.
Aquæ puræ, f℥iss.
Syrupi, fʒj.
Make a draught, with a tablespoonful of lemon-juice, repeating in four hours.

Dr. Joy.

405. ℞ Ammoniæ Sesquic. ʒj.
Aquæ, f℥vss.
Syrupi Zingiberis, fʒiij. Mix: mark No. 1.

℞ Aquæ, f℥iij.
Acidi Citrici, ʒj.
Mark No. 2. Two spoonfuls of No. 1 to be taken in effervescence with one spoonful of No. 2.

In the latter stage of Protracted Nervous Fevers.

Dr. Graves.

406. ℞ Ammoniæ Sesquicarb. gr. xv.
Aquæ destillatæ, f℥j.
Spirit. Myristicæ, fʒj.
Syrupi Aurantii, f℥ss.
Extr. Conii, gr. iij ad vj.
Make a draught: to be taken four times every day with a tablespoonful of fresh lemon-juice, while in a state of effervescence.

Sedative.—Dr. Copland.

407. ℞ Ammoniæ Sesquicarb. gr. xv.
Acidi Tartarici, ℈j.
Aquæ, fʒxj.
Syrupi Aurantii, fʒj. Make a draught.

LOTIONS, &c.

408. ℞ Liq. Ammoniæ Acetatis, f℥vj.
Spir. rectificati, f℥ij. Make a lotion.
To Hard and Inflamed Breasts, &c.—Dr. CLARK.

409. ℞ Liq. Ammoniæ Acet. f℥iij.
Spir. rectificati, fʒiv.
Aquæ Rosæ, f℥iv. Make a lotion.
In Lichen, &c.—Dr. BURGESS.

410. ℞ Liq. Ammoniæ Acet. f℥ij.
Acidi Hydrocyanici dil. fʒj.
Tinct. Digitalis, fʒiij.
Aquæ Rosæ, f℥v.
Make a lotion: apply twice a day to the affected parts by means of a sponge.
In Pruriginous Affections of the Aged.—Dr. A. T. THOMSON.

411. ℞ Liq. Ammoniæ Acet. f℥vj.
Spir. Rosmarini, f℥ij
Aquæ, ℥xvj. Make a lotion.
Discutient.—R. G. HOLLAND.

412. ℞ Liq. Ammoniæ Acet. fʒvj.
Aquæ Sambuci, f℥vij. Make an eyewash.
In Ophthalmia.—Mr. WARE.

AMMONIÆ HYDROCHLORAS, VEL MURIAS.

Sal Ammoniac.

Hydrochlorate, or Muriate of Ammonia, is regarded as alterative or resolvent; and is used in inflammation of the mucous membranes, after its violence has subsided; particularly in bronchitis, when not attended with much fever, pain, or irritability; and in a great variety of chronic diseases. It increases the action and improves the secretions of the mucous membranes, especially that of the lungs. It is also described as refrigerant, antiseptic, and tonic. The dose is from 5 to 20 grains every two or three hours. Still larger doses have been given in intermittent fevers, and in chronic enlargement of the prostate. But its use requires caution in persons of feeble constitution, especially those subject to hæmorrhage.

413. ℞ Aquæ destillatæ, f℥ij.
Ammoniæ Hydrochl. gr. viij–xij.
Tinct. Opii, gutt. ii–iij.
Extracti Glycyrrhizæ liq. ʒiss.

Mix: give a teaspoonful every two or three hours for a child 1 or 2 years of age.

Dr. Meigs.

414. ℞ Ammoniæ Muriatis, ʒj.
Syrupi Hemedesmi, f℥ss.
Aquæ Cinnamomi, f℥viiss.

Mix: make a mixture, of which take two tablespoonfuls every six hours.

In Adynamic Fevers, and Subacute Laryngitis.—Dr. Neligan.

415. ℞ Ammoniæ Muriatis, gr. xij.
Decocti Cinchonæ, f℥iss.

Make a draught: to be taken twice a day.

In Chronic Rheumatism.—Dr. H. W. Fuller.

416. ℞ Ammoniæ Hydrochlor. ʒij.
Extr. Glycyrrhizæ, ʒiij.
Antimonii Potassio-tart. gr. ij.
Aquæ destillatæ, f℥viij.

Make a mixture, of which take a tablespoonful every second hour.

[The Antim. Potassio-Tart. to be omitted when it has made a sufficient impression on the disease.]

In Pleurisy, Subacute Pneumonia, Mucous Congestion, &c.

Sir Geo. Lefevre.

417. ℞ Ammoniæ Muriatis, ʒiss.
Acidi Muriatici, fʒss.
Decocti Hordei, lbj.

Mix: take three tablespoonfuls every second or third hour.

Dr. Copland.

418. ℞ Ammoniæ Muriatis, ʒij.
Aquæ Menthæ,
Aquæ flor. Aurantii, ana f℥iij.

Mix: to be taken in two doses, at intervals of two hours, followed by a cup of coffee.

In Intermittent Fever.—M. Aran.

419. ℞ Ammoniæ Muriatis, gr. iv.
Liq. Ammon. Acetatis, fʒij.
Misturæ Camphoræ, f℥j.
Syrupi Limonis, fʒj.

Make a draught: to be taken every fourth hour.

In Typhoid Fevers.—Dr. Copland.

420. ℞ Ammoniæ Muriatis, gr. xv.
Gummi Acaciæ, ʒss.
Infusi Anthemidis, ℥iij.
Vini Antimon. q. ʒj.
Extr. Glycyrrhizæ, ʒij.
Mix: half a spoonful every two hours to a child of 5 or 6 years old.

In Dysentery and Catarrhal Affections.—TORTUAL.

421. ℞ Ammon. Hydrochl. gr. x.
Extr. Taraxaci, ʒss.
Decocti Aloes, comp.
Mist. Gentianæ comp. ana ʒv.
Sodæ Potassio-tart. ʒj.
Tinct. Lavand. comp. ♏xx.
Make a draught: to be taken in the morning, and, if occasion calls for it, it can be repeated at noon.

In Torpid Liver, with Uterine Disease.—Dr. G. CORFE.

422. ℞ Ammoniæ Mur. ℈ij.
Potassæ Nitratis, ℈iv.
Aquæ Rubi Idæi, ℥vj.
Syrupi fl. Aurantii, ʒiij. Mix: a spoonful every two hours.

In the early stage of Rheumatic, Exanthematic, and Catarrhal Fevers. CLARUS.

423. ℞ Ammon. Mur.
Extr. Glycyrrhizæ, ana ʒj.
Decocti Althææ, f℥vj.
Oxymel. simpl. (*vel* Scillæ), ℥j.
Make a mixture: take two tablespoonfuls three times a day.

In Catarrhal Affections.—Dr. COPLAND.

424. ℞ Ammoniæ Muriatis, ʒij.
Camphoræ, gr. vj.
Flor. Arnicæ, ʒss.
Sacchari albi, ʒvj.
Mix: make a powder. Let it be given in glass, a teaspoonful three or four times a day.

As an Expectorant and Emmenagogue.—M. BERENDS.

425. ℞ Ammoniæ Muriat.
Extr. Glycyrrhizæ, ana ℈j.
Ext. Taraxaci, q. s., to form a bolus.
Make 12 such doses. One may be taken every second or fourth hour.

In Scirrhus of the Prostate, &c.—SOBERNHEIM.

426. ℞ Ammoniæ Muriatis, ʒss.
Sulphuris loti, gr. xv.
Extr. Dulcamaræ, q. s.
Make four boluses. Take one every second hour.

In Chronic Pulmonary Catarrh.—FISCHER.

427. ℞ Ammoniæ Muriatis, ʒss.
Pulv. Opii, gr. x.
P. Digitalis,
P. Scillæ, āā ℈j.
Mix: divide into 30 pills. Take one every sixth hour.
In early stage of Phthisis.—Dr. H. GREEN.

428. ℞ Decocti Papaveris, Oj.
Ammoniæ Mur. ʒvj.
Make a lotion: linen rags dipped in it to be kept applied to the part.
To Milk Breasts.—Dr. CLARK.

429. ℞ Ammoniæ Muriatis, ʒij.
Acidi Acetici diluti, f℥vj.
Spir. Camphoræ, f℥ij. Make a lotion.
In Sprains, Contusions, &c.—Dr. JOY.

430. ℞ Ammoniæ Mur. ʒij.
Aquæ, f℥ij.
Spir. Rosmarini, ℥ss. Make a lotion.
For Unbroken Chilblains.

431. ℞ Ammoniæ Muriat. ℥ss.
Aquæ commun. ℥x. Dissolve, and add
Aceti Scillæ, ℥ij. Make a lotion.
In Hydrocele of Children, &c.—GRAEFE.

432. ℞ Ammoniæ Mur. ℥j.
Spir. rectificati, f℥j.
Aquæ, f℥xv. Make a lotion.
Dr. HOOPER.

433. ℞ Ammoniæ Mur. ʒj.
Liq. Ammon. Acet. f℥ij.
Aquæ, f℥iv.
Make a lotion: to be kept constantly applied.
In Hydrocele of Children.—Mr. BRANSBY COOPER.

434. ℞ Ammon. Hydrochlor. ʒj.
Aquæ fontanæ, f℥v.
Spir. rectif. f℥j. Mix: make a lotion.
In Swelled Testicles, &c.—Dr. A. T. THOMSON.

435. ℞ Ammon. Mur. ʒiiss.
Tinct. Arnicæ, ʒiiss.
Aquæ Rutæ, ℥x.
Aceti Rutæ, ℥v. Make a lotion.
In Hydrocele of Children.—CARUS.

436. ℞ Ammon. Mur. ʒij.
Liq. Ammon. Acet. f℥v.
Spirit. Vini rectif. f℥j. Make a lotion.
For the same.—Sir A. COOPER.

437. ℞ Ammon. Hydrochl. ℥ss.
Acidi Acetici diluti,
Spir. rectificati, ana f℥ss.
Misturæ Camphoræ, f℥xv. Make a lotion.

Dr. DRUITT.

438. ℞ Amygd. dulc. excort. ℥j.
Aquæ flor. Aurant. ℥ij.
Aquæ Rosæ, ℥viij. Make an emulsion, and add
Ammon. Muriatis, ʒj.
Tincturæ Benzoini, ʒij. Make a cosmetic lotion.

In Pimples and Dryness of the Skin.—HERRMAN.

439. ℞ Ammoniæ Muriat. gr. xv.
Camphoræ pulv. ℈j. Rub together, and add
Decocti Cinchonæ, f℥vi. Make a gargle.

In Putrid Sore Throat.—Dr. COPLAND.

440. ℞ Rad. Pyrethri cont. ℥j.
Aquæ ferventis, f℥xij.
Macerate for an hour, strain, and add to the liquor
Ammoniæ Mur. ʒiij.
Aceti communis, ℥iij. Make a mouth wash.

VAN SWIETEN.

441. ℞ Ammon. Mur. pulv.
Potassæ Nitratis pulv. ana ʒj.
Pulv. Capsici, ʒss.
Mix well, to be applied by means of a camel-hair pencil.

In Elongated Uvula.—Dr. B. GRANVILLE.

AMMONIÆ NITRAS, PHOSPHAS, SULPHAS, &c.

The remaining Ammoniacal Salts employed in medicine are:

Ammoniæ Nitras. Nitrate of Ammonia is refrigerant and diuretic. Dose, from 3 to 20 grains, in slight inflammations of mucous membranes, catarrhal and rheumatic fevers, &c. Equal parts of nitrate of ammonia, carbonate of soda, and water form a powerful freezing mixture.

Ammoniæ Sulphas. Sulphate of Ammonia is diuretic, stimulant, and resolvent. Dose, 15 to 30 grains.

Ammoniæ Nitro-Sulphas. Nitro-sulphate of Ammonia is said to be useful in typhoid fevers. Dose, about 12 grains.

Ammoniæ Phosphas. Phosphate of Ammonia has been used with success in some cases of rheumatism. Dose, 3 to 10 grains. Dr. Edwards gives 10 grains every eight hours.

Ammoniæ Succinas. Succinate of Ammonia is antispasmodic.

It is usually given in the form of Liq. Ammoniæ (*vel* Cornu Cervi) Succinatus, of which a few drops are a dose.

Ammoniæ Hydro-Sulphas. The Hydro-sulphuret of Ammonia, and the Sulphuretted Hydro-sulphuret (*Liq. Fumans Boylii*) are poisonous in large doses; in small doses they produce nausea, reduce the pulse, and promote the secretion of the skin and lungs. They have been used in catarrhal complaints, diabetes, and gout; but are now rarely prescribed. Dose, from 4 to 8 drops.

442. ℞ Ammoniæ Nitratis, ʒss.
Aquæ destillatæ, ℥iij.
Syrupi Althææ, ℥j.
Mix: a dessertspoonful every two hours.

In Fevers and Dropsies.

443. ℞ Liq. Vol. Cornu Cervi, ʒiv.
Acid. Succinici, q. s. to saturate.
Sp. Ætheris Sulphurici, ʒiv.
Mix: twenty to forty drops in a glass of sugared water two or three times a day. [Eller's Liquor Arthriticus.]

In Gout and Inveterate Rheumatism.—NIEMANN.

444. ℞ Ammoniæ Phosphatis, ℈ss.
Aquæ Cinnamomi, f℥j.
Make a draught, to be taken thrice a day.

In Acute and Subacute Rheumatism.—Dr. BUCKLER (U. S.).

AMMONIACUM (*Gummi*).

Gum Ammoniac is the concrete juice of an umbelliferous plant, Dorema Ammoniacum. It is stimulant, expectorant, deobstruent, diuretic, diaphoretic, and emmenagogue; and is chiefly used as an expectorant in affections of the chest not attended with inflammation; and in visceral obstructions. *Externally*, it is applied as a discutient and resolvent to indolent tumors.

Dose of the gum, 5 to 30 grains; of *Mistura Ammoniaci*, 4 to 8 drachms.

Emplastrum Ammoniaci and *Emp. Ammon. cum Hydrarg.* are the usual forms for outward application.

445. ℞ Misturæ Ammoniaci, f℥viij.
Vini Antimonii Potassio-tart. fʒj.
Make a mixture: dose, 2 or 3 spoonfuls.

Expectorant.—Dr. PEARSON.

446. ℞ Mist. Ammoniaci, f℥v.
Oxymel. Scillæ, f℥ss.
Vini Antimon. ♏xxj.
Aceti destillati, fʒiij.
Mix: take a tablespoonful frequently.
In Humoral Asthma, Chronic Cough, &c.—Dr. AINSLIE.

447. ℞ Pulv. G. Ammoniac. ʒj.
Oxymellis Scillæ, ℥ij. Rub up together, and add
Ovi unius vitellum.
Aquæ Menth. Puleg. ℥vj.
Aquæ Menth. pip. ℥iv.
Mix: to be taken during the day by a tablespoonful at a time.
In Catarrh.—TROUSSEAU and REVEIL.

448. ℞ Mist. Ammoniaci, f℥ivss.
Liq. Antimon. Tart. fʒiv.
Tinct. Camphoræ comp. f℥ss.
Syrupi Tolutani, f℥j.
Mix: take a spoonful occasionally.
In Chronic Pituitous Asthma.—Dr. COPLAND.

449. ℞ Mist. Ammoniaci,
Aquæ Pulegii, ana fʒvj.
Spir. Ammon. arom.
Syrupi Scillæ, ana fʒss.
Make a draught, to be taken twice a day.
As a stimulating Expectorant.—Mr. BRANDE.

450. ℞ Ammoniaci, ℈iiss.
Acidi Nitrici, fʒij.
Aquæ destil. f℥viij.
Add the distilled water to the acid, and make an emulsion with the gum; a teaspoonful two or three times a day.
In Chronic Catarrh of elderly persons.—Dr. ELLIS (U. S.).

451. ℞ Ammoniaci, ʒj.
Acidi Nitrici diluti, f℥j.
Aquæ, f℥iij. Triturate together until an emulsion is made, and add
Syrupi, fʒij.
Mix: take a dessertspoonful in some demulcent liquid.
Expectorant and Tonic.—Dr. PARIS.

452. ℞ Mist. Ammoniaci,
Mist. Amygdalæ, ana fʒiv.
Aceti Scillæ, fʒj.
Tinct. Opii, ♏iij.
Make a draught, to be taken every third hour.
In Catarrhal Cough.—Dr. GREGORY.

453. ℞ Mist. Ammoniaci, f ℥vj.
Sodæ Carbonatis, ʒss.
Tinct. Camphoræ comp. f ℥ss.
Tinct. Hyoscyami, f ℥j.
Vini Ipecacuanhæ, fʒij.
Make a cough mixture, of which take a tablespoonful for a dose.
In Chronic Bronchitis.—Dr. GRAVES.

454. ℞ Mist Ammoniaci,
Aquæ Cinnamomi, ana f ℥iij.
Cetacei (vitel. ovi sol.) ʒij.
Syrupi Tolutani, f ℥j.
Mix: take a wineglassful morning and evening.
As an Expectorant, in Phthisis, &c.—Dr. E. G. CLARK.

455 ℞ Misturæ Ammoniaci, ℥vij.
Oxymel. Scillæ, fʒvj.
Tinct. Camphoræ comp. ʒiv.
Make a mixture: take two spoonfuls every second or third hour.
In Chronic Bronchitis.—Sir. H. HALFORD, Bart.

456. ℞ Mist. Ammoniaci,
Mist. Amygdalæ, ana fʒvj.
Tinct. Scillæ, ♏x. Mix, for a draught.
Mr. BRANDE.

457. ℞ Mist. Ammoniaci,
Aquæ Cinnamomi, ana f ℥iss.
Syrupi Tolutani, f ℥ss.
Tinct. Castorei, fʒij.
Tinct. Opii, ♏v.
Make a mixture, of which take a tablespoonful frequently.
In Hooping Cough, &c.—Dr. PARIS.

458. ℞ Gummi Ammoniaci, fʒj.
Oxymel. Scillæ, ℥j.
Vini Ipecacuanhæ, fʒj.
Aquæ fl. Sambuci, f ℥ivss.
Syrupi Papaveris, ʒij.
Mix: let the patient take a spoonful at appropriate hours.
In Chronic Pectoral complaints.—Dr. COPLAND.

459 ℞ Mist. Ammoniaci, f ℥viss.
Tinct. Camphoræ comp. fʒvj.
Liq. Volat. cornu cervi, fʒiij.
Tinct. Scillæ, ʒiij.
Make a mixture: a tablespoonful now and then.
In Chronic and Asthmatic Cough.—Dr. WARREN.

460. ℞ Ammoniaci, ʒj.
Sagapeni, ʒij.
Tinct. Aloes comp. q. s.
Make into 4-grain pills; take two twice a day.
In Amenorrhœa, &c.—BORIES.

461. ℞ G. Ammoniaci, ʒj.
Scillæ recentis, ℈j.
Pulv. Ipecac. comp. ʒss.
Hydrarg. chloridi, gr. vj.
Mix: make into a mass, and divide into 24 pills; two may be taken every 4 hours.

In Chronic Cough.—Dr. LATHAM.

462. ℞ G. Ammoniaci, ʒss.
Pil. Scillæ comp. ʒss.
Extr. Hyoscyami, gr. xij.
Extr. Papaveris, gr. xij.
Make into 24 pills; take one twice a day.

In Chronic Coughs, &c.—Dr. BOISRAGON.

463. ℞ Ammoniaci, ʒj.
Saponis duri, ʒiiss.
Aloes extracti, gr. xv.
Assafœtidæ, ʒss.
Pulv. Rhei, ʒj.
Croci pulv. ʒss.
Syrupi, q. s. Make into 80 pills; take two twice a day.

Deobstruent.—RECAMIER.

464. ℞ Ammoniaci, ʒj.
Scillæ pulv. ℈j.
Saponis Venet. ℈ij.
Syr. Tolutani, q. s.
Make into 24 pills, of which 3 may be taken morning and night.

In Peripneumonia Notha.—Dr. E. G. CLARKE.

465. ℞ Emplastri Picis, 2 parts.
Emplastri Ammoniaci,
Emplastri Opii, each 1 part.
Mix: make a plaster of an appropriate size, to be placed between the shoulder blades.

In Cough.—Dr. COPLAND.

AMYGDALÆ. *Almonds.*

Sweet Almonds are the kernels of Amygdalus communis (dulcis). They are emollient and demulcent, and are used in the form of emulsion, in catarrhal complaints, in dysentery, and in strangury, calculus, and other affections of the urinary organs, to lessen the acrimony of the secretions. Milk of almonds is less frequently used alone than as a vehicle for more active remedies. (See Potassæ Nitras, Opium, Scilla, &c.) The *expressed oil* is emollient and slightly laxative. It may be formed into an emulsion with mucilage, or alkalies. *Confectio*

Amygdalæ is used to prepare *Mistura Amygdalæ;* the dose of the latter may be from 1 to 2 or 3 ounces. Of *Oleum Amygdalæ,* 1 to 8 drachms.

466. ℞ Misturæ Amygdalæ, Oj.
Syrupi Papaveris, f℥x.
Make a mixture, for an ordinary drink.
In Calculous Disorder, Strangury, &c.—Dr. E. G. Clarke.

467. ℞ Mist. Amygdalæ, f℥x.
Vini Ipecac. ♏vj.
Syr. Papaveris, f℥ss.
Make a draught, to be taken thrice a day.
In Catarrhal Cough.—Dr. G. Gregory.

468. ℞ Mist. Amygdalæ, f℥v.
Liq. Ammoniæ acet. f℥j.
Spir. Ætheris Nitrici,
Tinct. Croci, ana f℥j.
Make a mixture: take a tablespoonful three times a day.
In Catarrh.—Dr. Clutterbuck.

469. ℞ Mist. Amygdalæ, f℥vij.
Mucil. Acaciæ, f℥j.
Pulv. Ipecac. comp. ℈j.
Mix: take two spoonfuls every third hour while the cough is troublesome.
In Catarrhal Cough.—Dr. Latham.

470. ℞ Olei Amygdalæ, f℥iss.
Vitellum Ovi unius.
Aquæ fl. Aurantii, f℥v.
Mucilag. Acaciæ, f℥ss.
Vini Ipecacuanhæ, f℥iss.
Syr. Althææ (*vel* simpl.) f℥ss.
Make a mixture: a tablespoonful frequently.
In Catarrhs.—Dr. Copland.

471. ℞ Acaciæ pulveris, ℥ss.
Aquæ destillatæ, f℥ss. Mix, and add by degrees,
Olei Amygdalæ, f℥iij. Rub up together, and add
Aquæ destil. f℥iij.
Aquæ Rosæ, f℥iss.
Syrupi, f℥iij.
Mix: take one or two spoonfuls frequently.
In Catarrh, Urinary Irritation, &c.—Mr. Brande.

472. ℞ Olei Amygdalæ, f℥ij.
Syrupi Papaveris,
Syrupi Tolutani, ana f℥j.
Pulv. Sacchari, ℥ij.
Make a thick syrup, of which the patient may suck frequently, the cough being troublesome.
In the Cough of Measles, &c.—Dr. E. G. Clarke.

473. ℞ Olei Amygdalæ,
Syrupi Violæ, ana ℥j.
Mix: take two spoonfuls every third hour.

Dr. Harding.

474. ℞ Mellis despumati,
Olei Amygdalæ, ana ℥j.
Syr. Rhœados, ℥ss.
Aceti Scillæ, ʒij.
Syrupi Tolutani,
Mucil. Acaciæ, ana ℥ss. Mix.

In Coughs, &c.—Dr. Joy.

475. ℞ Olei Amygdalæ,
Pulv. Acaciæ,
Syr. Althææ, ana ʒij.
Aquæ Cinnamomi, ℥ss.
Aquæ Fœniculi, ℥j.
Mix: one or two teaspoonfuls to be given every hour.

In Infantile Diarrhœa.—Richter.

476. ℞ Olei Amygdalæ, f℥j.
Acaciæ pulveris, ʒij.
Aquæ destil. f℥vj.
Syrupi Papaveris, f℥ss.
Rub the oil up diligently with the gum, then by degrees add the water and syrup. Take a tablespoonful frequently during the day.

In Catarrh.—Dr. G. Gregory.

477. ℞ Olei Amygdalæ,
Mellis, ana ℥j.
Succi Limonis, ℥ss.
Syrupi Tolutani,
Syrupi Scillæ, ana ʒij.
Mix: make a thick syrup. Take a tablespoonful frequently.

In Catarrh.—Dr. Joy.

478. ℞ Olei Amygdalæ, f℥ss.
Aquæ Rosæ, f℥ij.
Liquor. Potassæ, fʒij. Mix, by shaking, and add
Syrupi, f℥ss.
Aquæ destillatæ, f℥v.
Make a mixture, of which two ounces may be taken for a dose.

In Catarrh, and in Renal and Urinary Irritation.
Mr. Brande.

479. ℞ Olei Amygdalæ,
Aquæ destillatæ, ana ℥ss.
Liq. Ammoniæ Sesquicarb. ♏xx.
Make a draught: to be taken every morning on an empty stomach.

In Worms.—Dr. Clarke.

The *Bitter Almond*, Amygdala amara, is the product of a variety of the Amygdalus communis, but contains, in addition to the constituents of the sweet almond, a peculiar principle, *Amygdaline*, which gives rise, when triturated with water, to hydrocyanic acid and volatile oil of bitter almonds. By distillation with water, *Aqua Amygdalæ amaræ* and *Oleum essentiale Amygdalæ amaræ* are obtained. These are sometimes used in the same cases as prussic acid. A few bitter almonds are sometimes added to the sweet in making emulsions, on account of their sedative properties, as well as for the flavor.

Aqua Amygdalæ amaræ is made of very different degrees of strength; and as no form is given for it in the British pharmacopœias, it is necessary for the prescriber to specify the kind intended. That of the Prussian pharmacopœia contains two-thirds of a grain of pure prussic acid in an ounce, which is about the average of the Continental preparations. Dose, from 10 to 30 drops, sometimes increased to 60. A formula for a much weaker kind has lately been introduced into the United States pharmacopœia. A still weaker kind is sometimes sold under the name of *black cherry water*. The leaves and kernels of the *Peach* (Amygdalus Persica) have similar properties. The flowers are laxative.

480. ℞ Amygdalæ dulc. excort. ʒvj.
Amygd. amaræ excort. ʒij.
Aquæ, f℥xvj.
Make an emulsion: take two spoonfuls twice or thrice a day.
Sedative and Demulcent.—BERAL.

481. ℞ Emuls. Amygd. dulc. (ex. Am. dulc. ʒij.) ℥j.
Amygdalinæ, gr. xvij.
Dissolve. Dose, from ten to thirty drops.
In the same cases as Ac. Hydrocyanicum.—WOEHLER.

482. ℞ Ol. essent. Amygd. amaræ, gtt. xx.
Spirit. Vini rectificati, ʒiij. [fʒiv.]
Mix: from ten to twenty drops three times a day.
In Facial Neuralgia.—RADIUS.

AMYLUM. *Starch.*

Wheat starch and the starches of other plants (as of potato, arrow-root, &c.) are demulcent and slightly nutritive. They are also used in enemata, in irritated states of the rectum; the powder is dusted on the skin to absorb irritated secretions, and to allay inflammation in some affections of the skin. It is much employed in the nursery for the excoriations of infants. Starch is an antidote for poisoning by iodine. The only officinal preparations are *Decoctum Amyli* and *Trochisci Amyli.*

483. ℞ Pulv. Amyli, ʒx.
Pulv. Sodæ Carbonatis, ʒj.
Mix: make a powder, to be applied to the affected part.
In some Skin Diseases.—DEVERGIE.

The fæcula or starch of potato, arrow-root, tous-les-mois, &c. have similar properties, but are more frequently employed as a mild article of diet.

ANETHUM. FŒNICULUM. ANISUM. CARUI.

These aromatic seeds, or rather fruits, are placed together, as their properties and uses are similar. The plants which produce them belong to the natural order *Umbelliferæ.*

Dill seed is the fruit of Anethum graveolens; *Anise seed*, of Pimpinella Anisum; *Fennel seed*, of Fœniculum dulce [officinale, *D.*]; *Carraway*, of Carum Carui. They are mildly stimulant and carminative; and are used in flatulent disorders, particularly of children; and as vehicles and correctives of more active or less agreeable remedies, especially to cover the taste, and prevent the griping effects of purgatives.

The doses of *Aqua Anethi*, *Aqua Fœniculi*, *Aqua Anisi*, and *Aqua Carui* are from half an ounce to two or three ounces for adults; or from a teaspoonful to a dessertspoonful for children. *Infusum Fœniculi*, *Infusum Anisi*, and *Infusum Carui*, the same.

Spiritus Anisi and *Sp. Carui* are used for the same purposes, in doses of one or two drachms; but for children the simple waters are preferable. *Tinctura Carui comp.* (Guy's H.) 1 to 4 drachms.

The dose of *Oleum Anethi* is from 2 to 4 drops; of *Oleum Fœniculi*, *Ol. Carui*, and *Ol. Anisi*, from 2 to 8 drops. *Oleosaccharum Anisi, &c.*, 20 to 30 grains. Of the powdered seeds, from 10 to 30 grains.

484. ℞ Semin. Anisi,
Semin. Fœniculi, ana gr. ij.
Pulv. Croci, gr. j.
Magnesiæ, gr. viij.
Sacchari albi, gr. vij.

Mix: make a powder. Take one-half immediately, and the balance after the lapse of an hour.

In Tormina of Infants.—Dr. COPLAND.

485. ℞ Radicis Fœniculi,
Semin. Fœniculi, ana ℥ij.

Cut, bruise, and mix. [Two or three spoonfuls to be boiled for some time in a quart of water, and the strained decoction taken by glassfuls.]

To promote the Secretion of Milk.—RADIUS.

486. ℞ Infusi Anisi, ℥iv.
Sacchari albi, ʒij. Mix: by teaspoonfuls.

In Flatulence of young Children.

487. ℞ Olei Anisi, gutt. iv.
Sacchari albi, ℈ss. Mix intimately, and add
Aquæ, f℥ij.
Pulv. Rhei, ℈ss.
Magnesiæ Carb. ℈j.
Tincturæ Opii, gutt. iv.
Sp. Ammon. fœtidi, gutt. x.

Mix: take a dessertspoonful every third hour.

In Infantile Convulsions.—Dr. BRERETON.

488. ℞ Olei Anisi, ♏xij.
Sacchari albi, ʒj.
Tinct. Zingiberis, fʒij.
Aquæ Menthæ pip. f℥viiss. Mix. Dose, three spoonfuls.

Carminative.—Dr. AINSLIE.

489. ℞ Sodæ Bicarbon. gr. viij.
Olei Anisi, gtt. j.
Syrupi Aurantii, ʒj. Rub up together, and add
Aquæ Anethi (*vel* Fœniculi), f℥j.

Take a teaspoonful as occasion requires.

As a Carminative for Children.

490. ℞ Seminum Anisi contus. ʒiss.
Fol. Melissæ, ʒj.
Aquæ calidæ, lbij.

Infuse for a fourth of an hour, strain, and add as much sugar as may please.

Carminative.—Dr. COPLAND.

ANGELICA.

The Garden Angelica, Angelica Archangelica (Nat Ord. *Umbelliferæ* or *Apiaceæ*), is stimulant, carminative, and tonic. The seeds and roots are the parts principally used; the latter retain their pungency longer. Dose of the powdered root, 10 to 20 grains; *Aqua Angelicæ*, an ounce; *Extractum*, 5 to 15 grains; *Infusum*, by spoonfuls; *Tinctura*, a drachm; *Spiritus Angelicæ*, and *Sp. Angel. Comp.* from half a drachm to 2 drachms.

491. ℞ Pulv. rad. Angelicæ, ℈j.
Pulv. Cinchonæ, ʒss.
Make a powder: to be taken every third hour.
In Intermittent Fevers.—Dr. Castle.

492. ℞ Angelicæ rad. ʒx.
Aquæ, Oiij.
Boil to two pints and strain. A wineglassful every three hours, as a sudorific and cordial.
In Typhus Fever.—Dr. Castle.

493. ℞ Rad. Angelicæ, ℥ij.
Rad. Serpentariæ, ℥ss.
Flor. Sambuci, ℥j.
Potas. Subcarbon. ʒiij.
Aquæ ferventis, lbij. Macerate for three hours and strain.
Liquoris colati, f℥iss.
Sp. Juniperi comp. fʒj.
Vini Opii, ♏x. Make a draught.
In Atonic Dropsy.—Dr. Copland.

ANTHEMIS. *Chamomile.*

The dried flowers of common Chamomile, Anthemis nobilis (Nat. Ord. *Compositæ*), are stomachic and tonic; and are used in dyspepsia and general debility. The *warm* infusion is used to promote the action of emetics. *Externally*, the hot decoction or infusion, or the flowers themselves moistened with hot water, are applied to relieve pain, &c. Dose of the powdered flowers, from five to thirty grains; *Infusum Anthemidis*, one to three ounces; *Extractum*, five to twenty grains; *Aqua*, one to eight drachms; *Oleum volatile*, one to four drops. *Decoctum Chamomæli comp.* is used in fomentations and clysters.

494. ℞ Pulv. Anthemidis, ℈ss.
Pulv. Piperis longi, gr. iij.
Pulv. Aloes, gr. j.
Mix: make a powder, to be taken every night.
In Flatulency and Eructations.—Dr. HEBERDEN.

495. ℞ Pulv. Anthemidis, ℈j.
Pulv. Myrrhæ, gr. v.
Pulv. Rhei, gr. iij.
Mix: make a powder, to be taken twice a day.
Stomachic and Tonic.—Dr. BABINGTON.

496. ℞ Pulv. Anthemidis, gr. xvj.
Pulv. Rhei, gr. viij.
Pulv. Zingiberis, gr. j. Make a powder.
Stomachic and Laxative.—Dr. A. T. THOMSON.

497. ℞ Pulv. Anthemidis, ℈j.
Potassæ subcarb. ℈ss.
Calc. Antimonii, ℈ss. Make a powder.
In Intermittents.—Dr. MORTON.

498. ℞ Anthemidis pulv. ℈ss.
Aquæ Menthæ pip. f℥iss.
Tinct. Cardam. comp. fʒiss.
Make a draught: to be taken thrice a day.
In Agues.—Dr. E. G. CLARKE.

499. ℞ Pulv. Anthemidis,
Pulv. Myrrhæ, ana ℈j.
Potas. subcarbon. ℈ss.
Make a powder: to be taken every sixth hour.
In Intermittent Fevers.—Dr. MEAD.

500. ℞ Pulv. Anthemidis, ℈j.
Syrupi, q. s.
To make a bolus: to be swallowed every third hour.
In Intermittents.

501. ℞ Pulv. Anthemidis,
Pulv. Cinchonæ, ana ℥j.
Pulv. Zingiberis, ℈ij. Mix, and add
Syrupi, q. s. Make an electuary: take ʒj thrice a day.
In Convalescence from Acute Diseases.—Dr. BLANE.

502. ℞ Flor. Anthemidis, ʒj.
Cort. Aurantii exsic. ʒij.
Aquæ destil. frigidæ, Oj.
Rub together in a mortar, and after an hour, strain. A wineglassful twice a day.
In simple Indigestion.—Dr. A. T. THOMSON.

503. ℞ Flor. Anthemidis, ℥ss.
Sem. Anisi cont. ʒiij.
Fol. Menthæ vir. ℥ss.
Carophyl. cont. ʒj.
Aurantii cort. sic. ʒij.
Aquæ ferventis, Oiss.
Macerate for an hour and strain: take a wineglassful frequently.
In Flatulent Dyspepsia, &c.—Dr. COPLAND.

504. ℞ Extracti Anthemidis, ʒij.
Ol. ess. Anthemidis, gutt. xij.
Pulv. Anthemidis, q. s.
Make into 120 pills: from eight to ten to be taken daily.
In Dyspepsia, &c.—THEUR.

505. ℞ Extr. Anthemidis, ʒj.
Assafœtidæ, ʒss.
Pulv. Rhei, ℈j.
Make into a mass, and divide into 30 pills: take three twice a day.
In Flatulent Dyspepsia.—Dr. AINSLIE.

506. ℞ Extr. Anthemidis, ℈ij.
Aloes Socot.
Zingiberis pulv. ana ʒss.
Mix, and divide into 20 pills: take one or two an hour before dinner.
In Indigestion.—Dr. HOOPER.

507. ℞ Infusi Anthemidis, f℥j.
Spir. Camphoræ, fʒj. Make a lotion.
In unhealthy Ulceration from Blisters, and in Typhus.
COLLES.

508. ℞ Infusi Anthemidis, ℥xij.
Olei Lini. (*vel* Olivæ), ℥ij. Make an enema.

℞ Infusi Anthemidis, fOss.
Sodæ Sulphatis, ℥j. Make an enema.

ANTHRACOKALI. A. SULPHURETUM.

These compounds are used as alteratives, in herpetic eruptions, and in scrofulous and rheumatic affections. Dose, 1½ to 2 grains three times a day.

509. ℞ Anthracokali simpl. gr. ij.
Magnesiæ carb. gr. v.
Make a powder: make three such doses. Give one every eight hours.
In Tetters.—POYLA.

510. ℞ Anthracokali simpl. ℈j.
Pulv. Glycyrrhizæ, ℥ss.
Mix: make a powder. Take a teaspoonful three or four times a day.
In Chronic Eczema, Impetigo, &c.—RADIUS.

511. ℞ Anthracokali Sulphur. gr. ij.
Sulphur. Sublim. gr. iv.
Magnesiæ Carbon. gr. iij.
Make a powder: to be taken every eighth hour.

In Tetters, Psora, &c.—POYLA.

512. ℞ Anthracokali simpl. gr. ij.
Hydr. Chloridi, gr. $\frac{1}{8}$.
P. Glycyrrhizæ, gr. iij.
Three of these doses may be given during the twenty-four hours.

In Syphilitic Eruptions.—POYLA.

513. ℞ Anthracokali, ℈ij.
Ext. Glycyrrhizæ,
Pulver. ejusdem, ana q. s.
Make 40 pills: take from two to six, three times a day.

In Lupus, Chronic Eczema, Impetigo, Psoriasis, and Lepra.
BLASIUS.

ANTIMONIUM.

The preparations of Antimony are alterative, diaphoretic, and emetic: in some cases they prove purgative. They are also employed, especially the potassio-tartrate, as contra-stimulants to subdue inflammation. The potassio-tartrate is also used as an external counter-irritant. The following are the officinal preparations and their doses:

Antimonium Metallicum. Regulus or metallic antimony was formerly cast into little balls, as *perpetual pills*, which served for a purgative.

Antimonii Tersulphuretum (formerly sesquisulphuretum, and sulphuretum nigrum), finely levigated, is alterative and diaphoretic. Dose, from five to thirty grains.

Antimonii Oxysulphuretum. [Ant. sulphuretum præcipitatum, D.; Ant. Sulph. aureum, E.] Precipitated or Oxysulphuret of Antimony. Dose, as an alterative and diaphoretic, one to three grains; as an emetic, five to fifteen grains.

Kermes Mineral is very similar to the last, and is used in the same manner.

Antimonii Oxydum. The dose is variously stated, and its effects probably uncertain. Mr. Tyson says, when prepared by his method (adding the chloride to water and treating the precipitate with sol. of carb. of ammonia), the dose is from one-tenth to one grain, and that the latter often vomits and purges. Other authors state the dose to be from two to five grains.

Antimonium Calcinatum. Calx Antimonii lota. Uncertain; but less active than the preceding. It was formerly prescribed in doses of five to ten grains or more. It is an antimoniate of potash.

Pulvis Antimonii Compositus. Antimonial powder. Dose, as an alterative, one to three grains; as a diaphoretic, three to eight grains. In large doses it is emetic and purgative. *James's Powder* is nearly the same, but with some unascertained difference in the mode of preparation.

Antimonii Vitrum ceratum. Formerly used in dysentery. Dose, four to ten grains.

Antimonii Tannas. As a contra-stimulant, three to eight grains.

Antimonii Potassio-tartras. Emetic Tartar. This is the most certain and generally used preparation of antimony. Dose, as an emetic, one to three grains; as a diaphoretic, one-twelfth to one-sixth of a grain; as an expectorant, one-sixteenth of a grain; as a contra-stimulant, from one to three grains, repeated every four hours for six times. Dr. Pereira recommends to commence with half a grain, and gradually increase the dose.

Vinum Antimonii Potassio-tartratis. Antimonial wine is given as a diaphoretic, from twenty to thirty minims every hour; as an emetic for children, half a drachm to a drachm every quarter of an hour until it operates.

Antimonii Terchloridum. Butter (or Chloride of) Antimony. It is used as a caustic only.

514. ℞ Antimonii Tersulphur. lævig. ʒss.
Magnesiæ Carbonatis, gr. v.
Cinnamomi pulv. gr. iv.
Sacchari albi, ʒss.
Make a powder: take half, morning and evening.
In Scrofula, Cutaneous Diseases, &c.—RADIUS.

515. ℞ Antim. Sulphur. nigri,
Hydrargyri Sulphureti nigri, ana ℈j.
Confectionis Aurantii, q. s.
Make a bolus: to be taken morning and night.

516. ℞ Antimonii Oxysulphureti,
Pulv. Ipecacuanhæ comp. ana ʒj.
Guaiaca Resinæ, ʒij.
Theriacæ, q. s. To make 60 pills: one every six hours.
In Skin Diseases.—Dr. CHEYNE.

517. ℞ Antimonii Oxysulphureti, ℈ss.
Sacchari albi, ʒij.
Sulphuris præcipitati, ℥j.
Olei Limonis, ♏xx.
Mix: make a powder. Take ʒss twice a day.
In Chronic Rheumatism, Skin Diseases, &c.

518. ℞ Antimonii Oxysulphureti, ℈ss.
Sulphuris sublimati, ʒiss.
Guaiaci Resinæ, ʒj.
Extr. Conii, ʒj.
Sacchari fæcis, q. s. Divide into 60 pills.
In Chronic Catarrhal Affections.—Dr. JOY.

519. ℞ Antimonii Oxysulphureti,
Hydrargyri Chloridi, ana ʒss.
Ammoniaci, ʒj.
Bals. Peruviani, q. s.
Make 30 pills: take one or two every night.
In Scrofula.—Dr. DUNCAN.

520. ℞ Antimonii Oxysulph.
Camphoræ tritæ, ana gr. vj.
Acid. Benzoici, ʒss.
Oleosacchari Anisi, ʒj.
Mix: make a powder, and divide into six equal parts. Take one every two hours.
In the second stage of Pneumonia.—BERENDS.

521. ℞ Kermetis Mineralis, ℈j.
Extracti Dulcamaræ, q. s.
Make 40 pills: take one every hour.
In Chronic Catarrh.—SOBERNHEIM.

522. ℞ Kermetis Mineralis, gr. iss.
Ipecacuanhæ pulv. gr. v.
Mix well, and divide into 6 powders. Take one every four hours.
In Hooping Cough.—MONTPELLIER HOSP.

523. ℞ Kermetis Mineralis, gr. j.
Camphoræ tritæ, gr. ij.
Pulv. Gummosi, ℈j.
Mix: make a powder. To be taken every second hour.
In Typhoid Pneumonia.—PHŒBUS.

524. ℞ Antimonii Oxidi, ʒiss.
Morphiæ Muriatis, gr. iss.
Confectio. Rosæ, q. s.

Make 24 pills, of which take two every three hours.

In Chronic Rheumatism, and Cutaneous Diseases.
DR. NELIGAN.

525. ℞ Lohoch albi (*vel* Mist. Amygdalæ), ℥v.
Antim. Oxidi albi, ʒss.

Mix: the whole to be taken, in divided doses, during 24 hours.

In Febrile Pulmonary Catarrh.—M. TROUSSEAU.

526. ℞ Antimonii Protoxidi (Tyson's), gr. ij.
Potassæ Sulphatis, gr. ix.
Calcis phosphatis præcip. gr. ix.

Mix: dose, from five to ten grains.

As a Diaphoretic, &c.—MR. TYSON.

527. ℞ Antimonii Sesquiox. ℈j.
Nitratis Potassæ, ʒj.
Pulv. Ipecac. comp. ʒss.

To be mixed and made into a very fine powder, and divided into seven equal parts, of which one may be administered each hour.

DR. PEREIRA.

528. ℞ Calc. Antimonii,
Potas. Carbon. ana ℈ss.
Pulv. Anthemidis, ℈j.

Make a powder, to be taken every sixth hour during the space of two or three days.

In Intermittents.—DR. MORTON.

529. ℞ Pulv. Antimonii comp. gr. xij.
Pulv. Tragac. comp. ℈ij.

Mix well, and divide into four powders. Take one every fourth hour.

As a Diaphoretic.—DR. JOY.

530. ℞ Pulv. Antimonii comp. gr. iij.
Hydr. Chloridi, gr. ss.
Extracti Hyoscyami, gr. iss.

Make a pill, to be taken every third hour.

In Acute Rheumatism, and mild Febrile Affections, with a harsh dry skin. DR. NELIGAN.

531. ℞ Pulv. Antimonii comp. gr. ij–v.
Camphoræ rasæ, gr. ij–iv.
Extr. Hyoscyami, gr. iv–vij.
Syr. Papaveris, q. s.

Make three pills, to be taken just before hour of sleep.

At the commencement of Brain Fever.—DR. COPLAND.

532. ℞ Pulver. Jacobi, gr. vj.
Hydrarg. Chloridi, gr. iij.
Extr. Hyoscyami, gr. iv.

Mix: make two pills, to be taken just before hour of sleep. [To be followed by an aperient draught in the morning.]

In recent Catarrhs.—Dr. G. GREGORY.

533. ℞ Pulv. Jacobi,
Pil. Aloes et Myrrhæ,
G. Guaiaci, sing. ʒiiss.
Tinct. Castorei, q. s.

Make 96 pills: take three or four every night; and take a teaspoonful of vinegar of squills every morning, in a tablespoonful of cinnamon water.

In Dropsy, &c.—Dr. JAMES.

534. ℞ Pulv. Jacobi, gr. v.
Hydrarg. Chloridi, gr. j.
Pulv. Ipecac. gr. ij.
Confect. Rosæ, q. s.

Make two pills: to be taken just before usual hour of sleep.

Diaphoretic.—Dr. HOOPER.

535. ℞ Pulv. Jacobi, gr. viij.
Hydr. Chloridi, gr. iv.
Opii pulv. gr. j.
Conf. Rosæ, q. s.

Mix, and divide into four pills, of which take one every six hours with a saline draught.

In Inflammation of the Lungs.—Dr. G. GREGORY.

536. ℞ Pil. Plummeri, gr. xviij.
Pulv. Jacobi veri, gr. xij.
Sapon. Castil. gr. xxiv.

Mix: divide into twelve pills. Two every night.

In Bilious Dyspepsia.—Dr. ROSS.

537. ℞ Antimonii Potassio-tart. gr. j.
Ipecacuanhæ pulv. ℈j. Make an emetic powder.

Dr. HOOPER.

538. ℞ Antim. Potassio-tart gr. iij.
Aquæ ferventis, ℥vj.

Dissolve: take f℥j every quarter of an hour, until vomiting is induced.

Dr. PEARSON.

539. ℞ Antim. Patassio-tartr. gr. j.
Decocti Hordei, Oij.

Mix: the whole to be taken in twenty-four hours. To be followed, as soon as it has sufficiently acted, by tonics. No local applications.

In Erysipelas.—Dr. WALSHE.

540. ℞ Antim. Tart. gr. ¼.
Decoct. Hordei, Oij. Dissolve, and add
Syrupi, ℥iij.
To be taken by glassfuls in the course of the day.

A nauseating drink in Inflammation of the Eyes and Ears.
TROUSSEAU and REVEIL.

541. ℞ Antim. Potassio-tart. gr. j.
Emulsio. Amygdalæ amaræ, ℥vj.
Mix: take three spoonfuls every third or fourth hour. [When the inflammation subsides, the same medicine to be continued at longer intervals.]

In Pneumonia, after bleeding, and calomel and opium.
DR. A. T. THOMSON.

542. ℞ Antim. Potassio-tart. granum.
Potassæ Nitratis, ʒij.
Misturæ Amygdalæ, f℥xij.
Tinct. Camphoræ comp. f℥ss.
Make a cough mixture, of which a tablespoonful may be given every hour.

In Bronchitis, &c.—DR. GRAVES.

543. ℞ Antim. Potassio-tartr. gr. j.
Tincturæ Opii, ♏xx.
Aquæ destillatæ, f℥j.
Mix: a teaspoonful every, or every alternate, night.

In Hooping Cough.—SIR W. WATSON.

544. ℞ Antim. Potassio-tart. gr. ij.
Magnes. Sulphatis, ℥ss.
Aquæ puræ, f℥x.
Mix: the dose for an adult is a tablespoonful; for a child of two years, a teaspoonful; repeated every half hour.

In Cholera.—DR. BILLING.

545. ℞ Antim. Potassio-tartr. gr. ij.
Aquæ destillatæ, f℥vij.
Aquæ Lauro-cerasi, fʒij.
Syrupi simplicis, fʒvj.
Make a mixture, of which a tablespoonful may be given every two hours. [With antiphlogistic treatment.]

In Acute Catarrh and Bronchitis.—DR. NELIGAN.

546. ℞ Antimonii Potassio-tartr. gr. iv.
Tincturæ Opii, fʒj.
Misturæ Camphoræ, f℥viij.
Make a mixture: a tablespoonful to be given every second hour.

In Delirium Tremens, and in the advanced stage of continued Fevers, with sleeplessness and extreme nervous excitement.
DR. GRAVES.

547. ℞ Antim. Potassio-tart. gr. ij.
Moschi, gr. xxx.
Mucilaginis Acaciæ,
Syrupi simplicis, ana f℥j.
Aquæ, f℥x. Mix: take f℥ss every hour.

In the same cases, where Opium is inadmissible.—Dr. GRAVES.

548. ℞ Antim. Potassio-tart. gr. iij.
Tincturæ Opii, fʒss.
Aquæ puræ, f℥vj.
Mix: dose, a tablespoonful every half hour, or at greater intervals until the delirium has ceased.

In Delirium Tremens, and other cases of nervous excitement where depletion is inadmissible. Dr. DRUITT.

549. ℞ Antimonii Potassio-tartr. gr. vj.
Aquæ Cinnamomi,
Aquæ destillatæ, ana f℥viij.
Syrupi Althææ, f℥ij.
Make a mixture, of which a sixth portion may be given every second hour.

In Pneumonia, Acute Rheumatism, &c.—Dr. JOY.

550. ℞ Antimonii Potassio-tart. gr. j.
Aquæ destillatæ, f℥iss.
Syrupi simplicis, f℥ss.
Mix: one, two, or three teaspoonfuls every quarter of an hour until vomiting is produced.

As an Emetic, in the Inflammatory Complaints of Children.
DRS. EVANSON and MAUNSELL.

551. ℞ Antim. Potassio-tartr. gr. j.
Aquæ destillatæ, f℥viij.
Mix: take f℥j every hour. [The same mixture to be repeated at intervals of four and afterwards of six hours.]

In Chorea, from fright, &c.—Dr. SETH THOMPSON.

552. ℞ Antim. Potassio-tart. gr. ij.
Aquæ puræ, f℥vj.
Tinct. Opii, f♏xx.
Make a mixture, of which a spoonful may be given every hour until nausea or vomiting supervenes.

In rigidity of Os Uteri, in Labor.—Dr. HARDY.

553. ℞ Antim. Potassio-tart. gr. ij.
Potassæ Nitratis, ʒss.
Aquæ, f℥xij.
Spt. Ætheris Nitrici, ℥j. Mix.

554. ℞ Antim. Potassio-tartr. granum.
Misturæ Amygdalæ, f℥xij.
Potassæ Nitratis, ʒij.
Tinct. Hyoscyami, fʒiss.
Tinct. Digitalis, fʒss.
Mix: one tablespoonful every hour.

In Bronchitis, with Dropsy of the Chest.—Dr. GRAVES.

555. ℞ Antim. Potassio-tartr. gr. j.
Mist. Amygdalæ, f℥xij.
Potassæ Nitratis, fʒij.
Tinct. Camphoræ comp. f℥ss.
Make a mixture, of which take a tablespoonful every hour.

In Bronchitis.—Dr. GRAVES.

556. ℞ Vini Antimon. Potassio-tartr. ♏xxx.
Vini Ipecacuanhæ, ♏x.
Tinct. Camphoræ comp. ♏xx.
Mucilag. Acaciæ, fʒvij.
Mix: give two teaspoonfuls every four hours, for a child of four years.

In Hooping Cough.—Dr. WEST.

557. ℞ Vini Antimon. P.-tart. f℥j.
Syrupi Papaveris, f℥j.
Aquæ, f℥vj.
Mix: take two or three spoonfuls for a dose.

Dr. HOOPER.

558. ℞ Vini Antimonii Pot.-tart. fʒij.
Liq. Ammoniæ Acetatis, f℥j.
Syr. Tolutani, fʒvj.
Aquæ fontanæ, f℥iv.
Mix: dose, a sixth part every fourth hour.

In recent Catarrh.—Dr. G. GREGORY.

559. ℞ Aquæ fontanæ, f℥vss.
Sacchari puri, ʒiss.
Vini Antimonii P.-tart. fʒij.
Tincturæ Opii, guttas xx. Mix: take f℥j thrice a day.

Diaphoretic.—Dr. JAMES HAMILTON.

560. ℞ Antim. Potassio-tartr. gr. j.
Cretæ præparatæ, ℈ss.
Make a powder, to be taken in two spoonfuls of some appropriate vehicle. [It frequently vomits, procures a stool, and produces diaphoresis.]

In Fevers.—Dr. E. G. CLARKE.

561. ℞ Antimonii Potassio-tart. gr. j.
Cretæ præparatæ,
Sacchari albi, āā ʒss.
Mix with the greatest accuracy, and divide into ten equal parts, of which take one every second or third hour.

Diaphoretic.—Mr. BRANDE.

562. ℞ Antim. Potassio-tart. gr. j.
Pulv. Ipecacuanhæ, gr. x.
Pulv. Opii, gr. ij.
Pulv. Glycyrrhizæ, ʒj.
Mix well, and divide into ten powders.

Expectorant.—Dr. HOOPER

563. ℞ Antim. Potassio-tart. gr. j.
Hydrarg. cum Creta, gr. xij.
Sacchari albi, ʒj.
Mix, and make eight powders. One powder two, three, or four times a day.

In Bronchitis of Children, and Skin Affections.—Dr. HOOPER.

564. ℞ Antim. Potassio-tart. ℈ij.
Tinct. Cantharidis, f℥j.
Aquæ Rosæ calidæ, f℥ij. Dissolve: make an embrocation.

As a Counter-irritant (when the ointment fails).—Dr. JOY.

565. ℞ Antim. Pot.-tart. ℈j.
Aquæ destillatæ, f℥j. Make an embrocation.

Sir W. BLIZARD.

566. ℞ Antim. Tart. ʒss.
Unguent. Hydrarg. ʒj.
Axungiæ, ʒvij.
Mix: the size of a nut to be rubbed in night and morning over the epigastric region.

For Chronic Inflammatory Dyspepsia.—Dr. ROSS.

567. ℞ Pulv. Aloes, gr. iij.
P. Antim. Tart. gr. ¾.
Butyri Cacao ʒij.
Mix: make a suppository. One to be introduced every day until a severe pain is felt round the margin of the anus.

To recall a suppressed hæmorrhoidal discharge.

TROUSSEAU and REVEIL.

ANGUSTURA. See CUSPARIA.

APARINE. See GALIUM APARINE.

ARCTOSTAPHYLOS. See UVA URSI.

APOCYNUM CANNABINUM.

Apocynum Cannabinum (Nat. Ord. *Apocynaceæ*) is known in America under the name of Indian Hemp, but must not be confounded with Cannabis Indica. The root is emetic and cathartic, and sometimes acts as a diuretic, diaphoretic, and expectorant. Dose of the powdered root as an emetic and cathartic, fifteen to twenty grains. *Decoctum rad. Cannabini,* one to two ounces three times a day in Dropsies. *Extractum,* three or four grains three times a day.

568. ℞ Decocti Apocyni, f℥xv.
Syr. Aurantii, f℥j.
Mix: take a wineglassful twice or thrice a day.

In Dropsy.

ARGEMONE MEXICANA.

The yellow Mexican Thistle, or Prickly Poppy (Argemone Mexicana, Nat. Ord. *Papaveraceæ*), contains a milky juice which is applied to cancers, spots on the cornea, and eruptions on the skin; also to repress proud flesh. The seeds are narcotic and emetico-cathartic. The oil expressed from the seeds, in the dose of thirty drops, produces profound sleep, and afterwards relieves the bowels. It has been proposed by Dr W. Hamilton as a remedy for Cholera.

569. ℞ Sem. Argemonis Mexicanæ, ʒij
Sacchari albi, ʒij.
Aquæ puræ, f℥viij.
Make an emulsion, of which take a tablespoonful every half hour.

In Dry Bellyache.—Dr. AFFLECK.

570. ℞ Succi Argemonis Mexicanæ, ℥viij.
Succi Jatrophæ multifidæ, ℥viij.
Saponis Hispanici, ℥j.
Spirit. Sacchari (Rum), ℥iij.
Mix: expose it to the sun till sufficiently thickened to spread on lint. Apply this to the diseased part, previously bathed with a decoction of berries of French physic nut.

A CREOLE remedy for *Cancer.*

ARGENTUM.

Silver in fine powder has been used, in frictions on the tongue, as an antisyphilitic remedy, by M. Serres, but the chloride is more active.

The Oxide, Cyanide, Chloride, Iodide, and Nitrate of Silver are tonic and antispasmodic; and are used in epilepsy, chorea, passive hæmorrhages, gastrodynia, &c. M. Serres lauds the preparations of silver in syphilis, but others have not found them effectual.

Nitrate of Silver, both solid and in solution, is much used as a stimulant, vesicant, and escharotic in various surgical diseases. It is supposed to arrest the progress of erysipelas and other inflammations of the skin, &c. Mr. Higginbottom, who has much extended its use, says it is not strictly a *caustic.* We must refer to his work for directions for its use in the various cases in which he recommends it.

Oxide of Silver is much recommended as a sedative and tonic by Dr. B. Lane, Sir James Eyre, and others, as a remedy for dyspepsia and painful affections of the stomach, as gastrodynia, pyrosis, &c., when the tongue is not red; also in uterine hæmorrhage, hæmoptysis, &c. In chronic diarrhœa, especially of children, it has also been found useful. The dose in stomach affections is from a quarter of a grain twice or three times a day, increased to one-third or half a grain, and, if necessary, to a grain. In obstinate relaxation of the bowels, and in that case alone, Sir James Eyre recommends the addition of a small portion of opium. In hæmorrhage the dose may be from half a grain to a grain or more.

Cyanide of Silver is supposed to combine the sedative operation of cyanogen with the tonic of the metal. Dose, one-tenth or one-twelfth of a grain.

Iodide of Silver is recommended by Dr. Patterson as not likely to discolor the skin. Dose, half a grain to one grain.

Chloride of Silver is less active. Dose, half a grain to five grains. In epilepsy, three grains three or four times a day.

Ammonio-Chloride of Silver, from one-fourteenth of a grain; rarely used.

Nitrate of Silver is given in doses varying from one-sixth of a grain to two or three grains. For *external uses*, solutions containing from a quarter of a grain to eight scruples, to an ounce of distilled water. The ointments also vary, containing from one grain to one drachm of the nitrate in an ounce of ointment.

571. ℞ Argenti Oxidi, gr. ¼.
Pulv. Tragac. comp. gr. v.
Mix: make a powder. To be taken three times a day.

In passive Hæmorrhages, painful Dyspepsia, Chorea, &c.

SIR JAMES EYRE.

The above is the *usual* dose with which Sir James commences, gradually increasing it if required. In some cases, however, he commences with half a grain; but in *no case* has he given more than one grain three times a day.

572. ℞ Argenti Oxidi, gr. iij.
Micæ panis, ʒj.
Make 12 pills: take one or two, three times a day.
In the same cases.—Sir JAMES EYRE.

573. ℞ Argenti Oxidi, gr. ij ad gr. vj.
Mucilaginis Acaciæ, f℥j.
Aquæ destillatæ, f℥iij.
Make a mixture: take f℥ss three times a day, first shaking the phial.
In the same cases.

574. ℞ Oxidi Argenti, gr. ix.
Opii pulv. gr. ij.
Extracti Anthemidis, q. s.
Mix, and divide into 12 pills. Take one three times a day.
In Menorrhagia.—Dr. THWEATT.

575. ℞ Oxidi Argenti, gr. vj.
Extr. Absinthii, ʒj.
Mix, and divide into 12 pills, of which one may be taken three times a day.
In Epilepsy, Angina, Chorea, &c.—Dr. NELIGAN.

576. ℞ Oxidi Argenti, gr. vj.
Pulv. Rhei, gr. xviij.
Ext. Conii, ℈ij. Make 18 pills: take one three times a day.
In severe Gastrodynia, &c.—Mr. STOWE.

577. ℞ Argenti Oxidi, gr. vij.
Extr. Hyoscyami, ℈j. Make 14 pills: take one twice a day.
J. H.

578. ℞ Oxidi Argenti, gr. iv.
Extr. Humuli, gr. xxiv.
Mix: make 12 pills. Take one three times a day, drinking afterward a wineglassful of an infusion of chiretta.
In obstinate Chronic Diarrhœa.—Dr. TUNSTALL.

579. ℞ Argenti Cyanidi, gr. j.
Pulv. Iridis, gr. ij.
Triturate in a glass mortar, and divide into ten equal parts. One to be rubbed on the tongue.
In Syphilis.—Dr. SERRES.

580. ℞ Argenti Iodidi,
Potassæ Nitratis, ana ℈ss.
Rub up together, and make a very fine powder, then add
Pulv. Glycyrrhizæ, ʒss.
Sacchari albi, ℈j.
Mucilag. q. s.
Make 40 pills, of which the patient may take one three times a day.
In Gastralgia, Pyrosis, Chorea, &c.—Dr. PATTERSON.

581. ℞ Argenti Chloridi, gr. j.
Pulv. Iridis, gr. ij.
Rub up together, and divide into 8 or 10 powders. One to be rubbed on the tongue. [Argenti Ammonio-chloridum is used in the same manner.]

In Syphilis.—M. SERRES.

582. ℞ Argenti Chloridi, gr. xv.
Sodii Chloridi, ʒj.
Amyli, gr. xv.
Pulv. Acaciæ, gr. xv.
Aquæ, q. s. Make 100 pills.

583. ℞ Argenti Chloridi, gr. xxxvj.
Pulv. Acaciæ,
Cons. Rosæ, ana q. s.
Make 12 pills: take one three times a day.

In Chronic Dysentery, and Epilepsy.—Dr. PERRY.

[The quantity of Chloride to be increased to 1 drachm (in 12 pills) in Epilepsy.]

584. ℞ Argenti Chloridi, gr. xxxvj.
Quinæ Muriatis, gr. xviij.
Mannæ, gr. viij.
Mix: make into a mass with mucilage, and divide into 12 pills, of which take one every six hours.

In the early stage of Phthisis, and in Dyspepsia in debilitated habits. Dr. NELIGAN.

585. ℞ Argenti Ammonio-chloridi, gr. j.
Pulv. Iridis, gr. ij. Rub up together, and add
Conservæ, q. s. Make 14 pills.

M. SERRES.

586. ℞ Argenti Nitratis cryst. gr. ¼ to ½.
Aquæ destillatæ, ℥ij.
Gummi Acaciæ, ℈ij.
Sacchari albi, ʒij.
Mix: a teaspoonful or two every two hours.

In obstinate Diarrhœa.—Dr. CANSTATT.

587. ℞ Argenti Nitr. cryst. gr. ⅙ ad ⅓.
Aquæ destillatæ, ℥j.
Syrupi simpl. ʒv.
Make a mixture: to be taken by spoonfuls in the course of the day.

In Chronic Diarrhœa (of Children).—M. TROUSSEAU.

588. ℞ Argenti Nitratis, gr. iij.
Opii pulv. gr. iij.
Pulv. Rhei,
Extr. Humuli, ana gr. xij.
Mix: make 12 pills. Take one three times a day.

In Pain and Tenderness of the Stomach, and other affections of mucous membranes. Dr. A. HUDSON.

589. ℞ Argenti Nitratis, gr. ij.
Extr. Humuli, ℈j.
Extr. Hyoscyami, gr. xij.
Rub well together, and divide into 8 pills. Take one three times a day.

In Pyrosis, Dyspeptic Palpitation, &c.—Dr. JOY.

590. ℞ Argenti Nitratis, gr. j.
Camphoræ, gr. xxiv.
Opii Extracti, gr. iij.
Spirit. rectificati, ♏iij.
Make 6 pills: take one three times every day.

In Spasmodic Diseases.—Dr. A. T. THOMSON.

591. ℞ Argenti Nitratis, gr. ix.
Pil. Aloes cum Myrrhâ, ℈ij.
Make 12 pills: take one twice a day.

In Chorea.—Dr. COPLAND.

592. ℞ Argenti Nitratis, gr. ij.
Fellis Bovini inspissati,
Extr. Anthemidis, ana ʒss.
Mix, and divide into 12 pills, of which one may be taken morning and noon.

In painful affections of the Stomach, without organic disease. Dr. NELIGAN.

593. ℞ Argenti Nitratis,
Extr. Gentianæ,
Pulv. Calumbæ, ana gr. xij.
Mix well, and divide into 12 pills, Take one twice a day or oftener.

In Epilepsy, Chorea, &c. [These contain 1 gr. N. S. in each.]

594. ℞ Argenti Nitratis cryst. ℈ss.
Opii puri, gr. vj.
Extracti Conii, ʒij.
Extracti Glycyrrhizæ, ʒj.
Mix: make into pills of two grains each. Take from two to five every day.

In the same case.—HEIM.

595. ℞ Argenti Nitratis, gr. ij.
Ext. Lupuli, ℈j.
Ext. Hyoscyami, gr. xij.
Make a mass, and divide into 8 pills. Take one three times a day.

Dr. HOOPER.

596. ℞ Argent. Nit. gr. iij.
Pulv. Opii, gr. iij.
Pulv. Rhei, gr. xij.
Ext. Humuli, gr. xij.
Mix, and divide into 12 pills. Take one three times a day.

In Palpitations of the Heart depending on Dyspepsia. Dr. ROSS.

597. ℞ Argent. Nit. gr. x.
Ext. Hyoscyami, ʒj.
Bismuthi Nit. ʒiss.
Mix: make into 40 pills. Take one night and morning.
In Chronic Gastritis.—Dr. H. GREEN.

598. ℞ Argent. Nit. gr. x.
Ext. Conii, *vel*
Ext. Lupuli, ʒj.
Pulv. Capsici,
Quinæ Disulph. āā ℈ij.
Mix: divide into 40 pills. Take one twice or thrice a day.
In obstinate forms of Dyspepsia.—Dr. H. GREEN.

599. ℞ Argent. Nit. gr. x.
Ext. Lupuli, ʒj.
Bismuthi Nit. ℈iss.
Quinæ Disulph. ℈ij.
Mix: make 40 pills. Take one twice or thrice a day.
In Gastralgia with Pyrosis.—Dr. H. GREEN.

600. ℞ Argenti Nitratis, gr. xij.
Tinct. Gentianæ comp. f℥iij.
Take a teaspoonful thrice a day.
In Leucorrhœa, &c.—Dr. A. HUDSON.

601. ℞ Argenti Nitratis, gr. vj.
Opii pulv. gr. iss.
Make 6 pills: take one after each liquid evacuation, or every hour.
In the rice-water purging of Cholera.—Mr. G. ROSS.

602. ℞ Argenti Nitratis, gr. vj. [gr. iv ad xv.]
Aquæ destillatæ, ℥xij. Make an enema.
In Acute Dysentery.—M. TROUSSEAU.

603. ℞ Argenti Nitratis, ʒj.
Aquæ destillatæ, f℥j.
Make a solution: to be applied with a camel-hair pencil.
In Excoriations of the Back, in tedious illnesses.
Dr. A. T. THOMSON.

[The same solution is applied to the sore edges of *Scorbutic Gums* (FOX); to *Erysipelas; Lupus; Porrigo, &c* (Dr. A. T. Thomson). A weaker solution, ten grains to an ounce of water, is used to *prevent* bed-sores.]

604. ℞ Argenti Nitratis, ℈iv.
Aquæ destillatæ, fʒiv.
Acidi Nitrici, gutt. vj.
Make a solution: to be applied two or three times a day over the inflamed surface, and for two or three inches beyond it, to arrest the spreading of
Phlegmonous and Traumatic Erysipelas.—Mr. HIGGINBOTTOM.

605. ℞ Argenti Nitratis, ℈j ad ℈iv.
Aquæ destillatæ, f℥j.
Dissolve: to be applied by means of a sponge affixed to a whalebone rod to the fauces, pharynx, epiglottis, and larynx.
In Affections of the Throat; particularly follicular disease of the Larynx. DR. HORACE GREEN.

[When ulceration exists, Dr. G. states that the solution should not contain less than ℈ij of the nitrate. A similar solution, containing from eight to forty grains of nitrate to an ounce of water, is used by Dr. E. Watson, Dr. Wagstaff, M. Latour, and others, in Hooping-Cough, Hoarseness, Diphtherite, Croup, &c. But Dr. E. Watson considers it improper in acute exudative croup; and only suitable in asthenic laryngeal inflammation; and that the strength should vary inversely to the intensity of the inflammation.]

606. ℞ Argenti Nitratis, gr. j.
Aquæ destillatæ, f℥j. Make a mouth-wash.
In Aphthæ.—DR. A. T. THOMSON.

607. ℞ Argenti Nitratis, gr. iiss.
Aquæ destillatæ, f℥j. Dissolve, and make an injection.
In Fistulous Sores.—DR. A. T. THOMSON.

608. ℞ Argenti Nitratis, gr. iiiss.
Aquæ destillatæ, f℥viij. Make a lotion.
For old Sores.—HAHNEMANN.

609. ℞ Argenti Nitratis, gr. iv.
Aquæ destillatæ, ℥j.
Make an eyewash: one drop to be applied to the eye by a camel-hair pencil, and repeated in five or six hours when the symptoms return.
In Catarrhal Ophthalmia.—DR. MACKENZIE.

610. ℞ Argenti Nitratis, ℈ss.
Aquæ destillatæ, f℥j.
Make an eyewash: one or two drops to be introduced into the eye every second day.
In Egyptian Ophthalmia.—DR. RIDGEWAY.

611. ℞ Argenti Nitratis, gr. iv.
Aquæ destillatæ, f℥j. Make an eyewash.
In Superficial Ulcers of the Cornea.—MR. MACKENZIE.

612. ℞ Argenti Nitratis, gr. viij.
Aquæ destillatæ, ℥iv. Make a gargle.
In Nurse's Sore Mouth.

613. ℞ Argenti Nitratis, gr. ij.
Aquæ destillatæ, f℥viij. Make an injection.
MR. DRUITT.

614. ℞ Argenti Nitratis, gr. ¼ to gr. j.
Aquæ destillatæ, ℥j. Make an injection.
In Gonorrhœa.—MR. CARMICHAEL.

[Some writers direct much stronger solutions. Mr. C. begins with a quarter of a grain, increasing the strength as it can be borne; but finds this to be seldom the case with a full grain.]

615. ℞ Argenti Nitratis, gr. iv ad xvj.
Aquæ destillatæ, f℥iv.
Make an injection: to be thrown into the bladder daily.

In Chronic Inflammation of the Bladder.

Dr. R. L. M'Donnel.

616. ℞ Argenti Nitr. in pulv. subtil. p. j.
Sacchari purificati, p. v.
Rub together: to be inhaled from a proper apparatus.

In Affections of the Air-passages.—Dr. Wagstaff.

617. ℞ Argenti Nitr. gr. iij ad x.
Liq. Plumbi diacet. ♏x–xx.
Cerati Cetacei, ʒj.
Mix: the size of a pin's head to be put within the eyelids, and repeated according to the degree of inflammation produced.

In Opacity of the Cornea.—Mr. Guthrie.

618. ℞ Argenti Nitratis, gr. iv.
Adipis præparati, ʒss. Make an ointment.

Dr. Druitt.

[M. Serres uses, for syphilitic ulcers, one scruple of oxide, or half a scruple of iodide or cyanide of silver, to one ounce of lard.]

ARMORACIA.

The fresh root of Horse-radish, Cochlearia Armoracia (Nat. Ord. *Brassicaceæ*), is used as a condiment on account of its pungency; as a medicine it stimulates the stomach, and increases the secretions, especially the urine. *Externally*, it is rubefacient. It yields, on distillation with water, a volatile oil, which is identical with that of mustard, and may be employed for the same purposes. Horse-radish is used in weakness of the stomach, and in paralytic, dropsical, rheumatic, and scorbutic complaints; also in hoarseness, and in chest affections unattended with inflammation.

Dose of the fresh root, half a drachm; of *Infusum Armoraciæ*, two ounces; *Spiritus Armoraciæ*, one to four drachms; *Syrupus Armoraciæ*, a drachm; *Syrupus Antiscorbuticus*, four drachms.

619. ℞ Rad. Armoraciæ, rec.
Sem. Sinapis cont. ana ʒiij.
Aquæ ferventis, Oj Macerate for an hour and strain.
Colaturæ, ℥vij.
Spir. Ammoniæ, arom. ʒiss
Spir. Pimentæ, ʒiij.
Mix: take two tablespoonfuls three times a day.

In Paralysis.—Dr. COPLAND.

620. ℞ Rad. Armoraciæ, cont. ℥ij.
Sem. Sinapis, ʒij.
Rad. Valerianæ, ʒij.
Rad. Rhei incisæ, ℥ss.
Vini rubri, Oiss.
Digest, and strain: a wineglassful occasionally.

Stimulant and Aperient.—Dr. HOOPER.

621. ℞ Inf. Armoraciæ comp. fʒix.
Tinct. Ammoniæ comp. ♏viij.
Syrupi Zingiberis, fʒj. Make a draught.

Stimulant.—Dr. PARIS.

622. ℞ Infusi Armoraciæ, ℥v.
Spir. Armoraciæ comp. ʒiv.
Tinct. Capsici, ʒij. Make a gargle.

In Catarrhal Deafness, and enlarged Tonsils.—Dr. FOSBROKE.

ARNICA. *Leopard's Bane.*

The root, leaves, and flowers of Arnica Montana (Nat. Ord. *Asteraceæ*), are used; but the dried flowers are alone officinal in the Prussian pharmacopœia, and are generally preferred. Many virtues are ascribed to Arnica; but its principal action is as a cerebro-spinal stimulant: it is also irritant to the stomach and bowels, and is supposed to be diuretic, diaphoretic, and emmenagogue. It is much employed, especially in Germany, to obviate the effects of severe falls, bruises, &c., on the brain and nerves; also in amaurosis, paralysis, and other nervous affections. In the latter stage of hydrocephalus and typhus fever, and in numerous other cases, it has also been recommended. *Locally*, it is applied in lotions for contusions, and in affections of the brain.

Dose of the powdered flowers, five to fifteen grains; of the root, ten to thirty. *Infusum Arnicæ*, half an ounce; *Extractum Arnicæ*, five to ten grains; *Tinctura Arnicæ*, thirty drops; *Oleum essentiale*, one to two drops.

623. ℞ Infusi Arnicæ (ex ʒj flor.) f℥iv.
Syrupi Croci, fʒvj.
Ætheris Sulph. gutt x.
Mix: a tablespoonful every hour, to a child above two years old.
In Hydrocephalus.—Dr. URE.

624. ℞ Flor. Arnicæ, ʒss.
Ammoniæ Mur. pur. ʒij.
Camphoræ tritæ, gr. vj.
Sacchari albi, ʒvj.
Mix: make a powder. A teaspoonful three times a day.
Expectorant and Emmenagogue.—M. BERENDS.

625. ℞ Flor. Arnicæ, ʒss.
Aquæ ferv. q. s. ad col. ℥viij.
℞ Colaturæ, ℥viij.
Syr. Aurantii, ℥ss.
Sp. Ætheris Nitrici, gtt. vj.
Mix: take a tablespoonful every second hour.
In the latter stage of Hydrocephalus.—GOELIS.

626. ℞ Tinct. Arnicæ, f℥ss.
Infusi Acori Calami, f℥viiss.
Mix: take an ounce every three or four hours.
In nervous Headache, and old Paralytic cases.
Dr. NELIGAN.

627. ℞ Infusi Arnicæ (ex ʒij. rad.) ℥vj.
Ætheris Sulphurici, ℈ij.
Mix: a spoonful several times a day.
In Nervous Affections.—BRERA.

628. ℞ Pulv. Arnicæ,
Pulv. Camphoræ, ana gr. iv.
Cons. Rosæ Caninæ, q. s.
Make a bolus: to be taken every sixth hour.
Dr. COPLAND.

629. ℞ Flor. Arnicæ, ℥j.
Aquæ, Oiiss. Boil to a pint and a half, and add
Syrupi Zingiberis, ℥ij.
Mix: take from f℥ij to f℥iij, every second hour.
In Paralysis, Articular Rheumatism, &c.—SWEDIAUR.

630. ℞ Flor. Arnicæ,
Rad. Serpentariæ, ana ʒij.
Decocti Cinchonæ ferv. ℥ix.
Infuse, strain, and to eight ounces, add
Ætheris Sulphurici, ʒss.
Syrupi, ʒj. Mix: two tablespoonfuls every two hours.
As a Stimulant to the Nervous System.—BRERA.

631. ℞ Inf. Arnicæ (ex ʒvj flor.) ℥vj.
Camphoræ, ℈j.
Mucilag. Acaciæ, ℥j.
Make an emulsion: take a tablespoonful every second hour.

HORN.

632. ℞ Infusi Arnicæ, f℥viiss.
Potass. Carbon. ʒj.
Tinct. Lavand. co. ʒiss.
Mix: take a tablespoonful three times a day.

DR. COPLAND.

633. ℞ Pulv. flor. Arnicæ, ʒiij.
Pulv. Cinchonæ, ℥ss.
Pulv. Serpentariæ, ʒiij.
Conf. Aromat. ʒj.
Syrupi Aurantii, ℥v.
Mix: take from fʒj to fʒij, every two hours.

DR. COPLAND.

634. ℞ Rad. Arnicæ,
Rad. Calumbæ, ana ʒij. Pour in
Aquæ ferventis, q. s. To strain off seven ounces.
Syrupi Aurantii, ℥j. Mix: a spoonful every three hours.

In Atonic Diarrhœa.—BERENDS.

635. ℞ Flor. Arnicæ, ʒvj.
Herbæ Rutæ, ℥j.
Aquæ ferv. f℥xij.
Macerate, and strain, to make a fomentation.

For Black Eye, &c.—GRAEFE.

636. ℞ Tincturæ Arnicæ, ʒij.
Aquæ destillatæ, ℥iv. Make a lotion.

For Contusions, &c.

ARSENICUM.

Arsenic in its metallic state is not administered medicinally. All its soluble preparations are violently poisonous; and its insoluble preparations are probably all so far acted upon by the fluids of the stomach as to become so. They are employed in medicine as alteratives, and febrifuges or antiperiodics; but their effects require to be very carefully watched. Arsenious Acid (formerly termed white arsenic) and its solution with potash (Liq. Potassæ Arsenitis) are generally preferred in this country; they are principally used in obstinate chronic diseases of the skin; but also in intermittent fevers and other periodic diseases. Arsenic is contraindicated when there is a quick pulse and a hot skin.

The dose of *Acidum Arseniosum* is from one-sixteenth to one-eighth of a grain; some practitioners prefer it to the following solutions in periodical diseases. *Liquor Potassæ Arsenitis* (Fowler's Solution) is given in doses varying from three to fifteen minims. Mr. Hunt recommends it not to be given in increasing doses, but five minims to be given three times a day, on a full stomach; and the dose reduced as soon as the conjunctiva is affected. He never finds it necessary to exceed this dose, in skin diseases. The other preparations and their doses are:

Liquor Arsenici Chloridi, 3 to 10 drops.
——— *Ammoniæ Arseniatis*, from 20 drops.
——— *Sodæ Arseniatis*, from 12 drops.
——— *Arsenici Periodidi*, 20 drops.
——— *Arsenici et Hydrargyri Hydriodatis*, from 10 to 30 minims.
Pilulæ Arsenici (Asiaticæ), one pill.
Quinæ Arsenias, 1-10th to ¼th of a grain.
——— *Diarsenias*, ⅓d of a grain.
Potassæ Arsenias, 1-16th to ⅛th of a grain.
Sodæ Arsenias, 1-12th of a grain.
Iodidum Arsenici, 1-10th of a grain.

637. ℞ Acidi Arseniosi, gr. j.
Sacchari puri, ℈ss.
Rub together to a very fine powder, and add
Micæ panis, q. s.
Mix well, and divide into 20 equal pills. Take one twice a day.
In Chronic Skin Diseases, Intermittents, &c.—Dr. Wood.

638. ℞ Acidi Arseniosi, gr. ij.
Strychninæ, gr. j.
Extr. Aconiti, gr. viij.
Pulv. Opii, gr. v.
Mix well, and divide into 16 pills. One every six hours, or four in twenty-four hours. If nausea ensues, give half a pill only.
In Neuralgia of the Bladder, &c.—Dr. S. D. Gross.

639. ℞ Acidi Arseniosi, gr. ij.
Opii pulv. gr. viij.
Saponis duri, ℈j.
Mix accurately, and divide into 24 pills. Take one once or twice a day.
Dr. A. T. Thomson.

[Dr. Barton directs 32 grains of soap, and to divide the mass into 32 pills.]

640. ℞ Acidi Arseniosi, gr. j.
Piperis nigri, ℈ss.
Rub up together for half an hour, then add
Mucil. Acaciæ, q. s.
To make 15 equal pills. Take one once or twice a day.
In Elephantiasis, Lepra, &c.—ASIATIC PILLS.

641. ℞ Liquor. Potassæ Arsenitis, f℥iv.
Liquor. Iodinei comp. (U. S.) f℥j. Mix: dose, five drops.
DUHAMEL.

642. ℞ Liq. Potassæ Arsenitis, fʒss.
Liq. Potassæ, fʒj.
Infusi Gentianæ co. f℥vij.
Sp. Ætheris Nitrici, fʒij.
Mix: make a mixture, of which take two tablespoonfuls three times a day.
In Psoriasis.—Dr. S. WRIGHT.

643. ℞ Liq. Potassæ Arsenitis, ♏iv.
Decocti Cinchonæ, fʒx.
Syrupi Aurantii, ʒij.
Tincturæ Opii, ♏v.
Make a draught: to be taken twice a day after food.
In Chronic Eczema and Pityriasis.—Dr. BURGESS.

644. ℞ Liq. Potassæ Arsenitis, fʒss.
Infusi Quassiæ, f℥v.
Tinct. Lupuli, f℥j.
Make a mixture: take a sixth part twice a day.
Dr. HOOPER.

645. ℞ Liq. Potassæ Arsenitis, ♏iv ad x.
Misturæ Camphoræ, fʒxss.
Spir. Ætheris comp. fʒss.
Syrupi Croci, fʒj.
Mix: make a draught, to be taken thrice a day.
In Epilepsy.—Dr. A. FRAMPTON.

646. ℞ Liq. Arsenitis Potassæ, ♏xx ad xxx.
Syrupi Simplicis, fʒiij.
Tinct. Cardam. comp. fʒiij.
Aquæ destillatæ, f℥vss.
Dose, f℥j, immediately after food.
Dr. DRUITT.

647. ℞ Liq. Potassæ Arsenitis, fʒj.
Vini Antimonii Potassio-tart.
Vini Ipecacuanhæ,
Liquor. Potassæ, ana fʒiiss.
Aquæ destillatæ, ad f℥xij.
Make a mixture, of which f℥j may be taken thrice a day.
In Hay Fever.—Dr. F. W. MACKENZIE.

648. ℞ Liquor. Potassæ Arsenitis, fʒij.
Liquor. Ammoniæ Hydrosulphatis, ♏xx.
Tinct. Hyoscyami, fʒij.
Infusi Buchu, f℥viij.
Mix: take a tablespoonful every fourth hour.

In Diabetes.—Mr. J. HOGG.

649. ℞ Arseniatis Ammoniæ, granum.
Aquæ destillatæ, f℥j.
Mix: take from twelve to twenty-four drops every day, gradually increasing the dose to fʒj.

In Skin Diseases, &c.

650. ℞ Arseniatis Sodæ, gr. j.
Aquæ destillatæ, f℥j.
Take from twelve to thirty drops during the day.

In Chronic Skin Diseases, &c.—Dr. PEARSON.

651. ℞ Sodæ Arseniatis, gr. ij.
Aquæ destillatæ, q. s. Dissolve, and add
Guaiaci pulv. ʒss.
Antimon. Oxysulphur. ℈j.
Mucilag. Acaciæ, q. s.
Mix with great care, and divide into 24 pills.

In Chronic Skin Diseases, &c.—ERASMUS WILSON.

652. ℞ Ferri Arseniatis, gr. iij.
Extracti Humuli, ʒj.
Althææ pulv. ʒss.
Syrupi, q. s. Make 48 pills: take one every day.

In Cancerous Diseases, and Herpetic Ulcers.—M. BIETT.

653. ℞ Liquor. Potassæ Arsenitis, fʒj.
Aquæ destillatæ, f℥j. Make a lotion.

In mild cases of Lupus.—Dr. HOOPER.

654. ℞ Acidi Arseniosi pulv. ʒj.
Pulv. Sang. Draconis, ʒviij.
Hydrarg. Sulphur. rubri. ℥ij.
Mix: to be moistened with saliva or mucilage at the time of using

As a Caustic, for Cancers, Lupus, &c.—ROUSSELOT.

655. ℞ Acidi Arseniosi, gr. j. ad ij.
Hydrarg. Chloridi, gr. C. Make a powder.

As a Caustic.—Dr. BURGESS.

ARTEMISIA.

Several species of Artemisia (Nat. Ord. *Compositæ*, or *Senecionideæ*) are used in medicine; the principal of which are here grouped together.

1. *Artemisia Absinthium.* Common Wormwood. The dried tops are used as a bitter tonic, and vermifuge; also as an antiperiodic and emmenagogue. *Externally*, wormwood is used in discutient and antiseptic fomentations. The dose of the powdered herb is twenty to thirty grains. The officinal preparations and the doses are—

Aqua Absinthii, ½ to 1 ounce.
Extractum——, 5 to 20 grains.
Essentia———, 2 to 8 drops.
Infusum———, 1 to 2 ounces.
Ol. Essentiale, 2 to 4 drops.
Syrupus Absinthii, ½ to 1 ounce.
Tinctura————, ½ dr. to 2 drachms.
———————, comp., a drachm.
Vini Absinthii, 2 or 3 tablespoonfuls twice or three times a day.

Wormwood also forms part of *Species Amaræ*, *Species Anthelminticæ*, and *Sp. Aromaticæ* (P.).

Sal. Absinthii, formerly much used, was carbonate of potash, obtained from the ashes of wormwood; but is now considered identical with that derived from other sources.

2. *Artemisia maritima*, sea wormwood, has similar properties. It is less unpleasant, but seldom used.

3. *Artemisia vulgaris.* Mugwort. The fibrillæ and soft sound parts of the root, dried in the shade, and reduced to powder, or infused, have been recommended in epilepsy, infantile convulsions, chorea, hysteria, and amenorrhœa.

The dose of the freshly-powdered root is from thirty to sixty grains in twenty-four hours; or to children, a few grains, according to their age. Dr. Burdach gives to adults a heaped teaspoonful of the powder, in warm beer, promoting diaphoresis, and repeats it daily till the disease is removed. It is not proper for young persons in diseases connected with their growth. The dose of *Extractum Artemisiæ* is thirty grains; *Syrupus* and *Syrup Art. comp.*, two drachms to sixteen; *Aquæ Artemisiæ*, one to two ounces.

4. *Artemisia Abrotanum.* Southernwood. This has an aromatic smell; it is regarded as tonic, vermifuge, and antispasmodic; but is seldom used in this country, except in fomentations, and in washes to promote the growth of the hair.

5. *Artemisia Santonica.* Tartarian Southernwood. This is supposed to yield semen contra, the worm-seed of the shops; which, however, consists of broken flower-buds and their stalks. Worm-seed is given in doses of ten to thirty grains morning and evening for some days, followed by an active purge, as a remedy for round worms.

The active principle, *Santonine*, is used for the same purpose. Dose, three or four grains.

6. *Artemisia Chinensis*, Chinese Mugwort, is used in the preparation of *Moxas*.

656. ℞ Infusi Absinthii, ℥iss.
Sp. Cinnamomi, f℥ss.
Make a draught: to be taken every four or six hours.
In Weakness of the Stomach.—Mr. Brande.

657. ℞ Foliorum Absinthii,
Foliorum Rutæ,
Foliorum Sennæ,
Ras. Cornu Cervi, ana ℥ss.
Rad. Rhei, ʒj.
Triturate together to a very fine powder, of which take ʒij every morning in four doses, in some saccharine material.
In Worms.—Dr. G. Gregory.

658. ℞ Infus. Absinthii, f℥ij.
Infus. Gigartinæ, f℥iss.
Tinct. Valerianæ,
Syrupi Zingiberis, ana fʒij.
Mix: take a third portion every three hours.
To expel Lumbrici.—Dr. Neligan.

659. ℞ Extr. Absinthii, ℥ss.
Aq. Menthæ piper. ℥iv.
Tinct. Aurantii, ʒij.
Make a mixture: a spoonful three times a day.
In Debility of the Stomach.—Augustin.

660. ℞ Vini Absinthii, f℥iv.
Potass Carbonat. ʒj. Mix: take f℥j four times a day.
As a Diuretic and Resolvent.—P. P. Frank.

661. ℞ Pulv. Absinthii, ʒss.
Calomelanos, gr. vj.
Sodæ Muriatis, gr. xij.
Saponis Jalapæ, gr. xxiv.
Mellis despum. q. s.
Mix, and divide into two boluses. Take one in the morning, and the other after six hours, unless it has produced good stools.
To expel Lumbrici or Ascarides.—Dr. Neligan.

662. ℞ Ferri levigati. ʒj.
Extr. Absinthii, ʒij. Make 36 pills: take one thrice a day.
In Chlorosis, Worms, General Debility, &c.—SYDENHAM.

663. ℞ Ol. Volat. Absinthii, ʒss.
Spir. Ætheris Sulph.
Spir. Vini rect. ana ʒij.
Give the patient from twenty to thirty drops every two or three hours.

664. ℞ Infusi Absinthii,
Enema. Aloes, ana f℥iv.
Make an enema: one-half to be used.
To dislodge Ascarides in Children.—Dr. URE.

665. ℞ Speciei Amaræ, ℥iv.
Aquæ ferventis, Oiv.
Macerate, and strain. To be added to a bath.
In Debility of Children.—RADIUS.

666. ℞ Absinthii,
Fol. Lauri,
Fol. Rosmarini, ana ℥j.
Aquæ, lbv. Boil to four pounds, and strain.
As a Fomentation in Bruises and Strains.—MIALHE.

667. ℞ Pulv. Artemisiæ vulg. ℥j.
Pulv. Sacchari albi, ℥ij.
Mix: take a teaspoonful four times a day.
In Epilepsy.—BRESLER.

668. ℞ Pulv. Artemisiæ vulg. ʒj.
Pulv. Sacchari albi, ℈j
Make a powder: to be taken at bedtime in warm beer.
In Epilepsy.—LÖWENSTEIN.

669. ℞ Extr. alcoholici Artemisiæ, gr. iv.
Acaciæ pulv. ℈j.
Sacchari pulv. ʒiij.
Mist. Amygdalæ, ℥iij.
A teaspoonful every half hour, gradually increasing the dose to two teaspoonfuls.
In Infantile Convulsions.—KÖLREUTER.

670. ℞ Santoninæ (crystallizable principle of Semen Contra), gr. xv.
Pulv. Sacchari, ℥iss.
Mucilag. Tragacanthæ, et
Aquæ florum Tiliæ, q. s.
To make a mass of the proper consistence: divide into fifty lozenges. (Each lozenge contains 1-5th gr. Santonine.) 1–5 daily.
For Ascaris Lumbricordes.—TROUSSEAU and REVEIL.

ARUM.

The root of Wake-Robin or Cuckow-pint (*Arum maculatum*, Nat. Ord. *Araceæ*) is acrid, stimulant, and increases the secretions. It was formerly used in humoral asthma, chronic rheumatism, jaundice, obstructions, &c.

Dose of the recently powdered root, from ten to thirty grains; of the conserve, one or two drachms.

Arum triphyllum is used in America in chronic coughs, even of a consumptive character.

671. ℞ Rad. Ari pulv. ℥j.
Sem. Carui pulv. ℥ss.
Magnesiæ, ʒij. Mix: a teaspoonful in the morning.

In weakness of the Stomach, in gouty constitutions.—NICOLAI.

672. ℞ Pulv. Ari tryphylli, ʒj.
Pulv. Gummi Acaciæ, ʒiij.
Pulv. Sacchari, ʒij. Triturate together, and add while rubbing
Aquæ, ℥vj. Mix: take two spoonfuls twice or thrice a day.

In Chronic Catarrhs, Rheumatism, &c.—Dr. WOOD.

673. ℞ Rad. Ari triph. recent. ʒiss.
Spirit. Juniperi, Oj
Make a tincture: take a spoonful every morning in sweetened water.

In Consumption.—M. POITEVIN.

ASARUM. *Asarabacca.*

The root and leaves of Asarum Europæum (Nat. Ord. *Aristolochiaceæ*) are acrid, emetic, cathartic, and sternutatory; but now scarcely used except with the latter intention. For this purpose the *Pulvis Asari compositus* is commonly used.

Asarum Canadense, Canada Snakeroot, or Wild Ginger, is an aromatic tonic. Dose of the powder, twenty to thirty grains. It does not usually prove emetic or cathartic.

ASPARAGUS.

The roots and shoots of A. officinalis (Nat. Ord. *Liliaceæ*) are diuretic, aperient, and alterative or deobstruent; and allay inordinate action of the heart. They contain *asparagine*, on which these effects are supposed to depend. Used chiefly in dropsy, consumption, and palpitations.

Dose of *Decoctum Asparagi*, a teacupful three times a day; *Extractum*, twenty to sixty grains; *Syrupus*, from one to four ounces in the day in heart affections and phthisis.

674. ℞ Decocti Asparagi, ℥xvj.
Potassæ Acetatis, ℈j.
Mel. Scillæ, ℥ss. Mix: to be taken by cupfuls.

In Dropsies.—FOY.

675. ℞ Decocti Asparagi, lbj.
Potas. Nitratis, ʒij.
Sp. Ætheris Nitr. ʒiij.
Oxymel. Scillæ, ℥ss. Mix: to be taken as a common drink.

Diuretic and Cooling.—Dr. COPLAND.

676. ℞ Syrupi Asparagi, f℥viij.
Take a dessertspoonful morning and night.

In Palpitations.—Dr. FOSBROKE.

ASSAFŒTIDA.

Assafœtida is the concrete juice of Narthex Assafœtida (Nat. Ord. *Umbelliferæ*). It is antispasmodic, expectorant, moderately stimulant, and slightly laxative. It is much used in hysterical affections, in nervous debility, hypochondriasis, flatulent distention of the bowels, in the cough of old persons, hooping-cough, asthma, and other affections of the chest not attended with inflammation. As an enema it is advised in flatulent diseases of children, in typhoid fever, cholera, convulsions, &c.

Dose, five to twelve grains; *Pilulæ Assafœtidæ* (E.) ten to fifteen grains; *Pil. Assafœtidæ* (Guy's H.) three pills; *Pilulæ Aloes et Assaf.* ten to fifteen grains; *Pil. Galbani comp.* ten to fifteen grains; *Mistura Assafœtidæ*, half an ounce to one ounce; *Tinctura Assafœtidæ*, a drachm; *Spiritus Ammoniæ fœtidus*, thirty drops to a drachm.

The officinal preparations for local use are, Enema Assafœtidæ; Emplastrum Assafœtidæ.

677. ℞ Assafœtidæ,
Pulv. Valerianæ, ana p. æquales,
Syrupi et Tinct. Valerianæ, q. s.
Make a mass, and divide into 5-grain pills. Take two, twice a day.

In Nervous Affections.

678. ℞ Assafœtidæ, gr. iv.
Ammoniæ Sesquicarb. gr. v.
Spir. Armoraciæ comp. f℥ij.
Decocti Aloes, f℥x. Make a draught.

In muscular Atony of the Alimentary Canal.—Dr. PARIS.

679. ℞ Tinct. Assafœtidæ,
Tinct. Absinthii, ana ℥j.
Take sixty drops three times a day.

In Tape Worm.—HUFELAND.

680. ℞ Mist. Assafœtidæ, f℥vj.
Tinct. Valerianæ Ammon. f℥ij.
Spir. Æther. Sulphuric. f℥j.
Mix: make a mixture. Two tablespoonfuls every six hours.

In Hysteria.—Dr. THOMAS.

681. ℞ Assafœtidæ, ℨj.
Aq. Menthæ pip. f℥vss. Rub well together, and add
Tinct. Valerianæ Am. f℥ij.
Tinct. Castorei, f℥iij.
Ætheris Sulphurici, ℨj.
Mix: make a mixture. A tablespoonful every second hour.

In the Hysterical Paroxysm.—Dr. JOY.

682. ℞ Spir. Ammon. Fœtidi, ℨss.
Tinct. Hyoscyami, ♏x.
Syrupi Aurantii, ℥ss.
Spirit. Anisi, f℥j.
Acidi Hydrocyanici, dil. ♏v.
Aquæ, ℥j. Take a teaspoonful three times a day.

In Laryngismus Stridulus.—Dr. REID.

683. ℞ Sp. Ammon. Fœtidi,
Tinct. Valerianæ, ana f℥iij.
Mist. Camphoræ, ℥viss.
Syrupi Croci, f℥iij.
Mix: take three tablespoonfuls frequently.

In Hysteria, Flatulence, and various Nervous Diseases.
Mr. BRANDE.

684. ℞ Assafœtidæ,
Opii pulv.
Piperis nigri, ana gr. iss.
Make a pill: one to be bruised, and taken in a spoonful of brandy and water every half or three-quarters of an hour.

In Cholera.—[AN INDIAN SPECIFIC.]

685. ℞ Assafœtidæ, ℨj.
Castorei, ℈j.
Ol. Animalis (Dippel's), gutt. xx.
Tinct. Myrrhæ, q. s.
Make a mass: divide into 4-grain pills.

Antispasmodic.—T. H. LYON.

686. ℞ Assafœtidæ, ℈iss.
Extr. Anthemidis, ℈iij.
Pulv. Rhei, ℈j.
Mix: make a mass, and divide into 30 pills. Take three morning and evening.

In Dyspepsia with Flatulence.—Dr. AINSLIE.

687. ℞ Gum Assafœt. gr. xxxvj.
Pulv. Rhei, gr. xij.
Olei Cajuput, gtt. xij.
Mix: divide into 12 pills. Take two every night.

In Flatulency—Dr. ROSS.

688. ℞ Assafœtidæ, ʒj.
Morph. Sul. gr. iij.
Mix: make 30 pills, of which give one three or four times a day.

In disordered Menstruation with dry Cough.—Dr. H. GREEN.

689. ℞ Tinct. Assafœtidæ, fʒj.
Tinct. Opii, ♏x.
Ipecacuanhæ pulv. ℈ss.
Aquæ, f℥ij.
Make a mixture, of which take a teaspoonful every third hour.

In Hooping-cough.—Dr. R. REECE.

690. ℞ Mist. Assafœtidæ, ℥vss.
Tinct. Valerianæ Ammon. ʒiv.
Mix: make a mixture. Take a fourth part every fourth hour.

Antispasmodic.—Dr. JOY.

691. ℞ Assafœtidæ, ʒj. Rub up with
Liquor. Ammoniæ acet.
Aquæ destillatæ,
Aquæ Pulegii, ana f℥ij.
Syr. Papaveris. fʒij. Mix: take two spoonfuls for a dose.

In obstinate Spasmodic Cough.—Mr. BRANDE.

692. ℞ Assafœtidæ puræ, ʒj.
Olei Amygdalæ dulc. gutt. xx. Rub up together, and add
Mucilag. Acaciæ, ℥ij.
Syrupi Althææ, ℥j.
Mix: make an emulsion. Give a teaspoonful every two hours to a child of two to six years, shaking the bottle.

In Hooping-cough.—KOPP.

693. ℞ Tinct. Assafœtidæ, fʒss.
Tinct. Valerianæ comp. fʒss.
Ferri Sulphatis, gr. ij.
Mist. Camphoræ, f℥j.
Mix: make a draught, to be taken three times a day. Take at night, going to sleep.
Pil. Hydrargyri, gr. iij.
Ext. Coloc. comp. gr. iv.

In Hysterical Affections.—Dr. W. DUNCAN.

694. ℞ Tinct. Æthereæ Assafœtidæ, ♏xx.
Spir. Ammon. Arom. f℥ss.
Mist. Moschi, f℥j. Mix: make a draught.

In Hysteric and Spasmodic Colic.—Dr. NELIGAN.

695. ℞ Assafœtidæ colatæ, ʒij.
Liq. Ammon. Acetatis, ℥j.
Aquæ Menthæ, ℥iij.
Syr. Croci, ℥ss.
Mix: a teaspoonful to a tablespoonful, according to the age of the child, every two hours.

In Millar's (acute) Asthma.—MILLAR.

696. ℞ Mist. Assafœtidæ, f℥vss.
Spir. Lavandulæ comp. ℥ss.
Spir. Ammoniæ arom. fʒij.
Mix: take three spoonfuls thrice a day.

In Nervous Indigestion, Hysteria, &c.—Dr. AINSLIE.

697. ℞ Tinct. Assafœtidæ, ℥ss.
Tinct. Opii, fʒj.
Decocti Hordei, Oss. Make an enema.

In Flatulent Colic.—Dr. HOOPER.

698. ℞ Assafœtidæ, gr. vj–viij.
Ol. Amygdalæ dulc. ♏iv. Rub together, and add
Pulv. Acaciæ, ʒss.
Infusi Anthemidis, ℥j. Make an enema.

In Flatulent Colic.—Dr. URE.

[This is for an infant. For older children, use one scruple to half a drachm of Assafœtida.]

699. ℞ Assafœtidæ, ʒij.
Camphoræ rasæ, gr. xij. Rub up with
Decocti Avenæ, ℥viij; then add
Olei Terebinthinæ, ℥ss. Mix: make an enema.

In Pestilential Cholera.—Dr. COPLAND.

700. ℞ Assafœtidæ, ʒij. Rub up with
Decocti Papaveris, lbj. Strain, write: the clyster.

In Spasmodic and Hysterical Affections.—RADIUS.

701. ℞ Assafœtidæ, ʒiij. Rub up with
Lactis Vaccini, ℥v.
Strain through a linen cloth, and make an enema.

In Ascarides.—RUDOLPHI.

AURANTIUM. *Orange.*

The dried rind of the *Seville* or *Bitter Orange, C. Bigardia*, is a light bitter tonic, stomachic, and slightly astringent. It is much prescribed as an accompaniment to other medicines;

particularly the stronger bitters, quinine, neutral salts, &c., to render them less offensive to the palate or the stomach. Although regarded as a very safe remedy, large quantities of the peel have proved fatal to children.

Dose of the powdered peel, five to thirty grains; *Confectio Aurantii*, one to four drachms; *Infusum Aurantii*, one to two ounces; *Elixir Aurant. comp.*, a drachm; *Syrupus Aurantii*, a drachm to an ounce; *Tinctura Aurantii*, one to three drachms; *Oleum Cort. Aurantii*, one to three drops.

The juice of the Sweet Orange, *Citrus Aurantium*, is refrigerant, and is used for the same purposes as Citric Acid and Lemon Juice.

Orange Flowers, and their *distilled water and oil*, are the product chiefly of the bitter orange. They are fragrant, and chiefly used for their flavor and odor, but are also regarded as antispasmodic. The *leaves* are aromatic, tonic, and diaphoretic. Dose, twenty to sixty grains.

702. ℞ Cort. Aurantii, ℥ss.
Flor. Anthemidis, ℥j.
Infuse in two pints of cold water for twenty-four hours, and strain. Take a wineglassful frequently.

In Weakness of the Stomach, Flatulence, &c.—Dr. PERCEVAL.

703. ℞ Flavedinis Aurantii,
Radicis Rhei,
Potassæ Tartratis, ana ℥ss.
Olei Cajuputi, ♏iij. Mix: make a powder.

In Hypochondriasis, &c.—KLEIN.

704. ℞ Infusi Aurantii comp. f℥ix.
Acidi Hydrochlorici, dil. ♏xx.
Syrupi Zingiberis, f℥j.
Make a draught: to be taken every day, two hours before dinner.

Tonic.—Dr. PARIS.

[For other recipes containing Cortex Aurantii, see under Acidum Nitro-Muriaticum, Cinchona, Quina, Gentiana, &c.]

705. ℞ Pulv. fol. Aurantii,
Pulv. rad. Valerianæ,
Syrupi Aurantii, q. s.
Make an electuary: a teaspoonful occasionally.

In Epilepsy, and other Chronic Nervous Diseases.
SCHUBARTH.

706. ℞ Fol. Aurantii,
Rad. Rhei, ana ʒj.
Rad. Valerianæ,
Potas. Bitartr. ana ʒiij.
Mix: take half a teaspoonful twice a day.

Chorea, Epilepsy, &c.—CHOULANT.

AURUM. *Gold.*

The preparations of gold excite the secretions, sometimes salivate, and, if too freely given, produce great local and general irritation, and act as irritant poisons. They are classed among the special stimulants and alteratives, and are used by frictions on the tongue and gums, and endermically, as well as administered internally, in syphilis, scrofula, scirrhous and cancerous diseases, lepra, and amenorrhœa. Metallic gold, in a finely divided state, produces the constitutional effects of the remedy in a milder degree, without proving a local irritant. Of the salts of gold, the chloride of gold and soda (Auro-Sodii Chloridum, Sodii Auro-terchloridum, vel Auri et Sodæ Murias vel Hydrochloras) is most used. The preparations and their doses are:

Auri Pulvis, from $\frac{1}{4}$th of a gr. to 1 gr. (1-5th to $\frac{1}{2}$ a gr.—LEGRAND).

Auri Chloridum [*Terchloridum, vel Perchloridum,*] . . . . *Auro-Sodii Chloridum, vel Sodii Auro-Terchloridum,*	From 1-20th to 1-10th of a grain. In frictions, from 1-16th to 1-6th, gradually increased.
Auri Cyanidum, —— *Iodidum,*	From 1-15th to 1-10th of a grain.

—— *Sulphuretum*, 1-10th of a grain to a grain and a half.
Aurum Stanno Paratum (*Purple of Cassius*), 1-15th to 1-10th of a grain (?).
Trochisci Auri, and *Troch. Auri Cyanidi*, 1 to 4 daily.

Unguentum Auri is applied in frictions, and also to the surface from which the cuticle has been removed by a blister.

Syrupus Auri is also used topically.

707. ℞ Auri pulveris, gr. vj.
Amyli pulv. gr. xxxvj.
Mix, and divide into 12 parts. Take one four times a day.

REICKE.

708. ℞ Auri pulveris,
Lycopodii, ana gr. ij.
Mix: to be rubbed on the tongue and gums, in divided portions, during the day.

In Syphilis, &c.—REICKE.

709. ℞ Auri pulveris, ℈j.
Syrupi Acaciæ, ℥j. Mix.

In Syphilitic Ulceration.

710. ℞ Auri pulveris, gr. xv.
Axungiæ, ℥ss. Mix.

To obstinate Syphilitic Ulcers.—BOUCHARDAT.

711. ℞ Auri Terchloridi, gr. j.
Lycopodii præp. gr. xv.

Mix, and divide into 16 powders. One to be rubbed on the tongue and gums daily. Afterward the same quantity to be divided successively into twelve and ten powders.

In Syphilis.—CHRESTIEN.

712. ℞ Auri Chloridi, gr. j.
Extr. Aconiti alcohol. ℈ss.
Pulv. Glycyrrhizæ, ℈ij.
Syrupi, q. s.

Mix intimately, and divide into 20 pills, of which one is to be taken thrice a day.

In Secondary Syphilis, with much pain.—Dr. NELIGAN.

[We omit many other formulæ, as they resemble the following for the use of the *Chloride of Gold and Soda*, which is nearly as active as the simple chloride, and cheaper.]

713. ℞ Auro-Sodii Chloridi, granum unum,
Aquæ destillatæ, q. s. Dissolve, and add
Syrupi simplicis, f℥vj.

Mix: take a tablespoonful thrice a day.

CHRESTIEN.

714. ℞ Auro-Sodii Chloridi, gr. j.
Aquæ destillatæ, ℥ss.

Dissolve: six drops, gradually increased to fourteen, to be taken three times a day in water, or decoction of sarsaparilla.

In Secondary Syphilis.—LEHMANN.

715. ℞ Sodii Auro-terchloridi, gr. ij.
Mannæ duræ, ℈iiss.

Rub up well together, and form into 24 pills with mucilage, of which one is to be taken three times a day.

In Syphilitic Affections.—Dr. NELIGAN.

716. ℞ Auro-Sodii Chloridi, gr. iv.

In sufficient distilled water to dissolve it.

Extracti Dulcamaræ, ʒj.
Extracti Aconiti, ℈ss.
Pulveris Althææ, q. s.

Make 80 pills, of which take one three times a day.

In Venereal Skin Diseases, &c.—GRÖTZNER.

717. ℞ Auri et Sodæ Muriatis, gr. j.
Extr. Mezerei, ʒj. Make 60 pills.

MAGENDIE.

718. ℞ Auro-Sodii Chloridi, gr. ¼.
Lycopodii, gr. xv.
Mix thoroughly, and divide into 20 powders. One powder to be rubbed on the tongue and gums daily. The same quantity to be divided the next time into sixteen, then into twelve, and by degrees into three packets.

In Syphilitic Affections.—CHRESTIEN: TROUSSEAU.

719. ℞ Auro-Sodii Chloridi, gr. j.
Aquæ destillatæ, ℥iij. Make an eyewash.

In Chronic Ophthalmia.—JAHN.

720. ℞ Auro-Sodii Chloridi, gr. iiss.
Axungiæ, ʒiss.
The size of a bean to be introduced into the nostril in the evening.

In Scrofulous Swelling of the Nose.—KOPP.

721. ℞ Auro-Sodii Chloridi, gr. iij ad iv.
Axungiæ, ℥ss. Mix thoroughly, and make an ointment.

In Induration, Exostosis, &c., especially of Syphilitic origin.

GRÖTZNER.

722. ℞ Auri Teroxidi, gr. ivss.
Extr. Mezerei, ʒij.
Mix, and divide into 60 pills. Take two to ten every day.

HOSP. OF MONTPELLIER.

723. ℞ Auri Cyanidi, gr. j.
Lycopodii, gr. xv.
Mix, and divide into 16 powders. One daily in frictions on the tongue.

724. ℞ Auri Cyanidi, gr. iss.
Pastæ Cacao, ℥j.
Mix, and divide into 24 lozenges. One to three daily.

CHRESTIEN.

725. ℞ Auri Cyanidi, gr. j.
Extr. Mezerei, gr. iij. [gr. viij.—CHRESTIEN.]
Pulv. Althææ, q. s.
Make into 15 pills. Give at first one pill, then two, then three, daily.

In Syphilis, Scrofula, Amenorrhœa, &c.

POURCHE: CHRESTIEN.

[Aurum Stannoparatum and Auri Sulphuretum are given in powders and pills, as the other preparations.]

BALLOTA.

Siberian Woolly Ballota (*Ballota lanata*, Nat. Ord. *Labiatæ*) is sudorific and diuretic; and is used in gout, rheumatism, dropsies, &c. The dried plant is employed.

726. ℞ Decocti Ballotæ, ℥xv.
Syrupi Althææ, ℥j.
Mix: this quantity to be drunk in the course of the day.

RADIUS.

727. ℞ Decocti Ballotæ, ℥xvj.
Tinct. Cinnamomi, ℥ss.
Ætheris Sulphur. ʒj.
Mix: a wineglassful to be taken every three hours.

In Dropsy.—REHMAN.

BALSAMUM CANADENSE. See TEREBINTHINA.

BALSAMUM COPAIBA. See COPAIBA.

BALSAMUM PERUVIANUM.

Balsam of Peru is obtained from incisions made into the trunk of the Myrospermum of Sonsonate. It is expectorant and stimulant, acting especially on the mucous membrane; hence it is used in chronic catarrhs, and other non-inflammatory affections of the chest attended with debility; also in leucorrhœa, gonorrhœa, chronic rheumatism, amenorrhœa, &c. Dr. Van Ness gives it in half-drachm doses three times a day, in diabetes mellitus. *Externally*, it is used as a stimulant to unhealthy ulcers, to chilblains, chapped nipples, and to promote the growth of the hair.

Dose, ten to forty grains; of *Tinctura B. Peruviani*, one to two drachms.

728. ℞ Bals. Peruviani, ʒiv.
Olei Amygd. dulc. ʒvj.
Pulv. G. Acaciæ, ℥j.
Rub up together, and add, while rubbing,
Aquæ Rosæ, ℥iv. Mix: dose, a tablespoonful.

In Chronic Catarrhs, &c.

729. ℞ Bals. Peruviani, ʒij.
Mellis despumati, ℥j.
Rub up together diligently, and add gradually
Aquæ destillatæ tepidæ, ℥vij.
Take two to four spoonfuls, twice, thrice, or four times a day.

730. ℞ Bals. Peruviani, ʒij.
Vitel. ovor, No. ij. Rub up together, and add
Extr. Cinchonæ, ʒiv.
Mellis Rosæ, ℥vj. Mix: take a tablespoonful twice a day.

In Chronic Bronchitis.—DR. JOY.

731. ℞ Bals. Peruviani, ʒss.
Mucilag. Acaciæ, ʒij. Rub up together, and add
Aquæ Cinnamomi,
Aquæ destillatæ, ana ℥ss.
Mix: make a draught. To be taken three times a day.

In Chronic Asthma, Old Dry Cough, and Rheumatism.

MR. BRANDE.

732. ℞ Bals. Peruviani, ʒij.
Ovi unius Vitellum. Rub up together, and add
Aquæ Cinnamomi, f℥viss.
Tinct. Aloes comp. fʒiij.
Syrupi Croci, fʒij.
Make a mixture: take f℥iss. twice a day.

In a Sluggish state of the Bowels.—DR. PARIS.

733. ℞ Bals. Peruviani, ʒij.
Mellis despumati, ʒvj. Mix, and add by degrees
Misturæ Myrrhæ (Guy's H.) f℥vj.
Tinct. Aurantii, f℥j.
Make a mixture, of which take from one to two spoonfuls three or four times a day.

DR. COPLAND.

734. ℞ Bals. Peruviani, ʒss.
Vitelli ovi, q. s.
Aquæ Cinnamomi,
Aquæ puræ, ana f℥j.
Spir. Ammon. Arom.
Syrupi Croci, ana fʒj.
Make a draught. To be taken three times a day.

In Paralytic Cases.—DR. HUGH SMITH.

735. ℞ Ung. Ceræ albæ, ℥iiss.
Bals. Peruviani, ʒij.
Olei Lavandulæ, ♏xij. Make an ointment.

To promote the growth of the Hair.—DR. COPLAND.

736. ℞ Bals. Peruviani, ʒj.
Fellis Bovini, ʒiij. Mix: make a balsam for the ear.

In fetid discharges from the Ear.—DR. HUGH SMITH.

BALSAMUM TOLUTANUM.

Balsam of Tolu, which is obtained from Myrospermum Toluiferum (Nat. Ord. *Papilionaceæ*), has similar properties and uses to Balsam of Peru; being a balsamic stimulant, tonic, and expectorant. It is chiefly prescribed in pectoral complaints, after the inflammatory action is subdued.

Dose, ten to thirty grains; *Tinctura Tolutana*, half a drachm to a drachm; *Syrupus Tolutanus*, two to four drachms; *Trochisci Tolutani*, ad libitum.

737. ℞ Balsami Tolut. ʒiss.
Misturæ Acaciæ, f℥j. Rub up together, and add slowly
Aquæ destillatæ, f℥iv.
Tinct. Camphoræ comp.
Syrupi simplicis, ana fʒiij.
Mix: make a mixture, of which take two tablespoonfuls three times a day.

In the above Cases.—Dr. COPLAND.

738. ℞ Bals. Tolutani, ʒss.
Mucil. Acaciæ, fʒiv.
Aquæ, fʒv.
Aquæ Pimentæ, ʒiij. Make a draught.

In Chronic Mucous Discharges.

739. ℞ Syrupi Tolutani, ℥j.
Emulsionis Acaciæ, ℥viij.
Olei Amygd. dulc. ℥iss.
Mix: a spoonful to be taken frequently.

In Chronic Catarrhs.—NIEMANN.

BARIUM. BARYTA.

All the soluble salts of Barium are poisonous; in small doses they are used as alterative and deobstruent remedies, in scrofulous diseases [when attended by an irritable and febrile state of the system], cancer, skin-diseases, &c.; but require caution. The Chloride of Barium (*Barii Chloridum*, formerly *Barytæ Murias*) is most frequently used.

Dose, one to two grains, sometimes increased to five grains [NELIGAN]; usually in solution. The poisonous effects of an overdose should be combated, in the first instance, by sulphate of magnesia or of soda, or by dilute sulphuric acid. The other preparations and doses are:

Liquor Barii Chloridi, 5 to 15 minims.
Barii Iodidum, 1 to 3 or 4 grains.
Barii Bromidum, the same.

740. ℞ Solut. Barytæ Muriatis sat. ℥j.
Acidi Muriatici, gutt. iv.
Mix: begin with three or four drops, and gradually increase the dose to ten drops twice a day.

In Scrofulous and Cancerous Affections.—Dr. CRAWFORD.

741. ℞ Barii Chloridi, ʒss.
Aquæ destillatæ, ℥j.
Mix: give daily, to a child of three years, from five to twenty drops; to older children from ten to thirty drops; increasing the dose to fifty or sixty. [WENDT says from five to fifteen drops every three hours.]

In Scrofula.—HUFELAND.

742. ℞ Barii Chloridi,
Ferri Potassio-tartr. ana ʒss.
Aquæ Cinnamomi, ℥j. Dissolve, and add
Syrupi Aurantii, ℥j.
To a child of two or three years, give eight or ten drops every three hours, in gruel; to those of four to six years, give twelve to fifteen drops; and to older children twenty drops, at the same intervals.

In Scrofulous Affections, Glandular Obstructions, &c.

Dr. URE.

743. ℞ Barii Chloridi,
Extracti Conii, ana ʒss. Dissolve in
Aquæ destillatæ, ℥ss. Add
Vini Antim. Potassio-tart. ʒiss.
Mix: give fifteen drops, gradually increased to thirty, every three hours, shaking the bottle.

In Chronic Enlargement of the Testicle, &c.—Dr. WYLIE.

744. ℞ Barii Chloridi, ℈ss.
Tinct. Ferri Sesquichlor. fʒij.
Syrupi Aurantii, f℥ij.
Aquæ destillatæ, f℥viij.
Mix: give from half an ounce to an ounce, three times a day.

In Scrofula, with languid Circulation, and Debility.

Mr. BALMAN.

745. ℞ Barii Chloridi, ʒss.
Tinct. Cinchonæ, ℥ss.
Mix: ten to fifteen drops morning and night, shaking the bottle.

In Scrofulous Photophobia.—AMMON.

746. ℞ Barii Chloridi, gr. j.
Morphiæ Muriat. gr. iij.
Conf. Rosæ, q. s.
Make 12 pills. Take one three times a day.

In Chronic Diarrhœa and Dysentery.—Dr. A. WALSH.

747. ℞ Barii Iodidi, granum
Cinnamomi pulveris,
Sacchari albi, ana ℈iv.
Mix, and divide into eight equal parts. One to be taken three times a day.

In Scrofulous Diseases.—RADIUS.

BEBEERINA.

Bebeerine is an alkaloid derived from the bark of the Greenheart tree, Nectandra Rodiæ (Nat. Ord. *Rosaceæ*). It is tonic and febrifuge.

Dose of the sulphate, which is the only salt of Bebeerine generally employed, from two to six grains twice a day, as a tonic in ordinary cases of debility, &c.; or from ten to twelve grains twice a day in intermittent fevers, during the intermissions. Some give as much as fifteen grains.

748. ℞ Bebeerinæ Sulphatis, gr. xxxvj.
Confect. Rosæ, q. s.
Make a mass, and divide into 12 pills. One to be taken three times a day during the intermissions.
In Intermittent Headache.—Dr. GAIRDNER.

749. ℞ Bebeerinæ Sulphat. ʒij.
Confect. Rosæ, q. s.
Mix: make 24 pills. Take one, two, or three, three times a day.
In Intermittent Fevers.—Dr. CHRISTISON.

750. ℞ Bebeerinæ Sulph. gr. xvj.
Acid. Sulph. dil. ♏x.
Aquæ destillatæ, f℥iiiss.
Syr. flor. Aurantii, f℥ss.
Mix: make a mixture. Take two tablespoonfuls every six hours.
In Periodic Headache and Neuralgia.—Dr. NELIGAN.

751. ℞ Bebeerinæ Sulph. ʒss.
Acidi Sulphurici dil. ♏xxv.
Syrupi simplicis, f℥j.
Tinct. Aurantii, f℥j.
Aquæ, f℥iv. Mix: a tablespoonful three times a day.
Dr. CHRISTISON.

BELLADONNA.

The leaves and root of Deadly Nightshade (*Atropa Belladonna*, Nat. Ord. *Solanaceæ*) are powerfully narcotic, and in some cases act as a diuretic, diaphoretic, and laxative. It is employed to alleviate pains and quiet nervous excitement and spasm, in neuralgic and convulsive affections, as chorea, epilepsy, hooping-cough, tic douloureux; also, in rheumatism, dysmenorrhœa, &c. Also, as a prophylactic against scarlet fever. *Locally*, it is used to relieve pain, and to dilate the pupil of the eye. The vapor of its decoction is inhaled to relieve asthma.

This powerful remedy requires to be used with great caution. The occurrence of dryness and stricture of the fauces, giddiness, or dimness of vision, indicates the necessity of suspending its use.

Atropia, Atropine, the active principle of belladonna, is an energetic poison, seldom given as an internal remedy in this country.

The dose of the powdered leaves of belladonna is from one grain once or twice a day, gradually increased to two or three grains, carefully watching its effect. To children, one-eighth to one-fourth of a grain is given. The powdered *root* is preferred in Germany; the dose is somewhat less.

Extractum Belladonnæ, from a quarter to half a grain twice a day; or one-twelfth of a grain to a child.

Extractum Belladonnæ Alcoholicum (U. S. and Paris codex), from one-sixth to one-fourth of a grain.

Tinctura Belladonnæ (L.), from five to twenty minims, equivalent to half a grain to two grains of the dried leaves. Dr. Wood says from fifteen to thirty drops.

Atropia, and *Atropiæ Sulphas*, from a thirtieth to a sixth of a grain for an adult.

The following are for local use: *Cataplasma—Ceratum—Emplastrum—Linimentum—Lotio—Oleum—and Unguentum Belladonnæ—Solutio Atropiæ—Ung. Atropiæ.*

752. ℞ Extracti Bellad. Alcoholici, gr. ij.
Aquæ destillatæ, ℥j.
Dissolve: give a child as many drops as it is years old, morning and evening.

As a Prophylactic against Scarlatina.—Dr. FLEISHMANN.

753. ℞ Extracti Belladonnæ, gr. iij.
Aquæ Cinnamomi, ℥j.
Give two drops, morning and evening, to a child under one year of age, and one drop more for every additional year.

For the same purpose.—Dr. HARDY.

[It should be continued for at least fourteen days.—Dr. SCHNEEMANN.]

754. ℞ Extracti Belladonnæ, gr. j.
Acidi Hydrocyanici dil. ♏ij.
Misturæ Camphoræ, ℥j. Make a draught.

In Gastralgia.—Dr. STRANGE.

755. ℞ Succi Belladonnæ (cum 1-5 Sp. rect.) f℥iv.
Misturæ Camphoræ, f℥vij.
Syrupi Rhœados, f℥ss.
Mix: make a mixture, of which take a tablespoonful every six hours.

In Neuralgia, and Tic Douloureux.—Dr. NELIGAN.

756. ℞ Extracti Belladonnæ, gr. viij. ad xij.
Vini Ipecacuanha, fℨj.
Syrupi Senegæ, f℥ss.
Syrupi Tolutani, f℥iiiss.
Mix: a teaspoonful three or four times a day, with a mucilaginous acidulated drink.

In Catarrh.—Dr. ELLIS (U.S.).

757. ℞ Extracti Belladonnæ, gr. vj.
Glycyrrhizæ Rad. pulv. ℥ss.
Succi spiss. Sambuci, q. s.
Make 12 pills. Take from one to three for a dose.

Dr. COPLAND.

758. ℞ Extracti Belladonnæ, gr. iv.
Extracti Gentianæ, ℈j.
Mix well, and make 12 pills. Take one three times a day.

In flying Rheumatic Pains.—Dr. J. OSBORNE.

759. ℞ Extracti Belladonnæ, gr. v.
Pulv. Ipecacuanhæ, ℈ss.
Mix: make 20 pills. Take one every two or three hours until the pain ceases.

In painful Menstruation in full habits.—Dr. G. BIRD.

760. ℞ Extracti Belladonnæ, gr. v.
Zinci Sulphatis, ℈j.
Mix: make 20 pills. Take one every three hours until the pain ceases.

In the same, in Leucophlegmatic habits.—Dr. G. BIRD.

761. ℞ Ext. Belladonnæ, gr. viij.
Pulv. Camphoræ, ℨj.
Quinæ Disulph. ℈ij.
Mix: make 30 pills. One every hour or two until the pain ceases.

For painful Menstruation.—Dr. H. GREEN.

762. ℞ Ext. Belladonnæ, gr. viij.
Pulv. Ipecacuan. gr. x.
Zinci Sulph. ℨss.
Mix: make 30 pills. Take one every hour until the pain is relieved.

In Dysmenorrhœa.—Dr. H. GREEN.

763. ℞ Extracti Belladonnæ,
Pilulæ Hydrargyri,
Ipecacuan. pulv. ana gr. xij.
Mix: make 12 pills. One to be taken morning and evening.

In Cancerous Affections.—Dr. AINSLIE.

764. ℞ Rad. Belladonnæ pulv. gr. ij.
Rad. Ipecacuanhæ p. gr. iss.
Sulphuris loti,
Sacchari Lactis, ana ʒss.
Mix: make a powder, and divide into 8 parts. Take one three times a day.

In Hooping-cough. (For a child of three or four years.) KOPP.

765. ℞ Rad. Belladonnæ, gr. iv.
Rad. Glycyrrhizæ,
Sacchari albi, ana gr. xxxviij.
Rub up well together. Dose, from four to twenty grains twice a day.

DR. COPLAND.

766. ℞ Ipecacuanhæ rad. pulv. gr. ij.
Belladonnæ rad. pulv. gr. iij.
Zinci Oxidi, gr. vj.
Sacchari albi, ʒj.
Make a powder, and divide into 6 parts. One every two hours.

In Nervous Epilepsy.—BERENDS.

767. ℞ Rad. Belladonnæ pulv. ℈ss.
Rad. Rhei pulv. ℈ij.
Mix, and divide equally into 10 powders. Take one twice or thrice a day.

In obstructions, enlargement, and induration of Liver and Spleen; Jaundice, Palpitations, &c. HUFELAND.

768. ℞ Rad. Belladonnæ pulv. gr. vj.
Quinæ disulphatis, gr. vj–xij.
Sacchari albi, ʒij.
Mix: make a powder, and divide into 6 equal parts. Take one twice or thrice a day.

In Obstinate Quartan Agues.—RADIUS.

769. ℞ Belladonnæ fol. pulv. gr. ij.
Potassæ Nitratis, p. gr. xv.
Sacchari purif. gr. ix.
Make a powder. To be taken every day just before going to sleep.

In Chronic Rheumatism, Epilepsy, &c.—DR. A. T. THOMSON.

770. ℞ Fol. Belladonnæ sic. gr. xij.
Aquæ ferventis, ℥vj.
Macerate, and strain. Make an enema.

In Spasm of the Rectum, or Sphincter Vesicæ.—PITSCHAFT.

771. ℞ Extracti Belladonnæ, ℈j.
Aquæ puræ, f℥iv. Make a lotion.

DR. DRUITT.

772. ℞ Extracti Belladonnæ, ʒj.
Liq. Plumbi diacet. Oj. Mix: make a lotion.

GRAEFE.

773. ℞ Tinct. Belladonnæ, f℥ij.
Linim. Saponis cum Opio, f℥viij.
Make a liniment: to be used frequently.

In Neuralgic Pains, and painful Glandular Enlargements.
Dr. NELIGAN.

774. ℞ Extr. Belladonnæ,
Adipis præparati, ana ʒij.
Opii pulveris, ʒss.
Mix accurately: the size of a hazel-nut to be rubbed on the seat of pain three times a day during the exacerbations.

In Neuralgia.—Dr. DEBREYNE.

775. ℞ Unguenti Belladonnæ, ℥ij.
Camphoræ redactæ, ʒj.
Tinct. Camphoræ comp. fʒj. Mix: make an ointment.

In painful Hæmorrhoids, and Chordee.—Dr. NELIGAN.

776. ℞ Ext. Belladonnæ Alcoholici, gr. iss.
Ext. Opii, gr. ¾.
Mix. (Place in the center of a little pledget of carded cotton; fold it up so as to inclose the extracts, tie with a very strong thread, and have a double thread eight inches long attached.) To be introduced *per vaginam*, placed on the neck of the uterus, and retained for twelve to twenty-four hours.

In Neuralgia of Uterus.—TROUSSEAU and REVEIL.

777. ℞ Atropiæ, gr. ¾.
Sacchari puri, ʒiiss.
Mix intimately. Give a grain and a half, two or three times a day, to a child of five years.

In Hooping-cough.—BOUCHARDAT.

778. ℞ Atropiæ, gr. ij.
Spirit. rectificati, fʒj.
Aquæ destillatæ, fʒvij.
Make a solution. One drop to be applied to the inner surface of the lower eyelid.

To dilate the Pupil.—Mr. W. W. COOPER.

779. ℞ Atropiæ, gr. v.
Adipis præparati, ʒiij.
Otto Rosæ, gutt. j. Make an ointment.

In Neuralgia.—Dr. W. P. BROOKES.

BENZOINUM. ACIDUM BENZOICUM, &c.

Benzoin is the balsamic resin of Styrax Benzoin (Nat. Ord. *Styraceæ*). It is stimulant to the mucous membranes, and expectorant; its vapor is deodorant and antiseptic; and the acid obtained from it by sublimation (Acidum Benzoicum), besides its expectorant properties, is diuretic and useful in calculous disorders, especially in phosphatic deposits. The *Benzoates* of ammonia, potash, and soda are decidedly diuretic, and useful in dropsy, gouty concretions, &c. They are usually formed extemporaneously, by adding benzoic acid to the carbonated alkalies.

Benzoin has the property of preventing ointments becoming rancid. Its vapors are supposed to be useful in hooping-cough. It is an ingredient in cosmetic washes; and in balsamic tinctures as applied to wounds, &c.

Dose of *Benzoinum*, three to ten grains; *Acidum Benzoicum* (and its salts), three to thirty grains; *Tinctura Benzoini*, and *Tinct. B. comp.*, thirty drops to a drachm.

780. ℞ Tinct. Benzoini comp. f℥ss.
Acaciæ pulveris, ℥ss.
Tragacanthæ pulv. ʒj.
Aquæ Cinnamomi, f℥j.
Aquæ puræ, f℥iiss.
Mix: make a mixture, of which take a fourth part three times a day.
In Chronic Bronchitis.—Dr. HOOPER.

781. ℞ Tinct. Benzoini comp.
Acidi Sulphurici dil. ana fʒss.
Mix: thirty drops to be given on sugar.
To allay Vomiting.—Dr. E. G. CLARK.

782. ℞ Benzoini pulv. ʒj.
Ammoniaci pulv.
Myrrhæ pulv. ana ʒiss.
Extr. Gentianæ, ℈ij.
Terebinth. Venet. ʒiss.
Rhei pulveris, q. s.
Make a mass, and divide into 4-grain pills. Two pills twice a day.
In Hypochondriasis, Habitual Constipation, &c.—Dr. COPLAND.

783. ℞ Acidi Benzoici, gr. xij.
Extracti Papaveris, gr. xviij. Make 6 pills: one for a dose.
Expectorant.—Dr. PARIS.

784. ℞ Acidi Benzoici, ʒij.
Mannæ, q. s. Make 40 pills: two pills twice a day.
In Enuresis Nocturna.—Dr. J. DELCOUR.

785. ℞ Acidi Benzoici, ℈ij.
Make a powder, to be taken four times a day.
In Alkaline Urine, with deposition of Phosphates.
Dr. GARROD.

786. ℞ Acidi Benzoici, gr. xviij.
Sacchari albi, ʒj.
Olei Anisi, gutt. ij.

Mix, and divide into six powders. One powder every second hour.

Expectorant, in Chronic Bronchitis, &c.—NIEL.

787. ℞ Acidi Benzoici, ℈ij.
Bals. Tolutani, ℈j.
Tinct. Tolut. q. s.

Make a mass, and divide into 12 pills. One twice a day.

In Chronic Bronchitis, &c.

788. ℞ Acidi Benzoici, gr. vj.
Camphoræ pulv. gr. ij.
Sacchari albi, ℈j.

Make a powder: dispense three such doses. Let the patient take one every alternate hour.

DR. COPLAND.

789. ℞ Acidi Benzoici, gr. ix.
Decocti Pareiræ, f℥iss.
Morphiæ Acetatis, gr. ⅛.

Make a draught: to be taken twice a day.

In Mucous Urine, with copious deposit of Phosphates.

DR. GOLDING BIRD.

[Inf. Uvæ Ursi may be substituted for Dec. Pareiræ when the urine is plentiful; Inf. Chimaphilæ when the kidneys require stimulating; and Inf. Buchu when the skin also is inactive.]

790. ℞ Acidi Benzoici, ʒss.
Acaciæ pulv. ʒj. Rub up together, and add
Syrupi Amygdalæ, ℥ij.

Mix: make a linctus. A spoonful every two hours, shaking the bottle.

Expectorant.—BERENDS.

791. ℞ Acidi Benzoici,
Ammon. Sesquicarb. ana ℈j.
Aquæ ferventis, f℥vss. Dissolve, and add
Syrupi simpl. fʒiv.
Tinct. Hyoscyami, fʒiss.

Mix: three tablespoonfuls to be taken three times a day.

In Uric Gravel.—DR. GOLDING BIRD.

792. ℞ Sodæ Carbonatis, ʒiss.
Acidi Benzoici, ℈ij.
Sodæ Phosphatis, ʒiij.
Aquæ ferventis, f℥iv.
Aquæ Cinnamomi, f℥viiiss.
Tinct. Hyoscyami, fʒiv.

Make a mixture: two spoonfuls three times a day.

In Uric Gravel.—DR. GOLDING BIRD.

793. ℞ Benzoini contusi,
Styracis cont. ana ℈j.
Mix: to be thrown on hot cinders in the patient's room.

In Hooping-Cough.

[Blotting paper, soaked in a solution of niter and dried, and afterward brushed over with Tinct. Benzoini comp. and dried, is also burned for the relief of Cough, Hoarseness, and Hooping-Cough.]

BERBERIS. *Barberry Bark and Fruit.*

The *Bark of the root* of the common Barberry (*Berberis vulgaris*, Nat. Ord. *Berberidaceæ*) is tonic and deobstruent, and is chiefly used as a remedy for jaundice and dysentery. The dose of *Infusum Berberidis* is from one to two ounces twice a day.

The *Fruit* is cooling, antiscorbutic, and astringent, containing malic and citric acids. It is useful in fevers, bilious disorders, and scurvy.

Berberine, the active principle of the bark, is tonic, and in large doses laxative. It has been found useful in dyspepsia with functional derangement of the liver; and in convalescence from typhus, cholera, &c. Dose, four to ten grains; larger doses act as a purgative.

794. ℞ Infusi Berberidis, f℥viij.
Sodæ Carbonatis, ʒj.
Tinct. Calumbæ, fʒij.
Mix: two spoonfuls twice or thrice a day.

In Jaundice.—Dr. COPLAND.

795. ℞ Berberinæ, ʒss.
Extr. Anthemidis, ℈j.
Mix, and divide into 12 pills. One, two or three times a day.

In Indigestion, &c.

796. ℞ Syrupi Berberidis Succi, ℥iss.
Aquæ, Oiss. Mix, as a common drink.

In Fevers, &c.

797. ℞ Syr. Berberidis Succi, ℥ij.
Infusi Salviæ, ℥vj. Make a gargle.

In Sore Throat

798. ℞ Infusi Berber. cort. ℥vij.
Mellis Rosæ, ʒj. Make a mouthwash.

In Aphthous Ulcers of the Mouth

BISMUTHI NITRAS.

[B. TRISNITRAS, L. 1836; SUBNITRAS, DUB.]

Nitrate, or Subnitrate of Bismuth, is tonic and antispasmodic, with a special efficacy in painful affections of the stomach; as gastralgia, cardialgia, and pyrosis. It has also been recommended in the diarrhœa of typhus fever and consumption. In too large doses, as two drachms, it has acted as an irritant poison; but by some these occasional poisonous effects are attributed to the presence of arsenic, which it is apt to contain, unless the purified metal is used in its manufacture. M. Montserrat gives it to the amount of two and a half drachms in twenty-four hours without any ill effect.

The usual dose is from three to ten grains, twice or thrice a day, after meals.

799. ℞ Bismuthi Nitratis, gr. v.
Pulv. Tragac. comp. ℈ss.
Make a powder: to be taken three times a day. [The dose of bismuth to be gradually increased to eight or ten grains.]
In painful Affections of the Stomach.—Dr. YEATS.

800. ℞ Bismuthi Nitratis, ʒij.
Mucil. Acaciæ, q. s.
Make 36 pills. One to be taken every two hours.
In Gastrodynia.—Dr. JOY.

801. ℞ Bismuthi Nitrat. ʒss.
Magnesiæ Carbon. gr xlviij.
Elæo-sacchari Anisi, fʒiss.
Mix, and divide into 12 powders. One four times a day.
In Nervous Vomiting, &c.—KOPP.

802. ℞ Bismuthi Nitratis,
Acaciæ pulveris,
Sodæ Bicarbonatis, ana gr. iv.
Make a powder, to be taken three times a day.
In Irritative Dyspepsia.—Dr. G. BIRD.

803. ℞ Bismuthi Nitratis, gr. xij.
Ipecacuanhæ pulv. gr. ij.
Magnes. Carbonatis, ʒij.
Mix, and divide into twelve equal parts. One, three or four times a day.
In Rheumatic Gastrodynia.—CLARUS.

804. ℞ Bismuthi Nitratis, gr. viij.
Digitalis fol. pulv. gr. viij.
Testæ præparatæ, ℈iv.

Mix, and divide equally into eight powders. One, two or three times a day.

In Hooping-Cough.—RADIUS.

805. ℞ Bismuthi Nitratis,
Ext. Nucis Vom. alcohol. ana gr. ss.
Magnesiæ Carbon. gr. iij.
Sacchari albi, gr. xv.
Olei Menthæ piper. gutt. iij.

Mix: make a powder. Twelve such doses are to be made up. One every third hour.

In Spasms of the Stomach.—VOGT.

806. ℞ Bismuthi Nitratis, gr. xlviij.
Extr. Belladonnæ, gr. vj.
Olei Menthæ pip. gutt. xij.
Mucil. Acaciæ, q. s.

Make twelve pills. One, every fourth or sixth hou

In Gastralgia with Pyrosis.

807. ℞ Bismuthi Nitratis, ʒj.
Elect. Catechu, ʒij. Make 36 pills. One every hour.

In Choleriform Diarrhœa.—DEVILLIERS.

808. ℞ Bismuthi Nitratis, gr. viij.
Opii pulveris, gr. j.
Sacchari albi, ʒij.

Mix, and divide into four powders. One every two hours.

In Cholera.—AMMON.

809. ℞ Bismuthi Nitratis, ʒiiss.
Extr. Belladonnæ, gr. xv.

Mix, and divide into 40 pills. Two, morning and night.

In Gastralgia.—CAIZERGUE.

810. ℞ Bismuthi Nitratis, gr. viij.
Mucil. Acaciæ, fʒij.
Misturæ Amygdalæ, f℥j. Mix: make a draught.

Dr. PARIS.

811. ℞ Bismuthi Nit. gr. vj.
Magnes. Carb. gr. x.
Pulv. Acaciæ, gr. xx.

Mix. (Stir in a cup of boiled milk; when cool, stir up again, and administer twice or thrice daily, each dose to be immediately followed by 1-16th gr. of muriate of morphia in a tablespoonful of water.)

In Pyrosis.—Dr. GRAVES.

812. ℞ Bismuthi Nitratis,
Magnesiæ Carbonatis, ana ʒij.
Acidi Hydrocyanici dil. ♏xxiv.
Aquæ puræ, ad f℥vj. Take f℥j twice a day.

Dr. W. BUDD.

813. ℞ Bismuthi Nitratis,
Magnesiæ Carbon. ana ℈ss.
Mucilag. Acaciæ, f℥iss. Rub up, and add
Aquæ flor. Aurantii, f℥iiss.
Spir. Ammon. Arom. f℥j.
Aquæ puræ, f℥x.
Syrupi Tolut. f℥ss.

Make a draught: to be taken immediately, and to be repeated in three hours.

In Gastrodynia, with Flatulence.—Dr. COPLAND.

814. ℞ Bismuthi Nitratis,
Rhei pulveris,
Conf. Aromaticæ, ana ℈ij.
Aquæ Menthæ piper. f℥iv.

Make a mixture: a fourth portion to be taken twice a day.

In Habitual Constipation and Flatulence.—Dr. DRUITT.

815. ℞ Bismuthi Nitratis, ʒj.
Magnesiæ Carbon. ʒss.
Tinct. Hyoscyami, f℥iij.
Infusi Rhei, f℥viiss.

Mix: f℥j to be taken three or four times a day.

In Atony of the Stomach with Irritability.—Dr. W. STRANGE.

816. ℞ Bismuthi Nitratis, ʒij.
Quinæ Disulph. ʒss.
Olei Menthæ pip. gutt. xx.

Mix: make 36 pills. Two or three to be taken morning, noon, and night.

In Functional Atonic Dyspepsia.—Dr. BARBOUR (St. Louis).

817. ℞ Bismuthi Nitratis, ʒij.
Morphiæ Acetatis, gr. iij.
Syrupi, q. s.

Make 70 pills: two or three to be taken morning, noon, and night.

In Mucous Gastritis (Organic Indigestion).—Dr. BARBOUR.

818. ℞ Bismuthi Nitratis, ʒj.
Adipis præparati, ʒvij. Mix: make an ointment.

In Excoriations, Irritable Sores, &c.—Mr. BRANDE.

BISTORTA. *Snakeweed.*

The root of Bistort (*Polygonum Bistorta*, Nat. Ord. *Polygonaceæ*) is astringent; and is used in mucous discharges, passive hæmorrhages, &c.

Dose, in powder, twenty or thirty grains. *Decoctum Bistortæ*, a wineglassful; it is also used as a gargle or mouth-wash, and as an astringent injection.

819. ℞ Pulv. rad. Bistortæ, ʒij.
Pulv. rad. Ipecac. gr. vj.
Pulv. Cinnam. comp. gr. xij.
Mix, and divide into six powders. One to be taken three times a day.
In Chronic Diarrhœa.

820. ℞ Decocti Bistortæ, f℥vj.
Decocti Papaveris, f℥ij.
Acidi Tannici, gr. xviij.
Mix: make a liquid, of which a sufficient quantity may be injected into the vagina, through an ivory syringe, four times a day.
In Chronic Leucorrhœa.—Dr. NELIGAN.

821. ℞ Rad. Bistortæ,
Cort. fr. Granati, ana ʒiiss.
Aquæ ferventis, Oss. Infuse, strain, and add
Vini Opii, gutt. v. Make an enema.
In Chronic Diarrhœa.—M. BOUCHARDAT.

BORAX. ACIDUM BORACICUM.

Borax (Sodæ Biboras) is diuretic, antilithic, and emmenagogue. It was an ingredient in the old *Pulvis ad Partum* (Ed. ph. 1774); it requires to be used with caution during pregnancy. *Locally*, it is used as a detergent, especially in aphthous affections. Dose, five to thirty grains.

Mel Boracis of the pharmacopœia is chiefly used in aphthæ of children.

Boracic Acid was formerly prescribed as a sedative.

822. ℞ Boracis pulv. gr. xv.
Myrrhæ pulv. gr. xij.
Croci pulv. gr. iij.
Ol. Caryophylli, gutt. j.
Make a powder: to be taken once or twice a day.
Emmenagogue.—Dr. T. FULLER.

823. ℞ Boracis pulv. ℈ij.
Capsici pulv. ℈j.
Pil. Aloes cum Myrrhâ, ʒj.
Olei Sabinæ, q. s.
Make 30 pills, of which take two twice a day.
In Chlorosis.—Dr. COPLAND.

824. ℞ Boracis pulv. ℈ij.
Sulphuris præcip. ʒj.
Mucil. Acaciæ, q. s.
Make 24 pills, of which take three three times a day.
In Chlorosis, with Chronic Eruptions.—Dr. COPLAND.

825. ℞ Boracis pulv. gr. xxx.
Decocti Pareiræ, f℥xij.
Make a mixture, of which a wineglassful may be taken every six hours.
In Mucous Discharges from the Bladder, with Acid Urine.
Dr. Neligan.

826. ℞ Decocti Aloes comp. f℥i.
Boracis pulv. ℈j.
Tinct. Aloes comp. fʒj.
Tinct. Castorei, fʒj.
Tinct. Croci, fʒss.
Aquæ Cinnamomi, fʒij.
Make a draught: to be taken every night.
Emmenagogue.—Dr. Copland.

827. ℞ Boracis pulv. ʒj.
Aq. Amygdalæ amaræ, ʒj.
Aq. Melissæ (*vel* Menthæ), ℥iv.
Make a mixture: the whole to be taken by spoonfuls in the course of the day.
In Dysmenorrhœa.—Pitschaft.

828. ℞ Potassæ Bitartratis, ʒij.
Boracis pulv. ʒj.
Aq. Fœniculi, ℥viij.
Spir. Juniperi comp.
Spir. Ætheris Nitrici, ana fʒiij.
Syrupi Papaveris, f℥ss. Make a mixture.
As a Diuretic in Dropsies.—Dr. Copland.

829. ℞ Boracis Pulv. ʒj.
Sodæ Bicarbonatis, ʒss.
Potassæ Nitratis, ʒss.
Mix, and divide into 6 powders. One to be taken three times a day with a wineglassful of water.
In Lithic Deposits.—Dr. Druitt.

830. ℞ Infusi Lini comp. f℥iss.
Boracis pulv. ℈j.
Spir. Ætheris Nitrici, fʒss.
Syrupi Papaveris,
Syrupi Aurantii, ana ʒss.
Mix: make a draught. To be taken every third or fourth hour.
In Acne, with Dysmenorrhœa.—Dr. Copland.

831. ℞ Boracis pulv. ʒj.
Potas. Bitartr. ℥ss.
Sacchari albi, ʒij.
Aquæ, Oj. Make a mixture: take f℥ij every six hours.
In Erythema Nodosum.—Dr. Neligan.

832. ℞ Acidi Boracici, ʒj.
Mist. Camphoræ, ℥iv.
Syrupi Aurantii, ℥j.
Mix: take two spoonfuls every second or third hour.
In Cerebral Affections.—CHAUSSIER.

833. ℞ Boracis, ʒj.
Aquæ Rosæ,
Aquæ fl. Aurantii, ana ℥iij. Make a cosmetic lotion.
In Freckles, Tan, &c.—HUFELAND.

834. ℞ Boracis, ʒj ad ij.
Aquæ, Oj.
Make a lotion: to be applied by means of lint, frequently renewed night and day.
To Gangrenous Buboes.—Dr. EFFENBERGER.

835. ℞ Boracis, ʒss.
Aquæ Sambuci, f℥xiss.
Spir. Rosmarini, ℥ss. Make a lotion.
To allay Itching in Roseola.—Dr. NELIGAN.

836. ℞ Boracis, ℥ss.
Aquæ Rosæ, ℥viij.
Morphiæ Sulphatis, gr. vj. Mix: make a lotion.
In Pruritus Vulvæ.—Dr. MEIGS.

837. ℞ Boracis, ʒj.
Aquæ puræ, f℥iij.
Spir. rectificati, f℥ss. Make a lotion.
Sir A. COOPER.

838. ℞ Boracis, ʒj.
Aceti destillati, f℥ij. Make a lotion.
In Ringworm of the Scalp.—Dr. ABERCROMBIE.

839. ℞ Boracis, ʒij.
Cretæ præparatæ, ℥j.
Aquæ Rosæ, f℥iij.
Spir. Vini, f℥iij. Make a lotion.
To Sore Nipples.—Dr. JOHNSON.

840. ℞ Boracis, ʒss.
Aquæ Rosæ, f℥viij.
Acidi Hydrocyan. dil. fʒij. Make a lotion.
In Lichen Agrius.—Dr. NELIGAN.

841. ℞ Boracis, ʒj.
Aquæ Rosæ, f℥iv.
Tinct. Opii, ʒss. Make an eye-wash.
In Photophobia.—FRICKE.

842. ℞ Boracis, gr. xvj.
Aquæ Lauro-cerasi, ℥j.
Mucil. Cydonii, ʒj.
Mix: make an eye-wash. One or two drops to be applied to the eye.
In latter stage of Ophthalmia.—SICHEL.

843. ℞ Mellis Boracis, ℥j.
Tincturæ Myrrhæ, ʒj.
Mellis despum. ʒvij. Mix.
In Aphthæ.—Mr. BRANDE.

844. ℞ Boracis, ℥ss.
Mellis Rosæ, ℥j.
Aquæ puræ, f℥viss. Make a gargle.
Dr. HOOPER.

845. ℞ Boracis pulv. ʒij.
Aquæ Rosæ, f℥vij.
Mellis despumati,
Tinct. Myrrhæ, ana f℥ss.
Mix: make a mouth-wash, or gargle.
In Mercurial Salivation.—Mr. BRANDE.

846. ℞ Boracis pulv. ʒj.
Ung. Rosati (*vel* Sambuci albi) ℥j. Make an ointment.
In Chilblains, &c.—HUFELAND.

BROMINIUM. POTASSII BROMIDUM. *Bromine, and Bromide of Potassium.*

Bromine is very analogous to iodine in its medical properties, and is used in the same cases; particularly in enlargement of the spleen, in hypertrophy of the heart, chronic arthritis, goitre, scrofulous swellings, &c. It is a powerful irritant, and requires to be administered cautiously, and largely diluted.

Bromide of Potassium has the same properties and uses, but is much less irritant. Dose, three to ten grains. *Bromide of Iron*, two to eight grains; *Bromide of Calcium*, two to eight grains; *Bromide of Mercury* is given in the same manner as calomel; *Deuto-Bromide* as corrosive sublimate. *Unguentum Brominii compositum* and *Ung. Potassii Bromidii* are applied to disperse scrofulous swellings, and in chronic arthritis.

847. ℞ Brominii (pond.) ʒj.
Aquæ destillatæ, ℥v.
Shake up together until a solution is made. Dose, from three to six drops, in sugared water.
M. POURCHE.

848. ℞ Bromidi Potassii, gr. vj ad viij.
Aquæ Lactucæ (*vel* destill.) ℥iij.
Syrupi Althææ, ℥j.
Mix: to be taken by spoonfuls in twenty-four hours.

MAGENDIE.

849. ℞ Potassii Bromidi, ℈j.
Aquæ fl. Aurantii, ℥iiiss.
Syr. Aurantii, ℥ss.
Mix: make a mixture, of which a fourth part may be taken every sixth hour.

In Chronic Enlargement of the Spleen and Liver.

DR. NELIGAN.

850. ℞ Potassii Bromidi, gr. iij.
Misturæ Camphoræ, ℥j.
Mix: make a draught. To be administered three times a day.

In Hypertrophy of the Spleen.—DR. WILLIAMS.

851. ℞ Potassii Bromidi, ℈j.
Aquæ destillatæ, ℥vj. Mix: a teaspoonful every two hours.

In Herpes Scabidus, Chronic Eczema, and Impetigo Sparsa.

RADIUS.

852. ℞ Potassii Bromidi, ʒss.
Brominii, ♏viij.
Adipis præp. ℥j. Make an ointment.

BRUCIA. *Brucine.*

This vegetable alkaloid is analogous to strychnia in its effects, but less powerful. It is derived from the same sources, but especially from the bark of Strychnos Nux Vomica.

Dose of Brucine, one-third or half a grain, gradually increased to one and a half grain; or till some effect is produced. *Tinctura Bruciæ*, six to twenty-four drops. The salts of Brucia are probably rather more active.

853. ℞ Bruciæ puræ, gr. xij.
Conf. Rosæ, ʒss.
Mix accurately, and divide equally into 24 pills. Take from one to four.

In Paralysis and Lead Colic.—MAGENDIE.

854. ℞ Aquæ destillatæ, ℥iv.
Bruciæ purif. gr. v.
Sacchari albi, ʒij. Mix: a spoonful morning and evening.

BUCHU. [BAROSMA. DIOSMA, L. 1836.]

The dried leaves of Buchu [Barosma serratifolia, crenata, crenulata, Nat. Ord. *Rutaceæ*] are stimulant, diuretic, diaphoretic; with a special action on the mucous membrane of the bladder; restraining mucous discharges, and allaying irritation of that organ. It has also been recommended in dyspepsia, chronic rheumatism, dropsies, cutaneous affections, &c.

Dose of Buchu in powder, twenty to thirty grains; *Tinctura Buchu*, one to two drachms; *Infusum Buchu*, one to two ounces.

Externally, the Tincture of Buchu has been used to relieve local pains; and the powdered leaves are used by the Hottentots as a vulnerary.

855. ℞ Infusi Buchu, f℥viss.
Pulv. Tragac. comp. ℈ij.
Tinct. Buchu, f℥ss. Mix.

In Rheumatism, Affections of the Mucous Surfaces, &c.
Dr. Copland.

856. ℞ Liquoris Potassæ, fʒij.
Infusi Buchu, f℥viij.
Mix: take three spoonfuls three times a day.

In Red Gravel, and Paucity of Urine.—Dr. R. Reece.

857. ℞ Potassæ Bicarb. ℈j.
Tinct. Hyoscyami, fʒss.
Infusi Buchu, fʒxj.
Make a draught: to be taken twice a day.

In Mucous Urine, with Irritation of Bladder and Kidneys.
Dr. Golding Bird.

858. ℞ Infusi Buchu, f℥xv.
Potassæ Bicarbon. ʒiss.
Potassæ Nitratis, ℈ij.
Tinct. Hyoscyami, ʒiij.
Make a mixture, of which a wineglassful is to be taken three times a day.

In Dyspepsia with Acidity.—Sir James Eyre.

859. ℞ Infusi Buchu, f℥vij.
Spir. Ætheris Nitrici, fʒiv.
Liq. Potassæ, fʒij.
Tinct. Scillæ, fʒiij.
Make a mixture: three spoonfuls three times a day.

In Dropsical Affections.—Dr. R. Reece.

860. ℞ Infusi Buchu, f℥v.
Pulv. Tragac. ʒss.
Tincturæ Buchu, fʒiij.
Tincturæ Digitalis, ♏xxxv.
Extracti Conii, gr. xxvj.
Syrupi Tolutani, f℥ss.
Make a mixture: two tablespoonfuls three or four times a day.

In Chronic Bronchitis, with Tubercles.—Dr. Copland.

861. ℞ Fol. Buchu, ʒij.
Fol. Uvæ Ursi, ʒij.
Aquæ ferventis, f℥vj.
Macerate for two hours: strain, and add
Liquoris Potassæ, fʒj.
Tinct. Cinnamomi,
Tinct. Hyoscyami, ana fʒiij.
Mix: two spoonfuls three times a day.

In Chronic Cystitis.—Dr. DRUITT.

862. ℞ Infusi Buchu, ℥vij.
Tincturæ Buchu,
Spiritus Juniperi comp. ana f℥ss.
Mix. Dose, two-tablespoonfuls.

Diuretic.—Dr. HOOPER.

863. ℞ Infusi Buchu, f℥vij.
Potassæ Bicarbon. ʒj.
Tinct. Hyoscyami, fʒiiss.
Extr. Sarsæ fluidi, fʒiv.
Make a mixture: two tablespoonfuls three times a day.

In Irritable Bladder, with Acid Urine.—Mr. COULSON.

864. ℞ Infusi Buchu, f℥vij.
Tincturæ Buchu,
Tincturæ Cubebæ, ana fʒiv.
Mix: two tablespoonfuls three times a day.

In Chronic Diseases of the Bladder, Kidneys, and Prostate.
Dr. JOY.

865. ℞ Infusi Buchu, f℥vss.
Balsami Copaibæ, f℥ss.
Liquoris Potassæ, fʒss. Mix: f℥j three times a day.

In Chronic Inflammation of the Bladder.
Dr. R. L. M'DONNEL.

CADMIUM.

The Sulphate of Cadmium is used for the same purposes as sulphate of zinc, and in the same manner; but chiefly for outward use. Dose, from a quarter to three grains. *Externally*, as an astringent in collyria, &c.

866. ℞ Cadmii Sulphat. gr. vj.
Sacchari albi, ʒss.
Mix, and divide into 12 powders. One, three times a day.

867. ℞ Cadmii Sulphatis, gr. iij.
Aquæ destillatæ, ℥j.
To be dropped into the eye once or twice daily.

To remove Specks in the Cornea.—KOPP.

868. ℞ Cadmii Sulphat. gr. ij.
Tincturæ Opii,
Aquæ destil. ana ʒj.
Mix: a few drops to be instilled into the eye three or four times a day.
For the same purpose.—RUST.

869. ℞ Cadmii Sulphatis, gr. ij.
Axungiæ, ʒj. Mix: make an eye ointment.
For the same.—RADIUS.

CAJUPUTI OLEUM.

The volatile oil of Melaleuca minor (Nat. Ord. *Myrtaceæ*). It is a diffusible stimulant, carminative, antispasmodic, and sudorific; and is used in hysteria, spasmodic and pestilential cholera, flatulent colic, spasms of the stomach, chronic rheumatism, low fevers, &c. Dose, three to ten minims.

Externally, it is an ingredient in stimulating and anodyne liniments.

870. ℞ Olei Cajuputi, fʒj.
Misturæ Acaciæ, f℥ss.
Aquæ puræ, f℥vss.
Make a mixture. Dose, a tablespoonful.
Carminative.—SWEDIAUR.

871. ℞ Olei Cajuputi, ♏iij.
Sacchari albi, ℈ss. Rub up together, and add
Infusi Calumbæ, fʒix.
Tincturæ Calumbæ, fʒj. Mix: make a draught.
DR. PARIS.

872. ℞ Olei Cajuputi, ♏v.
Mucilag. Tragac. ʒj. Rub up together, and add
Infusi Caryophylli, f℥iss.
Tinct. Ammoniæ comp. ♏vj. Mix: make a draught.
In Hysterical and Nervous Affections.—DR. NELIGAN.

873. ℞ Infusi Caryophylli, f℥iss.
Spir. Pimentæ,
Spir. Rosmarini, ana fʒss.
Tincturæ Opii, ♏xx.
Olei Cajuputi, ♏x. Mix: make a draught.
Antispasmodic.—DR. COPLAND.

874. ℞ Olei Cajuputi, ♏iv.
Sacchari albi, gr. x. Rub up together, and add
Decoct. Aloes comp. fʒix.
Tinct. Jalapæ, fʒj. Make a draught.
Laxative and Carminative.—DR. PARIS.

875. ℞ Olei Cajuputi, gutt. iv.
Spir. Ætheris Nitr. ℈ij.
Infusi Anthemidis, Oss. Make an enema.

In Colic.—VOGLER.

876. ℞ Olei Ricini, f℥j.
Olei Olivæ, f℥ivss.
Olei Cajuputi, f℥ss.
Mix: make a liniment. To be rubbed on the chest twice a day.

In Phthisis.—Dr. C. J. B. WILLIAMS.

877. ℞ Linim. Camphoræ comp.
Linim. Saponis,
Olei Cajuputi, ana ℥j. Make a stimulating liniment.

Mr. BRANDE.

878. ℞ Camphoræ, ʒj.
Olei Cajuputi, ʒij.
Ætheris sulph. ℥j. Mix: make a liniment.

TORTUAL.

CALAMUS. *Sweet Flag.*

The root of Acorus Calamus (Nat. Ord. *Acoraceæ*) is an aromatic stimulant and stomachic. It rarely causes any febrile excitement. It has been used chiefly as an adjunct to other stimulants, and to bitter tonics; in atony of the stomach, and in indigestion in gouty subjects; in asthenic fevers attended with weakness of the digestive organs; and in agues. *Locally*, it is used in stimulating baths and lotions.

Dose of the powdered root, fifteen to forty grains; *Infusum Calami*, one to two ounces; *Tinctura Calami*, half a drachm to a drachm and a half.

879. ℞ Inf. Acori Calami, ℥iij.
G. Acaciæ pulv. ʒj.
Sacchari albi, ʒiij.
Mix: a teaspoonful every two hours. [For children.]

In Dyspepsia, and Asthenic Diarrhœa.—WENDT.

880. ℞ Infusi Acori Calami, ℥iss.
Quinæ disulph. gr. ij.
Tinct. Cinnamomi, f℥j.
Make a draught: to be taken every sixth hour.

In Flatulent Dyspepsia.—Mr. BRANDE.

881. ℞ Infusi Acori Calami, ℥iss.
Tinct. Calami, ♏xl. Make a draught.

Dr. COPLAND.

CALX. *Lime.* LIQUOR CALCIS. *Lime Water.*

Quick Lime, or Oxide of Calcium (Calx), and *Slaked Lime* (Calcis Hydras), are not administered in the solid state. *Lime Water* (Liquor Calcis) is given as an astringent, antacid, and alterative, in diarrhœa, vomiting, heartburn, and other irritations of the stomach and bowels from acidity. From its solvent power upon the mucus of the intestines it is used to dislodge worms. Added to new milk, it enables a milk diet to be tolerated when the stomach could not otherwise bear it. Milk is also added to lime water to render it less unpalatable.

Externally, Lime Water is applied to ring-worm of the scalp and other cutaneous affections; and as a lotion to foul ulcers. It has also been used as an injection in leucorrhœa, and ulceration of the bladder; and, mixed with olive or linseed oil, it is a common application to recent burns. Lime is sometimes used in the form of ointment.

882. ℞ Liquoris Calcis,
Lactis recentis, ana ℥iv.
Give a tablespoonful at intervals of half an hour, an hour, or two hours.
To allay Nausea and Vomiting.—Dr. WOOD.

883. ℞ Lactis recentis, Oss.
Liq. Calcis, f℥j ad f℥iss. Mix: for a drink.
Dr. PEARSON.

884. ℞ Liq. Potassæ, fℨij.
Liq. Calcis, ℥vj.
Mix: take two tablespoonfuls in a cupful of thin broth, when the acidity is troublesome.
Dr. JOY.

885. ℞ Liquor. Calcis, f℥iv.
Conf. Aromaticæ, ℨij. Rub up together, and add gradually
Aquæ Lauro-cerasi, ℨj.
Make a mixture: take two tablespoonfuls two or three times a day, first shaking the bottle.
In Cardialgia and Gastrodynia.—Dr. NELIGAN.

886. ℞ Inf. Gentianæ Co. ℥ij.
Aquæ Calcis, ℥ij.
Tinct. Hyoscyami, ℨj. Mix: f℥j two or three times a day.
In Heartburn.—Dr. ROSS.

887. ℞ Aquæ Calcis, ℥vij.
Spir. Amm. Arom. ʒss.
Tinct. Hyoscy. ʒss.
Magnes. Carb. ℈j.
Mix: make a draught. To be taken twice a day.

In Dyspepsia with Heartburn.—Dr. Ross.

888. ℞ Olei Olivæ, ℥j.
Syrupi Papaveris, ℥j.
Pulv. Acaciæ, ʒij.
Vitelli ovi, ʒiij.
Aquæ Calcis, Oij.
Tinct. Opii, ʒj.
Make an emulsion: a tablespoonful every two hours.

To allay pain in Calculous Disorders.—M. Tott.

889. ℞ Liquoris Calcis,
Olei Amygdalæ, ana ℥ss.
To be mixed well together; then add
Adipis præparati, ℥j. Mix: make an ointment.

In Irritable Ulceration from Blisters.
Drs. Evanson and Maunsell.

890. ℞ Liquoris Calcis,
Linim. Camphoræ,
Olei Olivæ, ana ℥j. Make a liniment.

Dr. Hooper.

891. ℞ Calcis Hydratis, ʒij.
Ung. Cucumeris, ℥ij.
Vini Opii, ʒij. Make an ointment.

In Hæmorrhoids.—M. Guibourt.

CALCIS CARBONAS. *Carbonate of Lime.*

Carbonate of Lime is used in the form of *Prepared Chalk* (Creta præparata), *Prepared Oyster Shells* (Testæ præparatæ), and *Precipitated Carbonate of Lime* (Calcis Carbonas precipitatum, (Dub.); also held in solution by excess of Carbonic Acid (Carrara Water). In either form it is antacid, and is generally regarded as astringent. It is used generally in the form of prepared chalk, in diarrhœas; and in heartburn and acidity of the stomach and bowels, when laxatives are undesirable.

Externally, prepared chalk is used to absorb acrid discharges from ulcers, burns, &c.

Dose of *Creta præparata*, ten to forty grains; *Testæ præparatæ*, the same; *Pulvis Cretæ compositus*, and *P. Cretæ comp.*

cum Opio, ten to twenty grains; *Trochisci Cretæ*, two to six lozenges.

892. ℞ Aquæ Carraræ,
Lactis recentis, ana f℥ij.
Make a draught: to be taken three or four times a day.
In Irritative Dyspepsia, with Cardialgia.—Dr. NELIGAN.

893. ℞ Liquor. Calcis, f℥iij.
Cretæ præparatæ, ʒss.
Aquæ Anethi, f℥iij.
Make a mixture: take two tablespoonfuls.
Antacid and Carminative.—Dr. DRUITT.

894. ℞ Misturæ Cretæ, f℥ij.
Confect. Aromaticæ, ℈ss.
Tinct. Opii, ♏ij. Make a draught.
In Diarrhœa.—Dr. PARIS.

895. ℞ Pulv. Cretæ comp. ʒss.
Mist. Acaciæ, fʒiij.
Aquæ Cinnamomi, ʒvij. Mix: make a draught.
In Diarrhœa.—Mr. BRANDE.

896. ℞ Misturæ Cretæ, ℥vj.
Tinct. Lupuli, f℥j.
Tinct. Cardam. comp. fʒvij.
Vini Opii, fʒj.
Make a mixture: take half an ounce every six hours.
In Diarrhœa from Acidity.—Dr. NELIGAN.

897. ℞ Cretæ præparatæ, ʒiss.
Acaciæ pulveris,
Sacchari albi, ana ʒj.
Tincturæ Opii, gutt. x.
Aquæ fontanæ, f℥iij.
Make a mixture: a teaspoonful to be taken frequently.
In Diarrhœa of Children.—Dr. DEWEES (U.S.).

898. ℞ Aquæ Cinnamomi, f℥iiiss.
Misturæ Cretæ, fʒvj.
Confect. Aromaticæ, ʒj.
Liquor. Opii sedat. ♏xv. Mix: a teaspoonful every hour.
In Diarrhœa of Children.—Dr. URE.

899. ℞ Liquor. Potassæ, ♏xx.
Misturæ Cretæ, f℥j.
Tinct. Calumbæ, fʒj. Mix: make a draught.
Antacid.—Dr. HOOPER.

900. ℞ Misturæ Cretæ, f℥iss.
Tinct. Catechu, fℨj.
Tinct. Opii, ♏x.
Mix: make a draught. To be taken every third hour, or after each liquid stool.

In Diarrhœa.—Dr. Joy.

901. ℞ Misturæ Cretæ, fℨvij.
Misturæ Ferri comp. fℨiij.
Ammoniæ sesquicarb. gr. v.
Make a draught: to be taken as occasion requires.

In Diarrhœa.—Dr. Paris.

902. ℞ Misturæ Cretæ, f℥viss.
Vini Ipecacuanhæ, fℨiss.
Tinct. Camphoræ comp. fℨvj.
Syrupi Tolut. fℨiij.
Mix: take two tablespoonfuls three or four times a day.

In advanced stage of Bronchitis, with Diarrhœa.
Dr. Copland.

903. ℞ Pulv. Cretæ comp. gr. xviij.
Sodæ Carbon. exsic. gr. vj.
Pulv. Tragacanthæ, gr. xij.
Mix, and divide into six equal parts, of which take one every second or third hour.

In Diarrhœa of Children.—Dr. Neligan.

904. ℞ Cretæ præparatæ, ℥j.
Olei Olivæ, ℨiij.
Adipis præp. ℥ss. Mix: make an ointment.

In Burns, with Acrid Discharge.—Dr. Druitt.

905. ℞ Carbon. Calcis præcipit. ℨij.
Cerati Galeni (*cold cream*), ℥ij.
Extr. Belladonnæ, ℈j.
Glycerinæ, fℨij. Mix.

Dr. Neligan.

Calx Chlorinata (*Chloride of Lime*). See Chlorinium.

CALCII CHLORIDUM. [CALCIS MURIAS; Ed. Ph.]
Muriate of Lime; or Chloride of Calcium.

Chloride of Calcium, formerly called Muriate or Hydrochlorate of Lime, is regarded as deobstruent or alterative, and tonic; it is given chiefly in scrofulous diseases, bronchocele, &c. In large doses it acts as an irritant poison. It is usually administered in solution.

Dose of *Liquor Calcii Chloridi, L.*, from twenty to sixty minims, in water, milk, or other mild liquid.

Externally, Chloride of Calcium is sometimes used as a resolvent.

[From the resemblance between the names of Calcii Chloridum and Calcis Chloridum, mistakes are apt to occur. In some printed formulæ they appear to have been confounded.]

906. ℞ Liq. Calcii Chloridi, ♏xx ad xxv.
Misturæ Camphoræ, f℥x.
Tinct. Camphoræ comp. f℥iss.
Make a draught: to be taken three times a day.

Dr. Copland.

907. ℞ Chloridi Calcii, ʒj.
Aquæ destillatæ, ℥iiss.
Mix: take a teaspoonful two or three times a day, in milk.

In Scrofula.—Mr. B. Phillips.

908. ℞ Calcii Chloridi cryst. ʒiv.
Aquæ destillatæ, ℥xvj.
Mix: a teaspoonful three or four times a day [in barley-water, or liquorice-tea].

In Chronic Eczema.—M. Cazenave.

909. ℞ Calcis Muriatis, ʒj.
Extr. Hyoscyami, ℈ss.
Aquæ destillatæ, ℥vj.
Syr. Glycyrrhizæ, ℥j.
Mix: a spoonful to be taken four times a day.

In Scrofulous Consumption.—Dr. Beddoes.

910. ℞ Calcii Chloridi, ʒj.
Extr. Conii, gr. xv.
Aquæ Cinnamomi, ℥ss.
Dissolve: give eight to sixteen drops, three times a day, to a child ten years old, shaking the bottle.

In Scrofula.—Phœbus.

911. ℞ Calcii Chloridi, ʒj.
Digitalis pulv. ʒij.
Acidi Acetici, ℈ij.
Adipis suilli, ℥j. Mix: make an ointment.

To Glandular Swellings.—Sundelin.

912. ℞ Chloridi Calcii,
Chloridi Sodii, ana ℥ss.
Aquæ fontanæ, lbss.
Pulv. Lini. q. s. Make a cataplasm.

In Scrofulous and White Swellings.—Swediaur.

CALCIS PHOSPHAS.

Phosphate of Lime, in the form of *Burnt Hartshorn*, was formerly used in medicine, in the form of Sydenham's *Decoctum Album*, and afterward of *Mistura Cornu usti.* The precipitated phosphate (Calcis Phosphas præcipitatum, Ph. Dub.) is now preferred. Dr. Beneke strongly recommends it in rickets, scrofula, diarrhœa, ulcerations and excoriations of the skin and bowels, and general waste of the tissues, of children; it also promotes the cicatrization of ulcers, and the union of fractures, where there is a deficient secretion of phosphate of lime.

Dose for adults, from four to six grains three times a day; for children, two or three grains three times a day, with meals.

It may be mixed with the food. Dr. B. cautions against giving it too freely in case of fractures, lest too abundant callus cause deformity of the bone.

Phosphate of Lime is a good basis for Tooth Powders.

913. ℞ Calcis Phosphat. præcip. ʒiv.
Acaciæ pulveris, ʒij.

Mix. Dose, for children, three or four grains; for adults, six to nine grains, three times a day, at meal times. [As a substitute for Mistura Cornu Cervi.]

914. ℞ Calcis Phosphat. præcip. gr. iv–vj.
Misturæ Cretæ, ℥j.

Make a draught: to be taken three times a day. For children, give a fourth part.

In Diarrhœa, with Emaciation, and Acidity.

915. ℞ Pulv. Calcis Phosph. gr. 15.
Bismuthi Nitratis, gr. 15.
Pulv. Sacchari, gr. 75.

Mix: divide in five powders. Take one night and morning.

In Chronic Diarrhœa of Children.—TROUSSEAU and REVEIL.

CALCII SULPHURETUM.

Sulphuret of Lime is alterative, stimulant, and diaphoretic, and sometimes prescribed in skin diseases, gout, and chronic rheumatism. Dose, four to eight grains, or to the amount of twenty grains as an antidote to metallic poisons. But its principal use is to form sulphur baths, as more economical than sulphuret of potassium. For this purpose two or three ounces are dissolved in the water, and afterward twenty to forty drops of sulphuric acid, or from half an ounce to an ounce of tartaric acid, are added.

916. ℞ Calcii Sulphureti, ʒj.
Dulcamaræ pulv. ʒij.
Mellis, q. s.
To make 6 boluses: take one three times a day.
In Gout and Rheumatism.—MOENCH.

917. ℞ Calcii Sulphureti, ʒij.
Decocti Althææ, ℥ij. Make a lotion.
In Crusta Lactea.—HAHNEMANN.

CALUMBA.

Calumba, or *Colombo,* is the sliced root of the Cocculus palmatus, a plant (Nat. Ord. *Menispermaceæ*) of Mozambique. It contains a bitter principle in some quantity. It is one of the best tonics that we possess, though inferior as a febrifuge to Peruvian bark. From this and others it differs in being a pure bitter, destitute of astringency, containing neither tannic nor gallic acids. Its infusion may therefore be used as a vehicle for Iron or soluble preparations of Mercury, which it will not precipitate. Or it may be given alone in dyspepsia, convalescence from fevers, debility from any cause, scrofula, gout, &c. The powder may be given in doses of ten grains to ʒss, three times daily.

Extractum Calumbæ, (P.) gr. 5–15.
Infusum Cal. (L.E.D.) ℥iss.
Tinct. Cal. (L.E.D.) ʒj–ʒiij.

918. ℞ Pulv. Calumbæ, ʒss.
Ferri Potass. Tart. ℈ij.
Mix, and divide into 4 powders. (One every three to four hours in syrup.)
DR. ELLIS.

919. ℞ Pulv. Calumbæ, ʒj.
Pulv. Rhei, ℈ij.
Ext. Anthemidis, ʒij.
Ol. Carui, ♏v.
Syrupi Croci, q. s.
To make 4-grain pills; four every day.
In Mania, with Amenorrhœa.—AUGUSTIN.

920. ℞ Rad. Calumb. contusæ, ℥j.
Rad. Zingib. contusæ, ʒij.
Aquæ bullientis, Oj.
Infuse for two hours, and strain. (A wineglassful cold, every two hours.)

In Chronic Diarrhœa.—Dr. ELLIS.

921. ℞ Pulv. Calumbæ, ℥ss.
Aquæ, ℥x. Boil to six ounces; then add
Cascarillæ, ʒij.
Boil together, and to the strained liquor add
Tinct. Aurant. ʒij.
Syrup. Cinnam. ℥j. Take a spoonful every hour.

In Chronic Diarrhœa.—BERENDS.

922. ℞ Pulv. Rhei,
Pulv. Calumbæ,
Pulv. Cinnam.
P. Sodæ Carb. āā gr. v.
Mix. (To be taken before dinner, or at bedtime, for a fortnight.)

In Irritable Dyspepsia.—Dr. SEYMOUR.

923. ℞ Rad. Calumb. incisæ et contusæ, ʒss. Infuse in
Aquæ bullientis, ℥iij. Strain, and add
Syrupi Cinchonæ, ʒx. Mix.

In Chronic Diarrhœa and Dyspepsia.—TROUSSEAU & REVEIL.

924. ℞ Radicis Calumbæ, ʒij.
Cort. Cinchonæ, ʒij.
Cort. Aurantii, ʒj.
Cort. Cinnamom. ʒj.
Semin. Coriand. ʒj.
Aquæ bullientis, Oij.
Mix: infuse for twelve hours, and strain. Dose, a wineglassful three times a day before food.

In Atonic Dyspepsia.—Dr. ROSS.

CAMBOGIA. *Gamboge.*

Gamboge, or Gutti, is the concrete resin of a species of Garcinia growing in Siam. It is a hydragogue cathartic, and vermifuge; but not often given alone, as it is apt to produce nausea, vomiting, and griping. In combination with other cathartics it operates more favorably. In dropsical affections it is often combined with bitartrate of potash; its solution with alkalies is diuretic.

Dose, as a full purgative, two to six grains; as an alterative, half a grain to two grains. *Pilulæ Cambogiæ Compositæ*, ten to fifteen grains; *Pil. Cambogiæ cum Scammonio*, one to three pills; *Tinctura Cambogiæ Alkalina*, thirty to sixty minims; *Tinct. Cambogiæ Ammoniata* (Swediaur's), a drachm. It requires to be used with caution.

925. ℞ Cambogiæ, gr. ij ad iij.
Sacchari purif. ℈j.
Triturate together thoroughly: make a powder. To be taken every third hour, until the bowels respond freely.

In Dropsy.—Dr. CULLEN.

926. ℞ Cambogiæ pulv. gr. v ad viij.
Potassæ Bitartrat. ʒss.
Triturate together: make a powder. To be repeated every second or third day.

In Desquamative Nephritis.—Dr. G. JOHNSON.

927. ℞ Cambogiæ, gr. v.
Liq. Ammoniæ, gutt. xx. Rub up together, and add
Syrupi Rhamni, ʒij.
Aquæ Fœniculi, ℥j. Make a draught.

In Dropsy.—HARTMANN.

928. ℞ Cambogiæ, ℈ij.
Potassæ Tartrat. ℥j.
Sacchari albi, ʒij.
Aquæ, ℥vj.
Make a solution: a tablespoonful every two or three hours, till it operates on the bowels.

In Ascites.—Dr. DEWEES (U.S.).

929. ℞ Cambogiæ, gr. iv.
Elaterii, gr. ss.
Spir. Ætheris Nitr. ʒij.
Aquæ, ad ℥iv.
Mix: take a tablespoonful every second hour.

In Dropsy.—Dr. CHAPMAN (U.S.).

930. ℞ Cambogiæ, gr. xij.
Aloes Socot. ʒss.
Potas. Bitartratis, gr. xxxvj.
Make 24 pills. Take two three times a day.

Purgative. (Resembles Morrison's Pills.)—H. J.

931. ℞ Pil. Cambogiæ comp. ℈ij.
Pil. Hydrargyri, ℈j.
Mix, and divide into 12 pills. Take two as occasion requires.

In Constipation, with deficient Bile.—Dr. NELIGAN.

932. ℞ Pil. Cambogiæ comp. ℥ss.
Sodæ Carbonatis,
Quinæ Sulphatis, ana gr. xv.
Olei Menthæ piper. gutt. vj.
Syrupi, q. s.
Make 12 pills. Take two or three going to bed.
Purgative and Tonic.—Dr. ASHWELL.

933. ℞ Cambogiæ,
Scillæ rad. ana gr. xij.
Saponis duri, ʒj.
Mix with sufficient spirits of wine to make a mass, and divide into 48 pills. Two pills to be taken four times a day.
In Dropsical Complaints.—PHŒBUS.

934 ℞ Cambogiæ, gr. viij.
Olei Juniperi, ♏iij. Rub up together, and add
Potass. Bitartratis, ℈j.
Scillæ pulv. gr. j.
Syrupi Zingib. q. s. To make a bolus.
In Dropsical Affections.—Dr. COPLAND.

935. ℞ Cambogiæ, ℈ss.
Ferri Sulphatis, gr. vj.
Sacchari albi, ℈j.
Olei Menthæ pip. gutt. iij.
Mix: make a powder; prepare six similar doses. One to be taken every four hours till they have sufficiently operated.
To expel Tape-Worms.—VOGT.

CAMPHORA.

Camphor is a peculiar concrete from the wood of Camphora officinarum (Nat. Ord. *Lauraceæ*). It is sedative, antispasmodic, and diaphoretic. It produces slight exhilaration without quickening the pulse; quiets nervous irritation and restlessness; and is supposed to lessen irritations of the urinary organs, from cantharides, &c. It is frequently combined with diaphoretics to increase their efficacy in febrile complaints, and in rheumatism after depletions; with the fetid gums and valerian, in hysterical and nervous complaints; with bark, in malignant fevers and gangrene, &c. Held to the nostrils it relieves cold in the head; and the vapor inhaled—by means of a tube containing pieces of camphor—(*Cigarra Camphoræ*) is said to be useful in affections of the chest. The vapor, combined with hot air or steam, is also applied to the skin (*Bal-*

neum Camphoræ). Camphor is also used in *liniments*, as an anodyne and stimulant.

Dose of Camphor, from one to fifteen grains; *Mistura Camphoræ*, one to two ounces; *Tinctura Camphoræ*, thirty to sixty minims; *Tinct. Camphoræ comp.*, one to three drachms. Camphor is readily powdered by rubbing it with a drop or two of rectified spirit.

936. ℞ Camphoræ pulv. gr. iij ad vj.
Spir. rectif. ♏ij. Rub up together, and add
Confect. Rosæ, gr. vj.
Make a bolus: to be taken every fourth or sixth hour.

In Typhus Fever, with muttering Delirium.

937. ℞ Camphoræ (ope spir. redactæ), ʒss.
Sacchari albi, ʒj.
Acaciæ pulv. ʒiss.
Mix: make a powder. To be divided equally into ten powders.

Dr. Copland.

938. ℞ Camphoræ pulv. gr. iv.
Ammoniæ Sesquicarb. gr. iij.
Extr. Hyoscyami, gr. iv.
Mucilag. q. s.
Make a mass, and divide into three pills. One to be taken every two hours.

In the advanced stage of Typhus Fever.—Dr. Hooper.

939. ℞ Camphoræ p. gr. xv.
Opii pulv. gr. iij.
Make six pills: two or three to be taken every night at bedtime.

To prevent Chordee.—Ricord.

940. ℞ Camphoræ, gr. ij.
Extr. Conii, gr. iij. Make a pill: to be taken at bedtime.

In the same.—Dr. M. Ryan.

941. ℞ Camphoræ p. gr. v.
Extr. Hyoscyami, gr. v.
Make two pills: to be taken at once.

In Puerperal Mania.—Dr. Gooch.

942. ℞ Camphoræ p. gr. iij.
Pulv. Jacobi, gr. iv.
Potas. Nitratis, ℈ss.
Extr. Hyoscyami, gr. vij.
Cons. Rosæ, q. s. To make a bolus.

In Cerebral Affections.—Dr. Copland.

943. ℞ Camphoræ pulv.
Extr. Lactucæ, ana ℈iis.
Mix: make into 20 pills. From four to six pills to be taken daily.

Anaphrodisiac.—M. Ricord.

944. ℞ Camphoræ pulv.
Potassæ Nitratis, ana ℈ss.
Opii pulv. gr. ij.
Antim. Potassio-tart. gr. ss.
Hydrurg. Chlor. gr. iss. Rub up thoroughly with
Syrupi, q. s. To make a bolus.

In Rheumatism.—Dr. E. G. CLARK.

945. ℞ Camphoræ redactæ, ʒij.
Mucil. Acaciæ, f℥j.
Aquæ destillatæ, f℥vij.
Make a mixture: a tablespoonful every four hours.

In Chronic Bronchitis of the old and debilitated.
Dr. NELIGAN.

946. ℞ Camphoræ redactæ, ʒj.
Lactis recentis, ℥vj.
Aquæ Pulegii, ℥ij.
Make a mixture: a tablespoonful every fourth hour.

In the same cases.—Dr. NELIGAN.

947. ℞ Camphoræ, gr. viij ad xvj.
Spirit. rectif. ♏vj. Rub up, and add
Sacchari albi,
Pulv. Acaciæ,
Magnesiæ Carb. ana ℈ij.
Aquæ puræ, f℥viiss. Make a mixture.

Dr. COPLAND.

948. ℞ Camphoræ pulv. gr. iij.
Acaciæ pulv. ʒss. Rub up together, and add
Mist. Amygdalæ, f℥iss. Make a draught.

949. ℞ Pulv. Camphoræ, gr. ix.
Ovi Vitelli, partem quartam. Rub up well, and add
Mucilag. simp. ℥vj.
Syrupi Morph. Sulph. ℥j.
Syrupi simp. ℥ss. Mix: a tablespoonful every hour.

In Catarrhs.—TROUSSEAU and REVEIL.

950. ℞ Camphoræ p. gr. xxv.
Amygd. dulc. decort. No. vj.
Sacchari puri, ʒiij.
Bruise thoroughly, then add by degrees
Aquæ Menthæ vir. f℥viiss.
Make a mixture: three tablespoonfuls every fourth hour.

In Hysteria.—Dr. HOOPER.

951. ℞ Camphoræ p.
Potassæ Nitratis, ana ℈j.
Vitell. ovi, q. s. Rub up together, and add
Aquæ flor. Aurantii, ℥iv.
Tinct. Hyoscyami,
Tinct. Conii, ana ʒj.
Make a mixture: a tablespoonful every three hours.

In Chordee.—Dr. JOY.

952. ℞ Pulv. Camphoræ, gr. iij ad vij.
Tinct. Calumbæ,
Spir. Cinnamomi, ana f℥iss. Dissolve, and add
Aquæ Menthæ viridis,
Aquæ Pimentæ, ana f℥v.
Make a draught: to be taken when the vomiting is urgent.
In Spasmodic Asthma, Vomiting, &c.—Dr. COPLAND.

953. ℞ Camphoræ, gr. xxv.
Spirit. rectificati, ♏v. Rub up, and add
Pulv. Acaciæ, ʒiv.
Syrupi Limonis, f℥ss.
Aquæ Menthæ vir. f℥viiss.
Make an emulsion: dose, three tablespoonfuls.
Dr. HOOPER.

954. ℞ Cinchonæ pulv. ʒss.
Camphoræ pulv. gr. v.
Make a powder: to be taken every third or fourth hour.
In Gangrene and Malignant Fevers.—HARTMANN.

955. ℞ Camphoræ (ope spir. red.) ʒj.
Vitell. ovi unius,
Decocti Hordei, f℥xiv. Mix: make an enema.
Dr. JOY.

956. ℞ Camphoræ p. ʒj.
Olei Olivæ, ℥ij. Mix: make an enema.
In Ascarides.—Dr. FOWLER.

957. ℞ Linim. Camphoræ comp.
Liquor. Ammoniæ, ana ℥j.
Tinct. Capsici, ʒiij.
Mix: make a liniment. To be rubbed on the thorax and epigastrium.
In Angina Pectoris.—Dr. COPLAND.

958. ℞ Linim. Camphoræ, ʒxij.
Olei Rosmarini, ʒss.
Tinct. Opii, ʒij.
Make a liniment: to be rubbed over the bowels.
In Flatulent Colic, &c.—Dr. COPLAND.

959. ℞ Olei Camphorati, ℥j.
Olei Terebinthinæ, ʒij.
Saponis mollis pur. ʒiv. Mix: make a liniment.
In Lumbago.—Dr. FRASER.

960. ℞ Camphoræ, ʒj.
Olei Palmæ, ℥j. Mix: make an ointment.
In Whitlow.—Dr. E. G. CLARK.

CANNABIS SATIVA. CANNABIS INDICA.

Indian Hemp is generally considered to be the same species as *Cannabis sativa* of Europe; but in the East it secretes a resin, and acquires peculiar properties which it does not possess in Europe. Indian hemp is narcotic, anodyne, and anti-spasmodic: it produces a peculiar kind of delirium and catalepsy. As a remedy, it has been tried in tetanus, hydrophobia, painful neuralgic and rheumatic affections, cholera, &c. But it acts less powerfully in Europe than in India. The resinous extract is imported from India; and its purification is directed in the Dub. pharmacopœia. A still purer preparation is used under the name of Cannabine.

Dose of *Extractum Cannabis*, two to ten grains; *Tinct. Cannabis*, from fifteen minims to a drachm or more. In *Tetanus*, a drachm is given every half hour. *Cannabina*, half a grain to a grain; two-thirds of a grain, in one case, acted as a powerful narcotic.

The seeds of *Common Hemp* are the only part used. They have been given in mucous discharges and jaundice.

961. ℞ Tinct. Cannabis resinæ, ♏xv.
Spirit. Vini rectif. ♏xlv.
Mix: make a draught. To be mixed with water at the moment of taking it.

In Neuralgia, Rheumatism, &c.—Mr. DONOVAN.

962. ℞ Tinct. Cannabis Indicæ, ʒss.
Mucil. Acaciæ, fʒj.
Aquæ puræ, f℥j.
Make a draught: to be taken every fifth or sixth hour.

In Sciatica and other Neuralgic Pains.—Dr. NELIGAN.

963. ℞ Tinct. Cannabis Indicæ, ʒj.
Mucil. Acaciæ, fʒij.
Aquæ Cinnamomi, f℥j.
Make a draught: to be taken immediately, and repeated at intervals of two hours, or more frequently if death threatens.

In Tetanus and Hydrophobia.—Dr. NELIGAN.

964. ℞ Extracti Cannabis Indicæ, ℈j.
Rub up in a warmed mortar with
Olei Olivæ, fʒj. Then add gradually
Mucilag. Acaciæ, fʒiv.
Aquæ puræ, f℥viiss. Make a mixture: dose, f℥iss.

Mr. BROMFIELD.

965. ℞ Sem. Cannabis sativæ, ℥iv.
Cerevisiæ, Oij. Boil, strain, and add
Sacchari, q. s. Take half a pint every morning.
In Obstinate Jaundice.—Dr. BUCHAN.

966. ℞ Sem. Cannabis sativæ, ʒiij–vj.
Amygd. amar. No. iv. Contuse, and rub up with
Aquæ, lbij. Make an emulsion, strain, and add
Syrupi Papaveris, ℥j.
The whole to be drank in the course of a day.
In Gonorrhœa, and Chronic Inflammation of the Mucous Membranes. TODD.

CANTHARIS. *Spanish Fly.*

Cantharides are an irritant poison; but have been administered in small doses as a stimulant, acting especially on the urinary organs. They are given in paralysis of the bladder, obstinate gleet, and more rarely as a diuretic in atonic dropsy; also in some skin diseases, as lepra and psoriasis; and in hooping-cough. Their most important use, however, is as the usual and most convenient basis of blistering compounds. They also enter into the composition of some stimulating and rubefacient liniments.

Dose of the powdered flies, from half a grain to two grains; of *Tinctura Cantharidis*, from ten minims gradually increased to forty; of *Extractum Cantharidis*, from a quarter to half a grain. These must be exhibited with caution. Both the external and internal use of Cantharides is apt to occasion strangury; which is alleviated by mucilaginous drinks, and in the opinion of some, by camphor.

The following officinal preparations are for external use:

Ceratum Cantharidis (L.), and *Unguentum Infusi Cantharidis*, for keeping blisters open; *Emplastrum Cantharidis*, *Emp. Canth. compositum*, *Emp. Olei Cantharidis*, *Epithema Vesicatorum*, and *Aceti Cantharidis*, for raising blisters; *Collodion Cantharidale*, *Tela vesicatoria*, for the same purpose. *Linimentum Cantharidis* (U. S.), *Unguentum Extracti, and Ung. Tinct. Cantharidis*, as stimulants and rubefacients.

967. ℞ Amygdal. dulc. decort. ℥j.
Cantharidum pulv. subt. ℈ss.
Sacchari puri, ℥ss.
Rub up well together, and add gradually
Aquæ tepidæ, f℥x.
Strain: take a tablespoonful every three hours.

In torpor of the Kidneys, and paralysis of the Bladder.

Dr. NELIGAN.

968. ℞ Cantharidis pulv. gr. j.
Sacchari albi,
Acaciæ pulveris, ana ʒij. Mix well, and add
Mist. Amygdalæ, ℥v.
Mix: make a mixture. A tablespoonful every two hours.

In Hooping-Cough (for children).—FRANKEL.

969. ℞ Tinct. Cantharidis, gutt. ij.
Tinct. Hyoscyami, ♏v.
Aquæ puræ, fʒx.
Make a draught: to be taken four times a day.

In Incontinence of the Urine.—Dr. GREGORY.

970. ℞ Tinct. Cantharidis,
Tinct. Camphoræ comp. ana ʒj.
Tinct. Cinchonæ comp. ʒx.
Mix: from thirty minims, gradually increased to a teaspoonful, three times a day.

In Hooping-Cough.—Dr. BEATTY.

971. ℞ Tinct. Cantharidis, ʒj.
Infusi Quassiæ, ℥vj. Take a sixth part three times a day.

Dr. HOOPER.

972. ℞ Tinct. Ferri Sesquichloridi,
Tinct. Cantharidis, ana ʒij.
Tinct. Capsici, fʒj.
Syrupi Croci, ʒij.
Aquæ Pimentæ, f℥vij.
Make a mixture: two spoonfuls three times a day.

Dr. DRUITT.

973. ℞ Tinct. Cantharidis,
Liquor. Potassæ Arsenitis, ana ℥ss.
Mix: take ten drops twice a day. [The dose to be gradually increased to ♏xv, carefully watching its effects.]

In Psoriasis.—Prof. BENNETT.

974. ℞ Zinci Sulphat. gr. xxiv.
Cantharidis pulv. gr. vj.
Rhei pulveris, ʒj.
Tereb. Venet. q. s.
Make 24 pills: two, three times a day.

Dr. DRUITT.

975. ℞ Cantharidis, p. gr. ij.
Camphoræ, ℈ss.
Extracti Hyoscyami, gr. vj.
Spirit. rectif. q. s. Make four pills. Take one, twice a day.
Dr. HOOPER.

976. ℞ Pulv. Cantharidis, gr. xij.
Extr. Hyoscyam. ʒj.
Argenti Nit. gr. x.
Quinæ Sulph. ℈ij.
Mix: make 40 pills. Take one night and morning.
In Leucorrhœa of Nervous Females.—Dr. H. GREEN.

977. ℞ Pulv. Cantharidis, ℈ij.
Ext. Conii, ʒj.
Hyd. Submur. ʒss.
Pulv. Ipecac. ℈j.
Mix: make a mass, and divide into 40 pills. Take one, three or four times a day.
In general Anasarca.—Dr. H. GREEN.

978. ℞ Tinct. Cantharidis,
Ætheris Sulphurici,
Spir. Camphoræ,
Tinct. Opii, ana ʒiv. Mix: make a liniment.
In Hysterical Pain in the Side.—Dr. ASHWELL.

979. ℞ Antim. Potassio-tart. ℈ij.
Aquæ Rosæ calidæ, ℥ij. Dissolve, and add
Tinct. Cantharidis, ℥j. To be rubbed on the spine and chest.
In Hooping-Cough.—Dr. G. GREGORY.

980. ℞ Aceti Cantharidis, ℥ss.
Aquæ Coloniensis, ℥j.
Aquæ Rosæ, ℥j. Mix: make a lotion.
In Alopecia.—Mr. ERASMUS WILSON.

981. ℞ Tinct. Cantharidis, fʒij.
Aquæ Sambuci, f℥xj.
Ess. Rosmarini (Dub.), fʒvj. Mix: make a lotion.
To promote the Growth of the Hair.—Dr. NELIGAN.

982. ℞ Balsami Nervini (Fr. codex),
Medullæ Bovinæ, āā ℥j.
Olei Amygdalæ, ʒv.
Acidi Tannici, ʒss.
Spir. Vini Gall. ʒiiss.
Tinct. Cantharidis, ʒss.
Mix: according to art: make a pomatum. To be rubbed in frequently.
To arrest Loss of Hair.—TROUSSEAU and REVEIL.

983. ℞ Tinct. Cantharidis, ℈iv.
Lin. Camphoræ comp. ℥iss.
Tinct. Opii, ʒiij.
Make an embrocation. To be rubbed over the abdomen.

In Colic.—Dr. JOY.

984. ℞ Tinct. Cantharidis, f℥iij.
Lin. Saponis, fʒxj. Make a liniment.

In Chilblains.—Mr. WARDROP.

CAPSICUM.

Capsicum, the fruit of *Capsicum fastigiatum* and other species (Nat. Ord. *Solanaceæ*), is a powerful stimulant, and is used in atony of the stomach, particularly in the dyspepsia of gouty and debilitated subjects; and as a condiment to prevent flatulence from a vegetable diet. It is also prescribed in intermittent and low fevers; and both internally and as a gargle in malignant sore throat. As a gargle, and in the form of lozenges, it is also useful in relaxed sore throat, and chronic hoarseness.

Dose of *Capsicum*, of good quality, two to eight grains; *Tinctura Capsici*, ten to sixty minims; *Trochisci Capsici*, one swallowed slowly two or three times a day. *Tinctura Capsici concentrata* is used as an external stimulant in chilblains, cholera, &c.

985. ℞ Pulveris Capsici, ʒj.
Micæ panis, ʒss.
Aquæ, q. s. Make 20 pills. One or two, twice a day.

986. ℞ Pil. Saponis comp. gr. iij.
Pulv. Capsici, gr. iij.
Olei Fœniculi, ♏ij. Make into two pills, for a dose.

In Flatulent Atonic Dyspepsia.—Dr. HOOPER.

987. ℞ Pulv. Capsici, ℥ss.
Pulv. Zingiberis, ʒij.
Pulv. Sacchari albi, ℥ij.
Mucil. Tragac. q. s.
Make 96 lozenges. One to be slowly swallowed three times a day.

In Catarrhal Deafness.—Dr. FOSBROKE.

988. ℞ Capsici pulv. ʒij.
Aquæ ferventis, Oss.
Macerate for two hours, and strain. A tablespoonful two or three times a day.

In Malignant Sore Throat.—Dr. PEREIRA.

989. ℞ Capsici pulv. gr. xvj.
Aquæ ferventis, ℥viij.
Macerate, and strain; to form a gargle.

Dr. CURRIE.

990. ℞ Pulv. Capsici, ℈ss.
Aquæ ferventis, f℥viij.
Macerate for two hours, strain, and add
Mellis Rosæ,
Tinct. Myrrhæ, ana ℥ss. Make a gargle.

Mr. BRANDE.

991. ℞ Tincturæ Capsici, f℥iij.
Aquæ, ℥vj. Make a gargle.

Dr. A. T. THOMSON.

992. ℞ Tinct. Capsici, ʒj.
Decocti Cinchonæ, ℥vj.
Make a gargle. To be used five or six times a day.

In Chronic Hoarseness of growing boys.—Dr. GRAVES.

993. ℞ Capsici pulv. ʒj.
Sodii Chloridi, ℈j.
Aquæ ferventis, ℥vj. Macerate, strain, and add
Aceti, ℥ss. Make a gargle.

In Malignant Sore Throat. (Used in the West Indies.)

994. ℞ Pulv. Capsici, gr. iss.
Aquæ ferventis, ℥ss.
Macerate, and strain. One drop to be instilled into the eye every morning and night, increasing the strength as it can be borne.

In Amaurosis.—MAUNOIR.

995. ℞ Tinct. Capsici, ℥ss.
Linim. Saponis, ℥iss. Make a liniment.

996. ℞ Tinct. Capsici, ℥ss.
Tinct. Opii, ℥ss.
Make an embrocation. Bandages to be rolled round the fingers, &c., and wet with the embrocation two or three times a day.

In Chilblains.—Dr. A. T. THOMSON.

CARBON. *Animal and Vegetable Charcoal.*

Charcoal is antiseptic, and tends to keep the bowels soluble, perhaps by its mechanical action. It is used in flatulent dyspepsia, and to correct fetid eructations and discharges. *Animal Charcoal* is also sometimes prescribed in scrofulous and cutaneous diseases. Perhaps in the form of bone (or ivory) black, it may owe its efficacy in rickets and scrofula, in part, to the bone-earth it contains. *Externally*, charcoal (generally wood-charcoal) is added to poultices, to correct the fetor of foul ulcers. It is also dusted on the skin in porrigo, or used in the form of an ointment.

Dose of Charcoal, ten to twenty or thirty grains.

997. ℞ Pulv. Carbonis Tiliæ, ℥j.
Syrupi Aurantii, ℥iij.
Make an electuary. One or two teaspoonfuls every two hours.
In Fetid Eructations.—SCHUBARTH.

998. ℞ Carbonis animalis,
Pulv. Glycyrrhizæ rad. ana ʒvj.
Mix: make a powder. Half or a whole teaspoonful twice a day.
In Rickets and Scrofula of Children.—RADIUS.

999. ℞ Carbonis animalis, gr. iij.
Ammoniæ mur. p. ℈j.
Extr. Conii, gr. ij.
Glycyrrhizæ rad. pulv. q. s.
Make a bolus. Take one three times a day.
In Swelled and Scirrhous Prostate.—MAGENDIE.

1000. ℞ Carbonis ligni,
Sodæ Bicarbonatis, ana ʒj.
Confect. Sennæ, ℥ij.
Make an electuary. A teaspoonful three or four times a day.
In Obstinate Constipation.—MITCHELL.

1001. ℞ Carbonis pulv. ʒiij.
Adipis, ℥j. Make an ointment.
In Tinea Capitis.—ALIBERT.

CARDAMOMUM. *Cardamom.*

Cardamom, the seed of *Elettaria Cardamomum* (Nat. Ord. *Zingiberaceæ*), is an aromatic carminative stimulant, less heating than many other spices. It is a frequent adjunct to other stimulants, to bitter tonics, and to purgatives.

Dose of the powdered seeds, five to twenty grains; *Tinctura Cardamomi* and *Tinct. Card. composita*, one to two drachms.

1002. ℞ Tinct. Cardam. compos. ʒvj.
Aquæ Cinnamomi, ℥vj.
Mix: take three spoonfuls two or three times a day.
In Atonic Dyspepsia.—Dr. AINSLIE.

1003. ℞ Tinct. Cardamomi comp. fʒij.
Spir. Ammoniæ Arom. ♏x.
Aquæ Carui, f℥j.
Syrupi, fʒj. Mix: make a draught.
A Stimulating Carminative.—Dr. JOY.

1004. ℞ Sem. Cardam. pulv. gr. iv.
Extracti Rhei, gr. ij.
Extracti Coloc. comp. gr. j.
Make two pills. To be taken twice a day.

Laxative and Carminative.—H. J.

CARYOPHYLLI. *Cloves.*

Cloves are the unexpanded flowers of *Caryophyllus aromaticus* (Nat. Ord. *Myrtaceæ*), and belong to the more hot and stimulating aromatics. They are given to correct flatulence, and excite languid digestion; but chiefly as an adjunct to bitter tonics, or as a corrective to purgatives.

Dose of powdered cloves, two to eight grains; of *Infusum Caryophylli*, one to two ounces; *Tinctura Caryophylli*, twenty to thirty drops; *Oleum Caryophylli*, two to six drops.

1005. ℞ Inf. Caryophylli, f℥ix.
Tinct. Cardam. comp. f℥j.
Spir. Myristicæ, f℥ss.
Spir. Ammoniæ arom. f℥ss.
Syrupi Zingiberis, f℥j. Make a draught.

Stimulant.—Dr. Paris.

1006. ℞ Olei Caryophylli, ℈j.
Tinct. Opii, ℥ss.
Ætheris Sulphurici, ℥j.
Mix: twenty to thirty drops to be added to last two or three doses of cinchona.

In Intermittent Fevers.—Horn.

1007. ℞ Inf. Caryophylli,
Aq. Menthæ piper. ana f℥iiiss.
Tinct. Cardamomi comp. ℥ss.
Sp. Ammon. arom.
Syr. Zingiberis, ana f℥iss.
Take a wineglassful twice a day, after food.

Dr. Latham.

1008. ℞ Olei Caryophylli, ℥j.
Olei Cajaputi, ℥j.
Opii pulveris,
Camphoræ, ana ℈ss.
Spirit. rectificati, q. s. Dissolve.

In Toothache.—Dr. Copland.

1009. ℞ Infusi Caryophylli, ℥viij–xij.
Tinct. Galbani, ℥iv. Make an enema.

Stimulant.—Dr. R. Reece.

CASCARILLA.

Cascarilla is the bark of *Croton Eleuteria* (Nat. Ord. *Euphorbiaceæ*), and belongs to the aromatic bitter tonics. It is prescribed when a gentle stimulating tonic is required; as in simple dyspepsia, dysentery, flatulent colic, and in diseases of debility generally, but especially of the stomach and bowels. It is often combined with other bitters and stimulants, and with metallic tonics.

Dose of the powdered bark, twenty to thirty grains; of *Infusum Cascarillæ*, one to two ounces; *Tinctura Cascarillæ*, one to three drachms; *Mistura Cascarillæ comp.* (Ph. Lond. 1836), one ounce to one and a half, in chronic affections of the mucous membrane of the lungs.

1010. ℞ Infusi Cascarillæ, f℥vss.
Tinct. Cascarillæ, f℥ss.
Make a mixture. Three tablespoonfuls for a dose, two or three times a day.
In Atonic and Flatulent Dyspepsia.—Mr. BRANDE.

1011. ℞ Infusi Cascarillæ, f℥viij.
Tinct. Cascarillæ,
Tinct. Zingiberis, ana fʒiv.
Mix: make a stomachic mixture. Two tablespoonfuls twice a day.
In Dyspepsia, with Loss of Appetite.—Dr JOY.

1012. ℞ Infusi Cascarillæ, ℥vij.
Sodæ Bicarbon. ʒiij.
Tinct. Cardamomi, ʒvj.
Mix: a wineglassful an hour or two before, and two hours after dinner.
Mr. ABERNETHY.

1013. ℞ Infusi Cascarillæ, fʒvj.
Aquæ Cinnamomi, fʒiij.
Pulv. Kino comp. ℈ss.
Syrupi Papaveris, ʒj.
Mix: make a draught. To be taken twice a day.
In Chronic Dysentery.—Dr. G. GREGORY.

1014. ℞ Infusi Cascarillæ, f℥vss.
Acidi Nitrici dil. fʒj.
Tinct. Lupuli, fʒiij.
Mix: make a mixture. Dose, two tablespoonfuls.
HOSP. FOR CONSUMPTION.

CASSIA.

The pods of *Cassia fistula* (Nat. Ord. *Leguminosæ*) yield a pulp which is laxative in doses of one or two drachms; larger doses of half an ounce to two ounces are purgative, but apt to produce flatulence and griping.

1015. ℞ Pulpæ Cassiæ, ℥j.
Potassæ Tartratis, ʒij.
Aquæ Cinnamomi, ℥iij.
Mannæ, ʒiss.
Mix: a tablespoonful every two or three hours until it operates.
As a Laxative for Children.—Dr. URE.

1016. ℞ Pulpæ Cassiæ, ℥j.
Aquæ ferventis, Oij. Macerate, strain, and add
Magnesiæ Sulphatis, ℥j.
Antim. Potassio-tart. gr. iij.
Mix: to be taken by wineglassfuls.
In Painter's Colic.—FRENCH HOSPITALS.

[The Bark of *Cinnamomum Cassia* is used for the same purposes and in the same manner as Cinnamon. See CINNAMOMUM. For Cassia Senna, see SENNA.]

CASTOREUM.

Castor is a peculiar secretion obtained from the Beaver, (*Castor Fiber*); it is a nervous stimulant, antispasmodic, and emmenagogue; and is prescribed in hysteria, epilepsy, and various nervous affections; especially when connected with irregularity of the uterine functions. The Russian Castor is more powerful than the American, but is very scarce.

Dose of Castor in powder, ten to twenty grains; *Tinctura Castorei*, one to two drachms; *Tinct. Castorei comp.*, one drachm.

1017. ℞ Castorei, ℈j.
Ammoniæ Sesquicarb. gr. v.
Opii pulv. gr. ss.
Syrupi, q. s.
To make 6 pills. To be taken at short intervals.
In Hysteria.—Dr. HOOPER.

1018. ℞ Castorei Rossici, ʒss.
Aquæ Pulegii, ℥iss.
Syrupi Croci, ʒij.
Liq. Ammon. Sesquicarb. ♏xx–xxx.
Make a draught. To be taken two or three times a day.
In Hysteria.—Dr. PEARSON.

1019. ℞ Castorei Ros. pulv. ʒij.
Valerianæ rad. pulv. ʒiv.
Camphoræ rasæ, ʒj. Mix accurately, and add
Syrupi Papaveris, q. s. Make 12-grain boluses.

In Hysteria.—Dr. COPLAND.

1020. ℞ Tinct. Castorei Ammon. fʒv.
Ætheris Sulphurici, fʒiij.
Misturæ Moschi, f℥vij.

Mix: make a mixture. A tablespoonful every two hours until the symptoms disappear.

In Cramp of the Stomach, Flatulent Colic, Hysteria, &c.
Dr. NELIGAN.

1021. ℞ Spir. Ammon. arom. ʒiij.
Spir. Lavandulæ comp. ʒiv.
Tinct. Castorei, ʒiv.
Misturæ Camphoræ, ℥vij.

Make a mixture. Three spoonfuls three or four times a day.

In the same cases.

1022. ℞ Tinct. Castorei, ʒj.
Ætheris Sulphurici, ♏x.
Tinct. Opii, ♏vij.
Aquæ Cinnamomi, ℥ss.

Mix: make a draught. To be taken three times a day.

In Typhus Fever.—Dr. HUNTER.

CATECHU.

Catechu is an extract from the wood of *Acacia Catechu* (Nat. Ord. *Leguminosæ*). It is tonic, and powerfully astringent; and is used in most cases in which astringents are indicated; as in passive hæmorrhages, particularly from the bowels or uterus; diarrhœa, with debility and relaxation of the exhalents; chronic dysentery; and in "all cases of increased mucous discharges where there is no inflammation present;" as in chronic cystirrhœa, leucorrhœa, gleet, chronic catarrh, &c. Also as a topical astringent in relaxed sore throat, ulcerations of the mouth, hoarseness, chapped nipples, &c.

Dose of *Catechu*, ten to thirty grains; *Infusum Catechu*, one to two ounces; *Electuarium*, one to six scruples; *Tinctura*, half a drachm to two drachms; *Trochisci*, one slowly swallowed, several times a day; *Pulvis Catechu compositus* (D.), half a drachm to one and a half drachms.

The Tincture is also applied to chapped nipples.

1023. ℞ Pulv. Catechu, gr. v.
Conf. Rosæ, q. s.
Make a bolus. To be taken morning and evening.
In Chronic Diarrhœa of Children.—Dr. URE.

1024. ℞ Catechu pulv. gr. xv.
Pulv. Cretæ comp. cum Opio, ℈j.
Mix: make a powder. To be taken every four hours.
In Diarrhœa.—Dr. JOY.

1025. ℞ Catechu extr. pulv. gr. xij.
Conf. Opii, gr. viij.
Pulv. Cretæ, gr. iv.
Syrupi Aurantii, q. s.
Make a bolus. To be taken twice, thrice, or more frequently during the day.
Dr. COPLAND.

1026. ℞ Misturæ Cretæ, f℥vss.
Tincturæ Catechu, fʒvj.
Mix: take two or three tablespoonfuls after each liquid evacuation.
In Diarrhœa (after a rhubarb aperient).—Mr. BRANDE.

1027. ℞ Catechu pulveris, ʒj.
Aquæ ferventis, f℥viij.
Macerate for an hour, and strain. Make an astringent lotion.
Dr. DRUITT.

1028. ℞ Cinchonæ pulv. ℥ss.
Catechu pulv. ℥ss.
Myrrhæ pulv. ʒij. Mix.
As a Tooth Powder, in Spongy Gums.—Dr. PARIS.

CEDRON.

The seeds of *Simaba Cedron* (Nat. Ord. *Simarubaceæ*) are principally celebrated as a remedy for the bites of serpents and for hydrophobia; they are also given in intermittent fevers, spasms of the stomach and bowels, colic, dyspeptic affections, and cholera.

Dose, in ordinary cases, one or two grains; as an antidote for the bites of serpents, five or six grains with a spoonful of brandy. In large doses (twenty to thirty grains) it is poisonous.

CERA. *Wax.* CETACEUM. *Spermaceti.*

Yellow Beeswax, and white wax (the same bleached), and spermaceti (obtained from the head of the spermaceti whale, *Physeter macrocephalus*), are chiefly used as the basis of cerates and ointments; but are also occasionally prescribed, especially the latter, as demulcents, in irritations of the respiratory and urinary organs, and of the bowels. Spermaceti is easily reduced to powder by the aid of a few drops of rectified spirit.

1029. ℞ Ceræ flavæ (*vel* albæ), ℨiij.
Saponis duri, ℨj.
Aquæ destillatæ, ℥j.

To be liquefied by a slow fire, stirring with a wooden spatula; then pour into a mortar, and add, little by little,

Aquæ puræ, Oiss.
Syrupi Althææ,
Spir. Cinnamomi, ana ℥j.

Rub intimately, to form a mixture. A wineglassful to be given frequently.

In Dysentery, &c.—Dr. MONRO.

1030. ℞ Cetacei pulv. ℥ss.
Sacchari conditi, ℥j.

Rub up together. A teaspoonful to be taken now and then.

In Tickling Coughs.

1031. ℞ Cetacei pulv. ℨij.
Olei Olivæ, ℨj. Rub up together; then add
Acaciæ pulv. ℨiv. Then add by degrees
Aquæ puræ, ℥iv. Mix: a tablespoonful frequently.

In Coughs.—Mr. W. PROCTER.

1032. ℞ Cetacei, ℨvj.
Vitellum Ovi unis. Beat up well; then add
Syrupi Tolutani, f℥iss.
Aquæ Pulegii, Oj.

Make a mixture, of which f℥j may be given three, four, or more times a day; adding to each dose, if circumstances require, half a scruple of Nitrate of Potassa, or thirty minims Tr. Camph. Comp.

In Coughs.—GUY'S HOSP.

1033. ℞ Cetacei, ℨvj.
Acaciæ pulv. ℨiij.
Sacchari albi, ℥j.

Rub up together carefully, adding, little by little,

Aquæ destillatæ, ℥iv.

Make a mixture. A spoonful every two hours.

In Coughs.—HUFELAND.

1034. ℞ Cetacei, ℨj.
Acaciæ pulv. ℨij.
Olei Amygdalæ, ℥j.
Syrupi Tolutani, ℥j.
Aquæ Fœniculi, ℥ivss. Mix.

In Coughs, &c.—Dr. COPLAND.

1035. ℞ Cetacei (vitel. ovi sol.) ℈j.
Pulv. Cretæ comp. gr. xv.
Aquæ destillatæ, f℥iss.
Spir. Myristicæ,
Syrupi Tolut. ana fʒj.
Make a draught: to be given every sixth hour. Add, as occasion may require, five grains of Potassæ Nitras.

In Diarrhœa of Small-pox.—Dr. E. G. Clark.

1036. ℞ Cetacei, ℈iss.
Pulv. Tragac. comp. ʒij.
Aquæ Pimentæ, f℥vss.
Vini Ipecac. fʒj.
Tinct. Camphoræ comp. fʒiij.
Make a mixture. Take two spoonfuls two or three times a day.

In Coughs.—Dr. A. T. Thomson.

1037. ℞ Cetacei pulv. ʒij.
Olei Amygdalæ, ʒiij.
Conf. Rosæ caninæ, ℥j.
Syrupi Papaveris, ʒvj.
Ipecacuanhæ p. ℈ss.
Acidi Sulph. dil. ♏xv.
Make a linctus. A teaspoonful every two or three hours when the cough is troublesome.

In recent Cough.—Dr. R. Reece.

1038. ℞ Cetacei,
Ceræ flavæ, ana ʒij.
Pulv. Tragac. comp.
Confectio Opii, ana ʒj.
Syrupi Papaveris, q. s. Make an electuary.

In Dysentery.—Dr. E. G. Clark.

CETRARIA. *Iceland Moss.* CETRARINA.

Iceland Moss (*Cetraria Islandica*, Nat. Ord. *Lichenaceæ*) is demulcent, tonic, and nutritive. It is principally prescribed in consumptive and other coughs, attended with debility and emaciation: also in chronic dysentery and diarrhœa. When designed merely as a demulcent and nutrient, the bitterness may be in great part removed by macerating it in warm water, or in cold water in which a little carbonate of potash or soda has been dissolved. The bitter principle, *Cetrarine*, is given in doses of two grains every two hours, in intermittent fevers.

Iceland Moss is generally given in the form of decoction or jelly.

Dose of *Decoctum Cetrariæ*, one to four ounces, three times a day; of *Gelatina Lichenis*, quarter of an ounce frequently, dissolved in warm milk; *Chocolata Lichenis*, at pleasure.

1039. ℞ Decocti Cetrariæ, f℥vss.
Acidi Nitrici dil. fʒj.
Syrupi Tolutani, f℥ss.
Tinct. Camphoræ comp. fʒj.
Make a mixture. Take a fourth part three times a day.

In Consumption.—Dr. FARRE.

1040. ℞ Decocti Cetrariæ, ℥xiss.
Acidi Sulph. dil. fʒiss.
Syrupi, fʒvj.
Tinct. Opii, fʒj.
Make a mixture. Take f℥ij three times a day.

Dr. A. T. THOMSON.

1041. ℞ Cetrarinæ,
Acaciæ pulv. ana gr. ij.
Make a powder. To be taken every hour, or every two hours.

In Intermittents.—Dr. DUNGLISON.

1042. ℞ Cetrarinæ, gr. xxiv.
Extr. Calumbæ, ʒss.
Mix, and divide into 12 pills. Take one every fourth hour.

In Intermittents.—Dr. NELIGAN.

CHIMAPHILA, or PYROLA UMBELLATA. *Winter green.*

Winter-green (*Chimaphila umbellata*, Nat. Ord. *Pyrolaceæ*) is a stimulating diuretic; it is also tonic, and moderately astringent. It is given in dropsy, and chronic affections of the urinary organs; and also in scrofulous ulcerations, and cutaneous diseases. It stimulates the kidneys more than uva ursi, but is less astringent.

Chimaphila is seldom given in substance.

Dose of *Decoctum Chimaphilæ*, two to four ounces, three or four times a day; *Extractum*, from ten to twenty or thirty grains; *Syrupus* (Procter's), half an ounce to an ounce. The decoction is a frequent vehicle for other remedies.

1043. ℞ Decocti Chimaphilæ, ℥vij.
Spir. Juniperi, ℥j.
Mix: two spoonfuls to be taken four times a day.

In Dropsy.

1044. ℞ Decocti Chimaphilæ, f℥xvj.
Liq. Potassæ Carb. fʒij.
Mix: take four spoonfuls three times a day.
In Dropsy, Red Gravel, &c.—Dr. JOY.

1045. ℞ Decocti Chimaphilæ, f℥xj.
Potassæ Bicarbonatis, ℈j.
Tinct. Hyoscyami, f℥ss.
Mix: make a draught. To be taken twice a day.
In Mucous Urine, with Inactive Kidneys.—Dr. G. BIRD.

1046. ℞ Inf. Pyrolæ, ℥vj.
Tinct. Cubebæ, ℥j.
Tinct. Scillæ, ʒiij.
Spir. Ætheris Nitr. ʒiij.
Mix: take three spoonfuls three times a day.
In Dropsy of the Chest.—Dr. R. REECE.

1047. ℞ Dec. Chimaphilæ, f℥vij.
Potas. Nitratis, ʒss.
Spir. Ætheris Nitr. f℥ss.
Spir. Juniperi comp. fʒiij.
Make a mixture. Take a tablespoonful every third hour.
In old Cases of Dropsy.—Dr. NELIGAN.

CHIRAYTA, or CHIRETTA.

Chirayta (*Agathotes Chirayta*, Nat. Ord. *Gentianaceæ*) is a bitter tonic, resembling gentian in its properties and uses. By Dr. Sigmond, and others, it is stated to be preferable to other vegetable tonics, as it promotes the healthy action of the liver, and never constipates the bowels. It is given in dyspepsia, especially when attended with flatulence, sluggishness of the bowels, nervousness, and disordered secretions. But it is improper where there is much excitement, and a rapid pulse. A purgative should precede its use. In India it is given in intermittent and remittent fevers; and after a course of mercury.

The dose of Chirayta in substance is twenty grains; of *Infusum Chiraytæ*, half to one ounce; of *Tinctura Chiraytæ*, a drachm, two or three times a day.

1048. ℞ Infusi Chiraytæ, ℥viij.
Sodæ Carbon. ʒj.
Mix: take two or three spoonfuls three times a day.
In Dyspepsia, with Acidity of the Stomach.—Dr. R. REECE.

1049. ℞ Infusi Chirettæ, f℥j.
Liq. Ammoniæ, ♏x.
Tinct. Aurantii, ʒij.
Make a draught. To be taken morning and noon.
In Dyspepsia, with Acid Eructations.—Dr. NELIGAN.

1050. ℞ Tinct. Chiraytæ, ℥ss.
Inf. Cinchonæ spissati, ʒij.
Inf. Cascarillæ, ℥viss.
Syrupi Aurantii, ʒvj.
Make a mixture, of which take two tablespoonfuls three times a day.
In Convalescence from Acute Diseases.—Dr. NELIGAN.

1051. ℞ Extracti Chiraytæ, ʒij.
Sodæ Carbon. exsic. ℈j.
Zingiberis pulv. gr. xv.
Mix, and divide into 36 pills. Take two twice a day.
In Indigestion with Acidity, or from Intemperance.
Dr. R. REECE.

CHLORINIUM. CALX CHLORINATA. LIQ. SODÆ CHLORINATÆ. *Chlorine; and Chlorinated Lime, and Soda.*

Chlorine, and also Chloride of Lime, and Chlorinated Soda, which owe their properties to it, are antiseptic and deodorizing; their solutions are sometimes administered as a stimulant and antiputrescent in typhus fever, epidemic dysentery, malignant scarlatina, chronic diseases of the liver; and the latter in some chronic affections of the mucous membranes. *Externally*, largely diluted, these solutions are applied as lotions to foul and indolent ulcers, and in some cutaneous diseases; also, as gargles in putrid sore throat; as mouth-washes in fetid breath from decayed teeth or ulcerated mouth; and in local baths, in hepatitis, &c.

Dose of *Liquor Chlorinii*, thirty minims to two drachms, freely diluted; *Liquor Sodæ Chlorinatæ*, twenty to thirty minims; *Calx Chlorinata*, from half a grain to three or four grains. Most vegetable infusions convert Liq. Chlorinii into Muriatic Acid: it should therefore be given in water, or not mixed with other ingredients long before taking.

For disinfecting sick-rooms, and the clothes, &c. of the patient, and deodorizing discharges, Chloride of Lime is generally used, one part being mixed with thirty or forty of water. Or the same proportion of water to Liquor Sodæ Chlorinatæ. The latter is preferable as an internal remedy.

1052. ℞ Liq. Chlorinii, fʒss.
Aquæ puræ, f℥iss.
Syrupi Papaveris, fʒss.
Make a draught: to be taken every sixth hour.

Dr. COPLAND.

1053. ℞ Solut. Chlorinii (Midd. Hosp.) ʒij.
Aquæ puræ, Oj.
Mix: take from one to two spoonfuls frequently during the day, according to the age of the patient.

In Scarlatina.—Dr. WATSON.

1054. ℞ Liq. Sodæ Chlorinatæ, fʒvj.
Potassæ Bicarbon. ʒiij.
Sodæ Potassio-tartr. ʒvj.
Spir. Ammon. Arom. fʒiv.
Aquæ puræ, f℥x.
Make a mixture, of which take a sixth part twice a day.

H. J.

1055. ℞ Liq. Sodæ Chlorinatæ, fʒiss.
Infusi Serpentariæ, f℥vj.
Syrupi Aurantii, f℥iss.
Mix: make a mixture. Take two tablespoonfuls every four hours.

In the Advanced Stage of Typhoid Fevers.—Dr. NELIGAN.

1056. ℞ Liq. Sodæ Chlorinatæ, ʒss.
Aquæ puræ, ℥iv.
Mix: to be taken by spoonfuls during the day, in the intermission.

In Intermittent Fevers.—GOUZEE.

1057. ℞ Calcis Chlorinatæ, gr. iv.
Aquæ puræ, ʒx. Rub up together, strain, and add
Syrupi, ʒij. Make a draught.

In Putrid and Scarlet Fever.

1058. ℞ Calcis Chlorinatæ, ʒss.
Opii pulveris, gr. x.
Mix: make 10 pills. Take one three times a day.

In Gangrene of the Lungs.—Dr. DUNGLISON.

1059. ℞ Calcis Chlorinatæ, gr. viij ad xvj.
Pulv. Tracag. comp. ʒiss.
Syrupi, q. s. Make 24 pills. Take two twice a day.

Dr. COPLAND.

1060. ℞ Calcis Chlorinatæ, ℈j.
Opii pulveris, gr. iij.
Mucil. Acaciæ, q. s.

To make 18 pills. One every two or three hours, gradually increasing the dose until ten or twelve are taken daily.

In Gonorrhœa.—GRAEFE.

1061. ℞ Calcis Chloridi, gr. x.
Aquæ puræ, f℥iiiss.
Tinct. Calumbæ, fʒij.
Syrupi, f℥ss.

Mix: a tablespoonful to be given every hour.

In Typhus Fever.—Dr. REID.

1062. ℞ Decocti Avenæ, f℥xij.
Calcis Chlorinatæ, ℈ss.
Sodii Chloridi, ʒj. Make an enema.

Dr. REID.

1063. ℞ Calcis Chlorinatæ, ʒij.
Aquæ destillatæ, ℥xj. Dissolve, strain; then add
Mellis Rosæ, ℥j.

Make a liquor, with which wash the gums frequently, holding the liquor in the mouth.

In excessive Salivation.—Dr. NELIGAN.

1064. ℞ Infusi Cinchonæ, f℥iij.
Liq. Sodæ Chlorinatæ, f℥j. Make a mouth-wash.

In Cancrum Oris.—Dr. A. T. THOMSON.

1065. ℞ Liq. Chlorinii, ℥ss.
Aquæ, ℥iv.
Syrupi, ℥ss.
G. Tragacanthæ, ℈ss. Make a gargle.

RATIER.

1066. ℞ Sodæ Chloridi liq. ℥iss.
Decoct. Cinch. flav. ℥v.
Mellis Rosæ, ℥iss.
Spiritus Caryophylli (first triturated with some sugar), gtt. iv.

Make a gargle.

To correct Fetor of the Breath.—TROUSSEAU and REVEIL.

1067. ℞ Calcis Chlorinatæ, ℥j.
Aquæ, Oiis. Rub up together, strain, and add
Acidi Hydrocyanici, ʒj. Make a lotion.

For Itch.—DERHEIMS.

1068. ℞ Calcis Chlorinatæ, ʒj.
Boracis pulv. ʒj.
Adipis, ℥j. Make an ointment.

For Chilblains.—TRUSEN.

CHLOROFORMYL. *Chloroform.* See ÆTHEREA.

CHONDRUS CRISPUS. *Carrageen.*

Irish or Pearl Moss (*chondrus crispus*, or *Fucus Crispus*) is nutritive and demulcent; and is rather an article of diet than of medicine. It is given in catarrhal diseases, hæmoptysis, irritations of the bladder and kidneys, diarrhœa, dysentery, &c. It should be washed in water before boiling it; the decoction may be taken almost *ad libitum.*

1069. ℞ Chondri Crispi, ʒij.
Lactis recentis, Oj.
Boil to the consistency of a jelly, and add
Sacchari albi, ℥j.
Amygd. Amaræ, No. 2.
Mix: the whole to be taken in the day.

In Consumptive Diseases.—RADIUS.

1070. ℞ Chondri electi, ʒss.
Aquæ, q. s. Boil to f℥vj, strain, and add
Sodæ Phosphatis, ʒiss.
Syr. Opii (*vel* Papaveris), ʒij.
Mix: take a tablespoonful every second hour.

In Hæmoptysis.—CLARUS.

1071. ℞ Chondri electi, ʒiss.
Aquæ, ℥xij. Boil to f℥vss, strain, and add
Syrupi Rubi Idæi, ℥iss.
Aquæ Amygd. am. conc. ♏xx.
Mix: the whole to be taken in the course of a day.

VON GRAEFE.

CINCHONA.

Peruvian Bark is obtained from several species of Cinchona. The kinds principally used are the yellow, the pale, and the red. The first is the most powerful; the pale is used where a lighter tonic is required; the red is now seldom employed. All of them are tonic and antiperiodic; and are used in intermittent fevers (after due evacuations, and during the intermissions), and in diseases of debility unattended with local inflammation, especially of the stomach or bowels; in acute rheumatism, after depletions; in the advanced stage of malignant fevers and exanthemata; in scrofula; in amenorrhœa; and in painful neuralgic affections recurring at stated intervals.

The dose of *Pulvis Cinchonæ* is from five grains to two drachms, according to the purpose intended, and the ability of the patient's stomach to bear it. As a general tonic, it is usual to begin with a few grains, and increase the dose, as may be practicable or necessary, to fifteen, twenty, or thirty grains. In intermittents the medium dose is a drachm, more or less frequently during the intermission. In acute rheumatism, Dr. D. Davis has successfully given, after bleeding, &c., from twenty to thirty grains, three or four times a day.

The two principal alkaloids on which the virtues of Peruvian Bark depend, Quinia and Cinchonia, are used as substitutes for the bark itself. Quinia and its salts will be noticed elsewhere. See QUINIA. The following are the officinal preparations of Bark, with their doses:

Decoctum Cinchonæ, 1 to 3 ounces.
Extractum ———, 5 to 20 grains.
——— *Calisayicum*, 1 to 4 grains.
Infusum Cinchonæ, ——— cum *Calce, et Magnesiæ*, } 1 to 3 ounces.
Infusum Cinch. spissatum, 10 to 20 minims.
Syrupus Cinchonæ concent. ½ ounce.
——— *vinosus*, 1 ounce.
Tinctura Cinchonæ, 1 to 3 drachms.
——— *Am.* ½ dr. to 1 drachm.
——— *comp.* 1 to 3 drachms.
Vinum Cinchonæ, 1 ounce.
——— *et Valerianæ*, 1 oz. every 8 hours.
Cinchoninæ Disulphas, &c., 3 to 5 grains.
——— *Syrupus*, a spoonful.
——— *Tinctura*, a drachm.
——— *Vinum*, a wineglassful.

The following are for outward use: *Ceratum Cinchonæ; Cataplasma Antisepticum; Pulvis Cinchonæ cum Myrrhâ; Unguentum Cinchonæ.*

1072. ℞ Cinchonæ pulv. ʒvj–xij.
Pulv. Cinnamomi comp. ℈ij–iv.
Mix, and divide into 12 equal parts. Take one-fourth every hour, so regulated that four doses shall be taken before the accession of the paroxysm.

In Agues, during the Intermission.—DR. A. FRAMPTON.

1073. ℞ Cinchonæ pulv. ℈j.
Cascarillæ pulv. ℈ss. Make a powder.

In Weakness of the Stomach.—Dr. PEARSON.

1074. ℞ Cinchonæ pulv. ℥ss.
Magnesiæ Sulphat. ʒvj.

Triturate together into a powder, and divide into four equal parts, of which one part may be taken every other hour, between the paroxysms. [When the fit is mitigated, give the bark alone to complete the cure.]

In Intermittents, when purgatives can be borne.
Dr. CLEGHORN.

1075. ℞ Cinchonæ flavæ p. ℥j.
Antim. Potass.-tart. gr. ij.
Opii pulv. gr. j.

Mix, and divide into 4 powders. One to be given every second hour.

In the Malignant Intermittents of Italy.—BRERA.

1076. ℞ Cinchonæ fl. pulveris,
Potas. Bitartratis, ana ℥j.
Pulv. Caryophylli, ʒss.

Make a powder. Dose, a drachm and a half every three hours.
PETRIE.

1077. ℞ Cinchonæ pulv. ℥ss.
Serpentariæ, ʒj.
Sodæ Bicarb. ℈ij.

Mix, and make 4 powders. Give one every second or third hour between the paroxysms.

In Obstinate Intermittents.—ELLIS.

[Many other combinations of bark might be given, containing from ʒss to ʒj of bark, with 1-12 of camphor, 1·6 or 1-8 of ginger or of cinnamon, 1-2 of valerian, &c.]

1078. ℞ Cinchonæ pulv. ℥j.
Syrupi Aurantii, q. s.

Make an electuary: a teaspoonful to be taken every hour, drinking after it a spoonful of wine.

In Intermittents.—TODE.

1079. ℞ Cinchonæ pulveris,
Anthemidis pulv. ana ℥j.
Zingiberis pulv. ℈ij.

Mix: make into an electuary, with syrup. Give ʒj three times a day.

In Convalescence from Acute Diseases.—Sir G. BLANE.

1080. ℞ Cinchonæ flavæ p. ʒvj.
Ammoniæ Mur. ʒij.
Cinnamomi pulv. ʒj.
Syr. cort. Aurantii, ℥iij.

Make an electuary: a large teaspoonful four times a day.

In Intermittents and Nervous Diseases.—VOGT.

1081. ℞ Cinchonæ flavæ p. ℥j.
Ferri Carbon. ʒss.
Syr. Zingiberis, q. s.
Make an electuary. Dose, a drachm twice or three times a day.

Dr. BARCLAY.

1082. ℞ Pulv. Cinchonæ flav. ℥iss.
Pulv. Valerianæ,
P. bacc. Junip. āā ʒij.
Mellis, q. s.
Mix, and make an electuary. (Dose, ʒss twice daily for adults; gr. viii for children.)

In Debility or Indigestion.—TROUSSEAU and REVEIL.

1083. ℞ Decocti Cinchonæ, fʒx.
Acidi Sulphurici dil. ♏v.
Syr. Aurantii,
Tinct. Cardam. comp. ana fʒj.
Make a draught: to be repeated at intervals of four or six hours.

Tonic.—Mr. BRANDE.

1084. ℞ Decocti Cinchonæ, fʒx.
Conf. Aromaticæ, ℈j.
Tinct. Cinchonæ comp. fʒj.
Make a draught: to be taken every fourth hour.

Tonic and Cordial.—Dr. HEBERDEN.

1085. ℞ Infusi Cinchonæ,
Infusi Rosæ, ana ℥iv.
Make a mixture; take three tablespoonfuls three times a day.

In Convalescence.—Dr. JOY.

1086. ℞ Decocti Cinch. pal. fervent. ℥viij.
Serpentariæ rad. cont. ʒij.
Let it stand for an hour, and to the strained liquor admix
Spirit. Cinnamomi, f℥j.
Acidi Sulphur. dil. fʒiss.
Make a mixture: take two spoonfuls every sixth hour.

Dr. PRINGLE.

1087. ℞ Infusi Cinchonæ, ℥vij.
Acidi Muriatici dil. ʒj.
Tinct. Capsici, ʒss.
Tinct. Serpentariæ, ʒiij.
Syr. Papaveris, ʒiiss.
Make a mixture: take two or three tablespoonfuls every four hours.

Dr. COPLAND.

1088. ℞ Extr. Cinchonæ, gr. v. Dissolve in
Decocti Cinchonæ, f℥iss, and add
Syrupi Aurantii,
Tinct. Cinchonæ comp. ana fʒss.
Mix: make a draught. To be taken two or three times a day.

Mr. BRANDE.

1089. ℞ Decocti Cinchonæ, ℥vij.
Liquor. Ammon. acet. ℨij.
Sp. Ætheris Nitr. ℨj.
Make a draught: to be repeated every four hours.
In Erysipelas of the Aged and Debilitated.—Dr. G. GREGORY.

1090. ℞ Decocti Cinchonæ, f℥xij.
Tinct. Cinchonæ, fℨj.
Acidi Nitrici dil. ♏ix.
Syrupi Aurantii, ℨj. Make a draught.
In Typhus Fever, &c.—Dr. A. T. THOMSON.

1091. ℞ Decocti Cinchonæ, ℥iiss.
Inf. Gentianæ comp. ℥j.
Tinct. Cascarillæ, ℨij.
Liq. Potassæ Carb. ℨij.
Make a mixture, of which two tablespoonfuls may be taken twice a day.
Dr. PEARSON.

1092. ℞ Decocti Cinchonæ, f℥viiss.
Ammon. Sesquicarb. ℨss.
Syr. Zingiberis, f℥ss.
Mix. Dose, a sixth part, two or three times a day.
Dr. DRUITT.

1093. ℞ Decocti Cinchonæ, ℥ij.
Tinct. Guaiaci Ammon.
Syrupi Croci, ana ℨj.
Make a draught: to be taken every sixth or eighth hour.
In Chronic Rheumatism.—Dr. HUGH SMITH.

1094. ℞ Cinchonæ pulveris,
Rhei pulveris, ana ℨss.
Magnesiæ Carbon. ℈j.
Confect. Aromat. ℈ss.
Aquæ Cinnam. ℥iss.
Make a draught: to be taken twice a day.
In Diabetes.—Dr. COPLAND.

1095. ℞ Cinchonæ rubræ (*vel* flavæ), ℥ss.
Confect. Opii, ℨj.
Succi Limonis, fℨij.
Vini Oporto, f℥iv.
Mix: a third part to be taken every third hour.
In Intermittents.—Dr. WOOD.

1096. ℞ Decocti Cinchonæ, ℨxj.
Extr. Sarsæ, ℨj.
Potassæ Iodidi, gr. iij.
Liq. Potassæ, ♏xv.
Make a draught: to be taken three times a day.
In Rheumatic Gout, in cachectic subjects.—Dr. H. W. FULLER.

1097. ℞ Decocti Cinchonæ,
Infusi Rosæ comp. ana ℥iiiss.
Mellis Rosæ, f℥j.
Tincturæ Myrrhæ, ʒij.
Acidi Hydrochlorici, ♏x. Make a gargle.

Mr. BRANDE.

1098. ℞ Extracti Cinchonæ, ʒij.
Aquæ puræ, ℥iv.
Olei Olivæ, ℥ss.
Tinct. Opii, gutt. xij. Make an enema.

In Agues (when the stomach will not bear bark alone).

Dr. LIND.

1099. ℞ Pulv. Cinchonæ, ʒiij–vj.
Decocti Avenæ, Oss. Make an enema.

Dr. R. REECE.

1100. ℞ Medullæ Ossium, ʒvj.
Ol. Amygdalæ dulc. ʒij.
Pulv. Cinchonæ rubræ, ʒj. Make an ointment.

In Porrigo Decalvans.—BIETT.

CINNAMOMUM.

Cinnamon, the bark of *Cinnamomum Zeylanicum* (Nat. Ord. *Lauraceæ*), is a grateful aromatic stimulant. Besides being cordial and carminative, it possesses a degree of astringency. It is prescribed in atonic dyspepsia, flatulence, diarrhœa, and vomiting; but more frequently as an adjunct to bitters, purgatives, and to vegetable and metallic astringents, than alone.

The dose of Cinnamon is from five to twenty grains; of *Aqua Cinnamomi*, half an ounce to one a half; *Confectio Aromatica*, ten to forty grains; *Pulvis Cinnamomi compositus* (*P. Aromaticus*, E. and D.), five to twenty grains; *Tinctura Cinnamomi*, and *Tinct. Cin. composita*, one or two drachms.

[*Cassia*, the bark of Cinnamomum Cassia, is used for the same purposes, in the same forms, and in similar doses.]

1101. ℞ Aquæ Cinnamomi, ℥ij.
Aquæ flor. Aurantii, ℥j.
Sacchari albi, ℈ij. Mix: a teaspoonful every hour.

In the Vomiting of Infants, without Inflammation.—WENDT.

1102. ℞ Pulv. Cinnamomi comp. ʒj.
Aquæ Menthæ viridis, ℥viiss.
Sp. Lavand. comp. ʒiij.
Sacchari purif. ʒij.
Mix: take f℥iss three or four times a day.

Dr. CURRIE.

1103. ℞ Tinct. Cinnamomi, ℥iss.
Aquæ Cinnamomi, ℥viij.
Ætheris Acetici, ʒiss.
Syr. Papaveris, ℥ss.
A spoonful every quarter or half hour.

In Hæmorrhage and Fainting, in Parturition.—SCHNEIDER.

1104. ℞ Confect. Aromaticæ, ℈j.
Mist. Camphoræ, ℥ss.
Aquæ Cinnamomi, ℥j. Make a draught.

Dr. PEARSON.

1105. ℞ Mist. Cretæ, ℥v.
Conf. Aromaticæ, ʒj.
Liq. Ammoniæ carb. ʒj.
Tinct. Opii, ♏xx.
Make a mixture, of which take two spoonfuls, as occasion may require.

In Simple Diarrhœa.—Dr. AINSLIE.

1106. ℞ Confect. Aromaticæ, gr. xv.
Liq. Calcis, ʒxj.
Magnesiæ Carbon. gr. vj.
Tinct. Lupuli, ʒj.
Mix: make a draught. To be repeated three times a day.

In Chronic Dysentery.—Dr. G. GREGORY.

1107. ℞ Spir. Vini Gallici,
Aquæ Cinnamomi, sing. ℥iv.
Vitel. Ovorum, No. ij.
Olei Cinnamomi, ♏v.
Mix: dose, f℥ss frequently repeated.

Mr. BRANDE.

[This only differs from Mistura Spiritus Vini (L.) in containing more oil of cinnamon.]

CITRUS.

For *Citrus Aurantium* and *C. Bigaradia*, *see* AURANTIUM.

Citrus Bergamia. The essential oil of the rind of the fruit is used, under the name of Essence of Bergamot, on account of its pleasant odor, in ointments, liniments, &c.

Citrus Limonum yields Lemons. *Lemon Juice* is treated of under ACIDUM CITRICUM. *Lemon Peel* is aromatic, stimulant, and stomachic. It yields an essential oil which is carminative and stimulant, but seldom used except for its pleasant odor. *Tinctura Limonis* is used to flavor mixtures, syrups, &c. Lemon

14

peel is an ingredient in Infusum Aurantii comp., and Inf. Gentianæ comp.

1108. ℞ Cort. recent. Limonum, No. j ad ij.
Aquæ frigidæ, Oij. Macerate for six hours, and strain.
As a diluting drink for Invalids.—Mr. BRANDE.

1109. ℞ Sem. Limonum, ʒij.
Aquæ, ℔ij. Make an emulsion, and add
Sacchari albi, ʒij.
Mix: half a cupful every two hours.
In Hysteria.—VON HILDEBRAND.

COCCULUS INDICUS.

The fruit of *Anamirta Cocculus*, E. [*Cocculus Suberosus*, D.]. It is poisonous, producing tetanic convulsions, and coma. It is only used medicinally as an external application, in the form of *Unguentum Cocculi*, in some diseases of the scalp, and to destroy vermin. It contains *Picrotoxia*, which is also used in the form of ointments in the same cases.

COCCUS. *Cochineal.*

Cochineal is an hemipterous insect which feeds on a species of Cactus (*Opuntia Cochinillifera*): it is chiefly used as a coloring ingredient; but has been supposed to possess anodyne and antispasmodic properties. It has been principally given in hooping-cough, in doses of a few grains; *Tinctura Cocci*, thirty drops to two drachms.

1110. ℞ Cocci pulv. ℈j.
Potas. Carbonatis, ʒj.
Aquæ ferventis, ℥viij.
Triturate together, and strain. A teaspoonful three times a day, for children.
In Hooping-cough.—Dr. ALLNATT.

1111. ℞ Cocci pulveris, ℈ss.
Potassæ Carbon. ℈j.
Aquæ, f℥iv. Triturate together, and add
Sacchari albi, q. p.
Dose, a teaspoonful to a tablespoonful, according to the age.
In Coughs.—Dr. LOBB. (1765.)

1112. ℞ Cocci pulv. ℈ss.
Sodæ Bicarb. ℈ss.
P. Belladonnæ rad. gr. iiss.
Sacchari purif. ℥j.

Mix, and divide into fifteen powders. Take one every day. [Gr. 1-6th of belladonna in each.]

In Hooping-cough.—M. VIRICEL.

COCHLEARIA.

For *Cochlearia Armoracia*, Horse-radish, see ARMORACIA.

Cochlearia officinalis, Scurvy Grass, is regarded as antiscorbutic and diuretic, but is not often prescribed. *Spiritus Cochleariæ* is sometimes used in washes for the mouth and gums.

Dose of *Succus Cochleariæ*, half an ounce to two ounces; *Spiritus Cochleariæ*, half a drachm to one drachm; *Syrupus*, half an ounce to one ounce.

1113. ℞ Aquæ Sambuci fl. ℥vj.
Spir. Cochleariæ, ℥ss.
Succi Limon. recent.
Syr. Rhœados, ana ℥ij.

Mix: two spoonfuls every three hours.

In Scorbutic Complaints.—VOGEL.

1114. ℞ Spirit. Cochleariæ, ℥iiss.
Succi Limonum,
Mucil. Cydonii,
Syrupi Mori, ana ℥ss. Make a mouth-wash.

In Scurvy of the Gums, &c.

CODEIA.

One of the alkaloids obtained from opium. It is weaker than morphia, but its dose and effects are not satisfactorily determined. *Syrupus Codeiæ* is used in hooping-cough; dose, a drachm.

COFFEA. CAFFEINA. *Coffee and Caffeine.*

Coffee (the seeds of *Coffea Arabica*, Nat. Ord. *Rubiaceæ*), in its raw state, possesses febrifuge properties. It contains a peculiar principle, *Caffeine* or *Theine*, identical with that contained in tea, and which has also been prescribed medicinally, more particularly for the relief of hemicrania.

The dose of *unroasted coffee* is a scruple of the powdered

berries every hour during the intermission of intermittent fevers. It is also given in the form of strong decoction; which is sometimes combined with lemon juice. [See No. 29, page 30.]

The dose of *Caffeine* is a grain, repeated every hour or two.

Roasted Coffee is exhilarant and antisoporific; and is used to counteract the effects of opium, alcohol, and other narcotic poisons. It is best prepared by percolation, with from one to two ounces of ground coffee to a pint of boiling water. It has also been found useful in hooping-cough and asthma; also to conceal the bitter taste of quinine; and, in some measure, that of sulphate of magnesia.

Dose of *Infusum Coffeæ tostæ*, a cupful; *Syrupus Coffeæ*, an ounce; *Syrupus Caffeinæ Citratis*, half a drachm to a drachm; *Trochisci Caffeinæ*, one frequently.

1115. ℞ Coffeæ (non tostæ), ℥j.
Aquæ, f℥xviij.

Boil to six ounces, and strain. The whole to be given in three doses during the intermission.

In Agues.—Dr. GRINDEL.

1116. ℞ Coffeæ tostæ, ℨvj.
Aquæ ferventis, Oss.

Make an infusion. The whole to be taken during the day.

In Albuminuria.—M. HONORE.

1117. ℞ Caffeinæ, gr. vij.
Aquæ destillatæ, ℥iij.
Acidi Hydrochlorici, gutt. ij.
Syr. flor. Aurantii, ℥ss.

Mix: a tablespoonful every hour or two, as required.

In Hemicrania, &c.

1118. ℞ Syrupi Caffeinæ Citratis, ℥j.
Infusi Theæ Viridis, ℥v.

Mix: a tablespoonful every two hours before, and every hour during the attack.

In Hemicrania or Periodic Headache.—M. HANNON.

COLCHICUM.

The seeds and bulb (cormus) of *Colchicum autumnale* (Nat. Ord. *Melanthaceæ*) are irritant, diuretic, and purgative. Colchicum frequently exercises an almost specific power in relieving the paroxysm of gout; it is also given in acute and chronic rheumatism; and by Mr. Haden and others its use has been extended to inflammatory affections generally. Its effects seem to be uncertain, and its use requires caution. Eigenmann recommends Vinum Colchici in gonorrhœa, with Tinct. Opii, low diet, and warm baths.

Dose of the powdered *cormus*, two to eight grains; of the *seeds*, two to five grains. The following are the principal preparations, with their usual doses:

Acetum Colchici, L. and E., 30 to 90 minims.
Oxymel Colchici, 1 to 2 drachms.
Extractum Colchici, ½ a grain to 2 grains.
Extractum Colchici Aceticum, the same.
Succus Colchici, from 5 minims to 10.
Pulvis Colchici compositus (HADEN), from 8 to 30 grains.
Syrupus Colchici, E. 1817, 1 to 2 drachms.
Tinctura Colchici, ½ to 1 drachm.
——————— *comp.*, 20 to 30 minims.
Vinum Colchici, 15 minims to one drachm.
——————— *sem.*, U. S., 30 to 90 minims.

In some cases as much as two drachms of the tincture or wine has been given.

1119. ℞ Pulv. Colchici, gr. iij.
Potassæ Sulphatis, gr. iv.
Potassæ Bicarbon. gr. iij.

Triturate together, and make a powder.

In Rheumatism, Gout, and Inflammatory Affections.

MR. HADEN.

1120. ℞ Pulv. Colchici, gr. i–ij.
Pil. Hydrargyri, gr. ij.
Pil. Galbani comp. gr. v.
Extracti Opii, gr. ss.

Make two pills. To be taken two or three times a day.

In Chronic Bronchitis.—DR. COPLAND.

1121. ℞ Aceti Colchici, ℥ss.
Magnes. Calc. ℈iv.
Syrupi Croci, ℥ss.
Aquæ Menthæ Vir. ℥v.

Make a mixture. A sixth portion every six hours.

In Gout, &c.—DR. JOY.

1122. ℞ Aceti Colchici, f℥ss.
Potassæ Acetatis, ℥ss.
Aquæ Fœniculi, f℥vij.
Spir. Juniperi comp. f℥ss.

Mix: two tablespoonfuls three times a day.

DR. HOOPER.

1123. ℞ Aceti Colchici, f℈j–ij.
Magnesiæ, gr. xv–xx.
Magnesiæ Sulphatis, ℈j–ij.
Aquæ Cinnamomi, f℈ix.
Syrupi, f℈j. Make a draught.

In the Paroxysm of Gout.—Sir CHAS. SCUDAMORE.

1124. ℞ Oxymel. Colchici, f℥j.
Tinct. Camphoræ comp. f℥j.
Sp. Ætheris comp. f℈iij.
Mist. Camphoræ, f℥vj.
Make a mixture. Two spoonfuls as occasion may require.

In Spasmodic Asthma, and Chronic Dyspnœa.—Dr. R. REECE.

1125. ℞ Extracti Colchici Acet. ℈j.
Pulv. rad. Althææ, q. s. Make forty pills. One for a dose.

Sir C. SCUDAMORE.

1126. ℞ Extr. Colchici Acet. gr. ij.
Pulv. Ipecac. comp. gr. v.
Make two pills. To be taken going to bed.

ST. GEO. HOSP.

1127. ℞ Extracti Colchici, gr. j.
Extracti Coloc. comp.
Pil Hydrargyri, ana gr. ij.
Make a pill. To be taken twice a day.

In Acute Rheumatism.—Dr. G. GREGORY.

1128. ℞ P. Colchici sem. ℈ss.
Calomelanos, gr. viij.
P. Digitalis,
P. Quin. Disul. ana gr. xv.
Ext. Colocynth. gr. viij.
Conf. Rosæ, q. s.
Mix: form a mass, and divide into twenty pills. (1-4 during the day, at the commencement of the attack.)

In Gout.—TROUSSEAU and REVEIL.

1129. ℞ Extr. Colchici Acet. gr. xij.
Pil. Hydrargyri, gr. xxx.
Extr. Hyoscyami, gr. xviij.
Mix: make twelve pills. Two every third night.

As a Cathartic in Gouty habits (followed by the draught No. 1130 next morning). Dr. NELIGAN.

1130. ℞ Succi Colchici, ♏x.
Magnesiæ Carb. gr. xij.
Spir. Cinnamomi, f℈ss.
Aquæ Cinnamomi, f℥iss.
Make a draught. To be taken in the morning. (To be preceded by the above pills.)

Dr. NELIGAN.

1131. ℞ Tincturæ Colchici sem.
Tincturæ Gentianæ, ana ʒiij.
Mix: from thirty to forty drops to be taken three times a day.
In Chronic Rheumatism.—BLASIUS.

1132. ℞ Vini Colchici, ♏xx.
Inf. Rhei, fʒx.
Potassæ Bicarb. ℈j.
Tinct. Cardam. comp. fʒj.
Make a draught. To be taken at bedtime.
Dr. DRUITT.

1133. ℞ Vini Colchici, ♏xxx.
Magnesiæ Carb. gr. xv.
Aquæ Cinnamomi,
Aquæ puræ, ana f℥ss.
Make a draught. To be taken in the evening.
In the Paroxysm of Gout.—Mr. BRANDE.

1134. ℞ Vini Colchici cormi, ♏xx.
Potassæ Sulphatis, ʒiss.
Sodæ Bidarb. ℈ij.
Aquæ Anethi, f℥iss.
Tinct. Calumbæ, fʒiss.
Make a draught with fifteen grains of tartaric acid dissolved in half an ounce of water, and take during effervescence.
Dr. COPLAND.

1135. ℞ Magnes. Sulphatis, ʒiij.
Magnes. Carbon. ℈ij.
Vini Colchici, fʒiss.
Syr. Rhœados, f℥ss.
Aquæ Menthæ pip. f℥iv.
Aquæ destillatæ, f℥iss.
Mix: take two tablespoonfuls twice a day.
In Hæmorrhoids.—Dr. G. GREGORY.

1136. ℞ Vini Colchici, f℥ss.
Spir. Ætheris Nit. fʒiij
Potassæ Acetatis, ʒij.
Aquæ, f℥iij.
Mix: a teaspoonful to be given every four hours. To promote the elimination of urea.
In the Delirium of Scarlatina, with deficient Urine.
Prof. BENNETT.

1137. ℞ Vini Colchici, f℥ss.
Magnesiæ Sulphatis, ʒiv.
Aquæ Menthæ, f℥vj.
Mix: take f℥iss three times a day. (A pill of opium and antimony at night.)
In Acute Rheumatism.—Dr. HUGHES.

1138. ℞ Vini Colchici, f℥ij.
Solut. Magnes. Bicarb. (Murray's or Dinneford's), f℥iss.
Syrupi Croci, f℥ij.
Misturæ Camphoræ, f℥ivss.
Mix: take two spoonfuls every fourth hour.

Dr. DRUITT.

1139. ℞ Vini Colchici, f℥ss.
Tinct. Rhei et Aloes, f℥j.
Spir. Myristicæ, f℥ss.
Infusi Rhei, f℥vj.
Make a mixture. Two tablespoonfuls every three or four hours until it operates.

As a Cathartic, in Gouty and Rheumatic habits.

Dr. NELIGAN.

1140. ℞ Vini Colchici, ♏xxx.
Magnesiæ Sulph. ℥iss.
Magnes. Carbon. ℈j.
Aquæ Menthæ pip. f℥x. Make a draught.

In Erysipelas.—Dr. BASHAM.

1141. ℞ Aquæ Menthæ pip. f℥vij.
Liq. Ammoniæ acet. f℥ij.
Vini Colchici, ♏xv.
Syrupi Mori, f℥j.
Mix: make a draught. To be taken three times a day.

In Chronic Rheumatism, with Œdema, &c.—Dr. G. GREGORY.

1142. ℞ Vini sem. Colchici, f℥ss.
Potas. Iodidi, ℥ij.
Liq. Potassæ, ℥ij.
Tinct. Zingiberis, f℥iss.
Mix: take a teaspoonful twice a day in tepid water. (The pills No. 1143 to be taken occasionally.)

1143. ℞ Extr. Coloc. comp. ℈iss.
Extr. Acet. Colchici, gr. x.
Extr. Hyoscyami,
Saponis Hispan. ana ℈j.
Make 20 pills. Take one, two, or three, according to circumstances, at bedtime.

Mr. HODGSON.

1144. ℞ Tinct. Colchici,
Tinct. Camphoræ, ana ℥ss. Make a liniment.

In Rheumatism.—Dr. LAYCOCK.

1145. ℞ Linim. Saponis, f℥j.
Vini Colchici sem. f℥ss. Make an embrocation.

Mr. HARVEY.

COLOCYNTHIS. *Bitter Apple.*

Colocynth (the decorticated fruit of *Citrullus* [*Cucumis*] *Colocynthis*, Nat. Ord. *Cucurbitaceæ*) is a drastic purgative, in excessive doses producing violent irritation; but in moderate doses, in combination with other purgatives, it usually operates effectually, without inconvenience or danger. The dose of the powdered pulp is from two to eight grains, mixed with gum or starch; but it is not often given in this form; *Pilula* (formerly *Extractum*) *Colocynthidis composita*, four to twelve or fifteen grains; *Pilulæ Colocynthidis et Hyoscyami*, E., one to three pills; *Pilulæ Catharticæ compositæ*, U.S., one to three pills; *Pil. Colocynthidis comp.* D., ten to fifteen grains. [We have retained the old name (Extractum Col. comp.) of the London preparation in many of the following prescriptions, as it is still best known by that term, and is distinguished thereby from the Pil. Col. comp. D.] *Extractum Colocynthidis*, two to five grains.

Colocynth is administered in habitual constipation, alvine obstruction, as a revulsive in affections of the brain, and in the various cases in which an effective purgative is required. Small doses have been regarded as diuretic and alterative; but it is not much used with this intention.

1146. ℞ Extracti Colocynthidis comp. ʒj.
Saponis duri, gr. x.
Olei Menthæ pip. gutt. j.
Make 12 pills. Take two or three, according to circumstances.
In Costiveness.—Dr. BABINGTON.

1147. ℞ Extracti Coloc. comp.
Extracti Gentianæ, ana ʒss. Make 12 pills.
Dr. HOOPER.

1148. ℞ Pil. Coloc. comp. ʒss.
Pil. Aloes cum Myrrhâ, ℈ij.
Mix, and divide into 16 pills. Take two, as occasion may require.
In Habitual Constipation.—Dr. JOY.

1149. ℞ Extr. Colocynth. comp.
Pil. Galbani comp. ana ʒss.
Mix, and divide into 12 pills. Take two twice a day.
In Dysmenorrhœa, &c.—Dr. ASHWELL.

1150. ℞ Extr. Coloc. comp.
Extr. Aloes Socotræ, ana ℨiss.
Saponis Hispan. ℨss.
Olei Caryophyll. gutt. xv.
Make 38 pills. Take three at bedtime, as may be requisite.

Dr. BAILLIE.

1151. ℞ Extr. Coloc. comp. ℈ij.
Ipecacuanhæ pulv. gr. vj.
Saponis duri, ℈ss.
Extr. Hyoscyami, ℨss.
Make 18 pills. Take two every day at bedtime.

Dr. COPLAND.

1152. ℞ Extr. Colocynth. comp. ℨj.
Scammonii p. gr. xxiv.
Sodæ Carb. exsic. gr. xij.
Olei Menthæ pip. gutt. iv.
Mix, and divide into 24 pills. Take one, two, or three, according to circumstances, at bedtime.

As an occasional Aperient.—H. J.

1153. ℞ Extr. Coloc. comp. ℈iv.
Scammonii pulv. ℈j.
Extr. Rhei, gr. xij.
Olei Cinnamomi, gutt. iv.
Saponis duri, gr. vj.
Mix: make 24 pills. Two pills at bedtime, twice a week, or as may be required.

Mr. VANCE.

1154. ℞ Pil. Coloc. comp. ℈ij.
Extr. Hyoscyami, ℈j.
Mix, and divide into 12 pills. Take one or two, as occasion requires.

Dr. HAMILTON.

1155. ℞ Extr. Coloc. comp.
Conf. Scammonii, gr. iiss.
Sodæ Carb. exsic. gr. ij.
Make 2 pills. To be taken every night.

H. J.

1156. ℞ Extr. Colocynth. comp. ℈j.
Extr. Opii, gr. j.
Ol. Cinnamomi, gutt. j.
Make 4 pills. To be swallowed immediately.

In Bilious Colic.—Dr. E. G. CLARK.

1157. ℞ Extr. Coloc. comp. ℨss.
Extr. Opii, gr. j.
Mix, and divide into 6 pills. Take one every alternate hour until they operate.

In Ileus.—Dr. JOY.

1158. ℞ Extr. Coloc. comp. ʒj.
Extr. Jalapæ, ʒss.
Sapon. duri, ʒj.
Olei Carui, ♏viij. Make a mass, and divide into 40 pills.

In Costiveness, in Bilious Habits.—Dr. FRAMPTON.

1159. ℞ Extr. Coloc. comp. ʒj.
Pil. Rhei comp. ʒss.
Sodæ Carb. exsic. gr. xij.

Make a mass, and divide into 24 pills. Take one, two, or three, according to circumstances, at bedtime.

As an occasional Purgative.—H. J.

1160. ℞ Extr. Colocynth. comp. ʒj.
Sulphur. sublimati, ℈ij.
Potassæ Sulphat. ℈iv.
Syrupi, q. s., to make 50 pills.

Dr. A. T. THOMSON.

1161. ℞ Extr. Coloc. comp. ℈j.
Pil. Rhei comp. ʒss.
Ipecacuanhæ p. gr. vj.

Make 12 pills. Take one or more, according to circumstances, at bedtime.

Dr. BARON.

1162. ℞ Extr. Coloc. comp. ℈ij.
Scammonii pulv. gr. xij.
Saponis duri, gr. vj.

Make a mass, and divide into 12 pills. One or more at appropriate intervals, according to circumstances, to excite proper action of the bowels.

Dr. PARIS.

1163. ℞ Extr. Coloc. comp. ʒj.
Pulv. Rhei,
Pilulæ Hydrargyri, ana ʒss.
Olei Carui, ♏xij.

Divide into 24 pills. Two or three for a dose.

Mr. BRANDE.

1164. ℞ Extr. Coloc. comp. ℈iiss.
Pil. Rhei comp.
Pil. Hydrargyri, ana gr. xxiv.
Sodæ Carb. exsic. gr. xij.

Mix, and divide into 24 pills. Take one, two, or three, according to circumstances, at bedtime.

H. J.

1165. ℞ Extr. Coloc. comp. gr. xvj.
Pil. Hydrargyri, gr. vj.
Extr. Hyoscyami, gr. viij.
Pulv. Capsici, gr. ij.

Mix, and divide into 6 pills. Take one or two, according to circumstances, at bedtime.

Dr. JOY.

1166. ℞ Extr. Coloc. comp. ℈j.
Extr. Jalapæ, gr. vj.
Pil. Hydrargyri, gr. viij.
Olei Cassiæ, gutt. iij.
Mix: make 10 pills. Take one, two, or three, according to circumstances, at bedtime.

In Indigestion, with Costiveness and deficient Bile.
Dr. JAS. JOHNSON.

1167. ℞ Extr. Coloc. comp. ℈ij.
Hydrarg. Chloridi, gr. xxiv.
Olei Cinnamomi, gutt. vj.
Make a mass, and divide into 24 pills. Take two, at bedtime, twice a week.

Mr. VANCE.

1168. ℞ Hydrarg. Chloridi, gr. xij.
Extr. Colocynth. comp. ʒss.
Olei Caryophilli, ♏viij.
Make 8 pills. Take two or three for a dose.

As an Active Cathartic.—Mr. BRANDE.

1169. ℞ Extr. Colocynth. comp.
Pil. Rhei compos. ana ʒss.
Calomelanos, gr. xij.
Olei Carui, ♏v.
Mix: make a mass, and divide into 24 pills. Take from one to three at bedtime.

In habitual Constipation, and at the commencement of Fevers.
Dr. JOY.

1170. ℞ Pil. Colocynth. comp.
Pil. Rhei comp. ana ℈ss.
Hydrarg. Chloridi, gr. iij.
Ol. Lavandulæ, ♏iv.
Make 5 pills. To be taken early in the morning.

A Stomachic Purgative.—Dr. A. T. THOMSON.

1171. ℞ Infusi Colocynthidis (ex ʒss pulpæ), ℥iv.
Spir. Ætheris comp. ʒss.
Syrupi Aurantii, ℥ss.
Mix: a tablespoonful every two hours.

In Atonic Dropsy.—WENDT.

1172. ℞ Tinct. Colocynthidis,
Tinct. Nucis Vomicæ, ana ʒij.
Tinct. Pyrethri, ℥ss.
Mix: forty drops three times a day in infusion of arnica.

In Paralysis of the Lower Limbs.—VOGT.

1173. ℞ Tinct. Colocynthidis (Prus. ph), ♏xx.
Inf. Sennæ cum Tamarindis, f℥ij.
Tinct. Cardam. comp. fʒss.
Make a draught. To be taken twice a day.

In Dropsical Cases.—Dr. NELIGAN.

1174. ℞ Pulv. Colocynth. ʒss.
Sodii Chlor. ʒj.
Mellis, q. s. Mix, and make a suppository.

TROUSSEAU and REVEIL.

CONIUM. *Hemlock.*

Hemlock (Conium Maculatum, Nat. Ord. *Umbelliferæ*) is a powerful narcotic poison. In medicinal doses it is given as an anodyne, sedative, antispasmodic, and deöbstruent; in scirrhous and cancerous diseases (as a palliative); in scrofulous and other unhealthy ulceration; in goitre; in pulmonary irritation, and hooping-cough; in neuralgia; chronic rheumatism; skin diseases; enlarged viscera, &c.

Dose of *Fol. Conii exsic.*, from two or three grains, gradually increased till slight nausea or giddiness is produced; *Fructus Conii*, from one-third of a grain gradually increased to three grains in the day; *Extractum Conii*, from two or three grains, carefully increased as above; *Pilula Conii composita*, three to five grains twice or thrice a day; *Tinctura Conii*, from twenty to forty minims; *Succus Conii* (five parts juice to one spirit), from fifteen to sixty minims. *Unguentum Conii* and *Emplastrum Conii* are anodyne and resolvent. *Conia* is the active principle.

1175. ℞ Fol. Conii exsic. ʒj.
Conf. Rosæ, q. s.
Make a mass, and divide equally into 20 pills. Dose, one, two, or more, twice a day.

In Consumption, Chronic Rheumatism, Lepra, &c.

DR. WITHERING.

1176. ℞ Extracti Conii, ʒj.
Pulv. fol. Conii, q. s.
Make pills, each weighing two grains. At first the patient may take one for a dose, morning and night; after awhile, he can take two, then three, or four; and finally, the dose can be increased gradually as much as possible.

In Scirrhous, Cancerous, and Scrofulous Affections.

STOERCK.

1177. ℞ Extracti Conii,
Pulv. Ipecacuanhæ comp. ana ʒj.
Mix, and divide into 30 pills. Take two, going to bed.

To quiet Cough and Bronchial Irritation.—MR. BRANDE.

1178. ℞ Extracti Conii, gr. xxxij.
Ipecacuanhæ pulv. gr. iv.
Morphiæ Muriatis, gr. j.
Make 8 pills. Take one, going to bed.
In Consumptive Cough.—Dr. JNO. HUTCHINSON.

1179. ℞ Extracti Conii, ʒss.
Scillæ pulv. ℈ss.
Ipecac. pulv. gr. v.
Mix: make 10 pills. Take one twice or three times a day.
In Chronic Bronchitis.—Dr. G. GREGORY.

1180. ℞ Extracti Conii (in vacuo præp.) ʒj.
Hydrargyri Chloridi, gr. viij.
Antim. Potassio-Tartr. gr. iss.
Camphoræ pulv. ʒss. Make 24 pills.
In Spasmodic Dysuria.—Mr. ALLARD.

1181. ℞ Extracti Conii, ʒj.
Hydrarg. Chloridi, gr. vj.
Mix: make 12 pills. Dose, one to two, twice or three times a day.
Mr. PEARSON.

1182. ℞ Extracti Conii,
Extracti Hyoscyami, ana gr. v.
Misturæ Acaciæ, fʒij.
Rub up together, until they are thoroughly mixed, and then add
Liq. Ammoniæ Acetatis,
Aquæ puræ, ana f℥ss.
Syrupi Rhœados, fʒj.
Make a draught, to be taken every fourth hour.
In Pulmonary Irritation.—Dr. PARIS.

1183. ℞ Extracti Conii, gr. v.
Mist. Amygdalæ, fʒxiv.
Syrupi Papaveris, fʒij.
Mix: take a dessertspoonful twice or thrice a day.
To quiet common or Spasmodic Cough.—Mr. BRANDE.

1184. ℞ Extracti Conii, gr. iij.
Magnes. Sulphat. ℈ss.
Aquæ Carui, fʒx.
Syr. Tolutani, fʒj.
Mix: make a draught. To be taken three times a day.
In Hooping-cough.—Dr. G. GREGORY.

1185. ℞ Extracti Conii, gr. xij.
Aluminis pulv. gr. xxv.
Aquæ Anethi, f℥iij.
Syrupi Rhœados, fʒij.
Make a mixture. Take a dessertspoonful every sixth hour. [For a child two or three years old.]
In the second stage of Hooping-cough.—Dr. G. BIRD.

1186. ℞ Extracti Conii, ʒss.
Sodæ Carbonatis, ʒss ad ʒj.
Decocti Glycyrrhizæ, f℥vss.
Spir. Pimentæ, fʒiij.
Mix: dose, f℥ss to f℥j, three or four times a day.
In Cancerous Diseases, &c.—Dr. COPLAND.

1187. ℞ Succi Conii, f℥ss.
Misturæ Camphoræ, f℥viiss.
Mix: dose, f℥ss every fourth hour. [The dose to be carefully increased until some constitutional effects are produced.]
In Rheumatic Pains, Facial Neuralgia, &c.—Dr. NELIGAN.

1188. ℞ Infusi Cinchonæ, f℥vj.
Liquor. Calcis, f℥ixss.
Tinct. Lupulinæ,
Succi Conii, ana fʒij. Mix: a wineglassful three times a day.
In Chronic Eczema of the aged.—Dr. NELIGAN.

1189. ℞ Extracti Conii, ʒj.
Aquæ, ad gradum 120° calefactæ, Oss.
Tincturæ Conii, fʒj.
Make a solution, of which the warm vapor is to be inhaled into the lungs by means of a funnel, for about six minutes at a time, three times a day.
In Irritable Coughs.—Dr. PARIS.

1190. ℞ Coniæ, granum,
Spir. rectificati, ♏x.
Aquæ, f℥ss.
Inhale the vapor, by means of heat, from a proper vessel.
HOSP. FOR CONSUMPTION.

1191. ℞ Coniæ, gr. iij.
Aquæ destillatæ, ʒv.
Spirit. rectificati, ℈ij. Make an eye-wash.
In Scrofulous Photophobia.—Dr. FRÖNMULLER.

1192. ℞ Extracti Conii, ʒj.
Aquæ destillatæ, ℥iij.
Rub up together, and macerate for an hour; then strain, and make a lotion.
Dr. DRUITT.

1193. ℞ Fol. Conii exsic. ℥j.
Aquæ, lbiiss.
Boil down to two pounds, and strain. For use as a fomentation.
In Scrofulous Ulceration, Cancer, &c.—Dr. JOY.

1194. ℞ Coniæ, gr. iij.
Adipis, ʒiv.
Make an ointment. [As a substitute for Unguentum Conii.]

CONFECTIO AROMATICA. See CINNAMOMUM.

CONTRAYERVA. See DORSTENIA CONTRAYERVA.

COPAIBA. *Balsam of Copaiva.*

Copaiva, a resinous juice from incisions in the stem of Copaifera multijuga and other species (Nat. Ord. *Leguminosæ*), is a diuretic, and a stimulant of the mucous membranes generally. In large doses it is laxative. It is prescribed in diseases of the urinary organs, especially gonorrhœa; also in chronic affections of the chest, and in hæmorrhoids. *Externally* it is applied to chilblains, and to indolent ulcers.

Dose, ten to sixty drops or minims, three times a day. It may be taken floating on any aromatic water; or on plain water, to which a little of any aromatic bitter tincture (as of orange-peel or gentian) is added after the balsam has been dropped on it. Or it may be formed into an emulsion, with mucilage, egg, or an alkaline solution.

Dose of *Oleum Copaibæ*, fifteen to thirty minims; *Resina Copaibæ*, ten to thirty grains; *Syrupus Copaibæ*, two to eight drachms.

1195. ℞ Copaibæ, ℥j.
Mucilaginis Acaciæ, ℥j.
Aquæ puræ, ℥vj.
Mix: make an emulsion. f℥j twice a day.

In Incontinence of Urine, from excessive use of Soda.

DR. URE.

1196. ℞ Copaibæ,
Sp. Lavand. comp. ana f℥ij.
Misturæ Acaciæ, f℥ss.
Syrupi, f℥iij. Rub up together; then pour in gradually
Aquæ puræ, f℥iv.
A tablespoonful twice a day, or two spoonfuls in gonorrhœa.

In Chronic Catarrh, Nephritic Affections, &c.

DR. WOOD (U. S.).

1197. ℞ Bals. Copaibæ, ℥ss.
Mucil. Acaciæ, ℥iv.
Aquæ Puræ, ℥v.
Aquæ Pimentæ, ℥iij. Mix: make a draught.

ST. BART. HOSP.

1198. ℞ Copaibæ,
Sp. Ætheris Nitrici, ana ℥j.
Mix: fifteen drops four times a day, gradually increasing the dose.

In Gonorrhœa.—Sir A. Cooper.

1199. ℞ Copaibæ,
Liq. Potassæ, ana f℥iij.
Mucil. Acaciæ, ℥j.
Aquæ Menthæ pip. ad f℥vj.
Make a mixture: f℥j three times a day.

In Gonorrhœa.—Mr. Milton.

1200. ℞ Copaibæ, f℥iij.
Solut. Alkalinæ (Brandish), f℥iss.
Rub up well together; then add, while rubbing,
Syrupi, f℥ss.
Olei Limonis, ♏xxx.
Make a mixture. A teaspoonful three times a day, in a wineglass of water.

In Gonorrhœa, &c.—Dr. Neligan.

1201. ℞ Copaibæ, ℥ss.
Cubebæ pulv. ℥ss.
Liq. Potassæ, ℨiss.
Mucilag. Acaciæ, ℥ss.
Aquæ destillatæ, ℥viiss. Mix: f℥j twice a day.

In the same.—Mr. Bransby Cooper.

1202. ℞ Copaibæ, ℥vj.
Tinct. Cubebæ, ℥j.
Spir. Ætheris Nitr. ℥iss.
Liq. Potassæ, ℥iss.
Aquæ destillatæ, ℥vj.
Mix: a teaspoonful three or four times a day, in water or linseed tea.

In the same.

1203. ℞ Copaibæ, ℨss–ℨj.
Bals. Peruviani, ℈ss.
Mucil. Acaciæ, ℨj.
Mist. Ammoniaci, ℨxj.
Tinct. Opii, gutt. x.
Make a draught. To be taken morning and evening.

In Consumption.—Sir A. Crichton.

1204. ℞ Copaibæ, ℨij.
Bals. Tolutanti, ℨiss.
Mellis optimi, ℥ij.
Tinct. Opii, ℨj.
Syrupi Tolut. ℥j.
Mix: a teaspoonful every noon and evening.

In Laryngeal Phthisis.—Sir A. Crichton.

1205. ℞ Copaibæ, f℥vj.
Ol. Terebinthinæ, f℥ij.
Mix: forty drops three times a day, in a wineglass of water.

Dr. Druitt.

1206. ℞ Copaibæ, ℥ij.
Cubebæ ℥ij.
Aluminis pulv. ℥j.
Extr. Opii, gr. v.
Dose, a drachm, increased to two drachms, night and morning.

In Gonorrhœa.—Dr. Dunglison.

1207. ℞ Bals. Copaibæ, ʒv.
Ovi unius vitellum. Rub up together; then add
Syrupi Menthæ, ℥ij.
Aquæ flor. Tiliæ, ℥iv. M.
To be taken in eight doses.

In Catarrhs.—Trousseau and Reveil.

1208. ℞ Copaibæ, ʒivss. Beat up with
Vitello Ovi unius, and add
Cubebæ pulv. ʒivss.
Confect. Rosæ, ℥ss.
Make an electuary. A teaspoonful three or four times a day.

In old cases of Gonorrhœa.—Vogt.

[See Cubeba for other Electuaries, &c.]

1209. ℞ Amygdal. decortic. ʒvj.
Altheæ rad. pulv. ʒj.
Catechu pulv. ʒss.
Bals. Copaibæ, ʒiij. Make an electuary.

1210. ℞ Ceræ Albæ, ʒj. Liquefy by a slow heat, and incorporate
Bals. Copaibæ, ʒiij.
Rhei rad. pulv. ʒvj.
Make a mass, and divide into pills. Fifteen grains to be taken several times a day.

In Chronic Gonorrhœa.—Simon.

1211. ℞ Copaibæ, ℈ij–vj.
Spir. Ammoniæ Anis. ʒss–ij.
Syrupi Aurantii, ℥iij.
Mix: a teaspoonful every two hours.

In Chronic Catarrh.—Kraus.

1212. ℞ Copaibæ, ℥ij.
Magnesiæ recens calcin. ʒj.
Rub up together, and set away until congealed. Divide into two hundred pills. From three to six pills three or four times a day.

1213. ℞ Copaibæ, ℥ss.
Acidi Benzoici, ʒj.
Vitelli Ovi, q. s.
Mist. Camphoræ, f℥vij. Mix: f℥j twice a day.

In Dysuria Senilis.—Mr. SODEN.

1214. ℞ Copaibæ, ℥ij.
Vitel. Ovi. No. 2. Rub up together, and add
Syrupi Tolutani, ℥ij.
Vini Albi, ℥iv. Make a balsamic mixture. Dose, f℥ss.

In Chronic Affections of the Urinary Organs.

Dr. T. FULLER.

1215. ℞ Bals. Copaibæ, ℥ij.
Liquor Potassæ, ℥iij.
Aquæ destillatæ, ℥vij.
Boil for a quarter of an hour, and then add
Spir. Ætheris Nitrici, ℥j.
Let it stand for two or three hours. Dose of the supernatant liquor, a dessertspoonful three times a day.

Dr. PEREIRA.

1216. ℞ Copaibæ, ʒj.
Mist. Acaciæ, ℥ss. Rub up together, and add
Aquæ Rosæ, ℥vj. Make an injection.

JOHN HUNTER.

1217. ℞ Copaibæ, f℥ss.
Tinct. Catechu, fʒvj.
Olei Juniperi, gutt. ij.
Mucil. Acaciæ, fʒiij.
Aquæ puræ, f℥v. Mix: two spoonfuls three times a day.

In Gonorrhœa.—Dr. DRUITT.

1218. ℞ Copaibæ, ʒij.
Mucil. Acaciæ, ℥ss. Mix: and add
Liquoris Calcis, ℥vj. Make an injection.

In Ulceration of the Urethra, Rectum, or Vagina.

Mr. ABERNETHY.

1219. ℞ Copaibæ, ʒvj.
Vitellum Ovi unius,
Decocti Papaveris, ℥ij. Make an injection.

In Gonorrhœa.—M. RICORD.

1220. ℞ Copaibæ (Vitel. Ovi sol.) fʒij.
Olei Olivæ, f℥ij.
Decocti Papaveris, Oss.
Tinct. Opii, fʒj. Make an enema.

In Suppression of Urine.—Dr. E. G. CLARK.

COPALCHI CORTEX.

The bark of Croton suberosum. It is a bitter tonic, grateful to the stomach, and possessing some efficacy as an antispasmodic. It may be administered in the same forms as cascarilla, in atony of the stomach and bowels, and in other cases requiring vegetable tonics.

Dose of *Infusum Copalchi*, one or two tablespoonfuls, three times a day; *Tinctura Copalchi*, one or two teaspoonfuls; *Extractum*, one or two grains.

CORIANDRUM.

Coriander Seed (the fruit of Coriandrum sativum, Nat. Ord. *Umbelliferæ*) is moderately aromatic. Its principal use is to cover the taste and correct the griping property of senna. Hence it is an ingredient in Confectio Sennæ; Infusum Sennæ, U. S.; Tinctura Sennæ composita, E., &c.

CORNUA CERVINA. *Hartshorn.*

Hartshorn shavings yield a jelly which is demulcent, but rather an article of diet than of medicine. *Burnt Hartshorn* consists chiefly of phosphate of lime; but the precipitated phosphate is now preferred to it for medicinal purposes. (See Calcis Phosphas.) *Spirit of Hartshorn*, as obtained by distilling hartshorn, or bones, is a solution of carbonate of ammonia, containing, as originally prepared, some empyreumatic animal oil; but what is now sold under the name may be regarded as identical with a solution of pure or carbonate of ammonia. See Ammonia, for prescriptions.

CORNUS. *Dogwood.*

The bark of Cornus circinata, and some other species, is used as an astringent bitter tonic; and has been proposed as a substitute for cinchona.

Dose of the powdered bark, one to three scruples; *Infusum Cornûs circinatæ*, one to two ounces; *Decoctum Cornûs floridæ*, a wineglassful.

1221. ℞ Extr. Cornus circinatæ, ℨiss.
Zingiberis pulv. ℈ss.
Sodæ Carbon. Exsic. ℈ss.

Mix, and divide into 24 pills. Two or three, an hour before dinner, and three hours after dinner, with a draught of water.

In Indigestion from Debility of the Stomach.—Dr. R. Reece.

1222. ℞ Ext. Cornus circ. ʒij.
Tinct. ejusdem, ʒvj.
Aquæ, f℥vij. Mix: three spoonfuls three times a day.
Dr. R. Reece.

CORTEX ALSTONIÆ.

The bark of Alstonia scholaris (Nat. Ord. *Apocyneæ*) is an aromatic astringent bitter; and has been given in bowel complaints, cholera, &c.

Dose of the powdered bark, three to five grains; or a teaspoonful of the tincture (made with three ounces of bark to a pint of proof spirit).

1223. ℞ Pulv. Cort. Alstoniæ, ℈ij.
Pulv. Ipecac. rad. gr. iij.
Pulv. Rhei,
Extr. Gentianæ, ana ℈j.
Mix, and divide into 24 pills. Two, twice a day.

CORTEX BRASILIENSIS.

This astringent bark is used in hæmorrhages and other discharges, but is especially recommended for the cure of gonorrhœa. A drachm of the powdered bark is given daily in divided doses; or one or two ounces of the decoction twice or thrice a day.

COTYLEDON UMBILICUS. *Navel-wort.*

The expressed juice of this plant, and the same inspissated to an extract, have obtained some reputation for the cure of epilepsy.

The dose of the fresh juice is from one to two ounces; of the *extract*, from half a drachm to a drachm twice a day.

1224. ℞ Ext. Cotyledonis Umbil. ʒiij.
Aquæ, ℥vj. Make a mixture: f℥j to f℥ij twice a day.
Mr. Salter.

CREASOTON. *Creasote, or Kreasote.*

Creasote is obtained from wood-tar. It has been tried as a remedy for various diseases; but has been found most efficacious in allaying vomiting, when unconnected with inflammatory conditions and structural disease of the stomach; it is particularly useful in relieving hysterical vomiting, and in that of pregnancy; sea-sickness has sometimes been relieved by it. It has also been tried in cases of neuralgia, diabetes, chronic rheumatism, consumption, &c.; but not always with benefit. *Locally*, creasote is styptic, and antiseptic; it frequently affords immediate relief in toothache; and is applied, in the form of ointments and lotions, to indolent and foul ulcers, burns, &c.

Dose of Creasote, from one to two drops, sometimes increased to five or more, in not less than a wineglassful of water; *Mistura Creasoti*, E., one to two ounces.

1225. ℞ Creasoti, ♏x.
Glycyrrhizæ rad. p. ʒj.
Mix: make a mass, and divide into 12 pills. One, three times a day.
In Neuralgia, Chronic Rheumatism, and Bronchitis.—Dr. JOY.

1226. ℞ Creasoti, ♏j–v.
Spir. Ammoniæ Arom. ♏xv. ad ʒj.
Aquæ, f℥iss.
Make a draught. When the pain is severe, add tinct. camphoræ comp. fʒj.
In Diarrhœa.—Mr. KESTEVEN.

1227. ℞ Creasoti, ♏vj.
Pulv. Tragacanthæ, ʒss.
Mist. Camphoræ, f℥vj.
Mix: a sixth part to be taken for a dose.
In obstinate Vomiting, &c.

1228. ℞ Creasoti, gutt. iij.
Belladonnæ pulv. gr. xij.
Mix: make 12 pills. One, three times a day.
In Vomiting in Pregnancy.—PITSCHAFT.

1229. ℞ Creasoti, ♏j.
Mist. Camphoræ,
Infus. Gentianæ, ana fʒvj. Make a draught.
Dr. DUNGLISON.

1230. ℞ Creasoti, ♏j.
Spir. Juniperi, ♏xx.
Aquæ destil. f℥j.
Make a draught. To be taken every second or third hour.
In Chronic Diarrhœa, with Vomiting.—Dr. NELIGAN.

1231. ℞ Creasoti, ʒj.
Extr. Glycyrrhizæ,
Galbani colati, ana ʒss.
Althææ rad. pulv. ʒij.
Make a mass, and divide into 120 pills. Six pills to be taken four times a day.
RIECH.

1232. ℞ Creasoti, ʒj.
Decocti Amyli, f℥xij. Make an enema.
In Camp Dysentery.—Dr. WILLMOTT.

1233. ℞ Creasoti, ʒss.
Aquæ destillatæ, Oj. Make a lotion.
In Itch, Impetigo Sparsa, &c.—Dr. DUNGLISON.

1234. ℞ Creasoti, ʒj.
Aquæ destillatæ, ℥x. Make a lotion.
As a preventive of Bed-sores.

1235. ℞ Creasoti, ♏x.
Aceti, fʒij.
Aquæ, f℥ij.
Make a lotion. To be applied with a camel-hair pencil.
To Cancers and Phagedænic Ulcers.—SHORT.

1236. ℞ Creasoti, gutt. ij.
Aquæ destillatæ, ℥ij.
Mix: make a lotion. To be applied with a camel-hair pencil.
To Inflamed Eyelids.—G. T. BLACK.

1237. ℞ Creasoti, ʒss.
Infusi Salviæ, Oj. Make a mouth-wash.
In Mercurial Salivation.—Dr. FAULCON.

1238. ℞ Creasoti, ♏iv.
Tinct. Galbani, fʒij.
Aquæ destillatæ, f℥ij. Make a lotion.
In Indolent Ulcers, with excessive discharge.—Dr. NELIGAN.

1239. ℞ Creasoti, ♏xx.
Liq. Potassæ, ʒij.
Sacchari albi, ʒij. Rub up together, and add
Aquæ destillatæ, f℥viij. Make an injection.
In Leucorrhœa.—Dr. ALLNATT.

1240. ℞ Creasoti, ʒss.
Carbon. Animalis pur. ʒj.
Sp. Vini rect. ʒiss.
Ung. Cetacei, ℥iss. Mix: make an ointment.
For Burns and Scalds.—Dr. SUTRO.

[For *children* it must be diluted with from two to four times its weight of spermaceti ointment.]

1241. ℞ Creasoti, gutt. x.
Adipis, ℥j.
Liq. Plumbi Diac. gutt. xij.
Extr. Opii, gr. iij. Make an ointment.
To broken Chilblains.—DEVERGIE.

1242. ℞ Creasoti, ♏v–xx.
Adipis, ℥ss. Make an ointment.

In Acne, Lepra, ill-conditioned Ulcers, &c.—Dr. JOY.

1243. ℞ Creasoti, ♏x.
Adipis, pp. ℥ij.
Opii pulv. gr. viij. Mix: make an ointment.

Dr. NELIGAN.

1244. ℞ Creasoti, gr. lxxv.
Tinct. Pyrethri, ʒiiss.

[Soak a little cotton in the mixture, and put it into the hollow tooth.]

For Toothache.—TROUSSEAU and REVEIL.

CRETA PRÆPARATA. See CALCIS CARBONIS.

CROCUS. *Saffron.*

Saffron (the stigmas of Crocus sativus, Nat. Ord. *Iridaceæ*) is reputed exhilarant, antispasmodic, and emmenagogue; but it is little depended upon for these purposes in this country. It enters into several tinctures, &c., but chiefly as a coloring ingredient. An infusion, of a drachm or less in a pint of water, is sometimes taken in debility of the stomach, and small quantities are given to children to promote the eruption of exanthemata: it has also been used as a collyrium.

Dose of saffron, from five to thirty grains.

CROTON TIGLIUM. See OLEUM TIGLII.

CUBEBÆ.

Cubebs, the fruit of Piper Cubeba (Nat. Ord. *Piperaceæ*), are carminative, stimulant, and diuretic. Their use is almost confined to the treatment of gonorrhœa. They should be recently ground, and in fine powder. The usual dose of powdered cubebs is from 2 to 6 scruples, commonly 1 drachm, three times a day; *Tinctura Cubebæ*, 1 to 2 drachms; *Oleum Cubebæ*, 10 to 30 minims; *Extractum Cubebæ* (TOLLER'S), 15 grains twice a day; *Extractum Cubebæ fluidum*, U. S., 10 to 20 grains.

1245. ℞ Cubebæ pulv. ℥j.
Sacchari albi, ʒij.
Mucil. Acaciæ, f℥ij.
Aquæ Cinnam. f℥vj.

Mix: two tablespoonfuls three times a day.

In Gonorrhœa and Gleet.—Dr. JOY.

1246. ℞ Cubebæ pulv. ℈ij.
Sodæ Bicarbonatis,
Potassæ Bitartr. ana ℈ss.
Mix: make a powder. To be taken three times a day.

In the same.—Dr. DRUITT.

1247. ℞ Cubebæ pulv. ℥ij.
Aluminis pulv. ℥ss.
Mix, and divide into nine powders. One three times a day.

In Gonorrhœa.—M. RICORD.

1248. ℞ Cubebæ pulv. ℥ss.
Mellis despumati, q. s.
Mix: a teaspoonful three times a day.

1249. ℞ Cubebæ pulv. ℥j.
Ergotæ pulv. ʒss.
Pulv. Cinnam. comp. ℈ij.
Sacchari albi, ʒj.
Mix, and divide into eight powders. One, three or four times a day.

In Leucorrhœa, Gleet, &c.—Dr. M. RYAN.

1250. ℞ Pulv. Cubebæ, ℥j.
Copaibæ, ʒj.
Pulv. Acaciæ, ʒj.
Syrupi Hemedesmi, q. s.
Make an electuary: fʒj to fʒij, three times a day.

In Gonorrhœa.

1251. ℞ Copaibæ,
Acaciæ pulv. ana ʒij.
Rub up together until well mixed; then add
Cubebæ pulv. ʒij.
Mix, and make into six boluses. One, three times a day.

1252. ℞ Cubebæ pulv. ℥j.
Acaciæ pulv. ℥ss.
Syrupi Papaveris, f℥j.
Aquæ Cinnamomi, f℥vij.
Make a mixture. A tablespoonful three or more times a day.

Dr. HOOPER.

1253. ℞ Cubebæ pulv. subt. ℥iss.
Copaibæ, ℥j.
Olei Menthæ pip. gutt. viij.
Spir. Ætheris Nitr. gutt. xv.
Sacchari pulv. q. s.
Make into a paste. The whole to be taken in four days, wrapped in wafer-paper.

In Gonorrhœa.—M. BOUCHARDAT.

1254. ℞ Pulv. Cubebæ, ℥iij.
Bals. Copaibæ, ʒx.
Magnes. calcin. ℥ss.
Syrupi Cydonii, q. s.
To form an electuary: make into boluses the size of a nut. Three to be taken three times a day.

In Gleet.—TROUSSEAU and REVEIL.

1255. ℞ Pulv. Cubebæ, ℥ss.
Confect. Sennæ, ʒij.
Syrupi, q. s. To form an electuary.

In the beginning of an attack of Gonorrhœa.—Dr. HOOPER.

1256. ℞ Cubebæ pulv. ℥j.
Aquæ ferventis, Oj. Make an injection.

Dr. DUNGLISON.

1257. ℞ P. Cubebæ, ℥j.
Extr. Belladonnæ, ʒj.
Aquæ ferventis, ℥xvj. Macerate, and make an injection.

M. CHEVALLIER.

CUMINUM.

Cumin seeds (the fruit of Cuminum Cyminum, Nat. Ord. *Umbelliferæ*) are stimulant and carminative.

Dose, ten to thirty grains. But they are seldom used except as an external stimulant, as in *Emplastrum Cumini.*

CUPRUM. *Copper* (compounds of).

The salts of copper are poisonous. In medicinal doses they are astringent, tonic, and emetic. *Externally*, they are caustic and detergent. The following are the principal compounds of copper employed in medicine:

Cupri Diacetas (verdigris), and *Cupri Acetas* (crystallized verdigris), are rarely used, except as external applications. The *Diacetate*, also termed Ærugo, is almost exclusively employed for the ointment and plaster. *Unguentum Æruginis* is applied to stimulate and cleanse ulcers, and is also recommended for recent burns; and for warts and corns. Ærugo is a frequent ingredient in corn plasters.

Cupri Ammonio-sulphas. Ammoniated copper is given as a tonic and antispasmodic, in epilepsy, chorea, &c.

Dose, from a quarter or half a grain, gradually increased to two or three grains. *Pilulæ Cupri Ammoniati*, E., contain half a grain in each. *Externally*, ammoniated copper is used in lotions, collyria, &c.

Cupri Sulphas. Sulphate of copper is given in doses of a quarter to one grain as a tonic and astringent; or five grains as a prompt emetic in poisoning by narcotics. But its use requires caution. *Externally*, it is used as a caustic to destroy fungous growths, and in astringent and detergent lotions, &c.

Cupri Carbonas (obtained by adding carbonate of soda to a solution of the sulphate) has been recommended as an outward application, in impetigo, eczema of the scalp, &c.

Cupri Nitras is used as a caustic.

1258. ℞ Cupri Ammoniati, gr. xij.
Extr. Gentianæ,
Pulv. Calumbæ, ana ʒss.
Mix thoroughly, and divide into 36 pills. Take one twice a day.
In Epilepsy and Chorea (after purgatives).—Dr. JOY.

1259. ℞ Cupri Ammoniati,
Extr. Cannabis Indicæ, ana ʒj.
Mix: divide into 24 pills. One three times a day.
In Epilepsy (as a palliative in hopeless cases).
Dr. J. GRIEVE.

1260. ℞ Cupri Sulphat. gr. j.
Syrupi Papaveris, ℥j.
Aquæ Anisi, ℥iij.
Make a mixture. A teaspoonful every four hours.
In Hooping-cough (of children).—Mr. CHAVASSE.

1261. ℞ Cupri Sulphatis, gr. iij.
Medullæ Panis, ʒj.
Make a mass: divide into 24 pills. One, three or four times a day.
In Epilepsy, Chronic Dysentery, &c.—Mr. BRANDE.

1262. ℞ Cupri Sulphat. gr. vj.
Myrrhæ pulv. gr. xij.
Cons. Rosæ, ℈ij. Make 12 pills. One every six hours.
In Chronic Diarrhœa; and Dysentery.—Dr. NELIGAN.

1263. ℞ Cupri Sulphatis, gr. v.
Pulv. Rhei, ʒss.
Extr. Gentianæ, ʒj.
Syrupi, q. s.
Mix thoroughly: make 20 pills. One or two, twice a day.
In Leucorrhœa, Chorea, &c.—Dr. JOY.

1264. ℞ Cupri Sulphatis, gr. viij.
Opii purificati, gr. j.
Extracti Papaveris, ℈ss.
Mix: make four pills. One, two or three times a day.
In Chronic Dysentery.—Dr. G. GREGORY.

1265. ℞ Cupri Sulphatis,
Ipecacuanhæ p. ana ʒj.
Syrupi, q. s.
Divide into 5-grain pills. Dose, from two to four every second, third, or fifth day, in the morning; alone, without any liquid.
In Phthisis.—SWEDIAUR'S *Dry Emetic.*

1266. ℞ Cupri Sulphat. gr. ss.
Opii pulv. gr. ss.
Confect. Rosæ, q. s. Make a pill. One, three times a day.
In Chronic Diarrhœa and Dysentery.—Dr. JOY.

1267. ℞ Cupri Ammoniati, gr. vj.
Aquæ, ℥iij. Dissolve; then add
Liq. Opii Sydenhami, gtt. x.
Syrupi simp. ʒx.
Mix: a teaspoonful three or four times a day.
In Chorea.—TROUSSEAU and REVEIL.

1268. ℞ Cupri Carbonatis, ʒj.
Adipis præparati, ℥ss. Make an ointment.
In Chronic Impetigo, and Eczema of the Scalp.—DEVERGIE.

1269. ℞ Cupri Sulphatis, ℈ss.
Aquæ destillatæ, f℥j.
Make a lotion. To be applied with a camel-hair pencil to the part affected; when dry, smear the part with spermaceti ointment. Repeat the application for two or three days, till the skin appears to be affected.
To prevent and cure Chilblains.—Dr. GRAVES.

1270. ℞ Cupri Sulphatis, gr. v.
Oxymelis, ℥ss.
Mix: apply it with a camel-hair pencil.
In Ulcerated Throat, Cancrum Oris, &c.—Mr. BRANDE.

1271. ℞ Cupri Sulphatis, gr. ½ ad ij.
Aquæ destillatæ, f℥j. Make an eye-wash.
Dr. DRUITT.

1272. ℞ Cupri Sulphatis, ℈ss.
Aquæ destillatæ, ℥j.
Spir. rectif. fʒj. Make a lotion.
In Chronic Molluscum.—Dr. NELIGAN.

1273. ℞ Liq. Cupri Ammoniati, ♏xx.
Tincturæ Opii, fʒss.
Aquæ Rosæ, f℥iv. Make a lotion.

1274. ℞ Cupri Acetatis, gr. v.
Liq. Plumbi diacet. f℥ss.
Aquæ Rosæ, f℥iv. Mix: make a lotion.

Dr. DRUITT.

1275. ℞ Cupri Sulphatis, gr. iv ad gr. viij.
Aquæ puræ, f℥viij. Mix: make an injection.

Sir A. COOPER, Bart.

1276. ℞ Cupri Ammoniati, gr. iv.
Aquæ puræ, ℥viij. Make an injection.

JESSE FOOT.

CURCUMA. *Turmeric.*

Turmeric is stimulant and carminative; but less so than ginger, to which it is allied, belonging to the Nat. Ord. *Zingiberaceæ*. The dose is from five to twenty grains twice a day, for flatulence. In India it is sprinkled on ulcers.

CUSPARIA. *Cusparia or Angustura Bark.*

Cusparia is supposed to be the bark of Galipea Cusparia (Nat. Ord. *Rutaceæ*). It has been used instead of cinchona in the intermittent fevers, bilious diarrhœa, and dysentery of tropical climates. In Europe it has not been found an adequate substitute for cinchona; but it is employed with benefit in atonic dyspepsia, chronic diarrhœa, and dysentery.

Dose of the powdered bark, five to thirty grains; *Infusum Cuspariæ*, one to two ounces; *Tinctura Cuspariæ*, one to two drachms.

1277. ℞ Pulv. Cuspariæ, gr. v.
Pulv. Rhei, gr. v.
Make a powder. To be taken an hour before dinner.

In Flatulence, with Nausea.—Mr. BRANDE.

1278. ℞ Cuspariæ contusæ, ℥j.
Caryophylli cont. ʒj.
Aquæ ferventis, Oj. Macerate for six hours, and strain.
Colaturæ, f℥iss.
Tinct. Catechu,
Syrupi Aurantii, ana fʒss.
Make a draught. To be taken three or four times a day.

1279. ℞ Infusi Cuspariæ, ℥vj.
Tinct. Cardam. comp. ʒvj.
Aceti destillati, ℥ij.
MIX: three tablespoonfuls to be taken three times a day.

In Indigestion, with dry tongue and irritation.

Dr. BAILLIE.

1280. ℞ Infusi Cuspariæ, ℥j.
Tinct. Catechu, ʒiss.
Ipecac. pulv. ℈ss. Mix: make a draught.

In Internal Hæmorrhage.—Dr. Joy.

1281. ℞ Infusi Cuspariæ, ℥vj.
Tinct. ejusdem, ℥ss.
Pulv. ejusdem, ℈j.
Tinct. Opii, ♏xx.
Spir. Lavand. comp. ♏xl.
Mix: four spoonfuls every four hours.

In Diarrhœa, with Exhaustion and Irritability.

Dr. E. G. Clark.

CYDONIUM. *Quince Seed.*

The seeds of the fruit of Cydonia vulgaris (Nat. Ord. *Pomaceæ*) yield a mucilage to water, which possesses the demulcent and emollient properties of mucilage of acacia. Its principal use is as a soothing application to inflamed eyes, excoriated and erysipelatous surfaces; and as a vehicle for borax, &c. in sores of the mouth and throat.

CYNARA. *Artichoke.*

The leaves of common artichoke (Cynara Scolymus, Nat. Ord. *Compositæ*) yield a bitter juice, which is diuretic, and was formerly given in dropsical complaints. The juice inspissated to an extract has been found to give very speedy relief in some cases of rheumatism, both acute and chronic; in gout; and in sciatica. The dose of the extract, according to Mr. Copeman, is two or three grains; but Dr. Badeley directs five grains, three times a day. A purgative should precede its use; but care should be taken not to give such doses of the extract as will disturb the bowels. The tincture is scarcely sufficiently active; but may be given in conjunction with the extract.

1282. ℞ Ext. Cynaræ, ʒj.
Sarsæ pulv. ʒss.
Ol. Sassafras, gutt. ij.
Make 20 pills. One, three times a day.

In Rheumatism, &c.

1283. ℞ Extr. Cynaræ, gr. v.
Misturæ Camphoræ, f℥xj.
Tinct. Cynaræ, f℥j.
Make a draught. To be taken three times a day.

In Rheumatic, Gouty, and Neuralgic Attacks.

Dr. BADELEY.

1284. ℞ Extr. Cynaræ, gr. v.
Misturæ Guaiaci, ℥iss.
Liq. Opii Sedat. ♏vj. Make a draught.

In the same cases.

DAUCUS CAROTA. *Carrot: the root and seed.*

The root of the cultivated carrot (Daucus carota sativus) is applied to foul, indolent, sloughing, and cancerous sores. If simply scraped, it is stimulant and deodorizing; if boiled and mashed, it is emollient and anodyne. The seeds of the wild carrot (Daucus carota sylvestris) are stimulant and diuretic.

Dose, thirty to sixty grains, in dropsy and chronic nephritic affections; or an infusion of half an ounce of the bruised seeds in a pint of water may be taken in the course of a day.

DELPHINIUM STAPHISAGRIA. *Stavesacre.* DELPHINIUM CONSOLIDA. *Larkspur.* DELPHINIA. *Delphine.*

Stavesacre seeds (D. Staphisagria, Nat. Ord. *Ranunculaceæ*) are emetic, cathartic, and vermifuge, in large doses acting as an irritant poison. They have been given in lepra, and chronic eczema; but their principal use is for destroying lice, and for curing the itch; for which purposes *Unguentum Staphisagriæ* or *Decoctum Staphisagriæ* are used. *Tinctura Staphisagriæ concentrata* (Turnbull's) is used externally in the same cases as veratria. M. Bazin employs an extract and tincture as internal remedies for eczema.

Larkspur seeds (D. consolida) have been given by Augustin in spasmodic asthma.

Dose of *Tinctura Delphinii*, ten to twenty drops three times a day.

Delphinia is the active principle of both the above, and has been used in neuralgic and rheumatic pains, and local paralysis, as a substitute for veratria.

1285. ℞ Sem. Staphisagriæ, ℥ss.
Aquæ, Oiss. Boil, strain, and add
Ext. Papaveris, ʒij.
Make a lotion. A small quantity to be applied to the parts affected.
In Itch.—RANQUE.

1286. ℞ Extracti Staphisagriæ,
Oxidi Zinci, ana ʒss.
Adipis, ℥j. Make an ointment.
In Chronic Eczema.—M. BAZIN.

1287. ℞ Sem. Staphisagriæ, p. ʒij.
Ung. Ceræ albæ, ℥j. Rub up well, and add
Glycerinæ, ʒj. Make an ointment.
In Itch.—Dr. NELIGAN.

1288. ℞ Extracti Staphisagriæ,
Extracti Dulcamaræ, ana ʒj.
Mix: make 40 pills. Four pills to be taken in the day, and the number gradually increased to twelve.
In Chronic Eczema.

1289. ℞ Delphiniæ puræ, gr. viij.
Adipis præparati, ʒij.
Make an ointment. To be rubbed over the seat of pain for ten to twenty minutes.
In Facial Neuralgia, &c.—Dr. A. TURNBULL.

1290. ℞ Delphiniæ puræ, gr. x ad xxx.
Spirit. rectificati, f℥j. Make an embrocation.
Dr. A. TURNBULL.

DIANTHUS CARYOPHYLLUS. *Clove Pink.*

The petals of Clove Pink are accounted stimulant, cordial, antispasmodic, and sudorific; but are now scarcely used except for their fine color and odor; on account of which *Syrupus Dianthi Caryophylli* is sometimes added to cordial, antispasmodic, and saline mixtures. A teacupful of an infusion of the dried petals (an ounce to a pint) has been given every four or six hours in typhus fevers.

DIGITALIS. *Fox-glove.*

Dried leaves of D. purpurea (Nat. Ord. *Scrophulariaceæ*). Narcotic, diuretic, and sedative; generally producing a marked diminution of the force and frequency of the heart's action.

Used to reduce inordinate vascular excitement in some fevers, inflammations, and hæmorrhages; in heart affections; as a diuretic in dropsies; and also as a remedy for phthisis, epilepsy, and scrofula. Its action must be carefully watched, and its use suspended as soon as it affects the head, the pulse, the stomach, or kidneys. Dose of the powdered leaves, from half or one grain, gradually increased to two or three grains. *Infusum Digitalis*, from two or four fluid-drachms to a fluid-ounce, sometimes increased to one and a half or two ounces. *Tinctura*, from ten minims, carefully increased to twenty or thirty. *Extractum*, half a grain to one grain. *Pil. Digitalis et Scillæ*, E., five to ten grains.

Unguentum Digitalis is applied to scrofulous sores. The tincture, mixed with soap liniment or a strong infusion of digitalis, is applied to the abdomen to produce diuresis in dropsy.

Digitalina. Digitaline is the active principle of fox-glove; it is said to be one hundred times as strong as the powdered leaves, and is used in the same cases.

Dose, one sixty-fifth of a grain, or one milligramme. It is prepared in the form of granules, each containing this quantity: the usual dose is from two to three of these granules per diem.

1291. ℞ Infusi Digitalis, f℥iv.
Tinct. Digitalis, fʒss.
Potassæ Acetatis, ʒj.
Tinct. Opii, ♏v.

Make a mixture. A tablespoonful to be taken twice or thrice a day.

In Dropsical Affections.—Dr. PARIS.

1292. ℞ Infusi Digitalis, fʒiv.
Potassæ Acetatis, ℈j.
Spir. Ætheris Nitrici, fʒj.
Aquæ Cinnamomi, fʒv.

Make a draught. One every six hours until the urine is increased, unless the pulse, head, or digestive organs be affected, when it should be instantly discontinued.

In Hydrothorax.—Dr. JOY.

1293. ℞ Infusi Digitalis, fʒij.
Sp. Ætheris Nitr. fʒss.
Decocti Scoparii, fʒx.

Make a draught. To be taken three times a day.

In Œdema.—Dr. BARCLAY.

1294. ℞ Infusi Digitalis, f℥iij.
Potassæ Acetatis, ʒiij.
Spir. Ætheris Nitr. f℥j.
Liq. Ammoniæ Acet. f℥ij. Mix: dose, a sixth part.
Dr. HOOPER.

1295. ℞ Infusi Digitalis, f℥viiss.
Potassæ Nitratis, ʒij.
Acidi Hydrocyanici dil. ♏xiv.
Syrupi Aurantii, fʒij.
Mix: a tablespoonful every two hours.
In Hypertrophy of the Heart, with excessive action.
Dr. COPLAND.

1296. ℞ Infusi Digitalis, f℥iv.
Potassæ Acetatis, ʒij.
Spir. Ætheris Nitr. fʒij.
Aquæ Cassiæ, f℥iss.
Make a mixture. A tablespoonful every fourth hour.
In Cardiac Dropsy.—Dr. A. KILGOUR.

1297. ℞ Infusi Digitalis, fʒiv.
Liq. Hydrarg. Bichlor. fʒj.
Aquæ Menthæ sat. f℥j.
Tinct. Cantharidis, ♏xx.
Mix: make a draught. To be taken two or three times a day.
In Chronic Anasarca.—Dr. SEYMOUR.

1298. ℞ Succi Digitalis, ♏xij.
Mist. Camphoræ, f℥j.
Syr. Aurantii, fʒij.
Acidi Hydrocy. dil. ♏j.
Mix: make a draught. To be taken two or three times a day.
In Nervous Palpitations.—Dr. NELIGAN.

1299. ℞ Tinct. Digitalis, ♏x–xx.
Mist. Camphoræ, fʒx.
Tinct. Calumbæ, fʒj.
Make a draught. To be taken twice a day.
In Palpitation, with Nervous Irritability.—Dr. PARIS.

1300. ℞ Succi Limonis, ℥ss.
Potassæ Carbon. ad saturandum.
Decocti Sarsæ, ʒx.
Tinct. Digitalis, ♏x–xxx.
Mucil. Acaciæ, ʒij.
Make a draught. To be taken every six hours.
In Acute Tubercular Phthisis.—Sir A. CRICHTON.

1301. ℞ Tinct. Digitalis, fʒiss.
Tinct. Hyoscyami, fʒj.
Mist. Camphoræ, f℥iv.
Make a mixture. A teaspoonful as occasion may require.
In Palpitation, with Hypertrophy of the Heart.—Dr. JOY.

1302. ℞ Tinct. Digitalis, ♏xv.
Potassæ Acetatis, ʒj.
Spir. Juniperi comp. fʒij.
Decocti Scoparii, fʒxiv.
Make a draught. To be taken twice a day.

In Anasarca.

1303. ℞ Tinct. Digitalis, ♏x.
Oxymellis Scillæ, fʒss.
Misturæ Camphoræ, ℥j.
Make a draught. To be taken every four hours.

In Chronic Bronchitis, with Heart Disease.—Dr. JOY.

1304. ℞ Tinct. Digitalis, ♏xv.
Aceti destillati, fʒj.
Syrupi, fʒj.
Aquæ puræ, f℥iss.
Make a draught. To be taken three times a day until twelve doses are taken.

In Hectic.—Dr. DRUITT.

1305. ℞ Tinct. Digitalis, fʒiij.
Tinct. Scillæ, fʒj.
Mix: take thirty drops every four hours.

In Dropsy.—HORN.

1306. ℞ Pulv. Digitalis, ʒj.
Assafœtidæ, ʒj.
Make into a mass, with a sufficient quantity of Comp. Spirits of Lavender; and divide into pills weighing each two grains. One to be taken every morning.

In Chronic Catarrh, Phthisis, and Heart Disease.
Dr. WITHERING.

1307. ℞ Pulv. Digitalis,
Pulv. Scillæ rad. ana gr. xij.
Extr. Hyoscyami, gr. xviij.
Divide into 12 pills. One or two to be taken every three hours.

In Asthma, &c.—Dr. JOY.

1308. ℞ Pulv. Digitalis, gr. vj.
Pulv. Camphoræ, gr. xv.
Extr. Hyoscyami, ℈iss. Make 12 pills.

In Maniacal and Spasmodic Affections.—Dr. COPLAND.

1309. ℞ Pulv. Digitalis,
Pulv. Scillæ, ana gr. ix.
Extr. Gentianæ, ℈j.
Olei Juniperi, gutt. viij.
Syrupi, q. s.
To form 12 pills. One to be taken three times a day.

In Dropsy.—Dr. PEARSON.

1310. ℞ Pulv. Digitalis, ʒj.
Pulv. Scammonii, ʒss.
Pulv. Scillæ, ʒss.
Extr. Juniperi [*vel* Taraxaci], q. s.

Make a mass, and divide into 30 pills. One pill three times a day, with a wineglassful of water in which niter has been dissolved in the proportion of ʒiv to a quart.

In Hydrothorax.—Dr. DEBREYNE.

1311. ℞ P. Digitalis fol.
Potassæ Nitratis, āā ʒss.
Pulv. Sacchari, ʒiiss.

Mix: divide into 40 powders. (1–4 daily for children; 4–10 for adults.)

In Inflammation of Lungs and Heart, and in Dropsies.
TROUSSEAU and REVEIL.

1312. ℞ Pulv. Digitalis, gr. vj.
Hydrarg. Chloridi, gr. xij.
Pulv. Sacchari albi, gr. xviij.

Mix well, and divide equally into 12 powders. Take one powder every six hours.

In Hydrocephalus.—Dr. MERRIMAN.

1313. ℞ Pulv. Digitalis, gr. xij.
Pulv. Myrrhæ, gr. xxiv.
Ferri Sulphatis, gr. xij.
Syrupi, q. s. Make 12 pills. One, three times a day.

In Amenorrhœa, with Epilepsy.—Dr. BRIGHT.

1314. ℞ Pulv. Digitalis, gr. xvj.
Hydrarg. Chloridi, ℈ss.
Pulv. Glycyrrhizæ, ℈j.
Olei Juniperi, q. s.

Make 8 pills. Two, every three or four hours.

In the early stage of Brain Fever.—BRERA.

1315. ℞ Extracti Digitalis, ʒij.
Adipis, ℥j.

Make an ointment. The throat to be covered with lint smeared with this ointment, and frequently renewed.

In Croup.—RUDERMACHER.

1316. ℞ Tinct. Digitalis,
Linim. Saponis comp. ana ℥j.

Mix: make a liniment. To be rubbed over the abdomen.

In Dropsy.—Dr. CHRISTISON.

1317. ℞ Fol. Digitalis, sicc. ʒiv.
Aquæ ferventis, Oj.

Macerate for an hour, and strain. Cloths wet with the infusion to be laid over the abdomen.

In Dropsy.—Dr. DUNCAN.

1318. ℞ Infusi Digitalis, f℥ij.
Liquor. Ammoniæ, fʒij.
Ol. Sem. Papaveris, fʒiv. Mix: make a liniment.

For the same purpose.—Dr. ROYLE.

1319. ℞ Digitalinæ, gr. ¼.
Kermetis Mineralis, gr. xv.
Ext. Digitalis, gr. xv.
Excipientis, q. s.

Mix: divide into 50 pills. (1–5 daily for children; 4–10 for adults.)

In Inflammatory Affections of the Lungs.
TROUSSEAU and REVEIL.

1320. ℞ Digitalinæ (in alc. sol.) gr. j.
Hydrarg. Sulph. rub. gr. xxv.
Hydrarg. Ammonio-Chloridi, ℈viij.
Tinct. Opii, ʒj.
Cerati Galeni (*cold cream*), ℥iiss. Make an ointment.

In Eczema, and other cutaneous diseases.—M. DUMONT.

DOLICHOS [MUCUNA] PRURIENS. *Cowitch.*

The hairs with which the pods of this leguminous shrub are thickly covered are employed to dislodge worms, more especially lumbrici; which they probably effect by mere mechanical irritation. The usual mode of administering Cowitch is to dip the pods in syrup, and scrape off the spiculæ with the syrup until a mixture is obtained of the thickness of honey; the dose of which is from a teaspoonful to a tablespoonful, every morning for three times, following the last dose by a purgative. The following are more precise formulæ:

1321. ℞ Dolichi Pubis, ℈ij.
Syrupi, ℥ss.

Mix: give a teaspoonful every morning for three days, and a dose of castor oil after the last dose.

To expel Lumbrici.—CORREA.

1322. ℞ Spiculæ Dolichi, gr. xij.
Limat. Stanni, gr. xij.
Syrupi, q. s. Make a bolus, to be taken night and morning.

Dr. AINSLIE.

1323. ℞ Dolichi pub. ʒj.
Theriacæ, ℥j.

Make an electuary. A teaspoonful every morning.

In Lumbrici and Ascarides.—Dr. JOY.

[A purgative should be given every second or third day.]

DORSTENIA CONTRAYERVA.

Contrayerva root is stimulant, tonic, and diaphoretic; and was once esteemed as an antidote to poisons, as well as a remedy for low and malignant fevers and exanthemata; and as a tonic in debility of the stomach.

Dose of the powdered root, fifteen to forty grains; of *Pulvis Contrayervæ compositus*, one to two scruples.

DULCAMARA. *Bitter-sweet.*

The dried twigs of Woody Nightshade, Solanum Dulcamara (Nat. Ord. *Solanaceæ*), are regarded as alterative, diuretic, sudorific, and feebly narcotic. It is chiefly prescribed in obstinate cutaneous disorders, especially those of a scaly character; also in scrofula, chronic rheumatism, chronic catarrh, &c.

Dose of *Pulvis Dulcamaræ*, twenty to sixty grains; *Decoctum Dulcamaræ*, two ounces, three times a day; *Extractum*, five to ten grains; *Syrupus*, half an ounce to an ounce.

1324. ℞ Decocti Dulcamaræ, f℥xj.
Liq. Potassæ, f℥ss.
Tinct. Chirettæ, f℥ss.
Mix: two tablespoonfuls to be taken three times a day.

In Skin Diseases.—Dr. NELIGAN.

1325. ℞ Extr. Dulcamaræ, ℈ss.
Decocti Althææ, ℥iij.
Vini Opii, gtt. ij.
Oxymellis, ʒiij.
Dose for a child of two years, a teaspoonful.

In protracted Cough.—GOELIS.

1326. ℞ Caul. Dulcamaræ,
Rad. Arctii Lappæ, ana ʒvj.
Rad. Glycyrrhizæ,
Lign. Sassafras,
Lign. Guaiaci, ana ʒij.
Aquæ, Oiss.
Boil sufficiently to strain to a pint. A wineglassful several times a day.

In Rheumatism, Syphilis, Cutaneous Affections, &c.

AUGUSTIN.

1327. ℞ Decocti Dulcamaræ,
Decocti Malvæ comp. ana Oss. Make a lotion.

In Skin Diseases, with much Irritation.—Dr. HOOPER.

ELATERIUM.

Extractum Elaterii (Elaterium, D. and E.) is the dried fæcula of the juice of the unripe fruit of a cucurbitaceous plant, Ecbalium Elaterium, or Momordica Elaterium. It is a powerful hydragogue purgative, sometimes prescribed in obstinate constipation, but more frequently in dropsical cases. In over-doses it acts as an irritant poison.

It is difficult to state the dose, as commercial elaterium varies so much in its strength. Some authors speak of one or two grains; but this can only refer to very inferior kinds. Dr. Pereira found that a quarter of a grain of *good* elaterium acted very powerfully; and that the dose was from one-sixteenth of a grain to half a grain.

Elaterina, Elaterine, the active principle of elaterium, is given in doses of one-sixteenth to one-eighth of a grain.

Dose of *Tinctura Elaterii*, sixty minims; *Sol. Elaterinæ*, thirty to forty minims.

1328. ℞ Extracti Elaterii, gr. j.
Extracti Gentianæ, ℈j.
Mix: make 8 pills. Dose, one or two pills.

Dr. Pereira.

1329. ℞ Extr. Elaterii, gr. j.
Extr. Coloc. comp. ℈iiss.
Extr. Hyoscyami, gr. xij.
Mix: make 12 pills. One, night and morning.

In Cardiac Dropsy (when diuretics fail).—Dr. A. Kilgour.

1330. ℞ Elaterii, gr. ss.
Hydr. Chloridi,
Pulv. Capsici, ana gr. ij.
Conf. Rosæ caninæ, q. s.
Make a pill, to be taken in the morning.

In Anasarca.—Dr. G. Gregory.

1331. ℞ Tinct. Elaterii, f℥j.
Syrupi Sennæ, f℥ss.
Syrupi Zingiberis, f℥j.
Aquæ Menthæ pip. f℥j.
Make a draught, to be taken first, and if it does not produce a copious soluble alvine evacuation, repeat in four hours.

In Ascites, in the robust, with no inflammatory tendency.

Dr. Neligan.

1332. ℞ Extr. Elaterii, gr. iij.
Cambogiæ, ℈ss.
Extr. Aloes,
Sagapeni, ana gr. xij.
Olei Carui, q. s.

Make a mass, and divide into 12 pills. Two, going to bed.

1333. ℞ Extr. Elaterii, gr. xv.
Potassæ Sulphatis, ℈j. Rub up together, and add
Saponis duri, ʒj.
Zingiberis, pulv. ʒiss.

Rub up with a sufficient quantity of water, and make a mass: to be divided into 60 pills. One to be taken every hour till the bowels are freely opened.

SPRAGUE.

1334. ℞ Extr. Elaterii, gr. j.
Spir. Ætheris Nitr. f℥ij.
Tinct. Scillæ, f℥ss.
Oxymellis Colchici, f℥ss.
Syrupi Rhamni, f℥j.

Dose, fʒj three times a day in water.

In Dropsical Complaints.—Dr. FERRIAR.

1335. ℞ Elaterinæ, gr. j.
Spir. Vini rectif. f℥j.
Acidi Nitrici, gutt. iv. Make a solution. Dose, ♏xxx.

Dr. MORRIES.

EMETINA. See IPECACUANHA.

ERGOTA. (SECALE CORNUTUM.) *Ergot of Rye.*

Ergot is the grain of rye corrupted by a parasitic fungus. Its presence in rye flour is supposed to be the cause of certain gangrenous and convulsive diseases which sometimes prevail where this grain is much used. As a medicine its principal use is to hasten parturition when retarded simply by insufficient uterine action. It is also believed to possess the power of restraining hæmorrhages, and has been recommended in amenorrhœa, leucorrhœa, gleet, chronic dysentery, incontinence of urine in old persons, &c.

The following are the preparations in use, and their doses:

Pulvis Ergotæ. (This should be freshly powdered.) Dose, five or six grains, repeated every few hours. In incontinence of urine, Dr. Ross prescribes from six to ten grains every morning in tepid water. For a woman in labor, the dose is fifteen to twenty grains, repeated once or twice at intervals of twenty or thirty minutes if required.

Infusum Ergotæ, D. In the above diseases, from half a drachm to a drachm; in labor, one to two ounces, repeated in half an hour.

Extractum Ergotæ aquosum (Bonjean's Ergotine), three to five grains every quarter of an hour in obstetric cases. In hæmorrhages, a scruple may be given in the course of a day.

Tinctura Ergotæ, D., ten to twenty minims; in labor, half a drachm to a drachm.

Tinctura Ergotæ Ætherea, L., ten to twenty minims.

Tinctura Ergotæ Ammoniata (Mr. Gore's), thirty drops.

Vinum Ergotæ, U.S., one to two drachms several times a day, in hæmorrhage, &c. In labor, two or three drachms.

Solutio Secalis Cornuti Ætherea (Dr. Rees's); fifteen to thirty minims, in labor.

Oleum Ergotæ (Dr. Wright's); ten drops every three hours, in diarrhœa, &c.; twenty to forty drops in parturition, and extreme hæmorrhage.

1336. ℞ Ergotæ pulv. ʒss.
P. Cinnam. comp. ℈ss.
Sacchari albi, ʒss.
Mix, and divide into 10 powders. One every second or third hour.

In Active Hæmorrhage.—Dr. M. Ryan.

1337. ℞ Ergotæ (recens red. in pulv.) ʒss.
Divide equally into 8 powders. One to be given every three hours, or the whole in twenty-four hours.

In Epistaxis and Hæmoptysis.—Dr. Spairani.

1338. ℞ Ergotæ pulv. ʒss.
Extracti Gentianæ, ʒj.
Mix, and make 15 pills. One, three times a day.

In Dysmenorrhœa.—Dr. Dewees.

1339. ℞ Pulv. Ergotæ, ʒss.
Syrupi, ℥ss.
Aquæ Menthæ, ℥j.
Mix: a third part to be taken every twenty minutes.

In Labor.—M. Soubeiran.

1340. ℞ Ergotæ contritæ, ʒj.
Aquæ, f℥iij.
Boil to f℥jss. Of the decoction, freed from sediment, give the third part three times in the course of an hour.

In Lingering Labor from Inaction of the Uterus, and in Hæmorrhage. Dr. JOY.

1341. ℞ Ergotæ pulv. gr. xlviij.
Olei Sabinæ, ♏xij.
Theriacæ, q. s.
Make an electuary.. A sixth part three times a day.

Emmenagogue in simple Atony of the Uterine Organs.
Dr. NELIGAN.

1342. ℞ Ergotæ cont. ʒss.
Aquæ ferventis, f℥iij.
Infuse, and to the strained liquor add
Pulv. Ergotæ, ℈ss.
Sacchari albi, ʒj.
Make a draught: to be repeated in twenty minutes if the uterus does not contract.

1343. ℞ Pulv. Ergotæ, gr. iij.
Plumbi Acet. gr. ij.
Opii pulv. gr. ¼.
Mucil. Acaciæ, q. s.
Make a pill, to be taken every second hour.

In Uterine Hæmorrhage.—Dr. FERGUSON (U. S.).

1344. ℞ Ergotinæ (Extr. Aquos.) gr. xij.
Syrupi Croci, f℥ss.
Aquæ Menthæ pip. f℥iiiss.
Mix: make a mixture. Two tablespoonfuls every quarter of an hour until effectual.

To Accelerate Delivery.—Dr. NELIGAN.

1345. ℞ Ergotinæ, gr. xvj.
Aquæ puræ, ℥iij.
Syrupi flor. Aurantii, f℥j.
A tablespoonful every three hours, in hæmorrhage; or every quarter of an hour, to excite expulsive pains.

BONJEAN.

1346. ℞ Ergotæ, gr. vj ad x.
Sacchari albi, ℈ss.
Make a powder: make six similar doses. One every ten minutes.

In Uterine Hæmorrhage.—LOEWENHARD.

1347. ℞ Pulv. Ergotæ, ʒij.
Aquæ, ℥xij. Boil and strain: make an enema.

To Accelerate Delivery.—FOY.

ERIGERON. *Flea-bane.*

Canada Flea-bane (Erigeron Canadense, Nat. Ord. *Compositæ*) is diuretic, tonic, and astringent; and is given in dropsical complaints, and diarrhœa.

Dose of the flowering tops, in powder, thirty to sixty grains; *Infusum*, two to four ounces; *Extractum*, five to ten grains.

An infusion of two other species, E. heterophyllum, and E. philadelphicum, is also given in nephritic and dropsical complaints, to the amount of a pint in twenty-four hours. But they are not prescribed in this country.

ERYNGIUM. *Eryngo-root.*

The root of Sea-Holly, Eryngium maritimum (Nat. Ord. *Umbelliferæ*), is a mild expectorant, and has been thought useful in consumption; it is also diuretic, deobstruent, and antiscorbutic. Candied Eryngo is used as a pectoral.

1348. ℞ Rass. Corn. Cerv. ʒij.
Rad. Eryngii,
Hordei perlati loti, ana ʒij.
Aquæ, Oiss. Boil to a pint, strain, and add
Syrupi Adianti, ℥j. A cupful to be taken frequently.
In Consumption.

[We have omitted the snails usually added in foreign formulæ.]

ERYSIMUM. *Hedge-mustard.*

This cruciferous plant partakes of the pungency of mustard and horse-radish; and is used as an antiscorbutic, and as a remedy for chronic hoarseness.

Dose of *Syrupus Erysimi*, and *Syr. Erysimi compositus*, half an ounce to two ounces. See No. 341, p. 77.

EUPATORIUM.

Several species of Eupatorium (Nat. Ord. *Compositæ*) have been employed in medicine: only two can be noticed here.

Eupatorium perfoliatum, Thoroughwort. The tops and leaves are used as a diaphoretic and tonic; in large doses it is emetic and purgative. It is given in intermittent, remittent, and typhoid fevers, general debility, and dyspepsia.

Dose, in *powder*, thirty grains; of the *cold infusion*, as a tonic, an ounce frequently. The warm infusion is taken more freely, the patient being kept warm in bed, to promote diaphoresis. As an emetic, the warm decoction is taken by cupfuls. Dr. Peebles gives a wineglassful of the warm infusion every half hour, until perspiration, nausea, or vomiting, are produced, for the speedy relief of influenza.

Eupatorium Cannabinum, Hemp agrimony, is diuretic, aperient, and deobstruent; and has been recommended in cachectic diseases, coughs, suppressio mensium, dropsy, jaundice, scurvy, &c. Rarely prescribed in this country. A decoction of the *root* is used in dropsy.

ETHER. See ÆTHEREA.

EUPHORBIA. *Spurge.*

The various species of Spurge contain an acrid milky juice. The dried juice of one or more species constitutes the Euphorbium of the shops, which is only used as an external irritant; and occasionally with seven parts of starch, as a rough sternutatory. The powdered root of *Euphorbia corollata* and *E. Ipecacuanha* are emetic and cathartic; dose, ten to fifteen grains, as a substitute for ipecacuanha.

Euph. Hypericifolia, Black Purslane, is used in menorrhagia, leucorrhœa, and diarrhœa. The seeds of *Euph. Lathyris* yield a purgative oil; dose, four to twelve drops.

1349. ℞ Euphorbii gummi-res. ʒj.
Olei Olivæ, ʒx.
Digest for ten days, and strain. Used in frictions.

In Paralysis.—VAN MONS.

1350. ℞ Euphorbiæ hypericif. sic. ℥ss.
Aquæ ferventis, f℥xvj.
Macerate for half an hour, and strain. A tablespoonful every hour until the symptoms abate. [In Menorrhagia, a wineglassful three times a day.]

In Dysentery and Diarrhœa.—Dr. ZOLLICKOFFER.

1351. ℞ Olei Euphorbii Lathyris, gutt. viij.
Acaciæ pulveris, ʒj.
Sacchari albi, ℥ij.
Aquæ, f℥iij. Make a draught.

As an Active Purgative.—PICHONIER.

FEL BOVINUM. *Ox-gall.*

The bile or gall of the ox is used as a tonic, laxative, and deobstruent; it is particularly recommended in disorders connected with a deficiency of bile. In obstinate costiveness it has proved successful, and is thought to possess the power of directly softening indurated fæces. It is also useful in dyspepsia attended with vomiting. Combined with opium, it is said to prevent the constipating and other undesirable effects of that drug. Another virtue attributed to its free use is the alleviation of pain in cancerous diseases.

Dose of the inspissated fresh gall, *Extractum Fellis*, five to ten grains; of the same reduced to dryness, *Fel desiccatum*, four to eight grains.

1352. ℞ Fel. Bovini desic. ʒj.
Spir. rectif. q. s.
Make 15 pills. One or two, two or three times a day.
In Habitual Costiveness.

1353. ℞ Extr. Fellis, ʒij.
Olei Carui, ♏x.
Magnes. Carbon, q. s.
Make 30 pills. Two, three times a day.
In Costiveness, from Deficiency of Bile.—Dr. CLAY.

1354. ℞ Extr. Fellis, ʒij.
Rhei pulv. ʒss.
Make 30 pills. From two to six pills daily.
In Inactivity of the Liver, Jaundice, Costiveness, &c.

1355. ℞ Fellis Bov. ʒiij.
Extr. Gentianæ, ʒij.
Rhei pulveris, ʒij.
Assafœtidæ, ʒj. Mix, and divide into 120 pills.
Dr. JOY.

1356. ℞ Fellis Bovini,
Assafœtidæ, ana ʒj.
Rhei pulveris, ℈j.
Syrupi, q. s. Make 40 pills. Two, twice a day.
In Epilepsy, &c.—Dr. COPLAND.

1357. ℞ Fellis tauri inspis.
Aloes extr. pur. ana ʒj.
Extr. Colocynth. comp.
Saponis Castil. ana ℈j. Mix: make 36 pills.
In Dyspepsia, with Costiveness.

1358. ℞ Fellis inspissati,
Extr. Aloes purif.
Extr. Gentianæ,
Saponis Venet. ana ʒss.
Mix: make 30 pills. Two, twice a day.
In Costiveness and Dyspepsia.—Dr. COPLAND.

1359. ℞ Fellis Bov. recentis, ℥ij.
Decocti Avenæ tenuis, f℥viij. Make an enema.
To soften Indurated Fæces.—Dr. ALLNATT.

1360. ℞ Fellis Bovini,
Linim. Saponis, ana ʒiij.
Make a liquid, to be dropped into the ear.
In Deafness, from Indurated Wax.—Dr. E. G. CLARK.

FERMENTUM CEREVISIÆ. *Yeast.*

Yeast is tonic, stimulant, antiseptic, and laxative; and has been given with good effect in typhoid fevers, scarlet fever, putrid sore throat, furuncular disease, &c. It has been given in doses of an ounce, frequently, in petechial typhus, by Dr. Jones Lamprey. Mr. Mosse, of Fareham, gives a tablespoonful for adults, or a smaller quantity for children, three times a day. with water, as a remedy for boils; Mr. Bennett, of Gateshead, gives one or two tablespoonfuls frequently, as an antiseptic and stimulant in scarlet fevers, &c. *Externally*, it is applied as an antiseptic and stimulant (*Cataplasma Fermenti*, L.).

1361. ℞ Fermenti Cerevisiæ, ℥ss.
Misturæ Camphoræ, f℥ij.
Make a draught, to be taken every third hour.
Dr. STOCKER.

[If required more aperient, add Tinct. Jalapæ; if too relaxing, a few drops Tinct. Opii.]

1362. ℞ Cerevisiæ Fermenti, ℥x.
Camphoræ pulv. ʒss.
Spir. Ætheris Nitrici, ʒiv.
Make a mixture: f℥j every second or third hour.
In Petechial Typhus, and Dysentery with fetid dejecta.
Dr. JONES LAMPREY.

FERRUM. *Iron.*

The general operation of the preparations of iron is as a tonic: they usually raise the pulse, heighten the complexion, and promote the secretions. They are unsuitable in an excited state of the circulation; and are most useful where there is debility and relaxation of the fiber, and languid circulation. They are prescribed for chlorotic anæmia, scrofula, enlargements of the liver and spleen, fluor albus, gleet, passive hæmorrhages, chorea, atonic dyspepsia, chronic dysentery and diarrhœa, tic douloureux, worms, &c. Headache, or a sense of fullness in the head, is an indication that they do not agree, or have been pushed too far. Purgatives should generally precede their administration.

As the preparations and compounds of iron are so numerous, it seems expedient to divide them into groups. External applications are placed at the end of the whole.

1. Those in which the iron is in a metallic state, or that of oxide, or carbonate.

Limaturæ Ferri, and *Lim. Ferri Lævigatæ*, 3 to 10 grains.
Ferri Pulvis, D. (Iron reduced by Hydrogen), 1 to 6 grains.
Ferri Protoxidum (this can only be prepared extemporaneously, as in No. 1370.)
Ferri Oxidum Nigrum, E. [*Magneticum*, D.], 10 to 30 grains.
Ferri Sesquioxidum, L. [*Oxidum rubrum*, E.], 10 to 60 grains.

Ferri Peroxidum hydratum, D. [*Ferrugo*, E.]. In the moist state, as an antidote for arsenic, it must be given by spoonfuls, frequently, diffused in water. It must be given at least to the amount of twelve times the weight of the poison swallowed.

Ferri Carbonas, D.; five to thirty grains. [A mixture of carbonate and sesquioxide of iron. When sulphate of iron is decomposed by a carbonated alkali, proto-carbonate of iron is formed, which has a strong tendency to pass into the state of sesquioxide; this change is partially retarded by saccharine and gummy matters, as in *Pil. Ferri comp.*, and *Mistura Ferri comp.*, which are intended as forms for administering the carbonate; but is more effectually accomplished in the next preparation.]

Ferri Carbonas cum Saccharo, 5 to 30 grains.
Mistura Ferri Composita, 1 ounce to 1 or 2 ounces.
Pilula Ferri Composita, 10 to 20 grains.
Pilula Ferri Carbonatis, 5 to 10 grains.
Aqua Chalybeata Aerata, a pint in divided draughts.
———— (*Bewley's*), 2 ounces.

1363. ℞ Ferri Limat. læv. gr. vj ad xij.
Testæ præparatæ,
Sacchari albi, ana ʒj.
Olei Limonis, gutt. j.
Mix, and divide into 6 powders. One, twice a day.

In Rickets.—BERENDS.

1364. ℞ Ferri pulveris, gr. iij.
Pulv. Acaciæ, gr. vj.
Cretæ præparatæ, gr. xij.
Calcis Phosph. præcip. gr. vj.
Mix, and divide into 6 powders. One, twice a day.

In the same.

1365. ℞ Ferri lævigati, gr. iij.
Magnes. Carbon. gr. xv.
Cinnamomi, gr. vj.
Sacchari albi, ʒj.
Mix, and divide into 6 powders. One, morning and evening.

In Atrophy of Children, and Rickets.—HUFELAND.

1366. ℞ Limat. Ferri læv. ʒj.
Extr. Absinthii, q. s.
Make into 4-grain pills. One to four, night and morning.

In Chlorosis, Dyspepsia, Worms, &c.—SYDENHAM.

1367. ℞ Ferri pulv. (red.) gr. xxxvj.
Pil. Aloes cum Myrrhâ, ʒj.
Olei Juniperi, ♏x.
Mix: make into a mass with mucilage, and divide into 24 pills. Two, three times a day.

In Chlorotic Amenorrhœa.—Dr. NELIGAN.

1368. ℞ Auri pulveris, ℈ij.
Ferri pulveris, ℈ij.
Pulv. Acaciæ, ʒss.
Mix: one for a dose. To be given in water slightly acidulated with dil. sulphuric acid.

As an Antidote for Corrosive Sublimate.—Dr. BUCKLER.

1369. ℞ Ferri pulv. (*Quevenne's*) vel.
Ferri Sesquiox. ℥ss.
Bismuthi Nit. ʒv.
Ext. Opii Aquos. gr. iij.
Syrup. gummos. q. s.
Mix, and divide into 125 pills. One to ten daily, during meals.

In Chlorosis, &c.—TROUSSEAU and REVEIL.

1370. ℞ Magnesiæ Calcinatæ, ℈ij.
Aquæ destillatæ, f℥vj Rub up together, and add
Pulv. Ferri Protosulph. ʒiv.
Tinct. Quassiæ, fʒij.
Mix, and divide immediately into 6 draughts. [The protoxide here formed is thought to be very efficacious. The draughts must be well secured from the air.]

Mr. DONOVAN.

1371. ℞ Ferri Oxidi Magnet. ʒss.
Potassæ Bicarbon, ℈j.
Make a powder, to be taken twice a day. [The bowels to be kept open with the pills No. 1152.]

H. J.

1372. ℞ Ferri Oxidi Magnet. ʒss.
Magnesiæ Sulphatis, ℈j ad ʒss.
Zingib. pulveris, gr. v.
Make a powder, to be taken twice a day.

H. J.

1373. ℞ Ferri Sesquioxidi,
Rhei pulveris, ana ʒj.
Pulv. rad. Calumbæ, ℈iv.
Pulv. Zingiberis, ℈ij.
Mix, and divide into 12 powders. One, three times a day.

In Tic Douloureux.—Dr. Joy.

1374. ℞ Ferri Sesquioxidi,
Confect. Aurantii, ana ℥j.
Syrupi Zingiberis, q. s.
Mix: make an electuary. A teaspoonful twice or three times a day.

In Neuralgia, &c.—Mr. Brande.

1375. ℞ Ferri Sesquioxidi,
Pulv. Cinnam. comp. ana ʒj.
Syrupi Aurantii, ℥j.
Mix: make an electuary. A tablespoonful three times a day.

Dr. Joy.

1376. ℞ Ferri Sesquioxidi, gr. x–xx.
Pulv. Aromatici, gr v.
Syrupi Zingiberis, q. s.
Make a bolus, to be swallowed two or three times a day.

Dr. Copland.

1377. ℞ Ferri Sesquioxidi, ℈ss.
Pulv. Valerianæ, ʒss.
Syrupi Zingiberis, q. s. To form a bolus.

Chlorosis, Hysteria, Chorea, &.—Mr. Brande.

1378. ℞ Ferri Sesquioxidi,
Extr. Conii, ana ʒj.
Make into 24 pills. Two, twice a day.

In Fluor Albus and Scrofula.—Dr. A. T. Thomson.

1379. ℞ Ferri perox. hyd. ℥ss.
Pulv. rad. Belladon. gr. iv.
Ext. Cichosii, ʒiiss.
Mix, and divide into 100 pills. One to ten daily, during meals.

In Chlorosis, with Gastralgia.—Trousseau and Reveil.

1380. ℞ Ferri Sesquiox.
Pulv. Calumbæ,
Bismuthi Nit. āā ʒiiss.
Mix, and divide into 20 powders. One night and morning during meals.
In Diarrhœa combined with Anæmia.—TROUSSEAU and REVEIL.

1381. ℞ Ferri Sulphatis, ℈j.
Sodæ Subcarbon. gr. xxv.
Ammon. Sesquicarb. ℈j.
Vini Aloes, f℥ss.
Spir. Myristicæ, fʒiij.
Aquæ destillatæ, f℥vij.
Mix: dose, f℥ss three times a day.
Dr. DRUITT.

1382. ℞ Ferri Sulphat. gr. xv.
Potas. Carbon. gr. xxv.
Aquæ Rosæ, f℥viiss.
Syrupi Aurantii, f℥ss.
Make a mixture. Two tablespoonfuls three times a day.
In Tic Douloureux, &c.—Mr. M'DONOUGH.

1383. ℞ Ferri Sulphat. gr. ij.
Ammon. Sesquicarb. gr. v.
Mist. Gentianæ comp. ℥j.
Make a draught, to be taken three times a day.
A mild Tonic and Stimulant.—Dr. W. DUNCAN.

1384. ℞ Extr. Rhataniæ, ʒiiss.
Ferri Sesquiox. ʒiiss.
Syrupi Tolutani, ℥xvj.
Mix: take a spoonful from four to six times a day. (Shake before each dose.)
In Blennorrhœa, &c.—RICORD.

1385. ℞ Myrrhæ pulv. ℈j.
Ferri Sulphat. gr. iss.
Sodæ Carbon. gr. iv.
Tinct. Croci, fʒj.
Aquæ Menthæ pip. f℥iss.
Make a draught, to be taken three times a day.
Dr. JOY.

1386. ℞ Misturæ Ferri comp. f℥iss.
Aquæ Cinnamomi, f℥ss.
Make a draught, to be taken three times a day.

1387. ℞ Misturæ Ferri comp.
Decocti Aloes comp. ana ℥iv. Take fʒj three times a day.
Emmenagogue.—Dr. DRUITT.

1388. ℞ Mist. Ferri co.
Infus. Quassiæ, āā ℥vj.
Mix: two tablespoonfuls twice a day. (To restore the tone of the stomach, after proper use of purges.)
In Atonic Dyspepsia.—Dr. ROSS.

1389. ℞ Pil. Ferri comp.
Pil. Aloes cum Myrrhâ, ana ʒj.
Mix: divide into 24 pills. Two or three, twice a day.

1390. ℞ Ferri Sul. cryst. ʒiiss.
Reduce to a powder, and dry by a heat graduated to 104° F.; then add
Potass. Carb. sicc. ʒiiss.
Mellis defæc. gr. lxxv.
Mix, and divide into 50 pills. One to ten during the day.
In Anæmia.—BLAUD.

1391. ℞ Ferri Carbon. Saccharati, ʒss.
Pulveris Myrrhæ, gr. xxiv.
Pulveris Aromatici, ʒss.
Mix: divide into twelve equal parts. One, three times a day.
In protracted Diarrhœa of Children.—Dr. NELIGAN.

1392. ℞ Ferri carb. cum Saccharo,
Sodæ Bicarbon. ana ℈ss.
Bismuthi Nitratis, gr. v.
Make a powder, to be taken three times a day. [After bleeding, counter-irritants, and gentle salivation.]
In Cirrhosis of the Liver.—Dr. D. J. CORRIGAN.

1393. ℞ Ferri Sulphatis exsic. ʒss.
Sacchari purificati, ʒiij.
Acidi Tartarici, ʒss. Mix, and divide into 12 parts.

℞ Sodæ Bicarbon. ʒij.
Sacchari purif. ʒiij.
Mix, and divide into 12 powders. One of each to be dissolved in half a glassful of water, then mixed, and drunk immediately.

2. Combinations of oxide of iron with the vegetable acids and with lactic acid.

Ferri Acetas (liquidus), 4 to 24 minims.
Tinctura Ferri Acetatis, 30 to 60 minims.
Tinct. Ferri Acet. Ætherea, 5 to 20 minims.
Ferri Citras, *Ferri Ammonio-Citras*, 4 to 8 grains.
Ferri et Quinæ Citras, 3 to 5 grains. *Syrupus*, 1 to 2 drachms.
Ferri Lactas, 1 to 5 grains. *Syrupus F. Lact.*, 2 to 4 drachms.
Ferri Malas impurum (Ext. Ferri Pomatum), 5 to 10 grains.
Ferri Tanas, 2 to 3 grains three times a day, gradually increasing the dose.
Ferri Valerianas, 1 or 2 grains.
Tinct. Ferri Aurantiaca, 30 to 40 minims.
Vinum Ferri, 1 to 4 drachms; children 10 to 60 minims.
Mistura Ferri Aromatica, 1 to 2 ounces.

1394. ℞ Ferri Citratis, gr. xij.
Syrupi Zingiberis, fʒiij.
Aquæ, f℥iiiss. Mix. Dose, f℥ss three times a day.
Dr. DRUITT.

1395. ℞ Ferri Citratis, ʒss.
Syrupi Aurantii, fʒv.
Aquæ fl. Aurantii, ʒiij.
Mix: a teaspoonful in a wineglassful of water two or three times a day.
In Rickets, &c.—Dr. G. GREGORY.

1396. ℞ Ferri Ammonio-Citrat. ʒj.
Aquæ fl. Aurantii, f℥viiss.
Syrupi simplicis, f℥ss.
Make a mixture. A tablespoonful every four hours.
Dr. NELIGAN.

1397. ℞ Ferri Citratis, ℈ij.
Acidi Citrici, ʒij.
Aquæ destillatæ, f℥viij. Make a mixture.

℞ Potassæ Bicarbon. ʒij.
Syrupi Aurantii, f℥j.
Aquæ destillatæ, f℥vij.
Make a mixture. Take two tablespoonfuls with an equal quantity of the above mixture, three times a day.
In Amenorrhœa, &c.—Dr. E. RIGBY.

1398. ℞ Ferri Citratis, ʒss.
Ammoniæ Sesquicarb. ʒss.
Tinct. Cardam. comp.
Syrupi simplicis, sing. fʒiij.
Mix: give a sixth part three times a day.
In Debility, with Acidity and Flatulence.—Dr. DRUITT.

1399. ℞ Ferri Ammonio-Citr.
Ammoniæ Sesquicarbon. ana gr. v.
Aquæ, ℥j.
Make a draught, to be taken every fourth hour. [The ulcers to be touched with Acid. Nitric. Dilutum.]
In Stomatitis Ulcerosa.—Dr. F. W. MACKENZIE.

1400. ℞ Ferri Ammonio-Citr. ʒiss.
Infusi Calumbæ, f℥xj.
Tinct. Cardam. comp. fʒvj.
Tinct. Lyttæ, ʒiiss. Mix: two tablespoonfuls twice a day.
Dr. G. BIRD.

1401. ℞ Ferri Ammonio-Citrat. gr. xvj.
Liq. Ammoniæ, fʒss.
Syrupi, fʒiij.
Misturæ Camphoræ, f℥vss.
Make a mixture. A fourth part twice a day.
Sir B. BRODIE.

1402. ℞ Ferri Ammonio-tart. ʒj.
Aquæ, f℥vss.
Syrupi simpl. f℥ss. Mix: f℥j three times a day.
In Albuminuria.—Dr. C. LEES.

1403. ℞ Ferri Ammonio-tart ℈ij.
Aquæ destillatæ, f℥vj.
Syrupi Hemedesmi, f℥ij.
Make a mixture. Two tablespoonfuls three times a day.

Dr. NELIGAN.

1404. ℞ Ferri Ammonio-tart. ʒss-ʒj.
Infusi Rhei, fʒxij.
Infusi Aurantii comp. f℥viiss.
Potas. Bicarb. fʒij.
Spir. Ammon. Arom. ʒiv. Mix: a sixth part twice a day.

H. J.

1405. ℞ Ferri Ammonio-tartr. ʒss.
Decocti Aloes comp. ℥ivss.
Aquæ, f℥ivss.
Spir. Ammon. Arom. fʒiv.
Liq. Potassæ, fʒij. Mix: a sixth part twice a day.

H. J.

1406. ℞ Ferri Potassio-tartr. gr. vj.
Pulv. Cinnamomi comp. gr. ij.
Mix: make a powder, to be taken three times a day.

As a Tonic for Children.—Dr. G. GREGORY.

1407. ℞ Ferri Potassio-tartr. ℈ss.
Pulv. Calumbæ, gr. xij.
Pulv. Aromatici, gr. iv.
Mix: make a powder, to be taken three times a day.

Dr. JOY.

1408. ℞ Ferri Potassio-tartr. gr. ij.
Pulv. Aromatici, gr. iss.
Sacchari albi, gr. ij.
Mix: make a powder, to be taken three or four times a day.

As a Tonic for Children.—Drs. EVANSON and MAUNSELL.

1409. ℞ Ferri Pot.-tart.
Potassii Iodidi, āā ʒiiss.
Aquæ Cinnamomi, fʒiiss.
Syrupi, ℥xvj.
Aquæ, ʒij.
Dissolve the salts in the water; add the syrup, and shake the phial. Two to six tablespoonfuls every day.

In Scrofula with Chlorosis.—TROUSSEAU and REVEIL.

1410. ℞ Vini Ferri, fʒij.
Infusi Gentianæ comp. f℥iss.
Tinct. Cinnamomi comp. fʒj. Make a draught.

Dr. G. CLARK.

1411. ℞ Vini Ferri, f℥ss.
Tinct. Aloes comp. fʒvj.
Tinct. Castorei, fʒij.
Mix: a teaspoonful in a wineglassful of infusion of chamomile flowers, three times a day.

Emmenagogue.—Dr. JOY.

1412. ℞ Vini Ferri, f℥iss.
Spir. Ætheris comp. ℥ss.
Mix: a teaspoonful three times a day in water.
In Dysmenorrhœa.—Dr. Locock.

1413. ℞ Ferri Malatis, ʒj.
Aquæ destil. ʒxij. Make a solution. Dose, fʒj.
Tonic.—Spielman.

1414. ℞ Tinct. Ferri Aurantiacæ, ℥iss.
Syrupi Hemedesmi, f℥ss. Mix. Dose, fʒj.
Mr. Gore.

1415. ℞ Misturæ Ferri Aromaticæ, f℥viij.
Spir. Ammon. Aromat. fʒij.
Potassæ Bicarbon. ʒiss.
Rhei pulveris, ℈ss. Mix: a tablespoonful twice a day.
H. J.

1416. ℞ Extr. Hyoscyam. ʒss.
Ferri Valerianat. ʒj.
Mix: divide into 30 pills. One, three times a day.
In Chorea and Neuralgia.—Dr. H. Green.

1417. ℞ Ferri Valerianatis, gr. xij.
Olei Sabinæ, ♏xij.
Mannæ, q. s. Make 6 pills. One, three times a day.
In Chorea, and other Nervous Disorders.—Dr. Neligan.

1418. ℞ Ferri Lactatis, ʒj.
Pulv. Glycyrrhizæ, ʒj.
Mellis, q. s.
To form 40 pills: from one to six to be taken daily.
In Debility and Indigestion.—M. Trousseau.

3. Compounds of oxide of iron with nitric, phosphoric, and sulphuric acid: compounds of iron with chlorine.

Ferri Pernitratis Liquor, D., 5 to 30 minims. Kerr's weaker Sol., 20 to 60.
Ferri Phosphas, 5 to 10 grains.
Ferri Biphosphas (Dr. Routh's), 1 or 2 grains twice a day.
Syrupi Ferri Biphosphatis, 12 to 24 minims.
Ferri Sulphas, 1 to 5 grains.
Ferri et Aluminæ Bisulphas (Sir James Murray's), 6 to 10 grains.
Ferri et Ammoniæ Sulpho-tartras (Aikin's), 1 to 6 grains.
Ferri Chloridum, 1 to 4 grains in the day.
Tinctura Ferri Sesquichloridi, 10 to 30 minims.
Tinct. Ferri Sesquichl. Ætherea, 5 to 20 minims.
Ferri Ammonio-chloridum, 3 to 15 grains.
Tinctura F. Ammonio-chloridi, 15 to 60 minims.

1419. ℞ Ferri Pernitratis Liquor. f℥iij.
Syrupi simpl. f℥v.
Aquæ destillatæ, f℥iij.
Mix: a tablespoonful every six hours.

In Chronic Mucous Diarrhœa, Leucorrhœa, &c.

Dr. NELIGAN.

1420. ℞ Ferri Subphosphatis, ʒss ad ℈ij.
Potassæ (*vel* Sodæ) puræ, gr. iij.
Extracti Aloes, gr. iv.
Pulv. Glycyrrhizæ, ℈ss.
Albuminis Ovi, q. s.
Make 12 pills. Two every three or four hours.

In Cancer.—Mr. CARMICHAEL.

1421. ℞ Ferri Phosphatis, gr. xxx.
Myrrhæ pulveris, gr. xij.
Sacchari puri, gr. vj.
Mix: divide into 6 powders. One, morning and noon.

In Scrofulous Diseases of the Bones, in Children.

Dr. NELIGAN.

1422. ℞ Ferri Sulphatis exsic.
Extracti Gentianæ, ana ʒss.
Make a mass, and divide into 12 pills. One or two, three times a day.

In Anæmia.—Dr. HOOPER.

1423. ℞ Ferri Sulphatis, gr. xij.
Myrrhæ pulveris, ℈ij.
Conf. Rosæ, q. s. Make 12 pills. One, three times a day.

In Phthisis.—Dr. JOY.

1424. ℞ Ferri Sulphatis, gr. vj.
Opii pulveris, gr. j.
Mucilag. q. s.
Make a mass, and divide into 12 pills. One to be taken every third hour.

In Hæmatemesis.—Dr. GRAVES.

1425. ℞ Ferri Sulphatis, ʒss.
Ext. Gentianæ, ℈j.
Piper. Cayen. ℈ij.
Olei Cassiæ, q. s.
Make 24 pills. Two, night and morning.

In weakness of Sight, with general debility.

Sir W. ADAMS.

1426. ℞ Ferri Sulph. gr. ij.
Pulv. Aloes, gr. j.
Pulv. Aromat. gr. v.
Mix: make 2 pills. To be taken three times a day.

In Gastrodynia (following meals).—Dr. ABERCROMBIE.

1427. ℞ Ferri Sulphatis exsic. ℈j.
Pilulæ Aloes cum Myrrhâ, ʒj.
Olei Rutæ, ♏vj.
Mix: make a mass, and divide into 24 pills. Two, twice a day.
In Chlorosis.—Dr. NELIGAN.

1428. ℞ Ferri Sulphatis, ℈j.
Extracti Cinchonæ, ʒj.
Divide into 20 pills. One, three times a day.
As a tonic in Scrofulous habits.—Mr. BRANDE.

1429. ℞ Ferri Sulphatis, gr. ij.
Acidi Sulp. diluti, gutt. x.
Sacchari albi, ʒj.
Aquæ f℥j. Mix: fʒj three or four times a day.
In the advanced stage of Cholera Infantum.
Dr. CHAPMAN.

1430. ℞ Ferri Sulphatis, gr. xij.
Acidi Sulphurici dil. fʒj.
Tinct. Cardamomi comp. f℥ss.
Infusi Rosæ comp. f℥vss.
Mix: two tablespoonfuls two or three times a day.
Dr. DRUITT.

1431. ℞ Ferri Sulphatis, ℈ij.
Aquæ Cinnamomi,
Aquæ destillatæ, ana ℥viij. f℥ij twice a day.
In Worms.—Dr. E. G. CLARK.

1432. ℞ Ferri Sulphatis, gr. xvj ad ʒss.
Magnes. Sulphatis, ʒvj ad ʒix.
Acidi Sulphurici dil. fʒiv.
Infusi Gentianæ comp. f℥viij.
Mix: a tablespoonful, twice a day, in water.
H. J.

1433. ℞ Ferri Sulphatis, gr. vj ad xij.
Magnesiæ Sulphat. ʒj–vj.
Acidi Sulphurici dil. fʒj.
Infusi Aurantii comp. f℥xij.
Mix: a sixth part twice a day.
H. J.

1434. ℞ Ferri Sulphatis,
Quinæ Disulphatis,
Extr. Anthemidis, ana ℈j.
Olei Anthemidis, gutt. vj.
Mix: make 20 pills. One, three times a day.
Dr. GOLDING BIRD.

1435. ℞ Ferri Sulphatis, ʒij–iij.
Acidi Nitrici, ʒiij.
Rub up together for a quarter of an hour, and add by degrees
Aquæ destil. f℥iss. Mix. Dose, five to twelve drops.
Mr. TYSON.

1436. ℞ Ferri et Aluminæ Bisulphat. gr. v.
Aquæ Cinnamomi, f℥iss.
Mix: make a draught, to be taken every second or third hour. [The dose of the salt may be gradually increased to ℈ss.]

In Diarrhœa, with Debility.—Sir JAMES MURRAY.

1437. ℞ Ferri Protochloridi, gr. xij.
Pulv. rad. Gentianæ, ℈j.
Mix: and divide into 12 pills. From one to four to be taken daily.

In Scrofulous Eruptions.—BIETT.

1438. ℞ Tinct. Ferri Sesquichlor. fʒij.
Syrupi Zingiberis, ℥j.
Aquæ, f℥vij.
Mix: two spoonfuls two or three times a day.

DR. DRUITT.

1439. ℞ Tinct. Ferri Sesquichlor. ♏xij.
Aquæ tepidæ, ℥iss.
Make a draught. Repeat every fourth of an hour until nausea supervenes, or the urine flows.

In Retention of Urine, and Dysuria.—DR. JOY.

1440. ℞ Tincturæ Ferri Sesquichlor. ♏v.
Infusi Quassiæ,
Aquæ Cinnam. ana fʒvj.
Tinct. Calumbæ, fʒj.
Mix: make a draught, to be taken morning and noon.

In Atonic Dyspepsia.—Mr. BRANDE.

1441. ℞ Tinct. Ferri Sesquichlor. ♏xx.
Infusi Quassiæ, ℥j. Make a draught.

In Hæmaturia.—Dr. G. JOHNSON.

1442. ℞ Tinct. Ferri Sesquichl.
Tinct. Cantharidis, ana fʒij.
Tinct. Capsici, fʒj.
Syrupi Croci, fʒiij.
Aquæ Menthæ, fʒvj.
Two spoonfuls two or three times a day. [After proper local and general treatment.]

In Acne Rosacea.—Dr. BURGESS.

1443. ℞ Tinct. Ferri Sesquichlor. f℥ss.
Infusi Quassiæ, f℥xiij.
Tinct. Calumbæ, f℥iss.
Magnes. Sulphatis, ℥ij. Mix: a wineglassful every morning.

In Impetigo, in the Old and Debilitated.—Dr. NELIGAN.

1444. ℞ Tinct. Ferri Sesquichl. f℥ss.
Aquæ, ℥viij. Make an enema.

For Ascarides.—Dr. DARWALL.

1445. ℞ Ferri Ammonio-chloridi, ʒiij.
Mucilag. q. s. Mix: and divide into 60 pills.

1446. ℞ Ferri Ammonio-chloridi, ʒj.
Aloes pulv. ʒss.
Extracti Gentianæ, ʒss.
Mix: and divide into 30 pills. Two, three times a day.

Tonic and Aperient.—Dr. JOY.

1447. ℞ Ferri Ammonio-chlor. ʒiss.
Extr. Conii, ʒj.
Pulv. Capsici, ʒss.
Extr. Aconiti, gr. iv.
Camphoræ rasæ, gr. xv.
Extr. Aloes purif. ℈j.
Syrupi, q. s.
Rub up well together, and divide into 48 pills. Three, three or four times a day.

In Cancer.—Dr. COPLAND.

1448. ℞ Tinct. Ferri Ammonio-chl.
Tinct. Humuli, ana ʒss.
Misturæ Camphoræ, f℥iss.
Make a draught, to be taken twice a day. Every night, going to bed, take a 5-grain pill Pil. Coloc. et Hyos. (Colocynth and hyoscyamus.)

In Indigestion, with Sluggish Bowels, and Nervous Irritation.
Sir H. HALFORD.

1449. ℞ Infusi Quassiæ, f℥ss.
Tinct. Ferri Ammonio-chlor. fʒss.
Ammoniæ Sesquicarb. gr. vj.
Syrupi Aurantii, fʒj.
Aquæ destillatæ, fʒvij.
Make a draught, to be taken two or three times a day.

For Hysterical Women.—Sir B. BRODIE.

4. Compounds of Iron with bromine, iodine, cyanogen, sulphur.

Ferri Bromidum, 1 to 4 grains.
Ferri Iodidum, 1 to 5 grains.
Syrupus Ferri Iodidi, 12 to 60 minims; Dr. THOMSON'S, 20 to 60 minims.
Ferri Iodidum Saccharatum, 6 to 24 grains.
Pilulæ Ferri Iodidi (U. S.), 1 to 2 pills; LESLIE'S, 1 to 3 pills.
Ferri Percyanidum, 2 to 6 grains.
Ferri Protosulphuretum; freely, as an antidote to corrosive sublimate.
Ferri Persulphuretum; for the same.
Syrupus Ferri Sulphureti, CAZENAVE'S, ½ an ounce.

1450. ℞ Bromidi Ferri, ℈ss.
G. Acaciæ pulv. ℈j.
Confec. Rosæ, gr. x.
Mix correctly, and make 20 pills. Two, morning and evening.

In Scrofula, Hypertrophy of the Heart, and as an Emmenagogue.
MAGENDIE.

1451. ℞ Ferri Bromidi, ʒj.
Ext. Glycyrrhizæ, q. s.
Make 60 pills. One or two, morning and evening.

In Scrofula, Hypertrophy of Womb, &c.—WERNECK.

1452. ℞ Ferri Bromidi, ʒj.
Syrupi fl. Aurantii, f℥ss.
Aquæ fl. Aurantii, f℥iss.
Mix: make a solution. A teaspoonful every six hours, in a wineglassful of bitter infusion.

In Secondary Syphilis, with Debility, and in Anæmia.
Dr. NELIGAN.

1453. ℞ Ferri Iodidi, gr. xv (*vel* Syr. F. Iod. fʒiij).
Tinct. Calumbæ, f℥j.
Aquæ destillatæ, f℥vij.
Mix: two tablespoonfuls two or three times a day.

In Chlorosis in Strumous Habits.—Dr. ASHWELL.

1454. ℞ Ferri Iodidi, gr. ij.
Ext. Glycyrrhizæ, gr. iij.
Make a pill, to be taken every night.

In Amenorrhœa, &c.—Dr. E. RIGBY.

1455. ℞ Syr. Ferri Iodidi, fʒj. (THOMSON'S?)
Olei Morrhuæ, ʒiij.
Aquæ, q. s.,
To make a draught, to be taken two or three times a day.

In Chronic Gout and Rheumatism, in exsanguineous habits.
Dr. H. W. FULLER.

1456. ℞ Syr. Ferri Iod. (THOMSON'S), fʒj. (or ♏xxxvj. L.)
Acidi Nitrici, ♏iij.
Tinct. Rosæ (SQUIRE'S), fʒj.
Infus. Aurantii comp. f℥iss. Make a draught.
Dr. A. T. THOMSON.

1457. ℞ Syrupi Ferri Iodidi, fʒij.
Syrupi Zingiberis, f℥j.
Aquæ destillatæ, f℥v. Dose, f℥ss three times a day.
Dr. R. M'GREGOR.

1458. ℞ Ferri Percyanidi, gr. xv.
Extracti Valerianæ, gr. xlv.
Make 24 pills. One, three times a day, with infusion of Valerian.

In Chorea.—M. FAIVRE D'ESSNANS.

1459. ℞ Ferri Percyanidi, gr. iij.
Syrupi, f℥j.
Make a draught, to be taken three times a day.

In Chorea and Epilepsy.—Dr. JOY.

1460. ℞ Ferri Percyanidi,
Pulv. Guaiaci, ana ʒss.
Mix, and divide into 12 powders. One, three times a day.

In Intermittents.—ELLIS.

1461. ℞ Ferri Percyanidi pulv. gr. v.
Mucilaginis, ʒij.
Aquæ, ℥ij. Make an enema, to be used daily.

For Ascarides of the Rectum.

5. For external use.

1462. ℞ Ferri Sulphatis, ℥j.
Aquæ destillatæ, f℥xvj.
Make a lotion. To be applied by compresses, renewed every two or three hours.

In Erysipelas.—Prof. VELPEAU.

1463. ℞ Ferri Sulphatis, ʒij.
Adipis, ℥j.

In Erysipelas.

1464. ℞ Ferri Sulphat ʒj.
Aquæ destillatæ, ℥viij. A lotion.

For Sore Nipples.—Dr. UNDERWOOD.

1465. ℞ Ferri Phosphatis, ʒij.
Ferri Arseniatis, ʒss.
Ung. Cetacei, ʒvj. Make an ointment.

Mr. CARMICHAEL.

1466. ℞ Ferri Limat. gr. xv.
Iodinii, gr. xv.
Aquæ destil. ℥vj. Boil together, strain, and add
Syrupi Acaciæ, ʒj. Make an injection.

In Gonorrhœa.—M. TROUSSEAU.

1467. ℞ Ferri Phosphatis, ʒiv.
Pulv. Conii, ʒij.
Mix: to be sprinkled on the surface of the sore.

In Open Cancers.—Dr. R. REECE.

1468. ℞ Ferri Iodidi, ʒj.
Adipis, ℥j. Mix.

PIERQUIN.

FICI. *Figs.*

Figs, the fruit of Ficus Carica (Nat. Ord. *Moraceæ*), are nutritive, demulcent, and somewhat laxative. *Externally,* boiled in milk or toasted, they are applied to gum-boils to promote suppuration. Figs are ingredients in decoctum hordei compositum, and confectio sennæ.

1469. ℞ Rad. Althææ, ℥j.
Ficorum, No. ij vel iij.
Aquæ, Oij.

Boil to a pint, and strain. Make an emollient gargle.

In Inflammatory Sore Throat, Fevers, &c.—Dr. BUCHAN.

FILIX MAS. *Male Fern.*

The root (rhizome) and buds of Nephrodium Filix Mas (Nat. Ord. *Filicales*) are anthelmintic, and especially successful in expelling the tape-worm. The rhizome should be collected in September, the buds in May.

Dose of the freshly powdered root, from one to three drachms; of *Tinctura Filicis Ætherea*, one to two drachms; *Extractum* vel *Oleum Filicis* (obtained by evaporating an ætherial tincture of the buds or roots), ten to thirty grains; *Decoctum Filicis*, four ounces.

1470. ℞ Decocti Filicis, ℥iv.
Ætheris Sulphurici, ʒj.

Make a draught: to be taken in the morning, and afterward, without delay, inject the following enema: Decocti filicis, f℥x, Ætheris, fʒj. After an hour, administer Ol. Ricini, f℥ij.

In Tape-worm.—BOUDIER.

1471. ℞ Pulv. rad. Filicis, ʒiij.

Divide into three doses. Write: one powder to be taken every hour stirred up in tea; taking between each dose two tablespoonfuls of castor oil. Solid food to be abstained from for some days previously.

In Tape-worm.—Dr. WAURUCH.

1472. ℞ Olei Filicis Maris, ♏xxx.
Mist. Amygdalæ, f℥ij.

Make an emulsion, and divide into two equal portions. Take one, going to bed, and the other, the morning following. [An active cathartic to be given in four hours after the second dose, if it do not purge.]

Dr. NELIGAN.

1473. ℞ Extr. Filicis rad. (per Æth.) ʒj.
Pulv. radicis Filicis, q. s.

To form 8 boluses. The patient having dined on broth only on the previous day, let him take in the morning, fasting, two boluses every quarter of an hour; and two hours after the last dose let him take two ounces of syrup of æther, and two hours later an emulsion with three (query two) drops of croton oil.

1474. ℞ Extr. Æth. Filicis Maris, ʒss.
Mellis Rosæ, ℥ss.
Take half on going to bed, the other half in the morning, fasting. [To be followed by a cathartic.]

Dr. DUNGLISON.

FRAXINUS. *Ash.*

The bark of Fraxinus excelsior, the common ash, has been used as a substitute for cinchona in larger doses; and the leaves have been proposed as a substitute for senna. More recently the leaves have been highly commended for the cure of rheumatism, rheumatic gout, &c. For the latter purpose, a drachm of the leaves, gathered in June, and carefully dried and pulverized, is infused in a pint of boiling water till cold, and strained. Of this infusion a teacupful may be taken twice a day.

As a *purgative*, half an ounce is infused for a dose.

FUCUS.

For *Fucus Crispus*, Irish Moss, see CHONDRUS CRISPUS.

Fucus Vesiculosus, bladder sea-wrack, was formerly used in goitre, and in scrofulous affections. Prepared in the same manner as burnt sponge, it was given in doses of five or ten grains, sometimes increased to sixty. The fresh fucus, bruised, is applied to scrofulous tumors.

Fucus (*Gigartina*) *Helminthocortos*, Corsican Moss, is given to expel worms, especially lumbrici. Mr. Farr thought it useful in cancer.

Dose of *Pulvis Helminthocorti*, twenty to sixty grains; *Decoctum*, one to two ounces; *Infusum*, a wineglassful; *Gelatina*, a drachm or more.

1475. ℞ Helminthocorti, ℥ss. Boil with
Aquæ puræ, ℥vj, and strain.
Collaturæ, ℥iv. Add
Mellis despumati, ℥j. Two spoonfuls morning and evening.

In Worms.—SCHUBARTH.

FULIGO LIGNI. *Wood-soot.* FULIGOKALI.

The use of wood-soot is nearly obsolete in this country, but it seems to be a favorite remedy with some practitioners on the continent. The more shining portions are selected. *Internally,* it is given in hysterical affections, chronic rheumatism, catarrh of the bladder, &c. *Externally*, it is applied for the cure of itch and various skin diseases, and to cancers. In chronic eruptions, the crusts should first be removed by emollient applications, &c. It has also been recommended as an application to burns.

Fuligokali is prepared from wood-soot in a similar manner to *Anthrakokali*, and is prescribed in similar cases and doses. Mr. E. Wilson finds it useful in psoriasis palmaris.

1476. ℞ Tinct. Fuliginis, f℥ss.
Misturæ Camphoræ cum Magnesiâ, f℥ss.
Syrupi Aurantii, ℥j.
Make a mixture: an ounce every hour until the spasms abate.

In Hysteria.—Dr. NELIGAN.

1477. ℞ Fulig. ligni, ʒj ad ʒiiss.
Coffææ tostæ, ʒiiss.
Aquæ ferventis, ℥ij.
Macerate for an hour, strain, and add
Syr. Absinthii comp. ʒx. To be taken in four doses.

To destroy Lumbrici.—M. TROUSSEAU.

1478. ℞ Fuliginis ligni, gr. xxx.
Pil. Assafœtidæ comp. ℈j.
Olei Valerianæ, ♏x.
Mix, and divide into 12 pills. Two, three times a day.

In Hysteric Neuralgia of Females.—Dr. NELIGAN.

1479. ℞ Extr. Fuliginis Aquosi, gr. iv.
Make a pill, to be given three or four times a day.

In Catarrh of the Bladder.—RADIUS.

1480. ℞ Fulig. ligni depur. ℥ij.
Aquæ, lbj.
Coque per sex sexagess. Filter through paper. The injection to be used twice a day.

In Catarrh of the Bladder.

1481. ℞ Fulig. ligni, ʒj.
Adipis, ℥ij. Make an ointment.

In Favus and Alopecia.—Dr. BURGESS.

1482. ℞ Fulig. ligni,
Adipis, ana ℥ss.
Extr. Belladonnæ, ʒj. Mix thoroughly.

Applied on Lint to Cancers.—BLAUD.

1483. ℞ Fulig. ligni, ℥j.
Aquæ, ℥v.
Boil for a quarter of an hour, and strain. Make an enema.

In Ascarides.—M. TROUSSEAU

1484. ℞ Fuligokali, gr. xv–xxx.
Adipis, ℥j. Rub up together, and make an ointment.
In Obstinate Cutaneous Affections.—GIBERT.

FUMARIA. *Fumitory.*

Fumitory, Fumaria officinalis (Nat. Ord. *Fumariaceæ*), is little used; yet most valuable therapeutic properties have been attributed to it. It has been used in jaundice, diseases of the eyes, scorbutic complaints, and severe chronic affections of the skin. Cullen found it useful in lepra, as well as in less intractable cutaneous diseases.

Dose of the *Pulvis Fumariæ*, ten to forty grains; *Extractum*, five to twenty grains; *Tinctura*, one or two drachms; *Succus*, two ounces.

1485. ℞ Fumariæ sic. manip. j.
Rad. Taraxaci, ℥j.
Rad. Glycyrrhizæ, ℥ss.
Aquæ, Oij.
Boil to one pint, and strain. A cupful to be taken two or three times a day.
In Obstinate Cutaneous Diseases.—Dr. T. CASTLE.

1486. ℞ Tinct. Fumariæ, ʒvj.
Sodæ Bicarbon. ʒiij.
Misturæ Camphoræ, f℥vj.
Two spoonfuls three times a day.
In Indigestion, with Nervousness.—Dr. R. REECE.

GALBANUM.

This fetid gum is the concrete juice of an undetermined plant; as a medicine it may be regarded as intermediate between ammoniacum and assafœtida. *Internally*, it is taken as a stimulant, expectorant, and antispasmodic. *Externally*, it is applied to promote suppuration, and soften induration.

Dose, five to twenty grains; but rarely alone. It is conjoined with aloes and chalybeates, in amenorrhœa, and sluggish bowels; with expectorants, in chronic affections of the chest; and with other fetids, in hysterical and spasmodical complaints.

Dose of *Pil. Galbani compositæ*, ten to twenty grains; *Tinct. Galbani*, one drachm to one and a half.

1487. ℞ Pil. Galbani comp.
Pil. Ferri compos. ana ʒj.
Make 24 pills. One, twice a day.

R. J. C.

1488. ℞ Pil. Galbani comp.
Pulv. Zingiberis, ana gr. ij.
Pil. Rhei comp. gr. v.
Olei Anthemidis, ♏j.
Make 2 pills, to be taken going to bed.

In Indigestion, with Flatulence.—Dr. G. GREGORY.

1489. ℞ Galbani, ʒij.
Aceti Scillæ,
Aquæ Fœniculi, ana f℥ij.
Liq. Ammoniæ acet. fʒij.
Ætheris Nitrici, fʒj.
Syrupi Althææ, f℥ss
Make a mixture. A tablespoonful three or four times a day.

In Humid Asthma.—JAHN.

1490. ℞ Ferri Sulphatis,
Potassæ Sulphatis, ana ʒj.
Galbani,
Assafœtidæ, ana ʒiss.
Ext. Gentianæ, ʒij.
Pil. Aloes cum Myrrhâ, ʒiij.
Theriacæ, q. s.
Beat into a mass, and divide into 150 pills. Two or three, two or three times a day.

In Chlorosis, with Anæmia and Palpitation.—Dr. COPLAND.

1491. ℞ Emplas. Galbani, ʒiij.
Camphoræ, ʒss.
Opii pulv. ℈j.
Ol. Carui, gtt. xx. Make a plaster.

In Tormina in Infants.—Dr. R. REECE.

1492. ℞ Tinct. Galbani,
Tinct. Castorei,
Spir. Ammoniæ Arom.
Tinct. Aloes comp. ana ℥ss.
Mix: two teaspoonfuls twice a day in ginger tea.

In Nervous Irritation, with Indigestion.—Dr. LUKE.

[For other Prescriptions, see No. 264, p. 66; No. 271, p. 67; No. 1149, p. 209.]

GALIUM APARINE. GALIUM VERUM.

The juice and decoction of common cleavers or goose-grass, Galium Aparine (Nat. Ord. *Rubiaceæ*), have long been used as an aperient, diuretic, and antiscorbutic remedy, especially in the treatment of dropsy, scrofula, scorbutic eruptions, congestion of the spleen, &c. The fresh herb mixed with lard is applied to glandular and scrofulous swellings, and to ameliorate the condition of cancerous and foul ulcers.

The dose of the expressed juice is four ounces, three times a day. Recently its use has been revived as a remedy for cutaneous diseases in the following form :

1493. ℞ Galii Aparinis, manip. ampl. j.
Aquæ, Oij.
Boil for a third of an hour, and strain. Half a pint to be taken three times a day.

In Lepra.—Dr. WINN.

The juice and decoction of *Galium verum*, yellow ladies bedstraw, is also a popular remedy for hysterical complaints and epilepsy; *externally*, it is applied to scrofulous sores.

1494. ℞ Galii veri, ℥ij.
Aquæ ferventis, Oiss.
Macerate, and strain. A wineglassful to be taken frequently, warm.

In Cerebral Affections.—CHAUSSIER.

GALLÆ. *Nutgalls.* ACIDUM GALLICUM, ET ACIDUM TANNICUM.

Galls are excrescences found on the Dyer's Oak, Quercus infectoria (Nat. Ord. *Corylaceæ*). They are powerfully astringent, in consequence of the large quantity of tannin they contain; but are not much employed as an internal remedy. *Externally*, in infusion or decoction, galls are used in astringent gargles, lotions, and injections; and ointments prepared with finely pulverized galls are much used as an application to piles.

Dose of *Pulvis Gallæ*, eight to sixteen or twenty grains; *Tinctura Gallæ*, one to two drachms; *Infusum Gallæ*, half an ounce to, one and a half. *Unguentum Gallæ*, *Ung. Gallæ comp.*, *Ung. Gallæ et Opii* are used almost exclusively as pile ointments.

1495. ℞ Infusi Gallæ, f℥iv.
Cretæ præp. ℥ss.
Tinct. Opii, fʒss.
P. Gum. Acaciæ, ʒj.
Mix: a tablespoonful every two hours.

ELLIS.

1496. ℞ Tinct. Gallæ, f℥ss.
Mist. Amygdalæ, f℥iss.
Mist. Acaciæ, f℥ss.
Aquæ fontis, f℥v.
Mix: a tablespoonful after each liquid evacuation.

In Colliquative Diarrhœa.—Dr. NELIGAN.

1497. ℞ Gallæ pulv. ʒj.
Camphoræ, ʒss.
Tinct. Opii, fʒij.
Cerati, ℥j. Make an ointment.

In Piles.—Dr. HOOPER.

1498. ℞ Morphiæ, gr. ij.
Olei Olivæ, fʒij. Rub up together, and add
Ung. Zinci, ℥j.
Pulv. Gallæ, ʒj. Mix.

In painful Hæmorrhoids.—Dr. PARIS.

1499. ℞ Gallæ pulv. ʒj.
Cupri Sulphatis, ℈j.
Adipis, ℥j.

For Ring-worm of the Scalp.—(AN INDIAN REMEDY.)

1500. ℞ Pulv. Gallæ, ʒij.
Aquæ ferventis, Oj. Macerate for half an hour, and strain.

As an Astringent Gargle, Lotion, or Injection.—TADDEI.

Gallic Acid, Acidum Gallicum; and *Tannic Acid*, or *Tannin*, Acidum Tannicum, are obtained from galls, and are now very generally employed in the same cases as the galls themselves. They are powerfully astringent, and efficacious in arresting hæmorrhages and other discharges. Tannic acid is the more powerful topical astringent, and is therefore preferred to restrain hæmorrhages from the stomach and bowels, as also in gargles, lotions, and injections. But it is doubtful whether it is taken into the circulation, except so far as it may be converted into gallic acid. The latter is preferred as a remote astringent, in uterine hæmorrhage, hæmoptysis, hæmaturia, &c.

The dose of either is from two to twelve grains: as a general tonic and peptic, and in chronic fluxes, two or three grains of tannic acid is sufficient; in urgent diseases, as hæmorrhage from the stomach or bowels, from five to ten grains. To children in rickets, half a grain to one grain. In cases of chylous urine, Dr. B. Jones gives as much as twenty grains of gallic acid three times a day.

1501. ℞ Acidi Gallici, ℈ij.
Morphiæ Hydrochlor. gr. j.
Mist. Acaciæ, q. s.
Make 16 pills. One, going to bed. [To be increased to two pills if necessary.]

In Night Sweats of Phthisis.—J. H.

1502. ℞ Acidi Gallici, ℈ss.
Infusi Aurantii comp. ʒxij.
Mix: make a draught, to be taken every sixth hour.

In Albuminuria.—Mr. SAMPSON.

1503. ℞ Acidi Gallici, gr. vij.
Pulv. Acaciæ, gr. iv.
Make a powder, to be taken three times a day.

Dr. G. BIRD.

1504. ℞ Acidi Gallici, ℈ij.
Syrupi, fʒij.
Aquæ destillatæ, f℥viij.
Mix. Dose, a sixth portion, every three or four hours.

In Passive Hæmorrhage.—Dr. DRUITT.

1505. ℞ Acidi Gallici, ℈j.
Mucil. Acaciæ, fʒij.
Aquæ destillatæ, f℥iiiss.
Syrupi Rhœados, fʒij.
Make a mixture: an ounce every two or three hours.

In Hæmorrhage from the Kidneys or Bladder.—Dr. NELIGAN.

1506. ℞ Acidi Tannici, gr. xij.
Conf. Rosæ, ʒss.
Mix, and divide into 12 pills. One every six hours.

In Colliquative Sweating and Diarrhœa of Phthisis.
Dr. NELIGAN.

1507. ℞ Acidi Tannici, ʒss.
Confect. Rosæ, q. s. Make 18 pills. One every hour.

In Hæmoptysis.—COTTEREAU.

1508. ℞ Acidi Tannici, gr. xv.
Extr. Rhataniæ, ʒss.
Syrupi, q. s.
Make a mass, and divide into 20 pills. From one to ten to be taken daily in

Colliquative Sweats, Chronic Diarrhœa, Hæmorrhages, &c.
TROUSSEAU.

1509. ℞ Acidi Tannici, ℈j.
Spir. Vini Gallici, ℥ss.
Misturæ Camphoræ, f℥vss. Mix: make a gargle.
In Salivation, Spongy Gums, and Relaxed Throat.
Dr. DRUITT.

1510. ℞ Acidi Tannici, gr. xxxij.
Aquæ destillatæ, f℥viij. Make an injection.
In Obstinate Blennorrhœa.—BERAL.

1511. ℞ Acidi Tannici, ʒj.
Mastiches, ʒj.
Spir. Æther. Sulph. ℥iss.
Make a solution. To be introduced on cotton into a hollow tooth.
In Toothache.

1512. ℞ Acidi Tannici, gr. ij.
Ung. Ceræ, ℥j.
Mix: to be applied by means of a camel-hair pencil.
In Pemphigus Gangrenosus.

1513. ℞ Acidi Tannici, ℈j.
Adipis præp. ℥j. Make an ointment.
In Porrigo Scutulata.—CAZENAVE.

1514. ℞ Acidi Tannici, ʒj.
Hydr. Sulphur. cum Sulphure, ʒj.
Ung. Zinci, ℥ij.
Cerati Plumbi comp. ℥ij.
CUTANEOUS HOSPITAL.

1515. ℞ Acidi Tannici, gr. iv–xij.
Cerati Galeni (*cold cream*), ℥j. Make an ointment.
In Chronic Eczema.—Dr. NELIGAN.

1516. ℞ Acidi Tannici, gr. viij.
Carbon. Plumbi, gr. xij.
Cerati Galeni, ℥j. Mix.

1517. ℞ Acidi Tannici, ʒss.
Tinct. Opii, fʒij.
Aquæ destillatæ, f℥viij.
Mix: make a gargle. To be used frequently.
Mr. J. R. MARTIN.

GAMBOGIA. See CAMBOGIA.

GELATINA. GLUTEN ANIMALE.

Animal Jelly (either in the form of the finest commercial glue, or of size, or of purified gelatine) is used in emollient baths; or to diminish the acrimony of saline and sulphurous baths.

Animal gluten is one of the numerous medicines which has had its short-lived day as a fashionable remedy for intermittent fevers.

Purified gelatine, isinglass, and calves'-foot jelly are much used as articles of diet for the sick, but are seldom met with in prescriptions.

The quantity of glue or purified gelatine for a bath is from twelve to twenty-four ounces; it should be dissolved by heat in a quart of water, and the solution added to the bath.

1518. ℞ Gelatinæ purif. ℥xij.
Aquæ, Oij.
Boil for a quarter of an hour, and add the solution to a bath.
Dr. BURGESS.

1519. ℞ Gelatinii præp. (*patent size*), lbvj.
Aquæ (caloris gradu 75° ad 92° F.) Cong. xxx.
In Skin Diseases.—Dr. NELIGAN.

1520. ℞ Glutinis Anim. albi, lbij.
Aquæ tepidæ, lbvj. Dissolve, and add
Potassii Sulphureti, ℥iv. To be poured into the bath.
In Scrofula and Gout.—DUPUYTREN.

1521. ℞ Glutinis opt. (Flanders' Glue), lbj.
Sodii Chloridi, lbj.
Aquæ ferventis, q. s. Make a solution: for a bath.
MIALHE.

GENTIANA. GENTIANINA. *Gentian and Gentianine.*

The dried root of Gentiana lutea (Nat. Ord. *Gentianaceæ*) is one of the most frequently prescribed of the vegetable bitter tonics. Besides its use as a stomachic and general tonic in dyspepsia, "unconnected with inordinate irritability of the stomach," and in states of exhaustion from chronic diseases, it has been given as a febrifuge, anthelmintic, and antiseptic, and also as a remedy for gout. *Externally*, the powder is sprinkled on sloughing ulcers.

Dose of *Pulvis Gentianæ*, ten to thirty grains; *Extractum Gentianæ*, five to twenty grains; *Infusum Gentianæ*, one to two ounces; *Mistura Gentianæ comp.*, one to two ounces; *Tinct. Gent. comp.*, one to two drachms; *Vinum Gentianæ*, three to eight drachms; *Gentianina* (a mixed substance), one to three grains.

1522. ℞ Infusi Gentianæ comp. f℥ix.
Tinct. Gentianæ comp. f℥ij.
Syrupi Aurantii, f℥j.
Make a draught, to be taken twice a day.

As a Tonic.—Dr. PARIS.

1523. ℞ Infusi Gentianæ co. f℥iij.
Aquæ Cinnamomi, f℥j.
Sodæ Bicarbon. ℈ij.
Make a mixture: one-fourth part, morning and noon.

In Dyspepsia, with Acidity.—Dr. JOY.

1524. ℞ Magnesiæ Carbonat. ℈j.
Infusi Gentianæ comp.
Aquæ Cinnamomi, ana f℥vj.
Mix: make a draught, to be taken before dinner, and on going to bed.

In Dyspepsia, with Acidity.—Mr. BRANDE.

1525. ℞ Inf. Gentianæ comp. f℥v.
Tinct. Cardam. comp. ℥j.
Sodæ Subcarb. ʒss.
Mix: make a mixture. Two spoonfuls morning and noon.

In Indigestion.—Dr. MATON.

1526. ℞ Inf. Rosæ. comp.
Inf. Gentianæ comp. ana f℥vj.
Tinct. Gentianæ comp. f℥j.
Acidi Sulphurici dil. ♏x.
Mix: make a draught, to be taken three times a day.

In Dyspepsia with Nausea, &c.—Mr. BRANDE.

1527. ℞ Tinct. Gentianæ comp. f℥iss.
Tinct. Zingiberis, f℥j.
Tinct. Camphoræ comp. ʒij.
Quinæ Sulphatis, gr. xv.
Make a solution. A teaspoonful three times a day, in a little toast water.

In Chronic Dysentery and Diarrhœa of hot climates.

Dr. JAS. JOHNSON.

1528. ℞ Infus. Gentianæ comp. f℥vss.
Ferri Sulphatis, gr. iv.
Magnesiæ Sulphatis, ʒj.
Acidi Sulphurici diluti, ʒss.
Syrupi, ʒij.
Tinct. Aurantii, fʒiss.
Mix: two tablespoonfuls twice a day.

In Asthenic Palpitation.—Dr. G. GREGORY.

1529. ℞ Inf. Gentianæ comp. ℥iss.
Vini Ferri, ʒij.
Spir. Lavand. comp. ʒj.
Make a draught, to be taken twice a day.

In Relaxed Stomach and Anorexia.—Dr. HUGH SMITH.

1530. ℞ Infusi Gentianæ comp. ℥vij.
Spir. Cinnamomi, ℥j.
Acidi Sulphur. diluti, ♏xx.
Three spoonfuls, one or two hours before dinner.

Dr. PEARSON.

1531. ℞ Inf. Gentianæ comp. fʒix.
Tinct. Sennæ comp. fʒij.
Potassæ Tartratis, ʒj.
Syr. Zingiberis, fʒj.
Make a draught, to be taken twice a day.

Dr. PARIS.

1532. ℞ Extr. Gentianæ,
Ammon. Sesquicarb. ana ʒj.
Mix: make 30 pills. Two, two or three times a day.

In Obstinate Heartburn in Gouty Habits.—Mr. BRANDE.

1533. ℞ Extr. Gentianæ,
Aloes purif. ana ʒj.
Saponis Castil. ℈iss.
Mix, and divide into 36 pills. One to three, as occasion may require.

A Stomachic Laxative.—Dr. COPLAND.

1534. ℞ Extr. Gentianæ, gr. xlviij.
Olei Carui, gutt. vj.
Mix, and make 12 pills. One, once a day, an hour before dinner.

J. B. M.

1535. ℞ Gentianæ, gr. vj.
Conf. Rosæ, q. s.
Make 6 pills. One or two for a dose.

MAGENDIE.

GEOFFROYA. *Cabbage-Tree Bark.*

This bark is derived from Geoffroya inermis, and sometimes from Geoffroya Surinamensis. It is purgative, emetic, and acro-narcotic; and is only used to expel round worms. Cold water must be avoided during its operation; excessive sickness and purging require to be relieved by warm water, afterward a dose of castor oil, and lastly of opium. Seldom prescribed.

Dose, in *powder*, ten to thirty grains; *Extractum*, three grains; *Decoctum*, half ounce or ounce, for adults; half a drachm to a drachm and a half for children.

GEUM. *Avens.*

Avens or Herb Bennet (Geum Urbanum, Nat. Ord. *Rosaceæ*) is astringent, tonic, and antiseptic. It has been used as a substitute for cinchona; in agues, a drachm of the powder being given every two hours in the intermissions. A wine-glassful of an infusion, made with half an ounce of the root to a pint of boiling water, is taken as a sudorific and tonic in the latter stage of continued fevers, in diarrhœas and dysenteries.

GLYCERINA. *Glycerin.*

This liquid has the property of maintaining its moist state when exposed to the air; and is used in lotions, &c. in various skin diseases, where the object is to keep the surface in a moist and soft state.

1536. ℞ Glycerinæ, ℥ss.
Aquæ destillatæ, Oss. Make a lotion.

In Cutaneous Diseases, to keep the Skin moist.

Mr. STARTIN.

1537. ℞ Glycerinæ puræ, f℥iv.
Boracis, ʒss ad ʒj.
Aquæ Rosæ, f℥viiss.

To Chapped Hands, &c.—Mr. STARTIN.

1538. ℞ Sodæ Carbonat. ℈j.
Aquæ fl. Sambuci, f℥viiss.
Glycerinæ, f℥ss.

To allay Itching in Eruptions of the Scalp.—Dr. NELIGAN.

1539. ℞ Glycerinæ puræ, f℥ij.
Misturæ Amygdalæ, f℥vj.
Aquæ Rosæ, f℥viij. Make a lotion.

Dr. NELIGAN.

1540. ℞ Pulv. Tragacanthæ, ʒij.
Aquæ Calcis, f℥iij.
Glycerinæ puræ, f℥j.
Aquæ Rosæ, f℥iij. Make a liniment.
In Superficial Burns, Excoriations, Chaps, &c.

1541. ℞ Camphoræ pulv. ℈ss.
Glycerinæ puræ, fʒj.
Ung. Ceræ albæ, ʒvij. Make an ointment.
To allay Itching.—Dr. NELIGAN

GLYCYRRHIZA. *Liquorice.*

The root of Liquorice, Glycyrrhiza glabra (Nat. Ord. *Leguminosæ*), is demulcent and pectoral; and is used in catarrhal complaints, and in irritations of the mucous membrane of the bowels and urinary passages. The foreign extract (*Spanish or Italian Juice*) is a popular remedy for coughs. *Extractum Glycyrrhizæ*, L., D., and E., is a purer preparation; its chief use is as an excipient for pills; or as an adjunct to nauseous, especially aloetic, medicines. The root and extract are also added to decoctions of acrimonious substances, to lessen their acrimony. As a pectoral, decoctum glycyrrhizæ is taken by wineglassfuls in the above cases.

1542. ℞ Extr. Glycyrrhizæ, ℥j.
Potassæ Carbon. ʒiij.
Croci, ʒss.
Aquæ ferventis, Oij.
Macerate over night, and strain. A little to be taken frequently.
In Catarrh.—Dr. T. FULLER.

1543. ℞ Pulv. Extr. Glycyrrhizæ,
Pulv. Acaciæ, anā ʒij.
Aquæ ferventis, f℥iv. Dissolve, and add
Vini Antim. Potassio-tart. fʒij.
Tinct. Opii, ♏xx.
Make a mixture. A tablespoonful to be taken occasionally.
In Catarrhal Affections.—Dr. WOOD.

GRANATUM. *Pomegranate.*

The *rind of the fruit* of the pomegranate (Punica Granatum, Nat. Ord. *Myrtaceæ*) is astringent, and has been used in the form of decoction, in the same cases as other astringents;

but more frequently in gargles, and as an injection for leucorrhœa. It has also been given in intermittents.

The *bark of the root* (Radix Granati) is used for expelling tape-worm. For this a wineglassful of the decoction is taken every two hours, till a pint is taken. Strict diet should precede its use; and if it should not operate, a dose of castor oil is to be given.

Dose of *Pulvis cort. fr. granati*, twenty to thirty grains.

1544. ℞ Granati fr. cort. ℥ss.
Lactis Vaccinæ rec. lbiv.
Mix: boil down to lbij. Three tablespoonfuls every three hours.
In Chronic Diarrhœa.—Dr. HOOPER.

1545. ℞ Extr. Alcoh. rad. Granati, ʒvj.
Aquæ Menthæ,
Aquæ flor. Tiliæ,
Succi Limon. ana ℥ij. A fourth part every four hours.
To expel Tape-worms.—DESLANDES.

1546. ℞ Ext. Granati corticis Alcoholici, ʒvj.
Syrupi suc. Limon.
Aquæ Menth. sat.
Aquæ flor. Tilæ, āā ʒij. Mix: a tablespoonful for a dose.
For Tape-worms.—TROUSSEAU and RÉVEIL.

1547. ℞ Pulv. cort. rad. Granati, ℥ss.
Divide into 6 powders. One every half hour until the third dose is taken.
In Tape-worm.

1548. ℞ Decocti cort. rad. Granati, lbj.
Syrupi Zingiberis, ℥j.
A third part every half hour, until three doses are taken; beginning early in the morning. [The bowels should be previously cleared by castor oil.]
In Tape-worm.—Dr. JOY.

1549. ℞ Decocti fruct. Granati, f℥vij.
Mellis Boracis, f℥j. For a gargle, to be used frequently.
In Aphthous Ulceration of the Mouth and Fauces.
Dr. NELIGAN.

1550. ℞ Granati fr. cort. ʒiij.
Aquæ, Oij. Boil to a pint and a half, strain, and add
Aluminis, ʒiss.
Make an injection, to be injected two or three times a day.
In Leucorrhœa.—Dr. R. REECE.

GUAIACI LIGNUM. GUAIACUM. *Guaiacum wood, and resin.*

The shavings of guaiacum wood or lignum vitæ (Guaiacum officinale, Nat. Ord. *Zygophyllaceæ*) are alterative and sudorific. It is given in the form of decoction, in scrofula, chronic cutaneous diseases, chronic rheumatism and gout, and in syphilitic diseases.

Dose of *Decoctum Guaiaci*, two to four ounces; the wood is also an ingredient in Dec. Sarsæ compositum, and in various forms of diet-drink; and in Aqua Calcis composita, D. 1807, the dose of which is the same as the decoction.

Guaiacum, or Guaiacum resin, is obtained from the wood of the tree. It is stimulant and diaphoretic, diuretic and cathartic. It is also regarded as emmenagogue. But it is principally used as a remedy for chronic rheumatism.

Dose of *Guaiacum*, ten to twenty grains; *Mistura Guaiaci*, from one to three tablespoonfuls, two or three times a day; *Tinctura Guaiaci*, and *Tinct. Guaiaci composita* (*Ammoniata*, E.), one to two drachms; *Extractum Guaiaci ligni*, ten to thirty grains.

1551. ℞ Pulv. Guaiaci, ʒiv.
Mucilag. Acaciæ,
Syrupi simpl. ana ℥j.
Aquæ Cassiæ, ℥vj. Mix: two spoonfuls three times a day.
In Cynanche Tonsillaris.—Dr. Morris.

1552. ℞ Pulv. Guaiaci, gr. xv.
Mucil. Acaciæ, fʒj. Triturate together, and add
Potassæ Nitratis, gr. v.
Aquæ Cinnamomi, f℥x.
Syrupi Papaveris, fʒss.
Mix: make a draught, to be taken three times a day.
In Chronic Rheumatism.—Mr. Brande.

1553. ℞ Extr. Guaiaci ligni,
Extr. Sarsæ alcohol. ana ʒj.
Mix, and divide into 40 pills. To be gradually increased from two to ten pills daily.
In Cutaneous Diseases, &c.—M. Trousseau.

1554. ℞ Guaiaci (res.) gr. x.
Pulv. Ipecac. comp. gr. v.
Potassæ Nitratis, gr. x.
Confect. Rosæ, q. s.
Make a bolus, to be taken at bedtime.
In Chronic Rheumatism.—Dr. Joy.

1555. ℞ Guaiaci res. gr. xij.
Olei Sassafr. ♏v.
Theriacæ, q. s.
Make a bolus, to be taken three or four times a day.
In Chronic Rheumatism, especially if of Syphilitic origin.
Dr. Neligan.

1556. ℞ Guaiaci (resinæ),
Potas. Bitart. ana ʒss.
Mix well, and make a powder, to be taken at bedtime.
In Rheumatism, &c.—Weickard.

1557. ℞ Pulv. Guaiaci, ʒss.
Pulv. Potassæ Nitratis, ℈j.
Make a powder, to be taken at bedtime. [Some warm gruel to be taken after it.]
In Rheumatism.—Dr. Monro.

1558. ℞ Guaiaci pulv. ʒj.
Tinct. Guaiaci Ammon. f℥ss.
Pulv. Acaciæ, ʒij.
Syrupi Croci, f℥ss.
Aquæ puræ, f℥v.
Make a mixture. A fourth part twice a day.
In Chronic Rheumatism.—Dr. Hooper.

1559. ℞ Tinct. Guaiaci Ammon. f℥j.
Mist. Acaciæ, fʒiv.
Potas. Bicarbon. ʒiij.
Tinct. Cinchonæ, f℥j.
Tinct. Hyoscyami, fʒiv.
Syrupi Aurantii, fʒiv.
Decocti Cinchonæ, f℥viiiss.
Mix: two tablespoonfuls three times a day.
Dr. Roots.

1560. ℞ Tinct. Guaiaci Am. fʒij.
Misturæ Camphoræ, fʒvj.
Mist. Acaciæ,
Syrupi simp. ana fʒj.
Make a draught, to be taken three times a day.
In Chronic Rheumatism.—Dr. Joy.

1561. ℞ Tinct. Guaiaci compositæ,
Tinct. Humuli, ana f℥ss.
Decocti Cinchonæ Pallidæ, f℥ij.
Make a draught, to be taken three times a day.

Dr. DRUITT.

1562. ℞ Tinct. Guaiaci Ammon. fʒij.
Mucil. Gum. Tragacanthæ, fʒvj.
Triturate together, and add gradually
Misturæ Amygdalæ, f℥ij.
Make a mixture, to be taken during the day, in divided doses.

In Chronic Gout, Rheumatism, and Cutaneous Diseases.

Dr. NELIGAN.

1563. ℞ Tinct. Guaiaci comp.
Mellis, ana ʒj. Rub up together, and add
Aquæ Pimentæ, fʒx.
Make a draught, to be taken three times a day.

Mr. BRANDE.

1564. ℞ Guaiaci pulv.
Magnesiæ Calcin. ana gr. x.
Make a powder, to be taken as occasion may require, in a glass of water.

In Rheumatic Pains.—Dr. E. RIGBY.

1565. ℞ Guaiaci (vit. ovi s.) ℈j.
Aquæ destillatæ, ℥j.
Liq. Ammon. acet. fʒij.
Syrupi, ʒj. Mix: make a draught.

In Rheumatism.—Dr. E. J. CLARK.

1566. ℞ Pulv. Guaiaci,
Potassæ Nitratis, ana ʒj.
Pulv. Ipecacuanhæ, gr. iij.
Opii pulveris, gr. ij.
Make a powder, and divide into four portions. One to be taken every three hours in syrup or molasses.

In Rheumatism and Gout, after sufficient depletion.

Dr. WOOD (U. S.).

1567. ℞ Tinct. Guaiaci comp. fʒj.
Tinct. Serpentariæ, fʒss.
Mucilaginis, ♏xx.
Decocti Mezerei, fʒviss.
Dec. Dulcamaræ, f℥j.
Make a draught, to be taken three times a day.

In Psoriasis Guttata.—Dr. NELIGAN.

1568. ℞ Pulv. Guaiaci, ʒij.
Pulv. Rhei, ʒj.
Sulphuris subl. ʒij.
Potas. Nitratis, ʒij.
Syrupi Papaveris, q. s.
Make an electuary. Dose, half a drachm to a drachm.

In Chronic Rheumatism.—MID. HOSP.

1569. ℞ Guaiaci res. pulv. ℥iv.
Potassæ Carbon. ʒiss.
Pimentæ pulv. ℥j.
Spir. tenuioris, f℥xvj.
Digest for a few days, and strain. A teaspoonful to be taken three times a day in milk or wine.
In Dysmenorrhœa, and Idiopathic Amenorrhœa.
Dr. DEWEES (U.S.).

1570. ℞ Guaiaci pulv. ℥j.
Hydr. Bisulphureti rubri, ʒvj.
Conservæ Absinthii,
Cons. Rosæ, ana ℥j.
Syrupi Zingiberis, q. s. To form an electuary. Dose, ʒj.
In Chronic Rheumatism.—Dr. DE VALLENGIN.

HÆMATOXYLON. *Logwood.*

The shaved or rasped wood of Hæmatoxylon Campechianum (Nat. Ord. *Leguminosæ*) yields a decoction and extract which are used in medicine as an unirritating astringent, in chronic diarrhœa and dysentery, and in cholera infantum.

Dose of *Decoctum Hæmatoxyli*, one to two fluid-ounces, or two or three drachms for a child of two years old; of *Extractum Hæmatoxyli*, ten to twenty grains.

1571. ℞ Ext. Hæmatoxyli, ℈ss.
Misturæ Cretæ,
Aquæ Cinnamomi, ana fʒvj.
Make a draught, to be taken two or three times a day.
In Diarrhœa.—Mr. BRANDE.

1572. ℞ Extr. Hæmatoxyli, ʒss.
Aquæ puræ, f℥ij.
Tinct. Opii, ♏ij. Two drachms, three times a day.
In Chronic Diarrhœa.—Dr. PARIS.

1573. ℞ Decocti Hæmatoxyli, f℥vj.
Tinct. Monesiæ, f℥j.
Syrupi Aurantii, f℥j.
Make a mixture. A tablespoonful after each liquid evacuation.
In Chronic Diarrhœa and Dysentery.—Dr. NELIGAN.

1574. ℞ Decocti Hæmatoxyli, f℥iv.
Vini rubri Lusitanici, f℥j.
Acidi Nitrici diluti, ♏x.
Tinct. Opii, ♏v.
Mix: a dessertspoonful four times a day.
In Chronic Diarrhœa.—Dr. GRAVES.

1575. ℞ Extr. Hæmatoxyli, ʒj.
Decocti Cinchonæ, f℥iij.
Aquæ Cinnamomi,
Syrupi Aurantii, ana f℥ss.
Mix: a dessertspoonful every hour.

In Diarrhœa of Children.—Dr. URE.

1576. ℞ Decocti Hæmatoxyli, f℥viij.
Aluminis pulv. ʒss. Make an astringent enema.

Dr. R. REECE.

HELENIUM. See INULA.

HELLEBORUS.

The root of *Helleborus niger*, or Christmas Rose (Nat. Ord. *Ranunculaceæ*), is a hydragogue cathartic, and emmenagogue. In over-doses it acts as an irritant poison. The diseases in which it has been recommended are, mania, hypochondriasis, dropsy, epilepsy, apoplexy, amenorrhœa, cutaneous diseases, &c. But it is now seldom prescribed.

Dose of *Pulvis Hellebori nigri*, five to ten grains; *Extractum Hellebori*, U. S., five to ten grains; *Pilulæ Tonicæ Bacheri*, one or two a day as a tonic, three or four as a drastic; *Tinctura Hellebori nigri*, a drachm twice a day.

Other species have been used in medicine. HELLEBORUS FŒTIDUS, Bear's-foot, is given as a vermifuge, but requires caution.

Dose of the *powdered leaves*, five to twenty grains, for a child from three to six years old; or a fluid-ounce of a *decoction* made by boiling a drachm of the dried leaves in eight ounces of water. *Syrupus Hellebori fœtidi*, a teaspoonful at bedtime.

Dr. Norwood, U. S., highly recommends HELLEBORUS VIRIDIS as a remedy for typhus and typhoid fevers, typhoid pneumonia, and in some convulsive diseases of children with febrile symptoms; but we are not aware that it is prescribed in this country.

1577. ℞ Tinct. Hellebori nigri, fʒiss.
Infusi Sennæ comp. f℥j.
Syrupi Zingiberis, fʒij.
Mix: make a draught. To be taken early in the morning.

In Mania, or Cephalalgia, with Torpid Bowels.

Dr. NELIGAN.

1578. ℞ Extracti Hellebori Alkalini,
Extr. Jalapæ Alkalini, ana ʒss.
Zingiberis pulv. gr. x.
Mix well, and divide into 15 pills. Three, once or twice a week.
In Melancholia.—Dr. R. REECE.

1579. ℞ Tinct. Hellebori nigri,
Tinct. Castorei,
Spir. Ætheris Nitrici, ana fʒij.
Mix: 30 minims three or four times a day as occasion may require.
In Melancholia.—Dr. E. J. CLARK.

1580. ℞ Syrupi Hellebori Fœtidi,
Tinct. Rhei comp. ana ℥j.
A teaspoonful at bedtime, to be repeated in the morning.
For Worms, in Children of two to six years old.—Dr. BISSETT.

HEMEDESMUS INDICUS. *Indian Sarsaparilla.*

The root of this plant has been proposed as a substitute for sarsaparilla; it has an aromatic odor, and contains a peculiar volatilizable acid. It is supposed to be useful in affections of the mucous membrane generally, as well as to possess the sudorific and alterative properties of sarsaparilla.

Dose of *Decoctum Hemedesmi*, a wineglassful two or three times a day; of *Syrupus Hemedesmi*, one to two ounces; *Infusum Hemedesmi* (two ounces in a pint of aqua calcis for an hour), a wineglassful three or four times a day.

1581. ℞ Liq. Potassæ, fʒss to fʒj.
Aquæ fl. Aurantii, f℥j.
Syrupi Hemedesmi, f℥v.
Two tablespoonfuls three times a day in decoction of barley.
In Gonorrhœa.—Mr. H. BELLINAYE.

1582. ℞ Decocti Hordei comp. f℥x.
Syrupi Hemedesmi, f℥ij.
Make a mixture: two tablespoonfuls now and then.
In Inflammation of Mucous Membranes.—Dr. NELIGAN.

1583. ℞ Syrupi Hemedesmi, f℥iv.
Tincturæ Tolutanæ, f℥ss.
Tinct. Camphoræ comp. fʒj.
Vini Ipecacuanhæ, fʒiij.
Aquæ, f℥iij.
Make a mixture: a tablespoonful every second hour.
In Chronic Bronchitis.—Dr. NELIGAN.

HORDEUM. *Barley.*

Pearled Barley (the decorticated seeds) is much used in the form of Decoctum Hordei, and Dec. Hordei compositum, as a mild demulcent and slightly nutritive drink, in catarrh, febrile complaints, &c. *Decoctum Malti* and *Extractum Malti* are considered more supporting, and have been given in chronic affections of the chest, diseases of debility, &c.

HUMULUS. See LUPULUS.

HYDRARGYRUM. *Quicksilver.*

The compounds of mercury are alterative, deobstruent, cathartic, antiphlogistic, anthelmintic, and antisyphilitic. They are all of them (with the exception, perhaps, of the sulphurets) capable of inducing a state of mercurialism, of which salivation is the prominent symptom. Their action requires to be carefully watched. Some of the preparations of mercury are corrosive poisons; and most of them are capable of doing serious injury when incautiously used.

Mercurials are supposed directly to promote the secretion of bile, or its flow into the intestines. They increase the effect of diuretics and diaphoretics. The following are the principal preparations, and their doses:

Pilula Hydrargyri: as an alterative, three to five grains; as a cathartic, eight to fifteen grains, but usually conjoined with purgatives, or followed by them; as a sialogogue, five grains three times a day, till the gums are affected, adding a little opium, if necessary, to prevent the pills from acting on the bowels.

Hydrargyrum cum Cretâ, and *Hydr. cum Magnesiâ:* these are mild preparations, yet capable of producing salivation by their continued use. Dose, five to thirty grains; or two to five grains for children. They are much employed in diseases of children attended with deficient biliary secretion.

Hydrargyri Protoxidum (*nigrum*, vel *cinereum*). Rarely used as an internal remedy in this country. On the continent it is given in infantile syphilis, cutaneous eruptions, and croup. Dose, from one-eighth to half a grain. The dose for an adult, prepared according to Mr. Tyson's method, is from a quarter of a grain to one grain.

Hydrargyri Deutoxidum (*Oxidum rubrum*). Dose, from quarter of a grain to half a grain. Rarely prescribed.

Hydrargyri Precipitatum Nigrum (Hahnemann's soluble mercury). From half a grain to a grain.

Hydrargyri Sulphuretum cum Sulphure (Æthiops Mineral). Alterative in skin diseases, scrofula, &c., and as a vermifuge. Dose, five to forty grains.

Hydrargyri Sulphuretum: this is also alterative and vermifuge. Dose, from five to thirty grains. It is used in fumigations, to produce speedy salivation.

Hydrargyri Chloridum (Calomel). It is impossible to specify here the cases in which this remedy is given, or the intentions it is designed to effect. Dose, as an alterative, half a grain to a grain, every or every other night; as an antiphlogistic, three to five grains; as a cholagogue cathartic, three to six grains; but as its operation is uncertain, it is usual to combine it with vegetable purgatives, or to follow it with a draught of salts and senna. In some cases, as in cholera, yellow fever, &c., calomel has been given in scruple doses. *Pilula Hydrargyri Chloridi composita*, five to ten grains; *Pilulæ Calomelanos et Opii*, one or two pills repeatedly.

Hydrargyri Bichloridum. Corrosive sublimate. A few grains are sufficient to cause death. It is given as an alterative, in lepra and other chronic cutaneous diseases, old ulcers, chronic rheumatism, visceral diseases, and in syphilis. Dose, from one-twentieth or one-sixteenth of a grain to one-eighth, two or three times a day. *Liquor Hydrargyri Bichloridi*, half a fluid-drachm to two drachms.

Hydrargyri Ammonio-chloridum (white precipitate). This is for outward use only.

Hydrargyri Bromidum (*Sub-bromidum*). A grain twice a day.

Hydrargyri Perbromidum; from one-twentieth to one-fourth of a grain.

Hydrargyri Bicyanidum; one-sixteenth to one-eighth of a grain.

Hydrargyri Iodidum (*flavum*, aut *viride*); one to three grains.

Hydrargyri Biniodidum (*rubrum*); from one-sixteenth to one-eighth of a grain.

Hydrargyri Acetas; from one-sixth of a grain to one grain.

Hydrargyri Proto-nitras; one-tenth of a grain.

Hydrargyri Phosphas; one-sixth to half a grain.

Hydrargyri Sulphas flavus; quarter to half a grain as an alterative; as a rough emetic, two to four grains; one grain with five of starch as an errhine.

Hydrargyri et Quinæ Chloridum; half a grain three times a day as a sialogogue.

Potassii Hydrargyro-Iodidum (Dr. Channing, U. S.) is employed as the iodide. It is soluble in water, and given in doses of one-twelfth to one-twentieth of a grain.

We shall arrange the prescriptions in the above order; except that the *external applications* will be more conveniently placed together at the end.

1584. ℞ Pilulæ Hydrargyri, ʒj.
Divide into 12 pills. One, three times a day.

In Syphilis, and Chronic Inflammation of the Liver.—Dr. JOY.

1585. ℞ Pil. Hydrargyri,
Extracti Rhei, ana ʒj.
Mix thoroughly, and divide into 30 pills. One, twice a day.

In Indigestion, with Confined Bowels, and Inactive Liver.
Mr. BRANDE.

1586. ℞ Pilulæ Hydrargyri, gr. x.
Pulv. Ipecac. comp. gr. v.
Mix, and divide into 3 pills. One every four hours. Administer a purgative enema.

In Jaundice, with tenderness of the Liver.—Dr. GRAVES.

1587. ℞ Pil. Hydrargyri, gr. iij.
Ext. Hyoscyami, gr. iij.
Ipecac. pulveris, gr. j.
Make 2 pills, to be taken every night.

Dr. DRUITT.

1588. ℞ Pil. Hydrarg. gr. ix.
Sodæ Carbonatis, gr. vj.
Extr. Taraxaci, gr. xij.
Extr. Hyoscyami, gr. iij.
Mix: make 6 pills. One every second or third day, half an hour before dinner.

In Pityriasis.—Dr. NELIGAN.

1589. ℞ Pil. Hydrargyri,
Pil. Aloes compos. ana gr. xxiv.
Syr. Zingiberis, q. s.
Mix, and divide into 10 pills. One every night at bedtime.

In Flatulent Indigestion, with Liver Derangement.
Dr. AINSLIE.

1590. ℞ Pil. Hydrargyri, gr. iij.
Pulv. Scillæ, gr. j.
Pulv. Digitalis, gr. j.
Make a pill, to be taken noon and evening.

In Ascites.—Dr. G. GREGORY.

1591. ℞ Pil. Hydrargyri, ℈j.
Ext. Coloc. comp. ʒss.
Mix, and divide into 10 pills. Two every other night, or as occasion requires.

Dr. JOY.

1592. ℞ Pil. Hydrarg. gr. iij.
Pulv. Ipecac. gr. ss–j.
Ext. Coloc. co. gr. ij.
Ext. Hyoscy. gr. ij.
Sapon. dur. gr. j.
Mix: make 2 pills, to be taken at bedtime. [To be followed in the morning by a draught of Senna and Taraxacum.]

In Duodenal Dyspepsia.—Dr. COPLAND.

1593. ℞ Ung. Hydrarg. fort. ʒj.
Pulv. Sarsæ rad. ʒj.
Mix, and divide into 40 pills. One, morning and evening. [To be afterward increased to four a day.]

In Secondary Syphilitic Affections.—M. CAZENAVE.

1594. ℞ Ferri Sesquioxidi, ʒj.
Hydrargyri, ʒij.
Conf. Rosæ rubr. ʒiij.
Rub up together until the globules can no longer be distinguished.

Tonic, Alterative, and Sialogogue.—Dr. COLLIER.

1595. ℞ Hydrarg. cum Cretâ, ʒj.
Pulv. Ipecac. comp. ℈ij.
Magnesiæ Carbon. ʒss.
Triturate well together. Four to six grains to be taken as a sedative for children.

Dr. COPLAND.

1596. ℞ Hydrarg. cum Cretâ, ℈ss.
Pulv. Cretæ comp. ℈j.
Pulv. Tragac. comp. ʒss.
Divide into 10 equal parts. One every fourth hour.

In Diarrhœa (for infants of four or six months old).—Dr. URE.

1597. ℞ Hydr. cum Cretâ, ʒss.
Ipecac. pulveris, ℈ss.
Rhei pulveris, ℈ij.
Pulv. Cinnamomi comp. ℈ss.
Sacchari albi, ʒj.
Mix, and divide into 10 powders. One, two or three times a day.

As a Deobstruent, for Infants.—Dr. JOY.

1598. ℞ Hydrarg. cum Cretâ, gr. ij.
Rhei rad. pulv. gr. iv.
Pulv. Cinnam. comp. gr. j.
Make a powder, to be taken once a week. Give twice a day ten minims of wine of iron in a little water.

In Cachexiæ of Children.—Dr. OKES.

1599 ℞ Hydrarg. cum Cretâ, gr. vj.
Pulv. Ipecacuan. gr. ij.
Sacchari purificati, gr. xij. A fourth part every six hours.

In Aphthæ of Infants.—Dr. G. GREGORY.

1600. ℞ Hydr. cum Cretâ, gr. xij.
Pulv. Scammonii, gr. xij.
Carbonatis Sodæ siccatæ, gr. vj.
Pulv. Cinnamomi comp. gr. xij.
Mix: divide into 6 equal portions. One every morning.

Alterative and Cathartic for Children, and in Worms.
Dr. NELIGAN.

1601. ℞ Hydrargyri cum Cretâ, ʒj.
Olei Terebinthinæ, fʒj.
Pulv. Acaciæ, ʒss.
Aquæ, f℥ij.
Mix: a teaspoonful to be taken every two hours.

In a form of Miasmatic Fever, of Children.
Dr. UPSHUR (U.S.).

1602. ℞ Hydrarg. Oxidi nigri (Tyson's), ʒj.
Confect. Rosæ, ʒiij.
Pulv. Anthemidis, ʒss. Mix: as a substitute for Blue Pill.
Mr. TYSON.

1603. ℞ Hydrarg. Precipit. nigri (Hahnemann's), ℈ij.
Pulv. rad. Glycyrrhizæ, ℈ij.
Make 40 pills. One to be taken morning and night, to be afterward increased to four a day.

In Syphilides.—M. CAZENAVE.

1604. ℞ Hydr. Oxidi rubri, gr. j.
Opii, tertiam grani partem,
Olei Caryophylli, ♏j.
Make a pill, to be taken at bedtime for a week.
Sialogogue.—JOHN HUNTER.

1605. ℞ Hydrargyri Chloridi, gr. x.
Scammon. pulveris,
Jalapæ pulv. ana ℈j.
Sacchari albi, ℈ij. Mix, and divide into ten equal parts.
As a Purge for Children.—Mr. BRANDE.

1606. ℞ Hydrargyri Chloridi, ℈ss.
Butyri recentis, q. s.
Make a bolus: to be placed at the root of the tongue.
In Apoplexy.—Dr. COPLAND.

1607. ℞ Hydrarg. Chloridi, gr. iij.
Pulv. Jacobi, gr. iij.
Extr. Coloc. comp. gr. iv.
Extr. Hyoscyami, gr. ij. Divide into 2 pills, for a dose.
Dr. JOY.

1608. ℞ Hydrargyri Chloridi, gr. iv.
Pulv. Antimonii comp. gr. viij.
Opii purificati, gr. j.
Mix, and divide into 4 pills. One every six hours with an effervescent saline draught.
At the Commencement of Fevers.—Dr. G. GREGORY.

1609. ℞ Extracti Colocynthidis, ʒss.
Pulv. Scammonii, ℈j.
Hydr. Chloridi, gr. xij.
Mix: make 12 pills. Take one at night, as often as the bowels are bound up.
Dr. PEREIRA.

1610. ℞ Hydrarg. Chloridi, gr. ij.
Jalapæ, gr. vj.
Pulv. Camphoræ, gr. iij.
Pulv. Zingiberis, gr. vj.
Olei Cassiæ, gutt. ij.
Make a powder, to be taken once or twice a week in gruel.
In Dysmenorrhœa.—Dr. ASHWELL.

1611. ℞ Hydrargyri Chloridi, ℈j.
Opii pulveris, gr. v.
Conf. Rosæ, q. s. Make 20 pills. One morning and night.
In Syphilitic Cases.—Dr. A. T. THOMSON.

1612. ℞ Hydrargyri Chloridi, gr. xij.
Pil. Gambogiæ comp.
Extr. Colocynth. comp. ana gr. xv.
Syr. Zingiberis, q. s.

Make 12 pills. Two at bedtime, as occasion requires.

In Obstinate Costiveness.—Dr. JOY.

1613. ℞ Hydrarg. Chloridi,
Extr. Colchici acet.
Aloes purificatæ, ana gr. j.
P. Ipecacuanhæ, gr. ij.

Make a pill, to be taken every four hours. [After two or three pills have been taken, give one or two doses of Decoct. Aloes compositum.]

In Gout.—Mr. A. WHITE.

1614. ℞ Hydrarg. Chloridi, gr. iv.
Extr. Colocynth. comp. gr. viij.

Make two pills, to be taken at bedtime.

℞ Mist. Gentianæ comp. f℥x.
Magnes. Sulphatis, ℥iij.
Tinct. Jalapæ, f℥j.
Spir. Ammon. arom. f℥ss.

Make a draught, to be taken in the morning.

In Torpidity of the Liver (in strong constitutions).
Dr. G. GREGORY.

1615. ℞ Hydrargyri Chloridi, gr. j.
Pulv. Digitalis, gr. ss.
P. Tragacanth. co. gr. vj.

Mix: make a powder. One every sixth hour, for a child of two or three years old.

In Hydrocephalus.—Dr. URE.

1616. ℞ Hydrargyri Chloridi, gr. xij.
Pil. Hydrargyri, gr. xxiv.
Pulv. Scillæ, gr. xxxvj. Mix, and divide into 12 pills.

Sir A. COOPER.

1617. ℞ Hydrargyri Bichloridi, gr. iv.
Opii purificati, gr. viij.
Extr. Guaiaci, ℥ss.

Make 24 pills. One pill three times a day, with compound Decoction of Sarsaparilla.

In Syphilis.—DUPUYTREN.

1618. ℞ Hydrargyri Bichloridi, gr. iij.
Alcoholis, q. s. Dissolve, and add
Extracti Conii, ℥j.

Mix, and divide into 60 pills. Six pills to be taken in the day, and the quantity gradually increased to nine or ten.

In Herpetic Eruptions.—KOPP.

1619. ℞ Hydrargyri Bichloridi, gr. j.
Gluten. veg. recent. gr. xv. Rub together, and add
Pulv. Acaciæ, gr. iv.
Pulv. Althææ, gr. viij.
Mix, and divide into 10 pills. One, twice a day.

1620. ℞ Hydrargyri Bichloridi, gr. j.
Aquæ destillatæ, ♏x. Rub up together, and add
Pulv. Digitalis, ℈j.
Extr. Glycyrrhizæ, ʒss.
Beat into a mass, and divide into 16 pills. One, twice a day after meals.

C. L.

1621. ℞ Liq. Hydr. Bichloridi, fʒj.
Tinct. Cinchonæ, fʒj.
Aquæ destillatæ, ℥j.
Make a draught, to be taken twice a day.

In Opacity of the Cornea.—Dr. J. C. Hall.

1622. ℞ Hydrarg. Bichloridi, gr. j.
Tinct. Opii, ʒj.
P. Gum Acaciæ, ʒiij.
Aquæ destillatæ, ℥vj.
Mix: a tablespoonful to be taken night and morning.

In Rheumatic Amaurosis.—Langenbeck.

1623. ℞ Hydrargyri Bichloridi, gr. j.
Tinct. Rhei,
Tinct. Cinchonæ, ana f℥j.
Mix: a teaspoonful to be taken twice a day.

Sir A. Cooper.

1624. ℞ Hydrargyri Bromidi (Per-bromidi), gr. ss.
Decoct. Dulcamaræ, f℥viij.
Mix: two tablespoonfuls to be given three times a day.

In Obstinate Secondary Syphilitic Eruptions.—Dr. Neligan.

1625. ℞ Hydrargyri Cyanidi, gr. vj.
Opii pulv. ℈ss.
Micæ panis, ʒj.
Mellis, q. s.
Make 96 pills. One to be taken morning and evening.

M. Parent.

1626. ℞ Hydrargyri Cyanidi, gr. viij.
Aquæ destillatæ, ℥viij.
Dose, one or two drachms a day in milk and water, or gruel.

In the same cases as Liq. Hydr. Bichloridi.—M. Parent.

1627. ℞ Hydrarg. Proto-iodidi, ʒss.
Extr. Lactucæ, ℈ij.
Extr. Guaiaci, ʒj.
Extr. Sarsæ, q. s.
Make 72 pills. One to be taken daily at first, afterward two.

M. Biett.

1628. ℞ Hydrarg. Protiodidi, gr. xv.
Ext. Opii Aquos. gr. iv.
Ext. Guaiaci, ʒj.
Conf. Rosæ, q. s.

Make a mass, and divide into 100 pills. One to four daily.

In Secondary and Tertiary Syphilis.

TROUSSEAU and REVEIL.

1629. ℞ Hydrarg. Iodidi, ℈j.
Aloes Socot.
Ferri Sulphat. exsic.
Myrrhæ pulveris, ana ʒss.
Olei Sabinæ, gutt. xx.

Mix, and divide into 24 pills. One, three times a day.

In Amenorrhœa.—Dr. BARBOUR.

1630. ℞ Hydrarg. Iodidi Viridis, gr. ij.
Hydrarg. cum Cretâ, gr. xij.
Pulv. Aromatici, gr. ix.

Mix, and divide into 6 powders. One, every morning. [For a child of two years old.]

In Cutaneous Eruptions of Infancy and Childhood.

Dr. NELIGAN.

1631. ℞ Hydrarg. Iodidi, gr. j.
Extr. Juniperi, gr. xij.
Pulv. Glycyrrhizæ, q. s.

Mix, and divide into 8 pills. Begin with two, morning and evening; afterward increase to three or four.

In Scrofula, with Syphilis.—M. BIETT.

1632. ℞ Hydrarg. Iodidi viridis, gr. iv.
Hydrarg. cum Cretâ, gr. xij.
Sodæ Carbon. exsic. gr. xij.
Pulv. Myrrhæ, gr. vj.
Mucil, q. s. Make 12 pills. One to be taken three times a day.

In Chronic Impetigo.—Dr. NELIGAN.

1633. ℞ Hydrarg. Biniodidi, gr. j.
Extr. Glycyrrhizæ, gr. xxxij.

Mix thoroughly, and divide into 16 pills. One, night and morning.

In Syphilis.—Dr. JOY.

1634. ℞ Hydrarg. Biniodidi (rubri), gr. j.
Extr. Sarsæ,
Extr. Gentianæ, ana ℈j.

Mix, and divide into 10 pills. One, three times a day.

In Psoriasis.—Dr. BURGESS.

1635. ℞ Hydrargyri Acetatis, ʒss.
Camphoræ pulv. ʒss.
Opii pulveris, gr. xxx. [℈ss Dr. Joy.]
Syrupi Papaveris, q. s.
Mix, and divide into 30 pills. One, night and morning.
In Syphilis.—Mr. Carmichael.

1636. ℞ Hydr. Acetatis,
Mannæ,
Acaciæ pulv. ana ℈j.
Aquæ Rosæ, q. s. Make 20 pills. Three at bedtime.
In Syphilis.—Keyser.

1637. ℞ Hydrarg. Phosphatis, gr. j.
Opii pulveris, gr. j.
Antim. Potassio-tartratis, gr. ¼.
Make a pill, to be taken every night.
Dr. Hunt.

1638. ℞ Hydrargyri et Quinæ Chloridi, gr. xv.
Opii pulveris, gr. vj.
Micæ panis, q. s.
Mix well, and divide into 30 pills. One, three times a day.
As a Sialogogue.—Dr. Hamilton.

External Applications.

The following preparations for external use are contained in the L., E., or D. pharmacopœias:

Unguentum Hydrargyri.
Ceratum Hydrargyri compositum.
Linimentum Hydrargyri.
Emplastrum Hydrargyri.
Emplastrum Ammoniaci cum Hydrargyro.
(These contain metallic mercury.)
Unguentum Hydrargyri Nitrico-oxidi.
Unguentum Hydrargyri Iodidi.
Unguentum Hydrargyri Iodidi rubri.
Unguentum Hydrargyri Ammonio-chloridi.
Unguentum Hydrargyri Nitratis.
Unguentum Hydrargyri Nitratis mitius.
Liquor Hydrargyri Pernitratis (D.).

Ointments.

1639. ℞ Ung. Hydrarg. fortioris, ℥j.
Rub a drachm of this ointment on the inside of the thigh, before the fire, every night, until ptyalism is produced.
To produce Salivation, in Syphilis, &c.—Dr. Pereira.

[To salivate children, spread diluted mercurial ointment on a flannel roller, and place it around one of the child's legs. It cures syphilis without any inconvenience, whereas very few children recover to whom mercury is given internally.]

1640. ℞ Ung. Hydrarg. ℥j.
Glycerinæ, ʒj.
Make an ointment. Smear the ointment over the inflamed parts, and over the sound parts beyond, twice in twenty-four hours.

In Erysipelas.—Dr. NELIGAN.

1641. ℞ Ung. Hydrarg. ℥j.
Pulv. Amyli, ʒij.
Mix: make an ointment. To be smeared over the parts, and renewed as it peels off.

To prevent Pitting in Small-pox.—Prof. BENNETT.

1642. ℞ Ung. Hydrarg. ℥ij.
Ammoniæ Muriatis pulv. ʒj. Mix well.

In Glandular Enlargements.—DUPUYTREN.

1643. ℞ Ung. Hydrarg. fort. ℥j.
Camphoræ, ʒss.
Pulv. Opii, ʒj.
Mix, and make an ointment. Rub into the affected side.

In Pleurisy.—Dr. BLAKISTON.

1644. ℞ Hydrarg. cum Cretâ, ʒss.
Cerati Cetacei, ℥j. Make an ointment.

In Excoriations of the Anus.—Dr. QUAIN.

1645. ℞ Hydrarg. Oxidi nigri, ℈ss.
Adipis suilli, ʒj. Mix thoroughly: make an ointment.

In Blennorrhœa of the Eyes.—BLASIUS.

1646. ℞ Hydrarg. Oxidi nigri, ℥j.
Adipis suilli, ℥xvj.
Subject to a temperature of 300° to 320° for an hour, stirring constantly; then remove and stir till cold.

(As a substitute for Ung. Hydrargyri. But it seems still undetermined in what state mercury penetrates the human skin.)

Mr. DONOVAN.

1647. ℞ Hydrarg. Binoxidi, ʒss.
Camphoris, gr. iv.
Axungiæ, ℥j. Mix: make an ointment.

In Papular Eruptions of the Face.—Dr. BURGESS.

1648. ℞ Hydrarg. Chloridi, ℈j to ʒj.
Adipis præparati, ℥j. Make an ointment.

In most Chronic Eruptions.—Dr. BURGESS.

1649. ℞ Hydrarg. Chloridi, ℈ss.
Adipis, ℥j. Mix: make an ointment.

In Chronic Herpes Labialis.—Dr. NELIGAN.

1650. ℞ Hydrarg. Protiodidi, gr. xij–xxiv.
Axungiæ, ℥j. Mix: make an ointment.

In Syphilitic Eruptions and Inveterate Scaly Diseases.
Dr. BURGESS.

1651. ℞ Hydrarg. Iodidi, ℈ij–℈iv.
Axungiæ, ℥ij. Mix: make an ointment.

To old Venereal Sores and Scrofulous Ulcers.—M. LUGOL.

1652. ℞ Hydrarg. Biniodidi, gr. xij.
Axungiæ, ℥j. Mix: make an ointment.

In Syphilitic Eruptions and Inveterate Scaly Diseases.
Dr. BURGESS.

1653. ℞ Hydrarg. Iodidi rubri, gr. xv.
Adipis, ℥ss. Mix: make an ointment.

In Lupus.—BLASIUS.

1654. ℞ Hydrarg. Iodidi rubri, ℈j.
Adipis, ℥iss. Mix: make an ointment.

To Venous Ulcerations.—M. BIETT.

1655. ℞ Hydrarg. Iodidi rubri, gr. xv.
Adipis, ℥ij.
Olei Bergamotæ, gtt. x. Mix: make an ointment.

In Chronic Cutaneous Affections.—M. BIETT.

1656. ℞ Unguenti Hydrargyri Biniodidi, ʒj.
Unguenti Picis liquidæ, ʒvj. Mix.

In Porrigo Scutulata.—Mr. ERICHSEN.

1657. ℞ Hydrarg. Iodidi rubri, in pulv. subtiliss. gr. $\frac{1}{8}$–$\frac{1}{2}$.
Adipis, ℈ij.
Ceræ albæ, gr. ij. Mix: make an ointment.

As an Eye Salve.—KOPP.

1658 ℞ Hydrarg. Protonit. ℈j.
Axungiæ, ℥j. Mix: make an ointment.

In Lepra and Psoriasis.—Dr. BURGESS.

1659. ℞ Unguenti Hydrarg. Nitratis, ʒj.
Olei Amygdalæ dulcis, ʒvij.
Mix: make an ointment. To be used twice a day.

To Hæmorrhoids.—Mr. COULSON.

1660. ℞ Hydrarg. Cyanidi, gr. xij (gr. xvij. BIETT).
Axungiæ, ℥j. Mix: make an ointment.

To Syphilitic Sores.—BRERA.

Plasters.

1661. ℞ Unguenti Hydrarg. ℥j.
Gum. Ammoniaci, ʒvj.
Extracti Belladonnæ, ʒiv.
Acidi Hydrocyan. dil. ♏xxx.
(Make a mass with the Ammoniac, and extract with a little water; mix the ointment and acid, and rub the whole together.)

As an application to Scirrhous and Scrofulous Tumors.

1662. ℞ Unguenti Hydrargyri, ℥j.
Olei Terebinthinæ,
Camphoræ, ana ʒij.
Cerati simplicis, ℥j. Mix well, and make a plaster.

As a rubefacient application over the region of the Liver, when blisters cannot be used. DR. ELLIS (U.S.).

Liniments.

1663. ℞ Unguenti Hydrargyri, ʒiv.
Olei Amygdalæ dulcis, ℥vj.
Tincturæ Opii, ʒiij.
Mix: make a liniment. To be used two or three times a day.

To Inflamed Ulcers of the Glans Penis.—ST. MARIE.

1664. ℞ Unguenti Hydrarg. Nitratis, ℥iss.
Cerati simplicis, ℥viiss.
Olei Olivæ, ℥v. Mix: make a liniment.

MANCHESTER INFIRMARY.

1665. ℞ Hydrarg. Acetatis, ʒj.
Olei Olivæ, ʒij.
Axungiæ, ʒvj. Mix well, and make a liniment.

In Herpes.—VAN MONS.

1666. ℞ Merc. Sublim. corros.
Camphoræ, ana gr. xij.
Alum. crud.
Sach. Saturni, ana ℈j. Mix by trituration, and add
Acet. concent. ʒij.
To this solution, poured in a glass vessel, add
Ætheris Sulph. ʒj, and shake up. (*Plenck's liniment.*)

For Syphilitic Condylomata.—DR. FRICKE.

Lotions.

1667. ℞ Hydrarg. Chlor. ʒj.
Aquæ Calcis, ℥xij. Mix, to form a lotion. (Black wash.)

To Venereal Sores.

1668. ℞ Hydrarg. Chlor. ʒj.
Liquoris Calcis, ℥vss.
Misturæ Acaciæ, f℥ss. Mix, to form a lotion.

To Indolent and Venereal Sores.—DR. HOOPER.

1669. ℞ Hydrarg. Bichloridi, gr. xv.
Liquoris Calcis, lbj. Mix: make a lotion. (Yellow wash.)
Externally to Syphilitic Sores.

1670. ℞ Hydrarg. Bichloridi, gr. ij.
Spiritus tenuioris, ℥j. Mix: make a lotion.
To prevent Bed-sores.—Sir B. BRODIE.

1671. ℞ Hydrarg. Bichloridi. gr. j.
Mist. Amygdalæ, ℥vj. Mix: make a lotion.
To Irritable Eruptions, as Lichen.—Dr. JOY.

1672. ℞ Hydrarg. Bichlor. gr. j–iij.
Emuls. Amygd. amar. ℥vj. Mix: make a lotion.
In Favus.—GOWLAND.

1673. ℞ Hydrarg. Bichlor. gr. j.
Acid. Hydrocyan. ʒj.
Emuls. Amygdalæ, ℥vj. Mix: make a lotion.
In Lichen.—Dr. BURGESS.

1674. ℞ Hydrarg. Bichlor. gr. ij.
Acidi Hydrocyan. ʒij.
Emuls. Amygd. amar. ℥x. Mix: make a lotion.
For Chronic Eruptions with Itching.—Dr. BURGESS.

1675. ℞ Hydrarg. Bichlor. gr. ij.
Acidi Muriatici, ♏ij.
Misturæ Camphoræ, ℥viij. Mix: make a lotion.
In Sycosis.—Dr. L. WRIGHT.

1676. ℞ Hydrarg. ʒss.
Acidi Nitrici, ℥j. Dissolve, and add
Aquæ puræ, lbiiss.
Mix: make a lotion. [Half an ounce to be applied every morning for three weeks, or till the complaint is cured.]
In Psora and Prurigo.—Dr. JOY.

1677. ℞ Ung. Hydrarg. Nitrat. ℥j.
Olei Coc. palmat. ℥ij.
Liquoris Calcis, ℥iij.
Mix: make a lotion. To be applied night and morning.
In Herpes of Children.—Mr. C. HOGG.

1678. ℞ Hydrarg. deutobromidi, gr. vj.
Aquæ destillatæ, Oj. Mix: make a lotion.
For Syphilitic Chancres.—WERNECK.

Collyria.

1679. ℞ Hydrarg. Bichlor. gr. j.
Aquæ destillatæ, f℥viij. Make an eye-wash.
Mr. MACKENZIE.

1680. ℞ Hydrarg. Bichlor. gr. ij.
Pulv. Opii, gr. x.
Aquæ Rosæ, ℥iv. Dissolve, and add
Mucilag. Cydoniæ, ℥ss. Mix: make an eye-wash.

VAN MONS.

Injections.

1681. ℞ Hydrarg. Bichlor. gr. j.
Aquæ destillatæ, ℥viij. Mix.

As an Injection in Gonorrhœa when the constitution is not very irritable. Mr. BRANSBY COOPER.

1682. ℞ Hydrarg. Bichlor. gr. iv.
Aquæ destillatæ, ℥viij. Mix: make an injection.

In Gonorrhœa.—Mr. WALLACE.

1683. ℞ Hydrarg. Bichlor. gr. iij.
Aquæ Rosmarini,
Aquæ destillatæ, ana ℥iij. Dissolve.

To be used as an Injection in Fistula Lachrymalis.—BEER.

Gargles.

1684. ℞ Hydrarg. Cyanidi, ℈ss.
Mellis Rosæ, ℥j.
Decoc. Hordei, Oj. Mix: make a gargle.

BRERA.

1685. ℞ Hydrarg. Cyanidi, ℈ss.
Decoc. Lini, vel.
Decoc. Althææ, Oj. Mix: make a gargle.

In Syphilitic Sore-throat.—M. PARENT.

Baths.

1686. ℞ Hydrarg. Bichlor. ʒij.
Glycerinæ, ℥ij.
Aquæ pluvialis (caloris grad. 90° F.) cong. xxx.
Dissolve, to make a mercurial bath.

In Syphilitic Eruptions.—Dr. NELIGAN.

1687. ℞ Hydrarg. Iodidi rubri, ʒj.
Sodii Chloridi, ℥ij.
Aquæ pluvialis (caloris grad. 96° F.) cong. xxx.
Mix: make a bath.

In Obstinate Syphilitic Eruptions.—Dr. NELIGAN.

Caustic Applications.

1688. ℞ Hydrarg. Bicyanidi, gr. iij.
Aquæ destillatæ, ℥j.
Mix: to be applied to the part repeatedly with a camel-hair pencil.

In Lupus.—M. CAZENAVE.

1689. ℞ Calomelanos, gr. cc.
Arsenici Oxidi albi, gr. j.
Mix thoroughly. A small quantity to be sprinkled over the surface in Lupus.

DUPUYTREN.

1690. ℞ Hydrarg. Nitrat. acidæ, ʒij.
Pulv. Tragacanthæ, q. s. To form a mass.

Caustic Paste for Cancer and Lupus.—Dr. NELIGAN.

1691. ℞ Hydrarg. Oxidi rubri,
Aluminis usti, ana ʒss.
Pulv. Sabinæ, ʒij. Mix.

As an application to Whitlow, Condyloma, &c.

1692. ℞ Cinnabaris,
Pulv. Sang. Draconis, āā ℥ss.
Pulv. Acid. Arsen. gr. xlv.
Mix accurately. (A powerful caustic, to be made into a paste with water or saliva at the moment of being applied.)

In Lupus, Cancer, &c.—ROUSSELOT.

Powders for outward use.

1693. ℞ Calomelanos,
Pulv. Sacchari, ana ʒss.
Pulv. Opii, gr. x. Mix. To be blown into the eye.

In Ulcers of the Cornea.—RADIUS.

1694. ℞ Hydrarg. Bichlor. ℈j.
Oxidi Zinci, ʒj.
Pulv. Amyli Ind. ℥j.
Mix. The part, previously well cleaned, to be repeatedly dusted with the powder.

For Ill-conditioned Ulcers, Eczema, &c.—Dr. KELLY (U. S.).

1695. ℞ Hydrarg. Oxidi Nitrici,
Amyli, ana ʒss.
Sacchari puri, ℥j.
Mix well, by rubbing together, and form a subtile powder. To be blown into the eye three or four times a day.

In Thickening of the Cornea.—Dr. NELIGAN.

1696. ℞ Hydrarg. Sulphatis, gr. j.
Pulv. Asarabaccæ, ʒiss.
Mix, and divide into 8 powders. One to be used as an errhine twice a day.

In Gutta Serena and Ozæna.—Dr. ELLIS.

Fumigations.

1697. ℞ Hydrarg. Sulphureti rubri, ℥ss.
Pulv. Olibani, ℥ij.
Mix: to be thrown on a red-hot iron, and the diseased parts (only) exposed to the fumes.

In Herpes and Venereal Pustules.—FOY.

1698. ℞ Hydrarg. Protonitratis, gr. xv.
Aquæ destillatæ, ℥vj.
Acidi Nitrici, gr. xv.
Dissolve. (Soak in this solution a piece of white blotting-paper, eight inches by six in size; dry, and fold into a cigarette; several times a day breathe gently into the bronchi eight or ten mouthfuls of the smoke.)

In Syphilitic Infections of the Pharynx and Larynx.
TROUSSEAU and REVEIL.

HYOSCYAMUS.

The leaves and seeds of the common Henbane (*Hyoscyamus niger*, Nat. Ord. *Solanaceæ*) are employed for their narcotic properties. There are two cultivated kinds, the biennial and the annual, the former being supposed to possess the most activity. The plant should be gathered when in full flower; the seeds collected when ripe. These are more active than the leaves, but are not so much employed. Hyoscyamus allays pain, and subdues nervous excitement. It rarely tends to produce sleep, except indirectly, nor does it confine the bowels, like opium. In large doses it causes delirium, coma, and death. It is used in irritable affections of the lungs, bowels, and other organs; as a general sedative in cases where opium is objected to on account of its stimulant or constipating effect; and externally as an anodyne.

The dose of the powdered leaves is from three to ten grains. Of the juice of the fresh plant, expressed and preserved, from half a drachm to one drachm.

Tinctura Hyoscyami, ℥ss–℥ij.
Extractum Hyoscyami, gr. iij–x.
Pilula Hyoscyami et Zinci (Paris Codex), gr. iij–x.
Cataplasma, *Emplastrum*, and *Oleum Hyoscyami* are intended for external use.

1699. ℞ Extr. Hyoscyami, gr. iij.
Extr. Conii, gr. ij.
Mix: make a pill. To be taken at bedtime.

DR. JOY.

1700. ℞ Extr. Hyoscyami, gr. iv.
Calomelanos, gr. j.
Mix: make a pill. To be taken every night.

Dr. JOY.

1701. ℞ Extr. Hyoscyami,
Extr. Conii,
Extr. Papaveris, sing. ℈j. Mix: divide into 12 pills.

Dr. DRUITT.

1702. ℞ Extr. Hyoscyami,
Camphoræ,
Lupulinæ, ana gr. iij.
Mix: make 2 pills. To be taken at bedtime.

In Simple Watchfulness.—Dr. STEWARD.

1703. ℞ Extr. Hyoscyami, gr. xij.
Camphoræ, gr. vj.
Spirit. rectif. ♏ij.
Rub together, and divide into 6 pills. Two every night.

Anodyne and Soporific.—Dr. JOY.

1704. ℞ Extr. Hyoscyami,
Sodæ Carbonatis exsic. ana gr. v.
Olei Juniperi, ♏ij.
Mix: divide into 3 pills. To be taken at bedtime.

In Red Gravel.—Mr. BRANDE.

1705. ℞ Camphoræ,
Ammon. Sesquicarb, ana gr. iij.
Pulv. Ipecacuan. gr. j.
Extr. Hyoscyami, gr. iv.
Mucilag. q. s. To form 3 pills. Dose, one or two.

Antispasmodic.—Mr. SAVORY.

1706. ℞ Opii, gr. iij.
Extr. Hyoscyami,
Extr. Conii, ana gr. xv.
Rub together to form a mass, to be divided into 6 pills, of which one may be taken disguised in starch, every night, to produce sleep.

Dr. PARIS.

1707. ℞ Opii crudi in pulv. subtiliss. ʒss.
Extr. Hyoscyami, ʒiiss.
Saponis duri,
Iridis flor. pulv. ana ʒj.
Rub up, and form a mass, to be divided into 60 equal parts. (Ten gr. of the mass contain one gr. of opium, and five of the extract of henbane.)

Anodyne.—Dr. COPLAND.

1708. ℞ Ext. Hyoscyami, gr. ij.
Ext. Gentianæ, gr. ij.
Pulv. Opii, gr. ¼.
Ext. Stramon. gr. ⅓.
Mix: make a pill, to be administered half an hour after taking food.

For Painful Indigestion.—Dr. Ross.

1709. ℞ Ext. Hyoscyami, gr. xv.
Ext. Stramonii, gr. iv.
Ext. Humuli, ʒj.
Morph. Sulph. gr. iss.
Mix: divide into 30 pills. One every half hour until the pain is mitigated.

In Painful Affections, where full doses of opium are contra-indicated. Dr. H. Green.

1710. ℞ Pulv. Ipecac. gr. viij.
Pil. Coloc. Co. ℈iss.
Extr. Hyoscyami, ʒss.
Fellis tauri inspiss. ℈j.
Rub together, and divide the mass into 24 pills, of which take one, two, or three, for a dose.

Anodyno-aperient.—Dr. Copland.

1711. ℞ Camphoræ, ʒss.
Spirit. rectif. q. s. Pulverize, by rubbing.
Sodæ Carbon. ʒiss.
Extr. Hyoscyami, ℈ij.
Saponis duri, ʒj.
Olei Juniperi, ♏xxx.
Pulv. Irid. flor. q. s.
To make a mass, to be divided into 30 pills. Three, night and morning, with infusion of linseed, or decoction of marshmallow, as an ordinary drink.

In Acute Bronchitis.—Dr. Copland.

1712. ℞ Succi Hyoscyami, ʒss.
Mist. Camphoræ, ʒj.
Syrup. Rhœados, ʒij.
Mix: make a draught. To be taken at bedtime, and to be repeated at alternate hours, if it does not produce sleep.

Dr. Neligan.

1713. ℞ Extr. Hyoscyami, gr. x.
Vini Antimonii, ʒij.
Mix: dose, 10 drops three or four times a day to an infant with hooping-cough.

Mr. Savory.

1714. ℞ Extr. Hyoscyami, gr. iv.
Tinct. Scillæ, ♏x.
Acidi Nit. ♏vj.
Aquæ, ʒx.
Mix: make a draught, to be repeated in three hours.

In Spasmodic Asthma.—Dr. Gregory.

1715. ℞ Extr. Hyoscyami, gr. iij–v.
Tinct. Scillæ, ♏x–xij.
Spirit. Anisi, ʒiss.
Aquæ Anisi, ℥iss.
Acidi Nitrici, ♏viij.
Mix: make a draught. To be taken every three or four hours, while the paroxysms of dyspnœa are urgent.

Dr. COPLAND.

1716. ℞ Tinct. Scillæ, ♏viij.
Acid. Nit. dil. ♏vj.
Extr. Hyoscyami, gr. v.
Syrup. Papaveris, ʒj.
Aquæ, ℥iss.
Make a draught, to be taken two or three times a day.

In Coughs.—Dr. PARIS.

1717. ℞ Tinct. Scillæ, ♏x.
Acid. Nit. dil. ♏vj.
Extr. Hyoscyami, gr. iij.
Mist. Camphoræ, ℥iss. Mix: make a draught.

During the Fit of Asthma.

1718. ℞ Tinct. Hyoscyami, ♏xxx.
Aquæ Cinnamomi, ℥j.
Syrupi simplicis, ℥ss. Mix: make an anodyne draught.

Dr. HOOPER.

1719. ℞ Tinct. Hyoscyami,
Spir. Ammon. Arom. ana ♏xx.
Mist. Gentianæ Co. ℥j.
Mix: make a draught. Three times a day.

In Phosphaturia.

1720. ℞ Emuls. Amygdalæ, ℥iss.
Potassæ Nitratis, gr. v.
Tinct. Camph. Co. ʒj.
Tinct. Hyoscyami, ʒss.
Mix: make a draught. Take at night.

In Troublesome Cough.

1721. ℞ Acidi Sulph. dil.
Tinct. Hyoscyami, ana ʒiss.
Tinct. Digitalis, ʒj.
Liq. Ammon. Acet.
Aquæ, ana ℥iv.
Mix: make a mixture. Two tablespoonfuls three times a day.

In Nervousness.—Dr. HOOPER.

1722. ℞ Quinæ Disulph. gr. iss.
Acid. Sulph. dil. ʒj.
Tinct. Digitalis, gtt. xx.
Tinct. Hyoscyami, ʒj.
Syrup. Papaveris, ℥ss.
Aquæ fontanæ, ℥iv.
Mix: make a mixture. A tablespoonful every fourth hour.

In the Fever of Phthisis.—Dr. GRAVES.

1723. ℞ Inf. Aurant. Comp. ℥x.
Spir. Menth. vir. ʒj.
Liq. Potassæ, gtt. x.
Magnes. Carb. ℈j.
Tinct. Hyoscyami, ʒss.
Extr. Humuli, gr. viij.
Syrup. Zingib. ʒj. Mix: make a draught.

To prevent Vomiting.—Dr. COPLAND.

1724. ℞ Extr. Hyoscyami, ʒss.
Saponis albi, ʒij.
Lini Olei, ℥vj. Mix: make a liniment.

In Glandular Swellings.—DUPUYTREN.

1725. ℞ Foliorum Hyoscyami,
Fol. Stramonii,
Fol. Dulcamaræ,
Fol. Sambuci, each, a handful.
Axungiæ, lbij.

Heat together until all moisture is evaporated, and strain the ointment.

As an Application to Frost-Bites and Chilblains.—SPIELMAN.

IBERIS AMARA. *Bitter Candy Tuft.*

The seeds of this plant have been lately recommended in cases of hydrothorax, cardiac hypertrophy, and dropsical disorders, as also in bronchitis. In large doses they are found to cause excessive nausea, giddiness, and diarrhœa.

1726. ℞ P. Iberis amaræ sem. gr. xij.
Potassæ bitart. ʒij.

Mix, and divide into 12 powders. One, twice a day. (The dose of Iberis may be gradually increased to gr. iv, except when it produces nausea or giddiness.)

In Asthma, Bronchitis, Hydrothorax, &c.—Dr. SYLVESTER.

ICHTHYOCOLLA. *Isinglass.*

Isinglass consists of the swimming bladder of various species of sturgeon (*Acipenser*) which inhabit the seas of Russia and other parts of the world. The part being extracted from the fish, it is either simply dried, or dried and cut up into shreds. By boiling these a very pure gelatine is extracted, which is useful in diet, and employed in medicine for its demulcent properties.

1727. ℞ Ichthyocollæ, ℥ij.
Aquæ, lbij. Boil to lbj; strain, and add
Lactis vaccini, lbij.
Sacchari, ℥j.
Mix. (A wineglassful frequently, as a demulcent and nutritive for delicate persons.)

Dr. HOOPER.

INDIGUM. *Indigo.*

Indigo is a blue dye obtained from several species of *Indigofera* (Nat. Ord. *Leguminosæ*) by allowing the plants to ferment in vats of water. It is used in medicine as an antispasmodic, having been particularly recommended in the treatment of epilepsy. Dose of the powder, one scruple two or three times a day, gradually increased to a drachm at a time.

Pulvis Indigi compositus (Radius), in doses of one drachm three times a day in epilepsy.

1728. ℞ Indigoferæ disperm. ℥j.
Syrupi simp. ℥ij.
Mix: make an electuary. Half a teaspoonful every night and morning. (The dose may be gradually increased until three or four drachms of Indigo are taken in a day.)

In Idiopathic Epilepsy.—Dr. JOY.

1729. ℞ Indigo pulv. subtiliss. ʒss.
Pulv. Aromat. gr. v.
Mix: make a powder. Four times a day.

HÔPITAL DE LA CHARITE.

1730. ℞ Indigo pulv. (aquæ guttis nonnullis subacti), ʒij–iv.
Pulv. Aromat. ʒss.
Syrupi simp. ℥j. Mix: make an electuary. Dose, ʒj to ʒij.

In Epilepsy, Hysteria, and Chorea.—PHŒBUS.

1731. ℞ Pulv. Indigi, gr. lxxv.
Assafœtidæ, gr. xv.
Castoris, gr. vij.
Mix: divide into 20 pills. One every hour.

PODRECA.

INULA.

Elecampane is the root of *Inula Helenium* (Nat. Ord. *Compositæ*). It is dried, and cut into slices of a grayish-yellow color, which have a bitter pungent taste, and aromatic odor. It is tonic and expectorant, and is chiefly employed in cases of chronic catarrh, and in combination with other medicines. The dose of the powder, which is rarely given alone, is from a scruple to two drachms. Of *Decoctum Helenii*, and *Decoctum Helenii compositum*, one ounce to a wineglassful. Of *Extractum Helenii* (Cottereau), one scruple to one drachm.

1732. ℞ Extr. Helenii, ʒij.
Vini Antimonii, ℥j.
Syrupi flor. Aurantii, ℥ss.
Mix: dose, twenty to thirty drops every three hours.

In Asthma and Chronic Catarrh.—JAHN.

1733. ℞ Extr. Helenii, ʒj.
Pulv. Digitalis,
Pulv. Ipecac. ana gr. x.
Pulveris Opii, gr. v.
Mix: make a mass, and divide into 2-grain pills. One every hour.

In Chronic Catarrh.—HEIM.

1734. ℞ Rad. Inulæ Helenii,
Rad. Glycyrrhizæ,
Croci Stigmatorum,
Rad. Iris Florent.
Sem. Anisi,
Hyssopi officinal, ana ℥ss.
Aquæ, lbij. Boil to lbjss; strain, and add
Tinct. Tolutanæ,
Syrup. Tolutanæ,
Mellis, ana ℥j.
Mix: from f℥j to f℥ij every four or six hours.

In Pulmonary Affections.—ELSNER.

1735. ℞ Inulæ Helenii, ℥j.
Cacum. Hyssopi, ʒiij.
Fol. Hederæ terrest. ʒij.
Aquæ, q. s. to form of the strained liquor f℥xij. Boil for the fourth part of an hour, and strain; and to the strained liquor add
Potassæ Subcarb. ʒj.
Syrupi Tolutani,
Syrupi Althææ, ana ℥j.
Mix: dose, f℥j to f℥ij three or four times a day.

In Chronic Catarrhs, Asthma, Chlorosis, and Amenorrhœa.
DR. COPLAND.

IODINIUM. POTASSII IODIDUM. *Iodine, and Iodide of Potassium.*

Iodine is a non-metallic element (equivalent 126), having a black color and metallic luster, which volatilizes at a temperature of 350° into a violet vapor, and combines with metals and other bodies in the same manner as Oxygen and Chlorine. It is soluble in 7000 parts of water, more soluble in a solution of Iodide of Potassium, and easily dissolved by most spirits and ethers. It is obtained from the residual liquor of Kelp. It forms the active ingredient in burnt sponge, a remedy used before iodine was known. Iodide of Potassium (or Hydriodate of Potash) is obtained by decomposing a solution of Iodide of Iron with one of Carbonate of Potash. It is a very soluble salt. Free Iodine produces a deep blue color with starch, by which test both it and its salts are easily recognized.

Iodine and Iodide of Potassium are alike in their action. Both operate as stimulants to the absorbent system, and are thus employed in simple hypertrophy of any of the organs, and to promote the removal of non-malignant swellings and tumors. They exert an almost specific influence over scrofulous disorders, and the various symptoms of secondary syphilis. Goitre is remarkably under their control, and they are sometimes beneficial in pulmonary phthisis, and in various skin diseases. Externally, as caustics and rubefacients, they are employed to disperse swellings, epecially those having a scrofulous origin; while in a milder form, as of lotions, ointments, and baths, they are used in local or cutaneous affections, as well as in the same disorders which benefit by their internal administration. Both of these substances, if given long to excess, produce atrophy; or if used in large doses, act as irritant poisons.

The dose of Iodine in substance is from one-eighth of a grain to one grain. Of Iodide of Potassium, three to fifteen grains, or more. Both must be given in solution, and considerably diluted.

The following preparations contain Iodine, without the Iodide of Potassium:

Amyli Iodidum, iodide of starch, a mild preparation. Dose, half a drachm, gradually increased.

Sulphuris Iodidum. See *Sulphur*.

Tinctura Iodinii (E. and U. S.). Dose, ten to twenty drops three times a day.

Ether Ioduretus [Majendie]. Dose, ten drops diluted.

The *Solutiones Iodinii* of M. Lugol are for internal and external use. (*See below.*)

Unguentum Iodinii (U. S.) and *Cataplasma Iodinii* (Dunglison) are applied to scrofulous tumors.

The following contain Iodine along with Iodide of Potassium:

Tinctura Iodinii Composita (L., D.). Dose, ten minims to one drachm.

Liquor Potassii Iodidi Compositus (L., D.). Dose, two to four drachms.

Liquor Iodinii Compositus (E.) is much stronger. Dose, five to fifteen minims.

Aquæ Ioduretæ [Lugol] are of several strengths.

The *Unguentum Iodinii compositum* (L., E., D.), the *Solutiones Iodinii, rubefaciens, et caustica*, and the Ioduretted baths, *Balnea Iodureta*, of Lugol, are for external application.

The following preparations contain the Iodide of Potassium without Iodine:

Liquor Potassii Iodidi [Majendie]. Dose, ten minims, increasing.

Unguentum (L., D.), *Emplastrum* (L.), and *Linimentum Potassii Iodidi* [Guibourt], are for outward use.

In the following prescriptions Iodine alone is given:

1736. ℞ Tinct. Iodinii, ʒj.
Aquæ destil. ℥vj.
Mix: one-sixth part for a dose, gradually increased.

In Secondary Syphilis.

1737. ℞ Olei Amygd. dulcis, ℥ss.
Olei Olivæ, ʒij.
Iodinii, gr. ½. Mix: a third part three times a day.

In Scrofula.—Dr. DUNCAN.

			A.	B.	C.
1738.	℞ Iodinii,	gr.	½ —	¾ —	1.
	Sodii Chlor.	gr.	12 —	12 —	12.
	Aquæ destil.		Oj. —	Oj. —	Oj.

Dissolve, to form an iodine drink. (Of three different strengths, to be used as occasion may require.)

In Scrofula, &c.—M. LUGOL.

1739. ℞ Iodinii, gr. ij–iv.
Aquæ destil. Oj. Mix: make a lotion.

In Scrofula.—M. LUGOL.

1740. ℞ Iodinii, ℈j.
Olei Olivæ, ℥j.
Rub together. To be rubbed on the abdomen.

In Diarrhœa and other Affections of the Bowels.
Mr. M. DIAMOND.

1741. ℞ Liniment. Sapon. C. ℥j.
Iodinii, gr. viij vel x. Mix

To Scrofulous Tumors, &c.—Dr. COPLAND.

1742. ℞ Tinct. Iodinii, ʒj.
Lin. Sapon. Co. ℥j. Mix: make a liniment.

MANSON.

1743. ℞ Tinct. Iodinii, ℥ss.
Pulv. Lini, ℥j.
Pulv. Avenæ, ℥iij.
Aquæ destil. q. s. to form a cataplasm.

To Scrofulous Tumors, &c.

1744. ℞ Tinct. Iodinii, part. ij.
Aquæ destil. part. iij. Mix: make an injection.

To be introduced into the Sac of a Hydrocele after the withdrawal of the Fluid. Dr. M'DONNELL.

1745. ℞ Tinct. Iodinii, ʒss.
Aquæ puræ, ʒiss.
Mix: make an injection. To be injected into the tunica vaginalis after the evacuation of the fluid; and retained there.

After the operation for Hydrocele, when it has to be performed for the second time. Mr. BRANSBY COOPER.

The following contain both Iodine and Iodide of Potassium:

1746. ℞ Liq. Iodidi Potass. Co. ʒj.
Mistur. Camphoræ, ℥j.
Make a draught, to be taken twice a day.

Alterative.—Dr. PARIS.

1747. ℞ Potass. Iodidi, ʒiv.
Iodinii, gr. ij.
Aquæ Menth. pip.
Aquæ flor. Aurant. ana ℥iij.
Mix: make a mixture. Five drachms three times a day.

In Epilepsy.—MAJENDIE.

1748. ℞ Iodinii, gr. ss.
Potass. Iodidi, ʒss.
Syrup. Papa. ℥ss.
Aquæ destil. Oss.
Mix: make a mixture. Two tablespoonfuls three times a day.

In Syphilis and Scrofula.—TYRELL.

1749. ℞ Iodinii, gr. ss.
Potass. Iodidi, ʒss.
Syrup. Papa. ℥ss.
Inf. Gentianæ Co. ℥x.

Mix: make a mixture. Two tablespoonfuls three times a day; with half a grain of Acetate of Morphia, every night.

Secondary Syphilis in Weakly Constitutions.

Mr. BRANSBY COOPER.

1750. ℞ Iodinii puri,
Potass. Iodidi, ana gr. vj.
Aquæ destil. ℥v–℥vj.
Alcoholis, ʒij.

Mix: make a mixture. To be administered by inhalation.

To be Inhaled by Phthisical Persons, by means of the proper Apparatus. Sir C. SCUDAMORE.

1751. ℞ Potass. Iodidi, gr. xxiv.
Iodinii, gr. j ad ij.
Aquæ Rosæ, ℥vj.

Mix: make an eye-wash. To be used four times a day.

In Scrofulous Ophthalmia.—MAJENDIE.

1752. ℞ Iodinii,
Potass. Iodidi, ana ℥j.
Spirit. rectif. ℥ij.

Mix: make a liniment for the chest.

In Phthisis.—Dr. THEOPHILUS THOMPSON.

1753. ℞ Tinct. Iodinii Co. ʒj.
Lin. Sapon. ʒvij.

Mix: make a liniment. To be used frequently.

To Glandular Enlargements, and Tumidity of the Abdomen in Children. Dr. UNDERWOOD.

1754. ℞ Iodinii, ℈j.
Potass. Iodidi, ʒj.
Cerati Cetacei, ℥ij. Mix: make an ointment.

To Scrofulous Ulcers.—Mr. C. HOGG.

1755. ℞ Iodinii, gr. xij.
Potass. Iodidi, ℈iv.
Olei Nicotianæ, gtt. iv.
Adipis præpar. ℥ij. Mix: make an ointment.

To remove Tetanic Rigidity of Muscles and Tendons.

Dr. DEWEES (U.S.).

1756. ℞ Iodinii, gr. xv.
Potass. Iodidi, ʒj.
Tinct. Opii, ʒij.
Aquæ destil. ℥ij. Mix: make a lotion.

To painful Scrofulous Ulcers.—LUGOL.

1757. ℞ Iodinii, ʒij.
Potass. Iodidi, ℥ss.
Aquæ destil. ℥viij. Dissolve: make an embrocation.

In Indolent Strumous Affections.—LUGOL.

1758. ℞ Iodinii, gr. ij–iv.
Potass. Iodidi, gr. iv–viij.
Aquæ destil. lbj.
Dissolve. (For internal use, and for injection into scrofulous abscesses, &c. This is the Solutio Iodinii of Lugol.)

LUGOL.

1759. ℞ Iodinii, ʒiv.
Potass. Iodidi, ℥j.
Aquæ destil. ℥vj.
Dissolve. (Lugol's rubefacient Iodine Solution.)

For External Use.—LUGOL.

1760. ℞ Iodinii, ℥j.
Potass. Iodidi, ℥j.
Aquæ destil. ℥ij.
Dissolve. (Lugol's Caustic Iodine Solution.)

For External Use.—LUGOL.

1761. ℞ Iodinii, ℥j.
Potass. Iodidi, ℥ij.
Aquæ destil. ℥ij.
Sp. Vini rectif. ℥ij. Mix: make a caustic lotion.

To be applied in Congestion or Erosion of the Cervix Uteri.
Dr. CHURCHILL.

1762. ℞ Solut. Iodinii rubefac. ℥j–℥iv.
Aquæ, cong. xl–l. Dissolve: make an iodurated bath.

In Scrofula, Secondary Syphilis, &c.—LUGOL.

These contain the Iodide of Potassium without Iodine:

1763. ℞ Potass. Iodidi, ʒss.
Inf. Quassiæ, ℥vj. Mix: one-sixth part three times a day.

In Secondary Syphilis.—Dr. HOOPER.

1764. ℞ Potass. Hydriod. ʒj.
Tinct. Lupul. ℥ss.
Tinct. Cinchon. Co. ℥iss.
Mix: make a mixture. A teaspoonful twice a day in a glass of water.

1765. ℞ Potass. Iodidi, ℈j.
Syrupi Aurantii, ℥j.
Aquæ florum Tiliæ, ℥v.
Mix: make a mixture. A tablespoonful night and morning in an infusion of hops.

In White Swelling, and Chronic Syphilis.—Dr. LISFRANC.

1766. ℞ Potass. Iodidi, gr. xv.
Spiritus rectif.
Ext. Dulcamaræ, ana ʒij.
Pulverized liquorice root, and water, sufficient to make 180 pills. Six two or three times a day.

In Scrofula, Goitre, &c.—VOGT.

1767. ℞ Potass. Iodidi, gr. v.
Infusi Lupuli, ℥ij.
Make a draught, to be taken every eighth hour.

Advanced Stages of Pneumonia, &c.—Dr. UPSHER (U. S.).

1768. ℞ Potass. Iodidi, gr. iij.
Inf. Aurant. Co. ʒx.
Tinct. Scillæ, ♏xv.
Syrupi Aurantii, ʒj.
Mix: make a draught. To be taken three times a day.

In Ascites.—Dr. GREGORY.

1769. ℞ Decoc. Sarsæ, lbij.
Potass. Iodidi, ʒj.
Syrup. Aurantii, ℥ij.
Mix: the whole to be taken in twenty-four hours.

MAJENDIE.

1770. ℞ Potass. Iodidi, ʒij.
Infusi Quassiæ, lbij.
Dissolve: a wineglassful three times a day.

In Sympathetic Vomiting.—Dr. SELKIRK.

1771. ℞ Potass. Iodidi, gr. ij.
Potass. Bitart. ℈j
Mix: make a powder. To be taken twice a day in a glassful of pure water.

Diuretic.—Dr. PARIS.

1772. ℞ Liq. Potass. Iodidi, gtt. xv.
Acid. Hydrocyan. dil. gtt. x–xij.
Aquæ Lactucæ, ℥iv.
Syrupi Althææ, ℥j. Mix: a tablespoonful every hour.

In Phthisis.—M. DEFERMON.

1773. ℞ Liq. Potass. Iodidi, gtt. xv
Aquæ Lactucæ, ℥iv.
Acid. Hydrocyan. dil. gtt. x.
Syrupi Althææ, ℥j. Mix: a teaspoonful every hour.

In Phthisis.—M. DEFERMON.

1774. ℞ Potass. Iodidi, gr. iij.
Liq. Antim. Potass.-tart. ♏x.
Decoc. Sarsæ, ℥j.
Tinct. Hyoscyam. ♏xv.
Mix: make a draught. To be taken three times a day.

In the Asthma of Phthisical Persons.
Dr. THEOPHILUS THOMPSON.

1775. ℞ Aquæ Lactucæ dest. ℥viij.
Aquæ Menthæ p. dest. ʒij.
Potass. Iodidi, ʒiv.
Syrupi Althææ, ℥j.
Mix: make an atrophic mixture. (Five drachms of this, increased, if necessary, to ten drachms, to be given morning and evening.)

In Cardiac Hypertrophy in Young Subjects.—MAJENDIE.

1776. ℞ Potass. Iodidi, gr. viij.
Decoc. Ulmi, ℥xij.
Decoc. Dulcamaræ, ℥iv.
Mix: a wineglassful to be taken every night at bedtime.

In Eczema.—Dr. NELIGAN.

1777. ℞ Potass. Iodidi, ʒss.
Tinct. Aurantii, ℥ss.
Syrupi Zingiberis, ℥ss.
Aquæ puræ, ℥v.
Mix: a tablespoonful with an equal quantity of water three times a day.

In Phagedænic Ulceration of Throat.—Dr. OKE.

1778. ℞ Potass. Iodidi, ʒss.
Tinct. Opii, ʒij.
Aquæ fontanæ, ℥xij.
Spirit. Ætheris Nit. ℥ss.
Tinct. Lavandulæ Co. ʒj.
Mix: two tablespoonfuls twice a day.

In Rheumatism.—Sir B. BRODIE.

1779. ℞ Potass. Iodidi, gr. xij–xv.
Ung. Hyd. ciner. ℥ss. Mix: make an ointment.

In Herpes Exedens.—BLASIUS.

1780. ℞ Hydrarg. Iodidi rub. gr. viij.
Potass. Iodidi, ℈ij.
Adipis, ℥j.
Mix: make an ointment. To be used two or three times a day. (If too irritating, more lard may be mixed with it. This contains the Hydrargyro-Iodide of Potassium.)

HILDRETH.

1781. ℞ Unguent. Potass. Iodid. ʒiss.
Axungiæ præparatæ, ℥iij. Mix: make an ointment.

In Scabies.—Dr. BURGESS.

1782. ℞ Potass. Iodidi, gr. x.
Aquæ destil. ℥j. Mix: make a lotion.

To the Eye, in diffuse Opacity from Corneitis.—Dr. JACOB.

1783. ℞ Potass. Iodidi, gr. ij–iv.
Extr. Hyoscyami, gr. v–viij. Mix: to form a suppository.

In Enlargement of the Prostate.—Mr. STAFFORD.

In the remainder the Iodide is conjoined with a caustic or carbonated alkali.

1784. ℞ Potass. Iodidi, gr. xij.
Liq. Potass. (Brandish's), ʒiv.
Aquæ destil. ℥iss.
Mix: f℥j or f℥ij in a glass of water three times a day.

In Tuberculous Mesenteric Disease.—Dr. BLAKISTON.

1785. ℞ Decoc. Sarsæ Conc. ℥ij.
Liq. Potass. ʒiij.
Potass. Iodidi, ℈ij.
Infus. Chiraytæ, ℥x.
Mix: two tablespoonfuls three times a day.

In Psoriasis of the Hands.—Mr. C. HOGG.

1786. ℞ Inf. Buchu, ℥viij.
Liq. Potass. ʒj.
Potass. Iodidi, ʒss.
Tinct. Hyoscyami, ʒij.
Mix: make a mixture. Two tablespoonfuls twice a day, with a purgative pill every morning, and an alkaline bath to be taken at bedtime.

In Chronic Rheumatism.—Dr. WRIGHT.

1787. ℞ Sodæ Bicarb. gr. xv.
Potass. Bicarb. ℈j.
Aquæ puræ, ʒx.
Potass. Iodidi, gr. j–ij.
Spir. Æth. Nitr. ʒss.
Syrupi simp. ʒj.
Mix: make a draught. To be taken twice a day, in effervescence with a tablespoonful of recent lemon-juice.

In Phthisis, along with the Inhalation of Iodine.
Sir C. SCUDAMORE.

1788. ℞ Iodidi Potass. ʒss.
Potass. Bicarb.
Sodæ Bicarb. ana ʒj.
Aquæ puræ, ℥vj.
Mix: f℥j twice a day with f℥ss of dandelion water.

Dr. W. BUDD.

1789. ℞ Liq. Potass. ♏xv.
Potass. Iodidi, gr. iij.
Tinct. Cinchonæ, ʒiss.
Decoc. Sarsæ, ℥iij.
Mix: take three times a day.

In Rheumatic Gout.—Dr. H. W. FULLER.

1790. ℞ Olei Morrhuæ, ʒiij.
Liq. Potass. ♏xx.
Potass. Iodidi, gr. iij.
Essent. Limonum, ♏viij.
Aquæ destil. ʒj.
Mix: make a draught. To be taken 3 three times a day.

In Chronic Rheumatism of Cachectic Subjects.
Dr. H. W. FULLER.

1791. ℞ Liq. Potass. ♏xv.
Potass. Iodidi, gr. iij.
Extr. Sarsæ, ʒj.
Decoc. Cinchonæ, ℥xj.
Mix: make a draught. To be taken three times a day.

In Rheumatic Gout in Cachectic Subjects.

Dr. H. W. Fuller.

IPECACUANHA. EMETINA. *Ipecacuan and Emetine.*

Ipecacuan is the root of the *Cephaelis Ipecacuanha* (Nat. Ord. *Cinchonaceæ*), a Brazilian plant. Taken in small doses it is expectorant and diaphoretic, having a specific action on the bronchial mucous membrane, so as to excite its secretion when it is too dry, or to alter and check an inordinate flow of mucus in catarrh. It relaxes the system, and causes sweating. In full doses, it proves an easy and safe emetic. It does not nauseate so much as tartar emetic, nor is it so rapid and irritating in its action as sulphate of zinc. In cases of narcotic poisoning, such an emetic as sulphate of zinc is preferred. But for all ordinary purposes, and as an emetic for children and delicate persons, ipecacuan is by far the best. On account of its expectorant action it is in constant use in catarrhs, being frequently combined with squill. As a diaphoretic, it is employed in febrile affections, often in conjunction with opium. It is given to produce vomiting in hooping-cough and asthma, and administered in smaller doses in dyspepsia and dysentery. The dose of the powder, as an expectorant, is one to two grains; as a diaphoretic, two to four grains; as an emetic, ten to twenty grains.

Emetina is the active principle to which Ipecacuanha owes its powers. Impure Emetina is sometimes used, but the pure alkaloid is preferable. It is employed as Ipecacuan, but in much smaller doses. One-sixteenth to one-fourth of a grain may be given, according as we desire an expectorant or an emetic effect.

The compound Ipecacuan or Dover's powder will be separately spoken of. The following preparations contain Ipecacuan without Opium:

Vinum Ipecacuanhæ. Dose, as expectorant and diaphoretic, ten to thirty minims. Emetic for adults, two to four drachms. Emetic for children, twenty minims to one drachm.

Syrupus Ipecacuanhæ (E.), as an emetic for infants, half a drachm to one drachm.

Decoctum Ipecacuanhæ (Soubeiran) is given in dysentery in two-ounce doses.

Extractum Ipecacuanhæ (Paris Codex). Dose, one to ten grains.

Trochisci Ipecacuanhæ (U. S.).

The prescriptions are arranged as follows:

1. Ipecacuanha (or Emetine), as an emetic for adults.

1792. ℞ Pulv. Ipecac. ℈j.
Pulv. Antim. P. tart. gr. j.
Mix: to be taken entire as an emetic, or in divided doses as sudorific and expectorant.

1793. ℞ Pulv. Ipecac. ℈j.
Vini Antim. Potassio-tartratis, f℥iij.
Aquæ Menth. sativæ (vel Pulegii), f℥ix.
Mix: make an emetic draught.

Dr. GREGORY.

1794. ℞ Pulv. Ipecac. ℈j.
Aquæ Menth. Pulegii, ℥iss.
Mix: make an emetic draught. To be taken at once and followed by frequent draughts of tepid water, or tepid infusion of chamomile flowers.

Dr. JOY.

1795. ℞ Ipecac. ℈j.
Vini Ipecac. (vel Antimonii), ʒij.
Aquæ, ℥j. Mix.

A Common Emetic.—Dr. A. T. THOMSON.

1796. ℞ Pulv. Ipecac. ℈j.
Sodæ Sesquicarb. gr. x.
Aquæ Menth. vir. ʒx.
Mix: make a draught to be taken at once. (To be followed by an antacid mixture and aperient pills.)

In Herpes Labialis.—Dr. GREGORY.

1797. ℞ Pulv. Ipecac. gr. xv.
Aceti Scillæ, ʒj.
Aquæ Menth. viridis, ℥j.
Mix: make an emetic draught.

In Spasmodic Asthma.—Dr. GREGORY.

1798. ℞ Pulv. rad. Ipecac. ʒj.
Ammon. Subcarb. ℈j.
Aquæ Menth. pip. ℥iiss.
Tinct. Capsici, ℈j.
Olei Anthemidis, ♏x.
Mix: make an emetic draught (excitant).

In Narcotic Poisoning, &c.—Dr. Copland.

1799. ℞ Emetinæ impuræ, gr. iv.
Aquæ flor. Aurant.
Aquæ puræ, ana ℥j.
Syrup. flor. Aurant. ℥ss.
Mix: make a mixture. A tablespoonful every half hour to produce vomiting.

Majendie.

1800. ℞ Emetinæ puræ, gr. ¼.
Pulv. Sem. Sinapis, gr. x.
Tinct. Armoraciæ, ʒj.
Vini Antimonii, ʒij.
Aquæ puræ, ℥iss.
Mix: make a draught to be taken at once.

A Powerful Emetic.

1801. ℞ Infusi flor. Tiliæ, ℥iij.
Emetinæ puræ, gr. j in
Acido Acetico solutæ.
Syrupi Althææ, ℥j. Mix.
(A tablespoonful every quarter of an hour, until vomiting is produced.)

Majendie.

1802. ℞ Emetinæ puræ, gr. j.
Acidi Acetici, ♏x. Dissolve, and add
Aquæ flor. Aurant. ℥iij.
Syrupi simp. ℥j.
Mix: make a mixture. A tablespoonful every quarter of an hour until vomiting is induced.

Dr. Joy.

2. Ipecacuanha as an emetic for children.

1803. ℞ Pulv. Ipecac. ℈j.
Aquæ ferventis, ʒv—infuse
Colaturæ, ʒiv, add
Oxymel. Scillæ, ℥ss.
Mix: a teaspoonful every ten minutes until it operates.

As an Emetic for Children.—Dr. Merei.

1804. ℞ Pulv. Ipecac. gr. xiij.
Antim. Potassio-tart. gr. j.
Syrupi, ʒij.
Aquæ destillatæ, ʒx.
Mix: make a mixture. ʒj to ʒij every 15 minutes until effectual. (Tepid drinks may be employed as soon as vomiting has commenced, but not before; else, by diluting the medicine, they may render it inefficacious.)

As a Common Emetic for Children.—Dr. Underwood.

1805. ℞ Vini Ipecac. ℥ss.
Syrup. simp. ℥ss.
Aquæ, ℥j.
Mix: one or two teaspoonfuls to be frequently given, until vomiting produced.

A Mild Emetic for Children.—Drs. EVANSON and MAUNSELL.

1806. ℞ Vini Ipecac. ℥ss.
Liq. Antim. Tart. ℥ss.
Syrupi simp. ʒij.
Aquæ, ℥j.
Mix: make a mixture. One, two, or three drachms frequently to produce vomiting.

Emetic for Young Children.—Drs. EVANSON and MAUNSELL.

1807. ℞ Emetinæ puræ, gr. ss.
Syrupi Mori, ℥j.
Aquæ puræ, ℥iij.
Mix: make a mixture. A teaspoonful every fourth of an hour until vomiting occurs.

3. Ipecacuanha as an expectorant and diaphoretic.

1808. ℞ Pulv. Ipecac.
Sapon. Venet. ana ʒss.
Mix: make 20 pills. One, three times a day.

Dr. RICHARDS.

1809. ℞ Pulv. Ipecac. gr. vj.
Pulv. Myrrhæ, gr. xij.
Pulv. Potassæ Nitratis, ʒss.
Mix, and divide into 4 powders. One every four hours.

A Stimulating Expectorant.—Dr. PARIS.

1810. ℞ Pulv. Ipecac.
Antim. Sulphureti aurei, ana gr. j.
Camphoræ, gr. iij.
Pulv. Acaciæ, ℈j. Mix well: to be taken every two hours.

In Deficient Expectoration in Pneumonia.—PHŒBUS.

1811. ℞ Vini Ipecac. ℥ss.
Aquæ Cinnamomi, ℥j.
Aquæ puræ, ℥ivss.
Mix: make a mixture. One-sixth to one-fourth part for a dose.

Bronchitis, &c.—Dr. HOOPER.

1812. ℞ Vini Ipecac. ℥iij.
Syrup. Tolut. ℥v.
Mucilag. Acaciæ ad ℥xvj. Mix: dose, a teaspoonful.

Chronic Coughs.

1813. ℞ Mist. Amygdalæ, ℥vj.
Vini Ipecac.
Potassæ Carb. ana ʒiss.
Mix: two tablespoonfuls in effervescence, with a spoonful of lemon-juice every third hour.

Expectorant.—Dr. Joy.

1814. ℞ Sodæ Carbonatis, ℈j.
Succ. Limonum, ℥ss vel q. s.
Vini Ipecac ʒss.
Misturæ Camphoræ, ℥j.
Syrupi, ʒss.
Mix: make a draught. To be taken twice a day.

Diaphoretic.—Dr. Paris.

1815. ℞ Vini Ipecac. gtt. xx.
Liq. Ammon. Acet.
Aquæ, ana ℥ss.
Mix: make a draught. To be taken three times a day.

Bronchitis in weak Patients.—Dr. Budd.

1816. ℞ Pulv. Ipecac. gr. j.
Pulv. Antim. Co. gr. iij.
Hydrarg. Chloridi, gr. ss.
Sacchari, gr. vj. Mix: make a powder.

Diaphoretic in Fevers.—Dr. Hooper.

1817. ℞ Pulv. Ipecac. gr. xij.
Calomelanos, gr. iv.
Confect. Rosæ, q. s. to make 8 pills. One every fourth or sixth hour.

In Acute Bronchitis with much Fever.—Dr. Joy.

1818. ℞ Pulv. Rad. Ipecac. gr. iij–iv.
Mucilag. Acaciæ,
Syrupi, ana ʒij.
Aquæ destillatæ, ℥j.
Potassæ Nitratis, gr. xv.
Mix: make a mixture. Two teaspoonfuls three times a day, or every fourth hour.

In Measles of Infants.—Dr. Thomas.

1819. ℞ Vini Ipecac. ʒiij.
Syrupi Tolutani, ʒv.
Mucilag. Acaciæ, ℥j.
Mix: make a mixture. A teaspoonful every hour or second hour.

For Children threatened with Croup or Bronchitis.
Dr. Cheyne.

1820. ℞ Decocti Senegæ, ʒiijss.
Oxymel. Scillæ, ʒij.
Vini Ipecac. ʒij.
Antim. Tartar. gr. j.
Mix. (Dose, ♏x–xx every quarter of an hour, to an infant, to produce vomiting, or every two hours as an expectorant.)

In Croup, &c.—French Hosp.

4. Ipecacuanha with opium or poppies as expectorant or diaphoretic. (See also *Pulv. Ipecac. Co.*)

1821. ℞ Sodæ Carbonatis, ʒj.
Vini Ipecac. ℥ss.
Tincturæ Opii, ʒj.
Syrupi Tolutani, ℥ij.
Aquæ, ℥iss. Mix: make a mixture. ℥ss for a dose.
Bronchitis.—Dr. HOOPER.

1822. ℞ Syrupi Papaveris, ʒiiiss.
Acid. Sulph. dil. ʒiiss.
Vini Ipecac. ʒiss.
Oxymel. Scillæ,
Syrup. Tolutani, ana ʒij.
Aquæ, ad ℥viij.
Mix: make a mixture. A tablespoonful three times a day.
Dr. F. BIRD.

1823. ℞ Decocti Lichenis, ℥xj.
Vini Ipecac. ʒij.
Extr. Conii, ℈j.
Olei Anisi, ♏xij.
Syrup. Althææ,
Syrup. Papaveris, ana ʒiij.
Mix: make a cough mixture. Three or four tablespoonfuls four times a day.
Dr. COPLAND.

1824. ℞ Vini Ipecac. ʒij.
Aquæ, ℥j.
Mucilag. Gum. Ac. ℥ss.
Syrup. Limonis,
Syrup. Papaveris, ana ʒj.
Mix: take fʒj to fʒij every second hour.
In the Catarrhal Affections of Children.
Drs. EVANSON and MAUNSELL.

1825. ℞ Vini Ipecac. ʒiss.
Aquæ puræ, ℥iss.
Sodæ Bicarb. gr. xij.
Syrupi, ʒij.
Tincturæ Opii, gtt. iv.
Mix: take fʒj to fʒij every second hour.
In Hooping and Spasmodic Coughs of Children.
Drs. EVANSON and MAUNSELL.

1826. ℞ Sodæ Sesquicarb. gr. xxiv.
Vini Ipecac. ʒj.
Tincturæ Opii, ♏vj.
Syrupi, ʒiij.
Aquæ, ℥j. Mix: take a sixth part every six hours.
In Hooping-cough.—Dr. PEARSON.

1827. ℞ Tinct. Opii, ♏vj.
Vini Ipecac. ʒj.
Aquæ destillatæ, ℥j.
Syrupi Tolutani, ʒiij.
Sodæ Subcarb. gr. xxiv.
Mix. (A small teaspoonful to be given every six or eight hours.)

To Children in Hooping-cough.—Mr. SAVORY.

1828. ℞ Vini Ipecac. ʒij.
Tinct. Opii, ʒij.
Pulv. Potass. Nit. ʒiss.
Succi Limonis, ℥ss.
Mist. Camphoræ, ℥iv.
Mix. (Dose, ℥ij for adults; ʒss–ʒj for children.)

Diaphoretic.

5. Ipecacuanha in dysentery and dyspepsia.

1829. ℞ Pulv. Ipecac. Rad. ʒj.
Aquæ, ℥xij.
Boil to f℥vj. Four tablespoonfuls every six hours.

Chronic Dysentery.—Dr. JOY.

1830. ℞ Pulv. Ipecac. gr. ij.
Aluminis, gr. vj.
Syrupi Papaveris, q. s. to make two pills. One every four hours.

In Dysentery.—Dr. HOOPER.

1831. ℞ Pulv. Ipecac. gr. ij.
Confectionis Opii, ℈j.
Cretæ præparatæ, q. s.
Make 8 boluses, and give two night and morning.

In Dysentery.—ST. MARIE.

1832. ℞ Pulv. Ipecac. gr. ij.
Pulv. Aromatici, gr. x.
Syrupi Cinnamomi, q. s.
Make 2 boluses: one to be taken at bedtime.

In Dyspepsia.—CADET.

1833. ℞ P. Ipecacuanhæ,
Calomelanos, ana gr. iij.
Extr. Opii Aquosi, gr. iss.
Excipientis, q. s.
Mix, and divide into 10 pills. One, night and morning.

In Chronic Diarrhœa.—TROUSSEAU and REVEIL.

(See also RHUBARB.)

PULVIS IPECACUANHÆ COMPOSITUS. *Compound Ipecacuan Powder.*

This is also called *Pulvis Doveri*, or Dover's powder. Every ten grains contain one grain of ipecacuanha and one of opium, the rest being sulphate of potash. It is placed by itself, as being midway between ipecacuanha and opium, sharing the properties of both. Either of these separately will act on the skin, but combined they form one of the most valuable sudorifics that we possess. It may be employed generally in febrile cases, except where opiates are contraindicated, as by an irritable state of the stomach, excitement of the brain, furred tongue, and hot skin. It is very frequently given in catarrhal and rheumatic affections. It affords a useful means of administering opium in small quantities, as to children. But the proportion of opium it contains should be carefully borne in mind.

The dose of the powder is from five to ten grains.

The *Pilulæ Ipecacuanhæ et Opii* (E. P.) contain this powder. Dose, one to three pills.

The *Pilulæ Ipecacuanhæ cum Scillâ* (L. P.) consist of about half of this powder. Dose, five to ten grains.

Pilulæ Ipecacuanhæ et Opii (E.). Dose, five to ten grains.

1834. ℞ Pulv. Ipecac.
Pulv. Opii, ana gr. j.
Pulv. Sodæ Carbonatis, gr. xij.

Mix well by rubbing. Make a powder. One every eight hours. (This may be considered as a modification of Dover's Powder.)

In Spasmodic Asthma, Hooping-cough, &c.

Dr. A. T. THOMSON.

1835. ℞ Pulv. Doveri, ʒj.
Mist. Amygd. ℥vij.
Mucil. Acaciæ, ℥j.

Mix: take f℥j every three hours, or when the cough is troublesome.

In Catarrhal Cough.—Dr. LATHAM.

1836. ℞ Pulv. Ipecac. Co. gr. iv–vj.
Sodæ Tartarizatæ, ʒj.
Decocti Althææ, ℥iss.
Syrupi Limonis, ʒss.

Mix: make a draught. To be taken every fourth or sixth hour.

In Consumption.—Sir A. CRICHTON.

1837. ℞ Pulv. Ipecac. Co. gr. j.
Sacchari, ℈j.

Mix: make a powder, and divide into four parts.

To quiet young Infants.—Dr. HOOPER.

1838. ℞ Pulv. Ipecac. Co.
Hydrarg. c. Cretâ, ana gr. j.

Mix: make a powder. To be taken at bedtime.

In the Diarrhœa of Teething.—Dr. WEST.

1839. ℞ Pulv. Ipecac. gr. ¼.
Pulv. Doveri, gr. ss.
Sodæ Carbonatis sicc. gr. j.
Mix: make a powder. To be taken every second or third hour.

In Spasmodic Cough of Infants.

Drs. EVANSON and MAUNSELL.

1840. ℞ Sodæ Subcarb. exsic. gr. j.
Pulv. Ipecac. gr. ¼.
Pulv. Ipecac. Co. gr. j.
Pulv. Cinnam. Co. gr. j.
Pulv. Potass. Nit. gr. j.
Mix, and divide into 6 powders. One in some decoction of barley, or oatmeal, every three or four hours.

In the Diarrhœa of Children.—Mr. SAVORY.

1841. ℞ Pulv. Doveri, ʒj.
Pulv. Antim. Tart. gr. ij.
Pulv. Hydrarg. Chloridi, gr. viij.
Pulv. Jacobi veri, ʒj.
Pulv. Cinnamomi,
Pulv. Zingiberis, ana ʒij.
Pulv. Canellæ albæ, ʒj.
Mix, and divide into 8 powders. One to be mixed in a wineglass with a dessertspoonful of brandy, and twice or thrice as much of peppermint, cinnamon, or common water, and so drunk. This is to be given every ten or twenty minutes, according to the urgency of the case, or until the skin is bedewed with a copious sweat.

In Cholera.—Dr. RICHMOND.

JALAPA. *Jalap.*

This is the tuberous root of the *Ipomæa Purga*, a Mexican plant (Nat. Ord. *Convolvulaceæ*). It contains a peculiar resin, to which its cathartic property is owing. This resin is sometimes used alone. Jalap is an active drastic cathartic, producing copious watery evacuations. It irritates the intestines, and may cause nausea and griping. It is well fitted for use in constipation, and is safe for children. It must not be used during pregnancy, or when there is much irritation of the intestines. Being hydragogue, it is often of use in dropsies. It is sometimes given as a vermifuge.

The dose of the powder is from two to five grains for children; from ten to thirty grains for adults.

Extractum Jalapæ (L.), gr. v–℈j.
——————— *Alkalinum* (Durand), gr. iij–ix.

Pilula Jalapæ (Ph. Pruss.), gr. v–x.
———— *cum Colocynthide*, gr. v–x.
Pulvis Jalapæ compositus (L., E., D.), contains cream of tartar and ginger, ℈j–ʒj.
Tinctura Jalapæ, ʒj–ʒiij.
Syrupus Jalapinus (Paris Codex), ʒij–ʒiij.
Resina Jalapæ (E.), gr. iij–xij.
Mistura Jalapæ, dose, ℥iss.

1842. ℞ Pulv. Jalapæ,
Pulv. Rhei,
Pulv. Aloes, ana ℥j.
Saponis, ℥ij.
Syrupi Zingiberis, q. s.
Mix, and make into a pill-mass. Dose, twenty to thirty grains.

FOY.

1843. ℞ Pulv. Jalapæ, ℥iij.
Hydrarg. Chlor. ℥j.
Pulv. Zingiberis, ʒij. Mix: dose, four to twenty grains.

DR. COPLAND.

1844. ℞ Pulv. Jalapæ, gr. xij.
Calomelanos, gr. iij.
Potass. Sulphat. gr. vij.
Mix: make a powder. To be taken at night.

In disturbance of the action of the Liver.—DR. A. T. THOMSON.

1845. ℞ Pulv. Jalapæ, gr. x.
Pulv. Rhei, gr. v.
Calomelanos, gr. iij.
Pulv. Cinnam. Co. gr. ij. Mix: make a powder.

Strong Cathartic.—DR. JOY.

1846. ℞ Pulv. Jalapæ, ʒj.
Pulv. Scammonii, ℈j.
Pulv. Ipecac. ʒx. Mix: divide into 8-grain powders.

In Mucous Discharges.—DUMAS.

1847. ℞ Pulv. Jalapæ, ℈j.
Infusi Sennæ, ℥j.
Tinct. Sennæ,
Syrupi Zingib. ana ʒj.
Mix, and make a purgative draught.

.1848 ℞ Pulv. Jalapæ, gr. ij.
Pulv. Rhei,
Pulv. Cinnam. ana gr. j. Mix: make a powder.

Purgative for young Children.—MR. SAVORY.

1849. ℞ Pulv. Jalapæ, ℈j.
Potass. Bitart. ʒss.
Aquæ Cinnam. ʒxj.
Syrupi Zingiberis, ʒj.
Mix: make a cathartic draught.

DR. GREGORY.

1850. ℞ Pulv. Jalapæ, gr. xxv.
Tinct. Sennæ Co. ʒij.
Aquæ Menth. pip. ʒx.
Potass. Bitart. ʒj.
Syrupi Zingib. ʒj.
Mix: make a draught. To be taken every morning.

In Anasarca.—Dr. Gregory.

1851. ℞ Pulv. Jalapæ, ʒss.
Pulv. Ipecac. gr. v.
Hydrarg. Chlor. gr. v.
Pulv. Sacchari, gr. x.
Mix: from two to five grains every third hour, until catharsis is produced.

For Infants.—Drs. Evanson and Maunsell.

1852. ℞ Pulv. Jalapæ Co. ℥j.
Calomelanos, gr. x.
Mellis Rosæ, q. s.
Make an electuary. A teaspoonful every other morning, two hours before breakfast.

In Indigestion, and Morbid Conditions of the Liver.

1853. ℞ Pulv. Jalapæ,
Potassæ Bitart.
Ferri Carbonatis, ana ℥j.
Pulv. Zingiberis, ʒss.
Sacchari fæcis, q. s. to form an electuary.
Dose, ʒss to ʒj twice a day.

For Worms in Children.—Mr. Savory.

1854. ℞ Pulv. Jalapæ,
Pulv. Rhei,
Pulv. Calumbæ,
Pulv. Zingiberis,
Potassæ Bitart. sing. ʒj.
Ferri Sulphatis, gr. x.
Aquæ Menth. pip. ℥ixss.
Tinct. Sennæ Co. ℥ss.
Mix: two tablespoonfuls morning and noon.

In Congestion of the Spleen.—Mr. Twining.

1855. ℞ Extr. Jalapæ,
Pil. Rhei comp. ana ℈j.
Extr. Hyoscyami, gr. xv.
Extr. Conii, gr. v.
Mix: divide into 12 pills. Dose, one or two.

In Indigestion.—Dr. Gregory.

1856. ℞ Resinæ Jalapæ, gr. vj.
Ovi vitelli, semissem. Mix; then add
Mist. Amygdalæ, ℥vj.
Syrupi Althææ, ℥j. Mix. To be taken at once.

An agreeable Purge.—Trousseau and Reveil.

1857. ℞ Resinæ Jalapæ, gr. v.
Confect. Amygdalarum, gr. xxx.
Rub up together, and while rubbing add
Aquæ destil. ℥jss.
Mix: make a draught. To be taken at once.

In simple Constipation.—Dr. NELIGAN.

1858. ℞ Tinct. Jalap. ʒij.
Magnesiæ, ℈ij.
Aquæ puræ, ℥ij.
Mix. A draught to be taken every morning.

In Chlorosis.—Dr. HAMILTON.

1859. ℞ Tinct. Jalap. ʒvj.
Aquæ Canellæ, ʒij.
Sacchari, ʒj.
Mix: make a draught. To be taken as soon as possible.

In Scarlatina.—Dr. HAMILTON.

1860. ℞ Tinct. Jalap. ʒij.
Aceti Scillæ, ʒj.
Aquæ Menthæ, ℥j.
Mix: make a draught. To be taken three times a day.

Cathartic and Diuretic.—Dr. ELLIS.

1861. ℞ Pulv. Jalap.
Hydrarg. Sulphureti nigri, ana ʒij.
Pulv. Scammonii, ʒj.
Resinæ Jalapæ,
Pulv. Scillæ, ana ʒiss.
Syrupi Rhamni, q. s.
Mix, and make an electuary. Dose, ʒss to ʒj.

In Dropsy, or Lead Colic.—CADET.

JUGLANS REGIA. *The common Walnut Tree.*

The leaves of the common Walnut (Nat. Ord. *Juglandaceæ*) have been highly extolled by M. Negrier as a remedy in scrofulous affections. They are said to exert an alterative influence in the blood, to cause the disappearance of various chronic eruptions, and of other disorders traceable to a strumous cachexy. They have been especially recommended in scrofulous caries of the bones, in inflammation of the eyes, in chronic bronchitis, and in impetigo and eczema.

An *infusion*, a *decoction*, and an *extract* are the preparations chiefly employed. The juice of the unripe walnut shells is astringent. The *Extractum Juglandis immaturæ* is prepared from these.

Extractum Juglandis (foliorum); dose, three grains three times a day. · *Decoctum*, or *Infusum Juglandis*; dose, one to two ounces. The *Decoctum Juglandis Corticum* is sometimes employed as an astringent.

1862. ℞ Extr. Juglandis, gr. vj.
Syrupi simplicis, ℥j.
Mix: dose, for children, 2–3 pessertspoonfuls in the day; for adults, 1–2 ounces.

In Scrofula.—M. NEGRIER.

1863. ℞ Ext. Juglandis, ℈iv.
Pulv. foliorum Juglandis, ʒss.
Mix, and divide into 24 pills. Two, twice a day.

M. NEGRIER.

1864. ℞ Ext. Juglandis (foliorum), ℥j.
Adipis, ʒx.
Olei Bergamotæ, ♏iij. Mix: make an ointment.

To be used as a Friction in Scrofula.—M. NEGRIER.

1865. ℞ Extr. cort. Juglandis, ʒj.
Aquæ calidæ, ℥viij. Mix: make a gargle.

In Chronic Enlargement of the Tonsils.—Dr. BECKER.

1866. ℞ Extr. Juglandis immaturæ, ʒj.
Aquæ, ʒx. Dissolve: to be brushed over the affected parts.

In Chronic Congestion of the Tonsils.—Dr. BECKER.

JUNIPERUS. *Juniper.*

The common Juniper (*J. communis*, Nat. Ord. *Coniferæ*) is an erect evergreen shrub, of which the tops bearing the berries are the officinal part. The berries are globose, containing three seeds, of a purplish-black color when ripe, and possessing an aromatic odor and flavor like that of turpentine. Juniper is a stimulating diuretic and diaphoretic. It is chiefly employed as an adjuvant to other remedies, to increase the flow of urine in cases of dropsy. The dose of the berries is from one to three drachms.

Extractum Juniperi (Paris Codex), ʒj–ʒiij.
Oleum Juniperi (L., E., D.), an excellent diuretic, ♏iv–♏vi.
Infusum Juniperi (D.), ℥j–℥iij.
———— *comp.* (Parrish), dose, a wineglassful.
Electuarium Juniperi (Pharm. Sax.), ʒj–ʒiv.
Spiritus Juniperi comp. (L., E., D.), ʒij–ʒiv.

1867. ℞ Junip. baccarum, ℥iss.
Cremoris Tartari, ℥j.
Aquæ ferventis, Oj.
Infuse for an hour, and strain. A teacupful three times a day, with 40 drops of sweet spirits of niter.

In Dropsy.—Dr. ELLIS.

1868. ℞ Olei Juniperi, ʒss.
Ætheris Nitrici,
Tinct. Digitalis, ana ʒiij.
Mix: dose, twenty to thirty drops every three hours.

HUFELAND.

1869. ℞ Potas. Subcarbonatis, ʒj.
Infusi Gentianæ Co. ℥vij.
Spirit. Juniperi Co.
Tinct. Cardam. Co. ana ℥ss.
Mix: make a mixture. Three tablespoonfuls every fourth hour.

Diuretic.—Dr. JOY.

1870. ℞ Juniperi baccarum contrit. ℥ij.
Seminum Anisi contus. ʒij.
Aquæ ferventis, lbj.
Mix: after three hours, strain. A wineglassful frequently.

Diuretic.—Dr. HOOPER.

1871. ℞ Olei Juniperi, ℥iss.
Olei Anisi, gtt. vj.
Axungiæ, ℥ij. Mix well, and form an ointment.

In Tinea Capitis.—SULLY.

1872. ℞ Spirit. Juniperi, ℥ij.
Olei Caryophylli,
Adipis Myristicæ, ana ʒss. Mix, and make a liniment.

In Ecchymosis and Indolent Tumors.—AUGUSTIN.

KINO.

This is an extract obtained from trees of the genus *Pterocarpus* (Nat. Ord. *Leguminosæ*), but chiefly from the *P. marsupium*, a large tree growing in India. It occurs in small angular shining fragments, of a reddish-brown color, and very astringent to the taste. It is perhaps the most powerful of all the vegetable astringents, and contains about seventy per cent. of tannic acid. It is employed in diarrhœa and dysentery, to check the discharge in gonorrhœa and leucorrhœa, and to arrest internal bleedings. It is also employed externally as a styptic, as a local application to indolent ulcers, and is used in gargles to constringe relaxed uvula. The dose of the powder is from ten to thirty grains.

Tinctura Kino (L., E.), one to two drachms.

Pulvis Kino Compositus (L.) contains in twenty grains one grain of *opium*. It is used as astringent and anodyne in chronic diarrhœa and dysentery, in doses of ten to twenty grains.

Pulvis Catechu Comp. (D.) contains Kino.

Infusum Kino (Wood), dose, one ounce.

Pil. Kino Comp. (Ellis) contains Opium; one every four hours, in diarrhœa, &c.

1873. ℞ Kino, ℈ij.
Camphor. rasæ et subactæ, ʒss.
Oxidi Zinci, ℈ss.
Confect. Aromat. ℈j.
Mix: divide into 20 pills. Two, night and morning.

In Diabetes.—AUGUSTIN.

1874. ℞ Pulv. Kino, ʒvj.
Pulv. Aluminis,
Pulv. Cinnamomi, ana ʒij.
Syrupi, q. s. to form an electuary.
Dose, a dessertspoonful occasionally.

In Diarrhœa.—Mr. SAVORY.

1875. ℞ Pulv. Kino Co. gr. x.
Pulv. Cretæ Co. gr. xv.
Syrupi Zingib. q. s.
Mix: make a bolus. To be taken every sixth hour.

In Diarrhœa of old and enfeebled.—Dr. NELIGAN.

1876. ℞ Pulv. Kino Comp. gr. x.
Inf. Cascarillæ, ʒvj.
Aquæ Cinnamomi, ʒiij.
Syrupi Papav. ʒj.
Mix: make a draught. To be taken twice a day.

In Chronic Dysentery.—Dr. GREGORY.

1877. ℞ Pulv. Kino Co. gr. v–x.
Pulv. Cretæ Co. gr. xv.
Pulv. Opii, gr. ss.
Syrupi Zingib. q. s. to make a bolus. To be taken twice, thrice, or oftener during the day.

In Diarrhœa.—Dr. COPLAND.

1878. ℞ Kino, ʒj–ʒij.
Aluminis, gr. xx–xxx.
Aquæ ferventis, Oij.
Infuse for an hour, and strain: make an injection.

In Chronic Urethritis.—SWEDIAUR.

KOUSSO.

The dried flowers of *Brayera anthelmintica* (Nat. Ord. *Rosaceæ*) were first used in their native country, Abyssinia, as a remedy for tape-worm. They contain an extractive matter, in which tannic acid and a volatile oil have been discovered, and which is readily taken up by hot water. The remedy was introduced into Europe by Dr. Plieninger in 1834, but was not brought into general notice before the year 1850. The dose is bulky. For an adult, about half an ounce is infused in warm water, and taken thus, unstrained, being rendered more palatable by the addition of honey or a little lemon-juice. It may be followed by a dose of castor oil, but it will itself act as a drastic cathartic. The worm is generally voided after the first dose, entire or in fragments; but it has frequently been found that the head is left behind, so that the parasite is able to grow again in the intestine. Kousso was at first very dear, and difficult to be obtained, but it is now exported in considerable quantities from Aden. It has probably been overmuch praised.

1879. ℞ Florum Brayeræ, ℥j–℥iss.
Aquæ, ℥xvj.
Boil to one-half, and strain: to the strained liquor add sufficient honey to suit the taste. To be taken at one dose.

Dr. Plieninger.

KRAMERIA. *Rhatany.*

The root of *Krameria Triandra* (Nat. Ord. *Polygalaceæ*), a South American shrub, is known by this name. It is long and branching, of a reddish color, and has an astringent taste. The extract is also in frequent use, and resembles Kino. Rhatany is tonic and astringent. It may be used in the same cases as Kino, than which it is something less powerful. The extract contains about 43 per cent. of tannic acid. The dose of Rhatany in powder is from twenty to thirty grains.

Extractum Krameriæ (E.), from ten to thirty grains.

Infusum Krameriæ (L., D.), one to two ounces.

Syrupus Krameriæ (U. S.), half an ounce.

Tinct. Krameriæ (D.), and *Tinct. Rhataniæ aromatica*, dose one to two drachms.

1880. ℞ Pulv. rad. Rhataniæ, ʒiv.
Divide into 12 powders. One, twice a day.
In Fluor Albus.—Dr. MATON.

1881. ℞ Pulv. Krameriæ rad. ℥ss.
Aquæ, lbij.
Boil to lbjss; strain. Three tablespoonfuls every third hour.
Obstinate Diarrhœa.—Dr. JOY.

1882. ℞ Infusi Krameriæ, ʒxj.
Potass. Nitratis, gr. x.
Pulv. Ipecac. co. gr. v.
Syrupi Aurantii, ʒj.
Mix: make a draught. To be taken every four hours.
In Hæmoptysis.—Dr. THOMAS.

1883. ℞ Tinct. Rhatan. ℥j.
Aquæ Calcis, ℥vj. Mix: three spoonfuls three times a day.
In Diarrhœa.—Dr. REECE.

1884. ℞ Tinct. Matico, ʒvj.
Inf. Krameriæ, ℥vij.
Syrupi Croci, ʒij.
Mix: make a mixture; f℥ss every three or four hours.
In Chronic Mucous Diarrhœa, or in the Diarrhœa of Phthisis.
Dr. NELIGAN.

1885. ℞ Infus. Rosæ, ʒx.
Acid. Sulph. arom. ♏xv.
Tinct. Rhatan. (℥iij ad spir. tenuior. Oij.) ʒj.
Syrupi Rhœados, ʒj.
Mix: make a draught. To be taken three times a day.
A very grateful Tonic.—SPRAGUE.

1886. ℞ Rhatan. rad. contus. ℥iij.
Canellæ cort. contus. ℥ij.
Spir. tenuioris, Oij.
Digest for ten days, and strain through paper. (Tinct. Rhatan. Aromatica.)
SPRAGUE.

1887. ℞ Inf. Aurantii Co. ℥vj.
Tinct. Rhatan. arom.
Syrupi Zingiberis, ana ℥j.
Mix: make a mixture. Three tablespoonfuls three times a day, in weakness or flatulence.
Tonic and Astringent.—SPRAGUE.

1888. ℞ Ext. Rhataniæ, ʒss.
Confect. Ros. Gall. ℥iv.
Syrup. Papav. alb. ʒij.
Pulv. Catechu, gr. xv.
Mix: make an electuary. Dose, a teaspoonful.
In Diarrhœa, &c.—TROUSSEAU and REVEIL.

1889. ℞ Pulv. Krameriæ, ℥ss.
Calcis Carb. præcip. ʒij.
Pulv. Amyli, ʒx.
Mix: make a powder. (To be dusted over the part affected.)

In Eruptions of Pemphigus and Ecthyma.—Dr. NELIGAN.

1890. ℞ Pulv. Krameriæ, ʒij.
Pulv. Myrrh. ʒj.
Camph. ʒiv.
Carbonis Ligni, ℥j.
Spirit. Vini rect. ♏xx.
Rub up the Camphor with the Spirits, and then mix all together. A tooth powder.

Dr. A. T. THOMSON.

1891. ℞ Infus. Krameriæ rad. ℥vij.
Acid. Sulph. dil. ʒij.
Syrup. Rosæ Gall. ℥j.
Mix: make a gargle. To be used through a glass tube.

In Relaxation of the Uvula.—Dr. JOY.

1892. ℞ Infus. Rhatan. ℥viss.
Acid. Sulph. dil. ℥ss.
Syrupi Mori, ℥j. Mix: make a gargle.

For Relaxation of the Uvula and Fauces.—Dr. COPLAND.

1893. ℞ Tinct. Rhatan. ℥j.
Tinct. Opii, ʒij.
Tinct. Myrrh. ʒj.
Mist. Camph. ℥viss. Mix: make a lotion.

Locally, to bleeding from the Gums, attended with pain.
Mr. HARRISON.

LACTUCA. LACTUCARIUM. *Lettuce*, and *Lettuce-opium*.

The common garden lettuce, *Lactuca sativa* (Nat. Ord. *Compositæ*), is in frequent use as a salad, and its leaves are known to be possessed of slight narcotic properties. In these it is excelled by the *L. virosa*, a wild species. Lactucarium, called *Thridace* by the French, is the dried juice of the cultivated plant. When made by expression, or as a common extract, it possesses little power. The best is procured by cutting the stalks of the leaves while growing, and allowing the white juice which exudes to dry spontaneously. This Lactucarium resembles opium, though less active in its power of promoting sleep and allaying pain. Some have thrown doubt upon its powers. It does not confine the bowels like opium. It is particularly recommended for use in phthisis, and to allay irritability of the mucous membrane in catarrh. The dose of Lactucarium is from one to four grains. It is sometimes used externally.

Extractum Lactucæ (Paris Codex): dose, one to five grains.

Aqua Lactucæ (P. C.): half an ounce to two ounces.

Syrup. Lactucæ (P. C.) and *Syrup. Lactucarii* (P. C.): half an ounce to one ounce.

Pilulæ Lactucarii (Ellis): one every two hours, till sleep is procured.

Tinct. Lactucarii (E.): half a drachm to two drachms.

Trochisci Lactucarii (E.).

1894. ℞ Extr. Lactucæ,
Extr. Lupuli, ana gr. v.
Mix: make 2 pills. To be taken at bedtime.

Dr. Paris.

1895. ℞ Pil. Rhei Comp. ℈ij.
Extr. Lactuc. ℈j.
Mix: divide into 12 pills. One or two at night.

In Chronic Bronchitis.—Dr. Gregory.

1896. ℞ Ext. Lactuc. gr. iij.
Camph.
Extr. Hyoscyami, ana gr. ij.
Mix, and divide into 2 pills. To be taken every night at bedtime.

Mr. Stone.

1897. ℞ Morph. Acetatis, gr. iij.
Extr. Lactuc. gr. xxxij.
Olei Juniperi, gtt. viij.
Mucilaginis, q. s.
Mix: and divide into 8 pills. One every night.

Anodyne and Soporific.

1898. ℞ Extr. Lactuc. gr. xvj.
Extr. Papaveris albi, gr. xij.
Pulv. Aloes Co. gr. xviij.
Olei Cinnamomi, gtt. ij.
Mix: divide into 12 pills. Two every night.

Anodyne and Aperient.

1899. ℞ Succi spiss. Lactucæ vir. ʒss.
Pulv. Tragac. Co. ℈j.
Potass. Nitratis, ℈ij.
Mist. Amygdalæ, ℥iv.
Mix: make a mixture. A tablespoonful three times a day.

Anodyne.—Dr. Joy.

1900. ℞ Aquæ Lactucæ, ℥iv.
Aquæ florum Aurant. ʒij.
Syr. Pæoniæ, ʒj.
Syr. Belladonnæ, ʒij.
Liq. Ammoniæ, gtt. iij.
Mix: make a mixture. A tablespoonful every fourth hour.

In Pertussis.—Dr. PEYROTON.

1901. ℞ Lactucarii, gr. xxx.
Decocti Lichenis Islandic. ℥ij.
Mucilaginis, ℥ss.
Syrupi, ℥j. Mix. ℥j every two hours.

In Spasmodic Cough, Sleeplessness, Hysteria, &c.—BRERA.

1902. ℞ Lactucarii, ℈j.
Mucilag. Acaciæ, q. s. to reduce.
When perfectly mixed, pour on
Aquæ, ℥vj.
Syrup. Rubi Idæi, ℥ss.
Mix: make a mixture. Two spoonfuls every second hour.

In Spasmodic Cough, Sleeplessness, and Hysteria.
VON HILDENBRAND.

1903. ℞ Lactucarii, gr. vj.
Aquæ destill. ʒiij.
Mucilag. Cydoniæ, gtt. xx. Make an eye-wash.

In Catarrhal Ophthalmia.—RAU.

1904. ℞ Acidi Boracici, ʒij.
Lactucarii, ℈j. Solve in
Aquæ destill. ℥vj, et adde
Syrup. Papav. ℥ss.
Mix. Dose, a teaspoonful.

In Spastic Hæmoptysis.—ROTHANILL. (?)

1905. ℞ Tinct. Lactucarii, ʒj.
Aquæ destill. ℥j.
Aquæ Laurocerasi, ♏xx.
Syrupi simplicis, ʒij.
Mix: make a draught. To be taken in the morning and late in the evening.

Anodyne in Phthisis.—Dr. NELIGAN.

LAUROCERASUS.

The leaves of the common Cherry-laurel, *Cerasus Laurocerasus* (Nat. Ord. *Amygdaleæ*), yield a small quantity of Hydrocyanic Acid when distilled with water. The various preparations are used internally as sedative in cases of gastric neuralgia and dysentery, and applied externally to cancerous sores, burns, and other painful affections.

Aqua Laurocerasi (E., D.): dose, ten to forty drops.

Oleum Laurocerasi contains Prussic Acid, is poisonous, and of variable strength.

Infusum Laurocerasi (Cheston): for outward application to malignant ulcers.

1906. ℞ Aquæ Laurocerasi, ʒj.
Aquæ Menthæ pip. ℥ij.
Infus. Quassiæ, ℥iv.
Mix: ℥ss three times a day.

In Dysentery, &c.—AUGUSTIN.

1907. ℞ Aquæ Laurocerasi, ℥iv.
Etheris Sulph. ℥j.
Extr. Belladonnæ, ʒij. Mix: make a lotion.

In Neuralgia.—ROUX.

1908. ℞ Aquæ Laurocerasi, ℥iss.
Olei Amygdalæ, ℥ij.
Ceræ Albæ, ℥ss.
Liquefy the wax with oil, and mix with the laurel water, triturating well. Make an ointment.

As an application to Burns.—ROUX.

LAVANDULA. *Lavender.*

The flowers of the common Lavender, *L. vera* (Nat. Ord. *Labiatæ*), are well known on account of their fragrance, which is owing to a volatile oil, which may be separated by distilling them with water. *Lavandula Spica*, French Lavender, does not yield an oil of such good quality. Lavender is warm, aromatic, and carminative, and thus useful as a stimulant in debility from any cause, or as a corrective adjunct to other medicines.

Oleum Lavandulæ (L., E., D.): dose, five to ten minims.

Spiritus Lavandulæ, (E.), and *Tinctura Lavandulæ Composita* (L., D.): dose, half a drachm to two drachms.

Aqua Lavandulæ (P. C.), a perfume, and aromatic adjunct.

1909. ℞ Olei Lavandulæ,
Adipis Myristicæ,
Butyri Cacao, each, equal parts.
Mix: make an ointment.

To stimulate the growth of Hair.—Dr. GRIFFITH.

LINI OLEUM, ET FARINA. *Linseed Oil. Linseed Meal.*

The ground seeds of the common Flax (*Linum usitatissimum*, Nat. Ord. *Linaceæ*) form Linseed meal. The oil is expressed in the cold from the same seed. It is bland and sweet to the taste. It possesses the property of drying when exposed. The coverings of the seeds contain a large quantity of vegetable mucilage. To this oil and mucilage the meal owes its demulcent property, which makes it so useful, when mixed with hot water, to form a poultice, or soothing application to external parts, when injured or inflamed from any cause. Poultices are used to soothe pain and excitement, to promote the suppuration and resolution of swellings and inflammations, to restore healthy action in diseased surfaces, and to allay irritation by their emollient property and by guarding from the access of air.

Linseed oil, given internally, is laxative. It may be mixed with lime-water to form an application to burns and scalds. Linseed is also applied internally in the preparation of demulcent drinks, which are prescribed in catarrhs, inflammation of the bladder, &c.

Lini Oleum, as a laxative, half an ounce to one ounce.

Infusum Lini Comp. (L.), an ounce and a half, *ad lib.*

Cataplasma Lini (L.), and *Cataplasma Emolliens* (Paris Codex), form excellent poultices.

Linimentum Lini Olei (Ainslie) is a good application to burns.

1910. ℞ Infus. Lini Co. ℥iij.
Olei Olivæ, ʒij.
Vitelli Ovi unius.
Syrupi Althææ, ℥j.
Make a mixture. A tablespoonful frequently.

Demulcent in Ardor Urinæ, &c.—Dr. NELIGAN.

1911. ℞ Infus. Lini Comp. ℥ivss.
Tinct. Camph. Co. ʒiij.
Aquæ florum Aurant. ʒix.
Mix: two tablespoonfuls three times a day.

As a Demulcent in Coughs.—Dr. GREGORY.

1912. ℞ Olei Lini, ℥ij.
Infus. Lini, ℥viij. Mix: make an enema.

Emollient and Laxative.—SWEDIAUR.

1913. ℞ Flor. Anthemidis,
Sem. Lini contus, ana ℥ss.
Aquæ fervidæ, ℥vj. Macerate and strain; then add
Opii, gr. vj–xvj. Mix: make an enema.

Emollient and Anodyne.—Dr. COPLAND.

1914. ℞ Hordei farinæ,
Lini farinæ, each, equal parts.
Decoct. Malvæ seu Althææ, q. s.

(Rub the meal in the decoction, and cook it to a fit consistence, frequently stirring it. The poultice must be applied between two cloths.)

A common Emollient Application.—TROUSSEAU and REVEIL.

LINUM CATHARTICUM. *Purging Flax.*

This diminutive plant grows plentifully in dry situations throughout Europe. It is used as a cathartic, and is tolerably active in its operation, though not dangerous. The powder of the dried plant may be given in doses of one drachm or more.

Extractum Lini Cathartici (Dr. B. Lane): dose, five to ten grains twice a day, as laxative and diuretic.

1915. ℞ Lini Cathartici, herbæ recentis, ʒiij.
Aquæ ferventis, ℥ij.
Digest for two hours in a closed vessel, strain, and add
Tinct. Cardam. Co. ʒj. Make a draught.

In simple Constipation.—Dr. NELIGAN.

LOBELIA.

The *Lobelia Inflata* (Nat. Ord. *Lobeliaceæ*) is a small plant common in the United States of America. The whole plant, dried, is used in medicine, and owes its activity to a peculiar alkaloid. In small doses it is diaphoretic and expectorant; in larger doses, antispasmodic, sedative, and emetic. Like tobacco, it is poisonous when given in large quantities. It may be used to relax the muscles in strangulated hernia, &c.; but it is chiefly employed in spasmodic asthma. It may be given in one large dose to produce vomiting, or, more safely, in small doses gradually increased. In the latter case, one to five grains of the powder may be given three times a day.

Infusum Lobeliæ (Ellis), given to produce vomiting, half an ounce every half hour.

Extractum Lobeliæ, one to two grains.

Tinctura Lobeliæ (L., E., D.), half a drachm to two drachms.

Tinctura Lobeliæ Ætherea (L., E.), ten minims to one drachm and a half.

Acetum Lobeliæ (Procter), half a drachm to a drachm.

Syrupus Lobeliæ (Procter), one to two drachms.

1916. ℞ Pil. Ipecacuan Co. ʒj.
Styracis colati, ʒss.
Pulv. Lobeliæ, gr. xij.
Mix: divide into 24 pills. Two, every six hours.

In old cases of Bronchitis and Humoral Asthma.

Dr. Neligan.

1917. ℞ Tinct. Lobeliæ, ʒj.
Decocti Malvæ, ℥vj.
Mix: make a mixture. A spoonful to be taken every two or three hours.

As an Expectorant.—Radius.

1918. ℞ Tinct. Lobeliæ, ℥ss.
Aquæ Anethi, ℥ij.
Aquæ puræ, ℥iv.
Mix: make a mixture. One-sixth part for a dose.

In Asthma.—Dr. Hooper.

1919. ℞ Tinct. Lobel. Æth. ʒij.
Mist. Amygdal. ℥viss.
Succi Conii, ʒij.
Syrup. Hemidesmi, ℥j.
Mix: make a mixture. A tablespoonful every three hours.

In Asthma and Paroxysmal Coughs.—Dr. Neligan.

LUPULUS. LUPULINA. *Hops*, and *Lupuline.*

Hops are the strobiles or dry catkins of the common Hop, *Humulus Lupulus* (Nat. Ord. *Urticaceæ*). They are cultivated chiefly on account of their use in the making of malt liquors, but are likewise used in medicine. They are tonic, aromatic, and slightly soporific. They contain a bitter principle and a volatile oil. At the bases of, and between the leafy scales, is contained a yellowish powder, in which most of the active property resides. This, when separated, is called Lupuline. Hops and Lupuline are employed in various cases where a stimulant tonic is desirable; and a pillow of hops has been used to procure sleep, which it may do by means of its odor. The dose of powdered Hops is from half a drachm to a drachm; of Lupuline, from six to ten grains.

Extractum Lupuli (L.), five to twenty grains.

Infusum Lupuli (L.), one to two ounces.

Tinctura Lupuli (L., E.), and *Tinctura Lupulinæ* (D.), half a drachm to two drachms.

Syrupus Lupulinæ (Foy), half an ounce to an ounce.

Unguentum Lupulinæ (Soubeiran) is employed to appease the pain of cancerous ulcers.

1920. ℞ Lupulinæ, gr. viij.
Mucilaginis, q. s. Make 2 pills, to be taken at bedtime.
In the watchfulness of Mania, &c.—Dr. NELIGAN.

1921. ℞ Extr. Lupuli,
Extr. Lactucæ,
Camphoræ, ana ℈j.
Mix: make 12 pills. Two, at the beginning of the pains, and repeat in two hours, or as occasion requires.
In Dysmenorrhœa.—Dr. RIGBY.

1922. ℞ Extr. Hyoscyami,
Camphoræ,
Lupulinæ, ana gr. iij.
Mix: make 2 pills. To be taken at bedtime.
In simple wakefulness.—Dr. J. B. STEWARD.

1923. ℞ Tinct. Lupuli, ℥j.
Infus. Rosæ, ℥v.
Acidi Sulph. dil. ʒj.
Mist. Camph. ℥ij.
Mix: make a mixture. Two tablespoonfuls twice a day.
In Menorrhagia.

1924. ℞ Lupuli Strobil. ℥iss.
Aquæ ferventis, Oj. Mix: to be used by inhalation.
In Phthisis.—Dr. THEOPHILUS THOMPSON.

MAGNESIA, ET MAGNESIÆ CARBONAS. *Calcined Magnesia, and Carbonate of Magnesia.*

This earth is the oxide of the metal Magnesium. The Carbonate is obtained by precipitating a solution of the Sulphate of Magnesia by one of Carbonate of Soda. Pure Magnesia is made by burning the Carbonate in a crucible. There are two kinds of Carbonate—heavy and light. The former is obtained by mixing strong solutions, at a high temperature; the light carbonate is made by mixing weak solutions in the cold. Both Magnesia and its Carbonate are white, tasteless powders, insoluble in water. Both form solutions with the acids, but the carbonate only effervesces while so doing. Magnesia and its Carbonate are similar in their actions on the system, and are not always distinguished by prescribers. Both are antacid, and act as mild laxatives on the bowels; but if given too often or too largely as purgatives, they are apt to accumulate and form masses in the intestines. As an antacid, Magnesia is given in dyspepsia, heartburn, pyrosis, gouty and lithic disorders. As a laxative, it is very safe in the various affections of children. Combined with rhubarb, it is given in diarrhœa, and as an ordinary purge. The dose of Magnesia is from three to five grains for infants; for adults, from ten grains to half a drachm, according to the action required.

Trochisci Magnesiæ (calcinatæ), U. S.

Trochisci Magnesiæ (carbonatis), E.

1925. ℞ Magnesiæ, ℈ij.
Pulv. Rhei, gr. xv.
Pulv. Zingiberis, gr. v.

Make a powder: to be taken as often as a day passes without a movement of the bowels.

In Habitual Constipation.—Dr. PARIS.

1926. ℞ Magnes. Carbon.
Potass. Supertartratis,
Sacchari, utriusque gr. x.

A powder, to be taken every morning.

In Anasarca.—Dr. HAMILTON.

1927. ℞ Magnes. Calcin. ℈ij.
Pulv. Rhei, ℈j.
Pulv. Cinnamomi, gr. x.

Mix: three or four grains every third hour to very young infants; six to ten grains from six to twelve months.

Drs. EVANSON and MAUNSELL.

1928. ℞ Magnes. Carb. ℈j.
Inf. Gentian. co. ℥xj.
Tinct. Cardam. co. ʒj.

Mix: make a draught, to be taken twice a day.

In Dyspepsia with Acidity.—Mr. SAVORY.

1929. ℞ Magnes. Calcin. ʒss.
Aquæ Menth. pip. ℥iss.
Tinct. Aurantii, ʒj. Mix: make a draught.

In Heartburn.

1930. ℞ Magnes. Calcin. ʒiss.
Pulv. Rhei, ʒj.
Pulv. Zingiberis, ℈j.
Aquæ Menthæ pip. Oj. Mix: dose, ℥ss three times a day.

In Dyspepsia and Hypochondriasis.—Dr. GREGORY.

1931. ℞ Magnes. Carb. ʒiss.
Ammon. Sesquicarb. ʒss.
Aquæ Menth. vir. ℥vss.
Tinct. Lavand. co. ʒij.
Spirit. Carui, ʒj.
Syrupi Zingiberis, ʒij.
Make a mixture. A tablespoonful as occasion requires.

Antacid in Cardialgia, &c.—Dr. PARIS.

1932. ℞ Magnes. Carbon. ʒiss.
Spirit. Æth. Sulph. co. ʒiij.
Tinct. Cardam. co. ℥ss.
Spirit. Anisi, ʒv.
Olei Carui, ♏viij.
Syrupi Zingiberis, ʒij.
Mist. Camph. ℥iss.
Aquæ Menth. vir. ℥v.
Mix: make a mixture. Two tablespoonfuls when there is great nausea or flatulency, first shaking the phial.

Dr. JOY.

1933. ℞ Magnes. ℈j.
Olei Carui, ♏iv.
Spirit. Amm. fœt. ♏xx.
Tinct. Opii, ♏v.
Syrup. simp. ℥ss.
Aquæ Menthæ, ℥iss.
Mix: make a mixture. A teaspoonful every four hours.

In Diarrhœa and Flatulence of young children, continuing after the use of purgatives. Dr. JOY.

1934. ℞ Magnes. Carb. ʒij.
Pulv. Rhei, ℈ij.
Spirit. Ammon. Arom.
Syrupi Zingiberis, ana ℥ss.
Aquæ puræ, ℥v. Mix: one-sixth for a dose.

In Gastralgia and Pyrosis.—Dr. HOOPER.

1935. ℞ Magnes. Sulph. ʒij.
Magnes. Carbon. ℈j.
Syrupi Zingiberis, ʒj.
Aquæ Anethi, ʒxi.
Mix: make a draught. This white draught is often retained by the stomach when every other form of purge is rejected.

Dr. DRUITT.

1936. ℞ Magnes. Carb. ʒj.
Magnes. Sulph. ʒiij.
Spirit. Amm. arom. ʒj.
Tinct. Hyoscyami, ʒj.
Aquæ Menth. sat. ℥iv.
Mix: a tablespoonful three times a day.

1937. ℞ Magnes. Carb. ℥ss.
Pulv. cort. Aurant.
Pulv. Sem. Fœniculi,
Pulv. Sacchari puri, ana ʒj.
Mix well, and divide into 10-grain powders. (One to be given to wet nurses, when their milk decreases.)

Mr. SAVORY.

1938. ℞ Magnes. Carb. ʒiss.
Pulv. rad. Rhei, ʒss.
Mist. Acaciæ,
Syrupi Zingiberis, ana ʒvj.
Aquæ Pimentæ, ℥ivss.
Mix: make a mixture. Two tablespoonfuls two or three times a day.

As a Laxative in Chorea.—Dr. THOMAS.

1939. ℞ Magnes. ustæ, ʒij.
Tinct. Jalap. ʒj.
Mucilag. Gum. Acac.
Syrupi,
Aquæ Cinnamomi, ana ℥ss. When well mixed, pour in Aquæ, ℥ivss.
Make a mixture: dose, f℥j three times a day.

In Chorea of young children.—Dr. T. HAMILTON.

1940. ℞ Magnes. Carb. ℈j.
Tinct. Cardam. Co. ʒij.
Aquæ Anethi, ℥ss.
Syrupi, ʒij.
Mix: a teaspoonful frequently during the day.

In the colic of Infants.—Dr. GREGORY.

MAGNESIÆ BICARBONAS. *Bicarbonate of Magnesia.*

This is not known in the solid form, but it occurs dissolved in water in the elegant preparation called *Fluid Magnesia.* This is made by forcing Carbonic Acid Gas into water in which Carbonate of Magnesia is suspended. This is dissolved by the action of the gas, and the soluble bicarbonate formed. This preparation is pleasant to the taste. It supplies us with a pleasant mode of administering magnesia, and is especially resorted to as an antacid in gouty and dyspeptic disorders. The dose of Dinneford's solution is from half an ounce to one and a half ounce. The following preparations, though much weaker, are similar:

Liq. Magnesiæ Carbonatis (Paris Codex, *Eau Magnésienne*): dose, two to ten ounces.

Liq. Magnesiæ Carbonatis aeratus (Paris Codex, *Eau Magnésienne gazeuse*): one to ten ounces. It contains less magnesia, and more carbonic acid.

1941. ℞ Aquæ Magnes. Bicarb. ℥ss.
Spirit. Lavand. co. ʒij.
Mix: make a draught. To be taken immediately, and repeated if necessary in half an hour.

In Heartburn.—Dr. NELIGAN.

1942. ℞ Solutionis Magnes. (ope acidi carbonici), ℥iss.
Tinct. Ferri Mur. ♏x–xxx.
Make a draught, to be taken three times a day, drinking afterward a wineglassful of cold or tepid water.

In Anæmia, Chlorosis, Nervous Palpitations, &c.—Dr. JOY.

MAGNESIÆ ACETAS ET CITRAS. *Acetate and Citrate of Magnesia.*

These are prepared in solution by dissolving carbonate of magnesia with just enough acetic or citric acid to saturate it. Half an ounce of citric acid is equivalent to about three and a half drachms of the carbonate. These compounds are agreeable to the taste. They are employed as laxatives in inflammations, and to form refrigerant drinks in fever.

The dose of the *Liq. Magnesiæ Citratis* (Rabourdin) is from six to twelve ounces. It acts as a purgative.

Liq. Mag. Citratis (U. S.): dose, three to four ounces.

1943. ℞ Magnes. Carbon. ʒj.
Syrupi Tolutani, ʒj.
Spirit. Myristicæ, ʒss.
Succi Limonis, ʒiij.
Aquæ, ʒix. Mix: make a draught.

Mr. BRANDE.

1944. ℞ Solutionis Magnes. Bicarbon. ℥iss.
Syrupi Aurantii, ʒj.
Mix: make a draught with fʒiij of lemon-juice, to be taken while effervescing.

MAGNESIÆ SULPHAS. *Sulphate of Magnesia.*

This salt is contained in sea-water, Seidlitz-water, and in Epsom and Cheltenham salts. It occurs in prismatic crystals, which are soluble in water, and have a bitter, nauseous taste. They must not be mistaken for sulphate of zinc or oxalic acid. Sulphate of magnesia in small doses is diuretic; in large doses, a hydragogue cathartic, acting effectively, but without irritation. Being cooling in its operation, it is particularly adapted for use in inflammatory disorders of all kinds. It is one of the most frequently used of all purgative medicines. It is very often conjoined with senna in the prescription of a cathartic dose. Dose, from one drachm to one ounce.

Aqua Seidlitzensis (Paris Cod.) is a solution charged with carbonic acid gas. Dose, half pint to one pint.

(The double salts formed by the sulphate of magnesia with the sulphate of iron and quinine, might, perhaps, be employed with advantage in medical practice; but the preparations which have hitherto been sold under these names are spurious.)

Pulvis salinus compositus (E.), dose, two drachms to half an ounce, and *Enema catharticum* (D.) contain sulphate of magnesia.

1945. ℞ Magnes. Sulph. ʒvj.
Mannæ optimæ, ʒij.
Aquæ destill. ℥iss. Mix: make an aperient draught.

Dr. Hooper.

1946. ℞ Magnes. Sulph. ℥j.
Potass. Bicarbon. ʒij.
Aquæ Menth. pip. ℥vss.
Syrupi, ʒij. Mix: make a cathartic mixture.

Dr. Paris.

1947. ℞ Magnes. Sulph. ℥iss.
Magnes. Carbon.
Sodæ Bicarbon. ana ℥ss.
Sodii Chloridi, ʒij.
Pulv. Zingiberis, ʒj.
Mix. (One or two teaspoonfuls in warm water at bedtime.)

In Dysmenorrhœa.—Dr. Ashwell.

1948. ℞ Flor. Anthemidis, ℥ij.
Rad. Zingib. concis. ℥j.
Aquæ ferventis, Oiss.
Macerate during the night, strain, and add
Magnes. Sulph. ℥ij.
Sodæ Sulph. ℥iss.
Potass. Sulph. ʒv.
Mix: take a wineglassful the first thing in the morning. (After each dose take an hour's exercise in the open air, and breakfast afterward.)

Saline Aperient.—Dr. Copland.

1949. ℞ Magnes. Sulph. ʒiv.
Aquæ puræ, ʒiv.
Infus. Rosæ comp. ʒiv.
Syrupi Aurantii, ʒj.
Mix: make a draught. To be taken every third hour.

Dr. GREGORY.

1950. ℞ Magnes. Sulph. ʒvj.
Infus. Rosæ acidi, ℥ij. Mix: make a draught.

To purge in mild Febrile and Inflammatory Affections.

Dr. NELIGAN.

1951. ℞ Magnes. Sulph. ʒss–ʒj.
Aqua Rosæ, ℥j.
Acid. Sulph. dil. ♏x.
Acid. Hydrocyan. dil. ♏iij.
Mix: make a draught. To be taken every fourth hour.

In Hæmoptysis.—Dr. THEOPHILUS THOMPSON.

1952. ℞ Magnes. Sulph. ʒj–ʒiv.
Syrupi Aurantii, ʒij.
Acidi Sulph. dil. ♏x.
Aquæ Anethi, ℥j.
Mix: make a draught. Antiphlogistic purge. To this draught may be added, in case of debility, one grain of Sulphate of Zinc, or Sulphate of Iron, or two grains of Quinine.

Dr. DRUITT.

1953. ℞ Magnes. Sulph. ℥j.
Antimonii Potass.-Tart. gr. j.
Spirit. Ætheris Nitrici, ʒij.
Aquæ Menthæ, ℥x.
Mix: three large tablespoonfuls every fourth hour.

An active nauseating aperient for robust persons.

Dr. DRUITT.

1954. ℞ Magnes. Sulph. ℥j.
Antim. Potass.-Tart. gr. ij.
Aquæ, ℥viij. Mix. An ounce every hour.

In Asiatic Cholera.—Dr. JEPHSON (U. S.).

1955. ℞ Magnes. Sulph. ℥ss.
Mannæ, ʒij.
Infus. Sennæ, ʒvj.
Tinct. Sennæ, ʒij.
Aquæ Menthæ vir. ℥j.
Aquæ destill. ℥ij.
Mix: make a mixture. Three tablespoonfuls every morning, and repeat in four hours, if necessary.

Mr. ABERNETHY.

1956. ℞ Mannæ, ʒij.
Magnes. Sulph. ℥ss.
Infusi Sennæ, ʒvj.
Tinct. Sennæ, ʒij.
Aquæ Menth. pip. ℥j.
Mist. Camphoræ, ℥ij.
Mix: make a mixture. Three or four tablespoonfuls early in the morning.

Mr. ABERNETHY.

1957. ℞ Magnes. Sulph.
Mannæ, ana ℥j.
Tamarindi pulpæ, ℥ss.
Decocti Hordei, ℥iij. Dissolve, and add
Antimon. Tartariz. gr. j.
Make a mixture. Two tablespoonfuls, until the bowels have responded two or three times.

As a laxative in Remittent Fever.—Dr. E. J. CLARK.

1958. ℞ Magnesiæ Sulphatis, ʒiv.
Acidi Sulph. dil. ʒj.
Ferri Sulphatis, gr. vj.
Infusi Aurantii, ℥xiss. Mix: a sixth part twice a day.

In Anæmia, &c.

1959. ℞ Magnes. Sulph. ʒij.
Mannæ, ʒij.
Emuls. Amygdalæ, ℥iv.
Mix: make a purgative mixture for an infant. (A dessertspoonful for a child from one to two years old.)

Mr. SAVORY.

1960. ℞ Magnesiæ Sulphatis, ʒij.
Syrupi Aurantii, ʒij.
Aquæ Carui, ʒvj.
Mix: fʒij every hour until the bowels operate.

Laxative for children of three years of age.—Dr. WEST.

1961. ℞ Magnesiæ Sulphatis, ʒj.
Tinct. Rhei, ʒij.
Aquæ Carui, ʒvij. Mix: a teaspoonful every six hours.

In Simple Diarrhœa of Infants.—Dr. WEST.

1962. ℞ Magnesiæ Sulphatis, ℥ss.
Tinct. Jalapæ, ʒj.
Acidi Nitrici, ♏ij.
Aquæ Menthæ vir. ℥ij. Mix: make a draught.

In disordered states of the Liver.—Dr. ELLIS.

MALVA. *Mallow.*

The leaves of the common Mallow, *Malva sylvestris* (Nat. Ord. *Malvaceæ*), contain a considerable quantity of mucilage, which they yield to water. Their decoction is sometimes employed for its demulcent and emollient properties. It is employed externally as a fomentation to wounds, tumors, and painful parts; or given internally as a drink in bronchitis, or in irritation of the intestinal canal or urinary organs.

Decoctum Malvæ Compositum, one to three ounces.

1963. ℞ Decoct. Malvæ co. ℥vj.
Syrupi Papaveris, ʒij.
Oxymellis Scillæ, ʒj.
Mix: a fourth part when the cough is troublesome.

MANGANESII SALES. *Salts of Manganese.*

The metal Manganese resembles iron. Its black binoxide is well known. This is employed by chemists in the preparation of oxygen and chlorine. It has been used medicinally in the treament of some cutaneous maladies, being applied in the form of ointment to the eruptions of scabies and herpes.

The salts of Manganese are said to resemble those of iron in their tonic powers, but differ from them in being destitute of any astringent properties. They have also been found by Ure, Gmelin, Hannon, and others, to exert a remarkable power in causing the secretion of bile, and to act in large doses as purgatives.

The chief preparations of Manganese which have been used in medicine are as follows:

Manganesii Binoxidum. Given internally in scabies and syphilis. Dose, three to twenty grains three times a day.

Manganesii Carbonas. Also insoluble. Used in the same cases and same doses.

Manganesii Sulphas. Given as an alterative in cutaneous diseases, in doses of five to ten grains. As a purge and cholagogue, in doses of one to two drachms.

Manganesii Acetas. Dose, as an alterative, five to ten grains.

In the *Manganesii et Ferri Sulphas*, and *Manganesii et Ferri Carbonas cum Saccharo*, the properties of iron and manganese are obtained together. They may be given in anæmia, amenorrhœa, jaundice, &c., in doses of five grains to one scruple.

The *Chloride*, *Iodide*, *Malate*, and *Tartrate* are sometimes used in the form of pills, in scrofula, anæmia, and various skin diseases.

Pilulæ Manganesii Carbonatis (Hannon): dose, four to ten grains daily.

Pilulæ Manganesii Iodidi (Hannon): one pill daily, increasing.

Pilulæ Manganesii Malatis (Hannon): three, five, or six, daily.

Pilulæ Manganesii Phosphatis, and *Pilulæ Manganesii et Ferri Sulphatis:* eight to thirty grains daily.

(Various syrups of the same salts are prescribed by M. Hannon. See POCKET FORMULARY.)

1964. ℞ Manganesii Binoxidi, ℥j.
Sodii Chloridi, ℥iij. Mix well, and add
Acidi Sulphurici, ℥j.
Aquæ, ℥ij.

(The Chlorine which is evolved from this mixture on the application of heat, forms a powerful local stimulant in certain cases of cutaneous disease, and in chronic rheumatism. The gas should be carefully confined to the part by the proper apparatus.)

Dr. HOOPER.

1965. ℞ Manganesii Carb.
Extr. Cinchonæ, ana ʒj.

Mix, and divide into 30 pills. One twice a day, before breakfast and dinner.

In Chlorosis.—M. HANNON.

1966. ℞ Manganesii et Ferri Carbonatis cum Saccharo, gr. iij.
Extr. Sanguinis Bovini (prepared by drying and powdering the blood), gr. xv.

Mix: make a powder. To be taken three times a day after meals.

In Anæmia of Children.—Dr. S. T. SPEER.

1967. ℞ Manganesii Sulph.
Sodæ Carb. ana ʒj.
Mellis, q. s. to form a mass. Divide into 4-grain pills. One, for a dose.

In Anæmic Disorders.—M. HANNON.

1968. ℞ Manganesii Sulph. ʒiv.
Vini Sem. Colchici, ♏xxx.
Aquæ Rosæ, ℥iv. Mix: make a draught.

Purgative in Gouty or Rheumatic habits.—Dr. NELIGAN.

1969. ℞ Manganesii Sulph. ℈j.
Magnesiæ Sulph. ʒij.
Syrupi Zingiberis, ʒj.
Aquæ, ℥iss.
Mix: make a draught, to be taken in the morning.

In Gouty cases, to produce a copious discharge of Bile.

DR. DRUITT.

1970. ℞ Manganesii Sulph. ʒiv.
Acidi Sulph. dil. ♏viij.
Infusi Sennæ co. ℥ij. Mix: make a draught.

In Dyspeptic Affections and Bilious Disorder.—DR. NELIGAN.

1971. ℞ Manganesii Phosph.
Pulv. Cinchonæ, ana ʒss.
Syrupi Catechu, q. s.
Divide into 4-grain pills. One, three times a day.

MANNA. MANNITA. *Manna and Mannite.*

Manna is the concrete juice of two species of *Ornus* (or *Fraxinus*), the *O. Europæa* and *O. rotundifolia*, both natives of Southern Europe. They belong to the Nat. Ord. *Oleineæ*. The variety called Flake Manna is the best. Manna has a sweetish and slightly bitter taste. It acts as a gentle laxative, though its operation sometimes causes flatulence. This purgative property is owing to a peculiar unfermentible sugar, called Mannite, which it contains. This may be extracted from it by boiling alcohol, and will precipitate in white needles on cooling. It is a very agreeable cathartic. Both Manna and Mannite are well adapted for use in the affections of children, in obstinate constipation, and in the disorders of weakly women, as phlegmasia dolens, ascites, or low peritonitis.

The dose of Manna for children is one to four drachms; for adults, one to two ounces. Mannite is given by M. Solon in doses of one to two ounces, dissolved in two to four ounces of aromatic water, and taken warm.

1972. ℞ Mannæ, ℥j.
Potassæ Bitartratis, ʒss.
Seri Lactis, ʒvj.
Mix: take one-half immediately, and the balance in two hours after.

DR. JOY.

1973. ℞ Magnesiæ Sulph. ℥j.
Mannæ, ʒvj.
Tinct. Sennæ, ʒiss.
Aquæ ferventis, ℥v. Mix: dose, a fourth, or half part.

DR. AINSLIE.

1974. ℞ Saponis Venet. ℈iv.
Olei Amygd. dul. ℥iss. Dissolve, and add
Mannæ purif. ℥ss.
Potassæ Supertart. ʒij.
Syrupi Althææ, ℥j. Mix: make an emollient linctus.
BRENDELL.

1975. ℞ Mannæ, ℥j.
Aquæ Fœniculi, ℥iij.
Spir. Ammon. co. gtt. xx.
Mix: a tablespoonful every hour.
In Infantile Catarrh.—Mr. SAVORY.

1976. ℞ Mannæ, ℥ss.
Mucilag. Acaciæ, ℥ss.
Syrupi Violæ, ʒij.
Aquæ Menthæ, ℥j.
Mix: make a mixture. One to two teaspoonfuls every third hour.
For Infants in the early months.—Dr. JOY.

1977. ℞ Mannæ, ʒvj.
Syrupi Sennæ, ʒiij.
Olei Amygd. dulcis, ʒij. Rub up well, and add
Aquæ Fœniculi, ʒij.
Sacch. albi, ʒiss. Make an electuary: dose, ʒj to ʒij.
Aperient for young Children.—Dr. COPLAND.

1978. ℞ Mannitæ, ʒss.
Aquæ Menthæ pip. ℥ss. Dissolve, to make a draught.
An excellent Laxative for Children.—Dr. NELIGAN.

MARRUBIUM. *Horehound.*

Marrubium vulgare (Nat. Ord. *Labiatæ*) is a small herb common in England. In the fresh state it has a strong and peculiar aromatic odor. Both fresh and dry, it has a bitter taste. The plant also contains much mucilage. These constituents have been the cause of its extensive use as a popular demulcent tonic in simple coughs. It is also a general tonic, laxative, and antispasmodic. The dose is from half a drachm to one drachm in powder.

Extractum Marrubii (Port. Pharm.). Dose, five to ten grains, as a febrifuge.

Infusum Marrubii, one to two ounces.

1979. ℞ Extr. Marrubii,
Extr. Graminis (couch grass), ana ʒij.
Decocti Taraxaci, ℥x.
Oxymellis Scillæ,
Syrupi Fœniculi, ana ℥ij.
Mix: a tablespoonful frequently.

In Pectoral Complaints.—AUGUSTIN.

1980. ℞ Marrubii herb. exsic. ℥ss.
Aquæ destill. fervent. Oss.
Macerate for an hour, and strain.

℞ Colaturæ, ℥iss.
Tinct. Camph. co. ʒj.
Extr. Glycyrrhizæ, gr. x.
Mix: make a draught. To be taken three times a day.

In Chronic Bronchitis with Inordinate Secretions.
DR. COPLAND.

MASTICHE. *Mastich.*

This is an oleo-resin, which exudes from the *Pistacia Lentiscus*, a tree which grows in the countries bordering the Mediterranean (Nat. Ord. *Terebinthaceæ*). It occurs in yellowish semi-transparent brittle tears, of a pleasant smell and taste. It is employed in the manufacture of varnish; and used in medicine as a masticatory in toothache and other complaints, and as an ingredient in stimulating tinctures used in affections of the mouth and gums. It is contained in *Tinct. Ammoniæ co.*

1981. ℞ Pulv. Mastiches,
Pulv. Cretæ, ana ʒij.
Pulv. Iridis rad. ℥ss.
Olei Rosæ, gtt. iij. Mix: make a dentifrice.

PHŒBUS.

1982. ℞ Pulv. Mastiches,
Pulv. Sandarachi, ana ʒij.
Pulv. Kino, gr. x.
Pulv. Opii, gr. ij.
Olei Rosmarini, gtt. viij.
Spir. Armoraciæ, q. s.
To make a paste. For the toothache.

To fill Decayed Teeth.—GASSICOURT.

MATICO.

The leaves of *Artanthe elongata*, a Peruvian plant (Nat. Ord. *Piperaceæ*), which are large and strongly veined, and spongy on the under surface, are extensively used in their native country for the purpose of arresting local hæmorrhages. The leaves are either applied whole, or dried and reduced to a coarse powder, and in that state pressed on to the bleeding part. Matico has been further recommended in this country as an astringent for internal use. Chemical analysis has shown that it contains an aromatic and a bitter principle; but nothing has been found which can give it a real astringent quality. Its reputation as a styptic may probably be owing to the mechanical properties of the leaf and its powder, which may enable it to arrest hæmorrhage in the same way as German tinder and other applications of the kind. (See ROYLE'S MATERIA MEDICA.)

Decoctum Matico (D.), and *Infusum Matico* (D.): dose, half an ounce to one and a half ounce three times a day.

Tinctura Matico (D.): half drachm to two drachms.

1983. ℞ Tinct. Matico, ʒvj.
Inf. Krameriæ, ℥vij.
Syrupi Croci, ʒij.
Mix: make a mixture. f℥ss every three or four hours.
In the Diarrhœa of Phthisis, &c.—Dr. NELIGAN.

1984. ℞ Pulv. Matico, ʒiij.
Pulv. Opii, gr. iij.
Adipis, ℥j. Mix: make an ointment.
To Hæmorrhoids.—Dr. YOUNG.

MATRECARIA. *Corn Chamomile.*

The flowers of the *Matrecaria Chamomilla* are smaller than those of the true Chamomile, which they much resemble (Nat. Ord. *Compositæ*). Like them they possess a bitter taste and aromatic odor, which is partly lost on drying. Matrecaria may be used as a demulcent tonic in the same manner as Anthemis.

MEL. *Honey.*

A sweet fluid, prepared by the *Apis mellifica*, or Honey Bee. It tends to concrete on keeping. It contains two kinds of sugar, one of which crystallizes, but the other does not. It is nutritious, demulcent, and laxative; but chiefly is used as a vehicle, as in *Mel Boracis*, *Mel Rosæ*. It is employed in gargles, and given as a demulcent in coughs.

Oxymel, which contains vinegar and honey, is employed as an expectorant, and to form with water a cooling drink in febrile affections. The dose of Oxymel is one to two drachms.

Hydromel, or honied water (one part in sixteen), forms an agreeably refrigerant and slightly laxative drink.

Ceromel, a mixture of wax and honey, is applied to ulcers.

1985. ℞ Mellis,
Butyri recentis, ana ℥ij.
Liquefy by a slow heat. A spoonful frequently.

Expectorant.—St. Marie.

1986. ℞ Lichenis Islandici, ℥ij.
Foliorum Hyssopi, ℥ss.
Hydromellis, ℔ij. Macerate for five days, strain, and add
Sacchari, ℥iij.
One or two spoonfuls occasionally in catarrh.

Foy.

MELISSA. *Balm.*

The *Melissa officinalis*, a small herb well known in gardens, has an agreeable lemon-like odor, and aromatic and bitter taste. It belongs to the Nat. Ord. *Labiatæ*. It is chiefly used in perfumery, but it is sometimes employed in medicine for its stimulant and carminative properties, in the same manner as Thyme and Marjoram.

Infusum Melissæ (Plenck): dose, one to one and a half ounce.

1987. ℞ Melissæ officinalis exsic.
Rad. Glycyrrhizæ cont. ana ʒiiss.
Sem. Anisi cont.
Sem. Fœniculi cont.
Sem. Coriandri cont. ana ʒss.
Aquæ bullientis, ℔ij.
Infuse for an hour, and strain. Dose, ℥j–ij.

Dr. Copland.

MENTHÆ. *The Mints.*

Three kinds of Mint, all common and well-known plants, are employed in Medicine. They belong to the Nat. Ord. *Labiatæ*, and are named *M. piperita* (Peppermint), *M. viridis* (Spearmint), and *M. Pulegium* (Pennyroyal). All contain volatile oils, the odors of which, though somewhat similar, are yet easily distinguished. That of Peppermint is peculiarly pungent. These oils are separated by distillation, and employed in medicine for their carminative and stimulant properties, especially in dyspepsia, flatulence, and diarrhœa. They are likewise used to flavor more unpleasant medicines, and to correct the griping action of a purgative dose. The distilled waters of the mints contain only these volatile oils. The infusions, decoctions, and extracts contain also a bitter principle, which is found in these plants, and which imparts to them tonic properties. The dried plants are rarely used alone, except in cookery.

Oleum Menthæ viridis, *piperitæ*, or *Pulegii:* dose, two to five minims.

Aqua Menthæ viridis, *piperitæ*, and *Pulegii:* used as carminative vehicles.

Spiritus Menthæ viridis, *piperitæ*, and *Pulegii* (L.): dose, half to two drachms.

Infusum Menthæ viridis (D.): one and a half ounces every two hours to allay sickness, &c.

1988. ℞ Spirit. Menthæ pip. ℥j.
Aquæ Menthæ pip. ℥iv.
Syrupi Althææ, ℥iij.
Olei Cinnamomi, gtt. iij.
Olei Menthæ pip. gtt. iij.

Mix: a spoonful every two hours, in convulsive hiccough.

ALIBERT.

1989. ℞ Aquæ Menthæ piperitæ,
Infusi Caryophylli, ana ℥iiiss.
Tinct. Cardam. co. ʒss.
Spirit. Ammon. Arom.
Syrupi Zingiberis, ana ʒiss.

Mix: a wineglassful twice a day, after meals.

In Dyspepsia.—Dr. LATHAM.

1990. ℞ Menthæ viridis fol. rec. ℥iv.
Sacchari purif. ℥xij.

Bruise the leaves in a stone mortar, then adding the sugar, bruise them together until the compound forms a uniform mass. Dose, ʒj.

SPRAGUE.

1991. ℞ Fol. Menthæ vir. exsic.
Rad. Glycyrrhizæ concis. et contus. ana ℥ss.
Sem. Anisi cont.
Sem. Coriandri cont. ana ʒj.
Aquæ ferventis, q. s. to make of the strained infusion Oj.
Add magnesia and white sugar for the tormina of infants: or sometimes Acid. Sulph. Aromat. fʒj in nausea and vomiting.

Dr. COPLAND.

MENYANTHES. *Buckbean.*

Menyanthes trifoliata (Nat. Ord. *Gentianeæ*) is an elegant aquatic plant, with ternate leaves, and common in England. The leaves are chiefly used, but all parts of the plant possess similar properties. Like Gentian and Centaury, which belong to the same natural order, Buckbean is tonic and astringent. In large doses it is cathartic. It is very bitter to the taste, and contains a tonic principle. The various preparations may be used in scorbutus, scrofula, atonic debility, and costive conditions of the bowels. The powder of the leaves or root may be given in doses of twenty to thirty grains.

Infusum Menyanthidis: dose, one to two ounces.

Extractum Menyanthidis (Guibourt): ten to fifteen grains.

1992. ℞ Extr. Menyanthidis,
Extr. Valerianæ, ana ʒij.
Saponis duri, ℥ss.
Pulv. Rhei, ʒiss.
Syrupi, q. s. to make 2-grain pills.
Take ten three times a day.

In costive conditions of the Bowels.—VOGEL.

1993. ℞ Menyanthidis foliorum, ℥ss.
Zingiberis rad. concisæ, ℈ij.
Aquæ ferventis, Oss.
Macerate in a closed vessel for two hours, and strain. (In doses of ℥j–℥iss united with Spir. Æth. Nit. ʒj–ʒij.)

In Rheumatism, Arthritic Affections, and Cachectic and Cutaneous diseases. Dr. COPLAND.

1994. ℞ Extr. Menyanthidis, ℥ss.
Aceti Scillæ, ℥ij.
Tincturæ Assafœtidæ, ℥ss.
Mix: dose, thirty drops three times a day.

Diuretic.—AUGUSTIN.

MEZEREUM. *Mezereon.*

This is the bark of the root of the *Daphne Mezereon* (Nat. Ord. *Thymeleæ*), an English shrub. It contains a crystalline substance called Daphnine, but owes its medicinal properties to an acrid resin. These properties are not possessed to any extent by the wood. Mezereon bark is powerfully irritant, reddening the external surface. Internally, it is a diaphoretic and diuretic; in large doses it produces extreme purging, and becomes a poison. It is employed in various cutaneous diseases as a stimulant diaphoretic; also in secondary syphilis and chronic rheumatic complaints. It has been used as a vesicant, being first soaked in vinegar. Also as a masticatory, two or three grains being chewed at a time. The dose of the bark, rarely given alone, is from one to ten grains. It is contained in Decoct. Sarsæ comp.

Extractum Mezerei has been used as an external irritant.

Decoctum Mezerei (D.): dose, four to eight ounces daily, in syphilitic disorders.

Unguentum Mezerei (Guibourt) is used as a stimulating application to ulcers.

1995. ℞ Mezerei cort.
Armoraciæ rad. ana ℥j.
Aceti destill. ferventis, Oss. Infuse for a week, and strain.
Lotion for Porrigo Decalvans.—Mr. E. WILSON.

1996. ℞ Mezerei, ʒij.
Dulcamaræ, ℥ss.
Arctii Lappæ rad. ℥ij.
Aquæ, Oiv. Boil to three pints, and add
Rad. Glycyrrhizæ, ʒij. Strain: dose, f℥ij–f℥vj.
In obstinate Syphilitic and Cutaneous diseases.—VAN MONS.

MONARDA. *Horsemint.*

The *Monarda punctata* (Nat. Ord. *Labiatæ*) is an American plant, and is used in American practice. It has yellow flowers, spotted with brown. The whole plant is aromatic, and contains a stimulant volatile oil, which has a powerful smell. It is used in infusion, in the same manner as Spearmint, being given chiefly in flatulent colic. It has been recommended as an emmenagogue. The oil may be given as a carminative, in doses of two to three drops on sugar. It acts as a rubefacient externally.

1997. ℞ Olei Monardæ, ℥ss.
Tinct. Camphoræ, ℥ij.
Tinct. Opii, ʒij. Mix: make a liniment.

In Rheumatism and Fevers.—Dr. ATLEE (U.S.).

MONESIA.

This is the extract of some South American tree, the name of which is not certainly known, but it is supposed to be a *Chrysophyllum* (Nat. Ord. *Sapotaceæ*). It is in thick brown cakes, having a powerful bitter-sweet taste. It is soluble in water. It possesses astringent properties, and has been used in France with much success as a remedy in leucorrhœa, menorrhagia, diarrhœa, &c. It has also been given in chronic bronchitis, and applied externally in powder to atonic ulcers. Dose, two to ten grains, frequently repeated.

Mistura Monesiæ (Neligan): dose, half an ounce.

Syrupus Monesiæ (Derosne): dose, half an ounce.

1998. ℞ Extr. Monesiæ, ʒss.
Syrupi, ʒx.
Aquæ, ℥iij. Mix: to be taken in four doses.

In Chronic Diarrhœa.—TROUSSEAU and REVEIL.

1999. ℞ Syrupi Monesiæ (calidi), ℥xvj.
Aquæ flor. Aurantii, ℥ss.
Extracti Papaveris, gr. xvj. Mix: dose, half an ounce.

DEROSNE.

2000. ℞ Monesiæ, ʒj.
Aluminis, gr. xxiv.
Confect. Aromat. ʒss.
Syrupi, q. s. to form 24 pills. Two, three times a day.

In Chronic Diarrhœa, Pyrosis, and Leucorrhœa.
Dr. NELIGAN.

2001. ℞ Monesiæ,
Aquæ, ana ℥j.
Ceræ albæ, ℥ij.
Olei Amygdalæ, ℥iv. Mix: make an ointment.

In Indolent Ulcers.—DEROSNE.

MORPHIA. See OPIUM.

MORRHUÆ OLEUM. *Cod-liver Oil.*

This oil is derived from the liver of the *Gadus Morrhua*, or common Codfish, immense quantities of which are annually captured on the coast of Newfoundland. *Asellus* is one of the Latin names for this fish, whence the oil has been named *Oleum Jecoris Aselli*. The oils met with in commerce vary in appearance from pale to dark brown, according to the degree of heat which has been employed in their extraction from the livers. They are, however, very similar in composition, though liable to adulteration with other animal and vegetable oils. Besides the ordinary constituents of oils, this oil contains a certain proportion of biliary matters, a minute proportion of iodine, and a still smaller quantity of phosphorus. A violet color is produced in it by adding to it, on a white slab, a few drops of strong sulphuric acid. This is caused by the biliary matters present in the oil. Cod-liver oil has a peculiar taste and odor, though the intensity of these properties varies in different specimens.

This remedy is used with great advantage in many cases of emaciation depending upon a cachectic or scrofulous condition of the system. The patient will frequently grow fatter under its use, and gain health in proportion. Cod-liver oil is so serviceable in pulmonary consumption, that it has been supposed to exert a specific action in this disorder. If given in the early stages, it may sometimes check the disease altogether. It is useful also in skin diseases; in impaired nutrition from chronic gout and rheumatism; in scrofulous atrophy of children, with affections of the bones and joints. Cod oil, as also other oils, has been used as a vehicle for iodine, iodide of potassium, and phosphorus. Cod oil, when prescribed alone, may be taken floating on aromatic water, wine, or some other agreeable vehicle, or it may be suspended in mucilage, or saponified by admixture with potash, or the carbonate of potash or soda, and in that condition dissolved in water.

The dose of the oil for children is from one to two drachms three times a day; for adults, one to two ounces, or more. It should be continued for some time, or else no really beneficial results can be obtained. It may be applied externally in rheumatic, neuralgic, and some local scrofulous affections.

2002. ℞ Olei Morrhuæ,
Mucilaginis Tragac. ana ℥ij.
Aquæ Menthæ pip. ℥iv.

Rub well together, and form a mixture. Two tablespoonfuls three times a day.

Dr. Neligan.

2003. ℞ Olei Jecoris Aselli, ℥viij.
Pulv. Acaciæ, ℥j. Mix: make an emulsion, and add
Syrupi Aurantii, ℥j.
Spir. Menthæ pip. ʒij. Mix: a tablespoonful twice a day.

Dr. Ranking.

2004. ℞ Olei Morrhuæ nigri, ℥iij.
Ovor. duor. vitellos. Mix well in a marble mortar, and add
Syrup. cort. Aurant. ℥iss.
Aquæ flor. Aurant. ℥iij. Mix: four spoonfuls daily.

In Rickets.—Trousseau and Reveil.

2005. ℞ Ol. Morrhuæ depuratæ, ℥viij.
Pulv. Acaciæ, ℥iij.
Aquæ Menthæ sat. ℥iij.
Syrupi, ℥xviiss. Mix. one to eight tablespoonfuls daily.

In Scrofulous Affections, especially Rickets.

Trousseau and Reveil.

2006. ℞ Olei Morrhuæ, ℥iss.
Creasoti, gtt. iv.
Pulv. Tragacanthæ co. ʒij.
Aquæ Anisi, ℥ivss.

Mix: dose, ℥j three times a day. In cases when the oil produces nausea.

Consumption, &c.—Dr. A. T. Thomson.

2007. ℞ Olei Morrhuæ, ℥ss.
Liq. Ammoniæ, ♏v.

Mix: to be taken three times a day. The dose to be gradually augmented to five or six times the quantity.

In Diabetes.—Dr. Bence Jones.

2008. ℞ Olei Morrhuæ,
Syrupi Aurantii,
Aquæ Anisi, ana ℥j.
Olei Calami, gtt. iij. Mix: three spoonfuls a day.

In Rachitis and Gouty swellings.—Phœbus.

2009. ℞ Olei Jecoris Aselli, ℥j.
Sol. Potassæ Carb. ʒij.
Syrupi Aurantii, ℥j.
Olei Caryophylli, ♏iv. Mix: a teaspoonful twice a day.

For Children.—Dr. Ranking.

2010. ℞ Olei Morrhuæ, ℥iv.
Aq. Potass. Carb. ℥ss.
Olei Limon. ʒij.
Aquæ Carui, ℥iiss.
Spirit. Carui, ℥ss.
Mix: make a mixture. Two tablespoonfuls three times a day.

Dr. NELIGAN.

2011. ℞ Olei Morrhuæ, ʒiij.
Liquor Potassæ, ♏xx.
Potassii Iodidi, gr. viij.
Aquæ destill. ʒvij.
Mix: make a draught. To be taken three times a day.

In cases of Chronic Rheumatism with Cachexia.

Dr. H. W. FULLER.

2012. ℞ Olei Morrhuæ, ℥vj.
Ferri Iodidi, gr. xij. Dissolve f℥ss to f℥j for a dose.

In Consumption and Scrofula.—Dr. HEADLAND.

2013. ℞ Olei Morrhuæ, Oj.
Phosphori, gr. j.
Dissolve slowly with heat. Dose, f℥ss–f℥j.

In Phthisis.—Dr. T. THOMPSON.

2014. ℞ Olei Morrhuæ, ℥j.
Olei Lavandulæ, ♏x.
Mix: to be rubbed on the chest night and morning, when the stomach will not tolerate the oil.

Consumption, &c.—Dr. T. THOMPSON.

2015. ℞ Olei Morrhuæ, ℥ss.
Liq. Potassæ, ʒss.
Adipis præp. q. s.
Mix: make an ointment. To be used frequently.

In Scrofulous Ulcerations, and obstinate Cutaneous diseases.

Dr. NELIGAN.

2016. ℞ Olei Morrhuæ,
Extr. Fuliginis ligni, ana ʒij.
Unguenti citrini, ʒj.
Medullæ Ossium, ℥vj. Mix: make an ointment.

In Scrofulous Ophthalmia.—CARRON.

2017. ℞ Olei Morrhuæ, ℥j.
Aquæ Ammoniæ, ℥ss. Mix: make a liniment.

BRACH.

2018. ℞ Olei Morrhuæ, ʒiv.
Liq. Plumbi, ʒij.
Ovi Vitelli, ʒiij. Mix: make a liniment.

As an application to Ulcers.—BREFELD.

2019. ℞ Olei Morrhuæ, ʒj.
Olei Juglandis, ʒij.
Mix: a drop or two to be introduced between the eyelids.
In Opacities of the Cornea.

MORUS. *Mulberry.*

The common Mulberry is the fruit of *Morus nigra* (Nat. Ord. *Urticaceæ*), a common tree in gardens. It is an agreeable fruit, and has a dark subacid juice. This juice is sometimes employed in medicine as a grateful refrigerant in febrile disorders, and expectorant in coughs. It is slightly laxative.

Syrupus Mori (L.) is used as a coloring ingredient, and as an addition to refrigerant drinks in fevers.

MOSCHUS. *Musk.*

This is an odoriferous secretion found stored up in peculiar bags or follicles in the Musk Ox, *Moschus moschiferus* (Order, *Ruminantia*). It exists only in the males. The best musk comes from China, and is very valuable as a perfume. It is in soft reddish-brown grains, which possess a strong and well-known odor, and a bitter, disagreeable taste. Musk acts medicinally as a diffusible stimulant and antispasmodic. Thus it is used to rouse the system in low cases of typhoid and other fevers; and to act upon the nerves in chronic spasmodic diseases, as hysteria and epilepsy. The dose in substance is five grains to a scruple, every three or four hours.

Mistura Moschi (L. 1836): one to two ounces.

Mistura Moschi Ammoniata (White): dose, one to one and a half ounces.

2020. ℞ Moschi,
Ammoniæ Carbonatis, ana gr. x.
Confectionis Rosæ, q. s. to make a bolus.
One every three hours.
In Mortification, attended with spasmodic action.—Dr. Ellis.

2021. ℞ Moschi,
Camphoræ, ana ℥ss.
Olei Cajeputi, ♏v, or sufficient to make a mass to be divided into 12 pills. Two, every second or third hour.
Stimulant and Antispasmodic.—Dr. Hooper.

2022. ℞ Moschi, gr. viij.
Pulv. Opii, gr. ij.
Camphoræ, gr. xxiv.
Syrupi, q. s. to make a mass to be divided into 6 pills. To be taken during the day.

In Hospital Gangrene.—DUPUYTREN.

2023. ℞ Moschi, gr. viij.
Mist. Camph. ℥j.
Sp. Æth. Oleos.
Sp. Amm. Arom. ana ʒss.
Mix: make a draught. Every third hour.

In the Prostration of Fever.—Dr. GRAVES.

2024. ℞ Moschi, gr. x.
Ætheris,
Tinct. Opii, ana gtt. xx.
Aquæ Cinnamomi, ℥j. Mix: make a draught.

Last Stage of Typhus.—Dr. HOOPER.

2025. ℞ Moschi, gr. xxiv.
P. rad. Valerian, ℈iss.
Camphoræ rasæ, gr. xv.
Conserv. Rosarum, q. s. to make three boluses. One every fourth hour.

Antispasmodic.—Dr. COPLAND.

2026. ℞ Misturæ Moschi, ℥iv.
Spirit. Æth. Sulph. co.
Syrupi Aurantii, ana ℥j. Mix: a sixth part for a dose.

Stimulant Antispasmodic.—Dr. HOOPER.

2027. ℞ Moschi, gr. x–℈j.
Tinct. Castorei, ʒij
Syrupi Zingiberis, ʒij.
Aquæ dest. ℥j. Mix: make a draught.

In Coma from Fever.—Dr. E. J. CLARK.

2028. ℞ Moschi, gr. x.
Pulv. Valerianæ, ℥ss.
Pulv. Amyli, ʒss.
Aquæ ferventis, ℥viij. Mix: make an enema.

Antispasmodic and excitant.—RADIUS.

MYRISTICA. *Nutmeg.*

This is the roundish kernel of the fruit of the *Myristica moschata*, or Nutmeg-tree (Nat. Ord. *Myristicaceæ*), a native of the Molucca Islands. The nutmeg is hard, of a grayish color, and veined with red. It has an aromatic odor and taste, and contains a peculiar volatile oil, besides a fatty principle.

To the volatile oil nutmegs owe their stimulant and stomachic properties; but they are seldom prescribed alone, being generally given with less agreeable medicines, in order to disguise their flavor. *Mace* is a peculiar texture covering the shell of the nutmeg. It also is aromatic, and is sometimes used in medicine. The fat or butter of nutmegs may be used in making ointments. It is contained in the *Emplastrum Picis* (L.).

The dose of powdered Nutmeg or Mace is ten to thirty grains; of the *Oleum Myristicæ*, one to three drops.

Spiritus Myristicæ (L., E., D.), one to four drachms.

Pulvis Aromaticus (U. S.), ten to thirty grains.

2029. ℞ Cornu usti,
Pulv. Myristicæ,
Lauri baccarum tost. ana gr. x.
Pulv. Glycyrrhizæ, ʒss. Mix: make a powder.

In the Hectic attendant on Scrofulous Affections.—AUGUSTIN.

2030. ℞ Pulv. Myristicæ,
Pulv. Calumbæ, ana ʒj.
Pulv. Salepi, ℈j.
Infusi Lini, ℥iv. Mix: make a stimulant enema.

AMMON.

MYRRHA. *Myrrh.*

This gum-resin is produced by the *Balsamodendron Myrrha*, a small tree belonging to the Nat. Ord. *Terebinthaceæ*. It acts upon the mucous tracts in the same manner as the balsams, checking their secretions when inordinate in quantity. It is also tonic and antispasmodic. It is given in atonic dyspepsia, in chlorosis, in amenorrhœa, and in chronic bronchitis. It is frequently conjoined with chalybeates and with aloes. Externally, the tincture is used in gargles; the powder in dentifrices, and as an application to foul ulcers. Dose of the powder, ten to thirty grains.

Decoctum Myrrhæ (D.), one to two ounces.

Mistura Myrrhæ (Guy's), one to one and a half ounce.

Tinctura Myrrhæ, half to one drachm.

Emplastrum Myrrhæ.

2031. ℞ Myrrhæ contritæ, gr. vj.
Pulv. Ipecacuan. gr. iij.
Potassæ Nitratis, ʒss.
Mix, and divide into 4 parts. One every four hours.
Expectorant.—Dr. PARIS.

2032. ℞ Pulv. Myrrhæ, ʒiss.
Pulv. Scillæ, ʒss.
Extr. Hyoscyami, ℈ij.
Aquæ, q. s. to make 30 pills. Two, night and morning.
In Chronic Catarrh.—Mr. SAVORY.

2033. ℞ Pulv. Myrrhæ, ʒj.
Pulv. Scillæ, ℈j.
Pulv. Ammoniaci, ʒss.
Ammon. Carb. ʒss.
Extr. Hyoscyami, ℈ij.
Mucilag. Acaciæ, q. s. to make a mass: to be divided into 40 pills. Two, three times a day.
In Phthisis and Chronic Catarrh.—Dr. JOY.

2034. ℞ Myrrhæ, ʒiss.
Benzoini, ℈ij.
Bals. Copaibæ, ʒj.
Extr. Glycyrrhizæ, ℈iv.
Mix: make 44 pills. Two, two or three times a day.
In Asthma and Chronic Bronchitis.—Dr. COPLAND.

2035. ℞ Ferri Subcarb. ʒss.
Pulv. Myrrhæ,
Extr. Aloes pur. ana ℈j.
Pulv. Rhei, gr. vj.
Syrupi Zingiberis, q. s.
Mix: make 18 pills. Two or three, twice a day.
In Amenorrhœa.—Mr. SAVORY.

2036. ℞ Myrrhæ elutriatæ, gr. xxiv.
Extr. Hyoscyami, gr. ix.
Sol. Magnes. Bicarb. ℥vj. Triturate together, and add
Vini Ipecacuanhæ, ♏xl.
Mix: two spoonfuls every six hours.
Dr. BARON.

2037. ℞ Myrrhæ pulv. ℈j.
Ferri Sulphat. gr. iss.
Sodæ Carbonatis, gr. iv.
Tinct. Croci, ʒj.
Aquæ Menthæ Pulegii, ℥iss.
Mix: make a draught. To be taken three times a day.
Emmenagogue.—Dr. JOY.

2038. ℞ Myrrhæ contritæ, ℈j.
Ferri Ammon. Chlor. gr. v. Rub up together, and add
Syrupi Zingiberis, q. s.

Make an electuary, to be taken twice a day.

Emmenagogue.—Dr. Paris.

2039. ℞ Tinct. Myrrhæ, ℥j.
Tinct. Hellebori, ℥ss.
Tinct. Cantharidis, ʒij.

Mix: in doses of thirty drops, in a little sugar and water, three times a day.

In Amenorrhœa.—Dr. Ellis.

2040. ℞ Tinct. Myrrhæ,
Aceti, ana ℥ij.
Mellis, ℥j.
Infusi Contrayrvæ, Oiss. Mix: make a gargle.

In Putrid Sore Throat, Scarlatina, &c.—Dr. Fothergill.

2041. ℞ Myrrhæ, ℥j.
Calcis vivæ, ℥ij.
Aquæ, Oij.

Mix: infuse for a few days, then decant. To be injected into fistulous ulcers.

St. Marie.

2042. ℞ Oxidi Zinci, gr. xx.
Cerat. Galeni, ℥j.
Tinct. Myrrhæ, ʒss. Mix: make an ointment.

To irritable Eruptions of the Skin.—Dr. Neligan.

Naphtha. See Spiritus Pyroxylicus.

NUX VOMICA. STRYCHNIA.

Nux Vomica is the round flattened seed of the *Strychnos Nux Vomica*, a tree which inhabits the East Indies. It is very bitter in taste, and possessed of active and dangerous properties. Both the bitterness and activity are chiefly owing to an alkaloid, Strychnia, which may be extracted from the seeds, and which is poisonous in an extreme degree. Another alkaloid exists in them, called Brucia, which resembles Strychnia, but is less powerful. Nux Vomica and Strychnia are powerful excitants of the spinal system of nerves, and thus cause convulsions when given in an over-dose. Either of them may be used to restore the power of muscular motion, when this has been lost on account of a clot on the brain, which has since become absorbed. But unless the nervous center has regained its sound condition, no good can be done. Strychnia may be applied locally in torpor or local paralysis of the muscular or sentient nerves. It is also used as a tonic in dyspepsia, and has been given as an aphrodisiac. The dose of the powdered seed is about five grains three times a day; of Strychnia, one-twentieth to one-twelfth of a grain, carefully watching its effects.

Preparations of Nux Vomica:

Extractum Nucis Vomicæ (L., E.): dose, half to three grains.

Tinctura Nucis Vomicæ (D., 1826): dose, five to ten minims, or more.

Preparations of Strychnia:

Strychniæ Murias (D.): dose, as Strychnia.

Strychniæ Acetas: dose, one-thirtieth to one-twentieth of a grain.

Strychniæ Hydriodas: dose, one-sixteenth to one-tenth of a grain.

Strychniæ Phosphas: dose, one-twentieth to one-twelfth of a grain.

Strychniæ Sulphas: dose, one-twentieth to one-twelfth of a grain.

Strychniæ Nitras: dose, one-twentieth to one-twelfth of a grain.

(Brucia may be given in the same cases as Strychnia, but is much weaker. Dose, quarter to one grain.)

Prescriptions for internal use, containing Nux Vomica.

2043. ℞ Pulv. Nucis Vomicæ, gr. xxx.
Confectionis Rosæ, q. s. to make 10 pills. One, twice or thrice a day, closely watching the effects.

In Paralysis.—Dr. Ellis.

2044. ℞ Extr. Nucis Vom. ℈j.
Extr. Glycyrrhizæ, ℈vij.
Mix, and divide into 80 pills. Two to four, three times a day.

In Paralysis.—Radius.

2045. ℞ Pulv. Acaciæ,
Pulv. Sacchari, ana gr. xij.
Pulv. Nucis Vom. gr. iij.
Mix: make a powder. One, every day.

In Diarrhœa and Dysentery.—Hufeland.

2046. ℞ Extr. Nucis Vom. gr. ss.
Fellis bovis, gr. v.
Extr. Aloes aquosi, gr. j.
Mix: make 2 pills. To be taken every night.

Dr. Wilson.

2047. ℞ Extr. Nucis Vom. gr. vj.
Extr. Rhei, gr. ix.
Aloes Barbadensis, gr. ix.
Mix well, and divide into 12 pills. One, going to bed.

In habitual Constipation.

2048. ℞ Ext. Nucis Vomicæ, gr. iij.
Pulv. Rhei, gr. xv.
Pil. Hydrarg. gr. x.
Ext. Gentianæ, ℈ij.
Mix: divide into 15 pills. (One, three times a day, half an hour after meals.)

In Bilious Dyspepsia.—Dr. Ross.

2049. ℞ Extr. Nucis Vom. gr. iij.
Fellis bovini inspiss. gr. vj.
Extr. Taraxaci, gr. xxiv.
Pulv. Myrrhæ, gr. xviij.
Mix, and divide into 24 pills. One, three times a day.

In Prurigo.—Dr. Neligan.

2050. ℞ Morphiæ Acet. gr. j.
Extr. Nucis Vom. gr. ij.
Olei Olivæ, gr. x. Dissolve, and add
Extr. rad. Hellebori nig. (Ph. Ed.) ℈j.
Pulv. Glycyrrhizæ, gr. viij.
Mellis, q. s.
Make into a mass, and divide into 12 pills. One, two or three times a day.

In Chlorosis and Amenorrhœa.—Dr. Copland.

2051. ℞ Extr. Nucis Vom. gr. vj.
Pulv. Rhei, gr. vj.
Ferri Carb. c. Sacch. gr. xij.
Pil. Hydrarg. gr. vj.
Pulv. Opii, gr. v.
Mix, and divide into 12 pills. One, twice a day.

In Diarrhœa from exhaustion.—Dr. Nevins.

2052. ℞ Extr. Nucis Vom. gr. ij–vj.
Aquæ Melissæ, ℥vj.
Mucil. Acaciæ, ℥ss.
Mix: two spoonfuls every second hour.

Von Hildenbrand.

2053. ℞ Pulv. Nucis Vom. ʒss.
Misturæ Acaciæ,
Aquæ Cinnamomi, ana ℥j.
Tinct. Cardam. co. ℥j.
Aquæ destillatæ, ℥iij. Mix; one-sixth part for a dose.

Stimulant to the muscular system, in cases of Paralysis.

Dr. HOOPER.

2054. ℞ Pulv. Nucis Vom. ʒj.
Aquæ, ℥viij. Boil to f℥vj, and add
Tinct. Opii, ʒj. ℥ss every two hours.

In Dysentery.—Dr. HOOPER.

2055. ℞ Extr. Nucis Vom. ℈ij.
Mucilaginis, ℥j.
Aquæ distillatæ, ℥vj.
Syrupi Althææ, ℥j.
Mix: a tablespoonful every second hour.

In the painful Colic of Epidemic Dysentery.—RICHTER.

2056. ℞ Pulv. Nucis Vom.
Bismuthi Nitratis,
Extr. alcohol. Nucis Vom. ana gr. ss.
Magnes. Carb. gr. iij.
Sacchari, gr. xv.
Olei Menthæ pip. gtt. ij.
Mix: make a powder. A powder every three hours.

In Cramp of the Stomach.—VOGT.

2057. ℞ Tinct. Nucis Vom. gtt. ij.
Aquæ Laurocerasi, ʒj.
Mix: ten drops in some appropriate vehicle, night and morning.

In the Vomiting of Pregnancy.—KROYLA.

2058. ℞ Tinct. Nucis Vom. ℥ss.
Tinct. Cinchonæ c. ℥iss.
Tinct. Calumbæ, ℥iss.
Mix: dessertspoonful in glass of water three times daily, one hour before meals.

For Intestinal Irritation occurring after meals.

Dr. J. S. NICOL.

2059. ℞ Tinct. Nucis Vom.
Tinct. Cantharidis,
Ætheris Phosphorati, ana ℈ij.
Mix: 30 drops, three or four times a day.

In Paralysis, &c.—VOGT.

2060. ℞ Tinct. Nucis Vom. ʒij.
Tinct. Cinchonæ, ʒvj.
Infusi Cinchonæ, ℥vij.
Mix: make a mixture. fʒj three times a day.

In Paralysis, consequent on Fevers and other Acute Diseases.

Dr. NELIGAN.

2061. ℞ Tinct. Nucis Vomicæ, ℥ss.
Syrupi Ferri Superphosph. ʒvj.
Aquæ Cinnamomi, ʒvj.
Mix: a teaspoonful in water, twice a day.

In Paraplegia.—Dr. WILSON.

Prescriptions for internal use, containing Strychnia.

2062. ℞ Strychniæ, gr. iij.
Alcoholis, ℥j.
Dissolve: dose, from six to twenty-four drops in any mixture or drink.

MAJENDIE.

2063. ℞ Strychniæ, gr. ij.
Extracti Valerianæ, q. s. to make a mass, to be divided into 32 pills. One early in the morning for five days, then one, morning and evening.

In Amaurosis.—FURNARI.

2064. ℞ Strychniæ, gr. j.
Quinæ Disulphatis, ʒss.
Conf. Rosæ Gallicæ, ʒj.
Rub up together until well mixed, and make a mass, to be divided into 20 pills. (One pill for a dose.)

Stimulant to the Muscular System in Cases of Paralysis.
Dr. HOOPER.

2065. ℞ Strychniæ, gr. j.
Pil. Rhei co. ʒj.
Pil. Hydrarg. gr. vj.
Olei Menth. pip. gtt. iv.
Mix well, and divide into 15 pills. One, twice a day.

In Dyspeptic, Neuralgic, and Hysterical Affections.
Dr. RYAN.

2066. ℞ Strychniæ, gr. ij.
Ext. Hyoscyami, ʒss.
Morph. Sulph. gr. iij.
Capsici pulv. ʒss.
Zinci Sulph. gr. xv.
Mix: make a mass, and divide into 30 pills. One, three or four times a day.

In Facial Neuralgia.—Dr. H. GREEN.

2067. ℞ Strychniæ, gr. j.
Spirit. rectif. ℥ss. Dissolve, and add
Spirit. Ætheris Nitrici, ℥iss.
Syrupi Rhœados, ℥j.
Aquæ, ℥v.
Mix: make a mixture. Dose, ℥ss three times a day.

Stimulant to the Muscular System in Paralysis.—Dr. HOOPER.

2068. ℞ Strychniæ, gr. j.
Acidi Nitrici dil. ʒj.
Aquæ, ℥xij. Mix: dose, f℥j three times a day.

In Irritability of the Stomach, with Phosphatic Urine.
Dr. G. Bird.

2069. ℞ Strychniæ, gr. j.
Aceti destillati, ʒj.
Make a solution: dose, ♏vj in spring water twice a day.

Tonic.—Dr. Paris.

2070. ℞ Strychniæ puræ, gr. j.
Aquæ destillatæ, ℥ij.
Acidi Acetici, gtt. iij.
Sacchari albi, ʒij.
Mix: a teaspoonful night and morning.

Majendie.

2071. ℞ Strychniæ Acet. gr. iij.
Alcoholis, ʒj.
Aquæ Cinnam. ʒvij.
Mix: five drops twice a day in some suitable vehicle.

In Paralysis, &c.—Luders.

Prescriptions for external use, containing Nux Vomica.

2072. ℞ Extr. Nucis Vomicæ, gr. viij.
Alcoholis, ℥ij.
Aquæ Ammoniæ fort. ℥ss. Mix: make a lotion.

Stimulating to Paralyzed Limbs.—Radius.

2073. ℞ Tinct. Nucis Vomicæ, ℥j.
Liq. Ammon. fort. ʒij. Mix: make a liniment.

To be rubbed on Palsied Parts, or on the Abdomen in Asiatic Cholera. Majendie.

2074. ℞ Tinct. Nucis Vomicæ, ℥j.
Aquæ Coloniæ (*Eau de Cologne*), ℥iij.
Mix: make an embrocation.

A Friction in Local Paralysis.—Trousseau and Reveil.

2075. ℞ Tinct. Nucis Vomicæ, ℥ss.
Essentiæ Camphoræ,
Essentiæ Carui, ana ʒij.
Aquæ destillatæ, ℥vij. Mix: make a stimulant lotion.

In Skin Diseases.—Dr. Neligan.

Prescriptions for external use, containing Strychnia.

2076. ℞ Strychniæ, gr. xvj.
Axungiæ, ℥j.
Triturate well together to form an ointment.

As a Friction for Paralyzed Parts.—Bouchardat.

2077. ℞ Strychniæ, gr. xxiv.
Olei Olivæ, ℥j.
Mix: make an eye-wash. Twelve drops, to be used four times a day.
In Amaurosis.—CUNIER.

2078. ℞ Strychniæ, ʒss.
Olei Olivæ, ℥iss.
Mix: ten drops to be rubbed over the temples three or four times a day.
In cases of Amaurosis, depending on Paralysis of the Optic Nerve. DR. NELIGAN.

OLEA EMPYREUMATICA. *Empyreumatic Oils.*

These are oily liquids, obtained by the destructive distillation of various substances. Those obtained from vegetable matters are numerous, but not much employed. Thus oils having stimulant properties are obtained by distilling Myrrh, Guaiacum-wood, and Box-wood. Those made by the destructive distillation of Belladonna and Hyoscyamus are narcotic in their action.

The *Oleum Cornu Cervi*, or Dippel's animal oil, is obtained by the distillation of hartshorn shavings. It is produced along with ammonia, from which it is separated, by rectification, by the destruction of the animal matters of the horn. It has a strong and disagreeable smell, and sharp acid taste. It acts as a stimulant and antispasmodic. In large doses it is very poisonous. It is diaphoretic, and of use in destroying intestinal worms. It has been given in chorea and tetanus, and applied as a rubefacient externally. Dose, five to ten drops.

2079. ℞ Olei Cornu Cervi, ʒj.
Ætheris Sulphurici, ʒxv.
Mix: fifteen to thirty drops for a dose.
As a Stimulant and Antispasmodic.—BERAL.

2080. ℞ Olei empyreumatici Cornu Cervi, ℥ij.
Olei Terebinthinæ, ℥vj.
Mix. Let the mixture stand for three days; then, distil f℥vj from a glass retort. Divide this into six small vials, well stoppered, and place them in a cold and dark place. Take fifteen minims (gradually augmented to a drachm) in a little Cinnamon water, every night and morning, for five or six weeks. (The bowels must previously have been well cleared out.)
For Tape-worm.—M. CHABERT.

2081. ℞ Olei Dippelii, ʒj.
Olei Amygdalæ, ʒvj.
Saponis Terebinthinæ, ʒiv. Mix: make a liniment.

As an exciting application, and for rubbing on the Abdomen in cases of Worms. SUNDELIN.

For various Oils, see MORRHUÆ OLEUM, RICINI OLEUM, TEREBINTHINÆ OLEUM, TIGLII OLEUM, &c.

OLIVÆ OLEUM. *Olive Oil.*

This oil is expressed from the fruits of the *Olea Europæa*, or common Olive-tree (Nat. Ord. *Oleineæ*), which is extensively cultivated in Southern Europe and Syria. It is bland and pleasant to the taste, and in considerable doses acts as a gentle laxative. It is also employed as a demulcent and emollient, both for internal and external use. The dose, as a cathartic, is about one ounce.

Enema Olei Olivæ (U. S.) is laxative and anthelmintic.

2082. ℞ Olei Olivæ, ℥j.
Mannæ, ℥iss.
Mucilaginis, ℥vj. Mix. Dose, three tablespoonfuls.

As a Laxative.

2083. ℞ Olei Olivæ, ℥viij.
Spirit. Ammon. Aromat. ʒij.
Mix: three spoonfuls, night and morning.

Anthelmintic.—Dr. ELLIS.

2084. ℞ Olei Olivæ, vel.
Olei Coc. Palmat. ℥iv.
Ceræ albæ, ℥iiss.
Cetacei, ℥ss.
Liquefy by a slow heat, and when cooled, take an ounce and rub it up diligently with half a drachm of calomel. Make an ointment.

For Ring-worm of the Scalp.—Mr. C. HOGG.

OLIBANUM.

This fragrant gum-resin is chiefly the produce of an Indian tree, Boswellia thurifera (Nat. Ord. *Terebinthaceæ*). It has been used in medicine to check excessive secretions from the mucous membranes, as in Bronchitis, Leucorrhœa, &c. It occasionally enters into the formation of plasters, but is not so much employed as it used to be in former times.

2085. ℞ Olibani, ℈j.
Pulv. Cort. Aurant. gr. iv.
Syrupi Tolutani, q. s. to make a bolus. To be taken in the evening, and followed in the morning by the following draught.
Tinct. Benzoin. co. ♏xl.
Syrupi Tolutani, ʒj.
Decocti Cinchonæ, ℥iss. Mix.
In Fluor Albus.—Dr. E. Clark.

OPIUM. MORPHIA.

Opium is perhaps the most important drug in the whole Materia Medica. It is the half-dried juice obtained by cutting the unripe capsule of the White or Eastern Poppy, *Papaver somniferum* (Nat. Ord. *Papaveraceæ*). There are many kinds of Opium in commerce. The Turkey or Smyrna Opium, which occurs in small irregular masses, covered outside with the capsules of a species of dock, is of excellent quality, and generally preferred. The various kinds of Opium produced in India are also very good.

Opium, applied externally, acts as a sedative, lulling pain. Given internally in moderate doses, it first produces some excitement, quickening of the pulse, and heat of skin. This effect is quickly followed by a tendency to sleep, and a diminution of sensibility. It abates or banishes pain, if present. It diminishes irritation, and relaxes the muscular system. It diminishes the secretion of the bowels, but increases that of the skin, acting as a sudorific. Taken continually in small doses, it causes a kind of intoxication, as in opium-eaters. Taken in an over-large dose, it is a dangerous narcotic poison, causing deep sleep, with contraction of the pupil of the eye, succeeded by coma and death.

When not contraindicated, it is the best anodyne and soporific with which we are acquainted. A state of high fever or inflammation forbids its use, as its primary operation is that of a stimulant. It is seldom given when there is a parched tongue and dry skin. In most cases of great pain or irritation, in moderate fever with a moist skin and no cerebral disorder, in delirium tremens, in cancer, in bronchitis (combined with camphor or ipecacuanha, as in Paregoric and Dover's powder), opium may be prescribed. It is given to check the discharge in dysentery and diarrhœa, as a diaphoretic in many cases, and as an antispasmodic in convulsive disorders. It may be combined with calomel in severe inflammations, as pleurisy; and Dr. Graves gave it in fevers with tartar emetic.

In cases of poisoning by opium, the stomach-pump should first be used, or an emetic of sulphate of zinc given; the patient must be kept awake by continual walking between attendants; after the vomiting, cold water may be poured on the face and chest, and an infusion of gall-nuts given, followed by brandy and coffee. Artificial respiration may succeed when all other means have failed.

Opium contains many peculiar chemical principles, but its narcotic properties are chiefly owing to one of these, the alkaloid *Morphia*. Of this, good opium contains about twelve per cent., in combination with Meconic acid. This morphia may be extracted from opium, and used separately, either in the pure form or in combination with various acids, with which it forms salts soluble in water and spirit. Morphia resembles opium in its action, but is rather less stimulating. It may be used in the same cases.

The usual dose of opium for the adult is about one grain, but as much as three grains may be given in urgent cases. It acts powerfully on children, and should be given to them either in very small doses, or not at all. The doses of the various preparations of opium and morphia are as follow:

Those enumerated first are for internal use.

Extractum Opii (L., E., D.), half of a grain to three grains.

Extractum Opii Vinosum (Paris Cod.), quarter of a grain to one grain.

Pilulæ Opii (E.), five to ten grains. (Contain one grain in five.)

Pilulæ Calomelanos et Opii (E.), five to ten grains.

Trochisci Opii (E.) contain each one-tenth of a grain of the extract.

Confectio Opii (L., E.), ten grains to one drachm. (One grain in thirty-six to forty-three.)

Linctus Opiatus (Guy's Hosp.), one drachm.

Tinctura Opii (L., E., D.), ten drops to half a drachm or more, for adults; dangerous for children.

Tinctura Opii Ammoniata (E.) contains in eighty drops one grain of opium.

Tinctura Opii Aromatica (Guibourt), five to fifteen minims.

Tinctura Opii Fœtida (Fulda), fifteen minims to one drachm.

Acetum Opii (E.), five to ten minims.

Acetum Opii (D.), ten to thirty minims.

Vinum Opii (L., E., D.), ten minims to one drachm. Used also as an application to the eyeball in ophthalmia.

Liquor Opii Sedativus (Battley), five to twenty minims.

Guttæ Nigræ ("Black Drop"), five to ten minims.

Syrupus Opii (Paris Codex), one to four drachms.

The following preparations, named after other substances, owe their chief activity to the opium which they contain. The compound powders of Ipecacuan and Kino, and the pills containing Ipecacuan, may be referred to in their places; the rest will be numbered here among the preparations of opium.

Pulvis Ipecacuanhæ Compositus.
Pulvis Kino Compositus.
Pilulæ Ipecacuanhæ Compositæ.
Pilulæ Ipecacuanhæ cum Scillâ.

(Vide pp. 319, 326.)

Pilula Saponis Composita (L., D.), five to ten grains. (Contains one grain in five.)

Pilula Styracis Composita (L., E.), five to ten grains. (One grain in five.)

Pulvis Cretæ Compositus cum Opio (L., E., D.), ten to thirty grains, in Diarrhœa. (One grain of opium in forty.)

Tinctura Camphoræ Composita (L., E., D.), or Paregoric, contains one grain of opium in half an ounce. It is frequently added to cough mixtures. Dose, half a drachm to half an ounce for adults, five to ten minims for children. This is also known as *Tinctura Opii Camphorata*, a name which had better be avoided in prescriptions, to prevent the possibility of mistakes.

The following preparations of Morphia are in frequent use:

Morphia, quarter to half a grain.

Morphiæ Acetas (L., E., D.), one-eighth to quarter of a grain.

Morphiæ Hydrochloras (L., E., D.), quarter to half a grain.

Morphiæ Hydriodas (Dr. Thompson), quarter to half a grain (?)

Morphiæ Sulphas (U. S.), one-eighth to quarter of a grain.

Liquor Morphiæ Acetatis (L., D.), five to twenty minims.

Liquor Morphiæ Hydrochloratis (L., E., D.), five to twenty minims.

Liquor Morphiæ Citratis (Majendie), six to thirty drops in a day.

Liquor Morphiæ Sulphatis (U. S.) contains one-eighth of a grain of the salt in one drachm.

Solutio Morphiæ Bimeconatis (Squire), five to thirty minims.

Syrupus Morphiæ Acetatis (D.), one drachm or more.

Syrupus Morphiæ Hydrochloratis (D.), one drachm or more.

Syrupus Morphiæ Sulphatis (Paris) is intended as a substitute for Syrup of Poppies; each ounce contains quarter of a grain.

Trochisci Morphiæ (E.) contain each one-fortieth of a grain of Morphiæ Hydrochloras.

Trochisci Morphiæ et Ipecacuanhæ (E.) contain the same quantity.

The remaining preparations are employed only for external use. (The opium clyster is necessarily included here.)

Enema Opii (L., E.).

Linimentum Opii (L., E., D.).

Emplastrum Opii (L., E., D.).

Unguentum Opii (L.).

Collyrium Anodynum (Paris Codex).

Unguentum Gallæ Compositum (L.), and

Unguentum Gallæ et Opii (E.), contain opium.

Prescriptions containing Opium for internal use.

2086. ℞ Pulveris Opii, gr. x.
Extr. Glycyrrhizæ, ʒj.
Mix, and divide into 80 pills. One, as required.
Diaphoretic and Expectorant.—WURTEMBURG PHARM.

2087. ℞ Pulveris Opii, gr. j.
Extr. Fellis Bovini, gr. v–viij. Mix, and divide into 2 pills.
As a non-constipating Opiate.—DR. BETHUNE.

2088. ℞ Pulv. Opii, gr. ¼.
Hydr. Chlor. gr. ij.
Mix: make a powder, to be taken three times a day.
In Pleurisy, with large effusion.—DR. BUDD.

2089. ℞ Opii Pulv. gr. ij.
Antim. Potassio-tart. gr. j.
Theriacæ, q. s. to make 4 pills. One, twice a day.
Rheumatism.—DR. JOY.

2090. ℞ Opii purificati, gr. j.
Hydrarg. Chloridi, gr. iv.
Pulv. Antim. Co. gr. viij.
Syrupi, q. s.
Mix, and divide into 4 pills. One, every six hours.
With effervescing draughts at the commencement of Fevers.
DR. GREGORY.

2091. ℞ Pulv. Ipecac. gr. iij.
Opii contrit. gr. j.
Potass. Nitratis, gr. x.
Rub up thoroughly into a powder, to be taken going to bed.
Diaphoretic.—DR. PARIS.

2092. ℞ Pulv. Opii, gr. iv.
Potassæ Nitratis,
Sacchari lactis, ana ʒiss. Mix, and divide into 6 powders.
Antispasmodic.—PHŒBUS.

2093. ℞ Pulv. Ipecac. rad. gr. iv.
Sodæ Carb. exsic. ℈ij.
Pulv. Opii, gr. ij.
Mix, and divide into 4 powders. One, every six hours.
In Spasmodic Asthma, and Pertussis of Adults.—DR. JOY.

2094. ℞ Pulv. Opii, gr. iv.
Extr. Hyoscyami,
Extr. Conii, ana gr. xv.
Mix, and divide into 10 pills. One at night.
Anodyne.—DR. ELLIS.

2095. ℞ Pulv. Opii, gr. iiss.
Moschi, gr. vj.
Camphoræ, gr. vj.
Mix: make a powder. To be taken in syrup.

In Tetanus.—Dr. W. AINSLIE.

2096. ℞ Pulveris Opii, gr. ij.
Moschi, gr. v.
Magnesiæ, gr. iv.
Sacchari lactis, gr. x.
Mix: to be taken every two to four hours.

In Delirium Tremens.—VOGT.

2097. ℞ Pulv. Opii, gr. x.
Camphoræ rasæ, ℈ij.
Ammoniæ Carbonatis, ℈iv.
Amyli, gr. xv.
Mix, and divide into 8 powders. One, every hour or two hours.

Antispasmodic.—SWEDIAUR.

2098. ℞ Extr. Opii, gr. x.
Antimonii Sulphureti præcipitati, gr. xij.
Potassæ Nitratis, gr. xxiv.
Syrupi, q. s. Mix: make 6 pills. One at night.

To cause Perspiration, and to ease pain in Rheumatism.
RECAMIER.

2099. ℞ Pulv. Opii, gr. iv.
Calomelanos, gr. vj.
Antim. Potassio-tart. gr. j.
Extr. Conii, ℈j.
Mix: make 8 pills. Two going to bed.

In Rheumatic Pains.—Mr. BRANDE.

2100. ℞ Pulv. Opii, gr. x.
Sacchari, ʒj.
Aquæ Cinnamomi, ℥vj.
Mix: make a mixture. A tablespoonful every two hours.

In Tetanus and Colica Pictonum.—Dr. ELLIS.

2101. ℞ Extr. Opii, gr. iij.
Camphoræ, gr. vj.
Syrupi, q. s.
Mix, and divide into 6 pills. One to three a day.

Anodyne and Antispasmodic.—FOY.

2102. ℞ Extr. Opii, gr. j.
Plumbi Acetatis, gr. iv.
Pulv. Hyoscyami, gr. viij.
Mix: make 8 pills. One, night and morning.

In Epilepsy—RECAMIER.

2103. ℞ Extr. Opii,
Hydrarg. Acetatis,
Camphoræ, ana gr. xij.
Syr. Papav. q. s. to make 30 pills. One, night and morning.

In Syphilis.—Mr. CARMICHAEL.

2104. ℞ Extr. Opii, gr. xij.
Extr. Valerianæ,
Moschi, ana gr. xxiv.
Mix: make 16 pills. (First one, then two, then three a day.)

In Hysteria.—FOY.

2105. ℞ Extr. Opii, gr. j.
Zinci Sulphatis, gr. iv.
Syrupi Acaciæ, q. s. to make 4 pills. Two a day.

In painful Mucous Discharges from Urethra or Vagina.—FOY.

2106. ℞ Extr. Opii, gr. lxxij.
Argenti Nitratis, gr. vj.
Moschi, gr. xlviii.
Camphoræ, gr. xcvi.
Mix: make 96 pills. One, morning and evening, gradually increasing the dose.

In Epilepsy and Paralysis.—FOY.

2107. ℞ Liq. Opii Battleii, ♏xij.
Aquæ Cinnamomi, ℥iss.
Mix: make a draught. Take at night.

In Fevers, &c.—Dr. THOMAS.

2108. ℞ Liq. Opii sedativi, ♏xx.
Syrupi Papav. Rhœados, ʒij.
Misturæ Camphoræ, ℥j. Mix: make a draught.

In Febrile and Inflammatory Affections.—Dr. NELIGAN.

2109. ℞ Tinct. Opii, ♏xxx.
Liq. Ammon. Acet.
Aquæ Cinnamomi,
Syrupi Zingiberis, ana ℥ss.
Mix: make a draught. To be taken at bedtime, or on the return of pain.

Dr. HOOPER.

2110. ℞ Tinct. Opii, ♏xxv.
Spirit. Ætheris Sulph. ♏xxx.
Syrupi Tolutani, ʒiss.
Mist. Camphoræ, ℥j. Mix: make an anodyne draught.

Dr. JOY.

2111. ℞ Tinct. Opii, ♏xx-xxx.
Tinct. Caryophylli, ʒij–℥ss.
Acidi Nitrici dil. ♏xx.
Aquæ Pimentæ, ℥j. Mix: make an anodyne draught.

Dr. COPLAND.

2112. ℞ Guttarum Nigrarum (Houlton's), ♏x.
Spirit. Ætheris Nitrici, ʒss.
Aquæ destillatæ, ℥j. Mix: make an anodyne draught.

FOY.

2113. ℞ Tinct. Opii, ʒj.
Tartari Emetici, gr. iv.
Mist. Camphoræ, ℥viij.
Mix: make a mixture. f℥ss every second hour.

In Typhus Fever.—Dr. GRAVES.

2114. ℞ Antim. Tart. gr. j.
Gum. Tragacanthæ, ℈j.
Aquæ communis, ℥vij.
Tinct. Opii, ♏xx.
Syrupi Papaveris, ʒvij.
Mix: make a febrifuge mixture. Dose, f℥j.

M. PEYSSON.

2115. ℞ Potassæ Carbonatis, ℈j.
Aquæ Menthæ viridis, ℥j.
Tinct. Opii, ♏xxv.
Syrupi Tolutani, ʒj.
Mix: make a draught. To be taken at bedtime with a tablespoonful of lemon-juice.

Soporific and Refrigerant.—Dr. HOOPER.

2116. ℞ Conf. Aromat. ℈j.
Conf. Opii, ℈ss.
Mist. Cretæ, ʒx.
Spir. Ammon. Arom. gtt. x.
Syrupi Zingib. ʒj. Mix: make a draught.

In Diarrhœa.

2117. ℞ Potassæ Bicarb. ʒj.
Acidi Hydrocyan. dil. gtt. xij.
Tinct. Opii, ʒj.
Mist. Camphoræ,
Aquæ, ana ℥iv. Mix: a sixth part three times a day.

In Dyspepsia with Irritable Stomach.—Dr. G. LYON.

2118. ℞ Liq. Opii sedativi, ʒj.
Tinct. Hyoscyami, ʒij.
Liq. Ammon. Acetatis, ℥iss.
Syrupi Tolutani, ʒij.
Mist. Camphoræ, ℥iv.
Mix: a sixth part two or three times a day.

In Severe Coughs.—Mr. MORGAN.

2119. ℞ Vini Opii, gtt. x.
Aquæ Cinnamomi, ℥j.
Aquæ Melissæ, ℥ij.
Tinct. Castoris, gtt. xx.
Syrupi Opii, ℥ss. Mix. Dose, a tablespoonful.

In Uterine Colic.—AUGUSTIN.

2120. ℞ Tinct. Opii, ʒj.
Acidi Sulph. dil. ʒj.
Mellis, ℥iss.
Mix: make a linctus. A teaspoonful when the cough is urgent.
In Cough of Phthisis.—Dr. THEOPHILUS THOMPSON.

Prescriptions containing Morphia, &c., for internal use.

2121. ℞ Morphiæ, gr. j.
Confect. Rosæ, q. s. to make a mass, to be divided into 6 pills.
MAJENDIE.

2122. ℞ Morphiæ Acetatis, gr. j.
Confect. Rosæ, gr. xvj. Mix, and divide into 8 pills.
MIALHE.

2123. ℞ Morphiæ Acetatis, gr. ss.
Extr. Hyoscyami, gr. iij.
Mix: make a pill. To be repeated in six hours.
In Mucous Enteritis.—Dr. GREGORY.

2124. ℞ Morphiæ Sulph. gr. ij.
Potassii Cyanidi, gr. iv.
Mucilag. q. s. to make 24 pills. One, every six hours.
In Neuralgia.—ROUGIER.

2125. ℞ Morphiæ Hydrochlor. gr. ¼.
Pilulæ Hydrarg.
Extr. Lupuli, ana gr. ij.
Mix: make a pill. To be taken at bedtime.
In Inflammatory Fever.—Dr. THOMAS.

2126. ℞ Morphiæ Acetatis, gr. j.
Pulv. Digitalis, gr. vj.
Extr. Pulsatillæ, gr. xij.
Sacchari, ʒj.
Mix, and divide into 36 powders. One, four times a day.
In the Cough and Sleeplessness of Consumptive Patients.
CADET.

2127. ℞ Morphiæ Acetatis, gr. xv.
Cupri Ammonio-sulphatis, ʒss.
Fellis inspissati,
Pulv. Quassiæ, ana ℈iv.
Mix, and divide into 100 pills. Take five, night and morning.
In Diabetes Mellitus.—BRENDT.
(The dose is very large.—ED.)

2128. ℞ Morphiæ Sulph. gr. j.
Pulv. Ipecacuanhæ, gr. iij.
Olei Amygdalæ, gtt. xij.
Extr. Aconiti, gr. ij.
Pulv. Glycyrrhizæ,
Mellis, ana quant. suff.
Mix: make 6 pills. One, every three or four hours.
BRERA.

2129. ℞ Morphiæ Acetatis, gr. xvj.
Aquæ destil. ℥j.
Acidi Acetici, ♏iij.
Spir. Vini, ʒiss. Mix. (In doses of from 5 to 30 drops.)

Anodyne.—Dr. Copland.

2130. ℞ Morphiæ grani quartam partem,
Syrupi Papaveris, ʒj.
Aquæ destillatæ, ℥j.
Mix: make a draught. To be taken at night.

Brera.

2131. ℞ Morphiæ Acetatis, gr. ⅓.
Aceti destil. ♏ij.
Aquæ florum Aurant. ʒij.
Aquæ destil. ℥j
Syrupi Aurant. ʒss. Mix: make a quieting draught.

Dr. Paris.

2132. ℞ Morphiæ Acetatis, gr. j–ij.
Inf. Gentianæ co. ℥vss.
Syrupi Aurant. ℥ss.
Dissolve and mix. A fourth part three times a day.

In Chorea of Adults.—Dr. Thomas.

2133. ℞ Solut. Morphiæ Acetatis, gtt. xx.
Lactucarii, gr. x.
Inf. Anthemidis, ℥v.
Syrupi Althææ, ℥ss. Mix. Dose, a spoonful.

Beral.

2134. ℞ Morphiæ Hydrochlor. gr. j.
Acidi Hydrochlor. dil. ♏v.
Acidi Hydrocyan. dil. ʒss.
Aquæ, ℥j.
Syrupi Scillæ, ℥j.
Mix: fʒj when the cough is troublesome.

In the Cough of Phthisis.—Dr. Theophilus Thompson.

2135. ℞ Liq. Morph. Acet. ♏j–ij.
Aquæ, ℥j.
Mix: make a draught. To be taken in the morning. (To be succeeded by the following:)

2136. ℞ Magnes. Sulph. ʒj.
Inf. Rosæ, ℥iss.
Acidi Hydrocyan. ♏j.
Syrupi Tolut. ʒj.
Mx: make a draught. To be taken early in the morning.

In Hæmoptysis.—Sir C. Scudamore.

2137. ℞ Codeinæ, gr. iss.
Aquæ Laurocerasi, ʒiiss.
Aquæ flor. Tiliæ, ℥iij.
Syrupi, ℥j. Mix: a tablespoonful every half hour.

For Pain and Sleeplessness.—Trousseau and Reveil.

Prescriptions containing Paregoric and other preparations, not generally named after opium.

2138. ℞ Tinct. Opii Camphoratæ, ℥ss.
Tartari Emetici, gr. j.
Nitratis Potassæ, ʒij.
Mist. Amygdalar. ℥xij.
Mix: make a cough mixture. A tablespoonful every hour, or when the cough is troublesome.

In Bronchitis.—Dr. GRAVES.

2139. ℞ Tinct. Camphoræ co. ♏xx.
Vini Ipecacuanha, ♏x.
Vini Antim. Tart. ♏xxx.
Mucilag. Acaciæ, ʒvij. Mix: fʒij every fourth hour.

In severe Coughs of Children of four years of age.
Dr. WEST.

2140. ℞ Tinct. Camphoræ co. ℥j.
Vini Antim. ℥ss.
Pulv. Acaciæ,
Extr. Glycyrrhizæ, ana ʒiij.
Aquæ, ℥vj.
Mix well. A tablespoonful every three or four hours.

In Catarrh.—Dr. DEWEES (U. S.).

2141. ℞ Syrupi simp. ℥ij.
Vini Antimonii,
Tinct. Camph. co. ana ʒj.
Tinct. Tolutani, ♏xij.
Mix: a teaspoonful in a decoction of barley three or four times a day, while the cough is troublesome.

For Children.—Mr. SAVORY.

2142. ℞ Pil. Saponis c. Opio, gr. xx.
Camph. rasæ et redactæ, ʒss.
Mucilag. q. s.
Mix, and divide into 12 pills. One, every sixth hour.

In Irritation of the Neck of the Bladder.—Dr. NELIGAN.

2143. ℞ Pil. Styracis comp.
Confect. Aromaticæ, ana ʒss.
Mix, and make 12 pills. Two every night.

In Diarrhœa.

Enemata, Injections, and Suppositories.

2144. ℞ Tinct. Opii, gtt. v–vj.
Inf. Valerianæ, ℥iij. Mix: make an enema.

For Spasms in Children.—SWEDIAUR.

2145. ℞ Tinct. Opii, ʒj.
Inf. Valerianæ, ℥x.
Mucilag. Acaciæ, ℥j. Mix: make an enema.

Antispasmodic.—Dr. COPLAND.

2146. ℞ Amyli, ʒj.
Aquæ calidæ, Oj.
Morphiæ Acetatis, gr. j. Mix: make an enema.
In Chronic Diarrhœa.—CADET.

2147. ℞ Mist. Acaciæ, ℥iij.
Olei Olivæ, ℥j. Mix, and add
Vini Opii, ♏xxx. Make an enema.
In Ardor Urinæ.—Dr. THOMAS.

2148. ℞ Liq. Opii sedativi, ♏xxx.
Inf. Valerianæ, ℥j.
Mucilag. Acaciæ, ℥ss. Mix: make an enema.
To allay pain in Cancer of the Womb.—Dr. ASHWELL.

2149. ℞ Extr. Opii, gr. ij.
Aquæ ferventis, ℥viij.
Dissolve, and strain through paper; then add
Hydrarg. Chloridi, ʒj.
Mucilag. Acaciæ, ℥j.
Mix: make an injection. To be used twice a day.
Mr. COULSON.

2150. ℞ Pulv. Opii, gr. iss.
Extr. Hyoscyami, gr. v.
Saponis Hispan. q. s. to make a suppository.
Anodyne in painful Affections of the Bowels.

2151. ℞ Opii, gr. xij.
Liq. Plumbi Diacet. gtt. xij.
Aquæ, ℥ix. Mix: make an injection.
In Gonorrhœa.—GIRTENNER.

2152. ℞ P. Opii, gr. iij.
Decoct. Lini sem. ℥vj. Mix: make an injection.
In painful Affections of the Urethra.
TROUSSEAU and REVEIL.

2153. ℞ Morphiæ, gr. ij.
Vitelli ovi unius,
Olei Anthemidis,
Olei Papaveris, ana ℥j. Mix: make an injection.
To ease pain in Earache, acute Gonorrhœa, and Hæmorrhoids.
BRERA.

The remaining prescriptions are *for external use only.*

2154. ℞ Opii pulv. ʒiss.
Pulv. Lini sem. ℥ss.
Aquæ puræ, Oiss.
Boil to a pint, then strain. Make a lotion, to be used while hot.
As an Application to bruised and painful parts.

2155. ℞ Extr. Opii, ʒij.
Aquæ ferventis, Oj. Dissolve, and strain.

As a Fomentation in Pruriginous Affections.—RADIUS.

2156. ℞ Morphiæ Sulph. gr. vj.
Boracis, ℥ss.
Aquæ Rosæ, ℥iij. Mix: make a lotion.

As an Application in Pruritus Vulvæ, washing first with tepid soap and water. MEIGS.

2157. ℞ Decoct. Lini seminum, ℥iv.
Croci stigmatorum, ʒj.
Vini Opii, ʒj.
Macerate the saffron in the decoction, strain, and add the wine of opium. Make an eye-wash.

In Ophthalmia.—FOY.

2158. ℞ Liq. Plumbi Diacet. ʒss.
Vini Opii, ʒj.
Aquæ Rosæ, ℥viij. Mix: make an eye-wash.

Ophthalmia.—Dr. HOOPER.

2159. ℞ Lin. Saponis co. ℥j.
Liq. Ammoniæ, ʒiij.
Olei Caryophylli, ʒj.
Tinct. Opii, ℥ss. Mix: make an anodyne liniment.

Dr. COPLAND.

2160. ℞ Olei Amygdalæ, ℥ij.
Camphoræ, ʒj.
Tinct. Opii, ʒss. Mix: make an anodyne liniment.

Mr. SAVORY.

2161. ℞ Ætheris Sulph. ʒiiss.
Tinct. Camphoræ, ℥iiss.
Tinct. Opii, ℥ss. Mix: make an embrocation.

In Flatulent Colic.—Dr. AINSLIE.

2162. ℞ Tinct. Opii, ʒij.
Liq. Ammoniæ, ʒj.
Tinct. Cantharidis, ʒiij.
Lin. Saponis, ʒx. Mix: make a liniment.

In Lumbago.—Dr. H. W. FULLER.

2163. ℞ Lin. Saponis co. ℥iss.
Liq. Ammoniæ,
Tinct. Cantharidis,
Tinct. Opii, ana ʒj. Mix: make a liniment.

In Colic, and other local pains.—Dr. JOY.

2164. ℞ Tinct. Opii,
Spir. Ammon. co.
Lin. Saponis co. ana ʒij.
Mix: make an embrocation. To be rubbed on the back and sides.

In Influenza.—Mr. EVANS.

2165. ℞ Tinct. Opii, ʒij.
Tinct. Lyttæ, ʒij.
Lin. Camphoræ co. ℥j.
Mix: make a liniment. To be rubbed on the chest.

In Hooping-cough.—Dr. WEST.

2166. ℞ Tinct. Opii, f℥j.
Spir. Camphoræ,
Liq. Ammoniæ, ana ℥ss.
Mix: make an embrocation. To be rubbed frequently over the region of the belly.

In mild Cholera.—Dr. THOMAS.

2167. ℞ Morphiæ, gr. iij.
Olei Amygdali, ʒj. Mix: make a liniment.

To be rubbed near the Eye in painful Affections of that organ. POLI.

2168. ℞ Syrupi Opii, ℥j.
Axungiæ, ℥iij.
Essentiæ Rosæ, ♏iv. Mix: make an ointment.

For Chapped Lips.—PIERQUIN.

2169. ℞ Opii, ʒss.
Extr. Conii, ʒj.
Ung. Resinæ, ℥ss. Mix: make an ointment.

To Gangrenous Ulcers.—CARUS.

2170. ℞ Opii pulv. subtiliss. ʒj.
Camphoræ rasæ, gr. xv.
Adipis præparatæ, ℥ss.
Mix: make an ointment. To be rubbed on the parts affected with spasm.

In Tetanus.—Dr. THOMAS.

2171. ℞ Ung. Hydrarg. fort. ʒiij.
Ung. Opii, ʒj.
Mix: make an ointment. To be used two or three times a day.

To Ulcers of the Sphincter Ani.—Mr. J. HILTON.

2172. ℞ Morphiæ Acet. gr. iv.
Ung. Hydrarg. ʒij.
Adipis, ʒij.
Mix: make an ointment. A piece of the size of a pea to be rubbed on the pubes.

In Cancer of the Uterus.—VON HILDENBRAND.

2173. ℞ Opii Pulv ℈ij.
Camphoræ, ʒss.
Picis Burgund.
Emp. Litharg. ana q. s. to form a plaster.

For Rheumatic and Neuralgic Pains of the Chest, Back, and Loins. Dr. GRAVES.

2174. ℞ Cataplasmatis simp. ℥v.
Liquoris Opii Sydenhami, ʒss.
Pour the laudanum upon the plaster, and apply it warm to the painful parts.

In Colicky Pains of the Belly.—TROUSSEAU and REVEIL.

ORCHIS. See SALEPA.

ORIGANUM. *Marjoram.*

The *Origanum vulgare* (Nat. Ord. *Labiatæ*) is a native plant, of a fragrant smell and pungent taste. It contains a volatile oil, which is separated by distillation, and possesses stimulant and carminative properties. The infusion of Marjoram has been employed as a tonic, diaphoretic, and emmenagogue. The dose of *Oleum Origani* is five to ten minims. *Infusum Origani*, one ounce to one ounce and a half.

OVUM. *Egg.*

The egg, which is so well known as an article of food, is produced by the hen of the domestic fowl, *Phasianus Gallus.* Within a calcareous shell it contains two parts, divided by a membrane, both fluid at first, but coagulated by heat. These are the white of egg (*albumen ovi*) and the yolk of egg (*vitellus ovi*). The former is important medicinally as being the best antidote to poisoning by any of the soluble salts of mercury or copper. The yolk of egg is a yellow oleaginous fluid, which forms an emulsion with water, and is of use in suspending many oily and other substances which cannot well be given in solution.

Oleum Vitelli Ovi (Paris Codex) is used as an application to sores and hæmorrhoids.

2175. ℞ Ovi vitelli unius,
Aquæ, Oij. Mix, and make an emulsion; then add
Salis communis, ʒss. Dissolve: for a drink.

In the Mesenteric Atrophy of Children.—HUFELAND.

2176. ℞ Ovi Vitelli, ℥ss.
Cetacei, ʒij.
Syrupi Althææ, ℥ss.
Aquæ Cinnamomi, ʒiss.
Aquæ destil. ℥iv. Mix: a tablespoonful frequently.

As a Demulcent in Coughs.—Dr. GREGORY.

2177. ℞ Vitelli Ovi unius,
Olei Lini, ℥ij.
Mix well, and make a liniment. (The white of egg is used to make a liniment in the same manner.)

As an Application to Burns.—RADIUS.

PAPAVER. *Poppy.*

This term is restricted to the ripe capsules of the poppy which produces opium—*P. somniferum*. They are globular in form, light, dry and brown outside; inside hollow, divided by numerous partitions, and containing numerous small seeds which yield a fixed oil. The capsules contain a narcotic principle, which is similar to opium. Their extract is used in the same cases as opium, but it is not so powerful. The decoction of poppies is much used as an anodyne fomentation to painful bruises and swellings. Besides the narcotic principle, it contains much mucilage, and some oil, derived from the seeds.

Extractum Papaveris (L., E.), two to ten grains.

Decoctum Papaveris (L., E., D.) is for outward use.

Syrupus Papaveris (L., E.), one to four drachms.

Cataplasma Papaveris, emollient and anodyne.

2178. ℞ Syrupi Papaveris,
Succi Limonum, ana ℥ss.
Confect. Rosæ, ℥j.
Mix: make a linctus. A teaspoonful, as required.

In Phthisical Cough.—Dr. THEOPHILUS THOMPSON.

2179. ℞ Syrupi Papaveris, ʒvj.
Oxymellis Scillæ, ʒiij.
Decoct. Hordei, ℥vj.
Mix: two tablespoonfuls three times a day.

In simple Catarrh.—Dr. W. AINSLIE.

2180. ℞ Syrupi Papaveris, ℥ij.
Mucilag. Acaciæ, ℥iss.
Conf. fruct. Rosæ Caninæ, ℥j.
Acidi Sulph dil. ʒij.
Mix: make a linctus. A teaspoonful frequently.

In Coughs.—Dr. COPLAND.

2181. ℞ Mucilag. Tragacanthæ, ℥iiss.
Oxymellis Scillæ, ℥ss.
Syrupi Papaveris, ℥j.
Mix: make a mixture. A tablespoonful to be swallowed gradually; frequently, when the cough is troublesome.

SPRAGUE.

2182. ℞ Mist. Camphoræ, ℥ix.
Potassæ Nitratis, gr. vj.
Spir. Æth. Sulph. C. ʒj.
Tinct. Opii, ♏x–xij.
Syrupi Papaveris, ʒij.
Mix: make an anodyne draught. To be taken at bedtime.
Dr. Copland.

2183. ℞ Tinct. Rhodii, ℥ss.
Mucilag. Acaciæ ver. ʒvj.
Triturate well, and add by degrees
Inf. Uvæ Ursi,
Syrupi Papaveris, ana ℥ij.
Mix: make a mixture. Dose, a fourth part, three or four times a day.
In Asthma, and in Chronic Catarrhs.—Dr. Copland.

2184. ℞ Mucilag. ℥v.
Decoct. Papaveris, Oj.
Albuminis Ovi, ʒj. Mix: make an injection.
In Acute Gonorrhœa.—Gassicourt.

PAREIRA.

This is the root of *Cissampelos Pareira*, a climbing shrub, of the Nat. Ord. *Menispermaceæ*. It has a slightly bitter taste, and is demulcent and tonic in its action. It has some diuretic power. It is used in diseases of the urino-genital system—as in gonorrhœa, leucorrhœa—but chiefly in chronic inflammation of the bladder, in which case Sir B. Brodie and others prefer it to Uva Ursi.

Extractum Pareiræ (L.), five grains to one scruple.

Decoctum Pareiræ, one to three ounces.

Infusum Pareiræ (L., E.), one to two ounces.

Tinctura Pareiræ (Brodie), half a drachm to a drachm.

2185. ℞ Inf. Pareiræ, ℥viij.
Acidi Nitrici dil. ♏xl.
Mix: make a mixture. Three tablespoonfuls three or four times a day.
In Phosphatic Urine.—Dr. Joy.

2186. ℞ Inf. Pareiræ, ℥viij.
Acidi Nitrici dil. ♏xl.
Tinct. Hyoscyami, ʒij. Mix: ℥j–℥iss for a dose.
In Chronic Inflammation of the Bladder, with Phosphatic Urine. Dr. Hooper.

2187. ℞ Acidi Benzoici, gr. ix.
Decoct. Pareiræ, ℥iss.
Acet. Morphiæ, gr. $\frac{1}{8}$–$\frac{1}{4}$. Mix: make a draught.
In Mucous Urine.—Dr. G. Bird.

PAULLINIA.

This is a dried paste, formed of the pounded seeds of *Paullinia sorbilis*, a climbing Brazilian plant (Nat. Ord. *Sapindaceæ*). It is much esteemed in South America as a tonic and astringent, and has been given in chlorosis, diarrhœa, and dysentery. It is generally mixed with chocolate, and may be taken almost *ad libitum* in this form. The dose of Paullinia is from ten to thirty grains.

Syrupus Paulliniæ (Gavrelle), half an ounce or more.

Pilulæ Paulliniæ (Gavrelle), five to ten at a dose.

2188. ℞ Pulv. Ext. Paulliniæ, gr. 75.
Divide in pulv. 10. (From one to five of them to be taken at the beginning of a periodical headache, and one night and morning for several days about the time of the expected return.)

TROUSSEAU and REVEIL.

2189. ℞ Paulliniæ, ʒvss.
Sacchari albi, lbiss.
Aquæ, q. s. to make a paste, which divide into 10-grain lozenges.

GAVRELLE.

PEPSINA. *Pepsine.*

This is a peculiar albuminous principle which exists in the digestive gastric juice of man and other animals. Rennet, a fluid obtained by macerating the fourth stomach of the calf in salt and water, owes to Pepsine its power of coagulating milk. Rennet has been given in diabetes by Dr. Nelson. Corvisart, Boudault, Ballard, and others have used the Pepsine in a solid form, mixed with starch, in cases of indigestion from deficient secretion and pain after food.

The "poudre nutrimentive" of Corvisart, *Pulvis Pepsinæ et Amyli*, is given (either neutral or with three drops of lactic acid to a dose) in doses of fifteen to twenty grains, just before a meal, or in the first spoonful of soup at dinner.

2190. ℞ Pulv. Pepsinæ et Amyli, ʒiss.
Syrupi Cerasi Acidi, ℥iij, ʒvj.
Digest for twelve hours. (A sixth part for a dose.)

CORVISART.

2191. ℞ Pulv. Pepsinæ et Amyli, gr. xv.
Morph. Hydrochlor. gr. 1-6th. Mix.

In Indigestion, with Painful and Sensitive Stomach. (This is the "poudre nutrimentive," No. 2.) CORVISART.

2192. ℞ Pulv. Pepsinæ et Amyli, gr. xv.
P. Strychniæ, gr. 1-24th. Mix.

In Indigestion with Atony. ("Poudre nutrimentive," No. 3.)

2193. ℞ P. Pepsinæ et Amyli, gr. xv.
P. Ferri (Quevenne), gr. j.
Mix: to be taken before meals.

Dr. BALLARD.

PETROLEUM.

Petroleum, Rock Oil, or Persian Naphtha, is a liquid bitumen which flows out of the earth in many parts of the world, as at Rangoon, in Barbadoes, in North America, &c. It is a stimulant antispasmodic, being also diaphoretic, and occasionally used for its anthelmintic properties. Externally applied, it is rubefacient, and enters into the composition of many stimulating liniments.

The dose is from half a drachm to a drachm.

2194. ℞ Petrolei, ℥ss.
Tinct. Assafœtidæ, ʒvj.
Mix: 40 drops three times a day.

In Tape-worm.—SCHWARTZ.

2195. ℞ Petrolei, ʒij.
Tinct. Scillæ, ʒj.
Spir. Juniperi, ʒvj.
Mix: make a diuretic mixture. (Dose, forty drops three times a day.)

In Dropsy.—VOGT.

2196. ℞ Petrolei, ℥ss.
Olei Terebinthinæ, ʒj.
Spir. Juniperi, ℥iv. Mix: make an embrocation.

To be rubbed on the Loins in Atony of the Urinary Passages, and Dropsy. RADIUS.

2197. ℞ Petrolei, ℥ss.
Spir. Lavandulæ, ℥j.
Tinct. Opii, ʒij. Mix: make a lotion.

To Frozen Limbs.—PHŒBUS.

2198. ℞ Petrolei, ʒiij.
Camphoræ, ℈j.
Ung. simplicis, ℥iss. Mix: make an ointment.

To Rheumatic Limbs, &c.—RADIUS.

PHELLANDRIUM. *Water Fennel.*

The seeds of the *Phellandrium aquaticum*, a common English plant (Nat. Ord. *Umbelliferæ*), have been occasionally employed for their real or supposed influence over pectoral complaints. They act, in large doses, as a narcotic poison. Dose, five to ten grains.

Infusum Phellandrii (Bird): dose, half an ounce.

2199. ℞ Sem. Phellandrii, ℥ss.
Alcoholis, ℥vj.
Macerate for 24 hours, and add
Vini Burgundiæ, ℥vj.
Macerate for 3 days, and strain. Dose, ten to sixty minims.

In Chronic Bronchial, and Pulmonary Affections.—MARCUS.

2200. ℞ Sem. Phelland. aquat. cont. ℥j.
Gummi Acaciæ, ℥j.
Aquæ ferventis, ℥ix.
Macerate and strain. To the strained liquor, add
Syrupi Althææ, ℥ss.
Vini Ipecac. ʒij.
Mix: two tablespoonfuls every three or four hours.

In Catarrh.—DR. COPLAND.

PHOSPHORUS.

Phosphorus is one of the chemical elements. It is semitransparent, generally yellowish in appearance, and of a waxy consistence. It easily bends. It is so readily combustible that it takes fire at the slightest friction. It has a garlic-like odor and taste. In large doses it is a powerful corrosive poison; in very small quantities it is employed as a diffusible stimulant. It may be given to rouse the vital powers in typhoid fever, in the latter stage of phthisis, and in exhaustion from any chronic disease. It has been recommended in gout and rheumatism. It is employed externally as an ingredient in various rubefacient liniments, which are rubbed on to paralyzed parts, and used in obstinate skin diseases. The dose is from one-tenth to one-twentieth part of a grain, but it must never be given in substance.

Æther Phosphoratus (Van Mons), five to ten minims three times daily, in some emollient liquid.

2201. ℞ Phosphori, gr. iij.
Olei Caryophylli, ♏xij.
Pulv. Glycyrrh. q. s.
Make a mass, and divide into 12 pills. One, twice a day. (Quantity of Phosphorus may be cautiously increased to a scruple.)

In Lupus, obstinate Scaly Diseases, and Syphilitic Tubercles. Dr. HOOPER.

2202. ℞ Phosphori, gr. iij–℈j.
Olei Caryophylli, ♏x–ʒj.
Mucilag. q. s.
Make 12 pills. One, twice a day.

In Lupus, Syphilitic Tubercle, and inveterate Scaly Diseases. Dr. BURGESS.

2203. ℞ Phosphori, gr. iv.
Olei Olivæ, ʒss.
Digest for 14 days in a darkened place, and then add
Olei Carui, ♏iv.
Dose, fifteen drops twice a day, cautiously increased, in almond emulsion.

Stimulant, in Phthisis, Skin Diseases, &c.—Dr. HOOPER.

2204. ℞ Phosphori puri, gr. ij.
Ætheris Sulph. ℥j.
Olei Valerianæ, ♏xij.
Mix: in doses of five to ten drops on sugar.

Dr. COPLAND.

2205. ℞ Phosphori, gr. ss.
Olei Succini, ℥ss.
Mix: ten drops, three times a day, in a wineglassful of cold water.

In Paralysis.

2206. ℞ Olei Olivarum opt. ℥viij.
Phosphori excisi, gr. xx.
Dissolve with heat, strain cold and make a liniment.

In local Paralysis, Marasmus, Rheumatism, and Chronic Arthritis. Dr. COPLAND.

2207. ℞ Phosphori, gr. vj.
Olei Amygdalæ, ℥j.
Ammoniæ Carb.
Camphoræ, ana gr. ij. Mix: make a liniment.

AUGUSTIN.

2208. ℞ Ætheris Phosphorati, ʒj.
Cerati (nihilo aquæ mixt.), ʒv. Mix: make an ointment.

In cases of Lupus, Syphilitic Tubercle, and Acne Rosacea. Dr. BURGESS.

2209. ℞ Phosphori, gr. ij–v.
Ætheris, q. s. Liquefy, and add
Camphoræ, ℈j.
Cerati albi, ℥ss. Mix: make an ointment.

In Lupus, Syphilitic Tubercle, and Acne Rosacea.

DR. HOOPER.

PIMENTA. *Allspice.*

This is the small unripe berry of *Eugenia Pimenta* (Nat. Ord. *Myrtaceæ*), an evergreen West Indian tree. The berries have an aromatic odor, and strong spicy taste. They contain a volatile oil. Both Pimenta and its oil are used as diffusible stimulants and stomachics, and employed to give an agreeable flavor to other medicines. The dose of the powder is from ten to forty grains.

Oleum Pimentæ, one to three minims.

Aqua Pimentæ (L., E., D.) is used as a vehicle.

Spiritus Pimentæ (L., E., D.), one to two drachms.

Tinctura Pimentæ (Swediaur), ten to twelve drops.

2210. ℞ Pulv. Pimentæ,
Pulv. Cinnamomi,
Pulv Croci, ana gr. iv.
Opii, gr. j.
Confect Rosæ, q. s. to make 2 boluses. One for a dose.

In Chronic Diarrhœa.—FOY.

PIPERES. *The Peppers.*

The berries of *Piper nigrum* and *Piper longum*, Black Pepper and Long Pepper (Nat. Ord. *Piperaceæ*), are used as condiments, on account of their pungent odor and fiery taste. They are both employed in medicine as stimulants. Black Pepper deprived of its dark skin forms White Pepper. Black Pepper has been given in gonorrhœa, in the same manner as cubebs; also used in intermittent fevers, and applied in ointment to ring-worm. It is given in confection in cases of internal piles, which it stimulates by passing over them in the bowel. Long Pepper is chiefly employed as a carminative adjunct to other medicines. Either this or the other may be made use of in the formation of a stimulant plaster. Their dose is from ten to twenty grains.

Piperine is the active principle of the peppers, and may be prepared from them. It is analogous in chemical nature to the resins. It has a bitter and acrid taste, and has been much used in Italy as a substitute for quinine in the treatment of intermittents. The dose is from two to ten grains.

Confectio Piperis (L., E., D.): dose, one drachm.

Oleum Piperis, one to three minims.

Tinctura Piperis, half a drachm to a drachm.

Unguentum Piperis nigri (D. 1826).

2211. ℞ Confect. Piperis nigri,
Confect. Cassiæ, ana ℥j.
Mix: make a confection. (Dose, ʒij, increased to ℥ss, two or three times a day.)

For Hæmorrhoids.—Dr. HOOPER.

2212. ℞ Confect. Piperis nigri, ʒj.
Assafœtidæ, gr. v.
Syrupi Zingiberis, q. s.
Make a uniform confection. Twice a day.

In Hæmorrhoids.—Dr. PARIS.

2213. ℞ Confect. Piperis nigri, ℈ij.
Sulph. loti, ℈j.
Aquæ Cinnamomi, ʒxj.
Mix: make a draught. To be taken in the morning.

In Hæmorrhoids.—Dr. GREGORY.

2214. ℞ Farinæ Sinapis, lbss.
Pulv. Piperis nigri,
Zingiberis Pulv. ana ʒj.
Syrupi, q. s. Make a cataplasm.

To be applied to the Pit of the Stomach in Colic, or to the Feet as a Revulsive. Dr. ELLIS.

2215. ℞ Pulv. Piperis nigri,
Galbani, ana ʒiij.
Picis nigræ, ℥ij.
Olei Bacc. Lauri, q. s. Mix: make a plaster.

Stimulating in Rheumatism.—AUGUSTIN.

2216. ℞ Pulv. Piperis longi,
Pulv. Zingiberis, ana ℥ss.
Albuminis Ovi, q. s. Mix well, and make a cataplasm.

Rubefacient in Pleurisy.—FOY.

2217. ℞ Piperinæ, gr. xij.
Extr. Gentianæ, q. s.
Mix, and divide into 12 pills. (One every hour, in the absence of fever.)

In Ague.—Dr. ELLIS.

2218. ℞ Pil. Hydrarg. gr. j.
Piperinæ,
Quinæ Disulph. ana gr. ij.
Syrupi, q. s.
Mix: make a pill. One, three times a day, for a few days, after the paroxysm has been checked by piperine.

HARTTE.

PIX BURGUNDICA. *Burgundy Pitch.*

The impure resin which exudes from some large trees of the Nat. Ord. *Coniferæ*, especially the *Abies excelsa* and *Pinus Palustris*, is known by the names *Abietis*, *Resina*, *Thus*, *Frankincense*, *&c.* When it is strained and purified it constitutes *Thus præparatum*, or *Pix Burgundica.* These substances are rarely used internally, but they are employed in the preparation of various plasters and ointments, used as rubefacient or strengthening applications. Such are the following:

Emplastrum Thuris (D.).
Emplastrum Picis (L., E.).
Emp. Picis Compositum (Lisbon Pharm.).
Ceratum Picis (Beral).

2219. ℞ Picis Burgundicæ, ℥v.
Mucilag. q. s.
Mix, and divide into 100 pills. (Six to eight, three times a day.)

In Cutaneous Affections.—ULRICH.

2220. ℞ Picis, ℥iv.
Ceræ flavæ, lbij.
Olei Olivæ, lbiss.
Resinæ flavæ, ℥iv.
Mellis, lbss.
Sapon. Castil. ℥j.
Liquefy together at a slow heat, and afterward stir assiduously until almost cooled; then add
Bals. Canad. ℥iv. Mix: make an ointment.

To Scrofulous Ulcers.—Mr. C. HOGG.

PIX NIGRA. PIX LIQUIDA. *Pitch* and *Tar.*

Tar (*Pix liquida*) is a blackish empyreumatic liquid, somewhat resembling turpentine, obtained by the slow combustion of various species of Pine. It is made largely in North America. Pitch (*Pix nigra*) is the solid mass left on evaporating tar.

Both are stimulant, diaphoretic, and alterative. Internally, they are chiefly used in cutaneous diseases, especially in lepra and psoriasis. Pitch has also been given in piles. Both tar and pitch are much employed in the formation of ointments and plasters, which are of use in stimulating diseased parts to a healthy action, or in affording protection where it is needed. (Tar-water has been given in chest affections, and many other diseases.)

The dose of tar is from half a drachm to a drachm. It may conveniently be given inclosed in capsules. The dose of pitch is from ten grains to half a drachm.

Aqua Picis liquidæ, one to two pints a day.

Unguentum Picis liquidæ (L., E., D.), used in porrigo and lepra.

Unguentum Picis [nigræ] (L.). A stimulant application to ulcers and cutaneous diseases.

Emplastrum Picis nigræ (Wirtemburg Pharm.).

2221. ℞ Picis nigræ, ʒj.
Pulv. Acaciæ, ʒss.
Mix, and divide into 20 pills. Two, every night.

In Hæmorrhoids.—Dr. WARDLEWORTH.

2222. ℞ Picis liquidæ, ʒj.
Farinæ tritici, q. s.
Make a mass, and divide into 4-grain pills.

Dr. G. B. WOOD.

2223. ℞ Picis liquidæ,
Pulv. Glycyrrh. ana ℥ss.
Mix, and make a mass. Divide into 4-grain pills. Two to six, three or four times a day.

In Lepra and Psoriasis.

2224. ℞ Ung. Picis liquidæ,
Ung. Sulph. ana partes æquales. Mix: make an ointment.

In Porrigo, Lepra, and Scabies.—PHARM. GUYENSIS.

PLATINI SALES. *Salts of Platinum.*

Platinum, like Gold, is insoluble in all fluids except Aqua regia. By this the *Bichloride of Platinum* is formed. Seventeen parts of this being added in solution to six parts of common salt, the *Chloroplatinate of Soda* is produced, and may be obtained on evaporation. These two salts have been used in medicine, and in their operation they much resemble the corresponding preparations of Gold. In large doses they are poisonous. They were found by Höfer to be very efficacious when given in syphilitic affections and rheumatism. They are also given as alteratives in skin diseases. The Chloroplatinate of Soda is less irritating than the Bichloride of Platinum. The dose of the Bichloride is from half a grain to a grain and a half; of the Chloroplatinate, one to three grains.

2225. ℞ Platini Bichloridi sicc. gr. iss.
Mucilag. Acaciæ,
Aquæ puræ, ana ℥iij.
Mix: make a mixture. To be taken by tablespoonfuls in the course of twenty-four hours.

HÖFER.

2226. ℞ Platini Bichloridi, gr. viij.
Guaiaci Resinæ, ʒj.
Pulv. Glycyrrh. q. s.
Make 20 pills. One to four, night and morning.

DR. DUNGLISON (U. S.).

2227. ℞ Platini Bichlor. gr. v.
Sodii Chloridi puri, gr. viij.
Mucilag. Acaciæ,
Aquæ puræ, ana ℥iij.
Mix: to be taken by spoonfuls in the twenty-four hours.

In old Syphilitic Diseases.—DR. DUNGLISON.

2228. ℞ Sodii Chloroplatinatis, ʒss.
Decoct. Papaveris, ℥viij. Mix: make an injection.

In Gonorrhœa and Leucorrhœa.—HÖFER.

2229. ℞ Platini Bichlor. ʒj.
Extr. Belladonnæ, ʒij.
Adipis, ℥iv. Mix: make an ointment.

An application to Indolent Ulcers.—HÖFER.

PLUMBI PRÆPARATA. *Preparations of Lead.*

The preparations of lead are used as astringents both externally and internally, and are also employed for their antispasmodic or sedative properties. They are poisonous in large doses. Applied to the surface in plasters and ointments, and in lotions to inflamed parts, they are given internally to check hæmoptysis and other forms of bleeding, as well as in fluxes from the bowels and the urino-genital organs. The acetate of lead is in the most frequent use.

Plumbi Oxidum Semivitreum. Semivitrified Protoxide of

Lead. Litharge. This is not used internally, but is employed in making plaster, which is a sort of soap containing oxide of lead instead of an alkali. Plasters are applied to tumors, local inflammations, and diseased parts generally, to resolve or protect them. Many ointments, cerates, and other local applications contain oxide of lead.

Plumbi Acetas. Acetate of Lead is the preparation generally adopted for internal use. In cases of hæmoptysis, hæmatemesis, diarrhœa, dysentery, it may be given in doses of three to five grains. It is used externally to form astringent lotions, injections, and ointments.

Plumbi Diacetas. Diacetate of Lead is formed by boiling the Oxide in a solution of the Acetate. Its solution constitutes Goulard's Extract of Lead. It is used to form cooling and astringent lotions to inflamed parts, collyria in various forms of ophthalmia, and injections in gonorrhœa and leucorrhœa.

Plumbi Carbonas. Carbonate of Lead. White Lead. Its powder has been used as an astringent, and mixed with lard to form a cooling ointment.

Plumbi Nitras. Nitrate of Lead resembles the Acetate in its action. It is contained in Ledoyen's Disinfecting Fluid.

Plumbi Chloridum. This is only used locally. It has been employed in an astringent wash to cancerous ulcerations.

Plumbi Iodidum. The yellow Iodide of Lead has been given internally as an alterative and resolvent in scrofulous affections, in doses of half to three grains. It is also applied in the form of ointment to indolent ulcers and strumous tumors.

Plumbi Nitro-saccharas. This salt has been proposed by Dr. Hoskins, of Jersey, as a solvent for urinary calculi, a certain quantity in solution being injected into the bladder for this purpose.

Plumbi Tannas. Tannate of Lead has been applied, in the form of ointment, to sloughing bed-sores; and has been recommended as an application to chapped nipples.

The following preparations of Lead are made according to prescribed formulæ:

Pilulæ Plumbi Opiatæ (E.), one to two for a dose. Each contains three grains of Acetate of Lead and half a grain of Opium. They are given in diarrhœa, dysentery, and severe internal hæmorrhages.

Pilulæ Plumbi Iodidi (Cottereau), one, gradually increasing to five, night and morning.

The remaining forms are for external use:

Emplastrum Plumbi (L., E., D.). Litharge, or Lead plaster. Diachylon Plaster.

Emplastrum Resinæ (L., E., D.). Resin, adhesive, or sticking plaster. Both this and the last are used for strapping, and to keep together the edges of wounds.

Unguentum Plumbi Compositum (L.).

Unguentum Plumbi Iodidi (L., D.). Applied to scrofulous swellings, &c.

Unguentum Plumbi Carbonatis (E., D.).

Emp. Plumbi Carbonatis (U. S.).

Unguentum Plumbi Acetatis (E., D.).

Ceratum Plumbi Acetatis (L.).

(The last two form admirable cooling applications to sores and irritable eruptions.)

Liquor Plumbi Diacetatis (L., E., D.).

Liq. Plumbi Diacet. dilutus (L.). Goulard Water. This is much employed as an astringent and cooling lotion to inflamed parts, and to form collyria, &c.

Ceratum Plumbi Compositum (L.) contains the solution of Diacetate of Lead.

Prescriptions for internal use:

2230. ℞ Plumbi Acetatis,
Pulv. Malvæ, ana ʒj.
Syrupi simplicis, q. s.
Make 36 pills. Four or five during the day.
To check Sweats in Phthisis.—RADIUS.

2231. ℞ Calomelanos, gr. j–ij.
Plumbi Acetatis, gr. ss–j.
Mix: divide into 4 powders. One, every three hours.
In Cholera Infantum.—DR. ELLIS.

2232. ℞ Plumbi Acetatis, ʒss.
Calomelanos, gr. v.
Confect. Rosæ, q. s. to make 10 pills. One, every two to four hours.

In Hæmatemesis.—Dr. Ellis.

2233. ℞ Plumbi Acetatis, gr. iij.
Pil. Saponis co. gr. ij.
Mix: make a pill. One, night and morning.

In Hæmoptysis.—Dr. Gregory.

2234. ℞ Plumbi Acetatis, gr. ½–ij.
Pulv. Ipecac. co. gr. v.
Pulv. Scillæ, gr. j–ij.
Mix: make a powder. Two or three times a day.

In the Bronchitis of Fever.—Dr. Henderson.

2235. ℞ Plumbi Acetatis,
Opii, ana gr. vj.
Sacchari albi, ʒj.
Mix, and divide into 12 powders. One, three or four times a day.

Diarrhœa, &c.—Dr. Hooper.

2236. ℞ Plumbi Acetatis, gr. iij.
Opii, gr. j.
Extr. Conii, gr. v.
Make a mass: divide into 2 pills. To be given twice a day, drinking some acidulated draught, until the tendency to hæmorrhage ceases.

In Hæmorrhages.—Dr. Paris.

2237. ℞ Plumbi Acetatis, gr. xviij.
Opii purificati, gr. ij.
Extr. Hyoscyami, gr. x.
Mix, and divide into 6 pills. One, every six hours.

In Hæmoptysis.—Dr. Gregory.

2238. ℞ Plumbi Acetatis, gr. ij.
Aceti distil. ʒss.
Aquæ, ad. ℥iss.
Mix: make a draught. [The Acet. Acid is to prevent the formation in the stomach of Carbonate of Lead, which is thought to produce Colic.]

In Hæmoptysis.—Dr. Theophilus Thompson.

2239. ℞ Plumbi Acetatis, gr. ij.
Opii, gr. ¼.
Extr. Hyoscyami, gr. iv.
Mix, and divide into 2 pills. To be given at proper intervals, and washed down with a little distilled vinegar and water. Half a grain of Nit. Silver may sometimes be added with advantage.

In the Diarrhœa of Phthisis.—Dr. Theophilus Thompson.

2240. ℞ Plumbi Acetatis, ℥ss.
Ferri Sulph. ʒiij.
Aceti,
Spir. rectif. ana ℥ij.
Aquæ Rosæ, ʒvj.
Mix: make a mixture. Dose, ʒss–ʒj in some proper vehicle.
In profuse Sweating, Diarrhœa, and Gonorrhœa.—GORMANN.

2241. ℞ Plumbi Iodidi, gr. iv.
Confect. Rosæ, q. s.
Make 12 pills. One, night and morning.
In Syphilitic Eruptions, &c.—Dr. HOOPER.

2242. ℞ Plumbi Iodidi,
Pulv. Digitalis, ana gr. vj.
Extr. Stramonii alcohol. gr. ij.
Sacchari, ʒj.
Mix, and divide into 24 powders. One, four times a day.
GASSICOURT.

Prescriptions for external use:

2243. ℞ Plumbi Acetatis, gr. j–iss.
Triturate into a very fine powder; and by means of a fine hair pencil first dipped into water, and then immersed in the powder, apply it to the internal surface of the eyelids.
In Granular Ophthalmia of the Eyelids.—Dr. J. C. HALL.

2244. ℞ Plumbi Acetatis, gr. viij.
Aquæ destil. ℥viiss.
Spir. rectif. ℥ss.
Acidi Hydrocyan. dil. ʒij. Make a lotion. Write *Poison.*
Impetigo.—Dr. PARIS.

2245. ℞ Plumbi Acetatis, gr. vj.
Aquæ puræ, ℥j.
Tinct. Opii, gtt. xxx–l.
Mix: make an enema. To be repeated according to the frequency of the discharges.
In Dysentery.—Dr. BATCHELDER.

2246. ℞ Plumbi Acetatis,
Extr. Belladonnæ, ana ʒj.
Axungiæ, ʒvj. Mix: make an ointment.
As an application to Fissure of the Anus.—FOY.

2247. ℞ Liq. Plumbi Diacet. ♏xx.
Aquæ, ℥iss. Mix.
To be used as an injection in Gonorrhœa.
Mr. BRANSBY COOPER.

2248. ℞ Decoct. Malvæ co. Oj.
Liq. Plumbi Diacet. ʒj–ʒij. Mix: make a lotion.
In Lichen, Eczema, Impetigo, &c.—Dr. HOOPER.

2249. ℞ Liq. Plumbi Diacet. ʒj–ʒij.
Inf. Althææ, ℥xvj. Mix: make a lotion.
In Lichen and Chronic Eczema.—Dr. Burgess.

2250. ℞ Liq. Plumbi Diacet. ʒj.
Acidi Acetici,
Spir. rectif. ana ℥ss.
Aquæ, ℥ix. Mix: make a lotion.
Astringent.—Dr. Hooper.

2251. ℞ Liq. Plumbi Diacet. gtt. xv.
Tinct. Opii, ʒss.
Aquæ florum Sambuci, ℥iss. Mix: make an eye-wash.
In Ophthalmia.—Dr. Rust.

2252. ℞ Liq. Plumbi Diacet. dil. ℥j.
Spir. Camphoræ, ℥iij.
Aquæ, Oj. Mix: make a lotion.
To old Ulcers.—Dr. Ellis.

2253. ℞ Liq. Plumbi Diacet. ♏xxxiv.
Aquæ Calcis, ℥iv.
Olei Olivæ, ʒij.
Mix: make an injection. [To be shaken before using.]
In Inflammation of the Prostate and Urethra.—Foy.

2254. ℞ Liq. Plumbi Diacet. ♏xl.
Vini Opii, ʒj.
Aquæ Rosæ, ℥vii. Mix: make a lotion.
In Eczema.—Dr. Burgess.

2255. ℞ Liq. Plumbi Diacet. ʒss.
Decoct. Hordei, Oj.
Syrupi simplicis, ℥j. Mix: make a gargle.
In Cynanche.—Radius.

2256. ℞ Liq. Plumbi Diacet.
Olei Olivæ, ana ℥j.
Aquæ Rosæ, ℥iv. Mix: make a liniment.
As an application in extensive Burns.—Knackstedt.

2257. ℞ Olei Olivæ, ℥ij.
Liq. Plumbi Diacet. ʒj.
Ætheris Sulph. ʒij.
Tinct. Opii, ʒj.
Mix: make a liniment. A rag moistened with this to be frequently applied to the inflamed part.
In Milk Abscess.—Dr. Dewees (U. S.).

2258. ℞ Liq. Plumbi Diacet. ʒj.
Aquæ Rosæ, ℥j.
Ung. Cetacei, ℥ij.
Liquefy the ointment, and rub up with the lead-water. Afterward mix both together with rose-water. Make an ointment.
For Chapped Hands.—Dr. A. T. Thomson.

2259. ℞ Cataplasmatis simplicis, ℥iv.
Liq. Plumbi Diacet. ℥j
Ammon. Hydrochlor. ʒss. Mix: make a cataplasm.
An application to indolent Tumors.—RADIUS.

2260. ℞ Plumbi Subcarb. ʒij.
Calcis præparat. ℥ss.
Cerati Galeni, ℥ij. Mix: make an ointment.
In Papular Eruptions.—Dr. BURGESS.

2261. ℞ Hydrarg. Protochlor. ʒij.
Aluminis exsicc.
Plumbi Subcarb. ana ℥ss.
Terebinth. Venet. ʒvj.
Cerati Cetacei, ℥iss. Mix: make an ointment.
In Porrigo Galeata.—BANYER.

2262. ℞ Plumbi Carbon, ℈j.
Acidi Nitrici dil. q. s. to dissolve it.
Aquæ destil. lbj.
Mix: make a lotion. To be used faithfully two or three times a day.
In offensive Vaginal Discharges.—Dr. O. WARD.

2263. ℞ Plumbi Chloridi, ʒj.
Aquæ, Oj. Mix: make a lotion.
As a Wash to Cancerous Ulcerations, and to painful Neuralgic Tumors. Mr. TUSON.

2264. ℞ Plumbi Iodidi, gr. xij.
Ung. Ceræ albæ, ℥j.
Chloroformylis, ♏viij ad xij.
Glycerinæ, ʒj. Mix: make an ointment.
In obstinate cases of Prurigo.—Dr. NELIGAN.

2265. ℞ Plumbi Tannatis (recentis), ʒvj.
Axungiæ, ʒxv. Mix: make an ointment.
To be applied to Bed-sores.—Dr. TOTT.

2266. ℞ Plumbi Nitro-saccharatis, gr. xij.
Acidi Acet. fort. ʒj.
Aquæ puræ, ℥xij.
Mix: make an injection. The whole is to be brought to the boiling point, and, while warm, from four to eight ounces are to be injected into the bladder, by means of a double-current caoutchouc catheter. Renew it in ten or fifteen minutes, as may be deemed proper.
To Decompose and Dissolve Phosphatic Calculi.
Dr. J. E. HOSKINS.

POTASSA. *Potash.*

This is the oxide of the metal Potassium. It is known in solution as Liquor Potassæ, and in the solid form as Potassa Fusa, or Caustic Potash. Potash is antacid and alterative.

Given internally in moderate doses, and much diluted with water, it counteracts acidity in the stomach, in the system, and in the secretions. It checks a tendency to lithic deposits, and is useful in gout and rheumatism, in both of which there is an excess of acid. It counteracts heartburn, gastralgia, flatulence, and dyspepsia, when depending on an excess of acid in the stomach and intestines. As an alterative, Potash is given in scrofula, in the first stage of phthisis, in various skin diseases, and in secondary syphilitic disorders. If too long continued, it tends to weaken the system; or if given in too large doses, or in too concentrated a form, it is a dangerous corrosive poison.

Solid Potash (*Potassa Fusa*, or *Potassæ Hydras*) is a powerful caustic, destroying the tissues with which it comes in contact, on account of its very strong affinity for water. As it rapidly deliquesces, its effect spreads to a considerable distance from the place where it is applied, so that when a limited action is desired, means must be taken to confine it. Caustic Potash is used to form issues, to destroy hair and warts, and to remove the unhealthy surface from sinuous, scrofulous, or syphilitic ulcers. It often gives great pain. It has been applied by some to the internal surface of the urethra in stricture.

The *Potassa cum Calce* is frequently employed in the formation of issues, being less deliquescent than simple Potash.

Liq. Potassæ may be given internally in doses of ten to forty minims for adults, or of one to five minims for young children.

The *Alkaline Solution* of Brandish is similarly employed.

2267. ℞ Liq. Potassæ, ʒj.
Liq. Calcis, ℥vj.

Mix: make a mixture. Take one or two tablespoonfuls when there is abundance of acid, or when there is a great deposit of gravel from the urine, a small cupful of the same.

In the Lithic Acid Diathesis.—Dr. Joy.

2268. ℞ Liq. Potassæ, ♏xxx.
Aquæ Menth. pip. ℥vij.
Tinct. Gentianæ, ℥ss.
Magnesiæ, ʒj.

Mix: make a mixture. Two dessertspoonfuls two or three times a day.

In Acidity of Stomach in Gouty habits.—Dr. Thomas.

2269. ℞ Liq. Potassæ, ♏xx.
Mist. Cretæ, f℥j.
Tinct. Calumbæ, ʒj. Mix: make a draught.

In Acidity of Stomach.—Dr. HOOPER.

2270. ℞ Liq Potassæ, ♏xv.
Inf. Serpentariæ, ʒix.
Tinct. Serpentariæ, ʒj.
Syrupi Zingiberis, ʒss.
Make a draught. To be taken twice a day.

In the Lithic Acid Diathesis.—Dr. PARIS.

2271. ℞ Solut. Alkalinæ (Brandish's), ʒv.
Inf. Chirettæ, ℥viij.
Spir. Anisi co. ʒiij.
Syrupi Aurantii, ℥j.
Mix: make a mixture. Two tablespoonfuls three times a day.

In the Lithic Acid Diathesis.—Dr. NELIGAN.

2272. ℞ Liq. Potassæ, ℥j.
Sodii Chloridi, ℥j.
Sodæ Phosphatis, ʒiss.
Aquæ, ℥iij.
Mix: make a solution. A little to be added to the ordinary drink, so as not to affect the taste.

In Dyspepsia with Acidity.—Dr. SPURGIN.

2273. ℞ Liq. Potassæ, ℥ss.
Decoct. Dulcamaræ, ℥xj.
Tinct. Chirettæ, ℥ss.
Mix: make a mixture. Two tablespoonfuls, three times a day.

In Skin Diseases.—Dr. NELIGAN.

2274. ℞ Sol. Alkalin. (Brandishii), ʒj.
Pot. Sulph. c. Sulph. ʒiss.
Aquæ destil. ℥ij.
Tinct. Aurantii, ʒj.
Mix: make a draught. To be taken early in the morning.

Cathartic in Skin Diseases.—Dr. NELIGAN.

2275. ℞ Liq. Potassæ, ʒij.
Extr. Sarzæ, ʒiij.
Syrupi Aurantii, ℥ss.
Spir. Anisi, ʒj.
Aquæ, ℥viij.
Mix: make a mixture. Two tablespoonfuls three times a day.

To the Nurse, in Infantile Herpes.—Mr. C. HOGG.

2276. ℞ Liq. Potassæ, ʒij.
Potassæ Nitratis, ʒij.
Spir. Æth. Nit. ʒiij.
Syrupi Scillæ, ʒvj.
Aquæ destil. ad ℥vj.
Make a mixture. A tablespoonful three times a day, in a wineglassful of water.

Diuretic.—Mr. FERGUSSON.

2277. ℞ Liq. Potassæ, ʒiij.
Mist. Acaciæ, ℥ij.
Pulv. Pip. Cubebæ, ℥j.
Aquæ puræ, ℥viiiss.
Syrupi Aurantii, ℥j.
Mix: three tablespoonfuls three times a day.

In Gonorrhœa.—Dr. THOMAS.

2278. ℞ Liq. Potassæ, ʒiiiss.
Potass. Iodidi, ℈j.
Pulv. Rhei, ℈ij.
Mist. Camphoræ, ℥vj. Mix: f℥j, three times a day.

In Gonorrhœa.—Mr. MILTON.

2279. ℞ Potassæ Causticæ, gr. ij.
Aquæ destil. ℥j. Mix: make an injection.

To be used at the commencement of Gonorrhœa.—GIRTANNER.

2280. ℞ Potassæ fusæ, ℈ij.
Aquæ destil. ℥iv. Mix: make a lotion.

In Chronic forms of Favus.—Dr. BURGESS.

POTASSÆ CARBONAS ET BICARBONAS. *Carbonate* and *Bicarbonate of Potash.*

The Carbonate, though somewhat less active, resembles Potash in its action on the system internally, but has much less caustic power. The Bicarbonate is still milder, and more pleasant to the taste. Both are extensively used as antacids in dyspepsia, gouty, lithic, and rheumatic disorders. They are also used as alteratives in glandular enlargements and mesenteric disease, and as antiphlogistics in various febrile and inflammatory complaints. Both (but especially the Bicarbonate) are used to form effervescing draughts, for which purpose Citric Acid is preferable to Tartaric. The *Aqua Potassæ effervescens* is a solution of the Bicarbonate into which Carbonic Acid has been forced under pressure.

The dose of either of the Carbonates is from ten grains to one drachm.

Liquor Potassæ Carbonatis (L., D.), ten minims to one and a half drachms.

Aqua Potassæ effervescens (E.), half a pint to a pint.

2281. ℞ Pulv. Potass. Carbon. ʒj.
Pulv. Acaciæ, ℥j. Incorporate well together.
Dose, ʒss–ʒj, dissolved in water.

In Engorgement of the Bowels.—GUIBOURT.

2282. ℞ Potassæ Subcarb. ʒss–ʒj.
Inf. Quassiæ, Oj.
Mix: dose, four glasses daily.

In Lichen, Prurigo, &c.—Dr. BURGESS.

2283. ℞ Potassæ Carbon. ʒj.
Aquæ Anethi, ℥iij.
Mix: ten to twenty drops form a dose for an infant.

In Convulsions caused by Intestinal Irritation.—Mr. SAVORY.

2284. ℞ Potassæ Carbon. ʒij.
Spirit Amm. Arom. ʒj.
Aquæ Cinnamomi, ℥iv.
Mix: dose, fʒj, as required.

In Pyrosis.—Dr. ELLIS.

2285. ℞ Potassæ Subcarb. ℈j.
Pulv. Rhei, gr. v.
Pilulæ Hydrarg. gr. iij.
Syrupi, q. s. to make 6 pills. One, twice a day.

In Gout with Hepatic Derangement.—Dr. W. AINSLIE.

2286. ℞ Potassæ Carbon. ʒij.
Vini Antimonii, ʒj.
Tinct. Opii, ♏xl.
Spir. Lavand. co. ʒij.
Aquæ destil. ℥iv.
Mix: a tablespoonful every hour or two.

Expectorant.—Dr. ELLIS.

2287. ℞ Gummi Acaciæ, ʒv.
Saponis Medic. ʒss.
Potassæ Subcarb. ʒij.
Potassæ Nitratis, ℈ij.
Inf. Juniperi, lbij. Mix: make a diuretic mixture.

May be given in Gout, with twice the quantity of Potash, some Stomachic Tincture, and Tincture of Colchicum.

Dr. COPLAND.

2288. ℞ Magnesiæ, gr. vj.
Potassæ Bicarb. gr. xij.
Potassæ Tartratis, gr. xv.
Mix: make a powder. To be taken every evening in a small glass of water.

In the Lithic Diathesis.—Sir B. BRODIE.

2289. ℞ Potassæ Bicarb. ʒj.
Inf. Buchu, ℥vj.
Mix: make a mixture. A fourth part every four hours.

In Gout.—Mr. HOSKINS.

2290. ℞ Inf. Calumbæ, ℥v.
Potassæ Bicarb. ʒj.
Tinct. Gentianæ co. ʒiij.
Make a mixture. Three tablespoonfuls at noon.

In Indigestion with Acidity.—Dr. BABINGTON.

2291. ℞ Potassæ Bicarb. ℈j.
Tinct. Hyoscyam. ʒss.
Inf. Pareiræ, ℥iss. Mix: make a draught.

In Mucous Urine.—Dr. G. BIRD.

2292. ℞ Potassæ Bicarb.
Ammon. Sesquicarbon. ana ʒss.
Aquæ Anethi, ℥viiss.
Dose, ℥iss twice a day. After breakfast and at bedtime.

In cases of Dyspepsia, Acidity and Turbid Urine.—Dr. DRUITT.

2293. ℞ Pot. Bicarb. cryst. ʒss.
Tinct. Cinnamomi,
Tinct. Vanillæ, āā ♏xv.
Syrupi simp. ℥ij.
Aquæ, ℥xxxij.
Mix: to be taken by cupfuls three or four times a day.

In Gout and Rheumatism.—TROUSSEAU and REVEIL.

2294. ℞ Potassæ Bicarb. ℈ij.
Inf. Anthemidis, ʒx.
Tinct. Opii, ♏v.
Syrupi, ʒj.
Make a draught, to be taken every 6 hours until three or four doses are taken; then, unless the bowels are moved of their own accord, some cathartic medicine is to be given; and the same alternation is to be made for a month.

In the Lithic Acid Diathesis.—Dr. PARIS.

2295. ℞ Inf. Gentianæ co. ℥viij.
Sodæ Bicarb.
Potassæ Bicarb. ana ℈ij.
Spir. Æth. Nit. ʒiij.
Mix: make a mixture. Two tablespoonfuls three times a day. Every night a 5-gr. compd. rhubarb pill. [At the same time a warm soda pediluvium may be used at bedtime.]

In Subacute Rheumatism.—Dr. WRIGHT.

2296. ℞ Potassæ Carbon. gr ij–vj.
Aquæ, ℥j.
Mix: make an eye-wash. To be dropped on the eye every two to four hours.

For Specks on the Cornea.—Dr. HINSLEY.

2297. ℞ Potassæ Carbon. ℥iv.
Aquæ tepidæ, lbccc. Mix: make an alkaline bath.

In Rheumatic or Eruptive Disorders.—Dr. JOY.

2298. ℞ Potassæ Subcarb. ℥iv–viij.
Aquæ, q. s. to form an alkaline bath. (Fourteen pailfuls.)

In Skin Diseases, with Itching.—Dr. BURGESS.

2299. ℞ Potassæ Carbon. ʒiij.
Sodii Chloridi, ʒij.
Aquæ Rosæ, ℥viij.
Aquæ flor. Aurant. ℥ij. Mix: make a lotion.

To Sunburn and Freckles.—SUNDELIN.

2300. ℞ Potassæ Subcarb. ʒij.
Aquæ destil. ʒij.
Mucilag. Amygd. amar. ℥viij. Mix: make a lotion.

In Lichen and Prurigo.—Dr. BURGESS.

2301. ℞ Potassæ Carbon. ℥j.
Liq. Opii sedat. ʒvj.
Aquæ Rosæ, ℥ix.
Mix: make an alkaline lotion. (Flannels wet with this to be laid over the affected joint.)

In Rheumatic Gout.—Dr. H. W. FULLER.

2302. ℞ Potassæ Carbon.
Saponis albi, ana ℥j.
Aquæ Sambuci, Oij. Dissolve, strain, and add
Ammon. Hydrochlor. ʒij. For a fomentation.

To Bruises.—CADET.

POTASSÆ TARTRAS, BITARTRAS, CITRAS, ACETAS.

Tartrate, Bitartrate, Citrate and *Acetate of Potash.* (*Effervescing Draughts.*)

The neutral Tartrate of Potash is in use as a cooling purgative. It is frequently combined with senna, to hasten its action and moderate its griping tendency. It reacts as an alkali upon the urine, as do also the Citrate and Acetate. Dose, one to six drachms.

The Bitartrate, Acid Tartrate, or Cream of Tartar, is but

sparingly soluble in water. It has an acid taste, and is used to form refrigerant drinks in fevers. In small doses it is diuretic; in large doses, a hydragogue cathartic, being frequently combined with some other laxative, as sulphur. Dose, as a diuretic, one scruple to one drachm; as a laxative, one to two drachms; as a strong purge, half an ounce to an ounce.

The Acetate is also diuretic in small, and cathartic in large doses. It is much used for both purposes in dropsy. It is likewise employed as alterative in various skin disorders, especially lepra, and in diseases of the liver. It has been given with much success in gonorrhœa. Dose, as a diuretic, one scruple to one drachm; as a cathartic, one drachm to half an ounce.

Citrate of Potash results from the decomposition of either of the carbonates by means of citric acid or lemon-juice. It is therefore given, along with the carbonic acid gas which escapes, in effervescing draughts. These constitute most agreeable refrigerant drinks in inflammatory disorders. They are diuretic and diaphoretic. They are also given when an alkaline action on the urine is required, as in the lithic diathesis; and to check irritability of the stomach, or control obstinate vomiting. Tartaric acid may be used instead of citric, but is apt to form the insoluble Bitartrate instead of Tartrate of Potash. In forming an effervescing draught containing Potash, the following proportions must be observed:

One scruple of Carbonate of Potash to eighteen grains of Citric or Tartaric Acid, or half an ounce of Lemon-juice.

One scruple of Bicarbonate of Potash to fifteen grains of Citric or Tartaric Acid, or three drachms and a half of Lemon-juice.

The *Pulveres Effervescentes* (E., D.) contain the carbonate and the acid in the proportion required to make the effervescing draught.

Potassæ Borotartras, soluble Cream of Tartar, is purgative in the same dose as the Bitartrate.

Acetate of Potash, as alterative, diuretic, and purgative.

2303. ℞ Potassæ Acetatis, ℥ss–℥j.
Syrupi simplicis, ℥iij.
Spir. Æth. Nit. ℥j.
Mix: make a mixture. (One drachm for a dose.)
Diuretic.—Dr. HOOPER.

2304. ℞ Potassæ Acetatis, ʒiv.
Liq. Potassæ, ʒij.
Spirit. Juniperi, ʒij.
Mist. Camphoræ, ad ℥vj. Mix: f℥j three times a day.
In Gonorrhœa.—Mr. MILTON.

2305. ℞ Potassæ Acetatis, ʒiv.
Pulv. Rhei, ʒj.
Spir. Æth. Nit. ʒiij.
Mist. Camphoræ, ad ℥vj. f℥j three times a day.
In Gonorrhœa.—Mr. MILTON.

2306. ℞ Potassæ Acetatis, ʒss–ʒj.
Tinct. Digitalis, ♏v.
Tinct. Canthar. ♏x.
Spir. Æth. Nit. ʒss.
Aquæ, ad ℥iss.
Mix: make a draught. To be taken three times a day.
Diuretic in Dropsy.—Dr. BUDD.

2307. ℞ Pulv. Scillæ, gr. xxx.
Potassæ Acetatis, ℥ss.
Oxymel. Scillæ, ʒij.
Mellis, ℥ss.
Olei Juniperi, ♏xx.
Mix: make an electuary, which take every six hours with an equal quantity of nutmeg.
In old cases of Anasarca.—Dr. NELIGAN.

2308. ℞ Potassæ Acetatis,
Oxymel. Scillæ, ana ʒj.
Aquæ flor. Tiliæ, ʒiv.
Vini Opii, gtt. xv.
Syrupi Althææ, ℥j. Mix: dose, f℥ss.
Diuretic and Sedative.—PIERQUIN.

2309. ℞ Potassæ Acetatis,
Extr. Taraxaci, ana ℥ss.
Extr. Conii, gr. x–xx.
Aquæ Fœniculi, ℥viss.
Syrupi Sarzæ,
Syrupi Sennæ, ana ℥ss.
Mix: two or three tablespoonfuls every four hours.
In Jaundice.—Dr. COPLAND.

Tartrate of Potash, as alterative, diuretic, and purgative:

2310. ℞ Potassæ Tartratis, ʒij.
Pulv. Rhei,
Pulv. Cort. Aurant. ana ʒj.
Olei Cajuputi, ℈j. Mix: fʒj three times a day.
In obstructions of the Portal System.—ST. MARIE.

2311. ℞ Pulv. Rhei, ℈ss.
Potassæ Tartratis, ʒj.
Confect. Aromat. ℈j.
Aquæ Menthæ viridis, ℥ij.
Mix: make a draught. To be taken every eight hours.
In Jaundice.—DR. E. J. CLARK.

2312. ℞ Potassæ Tartratis, ʒj.
Potassæ Nitratis, ʒss.
Mannæ, ℥j.
Decoct. Taraxaci, ℥vj. Mix: f℥j every two hours.
In Dropsy following Scarlatina.—PHŒBUS.

2313. ℞ Liq. Ammon. Carbon. ℥vj.
Potassæ Bitartratis, q. s. to saturate. Dose, fʒj.
Diuretic.—LEIPSIC PHARM.

Supertartrate (or *Bitartrate*) *of Potash*, as refrigerant, diuretic, and purgative:

2314. ℞ Potassæ Supertart. pulv. ℥ij.
Potassæ Nitratis, ʒiij. Mix, and divide into 12 equal parts.
Refrigerant.—Dr. COPLAND.

2315. ℞ Potassæ Bitartratis, ʒss.
Pulv. Scillæ, gr. ij.
Pulv. Zingiberis, gr. iv.
Mix: make a powder. To be taken every eight hours.
In Ascites.—Dr. A. T. THOMSON.

2316. ℞ Potassæ Bitart. ʒij.
Lactis vaccini ferventis, Oj.
Dissolve. Let the liquor cool, strain, and separate the serum; to this add sugar as much as desired, and let the patient drink as he feels inclined to.
Diuretic drink in Fevers, &c.—Dr. PARIS.

2317. ℞ Potassæ Bitart. ʒij.
Aquæ ferventis, lbij.
Corticis Limonis, et
Sacchari, to suit the taste. For an ordinary drink.
Diuretic drink.—Dr. JOY.

2318. ℞ Potassæ Nitratis, gr. x.
Potassæ Bitart. gr. xx.
Pulv. Acaciæ, gr. x.
Sacchari albi, ʒss.
Mix: make a powder. To be taken three or four times a day in barley-water.

Diuretic in Fevers and Dropsies.—Dr. HOOPER.

2319. ℞ Potassæ Bitart. ʒiv.
Acidi Boracici, ʒj.
Aquæ destillatæ, ℥xij.
Mix: make a mixture. A fourth part every third hour to produce copious liquid stools.

In Dropsical Effusions.—Dr. NELIGAN.

2320. ℞ Potassæ Bitart.
Extr. Marrubii, ana ʒij.
Aquæ Melissæ, ℥iij.
Mix: half to be taken morning and evening.

In Hæmorrhoids with Constipation.—AUGUSTIN.

2321. ℞ Potassæ Supertart. ℥iss.
Sulph. præcip. ℥j.
Sodæ Boratis, ʒiiss.
Syrupi Zingib. q. s. to make an electuary. One or two teaspoonfuls at bedtime.

Dr. COPLAND.

2322. ℞ Sulph. loti,
Potassæ Bitart. ana ℥j.
Pulv. Jalapæ, ʒj.
Pulv. Cinnam. co. ʒj.
Mellis, v. Theriacæ, q. s. to make an electuary. Dose, a teaspoonful or dessertspoonful two or three times a day.

Constipation.—Dr. HOOPER.

3323. ℞ Pulv. Jalapæ,
Pulv. Rhei,
Pulv. Scammonii, ana gr. v.
Pulv. Elaterii, gr. ss.
Potassæ Bitart.
Potassæ Sulph. ana ʒss.
Syrupi Zingib. q. s. to form a bolus.

Powerful Purge in Pulmonary Engorgement and Dropsy.
Dr. GRAVES.

Borotartrate of Potash:

2324. ℞ Potassæ Borotartratis, ℥ss.
Antim. et Potass. Tart. gr. j.
Aquæ, ℥iv. Mix: dose, a spoonful.

In Congestion of the Head.—RADIUS.

2325. ℞ Potassæ Borotartratis, ℥j.
Aquæ Menthæ viridis, ℥viij.
Spirit. Ætheris Nit. ʒij.
Oxymellis Scillæ, ℥j. Mix: dose, f℥j every second hour.
Diuretic.—SELIG.

Effervescing and refrigerant mixtures, containing *Citrate of Potash:*

2326. ℞. Potassæ Bicarbonatis, ℈j.
Tinct. Aurantii, ♏xv.
Aquæ, ℥j.
Syrupi, ʒj.
Mix: make a draught with a tablespoonful of lemon-juice. To be taken in a state of effervescence.
Dr. GREGORY.

2327. ℞ Potassæ Bicarb. ℈j.
Aquæ Cinnamomi, ʒx.
Tinct. Opii, ♏v.
Syrupi Cort. Aurant. ʒj.
Mix: make a draught. To be taken every hour in active effervescence with a tablespoonful of lemon-juice.
In Obstinate Vomitings.—Dr. THOMAS.

2328. ℞ Emuls. Amygd. ℥j.
Vini Ipecac. ♏x.
Potassæ Bicarb. gr. x.
Succi Limonis, ʒiij. Mix: make a draught.
Expectorant.—Mr. SAVORY.

2329. ℞ Potassæ Bicarbonatis,
Acidi Citrici, ana ℈j.
Syrupi Mori, ʒiij.
Aquæ destillatæ, ʒix. Mix: fʒij every sixth hour.
In Febrile Coughs of Children one year old.—Dr. WEST.

2330. ℞ Potassæ Bicarb. ℈j.
Succi Limonis, ℥ss.
Mist. Camphoræ, ʒvj.
Antim. Tartarizati, gr. ss.
Syrupi Cort. Aurant. ʒj. Mix: make a draught.
In Scarlet Fever.—Dr. FRAMPTON.

2331. ℞ Acidi Citrici,
Potassæ Bicarb. ana ʒj.
Syrupi Aurantii,
Spirit. Myristicæ, ana ℥j.
Aquæ destillatæ, ℥xij.
Mix: make a mixture. f℥j every 4 hours.
In Fevers and Inflammatory Sore Throats.—Mr. SAVORY.

2332. ℞ Potassæ Bicarb. ℈j
Acidi Citrici, gr. xviij.
Aceti Scillæ, ʒj.
Spirit. Ætheris Nit. ʒss.
Syrupi Limonum, ʒj.
Aquæ puræ, ʒx.
Mix: make a saline draught. To be taken every 4 hours.

In Peripneumonia.—Dr. GREGORY.

2333. ℞ Succi Limonis, ℥ss.
Potassæ Carb. ℈j, or enough to saturate the lemon-juice.
Aquæ Menth. pip. ℥j.
Antim. Tartarizati, gr. 1-12th.
Syrupi, ʒij.
Mix: make a draught. To be taken at once, and repeated in 3 hours.

In severe Intermittents.—Mr. DAWSON.

2334. ℞ Potassæ Subcarb. ℈j.
Succ. Limon. rec. ℥ss.
Mist. Camphoræ, ℥j.
Potassæ Nitratis, gr. x.
Syrupi Rhœados, ʒj.
Mix: make a draught. To be taken every fourth hour.

In Fevers, &c.—Dr. COPLAND.

POTASSÆ NITRAS ET CHLORAS. *Nitrate and Chlorate of Potash.*

The Nitrate of Potash is diuretic and refrigerant. It has been used abroad in acute rheumatism, doses of as much as an ounce at a time, in large quantities of barley-water, being prescribed. In England it is given in dropsies, to form a cooling drink in fevers, to check hæmoptysis, mitigate dyspnœa, and alleviate scalding in gonorrhœa. It has also been prescribed in scurvy by Dr. Garrod. Dose, five to twenty grains, as a diuretic; but in acute gonorrhœa or rheumatic fever, one drachm to one ounce is given, much diluted with water.

Chlorate of Potash resembles the Nitrate in its action. It is used as a refrigerant and diaphoretic, in colds, fevers, &c. It has been especially recommended by some in various forms of cachexia—as in cancrum oris, in chronic syphilis, in phthisis and scrofula, in typhoid and eruptive fevers—being supposed to exert a special power in purifying the blood. Some suppose that it acts in a chemical manner, in the same way as those preparations which contain free chlorine, which is obviously a mistake. Similarly erroneous is the notion that it affords a direct supply of oxygen to the system. Dose, ten to thirty grains.

2335. ℞ Potassæ Nitratis, gr. x.
Sacchari, ℈j.
Mix: make a powder. To be taken in a wineglassful of spearmint water. (The mint water should be quite cold, and the powder dissolved in it just before the moment of administration.)

An agreeable drink in Fevers.—Dr. Druitt.

2336. ℞ Potassæ Nitratis, ʒvj.
Pulv. Acaciæ, ʒiij.
Pulv. Glycyrrhizæ,
Pulv. Althææ, ana ℥iij.
Syrupi, q. s.
Make into 5-grain pills. Five to six, three times a day.

In Dysuria and Urethritis.—Foy.

2337. ℞ Potassæ Nitratis, ʒij.
Decocti Hordei comp. Oj. Mix: for an ordinary drink.

In Measles, and Fevers generally.—Dr. E. G. Clark.

2338. ℞ Salis Nitri, ʒss.
Decocti Hordei, a cupful.
Dissolve: take every hour and a half.

In Influenza.—Mr. Rowe.

2339. ℞ Potassæ Nitratis, ℥ss–℥j.
Decocti Hordei, Oiss.
Sacchari, q. s. to suit the taste.
The whole to be taken in the day, in divided doses.

In Acute Rheumatism.—Gendrin.

2340. ℞ Potassæ Nitratis, ℈j.
Aquæ Menthæ pip. ʒij.
Mist. Camphoræ, ʒix.
Syrupi, ʒj.
Mix: make a draught. To be taken every fourth hour.

In Rheumatism.—Dr. E. J. Clark.

2341. ℞ Potassæ Nitratis, ℈j.
Syrupi Papaveris, ʒij.
Aquæ destill. ℥ij.
Make a draught. To be taken at bedtime.

In Hæmatemesis.—Dr. E. J. Clark.

2342. ℞ Syrupi Papaveris, ℥j.
Potassæ Nitratis, ʒj.
Mist. Amygdalæ, ℥v.
Mix: f℥ss when the cough is troublesome.

Dr. Hooper.

2343. ℞ Potassæ Nitratis, gr. x.
Camphoræ, gr. vj.
Pulv. Acaciæ, gr. xxiv.
Mix: one-third to one-half at a dose.

FOY.

2344. ℞ Potassæ Nitratis, ʒj.
Camphoræ,
Confec. Rosæ, ana ʒss.
Mix: divide in 4-grain pills. Two to ten a day.

In Gonorrhœa.—GUIBOURT.

2345. ℞ Potassæ Nitratis, ℥ss.
Aceti,
Syrupi simp. ana ℥ij.
Aquæ destill. ℥xij. Mix.

To be used as a common drink in Fevers, &c.—Dr. HOOPER.

2346. ℞ Potassæ Nitratis, gr. x.
Mist. Camphoræ, ʒxj.
Syrupi Tolutani, ʒj.
Mix: make a draught. To be taken three times a day.

At commencement of Fevers.—Dr. THOMAS.

2347. ℞ Potassæ Nitratis, ℈j.
Ammon. Hydrochlor. gr. xij.
Mix: make a powder. To be taken two, three, or four times a day, in three ounces of water.

As a Diaphoretic in Inflammatory Fever.—Dr. THOMAS.

2348. ℞ Potassæ Nitratis, ʒiss.
Antim. Potassio-tart. gr. j.
Hydrarg. Chloridi, gr. iv.
Mix, and divide into 8 powders. One every second hour.

Diaphoretic in Fevers.—Dr. DEWEES (U. S.).

2349. ℞ Potassæ Nitratis, ʒij.
Acid. Nit. dil. ʒj.
Decoct. Hordei, lbij. Mix: to be taken during the day.

In early stage of Fever.—Dr. GRAVES.

2350. ℞ Potassæ Nitratis, gr. xv.
Pulv. Scillæ,
Pulv. Pimentæ, ana gr. x.
Mix: dose, x–xx gr. three times a day, as a diuretic.

Diuretic.—SWEDIAUR.

2351. ℞ Potassæ Nitratis, ℈ij.
Sodæ Bicarb. ʒss.
Vin. Antim. ʒij.
Syrupi Croci,
Spirit. Æth. Nitrici, ana ʒj.
Aquæ, ℥v. Dose, ℥iss every four hours.

Febrifuge.—Dr. DRUITT.

2352. ℞ Potassæ Chloratis, ʒss.
Syrupi, ʒiiss.
Aquæ destill. ʒxiiss.
Mix: to be given in the course of the day in tablespoonful doses.

In Cancrum Oris.—Mr. HUNT.

2353. ℞ Potassæ Chloratis, ʒj.
Syrupi Rhœados, ℥j.
Aquæ destill. ℥v. One-sixth for a dose.

Stimulant in Febrile Affections, and the Exanthemata.
Dr. HOOPER.

2354. ℞ Potassæ Chloratis, ℈j.
Aquæ Cinnamomi, ʒxj.
Tinct. Aurantii, ʒj.
Mix: make a draught. To be taken every third hour.

In Typhus Fever.—Dr. THOMAS.

2355. ℞ Potassæ Chloratis, gr. viij.
Sodii Chloridi, gr. xx.
Sodæ Bicarb. gr. xxx.
Mix: make a powder. One, every second or third hour.

In low Febrile Cases, and in Cholera.—Dr. STEVENS.

2356. ℞ Potassæ Chloratis, gr. x.
Spirit Æth. Nit. ʒj.
Aquæ puræ, ℥iss.
Mix: make a draught. To be taken at bedtime.

In an ordinary Cold in the Head.

2357 ℞ Potassæ Nitratis, ʒij.
Decocti Hordei, ℥vij.
Oxymel. simp. ℥j. Mix: make a gargle.

In Ulceration of the Throat.—Mr. BRANDE.

2358. ℞ Sodii Chloridii,
Potassæ Nitratis,
Ammoniæ Hydrochloratis, ana ℥ij.
Aquæ, q. s. to dissolve.
A mixture producing intense cold.

To Local Inflammations with Heat.—Dr. HOOPER.

2359. ℞ Potassæ Chloratis, ʒj.
Aquæ destil. ℥xij
Dissolve. To indolent sores as a lotion, and internally in three times its bulk of vehicle.

Dr. COPLAND.

POTASSÆ SULPHAS ET BISULPHAS. *Sulphate and Bisulphate of Potash.*

Sulphate of Potash (*Sal Polychrestum*) is contained in compound Ipecacuan powder, in which it is of use in effecting, by the hardness of its crystals, a perfect division of the other constituents. This salt is a mild laxative, and is frequently combined with a dose of rhubarb, as in the *Pulvis Rhei Salinus* (Guy's Hosp.). It is also used as an alterative in liver obstructions. Dose, as an alterative, ten to twenty grains; as a purgative, one to four drachms.

The Bisulphate is very acid to the taste, and much more soluble in water than the last. It is sometimes employed as a cathartic and antiphlogistic, or may be given with a carbonate to form an effervescing draught. Dose, ten grains to two drachms.

Potassæ Sulphas cum Sulphure (E.), made by deflagrating niter with sulphur, is a mild purgative. Dose, half a drachm to a drachm.

Pulvis Salinus Compositus (E.) contains sulphate of potash. Dose, two to four drachms.

Pulvis Potassæ Sulphatis cum Rheo (Ellis). Dose, half a drachm.

2360. ℞ Potassæ Sulphatis, ℨij.
Pulv. Rhei, ℈ij.
Olei Fœniculi, ♏vj.
Extr. Centaureæ benedictæ, q. s. to make 60 pills.
Five to six for a dose.

Purgative.—PHŒBUS.

2361. ℞ Potassæ Bisulphatis,
Sodæ Carbonatis, ana ℨj.
Dissolve separately in two ounces of water, mix and take while effervescing.

Refrigerant Laxative.—Dr. BARKER.

POTASSÆ BICHROMAS. *Bichromate of Potash.*

This is an irritant poison if given in large doses. It has lately been employed by some Continental practitioners in the treatment of syphilitic disorders, apparently with considerable success. The dose of this salt is from one-sixth to one-fourth of a grain.

2362. ℞ Potassæ Bichromatis, gr. xv.
Extr. Gentianæ, ℨiij.
Mix, and divide into 80 pills. One, night and morning. (Should nausea or vomiting be produced, some opium may be added.)

In Syphilis.—Dr. VICENTI.

POTASSII IODIDUM. See IODINIUM.

POTASSII BROMIDUM. See BROMINIUM.

POTASSII CYANIDUM. See ACIDUM HYDROCYANICUM.

POTASSII SULPHURETUM. See SULPHUR.

PRUNA. *Prunes.*

These are the dried fruit of the *Prunus domestica*, or cultivated Plum-tree (Nat. Ord. *Amygdaleæ*). They are chiefly obtained from France. They are used in medicine on account of their mild laxative properties, for which purpose their pulp is frequently combined with senna, cassia, or other medicines, to form a confection (as in *Conf. Sennæ*).

2363. ℞ Pruni domesticæ fruct. lbss.
Sennæ foliorum, ℥j.
Caryophyll. contus. ʒss.
Sacchari brunei, ℥j.
Aquæ ferventis, Oij.
Mix: macerate for two hours, strain. Dose, f℥iv, every three hours until effectual.

A gentle Laxative.—DR. JOY.

PYRETHRUM. *Pellitory.*

This is the root of *Anacyclus Pyrethrum* (Nat. Ord. *Compositæ*), a native of Spain and other countries. It has no smell, but is very acrid when chewed. It contains a principle called *Pyrethrine*. It is powerfully irritant. It has been given in paralysis and intermittents, but is chiefly employed as a masticatory, to promote the flow of saliva. It is employed in the form of lotions to chilblains, and parts affected with rheumatic pains.

Tinctura Pyrethri (Paris Codex) is intended for external use.

2364. ℞ Pyrethri rad. contrit.
Mastiches, ana ʒj.
Make two masses. To be chewed as a masticatory, the saliva to be spit out.

DR. PARIS.

2365. ℞ Tinct. Pyrethri, ʒvj.
Linim. Camphoræ, ʒiv.
Liquoris Ammoniæ, ʒij. Mix: make a liniment.

For Chilblains and Rheumatic Pains.—DR. COPLAND.

2366. ℞ Pyrethri contusi, ℥ss.
Camphoræ, ʒiij.
Opii, ʒj.
Olei Caryophylli, ʒij.
Spirit Vini rect. ℥vj. Mix, and strain after ten days.

To be applied upon Cotton in case of Toothache.—Mr. BRANDE.

2367. ℞ Pyrethri, ℥j.
Florum Spilanthi (*Para cress*), ℥iv.
Fol. Inulæ Italicæ, ℥j.
Spirit. Vini rect. ℥viij.
Macerate for fifteen days, express, and strain.

Odontalgic.

QUASSIA.

This is the wood of *Picræna excelsa*, a West Indian tree (Nat. Ord. *Simarubaceæ*). In ordinary cases it is a pure bitter tonic, being neither irritant nor aromatic. Like calumba and canella, it contains no tannin, and may thus be prescribed with salts of iron. It acts on animals as a narcotic, and Kraus states that its prolonged use will bring on dimness of sight in men. It is used as other simple bitters, as a tonic in dyspepsia, loss of appetite and strength, and simple debility after fevers or from any cause. Its infusion is frequently resorted to as a convenient vehicle for the preparations of mercury and iron, and for iodide of potassium. It is seldom or never given in substance.

Extractum Quassiæ (E.), five to ten grains.

Infusum Quassiæ (L., E., D.), one ounce to one ounce and a half.

Tinctura Quassiæ (E.), one to two drachms.

Tinct. Quassiæ comp. (E.), one to three drachms.

Vinum Quassiæ (Radius), three to four drachms.

2368. ℞ Infusi Quassiæ, ʒvj.
Tinct. Calumbæ, ʒij.
Aquæ Cinnamomi, ʒv.
Syrupi Aurantii, ʒj.
Mix: make a draught. To be taken two or three times a day.

Tonic.—Dr. PARIS.

2369. ℞ Ras. lign. Quassiæ, ℥ss.
Aquæ Calcis vivæ, ℥vij.
Let it digest for 24 hours. Strain, and add
Aquæ Menth. vir. ℥ij.
Syrupi Aurantii, ℥ss. Mix.

Tonic and Antacid.—Dr. COPLAND.

2370. ℞ Infusi Quassiæ, ℥iss.
Myrrhæ, gr. x.
Potassæ Sulphatis cum Sulphure, ℈iss.
Tinct. Cinnam. co. ♏xxx.
Mix: make a draught. To be taken twice a day.
In Hypochondriasis.—Dr. E. J. CLARK.

QUERCUS. *Oak Bark.*

The bark of *Quercus pedunculata*, the common Oak (Nat. Ord. *Amentaceæ*). The thin pieces are the best. Oak bark contains tannic acid, and is therefore astringent in its properties. The proportion of this principle is about sixteen per cent. The decoction may be used both internally and externally in hæmorrhages, fluxes, and all cases where an astringent is desirable. The powder and extract have been given in intermittents. The dose of the powder is from half a drachm to a drachm.

Extractum Quercûs (D. 1826), ten grains to two scruples.

Decoctum Quercûs (L., E., D.), an ounce and a half to two ounces.

2371. ℞ Pulv. Quercus cort. ℈j.
Pulv. Calami,
Pulv. Gentianæ, ana gr. v.
Mix: make a powder. To be taken every three hours.
In the Apyrexia of Intermittents.—AUGUSTIN.

2372. ℞ Decocti Quercûs, ℥iss.
Pulv. Gallarum, gr. x.
Tinct. Catechu, ʒss.
Tinct. Cardam. c. ʒj.
Syrupi Aurantii, ʒj.
Make a draught, to be taken twice a day.
Astringent.—Dr. PARIS.

2373. ℞ Quercûs corticis exterioris contusæ, ℥iss.
Aquæ ferventis, Oj.
Macerate for three hours and strain; then add
Pulv. Gallæ, ʒij.
Tinct. Cardam. co. ℥ij. Mix: a wineglassful for a dose.
Astringent.—Dr. HOOPER.

2374. ℞ Quercûs cort. contus. ℥ss.
Aquæ ferventis, ℥xiij. Macerate for an hour, and strain.

℞ Colaturæ, ℥xj.
Tinct. Catechu, ℥ss.
Tinct. Cardam. co. ℥j.
Syrupi Aurant. cort. ℥j.
Mix: make an astringent draught.

Dr. COPLAND.

2375. ℞ Decocti Quercûs corticis, Oj.
Aluminis, ʒj. Mix: make an astringent injection.

In Leucorrhœa, &c.—Dr. HOOPER.

2376. ℞ Decocti Quercûs, Oj.
Pulv. Aluminis, ʒss.
Spirit. Vini Gallici, ℥ij. Mix: make a gargle.

In Chronic Sore Throat with relaxed Uvula.

Dr. ELLIS (U. S.).

QUINA ET SALES. *Quinine and its Salts.*

Quina and Cinchonia are the two bitter alkaloids to which the medicinal properties of the Cinchona barks are owing. The yellow barks (as the Calisaya) contain most Quina; the red barks, most Cinchonia. They exist naturally in combination with Kinic acid. Quina is extracted from the bark by a chemical process, and being subsequently combined with sulphuric acid, forms the crystalline Disulphate of Quina, or common Quinine. In this form it is perhaps more used than any other medicine, except Opium. Though itself rather insoluble in water, it becomes very soluble on the addition of a drop of dilute sulphuric acid for each grain of Quinine in the mixture.

As a tonic in simple debility, and loss of appetite from atonic dyspepsia, Quinine is unrivaled. It is rarely given where there is much irritation of the stomach, or in high inflammatory fever. It has lately been highly recommended in typhoid fever, though its employment in this case was deprecated by the late Dr. Graves. It is the best antiperiodic with which we are acquainted. It may be given between the paroxysms of ague, in moderate or in large doses. It is useful in neuralgia and other affections, when marked by periodicity.

The Valerianate of Quina has been recommended as an antiperiodic. The Arsenite combines the antiperiodic action of Arsenious acid with that of Quinine. The Citrate of Quinine and Iron may be given in debility when attended with anæmia, or in facial neuralgia.

The ordinary dose of *Disulphate of Quina* is two grains three times a day. As much as ten grains, or more, may be given in particular cases.

(Quinidia is an alkaloid found in some kinds of bark, which much resembles Quina. What has been called *Amorphous Quinine* is impure Quinidia. It may be prescribed and used like Quinine.)

Tinctura Quinæ composita (L.): dose, one to three drachms.

Quinæ Arsenis: dose, one-fifth of a grain.

Quinæ Citras, one to five grains.

Syrupus Quinæ Citratis (Majendie), one to two drachms.

Ferri et Quinæ Citras, five grains.

Quinæ Ferrocyanas (Paris Codex), one to five grains.

Quinæ Iodidum (*Hydriodas*), two to three grains.

Quinæ et Ferri Iodidum, two to three grains.

Quinæ Hydriodas Iodureta, two to three grains.

Quinæ Murias (D.), one to two grains.

Quinæ et Hydrargyri Chloridum, half to one grain.

Quinæ Kinas, three to five grains.

Quinæ Lactas, three to nine grains in the day.

Quinæ Nitras (Paris).

Quinæ Phosphas.

Quinæ Sulphas (*neutra*). These three are prescribed as the Disulphate.

Quinæ Tannas, one to five grains.

Quinæ Tartras (Paris Codex), one to five grains.

Quinæ Valerianas (D.), half to one grain.

Cinchoniæ Disulphas and *Quinidiæ* (vel *Chinoidinæ*) *Disulphas* are prescribed in the same manner as common Quinine.

Prescriptions giving the common Disulphate of Quinine. (When sulphuric acid is combined with it, the neutral or soluble Sulphate is formed.)

2377. ℞ Quinæ Disulph. gr. iij–xji.
Pulv. Sacchari, ʒij.
Mix, and divide into 6 powders. One, night and morning.
In Nervous Debility and Intermittents.—RADIUS.

2378. ℞ Quinæ Disulph. gr. iij.
Sacchari albi, gr. vij.
Mix: make a powder. To be taken every three hours, during the absence of the paroxysm.

In Ague.—Dr. JOY.

2379. ℞ Quinæ Disulph. gr. ⅓.
Pulv. Chocolat. gr. vij.
Sacch. lactis, gr. ij.
Mix: make a powder. To be taken every three hours.

Antiperiodic or Tonic.—KOPP.

2380. ℞ Quinæ Sulph. gr. xxxij.
Syrupi simp. ℥viij.
Mix: make a Quinine syrup. Two teaspoonfuls two or three times a day.

Antiperiodic or Tonic.—Dr. COPLAND.

2381. ℞ Quinæ Disulph. gr. xv.
Pulv. Cinnam. ʒss.
Extr. Cinchonæ, q. s. to make 30 pills. Four, every fourth, third, or second hour.

Antiperiodic or Tonic.—HENSCHEL.

2382. ℞ Quinæ Disulph. gr. x
Acid. Sulph. dil. gtt. viij.
Aquæ Cinnam. ℥iiss.
Syrupi, ʒij.
Mix: make a mixture. Dose, a tablespoonful.

Dr. DUNGLISON (U. S.).

2383. ℞ Quinæ Disulph. gr. ij.
Mist. Camphoræ, ʒx.
Tinct. Aurant. ♏xx. Mix: make a draught.

Dr. GREGORY.

2384. ℞ Quinæ Disulph. (seu Acet.) gr. xij.
Alcoholis (seu Spirit. Æth. co.) ℥ss.
Tinct. Opii, gtt. xij.
Mix: twenty drops in some appropriate vehicle.

SCHMIDT.

2385. ℞ Quinæ Disulph.
Camphoræ,
Capsici, ana gr. iij.
Mucilaginis, q. s. to make 3 pills. To be taken night and morning.

To prevent Sickening in persons exposed to Malaria.

Dr. COPLAND.

2386. [℞ Hydrarg. Chlor. gr. iij.
Pulv. Rhei, gr. x. Mix: make a powder.

To precede the use of Quinine in treatment of Ague.

Dr. WATSON.]

2387. ℞ Quinæ Disulph. gr. iij.
Infusi Rosæ comp. ℥x.
Syrupi Aurantii, ℥ij.
Mix: make a draught. To be taken every third hour.
In Ague.—Dr. GREGORY.

2388. ℞ Quinæ Sulph. gr. ij–vj.
Morphiæ Sulph. gr. ss–j.
Mix, and divide into two, three, or four doses.
In Ague, &c.—MAJENDIE.

2389. ℞ Quinæ Disulph. gr. x.
Antim. Pot.-tart. gr. iij.
Mix well, and divide into 6 equal parts. One to be taken every two hours during the intermission.
In Ague.—Dr. DOMINIQUE GOLA.

2390. ℞ Quinæ Disulph. gr. j.
Pulv. Cinchonæ, gr. xv.
Pulv. Rhei,
Oleo-sacch. Menthæ, ana gr. v.
Mix: make a powder. Eight of these to be given.
In Intermittent Fever.—Dr. NAUMANN.

2391. ℞ Quinæ Disulph. gr. x.
Ext. Millefolii, q. s. to make four pills.
One for a dose, to be given on the days on which the fever is absent.
In Intermittents.—Dr. PFEUFER (Heidelberg).

2392. ℞ Quinæ Disulph. gr. xxxvj.
Pulv. Capsici, gr. xij.
Mist. Acaciæ, q. s.
Mix, and make 12 pills. One or two, every fourth hour, until four doses have been taken before the expected return of the paroxysm.
In Intermittents.—Dr. THOMAS.

2393. ℞ Quinæ Disulph. gr. xv. ad ℈j.
Acid Sulph. dil. ♏xv.
Aquæ Cinnamomi, ℥xv.
Syrupi, ℥j.
Tinct. Opii, ♏x.
Make a draught. To be taken either twelve or six hours before the expected onset of the paroxysm.
To put a stop to severe Intermittents.—Dr. VAN BUREN.

2394. ℞ Pulv. Opii, gr. j.
Quinæ Disulph. gr. iij.
Pulv. Sacchari,
Pulv. Acaciæ, ana gr. vj. Mix: make a powder.
To be taken a short time before the Paroxysm of Malignant Intermittents. NEUMANN.

2395. ℞ Quinæ Disulph. gr. iiss.
Hydrarg. Chloridi, gr. j.
Morphiæ Acet. gr. 1-6.
Syrupi, q. s.

Mix: make a pill. To be taken every third hour.

In ordinary Remittent Fevers.—Dr. GREGORY.

2396. ℞ Quinæ Disulph. gr. viij–xx.
Acid Sulph. dil. q. s.

To be taken in some aromatic draught two or three times a day.

In Typhoid Fever (recommended only in the later stages, when the pulse is comparatively quiet). M. LOUIS.

2397. ℞ Ipecac. pulv. gr. xv.
Antim. Tart. gr. j. Mix. To be taken at once, and afterward,
Quinæ Disulph. gr. v–x, every two hours, in some suitable vehicle.

(Dr. R. Dundas, the most strenuous advocate of this plan of treatment, recommends the dose of 10 grains, as below, or even more.)

In Typhus Fever.—Mr. EDDOWES.

2398. ℞ Quinæ Disulph. gr. xxx.

Divide into 3 powders. One every second hour. (The dose to be afterward diminished during convalescence.)

To arrest Typhus Fever.—Dr. DUNDAS.

2399. ℞ Quinæ Disulph. ʒss.
Calomelanos, ℈j.

Mix: make a powder. This to be given at once: an hour afterward, the same dose of Quinine with 5 grains of James' Powder; and in two hours more, ℥iss of Castor Oil.

In Yellow Fever.—Dr. W. J. CUMMINS.

If the dose be vomited at first, it is to be repeated, and a mustard plaster applied to the epigastrium.

2400. ℞ Quinæ Disulph. gr. v–x.
Antim. Tart. gr. $\frac{1}{8}$–$\frac{1}{4}$.

Mix: make a powder. To be taken three times a day in a decoction of barley or oatmeal.

In Continued Fever.—Dr. HEADLAND.

2401. ℞ Quinæ Disulph. gr. vj.
Pulv. Jacobi, gr. iv.

Mix: make a powder. To be taken three times a day.

In Remittent Fever.—Dr. McWILLIAMS.

2402. ℞ Quinæ Disulph. gr. xij–℈j.
Ferri Sulph. gr. ix.
Acid. Sulph. dil. ♏xl.
Aquæ, puræ Oiss.

Mix. A wineglassful every quarter of an hour, or hour, according to circumstances.

In Cholera.—Dr. BELL.

2403. ℞ Quinæ Disulph. gr. x.
Acid Sulph. dil. ♏x.
Aquæ destil. ℥j.
Mix: make a draught. A draught every six hours.

In Neuralgia.—Mr. C. Hogg.

2404. ℞ Quinæ Disulph. gr. xvj.
Infusi Valerianæ ℥vj.
Mist. Camphoræ, ℥iv.
Tinct. Valerianæ, ℥ss.
Mix: make a mixture. Four tablespoonfuls every third or fourth hour. A dose of blue pill and castor oil to be given occasionally.

In Intermittent Epilepsy.—Dr. Fosbrooke.

2405. ℞ Quinæ Disulph. gr. ij.
Pulv. Ipecac. gr. iij.
Pulv. Doveri, gr. iij.
Mix: make a powder. One every three hours. (So as to give 16 gr. of Quinine in twenty-four hours.)

In the Dysentery of Ceylon.—Dr. Cameron.

The remaining prescriptions show the great variety of ways in which the Disulphate of Quina may be combined when exhibited as a simple Tonic.

2406. ℞ Quinæ Disulph. ℈j.
Ext. Anthemidis, ʒj.
Mix, and divide into 20 pills. One or two, twice a day.

In Atonic Dyspepsia.

2407. ℞ Ext. Belladonnæ, ℈ss.
Quinæ Disul. ʒj.
Mix: make 30 pills. One, three times a day.

In Gastralgia.—Dr. H. Green.

2408. ℞ Quinæ Disulph. gr. xij.
Tinct. Aurantii, ℥j.
Infusi Rosæ co. ℥v.
Mix: make a mixture. One-sixth part for a dose.

Tonic.—Dr. Hooper.

2409. ℞ Quinæ Sulph. gr. ij.
Acid. Sulph. dil. ♏ij.
Spirit. Myristicæ, ʒj.
Aquæ destil. ʒx.
Mix: make a draught. To be taken once or twice a day.

In Atonic Dyspepsia, &c.—Dr. Copland.

2410. ℞ Quinæ Disulph. gr. vi.
Acid. Sulph. dil. ʒj.
Tinct. Cardam. co. ʒiij.
Aquæ Cinnam. ℥vss.
Mix: two tablespoonfuls twice a day.

In Spermatorrhœa.—Mr. Milton.

2411. ℞ Aquæ destil. ℥iss.
Quinæ Disulph. gr. iv.
Acid. Sulph. dil. ♏iv.
Syrupi Zingib. ℥ss.
Mix: one or two teaspoonfuls three times a day.

Tonic mixture for Children.

2412. ℞ Quinæ Disulph. gr. ij.
Acid. Sulph. Arom. ♏xvj.
Aquæ destil. ℥iss.
Syrupi Caryophylli, ℥ss.
Mix. Take from fʒj to fʒij, three times a day.

Tonic for very young Infants.—Dr. JOY.

2413. ℞ Quinæ Disulph. gr. xviij.
Magnesiæ Sulph. ʒj.
Acid. Sulph. dil. ʒiss.
Mist. Camphoræ, ℥x.
Mix. One-sixth part, three times a day.

H. J.

2414. ℞ Quinæ Disulph. gr. j ad ij.
Sodæ Carb. gr. iv ad v.
Sacchari, ℈j.
Mix: make a powder. A powder night and morning.

In Scrofulous Ophthalmia.—VON AMMON.

2415. ℞ Quinæ Disulph. gr. xvj.
Acid. Sulph. dil. ʒss.
Tinct. Aurantii,
Syrupi Aurantii, ana ʒiv.
Aquæ puræ, ℥vij.
Mix. Three tablespoonfuls every noon.

For Children.—Mr. COULSON.

2416. ℞ Quinæ Disulph. gr. iij.
Acid. Sulph. dil. gtt. vj.
Tinct. Aurantii,
Syrupi Zingib. ana ʒij.
Aquæ destil. ℥iij. Mix: a tablespoonful twice a day.

In the Cachexy of Children.—Dr. OKE.

2417. ℞ Quinæ Disulph. ʒss.
Acid. Nit. dil. ʒiij.
Tinct. Aurantii,
Syrupi Zingib. ana ʒvj.
Mix: a teaspoonful two or three times a day, in a wineglassful of water.

Mr. J. MORGAN.

2418. ℞ Quinæ Disulph.
Ferri Sulph.
Extr. Anthemidis, ana ℈j.
Olei Anthemidis, gtt. vj.
Mix: divide into 20 pills. One, three times a day.

Dr. G. BIRD.

2419. ℞ Quinæ Disulph. gr. xij.
Extr. Gentianæ, ℈j.
Pil. Rhei comp. ℈ij.
Pil. Hydrarg. gr. vj.
Mix: make into 12 pills. One, three times a day.

In Atonic Dyspepsia.—Dr. RYAN.

2420. ℞ Extr. Aloes, gr. xviij.
Pil. Hydrarg. gr. vj.
Extr. Rhei, gr. xviij.
Quinæ Disulph. gr. xij.
Mix: divide into 12 pills. One, at noon, and at bedtime.

Alterative Tonic and Aperient.—Dr. BARON.

2421. ℞ Quinæ Disulph. gr. x–xv.
Acid. Phosph. sic. ℈ij.
Pulv. Althææ, ℈iv.
Extr. Centaurii, ℈ij.
Mix, and form a mass: divide into 60 pills. From three to six, two or three times a day.

In Nervous Debility, with disposition to Hæmorrhage, as after Abortion. RADIUS.

2422. ℞ Quinæ Sulph. ʒss–ʒj.
Potassæ Sulph. ʒiss.
Gummi Galbani, ℈iv.
Extr. Gentianæ, vel Anthemidis, ʒj.
Pil. Aloes c. Myrrhâ, ʒiij.
Theriacæ purif. q. s. to make a mass to be divided into 120 pills. Two or three, two or three times a day.

Tonic and Aperient.—Dr. COPLAND.

2423. ℞ Quinæ Disulph. gr. ij.
Acid. Sulph. dil. gtt. ij.
Tinct. Opii, ♏x–xxx.
Aquæ, ℥iss.
Mix: make a draught. Every four, six, or eight hours

Delirium Tremens.—Dr. R. B. TODD.

2424. ℞ Quinæ Disulph. gr. xij.
Acid. Sulph. dil. ♏vj.
Tinct. Opii, ♏vj.
Aquæ tepidæ, ℥vj.
Mix: make an enema. (Wherever the state of the stomach does not admit of the exhibition of Quinine in the ordinary way.)

Dr. JOY.

Prescriptions containing the salts of Quinine which are not officinal in the London Pharmacopœia.

2425. ℞ Quinæ Arseniatis, gr. ⅛.
Aquæ destil. ℥iss.
Syrupi flor. Aurant. ʒj.
Mix: make a draught. One such draught every four hours for two days, to overcome the fever.

In Tertian Agues, when Quinine and Arsenic, given separately, have failed. Dr. NELIGAN.

2426. ℞ Quinæ Diarsenitis, gr. iv.
Micæ panis, q. s. to make 12 pills. One pill two, three, or four times a day.

In Lepra, and other Cutaneous Diseases.—Dr. KINGDON.

2427. ℞ Quinæ Diarsenitis, gr. iv.
Sacchari pulveris,
Pulv. Acaciæ, ana ʒss.
Mix, and divide into 12 powders. One, twice a day.

In Lepra, &c.—Dr. KINGDON.

2428. ℞ Ferri et Quinæ Citratis,
Extr. Gentianæ, ana ʒss.
Mix: form a mass. Divide into 12 pills.

Tonic.—Dr. HOOPER.

2429. ℞ Ferri et Quinæ Citratis, gr. xlviij.
Tinct. Aurantii, ℥ss.
Aquæ puræ, ℥vss. Mix: f℥ss twice a day.

Dr. W. BUDD.

2430. ℞ Ferri et Quinæ Citratis, ℈ij.
Pulv. Myrrhæ, gr. vj.
Syrupi Zingib. q. s. to make 12 pills. One, every day, an hour before dinner.

In Dyspepsia.

2431. ℞ Ferri et Quinæ Citratis, ʒiss.
Ammon. Carbonatis, ʒij.
Tinct. Aurantii, ℥ij.
Aquæ, ℥ij. Mix: a teaspoonful in water twice a day.

2432. ℞ Quinæ informis (amorphous), gr. ij.
Acidi Citrici, gr. j.
Syrupi Limonum, ʒj.
Aquæ destil. ℥j.
Mix: make a draught. To be taken three times a day.

In General Debility, and in Convalescence from Acute Diseases. Dr. NELIGAN.

2433. ℞ Quinæ Ferrocyanatis, gr. xxiv.
Mucilaginis, q. s. to make 12 pills. Two for a dose.

Mr. DONOVAN.

2434. ℞ Quinæ Ferrocyanatis, gr. iv.
Alcoholis, ʒj. Dissolve, and add
Mist. Camphoræ, ʒvij.
Mix: make a draught. Shake the phial before taking.
In Ague.—Mr. DONOVAN.

2435. ℞ Quinæ Muriatis, ℈j.
Aquæ Menthæ piperitæ, ℥ss.
Mix: twenty to sixty drops every two hours.
In Intermittents of Children.—RADIUS.

2436. ℞ Quinæ Muriatis, gr. viij.
Aquæ Fœniculi, ℥v.
Ætheris Muriatici, ʒj.
Sacchari, ℥ss. Mix: a spoonful every two hours.
In Intermittents.—RADIUS.

2437. ℞ Quinæ Muriatis, gr. xij.
Acid. Muriat. dil. ♏v.
Aquæ destil. ℥vji.
Syrupi flor. Aurant. ℥j.
Mix: make a mixture. Two tablespoonfuls three times a day.
In Chronic Debility.—Dr. NELIGAN.

2438. ℞ Hydrarg. et Quinæ Chloridi, gr. xv.
Opii, gr. vj.
Micæ panis, q. s. to make a mass, to be divided into 30 pills. One, three times a day.
To produce Salivation.—Dr. HAMILTON.

2439. ℞ Quinæ Kinatis,
Piperis nigri,
Extr. Absinthii, ana ʒj.
Mix: make 60 pills. Three every two or three hours.
In obstinate Intermittents.—RONANDER.

2440. ℞ Quinæ Lactatis, ʒss.
Extr. Juniperi, q. s. to make 20 pills. Two to six a day.
In Intermittents.—BOUCHARDAT.

2441. ℞ Quinæ Lactatis, gr. vij.
Aquæ Menthæ viridis, ʒv.
Syrupi Caryophylli, ʒj.
Aquæ, ℥iiiss.
Mix: to be taken in divided doses during the apyrexia.
In Intermittents.—BOUCHARDAT.

2442. ℞ Quinæ Valerianatis, gr. viij.
Mucilag. ʒij.
Aquæ, ad ℥iij. Mix: dose, ʒj–℥ss.
In Neuralgia.—Dr. DAVEY.

2443. ℞ Quinæ Valerianatis, gr. ix.
Extr. Gentianæ, gr. xxiv.
Mix: make 12 pills. One, three times a day.
In Nervous Debility and Hysteria.—Dr. NELIGAN.

2444. ℞ Quinæ Valerianatis, gr. vij.
Infusi Cascarillæ, ℥iv.
Mix: make a mixture. Half an ounce every six hours.

For Hysterical and Neuralgic Affections in debilitated habits.
DR. NELIGAN.

2445. ℞ Quinæ Valerianatis, gr. ix.
Liq. Taraxaci, ʒvj.
Tinct. Sumbuli, ʒij.
Infusi Lupuli, ℥v.
Mix: make a mixture. Two tablespoonfuls every noon.

2446. ℞ Quinæ Tannatis, gr. iij.
Mucilag. Acaciæ, q. s. to make a pill. One pill three times a day.

In Intermittent Neuralgia.—DR. W. BUDD.

RESINA. *Resin.*

This is the hard, yellow, semi-transparent residuum left after the distillation of the volatile oil from common turpentine. Melted, and shaken with water, it becomes white resin. Resin unites with alkalies to form soluble soaps. It is never given internally. It is employed as a stimulant ingredient in plasters, cerates, and ointments, giving also substance to them when required to protect a part.

Ceratum Resinæ (L.).

Unguentum Resinosum, vel *Resinæ* (E., D.).

Resin or Basilicon ointment acts as a mild stimulant to foul and indolent ulcers.

Emplastrum Resinæ (L., E., D.) is known as adhesive or sticking plaster.

Ceratum Resinæ compositum (U. S.).

2447. ℞ Pulv. Resinæ, ℥iv.
Pulv. Acaciæ,
Pulv. Carbonis, ana ʒj.
Mix: make a hæmostatic powder.

To check external Bleeding.—GUIBOURT.

2448. ℞ Resinæ albæ, ℥viij.
Elemi, ℥ij.
Terebinth. Venetæ,
Olei bacc. Lauri, ana ℥j. Liquefy together, and strain.

A good adhesive Plaster.—FOY.

RHAMNUS. *Buckthorn.*

The Berries of *Rhamnus catharticus*, the Purging Buckthorn (Nat. Ord. *Rhamnaceæ*), are used in the recent state as cathartic. The juice is separated from the fresh berries by expression, and combined with spirit to preserve it, or formed into a syrup with ginger and other aromatics. Buckthorn is a powerful hydragogue cathartic, but rather too strong and irritating for general use. It is chiefly used in dropsy. Dose, of the fresh berries, twenty to forty; of the expressed juice, half to one ounce.

Syrupus Rhamni (L., E.), half to one ounce.

2449. ℞ Syrupi Rhamni, ℥ss.
Tinct. Sennæ,
Tinct. Rhei, ana ʒj.
Aquæ Anethi, ʒvj. Mix: make a purging draught.

RHATANIA. See KRAMERIA.

RHEUM. *Rhubarb.*

The drug known by this name is the root of various species of *Rheum* (Nat. Ord. *Polygonaceæ*), some of which are cultivated in England; others are little known. What is called *Turkey Rhubarb* is the best in quality. It is obtained through Russia from some part of the Chinese empire. It is yellow and mottled in appearance, nauseous and gritty when chewed. It contains a bitter principle, Rheine, and some peculiar resinous matters. Rhubarb is a mild purgative, and is distinguished by its astringent and tonic action. It first opens the bowels, but its secondary effect is to confine them. It is thus well fitted for use in diarrhœa, but is not so appropriate in constipation, where a continuous aperient action is desired. Though it seldom irritates, it is not fitted for inflammatory or febrile cases. It is a good purge for infants. It may be given in the form of dinner-pills in atonic dyspepsia.

The ordinary dose of powdered rhubarb is from twenty to thirty grains.

Pulvis Rhei compositus (E., D.). Rhubarb and Magnesia.

Gregory's Powder. Dose for adults, one scruple to one drachm; for children, five to ten grains.

Pulvis Rhei salinus (Guy's H.), ten grains to one drachm.

Pilulæ Rhei (E.), five to fifteen grains.

Pilula Rhei composita (L., E., D.), ten grains to one scruple.

Pilulæ Rhei et Ferri (E.), ten to fifteen grains.

Pilulæ Rhei cum Opio (Bart. Hosp.), two in diarrhœa.

Extractum Rhei (L., E., D.), ten grains to half a drachm.

Extractum Rhei fluidum (Procter), fifteen drops to half a drachm.

Infusum Rhei (L., E., D.), one and a half ounce.

Infusum Rhei alkalinum (Copland), one ounce to one and a half ounce.

Mist. Rhei (Gregory), half ounce three times day.

Liquor Rhei, one drachm equals one ounce of infusion.

Tinctura Rhei (U. S.), one drachm to one ounce.

Tinct. Rhei composita (L., E., D.), stomachic, one drachm; purgative, half to one ounce.

Tinct. Rhei et Aloes (E.), half to one ounce.

Tinct. Rhei et Gentianæ (E.), stomachic, one drachm; cathartic, half to one ounce.

Tinct. Rhei et Sennæ (U. S.), Warner's Cordial. One to two ounces.

Tinct. Rhei Anisata (Copland), one drachm to one ounce.

Syrupus Rhei (U. S.). For children, one to two drachms.

Trochisci Rhei (Paris Codex), fifteen grains; two or three for a dose.

Rheum ustum, vel *tostum* (Procter). An astringent in diarrhœa. Dose, five to ten grains.

Rhubarb may be prescribed as a purgative or stomachic in an almost infinite variety of ways.

The following are examples of powders containing Rhubarb:

2450. ℞ Pulv. Rhei,
Pulv. Calumbæ, ana gr. x.
Pulv. Aromatici, gr. v.
Mix: make a powder. To be taken at bedtime.

As an aperient in Dyspepsia.—Dr. W. Ainslie.

2451. ℞ Pulv. Rhei, gr. xij.
Pulv. Ipecac. gr. ij.
Mix: make a powder. One, every morning.
In Hæmatemesis.—Dr. HAMILTON.

2452. ℞ Pulv. Rhei, gr. xij.
Hydrarg. Chloridi,
Pulv. Zingib., ana gr. iij.
Mix: make a powder. To be taken every other morning.
For Diarrhœa in Intermittents.—Dr. THOMAS.

2453. ℞ Pulv. Rhei, gr. xv.
Calomelanos, gr. iij.
Pulv. Zingib. gr. ij. Mix: make a powder.
Strong Cathartic.—Dr. JOY.

2454. ℞ Pulv. Rhei, gr. vj.
Potassæ Bitart. gr. xij.
Pulv. Cinnam. co. gr. iij.
Sacchari, ℈j. Mix: make a powder.
A gentle Purgative for Children.—Dr. JOY.

2455. ℞ Pulv. Rhei, ℈j.
Magnes. Carbonatis, ℈ij.
Pulv. Cinnam. gr. x.
Mix: three or four grains every third hour for children six months old. Six to ten grains for from six to twelve months old.
Drs. EVANSON and MAUNSELL.

Pills in which Rhubarb is combined with various other medicines.

2456. ℞ Pulv. Rhei,
Sodæ Carbonatis,
Ext. Gentianæ, ana ʒiss.
Mix: divide in pil. No. 60. 2–6 for a dose.
PHARM. GUYENSIS.

2457. ℞ Pulv. Rhei,
Pulv. Zingib. ana ʒss.
Extr. Anthemidis, ʒj.
Mix: divide into 30 pills. Three before every meal.
In Dyspepsia and Chlorosis.—Dr. A. T. THOMSON.

2458. ℞ Pulv. Ipecac. gr. x.
Pulv. Rhei, ℈ij.
Syrupi, q. s. to make 12 pills.
One or two every day after dinner.
In Dyspepsia.—Dr. BUDD.

2459. ℞ Pulv. Rhei, ℈iv.
Pulv. Ipecac. gr. xxiv.
Saponis, ℈ss.
Mix, and divide into 24 pills. One, three times a day.
Mild Aperient for congested states of the Intestines.
Dr. DRUITT.

2460. ℞ Pulv. Rhei, ʒj.
Pulv. Ipecac. gr. x.
Olei Carui, gtt. x.
Mucilag. Acaciæ, q. s. to make a mass to be divided into 20 pills. Two, every night.

In Constipation.—Dr. CHAPMAN.

2461. ℞ Pulv. Capsici, ʒj.
Pulv. Rhei, ʒij.
Sacchari fæcis, q. s.
Mix, and divide in pil. No. 60. Two or three before dinner.

In Dyspepsia.—PHARM. GUYENSIS.

2462. ℞ Pil. Rhei co. ℈iiss.
Pil. Hydrarg. ℈ss.
Mix: divide into 12 pills. Two, at bedtime, once a week.

In Dyspepsia.—Dr. G. BIRD.

2463. ℞ Pil. Rhei co. ʒss.
Pil. Galbani co. ℈j.
Mix, and divide into 10 pills. One or two, every night.

In Hysteria.—Dr. GREGORY.

2464. ℞ Pil. Rhei co.
Pil. Galbani co. ana ℈iss.
Mix: make 12 pills. (Pil. Scillæ co. to be substituted for the Comp. Galbanum pill when there is much dyspnœa.)

Dinner-pills, for use in the Dyspepsia of old persons.
Dr. DAY.

2465. ℞ Pil. Rhei co.
Pil. Sagapeni co. ana gr. v.
Mix, and make two pills. To be taken at bedtime.

Dr. PARIS.

2466. ℞ Pil. Rhei co. gr. v.
Pil. Galbani co.
Pulv. Zingib. ana gr. ij.
Olei Anthemidis, ♏j.
Mix: make two pills. To be taken at bedtime.

In Indigestion.—Dr. GREGORY.

2467. ℞ Pil. Rhei co. ʒj.
Pil. Galbani co. ʒss.
Pulv. Antimonii co. gr. xviij.
Olei Lavandulæ, gtt. iv.
Mix: make 24 pills. Two every night, or other night.

Alterative and Laxative.

2468. ℞ Pulv. rad. Rhei,
Aloes Socot. ana ℈iss.
Saponis Castil.
Pulv. Calumbæ, ana ℈j. Mix: make 20 pills.

Dinner-pills, for the Dyspepsia of old persons.—Dr. DAY.

2469. ℞ Pil. Rhei co. ʒj.
Pil. Aloes c. Myrrhâ,
Pulv. Zingib. ana ℈j.
Syrupi Zingib. q. s.
Mix, and divide into 20 pills. One or two every day, before dinner.
In Indigestion.—Dr. GREGORY.

2470. ℞ Pil. Rhei co. ℈ij.
Olei Crotonis, ♏j.
Pil. Coloc. co. ℈j.
Olei Carui, ♏ij.
Saponis, gr. iv.
Mix, and divide into 15 pills. One or two, at night.
In Indigestion.—Dr. GREGORY.

2471. ℞ Pulv Rhei,
Pulv. Myrrhæ, ana gr. xv.
Extr. Aloes, gr. vij.
Extr. Anthemidis, ℈iss.
Syrupi Zingib. q. s. to make 20 pills.
Two or three, an hour before dinner.
In Dyspepsia with Constipation.—Mr. SAVORY.

2472. ℞ Pulv. Rhei,
Sodæ Acetatis,
Fellis tauri insp. ana ʒij.
Pulv. Gum. Acaciæ, q. s. Make into a pill mass.
Resolvent.—PHARM. DANICA.

2473. ℞ Pil. Rhei co. ʒj.
Pulv. Scammonii, ʒss.
Pulv. Zingib. gr. x.
Olei Caryophylli, ♏iv.
Theriacæ, q. s.
Mix, and divide into 24 pills. One or two, as occasion requires.
Habitual Constipation.—DR. JOY.

Bolus and Electuary of Rhubarb.

2474. ℞ Pulv. Rhei, gr. x–xv.
Pulv. Cretæ co. gr. vij.
Pulv. Ipecac. co. gr. iij–vij.
Syrupi Zingib. q. s. to make a bolus.
To be taken at bedtime.
In Diarrhœa.—Dr. COPLAND.

2475. ℞ Magnesiæ,
Potassæ Supertart.
Flor. Sulphuris,
Pulv. rad. Rhei,
Pulv. flor. Anthem. ana gr. vj.
Syrupi Aurantii, ʒiij.
Olei Pimentæ, ♏ij.
Mix: make an electuary. For a dose.
Cathartic.—HECKER.

Draughts, or single doses of Rhubarb in a fluid form.

2476. ℞ Pulv. Rhei, ℈j.
Conf. Aromat. gr. xv.
Aquæ Menthæ pip. ℥iss. Mix: make a draught.

In Diarrhœa.—Dr. GREGORY.

2477. ℞ Pulv. Rhei, ℈j.
Potassæ Sulphatis, gr. xv.
Aquæ Menthæ pip. ℥iss. Mix: make a purging draught.

Dr. GREGORY.

2478. ℞ Mist Gentianæ co. ʒix.
Tinct. Rhei co. ʒij.
Tinct. Cubebæ, ʒj.
Mix: make a cathartic draught.

Dr. PARIS.

2479. ℞ Pulv. Rhei, gr. xv.
Magnes. calcin.
Conf. Aromat. ana ℈j.
Aquæ Menthæ pip. ℥iss.
Mix: make a purgative draught.

Mr. SAVORY.

2480. ℞ Pulv. Rhei,
Potassæ Sulphatis, ana ℈j.
Decoct. Aloes co.
Aquæ Menth. viridis, ana ʒvj.
Spirit. Ammon. Aromat. ℥ss. Mix: make a draught.

Cordial Aperient.—Dr. DRUITT.

2481. ℞ Pulv. Rhei, ℈j.
Conf. Aromat. ℈ss.
Spirit. Ammon. Arom. gtt. xxx.
Aquæ Cinnamomi,
Aquæ destill. ana ʒvj.
Tinct. Rhei, ℥j.
Mix: make a draught. To be repeated in six hours.

In Diarrhœa.

The remaining prescriptions are for various purgative mixtures containing Rhubarb.

2482. ℞ Pulv. Rhei, ʒj.
Magnes. ʒiss.
Pulv. Zingib. ℈j.
Aquæ Menthæ pip. Oj. Mix. Dose, ℥ss.

Tonic in Dyspepsia.—Dr. GREGORY.

2483. ℞ Rhei rad. contrit. ʒss.
Sodæ Subcarb. ʒj.
Decoct. Glycyrrhizæ, ℥v and ʒij.
Syrupi Aurantii, ʒvj.
Mix. Dose, from f℥ss to f℥j once, twice, or three times a day. (A pleasant and efficacious method of administering small doses of rhubarb in dyspepsia.)

SPRAGUE.

2484. ℞ Infusi Rhei,
Decoct. Aloes co.
Infusi Gentianæ co.
Infusi Caryophylli, ana ℥iss.
Make a mixture. A fourth part twice a day.

Dr. BRIGHT.

2485. ℞ Pulv. Rhei,
Bismuthi Nitratis,
Conf. Aromat. ana ℈j.
Aquæ Menth. piperitæ, ℥iv.
Mix. A fourth part twice a day.

In Habitual Constipation.—Dr. DRUITT.

2486. ℞ Tinct. Rhei,
Tinct. Gentianæ co. ana ℥ss.
Tinct. Cardam. co. ℥j.
Sodæ Boratis, ʒss.
Tinct. Zingib. ʒij.
Bismuthi Oxidi, ʒj.
Mix: make a mixture, of which, after shaking, take a dessertspoonful with a tablespoonful of cold water, three times a day, after taking food.

In Diarrhœa.—Dr. RICHMOND.

2487. ℞ Infusi Rhei, ℥ss.
Potassæ Bisulph. ʒss.
Tinct. Cinnam. co. ℥ss.
Syrupi Sennæ, ℥ss. Mix: fʒj every third hour.

Aperient for Infants.—Drs. EVANSON and MAUNSELL.

2488. ℞ Pulv. Rhei,
Magnes. ana ℈j.
Olei Anisi, gtt. ij.
Sacchari, ʒj.
Aquæ destill. ad ℥ij.
Tinct. Rhei, ʒj.
Spirit. Amm. Arom. ♏xij.
Mix: make a mixture. A teaspoonful, as occasion requires.

For the Flatulence of Infants.—Dr. UNDERWOOD.

2489. ℞ Potassæ Sulph. gr. xij.
Infusi Rhei, ʒvss.
Tinct. Aurantii, ʒss.
Aquæ Cinnamomi, ʒiss. Mix: f℥ss, as occasion requires.

Aperient for Children of three years of age.—Dr. WEST.

2490. ℞ Pulv. Rhei,
Sodæ Sesquicarb ana ʒss.
Aquæ Menthæ pip. ℥ij. ʒvj.
Syrupi, ʒij.
Make a mixture. A tablespoonful or dessertspoonful every night.

Alterative Purge for Children.—Dr. UNDERWOOD.

2491. ℞ Infusi Rhei, ℥ij.
Potassæ Bicarb. ℈j.
Syrupi Zingib. ʒij.
Aquæ Menthæ pip. ℥ij. Dose, ℥j twice a day.

For Children with Voracious Appetites and Red Tongues.
Dr. DRUITT.

RHŒAS. *Red Poppy.*

Papaver Rhœas is a common British plant (Nat. Ord. *Papaveraceæ*). The petals are mucilaginous, bitter, and very slightly narcotic. They are chiefly used for the coloring matter which they contain, but have been also given in the forms of infusion and syrup as an anodyne in the catarrhal affections of children and adults.

Syrupus Rhœados (L., E.), half to one ounce.

Infusum Rhœados (Cottereau). In catarrhal affections, ad libitum.

2492. ℞ Petalorum Rhœados, ℥ij.
Acidi Sulph. dil. gtt. xv.
Sacchari, ℥ij.
Decocti Hordei, Oj. Infuse, and strain.

To be taken freely in Catarrhal Affections.—ST. MARIE.

RHUS. See TOXICODENDRON.

RICINI OLEUM. *Castor Oil.*

Castor Oil is obtained by expression from the seeds of the *Ricinus communis*, a plant which grows in India and other parts of the world. It has a peculiar faint odor and taste. It differs from most other oils in being soluble in its own volume of alcohol. It is a mild laxative cathartic, seldom griping, and safe in operation. It is admirably adapted for an aperient in irritable conditions of the system, for weak persons, and women after their confinement. It is the best purge in peritonitis and dysentery; in inflammatory diseases of the urinary organs, or after the operation for lithotomy; and in obstruction of the bowels. It is well fitted for children. When used as an aperient in constipation, its dose may be gradually lessened.

The dose of the oil for children is from one to two drachms; for adults, half to one and a half ounce. It may be taken alone, or swimming on coffee, milk, or wine and water; or made into an emulsion with yolk of egg or mucilage.

Emulsio purgans cum Oleo Ricini (Paris Codex). Half an ounce may be given every hour until it operates.

2493. ℞ Olei Ricini, ℥ij.
Syrupi florum Persicæ, ℥j. Mix.

For Tape-worm.—M. BOURDIER.

2494. ℞ Olei Ricini, ʒvj.
Mucilag. Acaciæ, ʒij.
Aquæ Fœniculi, ℥ss.
Mix: make a draught. To be repeated as occasion requires.

Dr. THOMAS.

2495. ℞ Olei Ricini, ℥ss.
Mucilag. Acaciæ, q. s. Mix, in a mortar, and add
Aquæ Menth. pip. ℥j.
Tinct. Opii, ♏xv.
Mix: make a draught. To be taken as occasion requires.

In Colica Pictonum.—Dr. THOMAS.

2496. ℞ Olei Ricini, ʒvj.
Vitelli Ovi, q. s.
Aquæ Menth. pip. ʒx. Mix: make a cathartic draught.

Mr. SAVORY.

2497. ℞ Olei Ricini, ℥iss.
Vitellum Ovi unius. Mix well, and add
Aquæ Menthæ viridis, ℥v.
Syrupi Aurantii, ℥j. Mix: ℥j for a dose.

A Purge for Children and Delicate Persons.—Dr. HOOPER.

2498. ℞ Ricini Olei, ℥j.
Ovi Vitelli, semissem. Rub up together, and add
Aquæ florum Aurant.
Syrup. simp. āā ℥j
Aquæ, ℥vj. Mix.

An Agreeable Purge.—TROUSSEAU and REVEIL.

2499. ℞ Olei Ricini, ʒij.
Vitelli Ovi, q. s. Rub up thoroughly together, and while rubbing, add gradually
Aquæ Cinnamomi, ʒix.
Spirit. Myristicæ, ʒss.
Tinct. Sennæ,
Tinct. Jalapæ, ana ʒj. Make a cathartic draught.

Dr. PARIS.

2500. ℞ Olei Ricini, ℥j
Pulv. Sacchari, ℈j.
Syrupi simp. ʒj.
Tinct. Opii, ♏iv.
Aquæ flor. Aurantii, ʒvij.
Mix: to be shaken before taken. A teaspoonful every four hours.

In Diarrhœa of Children Teething.—Dr. WEST.

2501. ℞ Olei Ricini, ℥ss.
Aquæ destil. ℥j.
Spirit. Pimentæ, ʒj.
Liq. Potassæ, gtt. xx. Mix: make a draught.

Dr. J. Hamilton.

2502. ℞ Olei Ricini, ℥j.
Æth. Sulph. ʒij. Mix: a spoonful every two hours.

Anthelmintic in Tænia.—Radius.

2503. ℞ Olei Ricini, ℥iss.
Vitel. Ovor. ij.
Infusi Anthemidis, ℥vj. Mix: make a cathartic enema.

Radius.

2504. ℞ Olei Ricini, ℥iij.
Potassæ Carbonatis, ℈j.
Saponis, ʒj.
Aquæ ferventis, Oj. Mix, and make an enema.

In obstinate Constipation, &c.—Dr. Hooper.

ROSA CANINA. *Dog Rose.*

This plant is the Dog Rose both of the ancients and the moderns. It belongs to the Nat. Ord. *Rosaceæ.* The fruit, or hip, is the part used. It contains much saccharine matter, with a little vegetable acid. The hairy seeds within must be removed. A confection is then formed of the pounded fruits, which is chiefly valuable in the formation of pill masses, and as a vehicle for other medicines.

Confectio Rosæ caninæ (L., E.). An acidulous and refrigerant vehicle. Has been given as an astringent in diarrhœa and dysentery.

ROSA CENTIFOLIA. *Cabbage Rose.*

This is the sweet rose of the gardens, said to have been first introduced from the East.

R. Damascena, a variety of the same species, is cultivated in India and elsewhere, to yield the famous fragrant oil known as *Attar* or *Otto of Roses.* The fresh petals of the Cabbage Rose are distilled with water, or their volatile oil is mixed with it, to form Rose Water. It is a very agreeable vehicle, much used in lotions and collyria. The syrup made from the same petals possesses their color, and is also slightly laxative.

Aqua Rosæ (L., E., D.).

Syrupus Rosæ (L., E.). Slightly laxative. One to four drachms to infants.

Unguentum Aquæ Rosæ (U. S.). A cooling application. "Cold Cream."

Oleum Rosæ (E., D.). A scent.

Oleum Rosæ (Soubeiran). A solution of the last in olive oil, used as an application to chilblains, &c.

2505. ℞ Aquæ Rosæ, ℥iij.
Lactis crem.
Ovi Albuminis,
Syrupi Violæ, ana ℥j. Mix: make a mouth-wash.

An agreeable Cooling Wash.—St. Marie.

ROSA GALLICA. *Red Rose.*

The Red or French Rose is a native of Europe. Its buds are used in medicine, both when fresh and dry. They have a bright-red color, which they communicate to water, but not much scent. They contain some tannic and gallic acids, and are therefore used as astringents in various cases. An acid infusion is given, mixed with water, as a cooling drink, and employed in gargles. A confection is employed as a vehicle, in the same manner as confection of Dog Rose.

Infusum Rosæ compositum vel *acidum* (L., E., D.). Dose, one and a half ounce. This contains, in one pint, one and a half drachms of dil. sulphuric acid.

Confectio Rosæ (L., E., D.). Slightly astringent. One to two drachms.

Mel Rosæ (L., E.). A cooling and astringent ingredient in gargles. Applied to aphthæ of the mouth.

Syrupus Rosæ Gallicæ (E., D.). One drachm to half an ounce.

2506. ℞ Conf. Rosæ, ℥ij.
Syrupi Tolutani, ℥ss.
Syrupi Papav. ʒj. Mix. In doses of ʒj.

Astringent in Bowel Affections.—Foy.

2507. ℞ Infusi Rosæ co. ℥iiiss.
Tinct. Myrrhæ, ℥ss.
Sacchari puri, ℥ss.
Mix: make a gargle. To be used frequently.

For Relaxed Throat or Uvula.—Dr. Hooper.

2508. ℞ Mellis Rosæ, ℥ij.
Sodæ Biboratis, ʒij.
Tinct. Myrrhæ, ʒij.
Aquæ, ℥vj. Mix: make a gargle.

DR. JOY.

2509. ℞ Rosæ rubræ, ℥iss.
Foliorum Sumach, ℥j.
Vini Cydoniæ, ℥iv.
Aceti Vini rubri, ℥x.
Macerate for ten days, express and strain.

As a Styptic, and Application to Bruises.—VAN MONS.

2510. ℞ Petalorum Rosæ rubræ, ʒij.
Aquæ ferventis, Oss.
Digest and strain. For an enema, to be used every day. (To be employed cold. After a few days, ℈j of Ext. Krameriæ is to be added.)

In Dilatation of the Rectum.—DR. TEISSIER.

ROSMARINUS. *Rosemary.*

The *Rosmarinus officinalis* (Nat. Ord. *Labiatæ*) is an evergreen garden shrub, whose flowers and tops are employed in medicine. They have a fragrant odor, and bitter taste, their most important constituent being an aromatic essential oil. Rosemary is stimulant and carminative, and employed as an agreeable addition to medicines of more active properties. It is often added to liniments and lotions, and is much used for its scent by perfumers.

Oleum Rosmarini (L., E., D.), two to three drops, carminative.

Spiritus Rosmarini (L., E., D.). Employed in making soap liniment.

2511. ℞ Rosmarini, ℥j.
Olei Olivæ, ℥iij.
Heat till the water has evaporated, express, and strain.

As a stimulating Application.—PHARM. HISPAN.

2512. ℞ Rosmarini,
Thymi,
Salviæ,
Origani,
Menthæ, ana lbss.
Aquæ ferventis, Ovj. Infuse for 12 hours, strain, and add
Essent. Saponis, ℥iv.
Ammon. Hydrochlor. ℥ij.
Aquæ, q. s. to make an aromatic bath.

In Chronic Rheumatism, Cutaneous Disorders, and Dyspepsia.

FOY.

RUBIA. *Madder.*

The roots of the common Madder, *Rubia tinctorum* (Nat. Ord. *Rubiaceæ*), are chiefly used as a dye, on account of their red color. The plant is a native of South Europe. The root has a peculiar odor, and a bitter taste. It has been used as a diuretic; but it is still more esteemed as an emmenagogue. In the latter character, it has been strongly recommended by Dr. Home. The dose of the powder is from half to two drachms three times a day.

Pulvis Rubiæ compositus (Radius), ten grains to one scruple, in Rachitis.

Decoctum Rubiæ (Dewees). A wineglassful every three hours, shortly before the expected time of the menstrual discharge.

2513. ℞ Pulv. Rubiæ, ℥j.
Pulv. Macis, ʒij.
Aquæ, Oiss. Boil to Oj, strain, and add
Tinct. Aromaticæ, ʒij.
Syrupi Acidi Cit. ℥ij.
Mix: f℥iij three or four times a day.

In Amenorrhœa, Chlorosis, &c.—SWEDIAUR.

2514. ℞ Rubiæ tinctorum rad. ℥j.
Theriacæ, q. s.
Olei Sabinæ, ♏xij.
Mix: make an electuary. A sixth part three times a day.

Emmenagogue in Simple Atony of the Uterus.—Dr. NELIGAN.

RUTA. *Rue.*

The heavy, peculiar smell and antispasmodic properties of the *Ruta graveolens* are well known. It belongs to the Nat. Ord. *Rutaceæ.* It is ordinarily a stimulant, but in large doses it is narcotic, and cases of poisoning by it have occurred. It is useful in some kinds of hysteria, but is especially recommended in flatulent colic, given either by mouth or in a clyster. It is likewise employed as an emmenagogue, and has been prescribed in the convulsions of infants. Rue is also vermifuge. The powdered leaves may be given in doses of ten to twenty grains, three times a day. The fresh leaves are more active.

Their expressed juice may be given in doses of half to one drachm.

Oleum Rutæ (L., E.), two to five minims, rubbed up with sugar and water.

Confectio Rutæ (L.), one scruple to one drachm.

Tinctura Rutæ (Beral), half to one drachm to adults.

Syrupus Rutæ (Beral), half to two drachms in the flatulent colic of children.

2515. ℞ Succi foliorum Rutæ, ℥j.
Oxymellis Scillæ, ℥ss.
Mix: a teaspoonful frequently.

In Hysterical Affections.—PIERQUIN.

2516. ℞ Fol. Rutæ,
Fol. Sabinæ, ana ℥ss.
Aquæ fervidæ, q. s. Boil to f℥xvj, and add
Assafœtidæ, ʒij.
Olei Olivæ, ʒij. Mix: an enema.

In Hysteria.—Dr. COPLAND.

2517. ℞ Rutæ,
Sabinæ,
Absinthii, ana ʒiij.
Aquæ ferventis, Oj. Infuse, strain, and add
Olei Ricini, ℥ss. Mix: make an enema.

For Ascarides.—RADIUS.

SABADILLA. *Cevadilla.*

This consists of the small brown follicles and seeds of two plants, *Veratrum Sabadilla* and *Asagræa officinalis*, both of the Nat. Ord. *Melanthaceæ*. The seeds are very bitter, and contain an acrid principle, described beyond as the alkaloid Veratria. They are drastic cathartics and emetics, being also used to destroy and expel intestinal worms. The dose, which should be cautiously given, as the remedy is highly poisonous, is from five to ten grains of the powder.

Extractum Sabadillæ (Turnbull). Dose, one-sixth of a grain; used as a substitute for Veratria in tic douloureux.

Tinctura Sabadillæ (Turnbull), used as a stimulating lotion in rheumatism.

Unguentum Sabadillæ (Paris Codex), to destroy vermin.

2518. ℞ Pulv. Sabadillæ, gr. ij.
Ferri Sulph. gr. j.
Pulv. Santonicæ,
Magnesiæ, ana ℈ss. Mix: to be taken four times a day.

In Tænia.—RADIUS.

2519. ℞ Tinct. Sabadillæ, ℥j.
Tinct. Camphoræ, ℥ij.
Spirit. Rosmarini, ℥ss.

Mix: make an embrocation. To be applied to the painful parts on woolen cloths.

In Neuralgia and Muscular Pains.—Dr. NELIGAN.

SABINA. SABINÆ OLEUM. *Savine. Oil of Savine.*

The tops of the *Juniperus Sabina*, an indigenous shrub (Nat. Ord. *Coniferæ*), are possessed of powerful medicinal properties. They have an acrid taste, and unpleasant odor, and owe their activity to a volatile oil, which may be separated by distillation. Both Savine and its oil are powerfully stimulant, and irritant to the external surface. Ointment and cerate of Savine are thus employed for the purpose of keeping open blisters, when it is thought desirable to keep up the local irritation, and promote the discharge of serum. Given internally, in small doses, with care, it proves cathartic, emmenagogue, and stimulant to the uterus of the female. It should not be administered when there is any irritation of that organ. In large doses it is highly dangerous, acting as an irritant poison. It has been given by criminals to procure abortion, frequently with fatal consequences. The dose of powdered Savine is from five to ten grains.

Oleum Sabinæ, two to five drops.
Extractum Sabinæ (Paris Codex), three to six grains.
Infusum Sabinæ (Pereira), half ounce.
Tinctura Sabinæ (Soubeiran), ten to fifteen drops.
Unguentum Sabinæ (L., D.).
Ceratum Sabinæ (E.).

2520. ℞ Pulv. Sabinæ, ʒj.
Pulv. Zingib. ʒj.
Potassæ Sulph. ʒij.

Mix: divide into 6 powders. One, twice a day.

In Amenorrhœa.—Dr. ELLIS.

2521. ℞ Pulv. fol. Sabinæ, gr. vij.
Sodæ Boratis, ℈j.
Pulv. Zingib. gr. vij.
Make a powder: to be taken twice a day.

In Amenorrhœa, with a languid Pulse.—Dr. COPLAND.

2522. ℞ Olei Sabinæ, gtt. viij.
Mucilaginis Acaciæ, ℥j.
Misturæ Camphoræ, ℥iij.
Mix: make a mixture. A fourth part three times a day.

In Amenorrhœa.—Dr. E. COPEMAN.

2523. ℞ Pulv. Sabinæ,
Pulv. Æruginis, each, equal parts.
Make a powder. (To be dusted over the part affected.)

In Eczema, Herpes, and Simple Excoriations.—Mr. ACTON.

SAGAPENUM.

This is one of the fetid gum-resins, derived from some unknown species of the Nat. Ord. *Umbelliferæ.* It has an unpleasant odor and taste, and contains an ill-smelling volatile oil. It is stimulant and antispasmodic. Though now little used, it has been given as an emmenagogue, and as an antispasmodic in hysteria and epilepsy. The dose is from ten to thirty grains.

Sagapenum præparatum (L.) is freed from impurities.

Pilulæ Sagapeni comp. (L. 1836), ten to thirty grains.

2524. ℞ Pil. Sagapeni co. gr. xl.
Olei Rutæ, ♏xv. Make 12 pills. Two or three for a dose.

In the Flatulent Colic of Hysteria.—Dr. NELIGAN.

2525. ℞ Sagapeni, ʒss.
Aquæ Pulegii, ℥iss.
Spirit. Myristicæ, ʒij.
Syrupi Tolutani, ʒj.
Mix: make a draught. To be taken morning and evening. Add Spirit. Ammon. comp. ♏xx as occasion requires.

In Asthma.—Dr. E. J. CLARK.

SALEPA. *Salep.*

Salep is the horny tuber of some species of *Orchideæ*, cultivated in India and Persia. It is considered very nutritious, containing starch, mucilage, and gummy matters. Boiled with water or milk, it yields an agreeable drink for invalids, and may be employed as a vehicle for medicines of different kinds.

2526. ℞ Salepi pulv. gr. viij. Boil in sufficient water to dissolve it; then throw in
Rad. Ipecac. gr. iij. After a quarter of an hour, to a fluid-ounce of the strained liquor, add
Syrupi Papaveris, ʒj. (Now and then add Tinct. Opii, gtt. j.)
Mix: a teaspoonful every two or three hours to an infant under one year.

In Catarrhal Diarrhœa.—Dr. MEREI.

SALIX ET SALICINA. *Willow-bark* and *Salicine.*

The bark of several of the native species of Willow (Nat. Ord. *Amentaceæ*) has been used in medicine. It contains some Tannic acid, and a peculiar bitter principle, called Salicine. Its taste is bitter and astringent. It is tonic and antiperiodic, and has been used in cases of debility, and in intermittents, as a substitute for Cinchona bark. The Salicine prepared from it has likewise been used in nearly all the cases in which Quinine is so serviceable. But it is at least doubtful whether it can in any disorder be so safely relied upon as the other; and though its cheapness has been alleged in its favor, yet, on account of the largeness of the dose, it has proved to be absolutely the more expensive of the two. The dose of powdered Willow-bark is from half to one drachm; and of Salicine as a febrifuge, ten grains to two scruples. It is given in smaller doses as a simple tonic.

Decoctum Salicis (Niemann), one to two ounces.

Unguentum foliorum Salicis (Hufeland) is recommended as a mild dressing to foul ulcers.

2527. ℞ Cort Salicis contus. ℥iij.
Aquæ, Oij. Boil to Oj; then add
Caryophyll. contus. ʒss, and strain.

℞ Colaturæ, ℥vij.
Tinct. Aurantii, ʒvj.
Syrupi Aurantii, ʒij. Mix: a fourth part three times a day.

Tonic and Antiperiodic.—Dr. COPLAND.

2528. ℞ Polygalæ amaræ Radicis, ℥vj. Boil with
Aquæ puræ, ℥xij to ℥viij, and strain. To the strained liquor, add
Salicinæ, gr. viij-x. One to two spoonfuls every two hours

VON DEM BISCH.

2529. ℞ Salicinæ, gr. xij.
Sacchari, ℈ij.
Mix, and divide into 4 powders. One, three times a day.

KROMBHOLZ.

2530. ℞ Salicinæ,
Extr. Gentianæ, ana gr. xxiv.
Pulv. Glycyrrhizæ, q. s. to make 12 pills.

VAVASSEUR.

2531. ℞ Salicinæ, gr. xv.
Antim. Pot. Tart. gr. j.
Sacchari, ℈iss.
Mix, and divide into 10 powders. One every second hour.

STEGMAYER.

2532. ℞ Salicinæ, gr. xvi.
Inf. Gentianæ co. ℥vij.
Syrupi Hemidesmi, ℥j.
Mix: two tablespoonfuls three times a day.

Tonic in Convalescence from Acute Diseases of the Digestive Organs. Dr. NELIGAN.

SALVIA. *Sage.*

The common Sage, Salvia officinalis (Nat. Ord. *Labiatæ*), is a native of South Europe. The leaves have a warm, bitter, and astringent taste, with an agreeably aromatic odor. Sage is slightly stimulant, astringent, and tonic. It is used in gargles, and is said to abate the sweating in hectic fever. Dose, in powder, twenty to thirty grains.

Infusum Salviæ (Ellis) is given as a drink in fevers.

Acetum Salviæ (Beral) is mixed with water to form gargles.

2533. ℞ Herbæ Salviæ,
Sem. Sinapis, ana ℥ss.
Aquæ fervidæ, Oj. Macerate for an hour, and strain. To the strained liquor, add
Spirit. Armorac. c. ℥ij.
Mix: two or three spoonfuls three or four times a day.

Diuretic and Cordial.—Dr. COPLAND.

2534. ℞ Infusi Salviæ, Oj.
Acidi Sulph. diluti, ʒij.
Mellis Rosæ, ℥j. Mix: make a gargle.

In Relaxation of the Uvula.—RADIUS.

2535. ℞ Infusi Salviæ, Oij.
Tinct. Cinchonæ,
Syrupi Mori, ana ℥ss.
Spirit. Armoraciæ, ʒj. Mix: make a gargle.

For Relaxed Uvula.—CADET.

SAMBUCUS. *Elder.*

The Sambucus nigra is the common species in Europe, and the S. Canadensis in America. (Nat. Ord. *Caprifoliaceæ.*) The flowers have an agreeable odor, and are employed to form a gently stimulating ointment, as well as a distilled water, used in flavoring. The berries are diaphoretic and laxative, and the bark also is said to be purgative. The former are seldom used, except to make wine; the bark was given in dropsies by Sydenham.

Aqua Sambuci (L., E.) is used as a vehicle.

Acetum Sambuci (Soubeiran), employed in gargles.

Decoctum Sambuci corticis (Sydenham), half pint morning and evening in dropsies.

Unguentum Sambuci (florum), (L.).

Extractum baccarum Sambuci has been given as an alterative. One drachm to half ounce.

2536. ℞ Florum Sambuci, ℥j.
Aquæ fervidæ, q. s. to form of the strained liquor f℥vj, to which, add
Oxymel. simp.
Oxymel. Scillæ, ana ℥j.
Antimon. Tart. gr. ij. Mix: one spoonful every hour.

In Bronchitis.—Dr. AUGUSTIN.

2537. ℞ Succi spiss. Sambuci, ℥ss.
Aquæ destil. ℥viiss.
Potassæ Nitratis, ʒss.
Rub up the Elder with water to form a solution, in which dissolve the niter. A tablespoonful every two hours.

Refrigerant in Hæmoptysis, &c.—Dr. NELIGAN.

2538. ℞ Extr. baccarum Sambuci,
Pulpæ Pruni,
Syrupi Rhœados, ana ℥ij.
Potassæ Nitratis, ʒj.
Mix: two or three spoonfuls a day.

In Asthma.—ST. MARIE.

SANGUINARIA.

This is the rhizome or root of the Canadian Bloodroot, *Sanguinaria Canadensis* (Nat. Ord. *Papaveraceæ*). The powder has a faint odor, and an acrid taste. Its action appears to resemble that of Ipecacuanha. It is emetic and somewhat irritant. It has been combined with chloride of zinc as an application to cancer, in which case it can only act the part of a vehicle. Dose of the powder as an alterative and diaphoretic, one to five grains; as an emetic, ten to thirty grains. It is very little used in England.

Infusum Sanguinariæ (half ounce to sixteen ounces aq. bull.): dose, half ounce to one ounce as an emetic.

Pilulæ Sanguinariæ (Griffith), one to two as an alterative; five to ten as an emetic.

Tinct. Sanguinariæ (U. S.), half drachm to one drachm as an alterative; three to four drachms as an emetic.

SANTONICA. *Worm Seed.*

This consists of the minute dried flowers and tops of some unknown species of Artemisia (Nat. Ord. *Compositæ*), growing in northern Africa and Syria. It contains a volatile oil, and a peculiar principle called Santonine. To one or both of these it owes its anthelmintic powers. It is chiefly used for ascarides and lumbrici in children. It must be given with, or followed by, a brisk purgative. Twenty to thirty grains for children, one to two drachms for adults, may be made into an electuary with honey, and given night and morning.

2539. ℞ Sem. Santonicæ,
Extr. Tanaceti, ana gr. vj.
Ferri Oxidi, gr. iv.
Olei Valerianæ, gtt. j. Mix: make a powder.

Vermifuge.—AUGUSTIN.

2540. ℞ Pulv. Sem. Santonicæ,
Pulv. Tanaceti, ana ʒss.
Pulv. Rhei, gr. xij.
Pulv. Jalapæ, gr. viij.
Pulv. Sacchari, ℈iv.

Mix, and divide into 6 or 12 powders, according to the age of the patient. (2–3 powders daily till the worms are expelled.)

For Round Worms.—Dr. MEREI.

2541. ℞ Seminum Santonici,
Tanaceti cacum. ana ℥ss.
Pulv. Valerianæ,
Pulv. Jalapæ,
Potassæ Sulphatis, ana ʒij.
Oxymellis Scillæ, q. s. to make an electuary.

Dose, ʒj night and morning.

Anthelmintic.—Dr. HOOPER.

2542. ℞ Seminum Santonici,
Seminum Tanaceti, rudè contus. ana ℥ss.
Pulv. Valerianæ, ʒij.
Pulv. Jalapæ, ʒiss.
Potassæ Sulph. ʒij.
Oxymellis Scillæ, q. s. to make an electuary.

A teaspoonful every night and morning. (Its use should be continued for five or six days.)

Lumbrici Ascarides.—BREMSER.

2543. ℞ Rad. Valerianæ,
Herbæ Absinthii,
Herbæ Tanaceti,
Cacum. Santonicæ, ana ʒiij.
Aquæ fervidæ, ℥xij.

Macerate for two hours and strain. To the strained liquor, add
Salis communis, ℥ss. Make an enema.

Vermifuge.—DR. COPLAND.

SAPO. *Soap.*

Hard Soap (*Sapo*) should be made of Olive oil and Soda. Castile Soap is very pure, but common Soap contains resin, tallow, and other such materials. Soft Soap (*Sapo mollis*) should be made of Olive oil and Potash, but it frequently contains train oil and many impurities. Soap is a kind of salt formed with the alkali by Stearic, Oleic, Margaric, and other acids contained in fats. It is soluble in pure water. It acts upon the system much in the same way as the carbonates of the alkalies, being antacid and alterative. Soap has been given in large quantities to dissolve lithic acid calculi in the bladder. It is a frequent ingredient in pills, and renders the resinous parts of purgative medicines more soluble in the stomach juices. Compound Soap pill is merely a vehicle for Opium, of which it contains one grain in every five. Soap is used externally as a detergent in many cutaneous diseases, and gives lubricity to liniments and embrocations, being at the same time slightly rubefacient. It is also a common ingredient in cerates and plasters. For most of these purposes Hard Soap is used. The compound Sulphur ointment, as also many forms for pills, contain Soft Soap. Dose of Hard Soap, ten grains to one drachm.

Pilula Saponis composita (L., E., D.) contains one grain of Opium in five.

Linimentum Saponis (L., E., D.).

Ceratum Saponis compositum (L.).

Emplastrum Saponis (L., E., D.).

2544. ℞ Saponis albi, ℈ij.
Olei Carui, gtt. ij ad iij.
Syrupi, q. s.
Mix: make two boluses. One for a dose.

Purgative and Alterative.—SWEDIAUR.

2545. ℞ Pulv. Saponis albi, ʒij.
Extr. Fellis bovis, ʒj.
Mix, until a uniform mass is formed; then add
Pulv. Guaiaci Res.
Calomelanos, ana ʒss.
Pulv. Guaiaci Ligni, q. s. to make pills of 4 grains each.
One or two, night and morning.

In Gout.—VICQ D'AZYR.

2546. ℞ Saponis medic. ʒiv.
Gum. Ammoniac. ʒij.
Extr. Conii,
Extr. Aconit. Nap. ana ʒiss.
Pil. Aloes c. Myrrhâ, ʒj.
Beat into a uniform mass, and divide into 4-grain pills. Two, morning and night, increasing by one every day until fifteen or twenty are taken during the day.

In Glandular Tumors and Scirrhous Formations.
Dr. LOWASSY.

2547. ℞ Saponis Castil. ʒiiss.
Gum. Ammon. ʒj.
Extr. Aloes pur. gr. xv.
Assafœtidæ, ʒss.
Pulv. Rhei, ʒj.
Croci sativi, ʒss.
Syrupi, q. s.
Mix: make 84 pills. Two, twice a day.

Deobstruent.—RECAMIER.

2548. ℞ Linim. Camphoræ co.
Linim. Saponis co. ana ʒiss.
Olei Cajuputi, ʒj. Mix: make a liniment.

Rubefacient.—Mr. SAVORY.

2549. ℞ Linim. Saponis co.
Liq. Ammon. Acet. ana ℥j. Mix: make a liniment.

For Chilblains.—Dr. THOMAS.

2550. ℞ Saponis alb. ℥iv.
Aquæ destil. ℥xx.
Pulv. Camphor. ʒij.
Liq. Plumbi D. ℥ss. Mix.

BRISTOL INFIRMARY.

2551. ℞ Saponis medic. ℥j.
Alcoholis rect. ℥vj.
Aquæ destil.
Camphoræ, ana ℥j. Dissolve slowly by heat, and add
Olei Rosmarini, ℈iv.
Olei Thymi, ℈j.
Liq. Ammoniæ, ʒij. Mix well: make a liniment.

DR. COPLAND.

SAPONARIA.

The common Soapwort, *Saponaria officinalis*, has been occasionally used as an alterative, diuretic, and diaphoretic. It contains a peculiar principle called *Saponine.*

2552. ℞ Saponariæ fol. ℥ss.
Aquæ ferventis, Oj.
Infuse for half an hour, then strain, and add sugar to suit the taste. Dose, as much as pleases.

In most Chronic Diseases of the Skin.—DR. BURGESS.

SARSA. *Sarsaparilla.*

This name is applied to the roots of several species of *Smilax* (Nat. Ord. *Smilaceæ*) growing in the West Indies, Mexico, and South America. They are all more or less similar in their properties, but the Jamaica Sarsaparilla is generally preferred to the rest.

This drug is supposed to be tonic and alterative, and is sometimes diuretic and diaphoretic. Its advantage is most appreciated in cachectic and depraved conditions of the system, particularly when these depend upon an old venereal disorder. In such cases the patient is said to improve in strength, and to gain flesh under its use. It is generally given in the form of the compound decoction; and being rarely used except in company with other medicines, it is not easy to judge of its individual action. It is recommended in secondary syphilis, in skin diseases of various kinds, in phthisical and scrofulous disorders, in cachexia consequent on purulent discharges, &c. It is frequently employed as a vehicle for other medicines. The dose of the powder is half to one drachm three times a day.

Infusum Sarsæ (U. S.). Dose, one to four ounces three times a day.

Decoctum Sarsæ (L., E., D.), three to six ounces.

Decoct. Sarsæ compositum (L., E., D.), three to six ounces. A substitute for the "Lisbon diet drink."

Extractum Sarsæ (Paris Codex), ten to twenty grains.

Extractum Sarsæ Liquidum (L., E., D.). Contains spirit, and may be preserved for any time. Dose, half to two drachms, in water.

Liquor Sarsæ (Battley) is similar. One drachm equals half a pint of the decoction.

Syrupus Sarsæ (L., E.). Dose, four drachms, with water.

2553. ℞ Pulv. radicis Sarsæ, ℥j.
Pulv. Sodæ Carbonatis, ʒj.

Mix: divide into 12 powders. (One every three hours in a cup of comp. decoction of Sarsaparilla.)

In Scrofula.—Mr. CLINE.

2554. ℞ Pilulæ Hydrarg. gr. viij.
Extr. Taraxaci,
Extr. Sarsæ, ana ℈v.

Mix: make 18 pills. Three, four times a day.

Dr. COPLAND.

2555. ℞ Decoct. Sarsæ comp. ℥iv.
Acidi Nitrici dil. ♏xx–ʒj.
Tinct. Hyoscyami, ʒss.

Mix: make a draught. To be taken three times a day.

In Oxaluria and Syphilis.—Dr. DRUITT.

2556. ℞ Acidi Nitrici,
Acidi Muriat. ana ♏ix.
Extr. Sarsæ fluidi, ℥iss.
Aquæ destil. ℥vss.
Tinct. Cinchonæ co. ℥j.

Mix: dose, one-sixth part three times a day.

In Oxaluria.

2557. ℞ Decoct. Sarsæ concent. ℥j.
Liquor. Potassæ, ʒij.
Decoct. Senegæ, ℥iij.
Mellis, ʒiij.
Aquæ, ℥iv.

Mix: make a mixture. A dessertspoonful three times a day.

In Herpes circinatus of Children.—Mr. C. HOGG.

2558. ℞ Rad. Sarsæ Jamaicensis, concisæ et cōntusæ, ℥ij.
Rad. Glycyrrhizæ concisæ, ʒij.
Liq. Potassæ, ♏xl–ʒj.
Aquæ destil. ferventis, ℥x.
Tinct. Cardam. co. ʒiij.

Macerate for 24 hours, and strain. Take the whole during the day.

An Alterative in cases where Alkalies are admissible.

Dr. DRUITT.

2559. ℞ Sarsap. rad. concisæ et contus. ℥iss.
Glycyrrhizæ rad. contusæ, ℥ss.
Coriandri Sem. contus. ʒij.
Liq. Potassæ, ʒj (or without)
Aquæ ferventis, Oj.

Macerate for 24 hours in a vase closed lightly, and strain. A third part of the strained liquor three times a day.

SPRAGUE.

2560. ℞ Antimon. Sulphureti, ℥iv.
Aquæ communis, lbxij.
Rad. Sarsaparillæ, ℥iij.
Rad. Chinæ Orient.
Cort. ligni Buxi,
Ichthyocollæ, ana ℥iss.
Oxymur. Hydrarg. gr. iij.

Inclose the Antimony in a muslin bag; boil the whole, excepting the last, until the decoction is reduced to one-half; then strain, and add the Sublimate.

For a Drink in Syphilitic Affections. (*Tisane de Feltz.*)

2561. ℞ Cort. rad. Sarsaparillæ, ʒij.
Liq. Calcis, ℥viij. Macerate for 12 hours, and strain.

℞ Hujus colaturæ, ℥vij.
Syrupi cort. Sarsap. ʒvj.
Liq. Alkalini (Brandish's), ʒij–ʒiij.
Tinct. Aurantii, ℥ss.
Potassii Iodidi, gr. vj.
Potassæ Nitrat. ℈ij.

Mix: make a mixture. From two to four tablespoonfuls, with an equal quantity of warm milk twice a day.

Alterative Mixture for Phthisical Patients.

Sir C. SCUDAMORE.

2562. ℞ Extr. Sarsæ, ʒij.
Decocti Sarsæ, ℥xij.
Acidi Nitrici dil.
Tinct. Hyoscyami, ana ʒj.

Mix: a third part three times a day, along with this pill at bedtime:

℞ Pil. Hydrarg. gr. v.
Pulv. Opii, gr. ½. Mix.

In Syphilitic Ulcerations.—Mr. B. TRAVERS.

2563. ℞ Decocti Sarsæ comp. Oiss.
Carnis Bovini, lbss.
Boil together by a slow fire until an equally smooth mixture is formed, which is to be taken every day.
In Phagedænic Ulcerations.—Dr. EGAN.

SASSAFRAS.

The bark of the root of the *Sassafras officinale*, an American tree (Nat. Ord. *Laurineæ*), is possessed of stimulant and diaphoretic properties. It is an ingredient in the compound decoction of Sarsaparilla. It owes its powers to a volatile oil.

Oleum Sassafras. Dose, two to ten drops, as a carminative.

Infusum Sassafras (Niemann), as a diaphoretic drink.

Tinctura Sassafras. Dose, one to three drachms.

2564. ℞ Corticis Sassafras, ℥ss.
Rad. Glycyrrhizæ, ʒij.
Aquæ ferventis, Oj. Infuse: one-half night and morning.
In Scrofulous Complaints.—HUFELAND.

2565. ℞ Infus. Sassafras, ℥viij.
Extr. Glycyrrhizæ, ʒj.
Tinct. Aconiti, P. L. ♏x.
Syr. Tolut. ℥ss. Mix: dose, one-sixth part.
Irritable Cough.

SCABIOSA.

The whole plant of the common field Scabious, *Scabiosa arvensis* (Nat. Ord. *Dipsacaceæ*), has been occasionally employed for its supposed tonic and alterative properties. It is sometimes prescribed in skin diseases.

2566. ℞ Scabiosæ arvensis, ℥ss.
Aquæ ferventis, Oj.
Infuse for half an hour; then strain, and add enough sugar to suit the taste. Dose, ad libitum.
In most Chronic Diseases of the Skin.—Dr. BURGESS.

2567. ℞ Infusi Scabiosæ, Oj.
Acidi Nitrici dil. ℈ij.
Syrupi Malvæ, ℥iij. Mix: two spoonfuls every day.
In Porrigo.—M. BIETT.

SCAMMONIUM. *Scammony.*

This is the concrete juice of the root of *Convolvulus Scammonium*, a Syrian plant (Nat. Ord. *Convolvulaceæ*). Its active properties are owing to one or more peculiar resins which it contains. It is frequently adulterated with starch, chalk, and other matters. When pure, it is a powerful drastic purgative. It is more active than jalap, and less unpleasant to the taste. It must not be given in inflammatory conditions, or in irritable states of the intestines. It is often combined with rhubarb and aromatics, enters into the composition of many purgative pills, and is given with calomel to children. It is useful as a hydragogue in dropsies. Dose, for adults, five to ten grains; for children, three to five grains.

Pulvis Scammonii compositus (L., E., D.) is purgative in doses of ten to thirty grains.

Extractum sive Resina Scammonii (E.): five to ten grains.

Pilula Scammonii composita (Guy's Hosp.): two at a dose.

Confectio Scammonii (L., D.): one scruple to one drachm.

Mistura Scammonii (E.): three ounces for a dose.

Tinctura Scammonii (Paris Codex): half to one drachm.

Trochisci Scammonii (Bouriéres): one to two for a child.

2568. ℞ Pulv. Scammonii, gr. iv.
Hydrarg. Chloridi, gr. iij.
Sacchari albi, gr. v.
Mix: make a cathartic powder. (To be taken in a little honey.)
Dr. Hooper.

2569. ℞ Pulv. Scammonii, gr. viij.
Extr. Gentianæ,
Fellis Bov. inspiss. ana gr. xvj.
Mix, and divide into 8 pills. One or two, at bedtime.
Stomachic and Aperient.—Mr. Savory.

2570. ℞ Pulv. Scammonii,
Pulv. Aloes,
Hydrarg. Chlorid. ana gr. ij.
Mix: make 2 pills. To be taken at once.
At the commencement of Typhus Fever.—Dr. Cheyne.

2571. ℞ Gum. Res. Scammonii, gr. xv.
Sacchari albi, gr. x. Rub up thoroughly, and then add
Olei Carui, ♏iv. Make 6 pills: two every hour.
Dr. Copland.

2572. ℞ Gum. Res. Scammonii, gr. xij. Rub up with
Extr. Glycyrrhizæ, gr. xx.
Tinct. Rhei, ʒij.
Syrupi Zingib. ʒj.
Aquæ Cinnamomi, ℥j. Mix: make an aperient draught.
Dr. Copland.

2573. ℞ Scammonii contr. gr. ij.
Potassæ Sulphatis, gr. x.
Mist. Acaciæ, ʒij. Rub up together, and add
Mist. Amygdalæ, ℥j.
Spir. Myristicæ, ʒss. Make a cathartic draught.

Dr. PARIS.

2574. ℞ Pulv. Scammonii, gr. viij–xij.
Magnesiæ Carbonatis, ℈j.
Mist. Acaciæ, ʒij.
Syrupi Papaveris, ʒj.
Aquæ Pimentæ, ʒix.

Mix: make a draught. To be taken at bedtime, and repeated every other morning, if necessary.

Dr. THOMAS.

2575. ℞ Resinæ Scammonii, gr. v.
Conf. Amygd. gr. xxx. Rub up together, and while mixing, add
Aquæ destil. ℥iss.

Mix: make a draught. (The dose for children is one-third or one-half the above.)

In Simple Constipation.—Dr. NELIGAN.

2576. ℞ Pulv. Rhei,
Pulv. Scammonii,
Potassæ Sulphatis, ana gr. x.
Pulv. Aromat. gr. vj.

Rub up thoroughly together: divide into 6 powders. One every fourth hour, to produce a free, soluble evacuation of the bowels.

Mild Aperient for young Children.—Dr. JOY.

2577. ℞ Scammonii, ℈j.
Olei Amygdalæ, ℥j. Mix well, slowly, with heat; then add
Mucilag. Acaciæ, ℥j. One or two teaspoonfuls for a dose.

For Children.—SWEDIAUR.

2578. ℞ Pulv. Scammonii, ʒss.
Pulv. Cretæ, gr. xv.
Pulv. Cinnamomi, gr. v. Mix: dose, two to five grains.

In Constipation of Children.

SCILLA. *Squill.*

This is the bulb of the *Urginea Scilla* (Nat. Ord. *Liliaceæ*), a plant growing on the sea-coast of the Mediterranean. Being sliced and dried, it forms semitransparent slips, which have a bitter taste. In small doses it is expectorant and diaphoretic; in large doses, emetic and purgative. It is also diuretic. It contains an acrid principle, and in very large doses may prove poisonous. It is given as a diuretic in dropsies, but generally in combination with other medicines. It is chiefly used as an expectorant in chronic bronchitis, where there is not much fever, and often conjoined with Ipecacuanha, Paregoric, and other remedies. It is rarely given as an emetic. The dose of the powder, as an expectorant, is about one grain.

Pulvis Scillæ compositus (Guy's Hosp.): one scruple three times a day as a diuretic.

Extractum Scillæ (Paris Codex): one to three grains.

Pilula Scillæ composita (L., E., D.). Dose, five to fifteen grains.

Acetum Scillæ (L., E., D.): half to one drachm. As expectorant and diuretic.

Oxymel Scillæ (L.). Like the last.

Syrupus Scillæ (E., D.). Similar.

Tinctura Scillæ (L., E., D.): ten minims to half a drachm.

Syrupus Scillæ comp. (U. S.): twenty to thirty minims.

2579. ℞ Pulv. Scillæ, gr. xij.
Pulv. Ipecacuanhæ, gr. xxiv.
Mix, and divide into 6 powders. One, every second hour.
In Chronic Catarrh.—FOY.

2580. ℞ Scillæ rad. exsicc. gr. xij.
Potassæ Nitratis, ʒj.
Sacchari, ʒj.
Pulv. Cinnam. co. ʒss.
Mix: divide into 6 powders. One, twice a day.
Diuretic.—Dr. JOY.

2581. ℞ Pulv. Scillæ,
Pulv. Digitalis, ana gr. j.
Olei Juniperi, gtt. ij.
Sodæ Boratis,
Pulv. Glycyrrhizæ, ana ℈j.
Pulv. Cinnamomi, gr. ij.
Mix: make a powder. To be taken two or three times a day.
Diuretic.—RADIUS.

2582. ℞ Pil. Scillæ co. gr. v.
Pil. Hydrarg. gr. iij.
Mix, and divide into 2 pills. To be taken at night.
Diuretic.—Dr. BAILLIE.

2583. ℞ Pil. Scillæ co. gr. x.
Hydrarg. Chlor. gr. ij.
Mix: make 2 pills. To be taken every day.
In Dropsies and Chronic Chest Affections.—Dr. RYAN.

2584. ℞ Pil. Scillæ co. ʒj.
Hydrarg. Chloridi, gr. v.
Olei Juniperi, ♏j.
Mix, and divide into 20 pills. One, two or three times a day.

Diuretic in Dropsies.—Dr. HOOPER.

2585. ℞ Pil. Scillæ co.
Extr. Conii, ana ʒss.
Mix, and divide into 12 pills. One or two, two or three times a day.

In Chronic Cough.—Mr. SAVORY.

2586. ℞ Pil. Scillæ co. ʒss.
Pil. Ipecacuanhæ co. gr. xxiv.
Quinæ Disulph. gr. iv.
Mucilag. q. s. to form a mass, to be divided into 12 pills. One, twice a day.

In Chronic Cough.

2587. ℞ Pulv. Scillæ recentis,
Pulv. Ammoniaci, ana ʒss.
Pulv. Acidi Benzoici, ℈j.
Balsami Sulph. q. s. to make 24 pills, of which three are to be taken at bedtime, and also in the morning, if necessary.

In Asthma.—Dr. E. J. CLARK.

2588. ℞ Pulv. Scillæ, gr. xij.
Pulv. Ipecacuanhæ, gr. xij.
Extr. Taraxaci, ℈iij.
Pil. Hydrarg. gr. x.
Syrupi, q. s. to make 24 pills. Two, morning and evening.

In Dropsy.—Dr. W. AINSLIE.

2589. ℞ Pil. Scillæ co.
Pil. Colocynth. co. ana ℈ij.
Olei Crotonis, ♏vj.
Mix, and divide into 18 pills. Three, twice a week.

In Dropsy.—Dr. SELWYN (U. S.).

2590. ℞ Aceti Scillæ, ℥ss.
Oxymellis, ℥iss.
Mix: make a linctus. ʒj for a dose.

Bronchitis.—Dr. HOOPER.

2591. ℞ Oxymellis Scillæ,
Mist. Acaciæ,
Syrupi Althææ, ana ℥ss.
Make a linctus. To be employed frequently.

In Cough and Sore Throat.—Dr. PARIS.

2592. ℞ Potassæ Sulph cum Sulphure,
Pulv. rad. Jalapæ,
Pulv. rad. Valerianæ, ana ʒj.
Oxymel. Scillæ, ℥iv.
Mix. For an adult, f℥ss, four times a day. For a child, from fʒj to fʒij.

Vermifuge.—STOERK.

2593. ℞ Pulv. Myrrhæ, ʒj.
Pulv. Ipecac. gr. vj.
Oxymel. Scillæ,
Mucilag. Acaciæ,
Syrupi Althææ, ana ʒvj.
Make a linctus. A little to be taken frequently.

In Catarrh.—Dr. COPLAND.

2594. ℞ Potass. Supertart. contrit. ℥iij.
Juniperi cacum. et baccæ pulv. ℥j. Rub up well together, and add, while rubbing,
Pulv. Jalapæ, ʒij.
Oxymel. Scillæ, ℥ij.
Syrupi Zingib. q. s. to form an electuary.
Dose, ʒj–ʒiij two, three, or four times a day.

Diuretic.—Dr. COPLAND.

2595. ℞ Aceti Scillæ, ʒj.
Decocti Hordei, ℥v.
Syrupi Croci, ℥j.
Mix: make a mixture. A spoonful three or four times a day.

In Coughs.—Dr. W. AINSLIE.

2596. ℞ Oxymellis Scillæ,
Spirit. Ætheris Nit.
Tinct. Camph. co. ana ℥ss.
Mix. A teaspoonful when the cough is troublesome.

In Chronic Catarrh.—Dr. GREGORY.

2597. ℞ Oxymellis Scillæ,
Misturæ Acaciæ,
Syrupi Tolutani, ana ℥ss.
Tinct. Opii, ♏xx.
Mix: fʒj frequently during the day.

In Chronic Catarrh.—Dr. GREGORY.

2598. ℞ Tinct. Digitalis, ʒj.
Oxymellis Scillæ, ℥ss.
Tinct. Opii, ʒss.
Aquæ, ℥vss.
Mix: make a mixture. One-sixth part for a dose.

Expectorant.—Dr. HOOPER.

2599. ℞ Ext. Glycyrr. ʒij.
Potass. Nitrat. ʒss.
Syrupi Scillæ, ʒiij.
Morph. Acet. gr. j.
Aquæ, ℥iv.
Mix. A dessertspoonful twice a day.

Mr. H. CLARK.

2600. ℞ Potassæ Nitratis, ʒj.
Mist. Amygdalæ, ℥vj.
Spirit. Juniperi co. ℥iss.
Aceti Scillæ, ʒvj.
Mix: make a mixture. A tablespoonful as occasion requires.

Diuretic.—Mr. SAVORY.

2601. ℞ Ammon. Muriatis,
Succi Glycyrr. inspiss. ana ʒj.
Aquæ fontanæ, ℥v. Dissolve, and add
Vini Antimonii, ʒij.
Oxymel. Scillæ, ℥ss.
Mix: make a febrifuge mixture.

HECKER.

2602. ℞ Oxymellis simplicis,
Oxymellis Scillæ,
Syrupi Papaveris,
Spirit. Ætheris Nitrici, ana ʒij.
Acidi Nit. diluti, ♏xl.
Aquæ destil. ad ℥iij.
Two tablespoonfuls for a dose.

Dr. BABINGTON.

2603. ℞ Sodæ Sesquicarb. gr. xx.
Vini Ipecacuan. gtt. xv.
Tinct Scillæ, gtt. x–xx.
Aquæ, ad ℥iss.
Mix: make a draught. To be taken three times a day.

In Chronic Bronchitis.—Dr. BUDD.

2604. ℞ Aceti Scillæ, ʒss.
Spirit. Ætheris Nit. ʒj.
Decoct. Scoparii co.
Decoct. Senegæ, ana ʒv.
Make a diuretic draught. To be taken three times a day.

Dr. PARIS.

2605. ℞ Oxymellis Scillæ, ʒij.
Syrupi Papaveris, ʒj.
Tinct. Camph. co. ʒss.
Tinct. æther. Lobel. inf. ʒss.
Mist. Ammoniaci, ℥j. Mix: make a draught.

In the Fit of Asthma.—Mr. SAVORY.

2606. ℞ Tinct. Jalapæ, ʒij.
Aceti Scillæ, ʒj.
Aquæ Menth. vir. ℥iss.
Mix: make a diuretic draught.

Dr. COPLAND.

2607. ℞ Oxymel. Scillæ, ℥j.
Vini Antimonii, ʒij.
Mix: fʒj every fifteen minutes, until effectual.

Emetic in Catarrhal Affections of Children.
Dr. UNDERWOOD

2608. ℞ Tinct. Scillæ, ʒiss.
Sodæ Carbonatis, gr. xij.
Aquæ Fœniculi, ℥iss.
Syrupi Tolutani,
Syrupi Croci, ana ʒij.
Tinct. Camphoræ co. ʒss.
Mix: fʒj to fʒij every third hour.

In Chronic Bronchitis of Children.
Drs. EVANSON and MAUNSELL.

2609 ℞ Pulv. Scillæ,
Pulv. Polygalæ Senegæ, ana ℥j.
Aquæ, lbj. Boil, and strain; then add
Mellis despum. lbss.
Mix: make a syrup, to each ounce of which add a grain of tartar emetic. (Dose, according to age, from ten drops to a teaspoonful or more, every fifteen minutes, as an emetic for children; and every hour or two as an expectorant.)

In Pulmonary Affections of Children.
Dr. COXE'S *Hive Syrup.*

2610. ℞ Syrupi Scillæ,
Syrupi Papaveris, ana ʒij.
Decocti Senegæ, ʒj.
Aquæ Ammon. Acet. ℥ss.
Mix: fʒj to fʒij every second hour.

In advanced stages of Pneumonia in Children.
Drs. EVANSON and MAUNSELL.

SCOPARIUS. *Broom.*

The fresh tops of the *Cytisus* (*Spartium*, or *Sarothamnus*) *Scoparius* (Nat. Ord. *Leguminosæ*) have been long used in medicine. Broom has a bitter taste and peculiar odor. It is a good diuretic, and therefore used frequently in dropsies, alone or in combination. In large doses it proves cathartic and emetic.

Extractum Scoparii (made by evaporating the decoction): ten grains to half a drachm.

Infusum Scoparii (L. 1836). Dose, two to four ounces, three times a day.

Decoctum Scoparii (D.): one to two ounces.

Decoctum Scoparii compositum (L.). A good diuretic, in doses of one to three ounces.

2611. ℞ Florum Scoparii, ℥j.
Sacchari albi, ℥ij.
Rub up together and form a confection. Dose, ʒj to ʒij.
In Gout and Rheumatism.—VAN MONS.

2612. ℞ Spartii cacuminis concis. ℥j.
Aquæ, Oj. Boil to half a pint, and add
Spirit. Æth. Nit.
Syrupi Zingib. ana ℥j. A wineglassful for a dose.
Diuretic in Dropsies.—Dr. HOOPER.

2613. ℞ Infus. Scoparii, ℥iiiss.
Liq. Ammon. Acet. ℥ij.
Tinct. Scillæ, ʒij.
Tinct. Camph. co. ʒvj.
Make a mixture. Three tablespoonfuls every third hour.
Diuretic.—Dr. PARIS.

SENEGA. *Seneka.*

The root of *Polygala Senega*, a North American plant (Nat. Ord. *Polygalaceæ*). It is a very good stimulating expectorant and diaphoretic, and proves emetic in large doses. It is much used in the latter stages of Pneumonia, and in Chronic Bronchitis, especially in the old and debilitated, and is frequently combined with preparations of Ammonia in these complaints. It has been given as an emmenagogue, and as a stimulant in low and typhoid fevers. Dose of the powder, ten grains to one scruple.

Infusum Senegæ (E.): one to three ounces.
Decoctum Senegæ (L.): one to three ounces.
Pilulæ Senegæ (Radius): six to twelve, three times a day.
Syrupus Senegæ (U. S.): one to two drachms.

2614. ℞ Pulv. Senegæ, ℥ss.
Cremoris Tartari, ʒvj.
Magnesiæ, ʒij.
Mix: make a powder. Take ʒj twice a day.
In Pannus of the Eye.—RADIUS.

2615. ℞ Pulv. rad. Senegæ,
Sacchari albi, ana gr. xij.
Camphoræ rasæ, gr. ij.
Mix: make a powder. Dispense three such doses. One powder, at intervals of two hours.
In Chronic Affections of the Chest.—Dr. COPLAND.

2616. ℞ Pulv. Senegæ, gr. xxx.
Sodæ Carb. sicc. gr. vj.
Pulv. Scillæ, gr. j.
Sacchari puri, gr. xij.
Mix: divide into 6 powders. One every four hours.

In advanced stages of Hooping-cough and Bronchitis in Children. Dr. NELIGAN.

2617. ℞ Decoct. Senegæ, ℥iss.
Ammon. Carb. gr. v–x.
Mix: make a draught. To be taken three times a day.

In the Bronchitis of Old Persons.

2618. ℞ Decoct. Senegæ, ℥viss.
Mucilag. Acaciæ, ʒiv.
Syrupi Tolutani, ℥j.
Mix: make a mixture. Three tablespoonfuls every three hours.

In Catarrh with excessive Secretion and Debility.—Dr. JOY.

2619. ℞ Decocti Senegæ, ℥iij.
Mist. Amygdalæ, ℥vj.
Tinct. Opii, gtt. viij. Mix: f℥ij three times a day.

In Chronic Coughs.—Dr. BAILLIE.

2620. ℞ Decocti Senegæ, ℥iij.
Liq. Ammon. Acet.
Mist. Acaciæ,
Syrupi Papaveris, ana ℥j.
Mix; make a mixture. ℥j for a dose.

Chronic Bronchitis.—Dr. HOOPER.

2621. ℞ Decocti Senegæ, ℥iv.
Vini Antimonii, ℈ij.
Syrupi Althææ, ℥j. Mix: a teaspoonful frequently.

Expectorant in the Second Stage of Croup.—WENDT.

2622. ℞ Decocti Senegæ, ℥ij. ʒv.
Ammoniæ Carbonatis, gr. viij.
Tinct. Scillæ, gtt. xvj.
Syrupi Tolutani, ʒij.
Mix: fʒiij in milk, every fourth hour.

In advanced stages of Croup, in Children from three to four years old. Dr. WEST.

2623. ℞ Decocti Senegæ, ℥j.
Liq. Ammon. Acet. ʒss.
Syrupi Scillæ, ʒij.
Syrupi Papaveris, ʒij.
Mix. From fʒj to fʒij every three hours.

For very young Infants, in advanced stages of Pertussis and Chronic Bronchitis. Dr. JOY.

SENNA.

This name is applied to the dried leaflets of several species of *Cassia* (Nat. Ord. *Leguminosæ*), growing chiefly in Africa and India. The Alexandrian and Bombay Sennas are the most frequently used. Senna is the most commonly employed of all cathartics. It is sure and safe; rather heating in its operation, but less irritant than the drastic cathartics. It frequently causes nausea and griping. It is inappropriate when there is much irritation or fever; and is generally avoided in pregnancy, or during the existence of hæmorrhoids. It is in general quite safe in children and elderly persons, and useful in all cases in which we desire to unload the bowels by a tolerably active purge. It is generally combined with some saline cathartic. The dose of the powdered leaves (seldom given) is from half to two drachms.

Infusum Sennæ compositum (L., D.) is a good purge in doses of one to three ounces.

Infusum Sennæ cum Tamarindis (E.): one and a half to three ounces.

Infusum Sennæ cum Coffeâ (Foy). *Café au Séné.* Dose, three ounces.

Liquor Sennæ (see Pocket Formulary). One drachm equals one ounce of the infusion.

Syrupus Sennæ (L., E.): one to two drachms for children.

Tinctura Sennæ composita (L., E., D.): one drachm to half an ounce.

Confectio Sennæ (L., E., D.): one drachm to half an ounce. A mild laxative.

Enema catharticum (E., D.).

2624. ℞ Pulv. Sennæ,
Pulv. Guaiaci, ana equal parts.
(Two teaspoonfuls to be taken twice or thrice daily.)

In Jaundice.—AUGUSTIN.

2625. ℞ Pulv. Sennæ, ʒj.
Extr. Taraxaci, q. s. to make 30 pills. (Dose, five to eight.)

Alterative Purge.—HUFELAND.

2626. ℞ Confect. Sennæ, ℥j.
Sulph. sublim. ℥ss.
Syrupi Tolutani, q. s. to make an electuary. Two teaspoonfuls frequently.

In Hæmorrhoids.

2627. ℞ Potassæ Sulph. ʒiv.
Sulphuris sublim. ʒij.
Electuarii Sennæ, ℥ij.
Syrupi, q. s.
Mix: make an electuary. A dessertspoonful every night.

In Piles.—Dr. W. AINSLIE.

2628. ℞ Conf. Sennæ, ℥iss.
Pulv. Jalapæ, ʒss.
Sulph. ℥ss.
Syrupi Sennæ, q. s. to make an electuary, which is to be taken with an equal quantity of nutmeg three times a day, or until the bowels are well opened.

For Hæmorrhoids.—Dr. PARIS.

2629. ℞ Conf. Sennæ, ℥iss.
Potassæ Supertart. ʒij.
Pulv. Jalapæ, ʒss.
Syrupi, q. s.
Mix: make an electuary. A teaspoonful morning and evening, as occasion may require.

Dr. THOMAS.

2630. ℞ Electuarii Sennæ, ℥ij.
Pulv. Pot. Supertart. ℥ss.
Carbonatis Ferri, ʒij.
Syrupi Zingib. q. s. to make an electuary. Take ʒj in the middle of the day and at night.

In Habitual Constipation.—Dr. GRAVES.

2631. ℞ Confect. Sennæ, ℥iss.
Ferri Tartarizati, ℈ij.
Syrupi Zingib. ʒiij. Mix: make an electuary.

Mild Aperient and Tonic.—Dr. JOY.

2632. ℞ Infusi Sennæ co. ℥v.
Magnesiæ Sulph. ℥j.
Tinct. Sennæ,
Tinct. Jalapæ,
Syrupi Zingib. ana ʒiij. Mix: make an aperient mixture.

(The *black draught* of most hospitals, given in doses of ℥iss–℥ij, some hours after an aperient pill, powder, or bolus, to accelerate their operation, at the commencement of many inflammatory affections, &c.)

2633. ℞ Sennæ, ʒiij.
Theæ Bohea, ʒj.
Zingib. concis. ℈j.
Aquæ destil. ferv. ℥iv.
Macerate for an hour in a lightly closed vessel, and strain. Then,

℞ Colaturæ, ʒx.
Tinct. Sennæ,
Tinct. Jalapæ, ana ʒj.
Syrupi Sennæ, ʒj.
Make a draught, to be taken the first thing in the morning.

Black Draught.—Dr. PARIS.

2634. ℞ Infusi Sennæ co. ℥j.
Pulv. Rhei, ℈j.
Tinct. Sennæ,
Tinct. Card. co.
Syrupi Zingib. ana ʒj.
Mix: make a draught, to be taken the following morning. (To be preceded by a pill containing three grains of Blue Pill and two of Ipecacuanha, taken at bedtime.)

In Torpidity of Liver.—Dr. GREGORY.

2635. ℞ Infusi Sennæ, ℥j.
Tinct. Sennæ, ℥ss.
Confect. Scammonii, ʒj. Mix: make a purging draught.

Dr. E. J. CLARK.

2636. ℞ Magnesiæ Sulph. ℥ss.
Infusi Sennæ co. ℥iss.
Tinct. Sennæ co. ℥ss. Mix: make an aperient draught.

A strong Purge.—Dr. HOOPER.

2637. ℞ Pulv. Rhei, gr. x.
Potassæ Tart. ℥ss.
Infusi Sennæ comp. ℥iss.
Syrupi Aurantii,
Tinct. Cardam. co. ana ʒij.
Mix: make an aperient draught.

A good Purge for Robust Persons.—Dr. HOOPER.

2638. ℞ Infusi Sennæ, ʒx.
Pulv. Colchici, gr. viij.
Tinct. Jalapæ, ʒj.
Syrupi Mori, ʒj. Mix: make a cathartic draught.

In Acute Rheumatism.—Dr. GREGORY.

2639. ℞ Sennæ foliorum, ʒvj.
Zingib. concis. ʒss.
Extr. Glycyrrhizæ, ʒij.
Aquæ ferventis, ℥ix.
Infuse. After three hours, strain, and add
Spiritus Ammon. aromatici, ʒij.
Tinct. Sennæ,
Tinct. Cardamomi compos. ana ℥ss. (Dose, ℥iss.)

Common Purgative.—Dr. DRUITT.

2640. ℞ Olei Menth. vir. ♏x.
Olei Menth. pip. ♏v.
Sacchari purif. ʒiij. Mix: then add
Infusi Sennæ, ℥vij.
Sodæ Sulph. ℥j.
Tinct. Sennæ, ʒv.
Spirit. Ammon. arom. ʒiij.
Mix: make a mixture. A fourth part every three hours until the bowels operate.

Warm Saline Purge.—Dr. COPLAND.

2641. ℞ Infusi Sennæ cum Tamarindis, ℥iss.
Syrupi Rhei, ℥ij.
Spirit. Nucis Moschatæ, ℥ss.
Mix: make a mixture. Two tablespoonfuls every two hours until it operates.

In Simple Constipation of the Old and Debilitated.
Dr. NELIGAN.

2642. ℞ Infusi Sennæ, ℥ivss.
Tinct. Sennæ, ℥j.
Liq. Antim. Tart. ʒij.
Syrupi Rosæ, ʒij.
Mix: make a mixture. A wineglassful, to be repeated until the bowels are well opened.

At commencement of Ague.—Dr. E. J. CLARK.

2643. ℞ Infusi Sennæ co. ℥v.
Potassæ Tartratis, ℥j.
Tinct. Jalapæ,
Tinct. Sennæ co. ana ʒiij.
Syrupi Rhamni, ʒij.
Mix: a fourth part every four hours until the bowels are freely opened.

In Phrenitis.—Dr. GREGORY.

2644. ℞ Sodæ et Potassæ Tartratis, ℥ij.
Infusi Sennæ, ℥iv.
Infusi Lini, lbiss. Mix: f℥iv every hour.

In Hæmatemesis.—Dr. J. HAMILTON.

2645. ℞ Infusi Sennæ, ℥ij.
Magnes. Sulph. ʒv.
Infusi Lini, ℥iv. Mix: f℥ij every hour.

In Hæmatemesis.—Dr. J. HAMILTON.

2646. ℞ Infusi Sennæ,
Aquæ Pimentæ, ana ℥j.
Potassæ Tart. ʒij.
Tinct. Cort. Aurantii, ʒj.
Mix: one to two teaspoonfuls every three hours.

Purgative for Children.—Mr. SAVORY.

2647. ℞ Infusi Sennæ co. ℥xv.
Potassæ Tart. ʒij.
Extr. Glycyrrhizæ, ℈ss.
Tinct. Card. co. ʒj.
Spirit. Ammon. arom. ♏xij.
Make a mixture: dose, fʒij to fʒiv.

Purgative for Children.—Dr. UNDERWOOD.

2648. ℞ Infusi Sennæ, ℥j.
Aquæ Menthæ pip. ℥ss.
Mannæ, ʒij. Mix well; strain, and add
Magnesiæ, ℈j.
Tinct. Rhei, ʒj.
Syrupi Rosæ, ʒij.
Mix: make a mixture. Dose, from fʒj to fʒij every second or third hour until catharsis is produced.

Purgative for young Children.—Drs. EVANSON and MAUNSELL.

2649. ℞ Infusi Sennæ, ℥j.
Tinct. Sennæ, ʒij.
Tinct. Aurantii, ʒj.
Aquæ, ℥j.
Mix: make a mixture. Take from fʒj to fʒij every third hour until it operates.

For Infants.—Drs. EVANSON and MAUNSELL.

2650. ℞ Sennæ foliorum, ℥ss.
Aquæ ferventis, lbj. Macerate and strain. Add
Sodæ Sulph. ℥ss.
Vini Antim. P. Tart. ℥j.
Mix: make an enema.

In Painters' Colic.—Dr. JOY.

2651. ℞ Coffeæ tostæ,
Fructûs Sennæ, āā ℥ss.
(Make an infusion of the coffee in the usual way, then infuse the senna, strain, and mix. Take with milk and sugar, according to taste.)

An agreeable Purge for Children.—TROUSSEAU and REVEIL.

SERPENTARIA. *Serpentary. Virginia Snakeroot.*

This root is produced by the *Aristolochia Serpentaria*, and other species of the same genus, growing in North America (Nat. Ord. *Aristolochiaceæ*). It occurs in slender fibers with a knotted head, and has a camphoreous taste. Serpentary is an aromatic tonic and diaphoretic, in large doses laxative and nauseant. It was once much esteemed as an antiperiodic in agues. It is sometimes given in combination with various stimulants and diaphoretics, in typhoid and other fevers. The dose of the powder is from ten to thirty grains.

Infusum Serpentariæ (L., E.): one to two ounces every two hours in low fevers.

Tinctura Serpentariæ (L., E.): one to three drachms.

2652. ℞ Pulv. Serpentariæ, gr. xxiv.
Camphoræ, gr. xlviij.
Confect. Rosæ, q. s. to make 18 pills.
To be all taken during the apyrexia.

In Malignant Intermittents.—FOY.

2653. ℞ Infus. Serpentariæ, ʒix.
Ammon. Sesquicarb. gr. v.
Syrupi, ʒj.
Mix: make a draught. To be taken twice a day.

To produce Diaphoresis in Fevers, &c.—Dr. PARIS.

2654. ℞ Liq. Sodæ Chlorin. ʒiiss.
Infusi Serpentariæ, ℥vj.
Syrupi Aurantii, ℥iss.
Mix: make a mixture. Two tablespoonfuls every four hours.

In advanced stages of Typhoid Fever.—Dr. NELIGAN.

2655. ℞ Infusi Serpentariæ, ℥vj.
Tinct. Camph. co. ʒv.
Spirit. Ammon. aromat. ʒiiss.
Syrupi Aurantii, ℥j.
Mix. A fourth part every three or four hours.

Dr. COPLAND.

2656. ℞ Infusi Serpentariæ, ʒvj.
Mist. Camphoræ, ʒiv.
Syrupi Aurantii, ʒj.
Tinct. Cinchonæ co. ʒj.
Ammon. Sesquicarb. gr. iij.
Mix: make a mixture. To be repeated every six hours.

In Fevers with Collapse and Putrescence.—Dr. GREGORY.

2657. ℞ Rad. Serpentariæ, ℥ss.
Cort. Cinchonæ pulv. ʒvj.
Cort. Aurantii sicc. ʒij.
Aquæ, lbiss. Boil to lbj, and add to the strained liquor
Tinct. Cinnamomi, ℥j.

Aromatic Tonic.—Dr. COPLAND.

2658. ℞ Rad. Senegæ,
Rad. Serpentariæ, ana ℥ss.
Aquæ fervidæ, Oj. Macerate in a closed vase for an hour and strain. To the strained liquor add
Camphoræ, ʒss (first dissolved in Ætheris Sulph. ʒiij).
Aquæ Cinnam. ℥j.
Syrupi Altheæ,
Syrupi Papav. ana ℥ss.
Mix. Two tablespoonfuls every four hours.

Diaphoretic.—HECKER.

SIMARUBA.

This is the bark of *Simaruba officinalis* (or *amara*), a large tree growing in Jamaica and South America, and belonging to the Nat. Ord. *Simarubaceæ*. It much resembles Quassia in its medicinal action, as well as in habitat and botanic affinity. But it is not quite so pure a bitter, as it contains some mucilage, like Calumba, and also a trace of gallic acid. In large doses it irritates, causing vomiting and purging, like other bitters. It is used in all cases where a simple tonic is required. It is much employed in Germany during the latter stages of dysentery and diarrhœa. It is not given in substance.

Infusum Simarubæ (E., D.): one to two ounces as a tonic.

2659. ℞ Pulv. Simarubæ,
Pulv. Absinthii, ana ʒij.
Aquæ ferventis, Oj. Infuse for a quarter of an hour, strain, and add
Syrupi Gentianæ, ℥j. Mix. (In wineglassful doses.)

Foy.

2660. ℞ Pulv. rad. Simarubæ, ℥ss.
Corticis Granati cont. ʒij.
Aquæ ferventis, ℥xij.
Mix: let it stand for two hours, and then add to the strained liquor
Conf. aromat. ʒj.
Tinct. Cardam. c. ℥j.
Mix: make a mixture. Three tablespoonfuls three or four times a day.

Dr. Thomas.

2661. ℞ Inf. Simarubæ, ℥iss.
Acid. Nit. dil. ♏iv.
Infus. Caryophylli, ℥ss.
Tinct. Opii, ♏vj.
Mix. One or two teaspoonfuls three or four times a day, in a decoction of barley.

In the Diarrhœa of Children.—Dr. Baillie.

SINAPIS. *Mustard.*

Black Mustard seeds are yielded by *Sinapis nigra* (Nat. Ord. *Cruciferæ*). When bruised and mixed with water, they yield a pungent smell and taste, owing to the formation of an acrid volatile oil. White Mustard is produced by *Sinapis alba*, also an indigenous plant. The seeds contain an acrid principle, and a fixed oil. Mustard seeds are sometimes used internally in medicine, on account of their stimulant and carminative properties. They excite the stomach, and rouse the system, when either is weak or torpid. In a large dose they are emetic, acting speedily, and thus being appropriate in cases of poisoning. The seeds of mustard, given whole, stimulate the intestinal canal, and act as laxatives. But mustard is chiefly used externally, on account of its irritant and rubefacient properties. A mustard poultice is useful as a stimulant. Applied over the seat of an internal inflammation or local pain, it forms one of the best counter-irritants. It is particularly used in disorders of the chest, belly, and throat. Mustard lotions and ointments are used for local friction in paralysis, and as applications to chilblains, &c. A mustard footbath is of use to rouse the system in cases of paralysis, poisoning, or torpor from any cause. Dose of the flour, as a stimulant, one scruple to two drachms; as emetic, half an ounce to one ounce.

Cataplasma Sinapis (L.) is a good form for mustard poultice. Lukewarm water will suffice. When the mustard flour is good, it is wrong to use vinegar.

2662. ℞ Cataplasmatis Lini, ℥iv.
Farinæ Sinapis, ℥ss. Mix.

Milder Mustard Poultice.—Dr. Copland.

2663. ℞ Pulv. Sinapis, lbss.
Pulv. Capsici annui,
Pulv. Zingiberis, ana ʒj.
Acid. Acet. pyrolig. q. s. to form a cataplasm. Then add
Olei Terebinth. ℥ij. Mix.

Stronger Mustard Poultice.—Dr. Copland.

2664. ℞ Pulv. Sinapis, ʒij.
Aquæ ferventis, ℥xvj.
Mix: make an injection. Use daily.

In Carcinomatous Ulceration of the Womb.—Dr. Ashwell.

2665. ℞ Farinæ Sinapis, ℥iv.
Aquæ calidæ, q. s. Mix: make a footbath.

As a Derivative in Cerebral and other Diseases.—Beral.

2666. ℞ Farinæ Sinapis, ʒj.
Aquæ Angelicæ,
Aquæ Hyssopi, ana ℥vj.
Spirit. Armoraciæ, ℥ss.
Aquæ Ammon. Mur. ℈iv.
Mellis Rosæ, ℥iv. Mix: make a gargle.

Stimulant in Diseases of the Mouth and Throat.—Spielmann.

2667. ℞ Decocti Papaveris fervent. Oij.
Sinapis, ℥iij.

Mix. Place over the stomach and belly a woolen cloth, well imbued with this liquor warm, and afterward slightly pressed out; and renew it again and again, until the pain is relieved.

For Pain in the Stomach and Bowels.—Dr. PARIS.

2668. ℞ Sinapis Olei (volatilis), gtt. ij.
P. Gum. Acaciæ, ʒij.
Syr. Aurantii, ʒiv.
Aquæ, ℥vss.

Mix: make a mixture. A tablespoonful every second hour.

Stimulant.

2669. ℞ Sinapis contusæ, ℥j.
Lactis Vaccini, Oj.

Boil together, until the cheesy part remains coagulated; then strain the liquor.

℞ Of the strained liquor, a wineglassful.
Syrupi Zingiberis, ʒj.

Make a draught, to be taken two or three times a day.

Stimulant.—Dr. PARIS.

2670. ℞ Sem. Sinapis albæ cont.
Radicis Armoraciæ, ana ℥ij.
Corticis Aurantii, ℥ss.
Aquæ Aurantii, ℥ss.
Aquæ fontanæ, Oij.

Boil to Oj, and strain; make a decoction. A large wineglassful three times a day.

In old Palsy.—Dr. THOMAS.

SODÆ CARBONAS ET BICARBONAS. *Carbonate and Bicarbonate of Soda.*

An impure carbonate of soda is known under the names of Kelp and Barilla, the former obtained by burning sea-weed in Scotland, the other by the combustion of land plants growing on the sea-shore of the Mediterranean. The carbonate is also manufactured in large quantities from common salt. Its crystals tend to effloresce in the air. It is antacid and antilithic, being used in dyspepsia, heartburn, flatulence, gouty and rheumatic affections, and cases of lithic deposit in the urine. Though in large doses an irritant poison, it is less corrosive than the same salt of potash. It is diuretic and diaphoretic. It is given as an antiphlogistic in coughs and mild inflammations. By passing a current of carbonic acid gas through the carbonate in powder, the Bicarbonate of Soda is formed. It is used for the same purposes as the other, but is milder and less corrosive. It is more adapted for effervescing draughts. (See *Sodæ Citras.*) The dose of either of the carbonates is from one to ten grains for children, and ten grains to one drachm for adults.

Sodæ Carbonas exsiccata (L., E., D.): dose, five to twenty grains.

Liquor Sodæ Carbonatis (D.), one to two drachms.

Aqua Sodæ effervescens (E.), "Soda water." An agreeable antacid drink.

Trochisci Sodæ Bicarbonatis (E.).

The following prescriptions contain the Carbonate of Soda as given for internal use.

2671. ℞ Pulv. Cinchonæ,
Sodæ Subcarbonatis, ana partes æquales.
Mix: dose, from five grains to ℈ss, two or three times a day.
Dr. Copland.

2672. ℞ Pulv. Rhei, gr. vj.
Sodæ Carbonatis, gr. xv.
Pulv. Calumbæ, gr. iv.
Mix: make a powder. To be taken before dinner.
In the Gouty Diathesis.—Dr. Day.

2673. ℞ Sodæ Carbonat. sicc. ʒss.
Pulv. Myrrhæ, gr. xviij.
Pulv. Ipecacuanhæ, gr. iij.
Mix: divide into 6 powders. One every fourth hour.
Antacid in Chronic Diarrhœa and Dysentery.—Dr. Neligan.

2674. ℞ Sodæ Subcarb. exsic. ℈iiss.
Pulv. Rhei, ʒj.
Extr. Hyoscyami, ℈ij.
Mix: divide into 36 pills. Two, three times a day.
In Acid Dyspepsia.—Dr. Copland.

2675. ℞ Sodæ Subcarb. exsic. ʒj.
Saponis Castil. ℈iv.
Olei Juniperi, ♏v.
Syrupi Zingib. ʒss.
Mix, and divide into 30 pills. Two or three daily.
In Lithic Acid Deposits.—Mr. Savory.

2676. ℞ Sodæ Carbonatis, ʒij–℥ss.
Aquæ calidæ, Oij.
Dissolve: make a drink. To be taken ad libitum.
During the passage of Gall-Stones.—Dr. Prout.

2677. ℞ Sodæ Subcarb. ʒss–ʒj.
Decoct. Hordei, Oj. Dissolve: dose, four glasses daily.

In Lichen, Prurigo, and other Skin Diseases attended with Itching. Dr. Burgess.

2678. ℞ Sodæ Subcarb. ʒij.
Syrupi Violæ tricoloris, ℥xij.
Mix: a tablespoonful night and morning. (Apply at the same time to the part a poultice containing ʒj of Sulphur.)

In Impetigo.—M. Biett.

2679. ℞ Bismuth Trisnit.
Magnes. Carb.
Sodæ Carb. ana ʒj.
Tinct. Cardam. co. ℥ss.
Aquæ destil. ad ℥vj. Mix: a sixth part for a dose.

2680. ℞ Mist. Camphoræ, ℥viss.
Sodæ Subcarb. ʒiss.
Ammon. Carb. ℈j.
Tinct. Calumbæ, ℥ss.
Spirit. Anisi,
Tinct. Card. co. ana ℥ss.
Mix: make a mixture. Two tablespoonfuls two or three times a day.

In Cardialgia with Acidity.—Dr. Copland.

Bicarbonate of Soda given internally.

2681. ℞ Sodæ Bicarbonatis, gr. iij.
Pulv. Cinchonæ, ℈j.
Mix: make a powder. To be taken three times a day.

Tonic and Antacid.—Dr. Druitt.

2682. ℞ Sodæ Bicarbonatis, gr. iij.
Ferri Sesquioxidi, ℈j.
Pulv. Rhei, gr. iij.
Mix: make a powder. To be taken three times a day.

Tonic and Antacid.—Dr. Druitt.

2683. ℞ Sodæ Sesquicarbonatis, ℈j.
Pulv. Opii, gr. iij.
Mix: make a bolus. To be taken immediately. (To be washed down with another scruple of soda, in a wineglassful of water as hot as the patient can swallow it. In the evening another scruple with two grains of opium, if necessary.)

In Asiatic Cholera.—Dr. Maxwell.

2684. ℞ Sodæ Bicarbonatis, ʒij.
Misturæ Camphoræ, ℥viij.
Mix: make a mixture. Two tablespoonfuls every three hours. (A hot bath containing ℥ij of Carb. Soda may be used at bedtime.)

In Acute Rheumatism.—Dr. Wright.

2685. ℞ Sodæ Bicarb. gr. xv.
Acid. Hydrocyan. Scheelii, gtt. iss.
Mist. Camphoræ, ℥x.
Mix: make a draught. To be taken three times a day after meals.
In Acid Dyspepsia.—Dr. CHAMBERS.

2686. ℞ Sodæ Sesquicarbonatis, ʒss.
Ammon. Sesquicarb. gr. v.
Tinct. Calumbæ, ʒj.
Inf. Gentianæ co. ℥iss.
Mix: make a draught. To be taken twice a day.
In Cancer.—Sir A. COOPER.

2687. ℞ Sodæ Bicarbonatis, gr. x.
Infusi Calumbæ, ℥iss.
Aquæ Laurocerasi, ♏xij.
Creasoti, ♏j.
Mix: make a draught. To be taken every six hours, until three or four doses are taken, if necessary.
In Acidity of the Stomach with Vomiting.—Dr. NELIGAN.

2688. ℞ Sodæ Bicarbonatis,
Sulphuris præcipitati, ana ℈j.
Tinct. Lavand. co. ʒij.
Aquæ, ℥vj.
Mix: make a mixture. A fourth part every second or third hour.
In ordinary Diarrhœa preceding Cholera.—Mr. J. GROVE.

2689. ℞ Sodæ Bicarbonatis, ʒij.
Ammon. Carb. ℈ij.
Ext. Taraxaci, ℥ss.
Spir. Ætheris Nit. ʒvj.
Tinct. Cardam. co. ℥j.
Aquæ Menthæ pip. ad ℥xij.
Take f℥iss three times a day. (With some blue pill and Colchicum at bedtime.)
In Palpitation of the Heart.

The Carbonate and Bicarbonate of Soda for external use.

2690. ℞ Sodæ Carbonatis, gr. xij.
Aquæ destillatæ, ℥xij. Mix.
To be used as a wash in Acne and other Skin Diseases.
Dr. NELIGAN.

2691. ℞ Sodæ Sesquicarb. ʒij.
Aquæ, Oiss.
Mix: make a lotion. (Lint saturated with this liquid is to be placed over the affected part, and the whole covered with oiled silk.)
In Eczema.—Dr. BENNETT.

2692. ℞ Sodæ Carb.
Sodæ Biborat. ana ℥v.
Aquæ pluvialis (caloris grad. 76°–98° F.) Cong. xxx.
Dissolve. An alkaline bath.

In many Skin Diseases.—Dr. NELIGAN.

2693. ℞ Sodæ Carb. gr. xx–ʒj.
Axungiæ, ℥j. Mix: make an ointment.

In Eruptive Diseases of the Scalp.—Dr. NELIGAN.

2694. ℞ Sodæ Bicarb. gr. xx.
Adipis præp. ℥j.
Chloroformylis, ♏iv. Mix: make an ointment.

In Impetigo.—Dr. NELIGAN.

2695. ℞ Sodæ Carb. ʒx.
Calcis, ʒv.
Axungiæ, ℥v.
Mix: make an ointment. (*Pommade Epilatoire.*)

To remove Hair in the treatment of Porrigo favosa.
M. CAZENAVE.

SODÆ ACETAS, CITRAS, TARTRAS. *Acetate, Citrate, and Tartrate of Soda.* (*Effervescing Draughts.*)

The Acetate occurs in white foliaceous masses. It is efflorescent. It is a very soluble salt, and has a pungent and bitter taste. In small doses it is diuretic, and is used for this purpose in dropsies. In large doses it is cathartic. Dose, as a diuretic, one scruple to one drachm; as a purge, two to four drachms.

The neutral Citrate and Tartrate are formed when an effervescing draught is made of either of the carbonates with Citric or Tartaric Acid. Such a draught is an agreeable refrigerant and diaphoretic, and may be prescribed in the same instances as one containing potash. The following proportions must be observed in prescribing:

One scruple of Carbonate of Soda will require to neutralize it ten grains of crystallized Citric or Tartaric Acid, or two and a half drachms of Lemon Juice.

One scruple of Bicarbonate of Soda will require seventeen grains of Citric Acid, eighteen of Tartaric Acid, or four and a half drachms of Lemon Juice.

Pulveres effervescentes (E., D.). These must be kept in different colored papers, and consist of Tartaric or Citric Acid, and Bicarbonate of Soda (or Potash), in the proportion to form an effervescing draught when two are mixed in a tumbler of water.

2696. ℞ Sodæ Acetatis,
Pulveris Rhei,
Fellis bovis inspiss. ana ʒj.
Pulveris Acaciæ, ʒss.
Mix, and divide into 2-grain pills. (Dose, 10–15 twice a day.
Laxative.—AUGUSTIN.

2697. ℞ Sodæ Sesquicarb. gr. xx.
Syrup. Aurant. ʒj.
Aquæ, ℥iss.
Mix: make a draught. To be taken with half an ounce of lemon-juice.
To relieve Nausea and Vomiting.—Dr. JOY.

2698. ℞ Sodæ Bicarb. ʒss.
Sodæ Sulph. siccat. ʒj. Mix.

℞ Acidi Citrici, gr. xv.
(Dissolve each powder separately, mix the solutions in a tumbler, and drink while effervescing.)
Dr. A. T. THOMSON.

SODÆ BIBORAS. See BORAX.

SODÆ ET POTASSÆ TARTRAS. *Potassio-Tartrate of Soda.*

This is made by adding Cream of Tartar to a solution of Carbonate of Soda. It is called *Rochelle Salt.* It is a mild and cooling purgative, in small doses diuretic. It may cause some griping, if given alone, but it is generally combined with infusion of Senna. Or it may be given as a Seidlitz powder —*i.e.* in effervescence, with some tartaric acid and bicarbonate of soda. In either of these forms it is an antiphlogistic cathartic, less irritating than the Sulphates of Soda and Magnesia, and well adapted for use in inflammatory complaints, and for children and delicate persons. It acts upon the urine as an alkali. Dose, as a diuretic, one scruple to one drachm; as a cathartic, two drachms to one ounce.

Pulveres effervescentes aperientes (Ellis). Seidlitz powders, containing Rochelle salt along with Bicarbonate of Soda and Tartaric acid. Two are mixed in water, and taken during effervescence.

2699. ℞ Sodæ Tartarizatæ, gr. x.
Pulv. Rhei, gr iij–vij.
Mix: make a powder. To be taken every morning for two weeks.
In Enlargements of the Mesentery in Children.
Dr. FORDYCE.

2700. ℞ Sodæ Tartarizatæ, ℥j.
Aquæ Menthæ vir. ℥vj.
Aquæ Cinnamomi, ℥ij.
Mix: make a mixture. Two spoonfuls every hour until it operates.

2701. ℞ Tartratis Potassæ et Sodæ, ʒvj.
Jusculi bovini (beef tea), lbj.
Mix: make a solution. To be consumed in divided doses.

In Chorea of Children about nine years of age.
Dr. J. HAMILTON.

2702. ℞ Infusi Sennæ C. ℥ij.
Sodæ Potassio-tart. ℥ss.
Infusi Calumbæ, ℥iss.
Mix: make a solution. To be taken in two doses.

Dr. PARIS.

2703. ℞ Sodæ Tartarizatæ, ℥j.
Extracti Hyoscyami, gr. vj.
Syrupi Anthemidis, ℥j.
Aquæ, ℥vj.
Mix: make a mixture. A tablespoonful every hour.

In Constipation.—PHŒBUS.

2704. ℞ Sodæ Pot.-tart. ℥iij.
Sulph. præcip. ʒiij.
Potassæ Bicarb. ʒij.
Mix: make a powder. A teaspoonful every night, and two teaspoonfuls every morning in a wineglassful of lettuce water.

GASKOIN.

2705. ℞ Sodæ Potassio-tartratis, ʒiv.
Syrupi Zingiberis, ʒj.
Spiritûs Myristicæ, ʒss.
Aquæ, ad ℥iss. Mix: make a draught.

Mild Aperient.—Dr. DRUITT.

2706. ℞ Sodæ Potassio-tartratis, ℥ss.
Magnesiæ calcinatæ, gr. x.
Aquæ Menthæ pip. ℥j.
Mix: make an aperient draught.

Dr. HOOPER.

2707. ℞ Sodæ Potassio-tartratis, ʒij.
Sodæ Sesquicarb. ℈j.
Sacchari albi, ℥j.
Mix: make a powder. To be taken in a wineglassful of water, with a tablespoonful of lemon-juice.

Effervescent Aperient.—Dr. DRUITT.

2708. ℞ Sodæ Potassio-tartratis, ℥ij.
Sodæ Sesquicarb. ℈j.
Tinct. Lupuli, ♏xxx.
Aquæ destillatæ, ℥j.
Syrupi, ʒj.
Mix: to be taken with a tablespoonful of lemon-juice.

In Inflammatory Fever.—Dr. GREGORY.

2709. ℞ Sodæ Tartarizatæ, ʒij.
Sodæ Carbonatis, ℈ij.
Aquæ Anethi, ℥ss.
Inf. Anthem. ℥j.
Tinct. Calumbæ,
Tinct. Aurant. C. ana ʒj.
Mix: make a draught. To be taken in effervescence, with 15 grains Acid. Tart. in f℥ss of water.

Stomachic Aperient.—Dr. Copland.

SODÆ PHOSPHAS. *Phosphate of Soda.*

It is made by adding a solution of Carbonate of Soda to one of the Superphosphate of Lime obtained from bone earth. It occurs in large crystals, and its solution browns turmeric paper. This salt is an exceedingly mild saline cathartic, and, having very little taste, is less disagreeable than some others. It may be used in fevers and inflammations, even in inflammations of the bowels, and disorders of pregnant women.

Phosphate of Soda is one of the solvents for lithic acid. As an antilithic it may be given in gouty and rheumatic disorders, especially the former, and in all cases where there is tendency to a lithic deposit in the urine. It has also been used in rickets, with the intention of supplying phosphoric acid to be used in the reparation of bone. The dose, as an antilithic, or in rachitis, is from one to two drachms, often repeated; as a purgative, half an ounce to one and a half ounce, in gruel or broth.

2710. ℞ Sodæ Phosphatis pulv. ʒiv.
Divide into 12 powders. One, twice a day in water or decoction of oatmeal.

In Uric Acid Gravel.—Dr. G. Bird.

2711. ℞ Sodæ Phosphatis, ℥ss.
Decocti Chondri, ℥vj.
Syrupi Limonum, ℥ss. Mix: make a purging mixture.

In Inflammatory Disorders, and where a mild action is desired.
Radius.

2712. ℞ Sodæ Phosphatis, ʒiv.
Aquæ Menth. pip. ℥iij. Dissolve, then add
Ext. Sennæ fluidi, ℥ss.
Mix: make a mixture, of which take a tablespoonful every second hour until the bowels are moved.

In the mild Febrile Affections of Children.—Dr. Neligan.

2713. ℞ Sodæ Biphosphatis, gr. viij.
Acidi Benzoici, gr. ij. Rub up together, and add
Aquæ destillatæ, ʒix.
Make a draught, to be taken three times a day.

In the Lithic Acid Diathesis.—Dr. PARIS.

2714. ℞ Sodæ Carbonatis, ʒiss.
Acidi Benzoici, ℈ij.
Sodæ Phosphatis, ʒiij.
Aquæ Cinnamomi, ℥viiss.
Aquæ puræ, ℥iv.
Tinct. Hyoscyami, ʒiv.
Mix: make a mixture. Two tablespoonfuls three times a day.

Uric Acid Diathesis.—Dr. G. BIRD.

SODÆ SULPHAS ET BISULPHAS. *Sulphate* and *Bisulphate of Soda.*

The Sulphate, or Glauber's salt, is extensively produced in the manufacture of the carbonate from common salt. The Bisulphate, an acid salt, is obtained as a residue in making hydrochloric acid. The Sulphate is in long prismatic crystals, of a bitter taste, and very soluble in water. It acts as a cathartic in the same manner as Sulphate of Magnesia, than which it is rather more irritant. It may be used in much the same cases, but the dose required is greater, being from half an ounce to two ounces.

The Bisulphate is also a cooling purgative. It resembles the same salt of Potash. It may be given in doses of half a drachm to two drachms as a diuretic, or of two to six drachms as a purgative.

Sodæ et Magnesiæ Sulphas has been used as a laxative and diuretic, in doses of half a drachm to two drachms several times a day.

2715. ℞ Sodæ Sulphatis, ℈iv.
Pulv. Opii, gr. ij. Mix: make a powder.

In Hæmorrhages and Inflammations after bleeding.—RADIUS.

2716. ℞ Sodæ Sulph. exsic. ℥ss.
Pulpæ Tamarindi, ℥j.
Syrupi succi limonis, q. s. to make an electuary. Two teaspoonfuls every hour until the bowels are opened.

PHŒBUS.

2717. ℞ Sodæ Sulphatis, ℥ss.
Antimonii Potassio-tart. gr. j.
Aquæ, ℥iv. Mix: make an emetic and cathartic draught.

Dr. Joy.

2718. ℞ Sodæ Sulphatis, ʒv.
Infusi Rosæ acidi, ℥iss.
Acid. Sulph. dil. ♏ij. Mix: make a draught.

Antiphlogistic Cathartic.—Dr. Neligan.

2719. ℞ Sodæ Carbonatis, ℥iss.
Aquæ puræ, Oviiss.
Acidi Sulph. dil. ℥j.
Conf. Aromat. ℥iij.
Spir. Menth. pip. ʒiij. Mix.

As an Aperient Drink in Cardialgia, &c.—Dr. Barlow.

2720. ℞ Sodæ Sesquicarb. ʒij.
Ferri Sulphat. gr. iij.
Magnesiæ Carb. ʒj.
Aquæ, Oss.
Acid. Sulph. dil. ʒx.

Pour the water into a stone bottle, in which dissolve the salts; then add the acid, close the vessel, and place it in a cool place, or cool by placing the vessel in water.

An effervescing, tonic, and purgative drink.—Dr. Paris.

2721. ℞ Sodæ Sulphatis, ℥j.
Foliorum Sennæ, ʒiij.
Aquæ fervidæ, Oj.

Infuse, and strain. Make a purging enema.

Dr. J. Hamilton.

SODÆ SULPHIS et HYPOSULPHIS. *Sulphite* and *Hyposulphite of Soda.*

The Sulphite of Soda has been administered internally by Dr. H. Hassall and others, in cases of vomiting from Sarcina ventriculi. It seems likely that the acid juice of the stomach sets free the sulphurous acid of the salt, and that this acts by its chemical power of destroying fungous growths, such as that which is the cause of this disease. It may operate in the same manner when applied as a lotion to aphthous surfaces, where also there is a vegetable growth. The Sulphite has been recommended by Mr. Graham, on hypothetical grounds, in the treatment of Asiatic Cholera. Dose, half a drachm to one drachm, or one and a half drachm.

The Hyposulphite of Soda (well known from its use in photography as a solvent for iodide of silver) is used to destroy parasitic vegetables, in the same way as the Sulphite. It is also employed on the Continent as an alterative in skin diseases, and may be given as a purgative in the same manner as the Sulphate of Soda. Dose, as an alterative, ten grains to one drachm; as a cathartic, two drachms to half an ounce.

2722. ℞ Sodæ Sulphitis, ʒss.
Aquæ, ℥iss.
Mix: make a draught. To be taken three times a day. (The dose may be increased.)

In Yeasty Vomiting.—Dr. JENNER.

2723. ℞ Sodæ Hyposulphitis, ʒvj.
Infusi Quassiæ, ℥xij. Mix: take f℥ss three times a day.

In Sarcina Ventriculi.—Mr. R. NEALE.

2724. ℞ Sodæ Hyposulphitis, ʒxiss.
Sacchari pulv. ℥viij.
Aquæ destillatæ, Oij.
Dissolve, and form a syrup: one to four fluid-ounces every day. (Thirty parts contain one part of the hyposulphite.)

In Chronic cutaneous and Scrofulous Affections.
EMILE MOUCHON.

2725. ℞ Sodæ Hyposulphitis, ʒvj.
Aquæ Menthæ pip. ʒxiv.
Tinct. Cardam. co. ʒij. Mix: make a draught.

An active Cathartic in atonic Dyspepsia.—Dr. NELIGAN.

2726. ℞ Sodæ Sulphitis, ʒj.
Aquæ puræ, ℥j. Mix: make a lotion.

In Aphthæ of the Mouth.—Dr. JENNER.

2727. ℞ Sodæ Hyposulphitis, ℥ss.
Potassii Sulphureti, ʒj.
Aquæ destillatæ, ℥xiss.
Aquæ Laurocerasi, ℥ss. Mix: make a lotion.

In Scabies, Eczema, &c.—Dr. NELIGAN.

SODÆ HYPOCHLORIS. *Soda Chlorinata.* See CHLORINIUM.

SODÆ VALERIANAS. *Valerianate of Soda.*

Valerianic Acid is made by oxidizing Fusel oil, by means of Bichromate of Potash. It is then combined with solution of caustic soda to form this salt. This possesses both the odor and the properties of Valerianic acid. It may be used as an antispasmodic, but is chiefly employed in the manufacture of the other Valerianates.

SODII CHLORIDUM. *Chloride of Sodium.*

Common salt is obtained from the waters of the ocean, from mines on the land, or from salt springs. It is the most universal and indispensable of all condiments. Various cachectic disorders, worms in the intestines, &c. have resulted from its omission as an article of food. Its quantity in the daily food has been sometimes increased in cases of scrofula, phthisis, dyspepsia, and skin diseases. It acts as a most useful alterative, and seems to purify the blood.

Salt has been used, along with other salines, to form a saline injection into the veins in Asiatic Cholera. In large doses it acts as a purgative, in still larger it produces speedy vomiting. As an emetic it is given in cases of poisoning, and in the early stage of cholera. Externally, it is given in baths to imitate sea water; and applied as a rubefacient in a strong solution, or as a stimulant to chilblains. One, two, or more ounces, dissolved in a pint of water, form a useful aperient enema for cases of ascarides. Dose, as an alterative, half to one drachm; purgative, two drachms to half an ounce; emetic, one to two ounces in warm water.

Pulvis Salinus (E.), two to three drachms.

Aqua Selterana (Paris Codex) is an aerated water, in imitation of Seltzer water.

2728. ℞ Sodii Chloridi, ʒiij.
Pulv. Cocci Cacti, gr. xv.

Mix, and divide into 6 powders. (One every morning, and finally a dose of some purgative.)

Anthelmintic.—Dr. Rush.

2729. ℞ Sodii Chloridi, ℥iij.
Sodæ Phosphatis, ℥j.
Sodæ Carbonatis, ℥iss.
Sodæ Sulphatis, ℥ss.

Dissolve in a little water, and gradually dilute the solution with more water, testing it from time to time with a urinometer, until it has been lowered exactly to the density of 1·030 at 60° Fahrenheit Heat this solution lastly to 98° Fahr., when it will be ready for use.

For Injection into the veins in Asiatic Cholera.

Dr. G. Owen Rees.

2730. ℞ Sodii Chloridi, gr. xxxj.
Sodæ Phosphatis, gr. v.
Sodæ Carbonatis, gr. vj.
Sodæ Sulphatis, gr. j.
Aquæ destillatæ, ℥x.

Dissolve, and heat the solution to 98° Fahr., when it is required for use. (The density of this solution is 1·004 at 68° and between 1·000 and 1·001 at 98°. Its composition is as closely as possible the same as that of the serum of the blood deprived of its organic principles.)

For Injection into the veins in Asiatic Cholera.
Dr. W. MARCET.

2731. ℞ Sodii Chloridi, ℥ij.
Decocti Avenæ, Oj. Mix.

A Purgative Enema, or to destroy Ascarides.—Dr. HOOPER.

2732. ℞ Salis communis, ℥ij.
Aquæ puræ, ℥vj.
Aceti,
Spir. Vini Gallici, ana ℥iij. Mix: make a fomentation.

To Bruises.—VOGT.

2733. ℞ Salis communis, lbj.
Aquæ, Oiv. Throw into a bath, and add
Gelatinæ communis, lbij, previously dissolved in
Aquæ, Ovj. Make a bath.

In Scrofulous Affections.—FOY.

SPARTIUM. See SCOPARIUS.

SPIGELIA. *Pink Root.*

This is the root of *Spigelia Marilandica*, an American plant (Nat. Ord. *Spigeliaceæ*). It has a faint odor, and a peculiar unpleasant taste. It is a purgative, and powerful anthelmintic. It is thought to have some narcotic properties. When given for worms, it is either conjoined with, or followed by, a brisk cathartic. The dose is ten to twenty grains for a child, one to two drachms for an adult, repeated morning and evening for some days, and followed by an active purgative, as above stated.

Infusum Spigeliæ (U. S.): dose, half to one ounce for children, four to eight ounces for adults.

Extractum Spigeliæ fluidum (Procter), ten to twenty drops at a time, for children.

2734. ℞ Pulv. Spigeliæ, gr. x.
Calomelanos, gr. iv.

Mix: make a powder. (To be taken for two mornings in succession, and on the afternoon of the second day followed by a purge.)

Anthelmintic for children above four years of age.—Dr. ELLIS.

2735. ℞ Pulv. Spigeliæ,
Pulv. Sennæ, ana ℈ij.
Pulv. Sabinæ, gr. xij.

Mix: make a powder. (One every morning for three days, followed by a purge.)

For Adults.—Dr. ELLIS.

2736. ℞ Pulv. Spigeliæ, gr. x.
Pulv. Stanni, ʒij.
Syrup. Zingiberis, ʒss.
Mellis, q. s.

Mix: make a bolus. To be taken an hour before breakfast, and repeated for three days; afterward administer a purging mixture, to produce a free evacuation of the bowels.

In cases of Lumbrici.—Dr. NELIGAN.

2737. ℞ Spigeliæ rad. concis. ℥ss.
Sennæ foliorum, ʒij.
Aurant. cort. conc.
Santonici sem. contus.
Fœniculi sem. contus. ana ʒj.
Aquæ ferventis, ℥xij.

Macerate for two hours in a lightly-closed vessel, and strain. Dose, a wineglassful every morning early, on an empty stomach.

In Lumbrici.—SPRAGUE.

SPIRITUS PYROXYLICUS. *Medicinal Naphtha. Wood Spirit.*

This is obtained, along with acetic acid and tarry matters, in the dry distillation of wood. It is quite distinct from Acetone, or Pyroacetic Spirit (obtained by distilling dry acetate of lime). Its specific gravity, when rectified, is about ·813. It is a volatile inflammable liquid, with a peculiar ethereal odor. It is a diffusible stimulant, expectorant, and diaphoretic. It is recommended strongly by Dr. Hastings and others, both for internal use and for inhalation, in phthisis and chronic bronchitis. In large doses it is a dangerous narcotic. Dr. Hastings supposed that it was of use in supplying carbon and hydrogen to the system. The experience of others has shown that it is really of little use in acute or advanced cases of pulmonary consumption. Dr. Hastings has also used it in gout and rheumatism. M. Lavirotte has given it in diarrhœa and dysentery. The dose of the Naphtha is from ten to twenty drops three times a day at first, gradually increasing if nausea is not produced.

2738. ℞ Naphthæ medicinalis, ♏x.
Syrupi Aceti, ʒij.
Aquæ, ℥j. Make a draught. One every six hours.

Anodyne in Hectic of Phthisis.—Dr. NELIGAN.

2739. ℞ Naphthæ medicinalis, ℥j.
Liquoris Opii sedativi, ʒij.
Mix: fifteen drops to be taken three times a day in a little water.

In Acute Bronchitis with hectic symptoms.—Mr. PROCTER.

(Though Dr. Hastings, Mr. Procter, and others give this liquid the name of "Pyro-acetic Spirit," it has been found that the remedy employed is simply rectified wood-spirit.)

SPONGIA. *Sponge.*

Sponge is the horny skeleton of certain marine animals very low in the scale of life, and found attached to rocks. It is light, porous, and elastic, and is employed to compress wounds, and to form tents, and plugs to restrain hæmorrhage. When burnt, it constitutes *Spongia usta.* This contains a small proportion of iodine, and has therefore proved useful as an internal remedy in goitre and scrofula. The dose is bulky, being from one to three drachms or more. It may be made into an electuary.

Electuarium Spongiæ ustæ (Radius), two to four spoonfuls a day, in goitre.

2740. ℞ Spongiæ ustæ, gr. x.
Pulv. Rhei, gr. iv.
Mix: make a powder. To be taken morning and evening.

In Scrofula.—HULSE.

2741. ℞ Spongiæ ustæ, ʒiv.
Magnes. Carb.
Potassæ Nitratis,
Sacchari albi, ana ʒij.
Mix: make a powder. (ʒj three times a day.)

In Scrofula.—CLARUS.

STANNI PULVIS. *Tin Powder.*

Finely powdered Tin has been used as a vermifuge. It acts by mechanically irritating and dislodging the worms. It may be given, mixed with syrup, in doses of half an ounce for several mornings, followed by an active purgative. An ointment of tin powder has been used in hæmorrhoids. The Sulphuret and Oxide of Tin have also been used as anthelmintics. Either may be given in doses of ten to twenty grains. The Chloride is a violent acrid purgative, in doses of two grains.

2742. ℞ Stanni pulv. ℥j.
Confectionis Sennæ, ℥ij. Mix. Dose, ℥ss.
Anthelmintic.—Dr. HOOPER.

2743. ℞ Pulv. Stanni, gr. xv.
Sacchari albi, gr. x.
Mix. Take twice a day for ten days. Afterward give three grains of calomel going to bed, and a laxative draught next morning.
Vermifuge.—Dr. E. J. CLARK.

2744. ℞ Pulv. Stanni, ℥j.
Extracti Absinthii,
Pulv. Jalapæ, ana ʒj.
Syrupi Cichorii co. q. s. to make an electuary.
(To be taken in twelve doses.)
FOY.

STRAMONIUM. *Thorn Apple.*

Both the leaves and seeds of *Datura Stramonium* (Nat. Ord. *Solanaceæ*) are officinal. The seeds are the most powerful. The root also has been employed. Tho leaves and other parts have a rank narcotic odor, and bitter taste. The seeds are small, blackish, and acrid. Stramonium is a very powerful narcotic. It quiets the heart, lessens the number of respirations, allays pain, controls spasmodic action, and dilates the pupil. It seldom causes sleep, and does not confine the bowels. In large doses it causes delirium and death.

Stramonium is especially useful in painful and irritable states of the respiratory organs. It may be given to allay cough, and diminish pain in the chest, or to stop the advance of a paroxysm of spasmodic asthma. In the latter disease it may with advantage be smoked like tobacco. Two or three pipefuls of the dried herb may be used at a time. It contains an alkaloid, Daturia, to which its narcotic properties are owing. But by its combustion an empyreumatic oil is produced, which has also narcotic properties. The dose of the dry leaves is from two to five grains; of the powdered seeds, from half to two grains.

Extractum Stramonii (*seminum*) (L., E.). Dose, quarter to half a grain, carefully increasing.

Extractum Stramonii foliorum (U. S.), one to two grains, gradually increasing.

Tinctura Stramonii (D.), half a drachm three times a day.

Tinctura Stramonii ætherea (Soubeiran), two to three drops.

Vinum Stramonii (Van Mons), six to twenty drops.

The two next are used as anodyne applications.

Unguentum Stramonii (U. S.).

Oleum Stramonii (Cottereau).

2745. ℞ Fol. Stramonii contusi,
Fol. Salviæ contus. āā partes æquales.
(In sufficient quantity to fill a pipe, which is to be smoked by the patient, and renewed three or four times.)

In Spasmodic Asthma.—TROUSSEAU and REVEIL.

2746. ℞ Extracti Stramonii, gr. j.
Ext. Glycyrrhizæ, ʒj.
Mix, and divide into 6 pills. One, when the cough is urgent.

In Irritation of Larynx or Throat.—Dr. HOOPER.

2747. ℞ Ext. (foliorum) Stramonii, ʒj.
Saponis duri, ʒij.
Acaciæ gum. pulv. ℈j.
Glycyrrhizæ rad. pulv. ℈ij.
Mucilag. Tragacanthæ, q. s. to make a mass to be divided into 60 pills. Dose, one, night and morning; or, three times a day.

In Asthma.—Sir H. HALFORD.

2748. ℞ Extracti Stramonii, gr. ss.
Ext. Hyoscyami, gr. iv.
Mix: make a pill. To be taken at bedtime.

Dr. PARIS.

2749. ℞ Pulv. Scillæ,
Pulv. Ipecac. ana ℈j.
Ext. Stramonii, gr. v.
Ext. Lactucæ, gr. xv.
Mix, and divide into 12 pills. One, three or four times a day.

Expectorant in Bronchitis.—Dr. HOOPER.

2750. ℞ Pulv. Seminum Stramonii, gr. x.
Pulv. Camphoræ, ʒj.
Pulv. Sabinæ, ℈v.
Ext. Senegæ, ℈iv.
Mix, and divide into 2-grain pills. Six to be taken three times a day.

In Rheumatism.—VOGT.

2751. ℞ Ext. Stramonii,
Ext. Opii Aquosi, āā gr. viij.
Zinci Oxidi, ʒij.
Excipientis, q. s.

Mix: make a mass, and divide into 40 pills. One to eight in the twenty-four hours.

In Neuralgia.—TROUSSEAU and REVEIL.

2752. ℞ Tinct. Stramonii, ♏xv.
Aquæ destillatæ, ℥j.
Syrupi Limonum, ℥ss.

Mix: make a draught. To be repeated every three hours, until the pain is mitigated.

In Tic-douloureux, Sciatica, &c.—Dr. NELIGAN.

2753. ℞ Extracti Sem. Stramonii, gr. xij.
Vini Antimonii, ℥ss.

Dissolve: ten drops to be taken every three hours in some infusion.

In Spasmodic Disorders.—HUFELAND.

2754. ℞ Pulv. Sem. Stramonii, ℥j.
Spiritûs rectf. Oj. Infuse, strain, and add
Opii, ℥j.
Spiritus Camphoræ, ℥ij. Make a lotion.

For Rheumatic Limbs.—PIERQUIN.

2755. ℞ Ext. Stramon. fol. gr. iij.
Ext. Opii, gr. iss.
Aquæ Rosæ, ℥iv. Mix: make an eye-wash.

In Painful Affections of the Eye.—TROUSSEAU and REVEIL.

2756. ℞ Ext. Stramonii, ʒss
Morph. Hydrochlor. gr. ivss.
Ovi unius, vitellum.

Mix, and make a liniment. (Pledgets of tow dipped in this to be applied to the painful hæmorrhoidal tumors.)

For Ulcerated Piles.—TROUSSEAU and REVEIL.

STYRAX. *Storax.*

This is the concrete resinous juice of the *Styrax officinale*, a small tree belonging to the Nat. Ord. *Styraceæ*. It resembles in action the balsams of Peru, Tolu, and Benzoin, but is less frequently employed than any of these. It is an aromatic expectorant, and may be employed in chronic coughs and other pulmonary affections.

Styrax præparata (L., E.) is a spirituous extract; dose, ten grains to one scruple.

Pilulæ Styracis (E.) contain one part in four of Opium.

Pilula Styracis composita (L.) contains one grain in five of Opium. The Opium is, of course, the most active ingredient in these two pills.

Syrupus Styracis (Giordano). Expectorant in doses of one drachm to half an ounce.

2757. ℞ Styracis præparatæ,
Sodæ Bicarb.
Extracti Hyoscyami,
Confect. Rosæ, ana ʒss.
Mix: make a mass, and divide into 4-grain pills. Two, three times a day.

In Chronic Bronchitis.

SUCCINUM. ACIDUM SUCCINICUM. *Amber* and *Succinic Acid.*

Amber is a yellow fossil resin, and its powder is sometimes used in fumigations. By distilling it, an oil and an acid in crystals are obtained. The *Oleum Succini* is sometimes used internally as antispasmodic, in doses of five to ten minims. But being an active rubefacient and stimulant externally, it is chiefly used as an ingredient in liniments and embrocations. It is thus employed in chronic rheumatism and paralysis. In the form known as *Roche's embrocation* it is rubbed on the chest in hooping-cough. This oil, acted on by strong nitric acid, produces *Artificial Musk.* It is also an ingredient in the original *Eau de Luce.* Succinic acid is sometimes given internally as an antispasmodic, in doses of five to eight grains.

Tinctura Succini (Paris Cod.): dose, forty drops to one drachm.

Tinctura Succini ætherea (Beral), fifteen to thirty drops.

Tinctura Succini alkalina (Spielmann), twenty to forty drops.

Balsamum Succini (Radius), and

Linimentum Olei Succini (Parrish), are used as antispasmodic frictions.

2758. ℞ Olei Succini,
Bals. Copaibæ,
Terebinth. Venet. ana ℥j.
Mix. Take ♏x three times a day in any appropriate vehicle.

In Leucorrhœa, Gleet, Emissions, &c.—Dr. COPLAND.

2759. ℞ Olei Succini, gtt. lxxx.
Pulv. Acaciæ,
Pulv. Sacchari, ana ℥ss.
Tinct. Tolutanæ, ʒij.
Aquæ destillatæ, ℥iv.
Mix. Take f℥ss every second or third hour.

In Spasmodic Cough.—Dr. Ellis (U. S.).

2760. ℞ Olei Succini, ʒij.
Linim. Saponis co. ʒx.
Mix: make a liniment. (Similar to Roche's embrocation.) ʒj, at a time, to be rubbed into the back.

In Hooping-cough, &c.—Dr. Hooper.

2761. ℞ Olei Succi, ℥j.
Tinct. Opii, ʒiv. Mix: make a liniment.

In Neuralgia.—Dr. Joy.

2762. ℞ Olei Succini, ℥ss.
Tinct. Lyttæ, ʒj.
Spirit. Rosmarini, ℥iiiss.
Mix: make an embrocation. To be used at night.

As a Counter-irritant in Ophthalmia.—Mr. White Cooper.

2763. ℞ Spiritus Camphoræ, ℥ss.
Tinct. Opii,
Olei Succini, ana ʒij.
Olei Amygdalæ, ℥ss.
Mix: make a liniment. To be used night and morning.

Rubbed on the Chest in Hooping-cough.—Mr. Savory.

SULPHUR. SULPHURETA. *Sulphur* and *Sulphurets.*

Sulphur is well known under the various forms of *Sulphur sublimatum*, *S. lotum*, and *S. præcipitatum.* The latter is commonly adulterated with sulphate of lime. The Sulphurets of Potassium, Sodium, and Calcium are used in medicine, as well as those of Mercury and other metals. When acted upon by any acid, these compounds exhale sulphuretted hydrogen, a gas having the odor of rotten eggs. The same gas is contained in the water of sulphureous springs, as in that of Harrogate. Sulphur, when burnt, produces Sulphurous acid, an irritant and poisonous gas.

Sulphur is used internally as a laxative, being frequently united with cream of tartar and other mild purgatives, and often given in piles. Externally it is used as an ointment in skin diseases, particularly the itch, over which it exerts an almost specific influence; but also in acne, porrigo, and other cases. It is used sometimes in the form of a fumigation. It is given internally in small doses in the same skin disorders, and as a deobstruent in affections of the liver. It is diaphoretic and alterative. A combination of sulphur and oil is used to stimulate unhealthy ulcers.

The Alkaline Sulphurets are employed as alteratives, and as external applications, or baths, in the same disorders. By adding an acid to one of them, sulphuretted hydrogen is produced. This gas is soluble to some extent in water. Taken internally it is diaphoretic and alterative, being recommended in uterine and liver affections, and skin diseases. In the latter instance it may be applied to the whole surface in the form of a bath.

The dose of Sulphur as an alterative is five to twenty grains three times a day; as a purgative, one to three drachms. Either of the alkaline sulphurets may be prescribed in doses of from two to ten grains.

Confectio Sulphuris (D.), one to two drachms at night, for hæmorrhoids.

Potassii Ferro-sulphuretum (Ferrara P.), three to four grains.

Bolus Potassii Sulphureti (Brera), one every three hours in mercurial salivation.

Pilulæ Potassii Sulphureti (Griffith), two to five several times a day.

Electuarium Potassii Sulphureti (Phœbus), one drachm as an alterative for children.

Syrupus Potassii Sulphureti (Paris Codex), one drachm for croup in children.

The remainder are for external use, chiefly in scabies, herpes, and other cutaneous diseases. The first two are applied to ulcers.

Balsamum Sulphuris (L. 1824).

Balsamum Sulphuris Terebinthinatum (Van Mons).

Unguentum Sulphuris (L., E., D.).

Unguentum Sulphuris compositum (L.).

Ceratum Sulphuris (Paris Codex).

Lotio Potassii Sulphureti (Ellis).
Balneum Potassii Sulphureti (Beral).
Unguentum Potassii Sulphureti (Alibert).

The prescriptions below are classified according to the chemical condition of the Sulphur which they contain.

The following contain the Sulphur in an uncombined state (though in the Prescriptions 2768–2772 it will be liable to combine to some extent with the alkali, or alkaline earth, given with it).

2764. ℞ Sulphuris loti,
Pulv. Sacchari, ana ʒss.
Camphoræ rasæ, gr. vj.
Mix, and divide into 6 powders. One every hour.
In Mercurial Cachexy.—RADIUS.

2765. ℞ Flor. Sulphuris, ʒj.
Pulv. Sem. Fœniculi, ʒij.
Pulv. Glycyrrhizæ, ʒiv. Mix: a teaspoonful frequently.
In Catarrh.—PHŒBUS.

2766. ℞ Sulphuris sublimati, ʒiss.
Sacchari non purif.
Potassæ Bitartratis, ana ʒij.
Mix: make a powder. To be taken twice a day.
In Scabies, Impetigo, &c.—Dr. W. AINSLIE.

2767. ℞ Flor. Sulphuris, ℥ss.
Potassæ Nitratis, ʒij.
Potassæ Bitartratis, ℥j.
Pulv. Jalapæ, ʒss.
Pulv. Cinnam. co. ʒj.
Mix: make a powder. A teaspoonful every night, in some suitable vehicle.
In Hæmorrhoids and Psora.—Dr. RYAN.

2768. ℞ Sulphuris loti, ʒss.
Sodæ Carb. sic. ℈j.
Antim. Pot.-tart. gr. ⅙.
Mix: make a powder. To be taken night and morning.
In Acne.—Dr. THOMAS.

2769. ℞ Sulphuris sublimati, ℥j.
Sodæ Bicarb. ʒj.
Pulv. Ipecac. gr. v.
Mix: from ℈j to ℈ij in milk, at bedtime.
As a Laxative on Change of Life.—Dr. TILT.

2770. ℞ Sulphuris præcipitati, gr. xv.
Magnesiæ, ℈j.
Mix: to be taken at bedtime in a glass of milk or water.
Mild Aperient in Piles.—Dr. A. T. THOMSON.

2771. ℞ Sulphuris præcip. gr. j.
Hyd. Chloridi, gr. iss.
Cretæ præp. gr. v.
Syrupi, q. s. to make a pill. To be taken morning and night.

In Tinea Capitis.

2772. ℞ Sulphuris, ʒj.
Magnesiæ, gr. xv.
Rub up with mucilage of gum arabic, and add
Mist. Amygdalæ, ʒx.
Syrup. Zingiberis, ʒss. Make a cathartic draught.

Dr. Paris.

2773. ℞ Sulphuris præcipitati, ʒij.
Aquæ Fœniculi, ℥iij.
Aquæ Cinnamomi, ℥j.
Syrupi Opii, ℥ss. Mix: take f℥ss every second hour.

In Diabetes Mellitus.—Augustin.

2774. ℞ Sulphuris sublimati, ℥ss.
Potassæ Bitartratis, ʒiss.
Confect. Sennæ, ℥j.
Syrupi, q. s.
Mix: make an electuary. A teaspoonful at bedtime.

In Piles.—Dr. W. Ainslie.

2775. ℞ Potassæ Bitart. ℥ss.
Sulphuris, ℥j.
Confect. Piperis nig. ʒij.
Olei Carui, ♏vj.
Theriacæ, ℥iij.
Mix: make an electuary. A teaspoonful twice a day.

In Hæmorrhoids.—Dr. Joy.

2776. ℞ Sulphuris, ℥j.
Acid. Sulph. ʒj.
Axungiæ, ℥ij.
Mix: make an ointment. (One-fourth to be rubbed upon the body night and morning.)

In Scabies.—Dr. A. T. Thomson.

2777. ℞ Picis liquidæ, ℥iv.
Ceræ flavæ, ℥ss.
Dissolve by a slow heat, and, before cooling, add, while stirring,
Sulphuris, ℥j. Mix: make an ointment.

In Porrigo Scutulata, Impetigo Favosa, &c.—Dr. Joy.

2778. ℞ Sulphuris sublimati,
Ung. Picis liquidæ, ana ℥iss.
Saponis mollis,
Ammoniæ Muriatis, ana ℥ss. Mix: make an ointment.

In Porrigo.—Dr. Chapman.

2779. ℞ Sulphuris, ℥ss.

Evaporate upon a heated metallic dish in a close place, so that the vapor shall reach the affected parts.

For a Fumigation in Itch and other Skin Diseases.
Dr. BURGESS.

The following prescriptions give Sulphur in combination with Potash and Soda, or their metallic bases:

2780. ℞ Potassii Sulphureti, gr. xl.
Aquæ destillatæ, ℥vj.
Syrupi Hemidesmi, ℥ij.

Mix: make a mixture. A tablespoonful three or four times a day.

In Troublesome Cutaneous Diseases.—Dr. NELIGAN.

2781. ℞ Potassii Sulphureti, ℈j.
Potassæ Carbonatis, gr. x.
Aquæ Menthæ pip. ℥ij.
Syrupi Croci, ℥j.

Mix: a tablespoonful every second hour.

In Cutaneous Diseases.—PHŒBUS.

2782. ℞ Potassii Sulphureti, ʒiss.
Potassæ Bicarb. gr. x.
Olei Menthæ pip. gtt. ij.
Syrupi Aurantii, ℥ij.
Mucilag. ℥j. Mix: a teaspoonful every second hour.

Alterative in Scrofula.—LOCKSTAEDT.

2783. ℞ Sodæ puræ (prepared with alcohol), ʒj.
Aquæ destillatæ, ʒv. Liquefy by a slow heat, and add Sulphuris puri, as much as will be dissolved

℞ Liquoris, ℥j.
Syrupi, ℥xxxj.

Mix well, in a well-stoppered vessel. (Dose, ʒj–ʒij for infants, ℥j–℥iij for adults.)

Dr. COPLAND.

2784. ℞ Potassæ Sulphureti (recentis), ʒj.
Aquæ destillatæ, ℥iij.

Mix: make a lotion. To be used once a day.

In Pityriasis Capitis.—Mr. WINZAR.

2785. ℞ Sulphuris sublimati, ʒij.
Potassæ Subcarb. ʒj.
Aquæ, ℥xvj. Mix: make a lotion.

In Prurigo.—Dr. BURGESS.

2786. ℞ Potassii Sulphureti,
Saponis, ana ʒij.
Spirit. rectif. ℥j. Mix: make a lotion.

In Scabies and Porrigo Favosa.—Dr. HOOPER.

2787. ℞ Potassi Sulphureti,
Saponis albi, ana ʒij.
Liquor. Calcis, ℥vij.
Spirit. rect. ʒj. Mix: make a lotion.

In Porrigo Favosa and Psora.—Dr. Joy.

2788. ℞ Sulphuris, ℥v.
Potassæ Carb. ʒij.
Aquæ, ℥j.
Olei Olivæ, ℥iv.

Dissolve the potassa in the water, then add the sulphur. Make a liniment.

In Psora.—Hôpital St. Louis.

2789. ℞ Sulphuris sublimati, ℥ss.
Potassæ Subcarb. ʒij.
Axungiæ, ℥ij.

Mix: make an ointment. A fourth part to be rubbed into the affected parts night and morning.

In Scabies.—Helmerich.

2790. ℞ Sodii Sulphureti, ʒiij.
Saponis Hispanici, ℥ss.
Spiritus rectificati, ʒij.
Aquæ Calcis, Oj.

Mix: make a lotion. To be used twice a day.

In Chronic Eczema of the Scalp.—Biett.

2791. ℞ Magnes. Sulph. ℥ss.
Potassæ Supertart. ℈j.
Potassii Sulphuret. ʒj.

Rub up together, and dissolve in a gallon of water; for a bath.

Sulphur Bath in Skin Disease, &c.—Dr. Copland.

2792. ℞ Pulv. Sulphuris,
Sodæ Hyposulphitis, ana ℥ij.
Aquæ pluvialis, cong. xxx (heated to 86° Fahr.).

Dissolve: make a sulphur bath.

In Scaly Diseases of the Skin.—Dr. Neligan.

2793. ℞ Potass. Sulphureti, ℥ij–℥iv.
Aquæ communis, lbc–lbcc. Dissolve, and add
Icthyocollæ, lbj–lbij, dissolved in 10lb boiling water.

Sulphur and Gelatine Bath in Skin Diseases, &c.
Dupuytren.

In the two lotions below, sulphuretted hydrogen and sulphurous acid gases are employed in solution.

2794. ℞ Potassii Sulphuret. ℥iv.
Acidi Sulphurici, ℥ss.
Aquæ, ℥xxxij. Mix: make a lotion.

In Scabies.—M. Dupuytren.

2795. ℞ Aquæ saturated with sulphurous acid, ℥ij.
Aquæ puræ, ℥viij.
Mix: make a lotion. To be constantly applied to the scalp.
In Tinea Favosa.—Dr. W. JENNER.

SULPHURIS CARBURETUM. *Carburet of Sulphur. Sulphuret of Carbon.*

This is a light, colorless, volatile, inflammable fluid, with a penetrating odor, and tastes at first cool, afterward warm and acrid. It dissolves in spirits, but not in water. It is a solvent for camphor, sulphur, and phosphorus. It is a diffusible stimulant, diaphoretic, and emmenagogue. In large doses it is a dangerous narcotic. It was first used in medicine by Lampadius. It is chiefly employed as a sudorific in rheumatism. It is also used externally as an embrocation to rheumatic joints, and to the abdomen in after-pains. It is an anæsthetic when inhaled. Dose, two to five drops.

2796. ℞ Sulphuris Carbureti, ʒj.
Alcoholis, ℥ss.
Dissolve. 4–6 drops every two hours.
In Rheumatism.—WUTZER.

2797. ℞ Sulphuris Carbureti, ʒij.
Ætheris Sulph. ℥j.
Dissolve. A few drops to be taken on sugar.
LAMPADIUS.

2798. ℞ Sulphuris Carbureti, ℈j.
Lactis vaccin. ℥vj.
Sacchari, ʒij.
Mix: a tablespoonful four or more times a day.
In Hypertrophy of the Stomach.—CLARUS.

2799. ℞ Sulphuris Carbureti, ℥ss.
Ol. Amygd. dulcis, ℥j. Mix: make a liniment.
For old Gouty Nodes.—MANSFIELD and OTTO.

2800. ℞ Sulphuris Carbureti, ʒiij.
Olei Olivæ, seu
Lin. Ammon. co. ℥ij. Mix: make a liniment.
In Rheumatism.—WUTZER.

2801. ℞ Camphoræ, ʒij. Dissolve in
Sulphuris Carbureti, ℥ss, and add
Alcoholis, ℥j. Mix: make a liniment.
In Chronic Rheumatism.—LAMPADIUS.

SULPHURIS IODIDUM. *Iodide of Sulphur.*

This is used chiefly as an external application in various cutaneous affections, as in impetigo, prurigo, porrigo, and scrofulous eruptions. Its powder has been given internally in the same affections in one and a half grain doses. The inhalation of the vapor of this substance has been recommended in humoral asthma by Dr. Copland.

Unguentum Sulphuris Iodidi (L.). May be varied in strength according to circumstances.

2802. ℞ Pulv. Sulphuris Iodidi, gr. x.
Pulv. Acaciæ, ℥ss.
Mix, and divide into 6 powders. One, night and morning.
In Skin Diseases and Incontinence of Urine.—ESCOLAR.

2803. ℞ Sulphuris Iodidi, ℈j–℥ss.
Axungiæ, ℥j. Mix: make an ointment.
In Acne, Prurigo, and the Scaly Diseases.—Dr. BURGESS.

2804. ℞ Sulphuris, ℥ss–℥iss.
Iodinii, ℈j–ʒj. Mix: make a powder.
To be employed as a Fumigation in Skin Diseases, one-twelfth part at a time. Dr. HOOPER.

SUMBUL.

This is a root obtained lately from Central Asia, the produce of an unknown plant (probably of the order *Umbelliferæ*). It is in yellowish gray fragments, resembling pieces of inferior rhubarb. It has a strong musky smell, and contains a volatile oil. It is stimulant and antispasmodic. It has been used in asthma, hysteria, and epilepsy. The dose of the powder is from ten to thirty grains.

Tinctura Sumbulis (Lane): dose, ten drops to one drachm.

Tinctura Sumbulis ætherea (Lane), ten drops to one drachm.

2805. ℞ Tinct. Sumbul. ʒj.
Mist. Camph. co. ʒxj.
Mix: make a draught. To be taken two or three times a day.
In Epilepsy and Hysteria.—Mr. SAVORY.

2806. ℞ Tinct. Sumbul. ♏xxx.
Ext. Cotyledon. umbil. ʒj.
Aquæ puræ, ad ℥iss.
Mix: make a draught. To be taken three times a day.
In some forms of Epilepsy.—Dr. TODD.

TABACUM. *Tobacco.*

The leaves of the common Tobacco plant, *Nicotiana Tabacum* (Nat. Ord. *Solanaceæ*), are indebted for their peculiar properties to the presence in them of a volatile alkaloid, Nicotia, and also of an oil. Tobacco, given internally, acts as a narcotic and sedative, producing sickness and depression of the action of the heart. It is poisonous in large doses, and causes death by convulsions. It is too dangerous for general use. It has been given as an antispasmodic, to relax the muscular system, in hernia, constipation, and colic. It is slightly diuretic. It has been frequently administered by enema in cases of spasm and constriction of the bowels. Smoking tobacco has been found useful in preventing the fits of spasmodic asthma. The dose of powdered tobacco is from one to five grains.

Vinum Tabaci (E.) may be given internally in doses of ten to forty minims.

Enema Tabaci (L., E., D.) must be employed with great caution.

Infusum Tabaci (U. S.) is likewise used as an enema.

Unguentum Tabaci (U. S.) is applied to ulcers and eruptions of the head.

2807. ℞ Pulv. Tabaci, gr. ij.
Tartari Emetici, gr. j.
Pulv. Sacchari, ʒij.
Pulv. Acaciæ, ʒss.
Mix, and divide into 20 powders. One every second hour.

In Hooping-cough.—PETSCHAFT.

2808. ℞ Extr. Tabaci, ʒj.
Extr. Glycyrrhizæ, ℥j.
Aceti Scillæ, q. s. to form a mass: to be divided into 180 pills. 1–3 for a dose.

In Dropsy.—VAN MONS.

2809. ℞ Tabaci foliorum, ℥ij.
Aquæ ferventis, lbiv.
Mix: macerate for half an hour. A fomentation for the abdomen. (To be continued until dizziness or nausea supervene.)

In Acute Dysentery, Lead Colic, &c.—DR. JOY.

2810. ℞ Tabaci, ʒij.
Aquæ puræ, Oj. Boil to half a pint, and to the strained liquor, add
Potassæ Subcarb. ʒj.
Make a lotion: to be used frequently.

In Scald Head.—Dr. THOMAS.

2811. ℞ Tabaci foliorum, ℥j.
Axungiæ porcinæ, lbj.
Melt together, and simmer until the leaves become friable, then express.

AMST. PHARM.

TAMARINDUS. *Tamarind.*

This is the preserved fruit of the *Tamarindus Indica*, cultivated in the East and West Indies (Nat. Ord. *Leguminosæ*). It has a sweet sickly taste, and is used in medicine as a laxative. It may be made into a drink with milk, or, combined with other substances, into a confection. Tamarind whey forms an agreeable cooling drink in fevers.

Tamarindus præparatus (L.) consists of the finer parts of the pulp.

Infusum Tamarindi (Cottereau), and

Lac Tamarindi (Foy), are used as cooling drinks in fevers.

2812. ℞ Tamarindi pulpæ, ℥ij.
Aquæ ferventis, lbij.
Mix: macerate for a quarter of an hour. To be used as a common drink.

In Inflammatory Affections, where a gentle Aperient effect is required. Dr. JOY.

2813. ℞ Pulpæ Tamarindorum, ʒiv–ʒvj.
Potassæ Nitratis, ʒij–ʒiij.
Seri Lactis, Oiiss. Mix: every two hours a coffeecupful.

Febrifuge.—STOLL.

2814. ℞ Mannæ,
Conserv. Tamarind. ana ℥iss.
Seri Lactis, lbiss.
Digest, and strain. A wineglassful frequently.

Febrifuge drink.—Dr. COPLAND.

2815. ℞ Pulpæ Tamarindi, ℥iss.
Cremoris Tartari, ℥ss.
Syrupi Rubi Idæi, q. s. to make an electuary. Take ʒij night and morning.

Laxative.—RADIUS.

TANACETUM. *Tansy.*

The native *Tanacetum vulgare* has large yellow heads of flowers, and finely divided leaves. The whole plant has a peculiar smell, and bitter aromatic taste. It belongs to the Nat. Ord. *Compositæ.* It is employed as a stimulant tonic, and occasionally as an anthelmintic. Dose of the dried leaves, ten grains to one drachm.

Infusum Tanaceti (Niemann): dose, one to one and a half ounce. Used also as an injection for ascarides.

Extractum Tanaceti (Giordano), six grains to one scruple.

Oleum Tanaceti (Guibourt), one to five minims.

2816. ℞ Olei Tanaceti, ℈j.
Extr. Juglandis, ʒij.
Pulv. Althææ, q. s. to make 60 pills. Three to five every second hour.

Vermifuge.—RADIUS.

2817. ℞ Infusi Tanaceti, ℥iss.
Decoct. Geoffroyæ, ℥ss.
Syrup. Zingib. ʒj. Mix: make a draught.

Anthelmintic for Lumbrici.—Dr. NELIGAN.

2818. ℞ Tanaceti,
Absinthii, ana ℥ss.
Valerian. rad. contrit.
Corticis Aurantii, ana ʒij.
Aquæ ferventis, ℥viij.
Infuse for an hour, and make an enema. To be used morning and evening.

For Ascarides.—Dr. HOOPER.

TARAXACUM.

The root of the common Dandelion, *Taraxacum Dens leonis* (Nat. Ord. *Compositæ*), is slightly tonic, alterative, diaphoretic, and diuretic. It is used as a resolvent in various affections of the liver. Its action is somewhat like that of sarsaparilla. It is given in dyspepsia, in dropsy, in skin diseases, and cachectic disorders. The root should be used fresh, the juice being obtained by simple pressure, and then at once evaporated to an extract, or some weak spirit and water first added.

Extractum Taraxaci (L., E.), ten grains to half a drachm.

Extractum Taraxaci fluidum (Hooper), one to two drachms.

Decoctum Taraxaci (L., E.), one and a half to two ounces.

Pilulæ Taraxaci (Ellis): dose, one three times a day.

Pilulæ Taraxaci cum Hydrargyro (Ellis), one three times a day.

Mistura Taraxaci (Richter), one ounce every three hours.

2819. ℞ Extr. Taraxaci,
Saponis, ana ℥j.
Potassæ Acetatis liquidæ, q. s.

Mix, and divide into 4-grain pills. From four to six during the day.

Diuretic.—ST. MARIE.

2820. ℞ Pil. Hydrarg. gr. iv.
Pulv. Aloes, gr. j.
Extr. Taraxaci, gr. v.

Mix: make 2 pills. To be taken at bedtime.

In Bilious Dyspepsia.—Dr. ROSS.

2821. ℞ Liquoris Taraxaci, ℥j.
Decocti Sarsæ co.
Liquoris Calcis, ana ℥iiiss.

Mix: two tablespoonfuls three times a day.

In Amenorrhœa.—Dr. RIGBY.

2822. ℞ Extr. Taraxaci fluidi,
Extr. Sarsæ fluidi,
Tinct. Calumbæ, ana ℥ij.

A dessertspoonful three times a day in a wineglassful of infusion of chamomile.

Dr. BRIGHT.

2823. ℞ Extr. Taraxaci, ʒj.
Sodæ Carbonatis, ʒss.
Tinct. Cardam. co. ℥ss.
Infusi Calumbæ, ℥ij.
Aquæ Pimentæ, ʒiiiss.

Mix: make a mixture. One-sixth part for a dose.

Chronic Affections of the Liver.—Dr. HOOPER.

2824. ℞ Extr. Taraxaci, ʒiij.
Extr. Gentianæ, ʒj.
Sodæ Subcarb. ʒj.
Aquæ Aurantii, ℥vij.
Spirit. Æth. Sulph. co.
Syrupi Rosæ, ana ℥ss.

Mix: from f℥j to f℥jss three times a day.

Tonic and Deobstruent.—Dr. COPLAND.

2825. ℞ Extr. Taraxaci, ʒiv.
Aquæ calidæ, ℥viiss.
Magnes. Sulph. ʒvj.
Tinct. Rhei, ʒij.
Tinct. Zingib. ʒiiss.

Mix: make a mixture. Two tablespoonfuls night and morning. (The evening dose to be accompanied with a purgative pill.)

In Congestion of the Liver.—Mr. C. HOGG.

2826. ℞ Sulph. Magnes. ℥ij.
Sp. Amm. arom. ʒj.
Sp. Card. co. ℥iss.
Infus. Gent. co. ℥iiss.
Infus. Sennæ co. ℥vj.
Extr. Taraxaci, ℥ss.
Mix. A wineglassful every morning, with two purgative pills at night.
In Bilious Dyspepsia.—Dr. Ross.

2827. ℞ Extr. Taraxaci, ʒij.
Potassæ Bicarb. ʒj.
Spirit. Ammon. arom. ʒij.
Tinct. Calumbæ, ℥ss.
Tinct. Aurantii, ʒiij.
Aquæ, ℥vij. Mix: two tablespoonfuls twice a day.
Dr. Melsom.

2828. ℞ Rad. Taraxaci, ℥iv.
Potassæ Supertart.
Sodæ Boratis, ana ℥ss.
Aquæ, lbiij, or boil to lbj and add, as there may be occasion,
Spirit. Æth. Nit. vel
Tinct. Scillæ, vel
Spirit. Junip. co. vel
Oxymel Scillæ.
Dr. Copland.

2829. ℞ Rad. Taraxaci,
Herbæ Fumariæ,
Fol. Sisymb. Nasturt.
Fol. Chærophylli sylv. ana ℥j. Cut up the whole well together, and add
Seri Lactis, ℥xxxij. Boil for six minutes, and afterward macerate until cooled; then strain. To the strained liquor, add
Potassæ et Sodæ Tart. ℥ss–ʒvj.
Mellis optimi, ℥j.
Mix: two, three, or four wineglassfuls during the day.
Deobstruent Decoction.—Van Swieten.

TEREBINTHINÆ OLEUM. *Oil of Turpentine.*

This is obtained by distilling common Turpentine, the resinous exudation of many trees of the Pine tribe (Nat. Ord. *Coniferæ*), growing both in the new and old worlds. Its properties are well known. In its action on the system it is stimulant, diaphoretic, diuretic, purgative, and anthelmintic. Externally it is a rubefacient. It is also given as an astringent. As an anthelmintic it should be given in a large dose, and generally combined with castor oil; for if it fail to purge, it may produce dysuria and other unpleasant consequences, in attempting to leave the system by means of the kidneys. As a purgative it is highly useful in cases of tympanitic distention of the abdomen, and is employed in the acute stage of puerperal fever. In small doses it is given in many different diseases. Thus it is prescribed in dropsy and suppression of urine, to act as a diuretic; as a stimulant to the nervous system in neuralgia and epilepsy; as an astringent in various cases of internal bleeding, and to check the mucous discharge in gonorrhœa and leucorrhœa; also given in inflammation of the eye by Mr. Guthrie and others. The ordinary dose of Oil of Turpentine as a stimulant and diuretic is from ten to thirty minims; as a cathartic or vermifuge, half an ounce to two ounces, generally combined with castor oil. It may be given suspended in mucilage, or with yolk of egg.

Confectio Terebinthinæ (D.), half an ounce to four ounces, as an anthelmintic.

Mistura Terebinthinæ (Franks), half an ounce every three hours until it operates.

Linimentum Terebinthinæ (L., E., D.) is applied on lint to burnt and scalded surfaces.

Enema Terebinthinæ (L., E., D.) is an efficient antispasmodic in cases of tympanitis, and also a vermifuge.

In the following prescriptions, Oil of Turpentine is given in small doses as a stimulant diuretic, or antihæmorrhagic:

2830. ℞ Olei Terebinth. ʒij.
Ætheris Sulphurici, ʒiij.
Mix. Take fʒss three times a day in some vehicle.

To facilitate the passage of Gall-stones.—Dr. Day.

2831. ℞ Olei Terebinth. ℥j.
Ovi vitellum unius,
Sacchari, ℥ss.
Aquæ, ℥iv. Mix: one-fourth for a dose.

Stimulant in Chronic Rheumatism.—Dr. Hooper.

2832. ℞ Terebinth. Olei, ♏x–xx.
Mellis despumat. ʒij.
Tinct. Scillæ, ♏x.
Pulv. Cinnam. co. q. s. to make an electuary.
To be taken twice a day.

Diuretic.—Dr. Paris.

2833. ℞ Olei Terebinth. ℥ss.
Mellis, ℥j.
Pulv. Tragacanthæ, ʒij.
Tinct. Lavand. co. ℥ss.
Aquæ, ℥iv. Mix. One-fourth part for a dose.

Stimulant.—Dr. HOOPER.

2834. ℞ Olei Terebinth. ♏xxx.
Mucilaginis, ℥ss.
Sodæ Bicarb. ℈ss.
Aquæ destil. ℥j. Mix: make a draught.

In Rheumatism, Rheumatic Ophthalmia, Iritis, &c.
Dr. DRUITT.

2835. ℞ Spirit. Terebinth.
Spirit. Æth. Nitrici, ana ʒiij.
Mist. Camphoræ, ℥ss.
Tinct. Lavand. co. ʒij.
Mix: a teaspoonful every four hours in a wineglassful of water.

In Typhus Fever.—Mr. J. LAIRD.

2836. ℞ Olei Terebinth. rect. ℥j.
Vitellum Ovi unius. Rub up together, and add gradually
Mist. Amygd. ℥iv.
Syrupi Aurantii, ℥ij.
Tinct. Lavand. co. ʒiv.
Olei Cinnam. ♏iv.
Mix: make a mixture. Two tablespoonfuls three times a day.

In Iritis and Chronic Rheumatism.—Dr. JOY.

2837. ℞ Olei Terebinth. rect. ʒss.
Aquæ Cinnam. ℥j.
Olei Limonis, gtt. iv.
Syrupi simp. ℥ss. Mix: from fʒj to fʒij every third hour.

In protracted Diarrhœa and Flatulence in Children.
Drs. EVANSON and MAUNSELL.

2838. ℞ Olei Terebinth. ♏xx–lx.
Decoct. Uvæ Ursi, ℥iss.
Mix: make a draught. To be taken three or four times a day.

In Hæmaturia.—Dr. T. SMITH.

2839. ℞ Olei Terebinth. ♏xv.
Aquæ Menth. pip. ℥j.
Mix: make a draught. To be repeated in four hours.

In Internal passive Hæmorrhages.—Dr. JOY.

2840. ℞ Olei Terebinth. ♏xv–xl.
Mucilag. Acaciæ, ʒvij.
Spirit. Lavand. co. ʒj.
Mix: make a draught. To be taken every fourth, sixth, or eighth hour.

In protracted Menorrhagia.—Dr. ASHWELL.

2841. ℞ Infusi Rosæ, ℥vij.
Magnesiæ Sulphatis, ʒvj.
Mannæ, ʒiv.
Olei Terebinth. ʒiss.
Mix: two tablespoonfuls every four hours.

In Hæmoptysis, Hæmatemesis, &c.—Dr. SMITH.

2842. ℞ Olei Terebinth. ʒx.
Magnesiæ Sulph. ℥j.
Pulv. Uvæ Ursi, ʒj.
Mist. Camphoræ, ℥viij.
Mix: two tablespoonfuls every second hour.

In Hæmaturia.—Dr. SMITH.

2843. ℞ Olei Terebinth. ʒij.
Mist. Acaciæ, ℥ij.
Inf. Matico, vel
Aquæ Cinnam. ℥iv.
Tinct. Capsici, ♏xxx.
Mix: make a mixture. Take f℥j, as occasion requires.

In Hæmoptysis.—Dr. THEOPHILUS THOMPSON.

2844. ℞ Olei Terebinth. ℥ss.
Olei Ricini, ℥j.
Mucilaginis,
Sacchari, ana q. s.
Olei Caryophylli, gtt. iv.
Aquæ destill. ℥viij.
Mix: make a mixture. Two or three spoonfuls two or three times a day.

In Purpura Hæmorrhagica.—Mr. W. SMITH.

2845. ℞ Olei Terebinth. ʒss.
Tinct. Kino,
Syrupi Zingib. ana ʒj.
Aquæ Cinnam.
Aquæ mollis, ana ʒiij.
Mist. Acaciæ, q. s. to mix well together.
Make a draught. To be taken two or three times a day.

To restrain Hæmorrhage from Piles.—Dr. OKE.

2846. ℞ Olei Olivæ, ℥vj.
Olei Terebinth. ℥ij.
Ceræ flavæ, ℥j.
Bals. Peruv. ʒij.
Camphoræ rasæ, ʒiss.
Dissolve the oil, turpentine, and wax; then add the rest. (Nearly the same as the Balsam of Chiron, a long-celebrated medicine.) Dose, gr. x–ʒss.

In Hæmorrhages and Fluxes.

2847. ℞ Olei Terebinth. part. ij, and add, drop by drop,
Acidi Sulph. part. iss, heated in a glass vessel by means of the sand bath. To the cooled liquor, add gradually
Alcoholis, part. viij.
Macerate for seven days. (Dose, ʒss–ʒj in some fit vehicle.)

Astringent Balsam for Hæmorrhagic Diseases.—Dr. COPLAND.

In the following it is given in large or cathartic doses, in tympanitis, or as a vermifuge:

2848. ℞ Olei Terebinth. ℥j.
Olei Amygd. dulcis, ℥ss.
Mix: make a draught. (To be repeated in five minutes if the symptoms are urgent.)

In Uterine Hæmorrhage.—Mr. J. GRIFFITH.

2849. ℞ Ricini Olei,
Terebinth. Olei,
Mist. Acaciæ,
Aquæ Menth. pip. ana ℥ss. Mix: make a draught.

Tape-worm, and Tympanitis.—Dr. HOOPER.

2850. ℞ Olei Terebinth.
Olei Ricini, ana ʒiij.
Olei Cajuputi, ♏vj.
Magnesiæ Calcinatæ, ℈j.
Aquæ Menth. pip. ℥iss. Mix: make a draught.

To combat Tympanitis in Typhoid Fever.—Dr. JOY.

The two next are examples of Turpentine Enemata.

2851. ℞ Olei Terebinth. ℥j.
Pulv. Acaciæ, q. s. Mix, and add
Decocti Hordei, ℥xix. Make an enema.

In Distention of the Abdomen with Gas.—Dr. HOOPER.

2852. ℞ Olei Terebinth. ℥j.
Olei Olivæ, ℥iss.
Camphoræ rasæ, gr. xx.
Decoct. Avenæ, ℥viij. Mix: make an enema.

In Hysterical Tympanitis, &c.—Dr. COPLAND.

In the remainder, Turpentine is prescribed as an external application.

2853. ℞ Cerat. Plumbi co. ℥j.
Olei Terebinth. ʒss.
Mix: make an ointment. (To be applied in a semi-fluid state with a feather.)

In Ecthyma.—Dr. NELIGAN.

2854. ℞ Olei Terebinth. ʒj.
Olei Amygd. gtt. xij.
Axungiæ, ℥j. Mix: make an ointment.

In Scabies.—Dr. NELIGAN.

2855. ℞ Olei Terebinth. ʒiij.
Linim. Camph. co.
Linim. Saponis, ana ℥ss. Mix: make an liniment.

For Chilblains.—Dr. THOMAS.

2856. ℞ Olei Terebinth. ℥ss.
Acidi Sulphurici, ʒiss.
Olei Olivæ, ℥iss.
Mix: make a liniment. (Similar to Pearson's Liniment.)

Chronic Rheumatism, &c.—Dr. HOOPER.

2857. ℞ Liq. Ammoniæ, ℥ss.
Olei Olivæ, ℥j.
Olei Terebinth. ℥ss.
Olei Limonis, ʒss.
Agitate together until mixed. Make a liniment.

Dr. COPLAND.

2858. ℞ Terebinth. Olei, ʒiij.
Acid. Acet. fort. ʒss.
Aquæ Rosæ, ʒiss.
Olei Limonis, ♏v.
Ovi Vitelli, q. s.
Mix: make a liniment for the chest. (An imitation of the celebrated liniment of St. John Long.)

In Asthma.—Dr. GRAVES.

TEREBINTHINA CHIA. *Chio Turpentine.*

This is a semi-fluid resin obtained from the ***Pistacia Terebinthus*** (Nat. Ord. *Terebinthaceæ*). It contains a considerable quantity of a fragrant volatile oil, and resembles Oil of Turpentine in its action on the urinary and other organs, and in its power of checking mucous fluxes.

Dose, ten to thirty grains, or more, three times a day, made into pills with powdered gum arabic or liquorice root; or given in emulsion with yolk of egg or tragacanth mucilage.

2859. ℞ Terebinth. Chiæ, gr. v.
Saponis duri, gr. iv.
Pulv. Calumbæ, q. s. to make 2 pills.

Diuretic.—Dr. HOOPER.

2860. ℞ Terebinth. Chiensis,
Spermaceti, ana ʒij.
Pulv. Myrrhæ, ʒj.
Olibani pulv. q. s. to make 70 pills. One or two, every third or fourth hour.
In Bronchial Affections, &c.—Dr. COPLAND.

TEREBINTHINA VENETA. *Venice Turpentine.*

This is a fluid Turpentine obtained from the Larch, *Larix Europæa* (Nat. Ord. *Coniferæ*). It is similar in action to Oil of Turpentine, and may be used in gonorrhœa and other fluxes. It is sometimes used to form a purgative clyster in colic or obstinate constipation. Dose, ten to thirty grains three times a day, made up as the last.

2861. ℞ Terebinth. Venetæ, ℥ij.
Extr. Rhei, ʒiij.
Camphoræ, ʒij.
Mix, and divide into 4-grain pills. Three, three times a day.
In Gonorrhœa and Leucorrhœa.—ST. MARIE.

2862. ℞ Terebinthinæ, ℥ss.
Balsam. Tolut. ʒss.
Gum. Ammoniac. ʒj.
Ext. Opii Aquosi, gr. vj.
Excipientis, q. s.
Mix, and divide into 80 pills. Five, every day.
For Catarrh of the Bronchi or Bladder.
TROUSSEAU and REVEIL.

2863. ℞ Terebinth. Venetæ,
Cetacei, ana ℥ss.
Pulv. Myrrhæ, ʒij.
Pulv. Olibani, q. s. to make 3-grain pills. One every three hours.
In Chronic Catarrh.—CADET.

2864. ℞ Terebinth. Venetæ, ʒj–ʒiss.
Vitelli ovorum, q. s. Mix, and add
Aquæ Menth. pip. ℥ivss.
Mix: one or two spoonfuls, as occasion requires.
Against Worms, and Chronic Affections of the Mucous Surfaces. CLOSSIUS.

2865. ℞ Terebinth. Venetæ, ℥ss.
Vitelli Ovi unius,
Infusi Lini, ℥x.
Olei Napi sylv. ℥j. Mix: make an enema.
In Colic and obstinate Constipation.—NOSOCOM. EDIN.

THEA. *Tea.*

The best teas, both black and green, are derived from *Thea Viridis* (Nat. Ord. *Theaceæ*), a plant of Northern China. Besides its use as a daily beverage, infusion of tea may be employed as a pleasant vehicle for many other medicines. Containing some Tannin, it has been occasionally used for its mild astringent properties.

2866. ℞ Infusi Theæ viridis, ℥vj.
Liq. Plumbi diacet. ♏xij. Mix: make an injection.
In Gonorrhœa.—Dr. THOMAS.

THUS. *Frankincense.* See PIX BURGUNDICA.

TIGLII OLEUM. *Croton Oil.*

This oil is expressed from the seeds of the *Croton Tiglium* (Nat. Ord. *Euphorbiaceæ*), a plant which grows in the East and West Indies. Croton oil, like Castor oil, is soluble in alcohol. It is very acrid. It is used externally as a counter-irritant. Rubbed on the skin it produces redness, followed by a pustular eruption. Given internally it is a most powerful drastic cathartic, excelled in activity by none but Elaterium. Large doses may cause death with choleraic symptoms. It is a hydragogue, and often increases the urine. It is generally very speedy in action, but it is not certain. It is used in very obstinate constipation, in dropsy, and in apoplexy or paralysis where a speedy irritant action on the intestines is desired. In lock-jaw or mania, when the patient cannot or will not swallow, it will produce catharsis if a few drops are placed on the tongue. It is employed as a counter-irritant in inflammations of the chest. Dose, for an adult, one or two drops.

Sapo Crotonis (Foy): dose, one to three grains.

Pilulæ Crotonis (Reece), one for a dose.

Trochisci Crotonis (Soubeiran), six contain one drop.

Tinctura Crotonis (Soubeiran): dose, fifteen to twenty-five drops.

Mistura Crotonis (Ellis), one drachm every hour until it operates.

Linimentum Crotonis (D.) is used as a counter-irritant, as also are the following:

Ceratum Crotonis (Caventou).

Emplastrum Crotonis (Bouchardat).

Unguentum Crotonis (Ainslie).

2867. ℞ Olei Tiglii, gtt. v.
Saponis,
Pulv. Acaciæ, ana ℈j.
Mix, and divide into 20 pills. One to three for a dose.

SUNDELIN.

2868. ℞ Tiglii Olei, ♏ij.
Olei Caryophylli, ♏j.
Micæ panis, q. s. to make a pill. To be taken immediately, and to be repeated after the lapse of two hours, unless it has operated.

Dr. PARIS.

2869. ℞ Olei Tiglii, ♏j.
Pulv. Aloes, q. s. to make a pill.

Dr. HOOPER.

2870. ℞ Olei Tiglii, gtt. iij.
Pil. Colocynth. co. ʒj.
Mix, and divide into 12 pills. One, every three hours.

In Colic.—Dr. R. B. TODD.

2871. ℞ Olei Tiglii, ♏j.
Extr. Colocynth. co. gr. v.
Pulv. Rhei, q. s. Mix, and divide into 2 pills.

Dr. HOOPER.

2872. ℞ Extr. Colocynth. co. ʒj.
Olei Crotonis, ♏vj.
Olei Menth. pip. ♏v.
Mix: make 12 pills. One, for a dose.

In obstinate Constipation.—Dr. RYAN.

2873. ℞ Olei Tiglii, ♏ij.
Pil. Coloc. co. ℈j.
Pil. Galbani co. ℈ij.
Mix, and divide into 12 pills. Three, at night.

In Facial Neuralgia.—Dr. GREGORY.

2874. ℞ Saponis Crotonis, gr. vj.
Calomelanos, gr. xxx.
Pil. Coloc. et Hyoscyam. gr. xxiv.
Mix: divide into 12 pills. One, three times a day.

Cathartic in Spasmodic Diseases.—Dr. NELIGAN.

2875. ℞ Pulv. Opii, gr. iij.
Olei Crotonis, gtt. v. Mix: make a pill.

In Asiatic Cholera when a draught (see 2880) *cannot be given on account of the vomiting.* Dr. MCGREGOR.

2876. ℞ Olei Tiglii, ♏j.
Hydrarg. Chloridi, gr. iij.
Extr. Anthemidis, gr. v.
Syrupi, q. s.
Make 2 pills. One or two, every other morning.

In Epilepsy.—Dr. THOMAS.

2877. ℞ Olei Tiglii, gtt. ij.
Mucil. Acaciæ, ʒij.
Aquæ, ℥j. Mix: a fourth part every four hours.

Dr. DUNGLISON.

2878. ℞ Olei Crotonis, gtt. iij.
Olei Amygd. ℥ss.
Pulv. Acaciæ, ʒij. Rub up well, and add gradually
Syrupi flor. Aurantii, ℥j.
Aquæ Anthemidis, ℥v.
Mix: a tablespoonful to be given every two hours until it operates.

PHŒBUS.

2879. ℞ Olei Crotonis, gtt. iij.
Pulv. Acaciæ, gr. iij. Rub up together, and add
Syrup. simp. ℥ss.
Infus. Anthemidis, ℥iij. Mix: in one or two doses.

Strong Purge.—TROUSSEAU and REVEIL.

2880. ℞ Olei Crotonis, gtt. v.
Tinct. Hyoscyami, ʒj.
Pulv. Opii, gr. v.
Pulv. Acaciæ, ʒss.
Aquæ, ℥iss.
Mix, and make a draught. To be taken immediately.

In Asiatic Cholera.—Dr. McGREGOR.

2881. ℞ Olei Crotonis Tiglii, ʒiij.
Olei Olivæ, ʒv.
Mix: make a liniment. To be rubbed into the side at bedtime.

Dr. G. BURROWS.

2882. ℞ Olei Tiglii, ♏xx.
Lin. Camph. co. ℥j.
Mix: ʒij rubbed over the fore part of the neck night and morning until a full crop of pimples appear.

In Aphonia.—Dr. GRAVES.

2883. ℞ Tiglii Olei, ♏x.
Linim. Saponis, ℥j.
Tinct. Opii, ℥ss. Mix, and make a liniment.

Irritant in Chest Affections, &c.—Dr. HOOPER.

2884. ℞ Olei Crotonis, ʒiss.
Ol. Cajuputi, ʒj.
Olei Olivæ, ʒx.
Mix. Five minutes' friction night and morning over the epigastric region.

In Chronic Inflammatory Dyspepsia.—Dr. ROSS.

2885. ℞ Tiglii Olei, ♏x.
Adipis, ℥ss.
Mix: make an ointment. The size of a nut to be rubbed in two or three times a day until an eruption appears on the skin.
Counter-irritant in Laryngitis, Neuralgia, &c.—Dr. Joy.

TORMENTILLA. *Tormentil.*

The root of *Potentilla Tormentilla* (Nat. Ord. *Rosaceæ*), a small native plant, has been used for its astringent properties. It contains about 18 per cent. of tannic acid. It is given internally as an astringent tonic, and in hæmorrhages and fluxes from the bladder and bowels. Externally it is well adapted for astringent lotions, injections, and gargles. Dose, thirty grains to one drachm.

Extractum Tormentillæ (Amst. Pharm.), twenty to thirty grains.

Pulvis Tormentillæ compositus (Genev. Pharm.), ten to thirty grains.

Decoctum Tormentillæ (L.), one and a half ounce three times a day.

2886. ℞ Decoct. Tormentillæ, ℥ix.
Vini Ipecac. ♏xx.
Tinct. Opii, ♏x.
Make a draught. To be taken once or twice a day.
In the Diarrhœa of Phthisis.—Dr. Paris.

2887. ℞ Rad. Tormentillæ, ℥j.
Aquæ, ℥xij. Boil to 8 oz., strain, and add
Aluminis, ʒj.
Mellis, ℥j. Mix: make a gargle.
In Relaxed Throat.—Radius.

TOXICODENDRON. *Poison Oak.*

The leaves of the *Rhus Toxicodendron*, an American plant (Nat. Ord. *Terebinthaceæ*), have no odor, but possess a disagreeable acrid taste, and are very poisonous in large doses. It rouses the nervous centers in the same manner as Strychnia. Toxicodendron is chiefly used in cases of local paralysis, whether of sensation or motion, and may sometimes restore the lost power in the affected part. It has also been given in obstinate skin diseases, and in chronic rheumatism. Dose of the powdered leaves, one to three grains.

Extractum Toxicodendri (Paris Cod.), one grain, gradually increased.

Tinctura Rhois (Paris Codex), five drops, gradually increased.

Tinctura Toxicodendri (Neligan), half a drachm to a drachm.

2888. ℞ Extr. Toxicodendri, gr. lxxv. (?)
Confect. Rosæ, q. s. Mix, and divide into 25 pills. (One to sixteen daily.)

In Paraplegia without organic lesion; in Paralysis of the Bladder or Rectum. TROUSSEAU and REVEIL.

2889. ℞ Extr. Toxicodendri,
Camphoræ, ana gr. xv.
Extr. Arnicæ,
Extr. Valerianæ, ana ʒss.
Pulv. Calami, q. s. to make a mass, to be divided into 30 pills. One, three times a day.

In Hemiplegia.—BRERA.

2890. ℞ Tinct. Toxicodendri, ʒss.
Syrupi Papaveris, ʒj.
Syrupi Limonum, ʒss.
Aquæ, ℥iss.
Mix: make a draught. One every six hours.

For Acute Pains in Chronic Paralysis.—Dr. NELIGAN.

TRAGACANTHA. *Tragacanth.*

This is a white gummy exudation from several species of *Astragalus* (Nat. Ord. *Leguminosæ*), growing in Asia Minor. It consists for the main part of a kind of gum called Bassorine, which, though not soluble in water, swells up with it into a paste or mucilage. It is inodorous and has a bad taste. It is used as a demulcent in coughs, diarrhœa, &c., and employed for the formation of a mucilage by means of which insoluble powders may be suspended in water.

Mucilago Tragacanthæ (E.) is chiefly used, on account of its viscidity, to suspend matters insoluble in water.

Pulvis Tragacanthæ compositus (L.) is demulcent in doses of half a drachm to one drachm, or is mixed with water to form a mucilage.

Tragacanth is also employed to make lozenges and pastes.

2891. ℞ Pulv. Tragacanthæ, gr. xv.
Sacchari albi, gr. xij. Rub up, and add by degrees
Mist. Amygd. dulc. ℥ij.
Mist. Camphoræ, ℥iiiss.
Syrupi Althææ, ℥ss.
Mix: make a demulcent mixture.

Dr. COPLAND.

TUSSILAGO. *Coltsfoot.*

The whole herb of *Tussilago Farfara*, the Coltsfoot, a common English plant (Nat. Ord. *Compositæ*), abounds in mucilaginous matter. It is also slightly bitter. Its preparations are in use as mild demulcent tonics, and are chiefly used in coughs. It may be given in decoction, or formed into paste or lozenges.

Decoctum Tussilaginis: dose, one to three ounces.

Syrupus Tussilaginis (Paris Codex), one drachm to one ounce.

2892. ℞ Decoct. Tussilaginis,
Mist. Amygd. ana ℥iij.
Syrup. Hemidesmi, ℥ij.
Mix: make a mixture. Two tablespoonfuls at intermediate hours.

In Chronic Bronchitis.—Dr. NELIGAN.

2893. ℞ Herbæ Malvæ offic.
Herbæ Tussilaginis,
Rad. Althææ,
Rad. Glycyrrhizæ, ana ℥j.
Sem. Anisi, ℥ss.
Aquæ fervidæ, sufficient to cover.
Macerate and make a pectoral infusion.

Dr. COPLAND.

ULMUS. *Elm Bark.*

The inner bark of the common Elm, *Ulmus campestris* (Nat. Ord. *Ulmaceæ*), is the part used. It is slightly astringent, containing about three per cent. of Tannic Acid. It is also supposed to be alterative, and its decoction is given in chronic rashes and other cutaneous affections.

Decoctum Ulmi (L.) may be given in doses of three to four ounces three times a day.

2894. ℞ Corticis Ulmi, ℥iss.
Sem. Carui cont. ʒss.
Aquæ, Oiss. Boil to a pint.

Alterative Drink.—Sir E. WILMOT.

2895. ℞ Corticis Ulmi,
Radicis Lappæ,
Radicis Rumicis,
Dulcamaræ,
Fumariæ, singulorum, ʒij.
Aquæ bullientis, Oj. Infuse for four hours, then strain, and add
Syrupi Sarsæ, ℥j.
Mix: make a mixture. To be taken in twenty-four hours in divided doses.

In Chronic Exanthemata.—CADET.

UREA.

This is a soluble crystalline substance, obtained from the urine of man and animals. It has been much employed as a diuretic by certain French and continental practitioners, and is said to increase the secretion of urine in dropsy and anasarcous disorders, without producing any disturbance of the animal economy. Dose, ten grains to half a drachm or one drachm three times a day.

Nitrate of Urea is recommended by Dr. Kingdon as a diuretic in anasarca, in doses of one grain to one grain and a half three times a day.

2896. ℞ Ureæ, gr. xxxvj.
Syrupi Aurantii, ℥ss.
Aquæ destill. ℥vss.
Mix: make a mixture. Take f℥j every six hours.

In Anasarca, &c.—Dr. KINGDON.

2897. ℞ Potassæ Bitart. ℥ss.
Ureæ, ʒij.
Mellis, ℥ss.
Mix: make an electuary. To be taken three times a day, with an equal quantity of nutmeg.

Diuretic in Dropsy.—Dr. NELIGAN.

2898. ℞ Ureæ Nitratis, gr. iss.
Confect. Rosæ, q. s. to make a pill.
To be taken three times a day.

In Anasarca, &c.—Dr. KINGDON.

UVA URSI.

The leaves of *Arctostaphylos Uva Ursi* (Nat. Ord. *Ericaceæ*), a small evergreen shrub, are powerfully astringent, and contain about thirty-six per cent. of Tannic Acid. This drug seems also to exert a specific influence on the kidneys. Some assert that it has a diuretic action, while others dispute it. It is chiefly given in the latter stage of chronic inflammation of the bladder, when its use should be persevered in for some time. Dr. Prout used frequently to prescribe it along with Hyoscyamus. It is sometimes given in cases of irritation from the presence of a stone in the bladder. The dose of the powder is one scruple to one drachm every three or four hours.

Extractum Uvæ Ursi (L.): dose, five to ten grains, as a tonic, &c.

Decoctum Uvæ Ursi (L., D.), one to two ounces three times a day.

Syrupus Uvæ Ursi (Procter), one drachm to half an ounce for a dose.

2899. ℞ Pulv. Uvæ Ursi,
Pulv. Cinchonæ, ana ʒij.
Pulv. Opii, gr. iij.

Mix, and divide into six powders. One, twice a day in lime-water.

In Nephritic Complaints, and as an Antilithic.—FERRIAR.

2900. ℞ Pulv. Uvæ Ursi, ʒiij.
Acidi Tannici, gr. vj.
Pulv. Opii, gr. ij.

Mix: divide into 12 equal portions. One, three times a day.

In passive Hæmaturia, Albuminuria, and Chronic Catarrh of Bladder. Dr. NELIGAN.

2901. ℞ Extracti Uvæ Ursi, ʒij.
Sodæ Carb. ʒss.
Pulv. Cinnam. co. ℥ss.
Confect. Rosæ caninæ, ℥j.
Syrupi, q. s. to make an electuary.

A tablespoonful for a dose.

Diuretic in Chronic Inflammation of the Kidneys, &c. Dr. HOOPER.

2902. ℞ Decocti Uvæ Ursi,
Liquoris Calcis, ana ℥iv.

Mix: a wineglassful for a dose.

Antilithic, and in Chronic Cystitis.—Dr. HOOPER.

2903. ℞ Potassæ Bicarb. ℈j.
Tinct. Hyoscyami, ʒss.
Inf. Uvæ Ursi, ʒxj. Mix: make a draught.

In Mucous Urine.—Dr. G. BIRD.

2904. ℞ Uvæ Ursi, ℨiss.
Sodæ Carb. exsic.
Pulv. Cinnam. c. ana ℨss.
Conf. Rosæ, q. s.
Divide into six boluses. One, three times a day.

In Chronic Inflammation of Kidneys and Bladder.—Dr. JOY.

2905. ℞ Acid. Phosph. dil. ℨss.
Inf. Uvæ Ursi, ℥ij. Make a draught.

In Mucous Urine, with copious Deposits.—Dr. G. BIRD.

2906. ℞ Inf. Uvæ Ursi (ℨij to warm water Oss), ℨxiv.
Acid. Sulph. dil. ♏xx.
Tinct. Digitalis, ♏xv.
Syrupi Papaveris, ℨiss.
Mix: make a draught. To be taken three or four times a day.

In Laryngitis, Bronchitis, &c.—Dr. COPLAND.

2907. ℞ Foliorum Uvæ Ursi contus. ℥ss.
Aquæ ferventis, Oj. Macerate for three hours, and strain.
To seven ounces of this, add
Tinct. Kino,
Syrupi Zingiberis, ana ℥ss.
Mix: make a mixture. A wineglassful for a dose.

Astringent.—Dr. HOOPER.

VALERIANA. *Valerian.*

The root of the common Valerian, *Valeriana officinalis* (Nat. Ord. *Valerianaceæ*), is officinal on account of its antispasmodic properties. It has a strong and peculiarly disagreeable smell. It acts upon the nervous centers without materially affecting the secretions. It is used in epilepsy, hysteria, spasmodic cough, and dyspnœa, in dyspepsia, neuralgia, and as a vermifuge. The odor and medicinal properties of Valerian are due to a peculiar volatile oil, which contains an acid, Valerianic Acid, and may be separated from the root by distillation with water. This acid is also obtained by the artificial oxidation of oil of grain (Fusel oil), which is accomplished by distilling it with Bichromate of Potash and Sulphuric acid. Various Valerianates used in medicine are formed by means of this acid, and combine with its peculiar antispasmodic properties the medicinal action of the base with which it is united in each case. (See Quina, Zincum, &c.) The dose of the powdered root of Valerian is half a drachm to one drachm.

Infusum Valerianæ (L., D.), one to two ounces.

Tinctura Valerianæ (L., E., D.), half a drachm to half an ounce.

Tinctura Valerianæ composita (vel *Ammoniata*) (L., E.), half a drachm to two drachms.

Syrupus Valerianæ (Paris Codex), one drachm to half an ounce.

2908. ℞ Pulv. Valerianæ rad. ℈j.
Pulv. Cinnamomi co. gr. x.
Mix: make a powder. To be taken every four hours.
In Hysteria, Nervous Headache, &c.—Dr. JOY.

2909. ℞ Pulv. Valerianæ, ʒj.
Pulv. fol. Aurantii, ℈j.
Ammoniæ Muriatis, gr. ij.
Olei Cajuputi, ♏iv.
Mix: make a powder. ʒj four times a day, in hot tea.
In Epilepsy.—NIEMANN.

2910. ℞ Pulv. Valerianæ, ℈ij.
Castorei, gr. xv.
Oxidi Zinci, ℈j.
Olei Cajuputi, ♏v.
Syrupi simp. q. s.
Divide into 18 pills. Three, four times a day.
DUPUYTREN.

2911. ℞ Ferri Carb. gr. v–℈j.
Pulv. Valerianæ, ʒss.
Syrup. Zingib. q. s. to make a bolus.
In Hysteria, Anæmia, &c.—Dr. COPLAND.

2912. ℞ Pulv. Castor. opt. ʒij.
Pulv. rad. Valerianæ, ℥ss.
Camphoræ rasæ, ʒj. Mix accurately, and add
Syrupi Papaveris, q. s. to make a 12-grain bolus. To be enveloped in saffron powder.
Antispasmodic.—Dr. COPLAND.

2913. ℞ Pulv. Valerianæ,
P. foliorum Aurantii, ana ʒvj.
Syrupi Absinthii, q. s. to make an electuary. 2–3 teaspoonfuls a day.
SWEDIAUR.

2914. ℞ Infusi Valerianæ, ʒvj.
Tinct. Valerian. co. ʒj.
Mist. Camphoræ, ʒiv.
Mix: make a draught. To be taken three times a day.
In Hysteria.—Dr. GREGORY.

2915. ℞ Valerianæ rad. in pulv. cont. ℈j.
Misturæ Acaciæ, ʒj.
Infusi Valerianæ, ʒix.
Tinct. Valerianæ, ʒj.
Tinct. Castorei, ʒj.
Mix: make a draught. To be taken three times a day.

Antispasmodic.—Dr. PARIS.

2916. ℞ Tinct. Valerianæ comp. ℥ss.
Spirit. Juniperi comp. ℥ij.
Aquæ Pimentæ, ℥iiiss. A fourth part for a dose.

Stimulant.—Dr. HOOPER.

2917. ℞ Tinct. Valerianæ Ammoniatæ,
Spirit. Ammon. fœtidæ, ana ℥ss.
Spirit. Armoraciæ co. ℥ij.
Aquæ Pimentæ, ℥iij. Mix: a fourth part for a dose.

In Hysteria.—Dr. HOOPER.

2918. ℞ Tinct. Valerianæ, ʒj.
Acid. Sulph. dil. ♏x.
Tinct. Cinchonæ co. ʒj.
Aquæ, ℥j.
Mix: make a draught. To be taken two or three times a day.

In Hysteria.—Dr. ASHWELL.

2919. ℞ Tinct. Valerian. Ammon.
Spir. Ætheris comp.
Spir. Lavand. co. ana ʒss.
Tinct. Hyoscyami, ♏xx.
Mist. Camphoræ, ʒx.
Mix: make a draught. To be taken every second or third hour.

In Hysteria.—Dr. ASHWELL.

2920. ℞ Pulv. Valerianæ, gr. x.
Pulv. Rhei, gr. v.
Aquæ Menthæ pip. ʒx.
Ammon. Sesquicarb. gr. iij.
Tinct. Zingiberis, ♏xx.
Mix: make a draught. To be taken twice a day.

In Hysteria.—Dr. GREGORY.

2921. ℞ Tinct. Valerianæ,
Spir. Æth. Sulph. co. ana ʒij.
Chloroformylis, ʒj. (*Large dose.*—ED.)
Aquæ puræ, q. s. to make a draught.

In Delirium Tremens.—Dr. S. PRATT (U.S.).

2922. ℞ Infusi Valerianæ, ℥iv.
Quinæ Disulph. gr. x.
Vini Opii, ♏xx.
Syr. flor. Aurantii, ℥vj.
Mix: make a mixture. A tablespoonful every two or three hours.

In Typhoid Fever.—BROQUA.

2923. ℞ Olei Valerianæ, gtt. viij.
Spirit. Ammon. aromat. ʒj.
Aquæ, ℥iv.
Sacchari, ʒij.
Mix: a tablespoonful every second or third hour.

Dr. Ellis.

VANILLA.

The aromatic seed-pods of some American plants of the Nat. Ord. *Orchideæ*, particularly the *Vanilla aromatica*, have been used in medicine on account of their aromatic properties. Vanilla contains a volatile oil, and is used in cookery because of its agreeable flavor. It has also been given in epilepsy, hysteria, &c., as a diffusible stimulant, and its fluid preparations may be employed as pleasant vehicles for other medicines. The dose of the powder is from five grains to a scruple.

2924. ℞ Fructûs Vanillæ concis. et contus. part. j.
Alcoholis, part. vj.
Macerate slowly with heat for eight days, and strain. Dose, fʒj.

Nervine, Analeptic, Excitant.—Pfaff.

2925. ℞ Fructûs Vanillæ concis. et contus. ℥vj.
Potassæ Subcarb. ʒvj.
Aquæ destil. Oij.
Spirit. Vini tenuioris, Oiss.
Macerate slowly with heat for three days, and strain.

Agreeable Aromatic Vehicle.—Dr. Copland.

VERATRUM. *White Hellebore.*

The root stock of the *Veratrum album* (Nat. Ord. *Melanthaceæ*) is very acrid and poisonous. It is said to contain Veratria, and another similar alkaloid. It used to be employed as an active hydragogue cathartic, and was given in gout in the same manner as Colchicum. It is occasionally employed as an errhine, as its powder causes sneezing and increase of the nasal secretion. But it is generally used only externally, for the purpose of destroying vermin which infest the skin or hair. Dose, one to two grains.

Vinum Veratri (L.), ten minims may be given three times daily, in gout and rheumatism.

Pulvis Veratri compositus (Radius) is employed as an errhine.

Unguentum Veratri (U. S.) is used as a friction in Scabies.

2926. ℞ Pulv. Veratri, ℥ij.
Saponis mollis, ℥j.
Aquæ ferventis, q. s. to make an ointment. To be rubbed once a day upon the affected parts. After 2–3 such frictions a warm bath is to be used.

In Scabies.—BOUCHARDAT.

VERATRIA.

The fruit and seeds of two kindred plants, *Veratrum Sabadilla* and *Asagræa officinalis*, have been already mentioned under the name of Sabadilla. From these their active principle, the alkaloid Veratria, is prepared by a chemical process. It does not crystalize, and is but sparingly soluble in water, though readily in alcohol. It is extremely irritating to the nostrils, and has a bitter acrid taste. Internally it is emetic and purgative, in large doses poisonous. It has been given in rheumatism, and as a stimulant in nervous affections, in doses of one-twelfth to one-sixth of a grain. But it is chiefly employed as an external irritant. It sometimes dispels local neuralgic pains, and is useful in chronic gouty and rheumatic affections.

The *Muriate* and *Nitrate of Veratria* have been used by some. The *Sulphate of Veratria* has been proposed as a substitute for the *Eau Medicinale d'Husson.*

Pilulæ Veratriæ (Majendie), one to three for a dose.

Tinctura Veratriæ (Majendie), ten to twenty drops in water, in gout, &c.

Liquor Veratriæ Sulphatis (Cadet), one to two drachms, thrice daily in gout.

Lotio Veratriæ (Turnbull), and

Unguentum Veratriæ (Turnbull), are used externally in neuralgia and rheumatism.

2927. ℞ Veratriæ, gr. j.
Extr. Hyoscyami,
Pulv. Glycyrrhizæ, ana gr. x.
Mix, and divide into 12 pills. One, three times a day.

In Gout, Neuralgia, and Rheumatism.—Dr. TURNBULL.

2928. ℞ Veratriæ, gr. iv.
Alcohol. ♏vj.
Adipis, ℥ss. Mix well, and make an ointment.

In Neuralgia.—Dr. HOOPER.

2929. ℞ Veratriæ, gr. v.
Axungiæ, ℥ss.
Mix, and make an ointment. ʒss to be rubbed on every night with a horsehair glove, until severe tingling is produced.
In Sciatica.—Mr. C. R. Bree.

2930. ℞ Veratriæ (Morson's), gr. viij.
Olei Limonis, ♏x. Rub up together, and add
Adipis, ʒvij.
Hydrarg. Bisulphuret. ℈ss. Make an ointment.
Dr. G. Bird.

2931. ℞ Veratriæ puræ, gr. xxxvj.
Olei Olivæ, ʒss.
Adipis, ʒviiss.
Olei Bergamii, ♏x.
Olei Santalini, ♏ij. Mix: make an ointment.
In Neuralgic Rheumatism.—Dr. H. W. Fuller.

2932. ℞ Veratriæ, gr. ij.
Lin. Saponis co.
Spirit. Camphoræ, ana ℥iss.
Spirit. Amon. arom. ʒj.
Mix: make a liniment. A dessertspoonful every night to be rubbed in well behind the ears and around the throat.
In Neuralgia of the Face.—Mr. H. Neil.

2933. ℞ Veratriæ, ʒss.
Pulv. Opii, ʒj.
Axungiæ, ℥iss. Mix: make an ointment.
To Rheumatic Joints.—Dr. Dunglison.

2934. ℞ Veratriæ, ℈j.
Potassii Iodidi, ʒss.
Axung. ℥j. Mix: make an ointment.
To promote Absorption of Indolent Swellings.—Jourdan.

VINUM. *Wine.*

The various kinds of wine, when good and unadulterated, are often preferable to brandy and spirit as stimulants and cordials. They are considerably diluted, and therefore less dangerous than stronger liquors, and are more agreeable to the taste of most patients. But they sometimes agree ill with the stomachs of dyspeptic persons. Sherry wine is generally preferred for ordinary use. Port wine is often ordered to patients during convalescence, as it possesses some astringency, and is more tonic in its action. Effervescing wines are more exhilarant, and less narcotic than others. Acid wines may be used in a diaphoretic regimen. Wines form agreeable vehicles for many medicines.

All stimulant drinks must be avoided when there is fever with a full pulse, dry tongue, and hot skin. They are appropriate whenever the system appears to be in want of nervous power to enable it to bear up against a disease.

2935. ℞ Infusi Rosæ co. ℥v.
Vini rubri Hispanici, ℥ij.
Syrupi simp. ℥j. Mix.

For an Ordinary Drink in states of Debility.—Dr. HOOPER.

2936. ℞ Vini, ℥vj.
Ovor. duor. vitellos,
Sacchari purif. ℥ss.
Olei Cinnam. ♏iv.
Tinct. Capsici, ℈j.

Mix. Dose, f℥jss three, four, or more times a day, according to the degree of debility.

In cases of Debility, without High Fever.—Dr. COPLAND.

2937. ℞ Ovorum vitellos duor.
Olei Cinnam. gtt. xx. Mix, and add
Vini Madeirensis,
Aquæ Cinnam. ana ℥iij.
Aquæ destil. ℥ij.
Sacchari, ʒij. Mix: three or four spoonfuls for a dose.

In Convalescence from Low Fevers.—Dr. ELLIS.

2938. ℞ Vini Xerici, ℥ij.
Ovi vitellum unius,
Jusculi bovini (sine sale), ℥viij. Mix: an enema.

Restorative in Low Fevers, Tetanus, &c.—RADIUS.

VIOLA. *Violet.*

The flowers of the *Viola odorata*, or *Sweet Violet* (Nat. Ord. *Violaceæ*), have been used on account of their demulcent and mild laxative properties. In large doses they are emetic. The Syrup of Violets is employed as a laxative for infants. The root of the violet is emetic in half drachm to one drachm doses. The leaves and flowers of the *Viola tricolor*, or Wild Pansy, have been popularly supposed to possess alterative powers.

Confectio Violæ (Soubeiran), one drachm to half an ounce.

Syrupus Violæ (L. E.), one to two drachms to infants.

2939. ℞ Violæ odoratæ rad. ʒss.
Syrupi Scillæ, ʒj.
Mix: make a bolus. To be taken immediately, and repeated after an hour, if necessary.

Emetic.—Dr. NELIGAN.

2940. ℞ Mellis Violæ,
Mannæ, ana ℥ss.
Syrupi Violæ, q. s.
Make an electuary. A teaspoonful as occasion requires.

A mild Laxative for Children.—Dr. NELIGAN.

2941. ℞ Syrupi Violæ, ℥iiss.
Olei Amygd. dul. ℥j.
Syrup. Scillæ,
Syrup. Sennæ, ana ℥ss. Mix: make a linctus.

Demulcent and Aperient for Infants.—Dr. COPLAND.

2942. ℞ Violæ tricoloris fol. ʒx. Boil in
Lactis, ℥v, strain, and add
Syrupi Violæ tricol. ℥ij.
To be taken as a *tisane* night and morning for several weeks.

In Cutaneous Eruptions and Constitutional Syphilis.
TROUSSEAU and REVEIL.

ZINCI OXIDUM.* ZINCI CARBONAS. *Oxide and Carbonate of Zinc.*

These are both white insoluble powders. The former is preferred for use, but the Carbonate is often sold for it. The Oxide of Zinc is not often used internally, though it may be employed in nervous disorders in the same manner as the Sulphate. For this purpose two to ten grains may be given three times a day. Externally it is employed as an absorbent powder, being dusted over sores, excoriations, and eruptions. It forms a mild cooling ointment, which is applied to wounds, to ring-worm of the scalp, impetiginous pustular eruptions, and tarsal ophthalmia. The Carbonate, or *Prepared Calamine*, is much used to form plasters and cerates, and ointments for dressing wounds and ulcerations.

Pulvis Oxidi Zinci (Thomson), one every four hours in spasmodic cough.

* It was thought best to place these here before the other preparations of Zinc, although out of their strict alphabetical order.

Pilulæ Oxidi Zinci (Ellis), one, three or four times daily, in spasmodic disorders.

Unguentum Zinci (L., E., D.) is extensively used as a mild ointment.

Ceratum Calaminæ (L., E.) is also used as a dressing to ulcers and excoriations.

2943. ℞ Zinci Oxidi, gr. xij.
Magnesiæ calcinatæ, ʒss.
Pulv. Calumbæ, ʒj.
Rub up well together, and divide into 12 powders. One, three or four times a day.

In Diarrhœa.—De Haen.

2944. ℞ Zinci Oxidi,
Ext. Valerianæ,
Ext. Hyoscyami, ana ʒss.
Mix, and divide into 40 pills. (1–10 daily.)

In Obstinate Neuralgias.—Meglin.

2945. ℞ Pulv. Oxidi Zinci, ʒj.
Pulv. Opii, gr. x.
Pulv. Cinchonæ,
Pulv. Sem. Fœniculi, ana ℥j.
Mix: divide into 50 powders. One every second hour.

In Hooping-cough.—Augustin.

2946. ℞ Zinci Oxidi,
Extr. Gentianæ, ana gr. v. Mix: make 2 pills.

Tonic.—Dr. Hooper.

2947. ℞ Extr. Hyoscyami,
Pulv. Valerian. rad.
Zinci Oxidi, ana gr. j.
Make a pill: to be taken two or three times a day.

In Neuralgia.—Dr. Day.

2948. ℞ Zinci Oxidi,
Extr. Hyoscyami, ana gr. iv.
Mix, and divide into 2 pills. To be taken at night.

In the Night Perspirations of Phthisis.
Dr. Theophilus Thompson.

2949. ℞ Zinci Oxidi, ʒij.
Pulv. Amyli. ℥iv.
Mix: make a powder. To be dusted on the parts affected.

Eczema, Acne, Impetigo.—Cazenave.

2950. ℞ Zinci Oxidi, ʒij.
Camphoræ, ʒss.
Pulv. Amyli. ℥iv.
Mix: make a powder. To be dusted over the parts affected.

In Prurigo.—Cazenave.

2951. ℞ Unguent. Zinci, ℥ss.
Bals. Peruv. ʒj.
Pulv. Lapid. infern. ℈j. Mix: make an ointment.

For Syphilitic Chancres, during healing.—Dr. FRICKE.

2952. ℞ Zinci Oxid. gr. xij.
Calomelanos, gr. ix.
Camphoræ, gr. vi.
Butyri recentis, ʒij.
But. Cacao, ʒss. Mix: make an ointment.

For the Eyelids in Ophthalmia.—TROUSSEAU and REVEIL.

2953. ℞ Oxidi Zinci, gr. xx.
Cerat. Galeni (cold cream), ℥ij.
Ext. Belladonnæ, gr. xx.
Glycerinæ, ʒij. Mix: make an ointment.

To Irritable Eruptions with a copious discharge.
Dr. NELIGAN.

2954. ℞ Ung. Zinci, ℥j.
Liquor. Plumbi diacet.
Liquor. Opii sedat. ana ʒss.
Mix: make an ointment. To be applied to the affected part twice a day.

In External Piles.—Mr. COULSON.

2955. ℞ Zinci Oxidi,
Pulv. Calaminæ,
Pulv. Lycopodii, ana ℥j.
Pulv. Myrrhæ,
Plumbi Acet. ana ʒss.
Axungiæ, ℥iss. Mix: make an ointment.

To Extensive Burns.—Mr. SAVORY.

ZINCI ACETAS. *Acetate of Zinc.*

This occurs in small colorless soluble crystals, having a metallic taste. It is rarely given internally, but is well adapted for use in astringent lotions and injections, being milder and less irritating than the sulphate. It may be used as a collyrium in ophthalmia, or as an injection in gonorrhœa and leucorrhœa.

Tinctura Zinci Acetatis (D. 1226) is used to form injections and collyria, diluted with water.

2956. ℞ Zinci Acetatis, ℈j.
Aquæ destill. ℥vj.
Mix: a tablespoonful in mucilage every two hours.

In severe cases of Angina tonsillaris, occurring in Scarlatina, &c. Dr. PLANGE.

2957. ℞ Zinci Acetatis, ʒss.
Aquæ destill. ℥xvj. Mix: make a lotion.

In Ophthalmia.—Mr. WARE.

2958. ℞ Zinci Sulphatis, ʒj.
Plumbi Acetatis, ʒss.
Camphoræ, ℈j.
Aquæ Rosæ, ℥xij.
Dissolve, and strain. Make an eye-wash.

In Ophthalmia.—SPIELMANN.

2959. ℞ Tinct. Acetatis Zinci, ʒij.
Infusi Matico, ℥viiss.
Mucilag. Gum. Trag. ʒij.
Mix: make an injection. To be used frequently.

In advanced stages of Gonorrhœa, Gleet, and Leucorrhœa.
Dr. NELIGAN.

ZINCI CHLORIDUM. *Chloride of Zinc.*

The Chloride, or Butter of Zinc, is sometimes given in small doses as an antispasmodic, but is chiefly used externally. It is one of the most powerful caustics known. It is deliquescent, and destroys organic tissues by its great affinity for water. Its action causes great pain. It is used to destroy entirely the surface of a cancerous or phagedænic sore, or the dangerous eruption of Lupus. It is safer than arsenious acid for such purposes. A dilute solution may be used as a wash for foul ulcers or scrofulous sores, or as an injection in gonorrhœa.

Burnett's solution contains one pound of this chloride in five gallons of water. It is largely employed as a disinfectant and deodorizer; also to prevent the dry rot in wood, and to preserve animal matters from putrefaction. Lotions of Chloride of Zinc remove the unpleasant odor from cancerous and other sores. When used as a caustic, this chloride is generally made into a paste with flour, and it is sometimes combined with Chloride of Antimony.

Zinci Chloridi Liquor (D.) may be used as a caustic, or diluted with water to form a disinfecting solution.

2960. ℞ Zinci Chloridi, gr. ij.
Sp. Æth. Sulph. ℥ss.
Mix: five drops to be administered every four hours.

In Chorea, Epilepsy, &c.—HANKE.

2961. ℞ Zinci Chloridi, gr. j.
Aquæ puræ, ℥j.

Mix: make an injection. A small syringeful to be thrown into the urethra every six or eight hours, and the proportion of chloride gradually increased to three grains in the ounce.

In Gonorrhœa.—Mr. LLOYD.

2962. ℞ Zinci Chloridi, partem j.
Farinæ tostæ, partes ij ad iv.
Aquæ, q. s. to make a caustic paste. About 24–30 drops of water to each ounce of the chloride.

A Powerful Caustic.—CANQUOIN.

2963. ℞ Chloridi Zinci, ℨss.
Muriatis Antimonii liquidi, ♏xv.
Farinæ, ℨj.
Aquæ destill. q. s.

Make a mass, which will eat out the morbid part.

In Cancer and Lupus.—Dr. NELIGAN.

2964. ℞ Zinci Chloridi liquidi (*i. e.* zinc dissolved in strong hydrochloric acid), gtt. v.
Morphiæ Sulphatis, gr. ss.
Pastæ Tragacanth. ℨiij.

Mix: make a suppository. To be introduced into the vagina every other day.

In Cancer of the Uterus.—GAUDRIOT.

ZINCI CYANIDUM ET FERROCYANIDUM. *Cyanide of Zinc. Ferrocyanide of Zinc.*

The Cyanide is made by precipitating a solution of the Sulphate with one of Cyanide of Potassium. It is given in spasmodic affections in doses of one-quarter of a grain to six grains more.

The Ferrocyanide has also been employed by Schindler and others, being given in nervous and spasmodic disorders, in doses of one to four grains three times daily.

2965. ℞ Zinci Cyanureti, gr. vj.
Magnesiæ calcin. gr. iv.
Pulv. Cinnamomi, gr. iv.

Mix: make a powder. To be taken every fourth hour.

In Gastrodynia, Dyspepsia, and Dysmenorrhœa.
Dr. COPLAND.

2966. ℞ Zinci Cyanureti, gr. vj.
Magnesiæ calcin. gr. iv.
Pulv. capanellæ, gr. iij.

Mix: one powder every four hours.

In Neuralgia of the Stomach.—Dr. HENNING.

2967. ℞ Zinci Cyanidi, gr. xv.
Ext. Glycyrrhizæ, ʒij.
Mix: divide into 60 pills. One, three times a day.

KOPP.

2968. ℞ Zinci Cyanidi, gr. ¼–j.
Syrupi simp. ℥j. Mix.

Vermifuge.—MAJENDIE.

2969. ℞ Zinci Ferrocyanidi, gr. viij.
Sacchari, ʒj.
Mix, and divide into 12 powders. One, every second hour.

In Cardialgia.—ROSENSTEIL.

2970. ℞ Zinci Ferrocyanidi, gr. xv.
Pulv. Valerian. ʒss.
Ext. Valerian. q. s. and make 60 pills.
One, night and morning.

In Chorea.—ROSENSTEIL.

2971. ℞ Zinci Ferrocyanidi, gr. iv.
Aquæ destill. ℥ij.
Mix: a fourth part, four times a day.

LINCKE.

ZINCI IODIDUM. *Iodide of Zinc.*

This is sometimes given internally in small doses in scrofula. It acts externally as an astringent and alterative. It is used to form collyria in scrofulous ophthalmia, and an ointment is employed in the friction of chronic glandular enlargements. An *Iodide of Zinc and Morphia* has been described by M. Bouchardat, who gives it in doses of quarter and half grain in gastralgia.

Unguentum Zinci Iodidi (Ure) is employed as a friction to tumors.

Syrupus Zinci Iodidi (Thomson) contains fifteen grains in the ounce.

2972. ℞ Zinci Iodidi, gr. iv.
Aquæ destill. ℥vj. Mix: make an eye-wash.

2973. ℞ Zinci Iodidi, ʒj.
Adipis, ℥j. Mix: make an ointment.

Alterative Stimulant in Skin Diseases.—Dr. HOOPER.

ZINCI SULPHAS. *Sulphate of Zinc.*

This salt occurs in small colorless prismatic crystals of a styptic taste, and soluble in water. Internally, given in small doses, it is astringent, tonic, and antispasmodic. It is given as an astringent in fluxes and hæmorrhages; as a tonic in general debility, from whatever cause; and as an antispasmodic in hysteria, chorea, epilepsy, neuralgia, and gastrodynia. In large doses it acts suddenly as an emetic, without producing much nausea, and is therefore well adapted for use in cases of narcotic poisoning. Externally the Sulphate of Zinc acts as one of the best astringents known. It is used in collyria, in gargles for relaxed uvula, in injections in gonorrhœa, &c., in lotions to sores.

The dose as a tonic and antispasmodic is from two to ten grains. In epilepsy the dose must be gradually increased from a small quantity to as many grains as can be tolerated without producing vomiting. The dose as an emetic is from one scruple to one drachm.

Sulphate of Zinc is prescribed for internal use in the following prescriptions:

2974. ℞ Zinci Sulphatis,
Ext. Hæmatoxyli, ana gr. v. Mix, and divide into 2 pills.
Diarrhœa, &c.—Dr. HOOPER.

2975. ℞ Zinci Sulphatis, gr. ij.
Ext. Hyoscyami, gr. iv.
Mix, and divide into 2 pills. To be taken at night.
For the night Perspiration of Phthisis.
Dr. THEOPHILUS THOMPSON.

2976. ℞ Zinci Sulphatis, ʒss.
Extracti Conii, ʒj.
Syrupi Tolutani, q. s.
Mix: divide into 20 pills. One, three times a day.
In the Ulcerated Stage of Consumption.—Dr. GREGORY.

2977. ℞ Zinci Sulphatis, ℈ss.
Extracti Gentianæ, ℈ij.
Ext. Colocynth. co. ℈j.
Mix, and divide into 20 pills. Two, every night.
In Costiveness with Nervous Debility.—Dr. BABINGTON.

2978. ℞ Zinci Sulphatis, ʒj.
Extracti Gentianæ, ℈j.
Quinæ Disulphatis, ʒss.
Olei Anthemidis, gtt. vj.
Mix, and divide into 30 pills. One, three times a day.
Tonic.—Dr. GOLDING BIRD.

2979. ℞ Zinci Sulphatis, ℈j.
Ext. Gentianæ, ℈iv.
Ext. Anthemidis, ℈ij.

Beat into a mass, and divide into 40 pills. Two, twice a day, with the following draught:

℞ Inf. Gentianæ co. ℨx.
Acid. Sulph. Aromat. ♏xij.
Tinct. Zingiberis, ℨj. Mix.

Tonic.—Dr. COPLAND.

2980. ℞ Zinci Sulphatis, ℈j.
Aquæ Cinnamomi,
Aquæ puræ, ana ℥ss. Mix: make an emetic draught.

To produce Vomiting speedily, after Poisoning, &c.
Dr. HOOPER.

2981. ℞ Zinci Sulphatis, gr. xv.
Pulv. Ipecac. gr. xv.
Aquæ puræ, ℥iss.

Mix: make an emetic draught. (To be repeated in ten minutes, and then followed by large doses of calomel.)

In Dysentery and Cholera.—Mr. RICHARDSON.

2982. ℞ Zinci Sulphatis, ℈j.
Infusi Quassiæ, ℥v.
Tinct. Calumbæ, ℥j.

Mix: make a mixture. One-sixth part for a dose.

Tonic.—Dr. HOOPER.

2983. ℞ Zinci Sulphatis, gr. ij–iv.
Tinct. Cantharidis, ♏xx.
Aquæ puræ, ℥j. Mix: to be taken three times a day.

In Paraplegic Palsy.—Dr. BUDD.

2984. ℞ Zinci Sulphatis, gr. ij.
Vini Opii, ♏v.
Syrupi Tolutani, ℨj.
Mistura Amyg. ℨix.

Mix: make a draught. To be taken three times a day.

In latter Stages of Consumption.—Dr. GREGORY.

2985. ℞ Zinci Sulphatis, gr. vj.
Acidi Sulph. dil. ♏xxx.
Syrupi Aurantii, ℥ss.
Infusi Aurant. ℥vss.

Mix: two spoonfuls three times a day.

Tonic.—Dr. DRUITT.

2986. ℞ Zinci Sulphatis, gr. $\frac{1}{4}$–j.
Quinæ Disulph. gr. ij.
Inf. Rosæ comp. ℨx.
Tinct. Aurantii,
Syrupi Aurantii, ana ℨj.

Mix: make a draught. To be taken every fourth hour.

Dr. COPLAND.

The following prescriptions are for external use:

2987. ℞ Zinci Sulph.
Alum. ust.
Sodæ Bibor. āā gr. xv.
Pulv. Sacchari, ʒss.
Mix, and reduce to a very subtile powder.
Dry Collyrium for Ophthalmic Affections.
TROUSSEAU and REVEIL.

2988. ℞ Zinci Sulphatis, ℈j.
Aquæ Rosæ, ℥vij.
Oxymellis simplicis, ℥j.
Mix: make a gargle. To be used frequently.
DR. COPLAND.

2989. ℞ Zinci Sulphatis, gr. ij.
Vini Opii, ʒij.
Aquæ Rosæ, ℥vj. Mix: make a lotion. To the eyes.
In the Purulent Ophthalmia of Infants, after the Complaint has been subdued by Lotions of Nitrate of Silver.
MR. J. FRANCE.

2990. ℞ Zinci Sulphatis, gr. ij.
Aluminis usti, gr. iij.
Plumbi Acetatis, gr. ij.
Aquæ puræ, ℥j. Mix: make a lotion. To be used warm.
In Erysipelas and Paronychia.—DR. F. BROWN.

2991. ℞ Zinci Sulphatis, gr. x–℈j.
Spiritûs Camphoræ, ♏xx.
Aquæ destil. ℥j.
Mix: make an injection. A teaspoonful to be used three times a day.
In Gonorrhœa.—MR. J. L. MILTON.

2992. ℞ Zinci Sulphatis,
Acidi Tannici, ana gr. xv.
Aquæ Rosæ, ℥vj.
Mix: make an injection. To be used two or three times daily.
In Gonorrhœa.—M. RICORD.

2993. ℞ Zinci Sulph. gr. xxx.
Aquæ, Oss.
Dissolve: an enema to be used daily after an operation of the bowels.
For Hæmorrhoids.—DR. DAY.

2994. ℞ Zinci Sulphatis,
Plumbi Acetatis,
Camphoræ in pulv. (ope Spir. rectif.) contrit.
Opii duri contriti, ana gr. vj
Syrupi, ʒij. Rub up together, and add
Aquæ Rosæ, ℥vss.
Make a liquor: a sufficient quantity to be injected into the urethra four times a day by means of an ivory syringe.
In Gonorrhœa and Gleet.—DR. PARIS.

2995. ℞ Zinci Sulphatis,
Cupri Sulph. ana ʒj.
Aquæ Rosæ, ℥viij. Mix: make a lotion.

Styptic.—Dr. COPLAND.

ZINCI VALERIANAS. *Valerianate of Zinc.*

This salt has a strong odor and taste of Valerian. It has been much recommended as a powerful tonic and antispasmodic, and is given in neuralgia and hysteria, in doses of one to two grains.

2996. ℞ Zinci Valerianatis, gr. ix.
Pulv. Tragacanthæ, gr. xxx.
Mix, and divide into 12 pills. One, night and morning.

In Nervous Headache.—DEVAY.

2997. ℞ Zinci Valerianatis, ℈j.
Ext. Hyoscyami, ℈iss.
Mix: make 30 pills. One, two or three times a day.

In Facial Neuralgia.—Dr. H. GREEN.

2998. ℞ Zinci Valerianatis,
Quinæ Valerianatis, ana gr. j.
Extr. Gentianæ, q. s.
Mix: make a pill. To be repeated every hour.

In Epilepsy.

2999. ℞ Zinci Valerianatis,
Pulv. Castoris, ana ℈j.
Ext. Valerianæ, q. s., and make a mass; to be divided into 24 pills. Dose, one or two.

C. MARTINI.

3000. ℞ Zinci Valerianatis, gr. ¾.
Aquæ flor. Aurantii, ℥iss.
Mix: make a draught. To be taken three times a day.

In Hysterical Neuralgia.—Dr. NELIGAN.

3001. ℞ Zinci Valerianatis, gr. iss.
Aquæ destil. ʒvss.
Syrupi, ℥j. Mix: a dessertspoonful every half hour.

DEVAY.

3002. ℞ Zinci Valerianatis, gr. viij.
Tinct. Valerianæ, ʒij.
Aquæ flor. Aurantii, ℥iij.
Syrupi Hemedesmi, ʒij.
Mix: make a mixture. A tablespoonful every six hours.

In Hysteria and Chorea.—Dr. NELIGAN.

ZINGIBER. *Ginger.*

This is the rhizome of the *Zingiber officinale* (Nat. Ord. *Zingiberaceæ*), a native of the East and West Indies. Its active constituents are a volatile oil and soft acrid resin. It has an agreeable aromatic smell, and a warm burning taste. It is an excellent stimulant, carminative, and stomachic. It is often combined with purgative medicines to obviate their griping tendency. Externally ginger is rubefacient, and may even raise a blister. Ginger plasters have been applied with benefit in cases of local pain. Dose, ten grains to half a drachm.

Extractum Zingiberis Æthereum (Beral): dose, one to three grains.

Tinctura Zingiberis (L., E., D.), one to two drachms.

Syrupus Zingiberis (Guibourt), one drachm to half an ounce, as an addition to other medicines.

Trochisci Zingiberis (Soubeiran) are of use in dyspepsia.

3003. ℞ Tinct. Zingiberis, ʒij.
Spirit. Ammon. arom. ʒss.
Aquæ destill. ℥iss.
Mix: make a draught. To be taken three times a day.

In Acidity of Stomach and Heartburn.

3004. ℞ Zingiberis concis. rad. ʒiss.
Aquæ ferventis, Oss. Macerate for two hours in a lightly closed vase, and strain; then add
Tinct. Zingiberis,
Syrupi ejusdem, ana ℥ss. Mix.

A good Vehicle, and a grateful Aromatic in Flatulency.

Dr. Copland.

3005. ℞ Pulv. Zingiberis, ʒvij.
Pulv. sem. Sinapis, ʒj.
Aquæ ferv. q. s. to form a paste of uniform consistence, which is to be spread upon lint or leather, and applied to the affected part.

Stimulant to Local Pains.

INDEX OF DISEASES AND REMEDIES.

This Index is intended to assist the memory of the prescriber on the occurrence of any emergency. In most cases the remedies most to be relied on are mentioned first. The majority of the names are in Latin, to facilitate a reference to the body of the work. This reference will at once show the variety of ways in which each remedy may be prescribed, and the many modes of combining it with other medicines.

Acidity, Gastric.

Alkalies (Potassa, Soda, Ammonia, Lime, Magnesia, their carbonates and bicarbonates). Purgatives (Rheum, Aloes, Pilula Hydrargyri, Ricini Oleum). Tonics (Calumba, Cascarilla, Gentiana). Stimulants.

Acne. See Cutaneous Diseases.

Ague. See Fever, Intermittent.

Albuminous Urine. See Bright's Disease of Kidney.

Amaurosis.

Strychnia. Tonics. Purgatives. Blisters to temple.

Amenorrhœa.

Ferrum (Sulphate, Sesquichloride, Ammonio-citrate, Carbonate). Aloes. Gum-resins (Assafœtida, Myrrh, Ammoniacum, Guaiacum, Galbanum). Valeriana. Cantharides, Sabina, Ergota, with caution.

Anæmia.

Ferri præparata. Aloes and other purges. Tonics, Stimulants, and good living.

Anæsthetic agents.

Æther. Chloroformyl. Amyl. Freezing. Galvanism.

Anasarca. General dropsy.
Drastic purges (Jalapa, Scammonium, Tiglii Oleum, Elaterium, Hydrarg. Chlor.). Scilla. Colchicum. Scoparius. Salines (Potass. Acet., Bitart., &c.).

Aneurism, Aortic.
Digitalis. Purges. Low diet. Rest.

Angina Pectoris.
Opium. Digitalis. Moschus? Assafœtida?

Angina tonsillaris. See Cynanche, and Sore-throat.

Aphonia. Loss of voice.
Blisters. Cataplasma Sinapis. Stimulant gargles in simple relaxed throat. Mercury and Iod. Potassium in syphilitic cases.

Aphthæ. Thrush.
Potassæ Chloras. Mel Boracis. Liquor Sodæ Chlorinatæ. Liq. Calcis Chlorin. Washes of Rhatany, Catechu, &c.

Arachnitis. Inflammation of membranes of brain.
Drastic purges. Pil. Hydrarg. Shaving. Cold lotions or Ice to head. Darkness and Quiet.

Ascarides.
Purges (Castor oil, Jalap, Scammony, Aloes, Senna). Clysters of common Salt, of Assafœtida, Tanacetum, Quassia, Artemisia. Artemisia contra.

Ascites.
Drastics (Elaterium, Scammonium, Ol. Tiglii, Cambogia, Potassæ Bitart.). Salines. Pil. Hydrarg. Scilla. Digitalis. Taraxacum.

Asthma.
Change of air. Stramonium. Opium. Æther. Sp. Æth. Nit. Sp. Chloroform. Hyoscyamus. Antim. P. Tart. Ipecacuanha. Valeriana. Assafœtida. Scilla. Digitalis.

Bed-sores.
Plasters of Amadou, &c. Unguentum Plumbi. Alum poultice.

BLADDER, Inflammation of.
Pareira. Uva Ursi. Opium. Buchu. Copaiba.

BLEEDING. See Hæmorrhage.

BRIGHT'S DISEASE OF KIDNEY.
Purge (as Jalap) at morning. Diaphoretic (Dover's powder) at night. Hot-air baths. Cupping of loins for active inflammation. Pil. Hydrarg.

BRONCHITIS.
Vin. Antimonii. Ipecacuanha. Scilla. Potass. Bicarb. Purges.

BUBO.
Poultices. Emplast. Hydrarg. Ung. Plumbi. Ung. Plumbi Acet. Ung. Opii.

BURNS AND SCALDS.
Cotton-wool. Flour. Chalk. Linimentum Calcis. Lotions of Chlorinated Soda, Decoct. Lini sem. Simple Ointment.

CACHEXIA.
Animal food. Wine and stimulants. Change of air. Morrhuæ Oleum. Tonics.

CALCULOUS AFFECTIONS, with acid urine.
Potash, Soda, Lime, Magnesia, their carbonates and bicarbonates. Sodæ Phosphas. Ammoniæ Phosphas. Acidum Benzoicum. Uva Ursi. Buchu. Pareira.

CALCULOUS AFFECTIONS, with alkaline urine.
Acidum Nitricum. Acidum Hydrochloricum. Strychnia. Tonics. Stimulants. Uva Ursi, Buchu, Pareira.

CALCULI, BILIARY.
Soda, and its carbonates. Opium. Æther.

CANCER.
The Knife. Escharotic applications (Actual cautery, Zinci Chloridum, Antimonii Terchloridum, Potassæ fusa). Anodyne applications (Unguentum Opii, Cataplasma Opii, Ung. et Cataplasm. Belladonnæ, Carrot and Charcoal poultices). *To remove smell*, Liq. Sodæ Chlorin.

CANCRUM ORIS.
Potassæ Chloras. Borax externally.

CARDIALGIA. Heartburn. See Acidity, Gastric.

CARIES OF BONES.
Acidum Phosphoricum? Potassii Iodidum. Morrhuæ Oleum.

CATARRH.
Ipecacuanha. Scilla. Sp. Æth. Nit. Liq. Ammoniæ Acetatis et Citratis. Mist. Amygdalæ. Ammoniacum. Benzoinum. Myrrha. Tolu. Hyoscyamus. Camphor. Terebinth. Oleum. Salines. Purgatives. Tonics.

CEPHALALGIA. Headache.
Purgatives, Tonics, or Stimulants, according to cause.

CEREBRAL INFLAMMATION.
Drastics. Cold applications. Clysters of Tartar Emetic. Colocynth, &c. See Arachnitis.

CHANCRE.
Caustics (Argent. Nit., Potassa fusa, Acidum Nitricum). Lotio Hydrarg. Oxidi. Linim. Hydrarg. Ung. Hyd. Nitratis. Ung. Hyd. Nitrico-ox. Ung. Zinci.

CHAPS.
Glycerina. Honey. Mel. Boracis. Ung. Sambuci. Sapo Camphoratus.

CHILBLAINS.
Lotion of Iodine, Hydrochlor. acid, or Carb. Potash. Ointments of Alum, Camphor, Creasote, Henbane, Mustard, Borax.

CHICKEN-POCK.
Mild purges. Salines. Rest, and moderate support.

CHLOROSIS. See Anæmia.

CHOLERA, ENGLISH.
Castor oil. Rhubarb, Senna. Chalk. Catechu.

CHOLERA, MALIGNANT.
Rhubarb and Magnesia, as prophylactic. Sulphuric acid? Quinine? Emetic of Salt? Wine and Stimulants. Warm poultices to abdomen. Opium? Calomel?

CHOREA.
Ferri Carbonas, Ferri Ammon. Cit., Vinum Ferri. Cupri Sulphas, Cupri Ammon. Sulph. Liquor Potassæ Arsenitis. Valeriana, Assafœtida. Purgatives. Tonics.

COLIC. Pain in belly with flatulence, and without inflammation.
Purgatives (Rhubarb, Senna, Castor oil). Alkalies (Soda, Chalk, Magnesia). Turpentine. Assafœtida. Valerian. Ether. Warm fomentations. Plasters of Opium, Belladonna, Camphor, Turpentine. Clysters of Turpentine, Assafœtida, Tobacco.

COLICA PICTONUM. Lead colic.
Alumen. Acidum Sulphuricum. Magnes. Sulph. Ol. Ricini. Opium. Potassii Iodidum. Anodyne plasters.

CONDYLOMATA. Warts.
Caustics (Nit. Silver, Nit. acid). Lotions of Iodine, Carb. Potash, or Bichlor. Mercury. Ung. Hyd. Nit. Ox. Ung. Hyd. Nitratis.

CONSTIPATION.
Purgatives (Rheum, Aloes, Ol. Ricini, Colocynthis, Jalapa, Scammonium, Senna, Magnesia, Magnes. Sulph., Sod. Sulph., Sod. et Pot. Tart., Elaterium, Ol. Tiglii). Laxatives (Cassia, Prunum, Manna). Brown bread. Exercise. Cold bathing. Tonics (Cinchona, Calumba, Ferri Carb., &c.). Fel Bovis. Terebinthina.

CONSUMPTION. See Phthisis.

CONTUSIONS.
Lotion of Arnica. Lotions of Liq. Plumb. Diacet., Acetic acid, Sulph. Copper, Carb. Potash. Linimentum Calcis. Unguents.

CONVULSIONS. See Epilepsy, Hysteria, Chorea.

CONVULSIONS OF CHILDREN.
Castor oil. Tonics. Wine and water. Wholesome diet.

CORYZA. Cold in the head.
Sp. Æth. Nit. Salines (Pot. Chloras, Pot. Nitras). Sodæ Bicarb. Ipecacuanha. Mild purging. Warm bathing. Quina. Ammonia.

COUGH, CHRONIC.
Mist. Acaciæ. Mist. Amygdalæ. Oxymel Scillæ. Tinct. Campb. co. Mistura Sem. Cydoniæ. Myrrha, Tolu. Decoct. Cinchonæ with Ammonia. Ipecacuanha and Hyoscyamus. Syr. Papaveris.

CRAMP IN THE STOMACH. See Acidity, and Colic.

CROUP.
Leeches to throat. Warm bath. Vinum Antimonii, to keep up nausea. Cataplasma Sinapis. Hyd. Chlor., or Castor oil.

CROUP, SPASMODIC, of Infants.
Warm bath. Castor oil. Stimulants (wine). Tonics.

CUTANEOUS DISEASES.
Alkalies (Potash, Soda, their carbonates and bicarbonates). Sulphur, Potassii Sulphuretum, Sodii Sulphuretum, Ammon. Hydrosulph. Acidum Arseniosum, Liquor Potassæ Arsenitis, Liq. Arsenici terchloridi, Arsenici Iodidum, Liq. Hydrarg. et Arsenici Iodidi (Donovan's). Creasoton. Fuligokali, Pix nigra, Aqua Picis liquidæ. Hydrarg. Chlor., Hydrarg. Bichlor., Pil. Hydrarg. Antim. P. Tart. Brominium. Potassii Iodidum. Guaiacum, Sarsa, Mezereum. Oleum Morrhuæ. *Externally only*, Ung. Sulphuris, Ung. Creasoti, Ung. Picis nigræ, Ung. Hydrargyri, Ung. Hyd. Chlor., Ung. Hyd. Nit. Ox. Lotio Hyd. Ox., Lotio Hyd. Binox. Ung. Hyd. Am. Chlor., Ung. Iodin., Ung. Pot. Iodidi. Lotio Sod. vel. Pot. Carb. Liquor Calcis. Balneum Sulphurosum, &c.

CYNANCHE. Tonsillitis, or Quinsy.
Leeches. Poultices. Emetics. Nit. Silver to fauces. Guaiacum internally. Pot. Iodidum.

CYSTITIS. Inflammation of bladder.

(*When acute*) Leeches to perinæum or pubes. Castor oil. Warm bath. Opium. Pulv. Ipecac. co. (*When chronic*) Copaiba, Uva Ursi, Cubeba, Buchu.

DELIRIUM TREMENS.

Stimulants in moderation. Opium. Quina. Moschus. P. Ipecac. co. Antim. P. Tart.

DIABETES. Saccharine urine.

Animal food. Fats and oils. Exclude starch from diet. Gluten bread, Bran bread. Ammonia. Ammon. Hydrosulph. Cupri Ammon. Sulph. Tinct. Ferri S. Chlor. Catechu, Kino. Opium, Morphia. Colchicum.

DIARRHŒA.

Purgatives (Castor oil, Senna, Pil. Hydrarg., Rhubarb). Absorbents (Creta, Bismuthi Nit.). Aromatics (Cinnamomum, Myristica, Caryophyllus, Pimenta, Zingiber, Piper, Cubeba, Capsicum, Mentha piperita, Ol. Cajuputi). Astringents (Opium, Acidum Tannicum, Acidum Gallicum, Catechu, Kino, Krameria, Hæmatoxylum, Gallæ, Quercus, Tormentilla, Cupri Sulphas, Plumbi Acetas, Alumen, Acidum Sulphuricum). Cinchona, Quina, Calumba, Quassia. Antim. P. Tart. Ipecacuanha.

DIPHTHERIA. Malignant sore-throat, with formation of white membrane.

Nit. Silver to throat. Wine and support. Quina, et Cinchonæ præparata. Ammonia. Potassæ Chloras. Mel. Boracis. Liq. Sodæ Chlorinatæ. Salines. Sp. Æth. Nit., Sp. Æth. Chlor.

DROPSY. See Anasarca, and Ascites.

DROPSY, OVARIAN.

Potassii Iodidum. Liq. Iodinii. Ung. Iodinii. Pil. Hydrarg.

DYSENTERY.

Leeches, when acute. Warm fomentations. Pil. Hydrarg. Ol. Ricini. Opium, Morphia. Ipecacuanha, Pulv. Ipecac. co. Enema or suppository of Opium. Astringents (Plumb. Acet., Cupri Sulph., Acid. Tannic., Terebinthina).

DYSPEPSIA.
Purgatives (Ol. Ricini, Rheum, Aloes). Alkalies (Sod. Carb., Liquor Calcis, Magnesia, Magnes. Carb., Liq. Magnes. Bicarb.). Absorbents (Creta, Bismuthi Nit.). Aromatics (Cinnamomum, Zingiber, Capsicum, Cubeba, Coriandrum, Carui, Anisum, &c.). Tonics (Cinchona, Calumba, Artemisia, Gentiana, Ferri Carb., Acid. Sulph. dil., Argent. Nit.; Strychnia, small doses). Alteratives (Pil. Hydrarg., Hyd. c. Cretâ, Hyd. Chlor., Colchicum, Ipecacuanha, &c.). Acidum Lacticum. Pepsina.

DYSPNŒA. See Asthma.

DYSURIA.
Opium. Copaiba. Antim. P. Tart. Salines. P. Ipecac. co. Pareira.

EAR, INFLAMMATION OF.
Leeching. Poulticing, Warm Fomentations, Foment. of Decoct. Papav. Injection of Opium, Morphia, or Alum.

ECTHYMA. See Cutaneous diseases.

ECZEMA. See Cutaneous diseases.

ELEPHANTIASIS. See Cutaneous diseases.

EMPHYSEMA, GENERAL.
Pad over wound in lung. Bandage. Bleeding?

EMPHYSEMA OF LUNG. See Asthma.
Ether and Stimulants. Opium? Hyoscyamus, Stramonium. A dry bracing climate.

EMPYEMA. Effusion following Pleurisy.
Calomel and Opium. Tapping. Quinine.

ENDOCARDITIS.
Blistering. Antim. P. Tart. (to keep up nausea). Calomel and Opium. Leeching. Purgatives.

ENLARGEMENTS, GLANDULAR.
Apply Tinct. Iodin., Tinct. Iodin. co., Ung. Iodinii, or Ung. Pot. Iod. *Internally:* Potassii Iodidum. Ferri præparata. Aloes. Quina. Pil. Hydrarg.

ENTERITIS. Inflammation of bowels.
Leeches to abdomen. Warm fomentations. Ditto with Tinct. Opii or Decoct. Papav. Calomel and Opium. Castor oil. Warm enemata. Blistering, when chronic.

EQUINIA. Glanders.
Wine, Brandy, and support. Nitric acid? Quina?

EPILEPSY.
Purgatives (Aloes, Rhubarb, Castor oil). Wine and Stimulants. Good living and air. Quinine and tonics. Specific remedies (Argent. Nit., Argent. Ox., Zinci Sulph., Zinci Acet., Zinci Oxidum, Zinci Valerianas, Ferri præparata, Cupri Sulph., Cupri Ammon. Sulph., Liq. Pot. Arsen., Terebinthinæ Oleum, Cotyledon, Valeriana, Indigo).

EPISTAXIS.
Raise arms. Cold to nape of neck, or forehead. Plug nares. Injections of Alum, Sulph. Copper, or Sulph. Iron.

ERYSIPELAS.
Purgatives (Senna, Hyd. Chlor., Magnes. Sulph., Sod. et Pot. Tart.). Calomel and Opium. Leeches. Vinum Antimonii. Vinum Ipecac. *In low cases*, Wine, support, Quinine. *External applications*, Warm foment., Starch, Chalk, Magnesia, Nit. Silver. Cataplasma fermenti, or Lotio Sodæ Chlorin., or Cataplasma Carbonis, for gangrene.

ERYTHEMA.
Saline aperient. Cool lotion of Spirit, Ether, or Chloroform. Lotio Plumbi Diacet. Lotio Sodæ Carb.

EXCORIATIONS.
Dry powder (Chalk, Starch, Plumbi Carb.). Unguentum Aquæ Rosæ ("Cold cream"). Ung. Zinci, Ung. Plumbi Carb. Sapo Camphoratus. Glycerina.

EXANTHEMATA. See Fevers, Eruptive.

FACE, ERUPTIONS OF.
Alteratives (Pil. Hydrarg., Hyd. Bichlor., Aloes, Liq. Pot. Arsen., Sarsa, Potassii Iodidum). Cool washes (Sod.

Carb., Ammon. Hydrochlor., Pot. Nit., Aqua Rosæ, Aqua Amygdalæ, Lotio Plumb. Diacet.). Unguents.

FAINTING.

Ammonia to nostrils. Cold water to face and chest. Fresh air. Loose clothing.

FEVERS, ERUPTIVE.

Antim. P. Tart. Ipecacuanha, and Hyd. Chlor., in high fever. Salines (Potassæ Nitras, Potassæ Chloras, Ammoniæ Acetatis Liquor; Liq. Ammon. Citratis; Potassæ Tartras, Bitartras, Acetas; Pulveres effervescentes). Acid drinks (Acidum Nit. dil., Acid. Hydrochlor. dil., Acid. Sulph. dil., Juleperum Acidum, Acid. Cit., Acid. Tart., Succus Limonum). Purgatives (Magnes. Sulph., Sodæ Pot. Tart., Oleum Ricini, Jalapa, Pil. Hydrarg.). Diaphoretics (Salines, Sp. Æth. Nit., Sp. Chloroform, Ipecac., Pulvis Doveri; Opium, cautiously; Antim. P. Tart., in small doses). *In low cases*, Wine and support. During convalescence, Quina and Iron.

FEVER, INTERMITTENT. Ague.

Between paroxysms, Quinæ Disulphas; any salt of Quina, Cinchona, Quinidia; any preparation of Cinchona bark. Cusparia, Cascarilla, Calumba, Gentiana, Quassia, &c. *Taken continuously*, Liquor Potassæ Arsenitis, Liq. Arsen. Terchlor. Also preparations of Iron and Copper, and Chloride of Sodium. For enlarged spleen, Ferri Iodidum, Ferri Bromidum. Purgatives.

FEVER, TYPHOID.

Salines in early stage. Afterward, Wine and support. Liq. Ammoniæ, Sp. Ammon. Arom., Ammon. Carb. Acid drinks. Moschus. Camphora. Capsicum. Mist. Terebinthinæ. Cinchona and Quina when fever has abated. For Diarrhœa, Opium with caution, vegetable astringents. To head, shaving and cool lotions. To belly, warm applications, Cataplasma Sinapis, Cataplasm. Terebinth.

FISTULÆ. Burrowing ulcers.

Stimulating injections (Sol. Argent. Nit., Tinct. Iodin. co.,

Sol. Cupri Sul., Sol. Hyd. Bichlor., Tinct. Canth., Tinct. Myrrhæ).

FLATULENCE.

Purgatives (Rheum, Aloes, Pil. Hydrarg.). Cordials (Vinum, Tinct. Aurant., Tinct. Capsici, Pulv. Aromat., Conf. Aromat., Piperes, Menthæ, Zingiber, Cinnamomum, Coriandrum, Pimenta, Anisum). Assafœtida, Moschus. Alkalies (Ammonia, Soda, and their carbonates). Argent. Nit., Argent. Oxidum. Terebinthina, Enema, Terebinth.

FŒTOR OF BREATH.

Purgatives. Hyd. Bichlor. Acid. Nit. dil. Washes of Alum, Acid. Nit., Tannin. Lozenges of Catechu, Charcoal.

FROST-BITES.

If no gangrene, stimulating liniments. See Chilblains. If gangrene, Poultices and Emollient ointments.

GALL-STONES.

During passage, Bleeding, Leeches, Warm bath, Opium, Chloroform. *Afterward*, Calomel, Purgatives, Alkalies.

GANGRENE.

Wine and support internally. *Locally*, Poultices. Decoct. Papav. Decoct. Lini Sem. Linim. Opii. Stimulating lotions of Tinct. Myrrhæ, Ol. Terebinth., Vinum. Cataplasm or lotion of Sod. Chlorin. or Charcoal, for fœtor. Ung. Resinæ, Ung. Plumbi Acet.

GASTRALGIA. Gastrodynia, pain in the stomach.

For acidity, see above. Otherwise; Argent. Nit., Argent. Oxid. Bismuthi Nit. Opium, Aconitum, Conium. Wine and Cordials (see Flatulence). Aloes, Rheum.

GLANDS, ENLARGEMENT OF.

Internally, Liq. Iodinii. Potassii Iodidum. Ferri Iodidum. Oleum Morrhuæ. Cinchona, Quina, Saline purges. *Externally*, Tinct. Iodinii rubefaciens, Tinct. Iod. co. Emplastrum et Unguentum Iodinii, Emplast. et Ung. Pot. Iod., Emplast. et Linim. Hydrarg., Emp. Ammoniaci c. Hydrarg., Emp. Conii, Emp. Opii. Decoct. Papav., pro fotu.

GLEET. See Gonorrhœa.

GOITRE. See Glands, Enlargement of.

GONORRHŒA.

If high inflammation or fever, Rest, Abstinence, Leeching, Purging (Ol. Ricini, Pil. Hyd., Senna). Poulticing, Warm fomentations. When active inflammation has subsided, *internally*, Copaiba. Cubeba. Acid. Sulph. d. Argent. Nit. Acid. Tannic. Catechu. Opium. Tinct. Ferri Ses. Chlor. Cinchona. Salines, &c. *Locally*, injections of Nit. Silver, Sulph. Copper, Acet. Lead, Sulph. Zinc, Tannin, Opium, Iodine, Iodide Iron, &c.

GOUT.

Internally, Colchicum, its tincture, comp. tincture, Wine. Alkalies (Ammonia, Potash, and their carbonates). Pil. Hydrarg., Hyd. Chlor. Opium with a purge. Cinchona, Quina, in chronic cases. *Locally*, Cotton wool, Flannel. Warm pediluvia. Liniments of Opium, Belladonna, Conium. Lotion or foot-bath of Carb. Soda. Blister above joint.

GRAVEL. See Calculous diseases.

GUMS, Looseness or Bleeding of.

Tooth-powders of Alum, Catechu, Quinine, &c. Mouth-washes of same, of Sulph. Zinc, Tannin, Nit. Silver, Myrrh., Borax.

HÆMATEMESIS. Bleeding from Stomach.

Farinaceous diet. Cold drinks, and Ice. Pil. Hydrarg., Ol. Ricini, Aloes. Quinine. Acid. Sulph. dil. Ice externally in aggravated cases.

HÆMOPTYSIS. Spitting of Blood.

Bleeding in plethoric cases. A blister or mustard poultice to chest. Low diet. Cold drinks, or Ice. Rest. Antim. P. Tart. Acid. Sulph. dil. Plumb. Acet. Terebinthinæ Ol. Tinct. Opii. Catechu. Acid. Tannic. Tinct. Digitalis. Potassæ Nitras.

HÆMORRHAGE, INTERNAL. See Hæmatemesis, Hæmoptysis, &c.

HÆMORRHAGE, EXTERNAL. See Epistaxis, Purpura, Scurvy.

HÆMORRHOIDS. Piles.

Aloes, Rhubarb, Castor oil. Electuaries of Senna, Sulphur, Jalap. Tartrate Potash. Confection of Black Pepper, Ointments, Astringent, of Alum, Lead, Mercury, Ox. Mercury, Zinc, Gall, Tannin. Anodyne, of Opium, Belladonna, Morphia, Stramonium. Lotions, Astringent, of Sulph. Zinc, Diacet. of Lead, Bichlor. Merc., Sul. Copper, Nit. Silver. Anodyne, of Opium, Poppies, &c.

HEADACHE. See Cephalalgia.

HEART, INFLAMMATION OF. See Endocarditis, Pericarditis.

HAIR, LOSS OF.

Unguentum Cantharidis. Tinctura Cantharidis. Pomatum cum Quinâ. Lotio Hyd. Bichlor. Ung. Bals. Peruv.

HEMICRANIA.

Quina. Ferri præparata. Purgatives, if plethoric. Wine, if reverse. Valeriana. Spir. Æth. Sulph. co. Chloroformyl.

HEMIPLEGIA. See Paralysis.

HEPATITIS. See Liver, Inflammation of.

HERNIA. Rupture.

Reduction. Truss to keep in place. *When strangulated*, Hot bath, Opium, Chloroform, Tart. emetic to nauseate, Belladonna, Tobacco clyster, &c.

HERPES. See Cutaneous Affections.

HICCOUGH. See Acidity, and Flatulence.

HOOPING-COUGH.

Vinum. Antim. Tart. Vin. Ipecac., Pulv. Ipecac. co. Pulv. Jacobi ver. Ammonia, et Carb. Oxymel Scillæ. Spir. Æth. Nit. Potass. Bicarb. Cinchona, Quina. Assafœtida, Moschus. Bals. Tolut. Copaiba. *Externally*, Linim. Ol. Succini. Linim. Ammoniæ. Linim. Saponis. Linim. Opii. Emplast. Assafœtidæ, Emp. Belladonnæ.

HYDROPHOBIA.

After bite, Caustics (Actual Cautery, Chloride Zinc, Potassa fusa). *During paroxysm*, Ice to spine and cranium. Chloroform. Opium. Cannabis. Wine.

HYDROCEPHALUS. Water on the brain.
Potassii Iodidum. Ferri Iodidum. Quina. Vinum. Purgatives (Hyd. Chlor., Pil. Hyd., Jalapa, Ol. Ricini, Ol. Crotonis). Diuretics (Digitalis, Scilla). *Locally*, during fever, Cold applications. *When chronic*, Blistering, Mustard poultices, Stimulating liniments.

HYDROTHORAX. Water on the chest.
With general dropsy. See Anasarca.
After Pleurisy. See Pleurisy.

HYPOCHONDRIA.
Change of air and scene. Mild purgative course. Quina and tonics. Rem. for Dyspepsia.

HYSTERIA.
Mild purging. Aloes. Ferrum. Quina. Stimulants (Ammonia, Amm. Carb., Æther. Sulph., Spir. Æth. Nit., Assafœtida, Valeriana, Castoreum, Moschus, Sp. Succini). Ferri Zinci, et Quinæ Valerianates. Quina and tonics. Opium, Morphia.

IMPETIGO. See Cutaneous affections.

IRITIS.
Hyd. Chlor., Pil. Hyd. Leeching. Blisters to temple. Turpentine internally. Darkness.

ISCHURIA. Suppression of urine.
Bleeding, Hot bath, Opium. Ol. Ricini, Aloes. Pulv. Ipecac. co. Liq. Ammon. Acet.

ITCH. See Scabies.

JAUNDICE. See Hepatitis, and Gall-stones.
When no severe pain or fever, Emetics (Antim. Tart., Ipecacuanha); then Purgatives (Pil. Hyd., Hyd. Chlor., Jalapa, Magnes. Sulph.). Balneum Acid. Nitro-mur.

JOINTS, INFLAMMATION OF. See Gout, Rheumatism, Scrofula.

KIDNEYS, INFLAMMATION OF. See Bright's disease, and Calculous affections.

LABOUR, RETARDED.
If no obstruction, Ergota. Sodæ Biboras. Contrajerva.

LARYNGITIS.

Acute. Bleeding, Leeching. Tart. emet. Calomel and Opium. *Threatened suffocation,* Warm bath, Tracheotomy.

Chronic. Blisters. Cataplasm. Sinapis. Unguent. Antim. Tart. Nit. Silver, locally. Internally, Potassii Iodidum. Hyd. Chlor. *For Dyspnœa,* Opium Belladonna, Stramonium.

LEUCORRHŒA.

Internally: Ferri præparata. Potassii Iodidum. Copaiba. Terebinthina. Guaicum. Opium. Acid. Sulph. dil. and other astringents. *Locally,* Nit. Silver, Alum, Acet. Lead, Sulph. Copper, Sulph. Zinc, Tannin, Gallic acid., Tinct. Galls, Tinct. Catechu, Decoct. Quercûs, Tinct. Iodinii, Tinct. Opii.

LEPRA. See Cutaneous affections.

LIVER, INFLAMMATION OF.

Leeching and Cupping. Leeches to arms. Blisters, when fever has subsided. Ung. Hydrargyri, Linim. Hydrarg. Pil. Hydrarg., Hyd. Chlor. Magnes. Sulph., Aloes, Senna. Antim. P. Tart. Ipecacuanha. Rheum.

Chronic. Pot. Iod. Acid. Nit. dil. Balneum Nitro-muriaticum. Taraxacum.

LUMBAGO.

Rem. for Rheumatism (Alkalies, Purgatives, Colchicum). Potassii Iodidum. Aloes, Opii. Ung. Belladonnæ. Emp. Belladonn. Emp. Saponis c. Opio. Quina.

LUNGS, INFLAMMATION OF. See Pneumonia.

MAMMÆ, INFLAMMATION OF.

Ricini Ol. Salines. Poultices. Ung. Opii, Decoct. Papav., Ung. Belladon.

MANIA.

Cold douche, Shower-bath. Quiet. Purgatives. Opium. Belladonna.

MARASMUS.

Wine and good living. Oleum Morrhuæ. Quina and tonic. Ferri præparata.

MEASLES. See Fevers, Eruptive; and Cough.

MELANCHOLIA.

Tonics. Purgatives. Wine. Pil. Hydrarg. Aloes.

MENINGITIS. See Arachnitis.

MENORRHAGIA.

Leeching. Rest in recumbent posture. Cool acid drinks. Ice to vulvæ. Saline purgatives, Pil. Hydrarg. Astringents (Plumb. Acet., Alum, Acid Tan.), *externally and internally*. Quina, Steel, and Wine, for exhaustion.

MOUTH, AFFECTIONS OF. See Aphthæ, Cancrum oris, Fœtor, &c.

NEURALGIA.

Inflammatory. See Rheumatism, Gout. Warm fomentations. Decoct. Papav. Ung. et Linim. Opii et Belladonnæ.

Intermittent. Quina and tonics. Arsenic. Pot. Iodidum.

Chronic. Linim. et Ung. Opii aut Belladonnæ. Emp. Aconiti. Ung. Aconitinæ.

NERVOUS EXCITABILITY.

Assafœtida, Valeriana, Camphora, Moschus, Castoreum, Ammonia, Hyoscyamus, Opium. Ether Sulph. Quina and tonics. Ferri præp. Zinci præp. Argenti Oxidum.

NIPPLES, EXCORIATION OF.

Glycerina. Ung. Opii. Ung. Zinci. Ung. Plumbi Acet. Emplast. Opii, Emplast. Belladonnæ.

NODES. See Periostitis.

ONYCHIA. Whitlow.

Poulticing, Lancing. Removing edge of nail. Ung. Zinci, Ung. Hyd. Nit. Ox. Argent. Nit.

OPHTHALMIA. See Rheumatism, Scrofula.

Astringents (Unguent. vel Lotio Argent. Nitratis, Lotio Plumb. Diacet., Aluminis, Cupri Sulph., Zinci Sulph., Rosæ inf. co.; Ung. Zinci to lids). Anodynes (Vin. Opii, Decoct. Papav., Tinct. Belladonnæ). *Internally*, Pil. Hyd. Pot. Iod. Quina.

ORCHITIS. Inflamed testicle.

Acute. Leeching. Antim. P. Tart. Pil. Hyd. Ol. Ricini. Low diet.

Chronic. Strapping. Ung. Hyd. Potassii Iodidum or Pil. Hyd., internally.

OZÆNA.

Pil. Hydrarg. Potassii Iodidum. Injections of Argent. Nit., Alum, Acid. Tan., Liq. Calcis Chlor.

PALPITATION OF HEART.

Remedies for Inflammation; if none, Remedies for Acidity or Nervous excitability.

PARALYSIS.

Recent. Rest and Saline purgatives.

Chronic. Nux vomica, Strychnia. Hyd. Bichlor. Toxicodendron. Electricity. Arg. Nit. Phosphorus. Frictions of Arnica, Armoracia, Tinct. Nuc. vom., Sinapis, Cantharides.

PERICARDITIS. Inflammation of pericardium. See Rheumatism.

Acute. Bleeding, Cupping, or Leeching. Antim. P. Tart. repeatedly. Morph. Acet. Hyd. Chlor. repeatedly, and Opium; Saline purges. Blister, kept open.

Chronic. Blisters. Ung. Antim. P. Tart. Ung. Hydrarg. Pil. Hydrarg. Digitalis. Scilla. Colchicum. Alkalies. Quina.

PERIOSTITIS.

Fomentation of Poppies. Linim. Opii. Linim. Belladonnæ. Ung. Hyd., Ung. Pot. Iod., Ung. Iodinii. *Internally,* Pot. Iodidum. Pil. Hydrarg. Sarsa.

PERITONITIS. Inflammation of peritoneum.

Leeching. Hot fomentations. Decoct. Papav. Emp. Terebinthinæ. Antim. P. Tart. Hyd. Chlor. and Opium. Enema Terebinth., Enema Opii, Enema Ol. Ricini. *Chronic cases.* Blisters, Calomel, Purgatives.

PHRENTITIS. See Brain, Inflammation of.

PHTHISIS. Consumption.
Incipient. Change of air, bracing. Exercise. Morrhuæ Oleum. Quina. Potassii Iodidum. Ferri præparata.
Confirmed. See Remedies for Hæmoptysis and Sweating. Blisters to chest. Ung. Antim. P. Tart. Emetics occasionally. For cough, Opium, Squill, Conium, or Stramonium. For diarrhœa, Opium, Acidum Tannicum, Acid. Sulph. dil., Plumb. Acet., Cupri Sulph. For vomiting, Magnes. Sulph., Acid. Hydrocyan. dil., Creasote. Wine and support. Mild moist climate.

PLEURITIS. Inflammation of pleura.
Acute. Bleeding or leeching. Antim. P. Tart. repeatedly. Pil. Hyd., Hyd. Chlor. Senna, Magnes. Sulph.
Chronic, with effusion. Blisters. Hyd. Chlor., Pil. Hyd. Tapping. Quina. Wine and support.

PNEUMONIA. Inflammation of lung.
Acute. Antim. P. Tart. repeatedly. Pil. Hyd. or Hyd. Chlor.
Chronic. Blistering. Ung. Antim. P. Tart. Saline purges. Hyd. Chlor. Wine and Ammonia in low cases.

PORRIGO.
Wash head, cut away hair. Apply Acid. Sulph. dil., Acid. Acet. fort., Argent. Nit., Lotio Zinc. Sulph., Cupri Sulph., Plumb. Acet., P. Diacet., &c. Ung. Sulphuris, Ung. Sulph Iodidi. Sod. Hyposulph.

PLETHORA.
Purgatives. Low diet. Exercise.

PRURITIS. Itching.
Alkaline lotions (Carb. Soda, Carb. Potash, Sodæ Bibor.). Liq. Sodæ Chlorin. Decoct. Papav. Ung. Belladon.

PURPURA. See Scurvy.

PYROSIS. Water-brash.
Quina and tonics. Pills of Rhubarb and Aloes. Alkalies, if liquid vomited be acid. Acid. Sulph. dil., if it be

alkaline. Ferri præparata. Kino, Catechu, Acid. Tannic.

QUINSY. See Tonsils, Inflammation of.

RACHITIS.

Calcis Phosph., Magnes. Phosph., Acid. Phosph. dil. Ferri præparata. Quina and tonics. Iodide Potassium. Alkalies, and treatment for Scrofula.

RHEUMATISM.

Acute. Bleeding, Leeches. Antim. P. Tart. Hyd. Chlor. Opium. Morph. Acet. Pot. Bicarb. Pot. Nit. Succ. Limonis. Cotton wool and Alkaline lotions to joints.

Heart affection. See Pericarditis, Endocarditis.

Chronic. Alkalies (Pot. vel Sod. Bicarb.). Cotton wool and Alkaline lotions to joints. Cathartics (Hyd. Chlor. Senna, Colocynth, Sod. P. Tart., &c.). Salines. Diaphoretics. Ipecacuanha. Colchicum. Guaiacum. Pot. Iodidum. Quina.

RINGWORM. See Porrigo.

ROSEOLA.

Attention to teeth. Mild Aperients (Ol. Ricini, Senna, Rheum, Sod. P. Tart.). Ipecacuanha.

RUPIA.

Pot. Iodidum. Wine and generous living. Dec. Sarsæ. Quina. Poultices to scabs.

SALIVATION.

Leave off Mercury. Acid. Sulph. dil. Potassii Iodidum. Mouth-washes of Sulph. Copper, Catechu, Tannic acid, Borax. Ricini Oleum.

SCABIES. Itch.

Ung. Sulph., Ung. Sulph. co., Ung. Sulph. Iod. Ung. vel Lotio Sod. Carb. Ung. Sod. Hyposulph. Ung. Hellebori. Sulphur baths. Internally, Sulphur and Alkaline sulphurets.

SCARLATINA. See Fevers, Eruptive.

Saline purges. Potassæ Chloras. Liq. Sodæ Chlorin. Acid. Nit. dil. Gargle of Myrrh.

SCIATICA.
Aperients (Senna, Colocynth, Aloes). Warm bath. Friction. Terebinthina. Emp. vel Linim. Opii. Emp. Belladonnæ.

SCIRRHUS. See Cancer.

SCROFULA.
Fresh air, Exercise, Generous diet. Potassii Iodidum. Tinct. Iodinii co., internally, and externally to swellings. Ferri Iodidum. Ferri Carb., Ammon. Cit., Sesquichlor., &c.; Cinchona, Quina. Pil. Hyd. Occasional Aperients. Liquor Potassæ. Barii Chloridum. Morrhuæ Oleum. Conium?

SCURVY, or Purpura.
Mixed diet. Vegetable food, fresh. Milk. Succus Limonum, Acidum Citricum, other Vegetable acids. Tonics. Wine. Gargles and fomentations of Vinegar.

SEA-SICKNESS.
Chloroform (five drops in water). Creasote (three drops). Æth. Sulph., Sp. Æth. Nit. Wine, Brandy. Sp. Ammon. Aromat. Warm plasters to pit of stomach.

SLEEPLESSNESS.
Opium, Morphia, Liq. Morph. Bimec.; Morph. Acet., Hydrochlor. Syrup. Papav. Lactucarium. Camphora. Pillow of Hops.

SNAKEBITES.
Ammonia, internally and externally. Ether. Wine and support. Olivæ Oleum rubbed in. Cautery to bite.

SORE-THROAT. See Throat, Inflammation of.

SPASMODIC DISEASES. See Hysteria, Epilepsy, Nervous excitability.

SPLEEN, ENLARGEMENT OF. See Ague, and Scrofula.

SPRAINS.
Lotion of Tinct. Arnica. Lotions of Ammon. Hydrochlor., Nit. Pot., &c. Decoct. Papav. Linim. Opii. Emp. Opii, Emp. Belladonnæ. Bandaging.

STOMACH, AFFECTIONS OF. See Acidity, Flatulence, Dyspepsia, Gastralgia, Cancer, Hæmatemesis.

STRANGURY, or Dysuria.
Warm bath. Suppository or Enema of Opium. Nit. Pot. Sp. Æth. Nit.

SWEATING, PROFUSE. See Ague, and Phthisis.
Acid. Sulph. dil. Quina. Catechu. Hæmatoxylon. Ol. Ricini.

SYPHILIS.
To sore. See Chancre.
Primary forms. Pil. Hyd., Hyd. Chlor., and Lotio Hydrarg. Ox.
Secondary. Pot. Iodidum. Hyd. Bichlor.
Tertiary. Pot. Iodidum. Sarsa. Quina. Acid. Nit. dil. Wine and support. Alkalies. Auri præparata.

TAPE-WORM.
Brisk Cathartics (Senna, Colocynth, Jalapa, Scammonium, Hyd. Chlor., Ol. Ricini, &c.). Radix Filicis maris. Terebinthina. Brayera.

TOOTHACHE.
Extraction. Stopping. Warm fomentations. Bag of hot salt or sand. Tinct. Opii or Tinct. Belladonnæ to cheek. Pledget of cotton wool to tooth with Creasote, Chloroform, Tinct. Opii, or Tinct. Camph.

TESTICLE, INFLAMMATION OF. See Orchitis.

TETANUS.
Cold affusion. Opium, Morphia. Antim. P. Tart. Ice to spine. Belladonna, Conium, Cannabis, Hyoscyamus, Camphora, &c. Chloroform by inhalation. Ammonia. *In mild cases*, Quina, Wine, Aperients.

THROAT, INFLAMMATION OF. See Laryngitis, Diphtheria, Scarlatina, Phthisis, Syphilis.
Simple sore-throat. Cataplasma Sinapis. Flannel to throat, Sp. Æth. Nit. Saline purgative.
Atonic sore-throat. Nit. Silver topically. Gargles of Alum, Acid. Hydrochlor., Tannin, &c. Quina.

TINEA CAPITIS. See Porrigo.

TONSILS, INFLAMMATION OF. Tonsillitis, Quinsy.
Leeches and hot fomentations to throat. Antim. P. Tart. Ipecacuanha, P. Ipecac. co. Aperients (Pil. Hyd., Magnes. Sul., Ol. Ricini). Guaiacum. Nit. Silver, or Tinct. Iodine, to tonsils.

TENESMUS.
Purgatives (Ol. Ricini, Rheum). Ipecacuanha. Opium. Enema Opii. Assafœtida. Ammonia, Cordials.

TRISMUS. See Tetanus.

ULCERS.
Strapping. Bandaging. Poulticing. Ointment of Chalk. Ung. Zinci, Ung. Plumbi Acet. Emp. Plumbi vel Saponis, Emp. Resinæ. Stimulating applications (Ung. Argent. Nit., Cupri Sulph., Cupri Diacet.; Ung. Hydrargyri, Hyd. Nitratis, Hyd. Nit. Ox., Hyd. Ammon. Chlor., Lotio Hyd. Ox., Hyd. Binox., Plumbi Diacet., Ung. Mezerei). Astringents (Alumen, Ung. Gallæ, Acid. Tan., Zinci Sul.). Anodynes (Ung. et Emp. Opii et Belladonnæ, Ung. et Emp. Conii). Deodorizing (Ung. Carbonis, Lotio Calcis Chlor.). Caustics (Acid. Nit., Zinci Chlor., Argent. Nit., Potassa fusa).

URETHRITIS. See Gonorrhœa.

URINE, INCONTINENCE OF.
Cold bathing. Suppository or enema of Opium. Tinct. Canth. with Tinct. Hyoscyami. Alkalies. Tinct. Ferri S.-chlor.

URINE, RETENTION OF. See Ischuria.

URTICARIA.
Alkaline lotions (Sod. Carb. et Bicarb., Pot. Carb. et Bicarb.). Alkalies internally. Antim. P. Tart. Ipecacuanha. Rheum. Senna.

UTERUS, INFLAMMATION OF.
Warm fomentations. Opium, Morphia. Belladonna. Oleum Ricini. Inject. of Decoct. Papav.

Uvula, Relaxation of.
Quina. Ferri præparata, Nit. Silver or Tinct. Iodin. locally. Pulv. Alum. Astringent gargles. Excision.

Vomiting.
Attention to cause. Acid. Hydrocy. dil. Creasoton, Chloroformyl. Morphia. Bismuthi Nit. Alkalies. Quina.

Warts. See Condylomata.

Worms. See Tape-worm.
Cathartics (Hyd. Chlor., Jalapa, Scammonium, Senna, Colocynthis; Terebinthinæ Ol., followed by Ol. Ricini). Stanni Pulv. Macuna. Santonica. Spigelia. Brayera. Filix mas. Tanacetum. Assafœtida. Enema of salt.

Yellow Fever.
Emetic (Zinc. Sulph., Ipecacuanha, or Salt); followed by Hyd. Chlor., repeated doses. Tiglii Ol. Opium. Cold sponging. Astringents for hæmorrhage. Stimulants for collapse. During convalescence, Quina, or Cusparia.

CPSIA information can be obtained
at www.ICGtesting.com
Printed in the USA
LVHW101335160422
716387LV00003B/68

9 783752 590692